NUNS AND SOLDIERS

By the same Author

THE FLIGHT FROM THE ENCHANTER
THE SANDCASTLE
THE BELL
A SEVERED HEAD
AN UNOFFICIAL ROSE
THE UNICORN
THE ITALIAN GIRL
THE RED AND THE GREEN
THE TIME OF THE ANGELS
THE NICE AND THE GOOD
BRUNO'S DREAM
A FAIRLY HONOURABLE DEFEAT
AN ACCIDENTAL MAN
THE BLACK PRINCE
THE SACRED AND PROFANE LOVE MACHINE
HENRY AND CATO
A WORD CHILD
UNDER THE NET
THE SEA, THE SEA

Plays

A SEVERED HEAD (with J. B. Priestley)
THE ITALIAN GIRL (with James Saunders)
THE THREE ARROWS and THE SERVANTS
AND THE SNOW

Philosophy

SARTRE, ROMANTIC RATIONALIST
THE SOVEREIGNTY OF GOOD
THE FIRE AND THE SUN

NUNS AND SOLDIERS

Iris Murdoch

THE VIKING PRESS

NEW YORK

Copyright © Iris Murdoch, 1980
All rights reserved

First published in 1981 by The Viking Press
625 Madison Avenue, New York, N.Y. 10022

LIBRARY OF CONGRESS CATALOGING IN PUBLICATION DATA
Murdoch, Iris.
Nuns and soldiers.
I. Title.
PZ4.M974Nu   1981   [PR6063.U7]   823'.914   80-16935
ISBN 0-670-51826-3

Printed in the United States of America
Set in Baskerville

To
NATASHA and
STEPHEN SPENDER

ONE

'Wittgenstein —'

'Yes?' said the Count.

The dying man shifted on the bed, rolling his head rhythmically to and fro in a way that had become habitual only in the last few days. Pain?

The Count was standing at the window. He never sat down now in Guy's presence. He had been more familiar once, though Guy had always been a sort of king in his life: his model, his teacher, his best friend, his standard, his judge; but most especially something royal. Now another and a greater king was present in the room.

'He was a sort of amateur, really.'

'Yes,' said the Count. He was puzzled by Guy's sudden desire to belittle a thinker whom he had formerly admired. Perhaps he needed to feel that Wittgenstein too would not survive.

'A naive and touching belief in the power of pure thought. And that man imagined we would never reach the moon.'

'Yes.' The Count had often talked of abstract matters with Guy, but in the past they had talked of so much else, they had even gossiped. Now there were few topics left. Their conversation had become refined and chilled until nothing personal remained between them. Love? There could be no expression of it now, any gesture of affection would be a gross error of taste. It was a matter of behaving correctly until the end. The awful egoism of the dying. The Count knew how little now Guy needed or wanted his affection, or even Gertrude's; and he knew too, in his grief, that he himself was withdrawing, stifling his compassion, coming to see it as fruitless suffering. We do not want to care too much for what we are losing. Surreptitiously we remove our sympathy, and prepare the dying one for death, diminish him, strip him of his last attractions. We abandon the dying like a sick beast left under the hedge. Death is supposed to show us truth, but is its own place of illusion. It defeats love. Perhaps shows us that after all there is none. I am thinking

Guy's thoughts now, the Count said to himself. I do not think this. But then I am not dying.

He pulled back the curtain a little and looked out into the November evening. Snow had begun to fall again in Ebury Street, large slow flakes moving densely, steadily, with visible silence, in the light of the street lamps, and crowding dimly above in the windless dark. A few cars hissed by, their sound muted and softened. The Count was about to say, 'It's snowing,' but checked himself. When someone is dying there is no point in telling him about the snow. There was no more weather for Guy.

'It was the oracular voice. We felt it had to be true.'

'Yes.'

'A philosopher's thought suits you or it doesn't. It's only deep in that sense. Like a novel.'

'Yes,' said the Count. He added, 'Indeed.'

'Linguistic idealism. A dance of bloodless categories after all.'

'Yes. Yes.'

'But really, could I be happy now?'

'What do you mean?' said the Count. He was always, now, frightened that even in these sterile conversations something terrible might be said. He was not sure what he anticipated, but there could be something dreadful, a truth, a mistake.

'Death is not an event in life. He lives eternally who lives in the present. To see the world without desire is to see its beauty. The beautiful makes happy.'

'I never understood that,' said the Count, 'but it doesn't seem to add up. I suppose it's out of Schopenhauer.'

'Schopenhauer, Mauthner, Karl Kraus—what a charlatan.'

The Count looked surreptitiously at his watch. The nurse put a strict time limit on his conversations with Guy. If he stayed too long Guy began to ramble, the abstract moving on into the visionary, the mind-computer beginning to jumble its items. A little less blood to the brain and we are all raving lunatics spouting delusions. Guy's ramblings were to the Count unspeakably painful: the helpless still self-aware irrationality of that most rational of minds. What was it like within? It was the pain-killing drugs, of course, the cause was chemical. Did that make it better? It was not natural. But was death natural?

2

'Language games, funeral games. But—the point—is—'

'Yes?'

'Death drives away what rules everywhere else, the aesthetic.'

'And without that?'

'We can't experience the present. I mean dying does—'

'It drives away—'

'Yes. Death and dying are enemies. Death is an alien voluptuous power. It's an idea that can be worked upon. By the survivors.'

Oh we shall work, thought the Count, we shall work. We shall have time then.

'Sex goes, you know. A dying man with sexual desire—that would be obscene—'

The Count said nothing. He turned again to the window and rubbed away the misty patch which his breath had made upon the glass.

'Suffering is such muck. Death is clean. And there won't be any—*lux perpetua*—how I'd hate that. Only *nox perpetua*—thank God. It's only the—*Ereignis*—'

'The—'

'That one's afraid of. Because there is—probably—a sort of event—half an event—anyway—and one does wonder—what it will be like—when it comes—'

The Count did not want to talk about this. He cleared his throat but not in time to interrupt.

'I suppose one will die as an animal. Perhaps few people die a human death. Of exhaustion, or else in some kind of trance. Let the fever run like a storm-driven ship. And in the end—there's so little of one left to vanish. All is vanity. Our breaths are numbered. I can see the imaginable number of my own—just coming—into view.'

The Count continued to stand at the window staring at the huge slow illuminated snow flakes showering steadily out of the dark. He wanted to stop Guy, to make him talk about ordinary things, and yet he felt too: perhaps this speech is precious to him, his eloquence, the last personal possession of the breaking mind. Perhaps he needs me to make possible a soliloquy which soothes his anguish. But it's too fast, too odd, I can't play with his ideas like I used to. I am dull and I can't converse, or is my silence enough? Will he want to see me tomorrow? He has banished the others. There will be a last meeting. The Count came to Ebury Street every evening now, he had given up his modest social life. Soon there would be no more tomorrows anyway. The cancer was advanced, the doctor doubted whether Guy would last till Christmas. The Count did not look that far ahead. A crisis in his own life was approaching from which he carefully, honourably averted his eyes.

Guy was still rolling his head to and fro. He was a little older than the Count, forty-three, but he seemed an old man now, the leonine look quite gone. His mane of hair had been cut, more had fallen out. His scored forehead was a dome from which all else fell away. The big head had shrunk and sharpened, accentuating his Jewish features. A glittering-eyed Rabbinical ancestor glared out through his face. Guy was half Jewish, his forebears Christianized Jews, wealthy men, Englishmen. The Count contemplated Guy's Jewish mask. The Count's father had been ferociously anti-semitic. For this, and for much else, the Count (who was Polish) did constant penance.

Trying at last to assert ordinariness the Count said, 'Are you all right for books? Can I bring you anything?'

'No, the *Odyssey* will see me out. I always thought of myself as Odysseus. Only now—I won't get back—I hope I'll have time to finish it. Though it's so awfully cruel at the end. . . . Are they coming this evening—?'

'You mean—?'

'*Les cousins et les tantes.*'

'Yes, I imagine so.'

'They flee from me that some time did me seek.'

'On the contrary,' said the Count, 'if there is anyone whom you would like to see, I can guarantee that that person would like to see you.' He had picked up from Guy a certain almost awkward precision of speech.

'No one understands Pindar. No one knows where Mozart's grave is. What does it prove that Wittgenstein never thought we'd reach the moon? If Hannibal had marched on Rome after the battle of Cannae he would have taken it. Ah well. *Poscimur.* It sounds different tonight.'

'What does?'

'The world.'

'It's snowing.'

4

'I'd like to see —'
'The snow?'
'No.'
'Manfred?'
'No.'
'It's nearly time for the nurse.'
'You're bored, Peter.'

This was the only real remark which Guy had addressed to him tonight, one of the last precious signs, in the midst of that appalling privileged monologue, of a continuing connection between them. It was almost too much for the Count, he nearly exclaimed with pity and distress. But he answered as Guy required him to do, as Guy had taught him to do. 'No. It isn't boredom. I just can't pick up your ideas, perhaps I don't want to. And not to allow you to lead the conversation — would be fearfully impolite.'

Guy acknowledged this with the quick grimace which was now his smile. He lay quiet at last, propped up. Their eyes met, then shied away from the spark of pain.

'Ah well — ah well — she shouldn't have sold the ring —'
'Who — ?'
'*En fin de compte — ça revient au même —*'
'*De s'enivrer solitairement ou de conduire les peuples.*' The Count completed the quotation, one of Guy's favourites.

'Everything's gone wrong since Aristotle, we can see why now. Liberty died with Cicero. Where's Gerald?'
'In Australia with the big telescope. Would you — ?'
'I used to believe my thoughts would wander in infinite spaces, but that was a dream. Gerald talks about the cosmos, but that's impossible, you can't talk about everything. That one knows anything at all . . . is not guaranteed . . . by the game. . . .'
'What — ?'
'Our worlds wax and wane with a difference. We belong to different tribes.'
'We have always done so,' said the Count.
'No — only now — Oh — how ill's all here. How much I wish I could —'
'Could — ?'
'See it —'
'See?'

'See it ... the whole ... of logical space ... the upper side ... of the cube. ...'

Through the door which Guy's wife Gertrude had quietly opened, the Count could see the Night Nurse sitting in the hall. She rose now and came promptly forward, smiling, a sturdy brunette with almost dusky red cheeks. She had changed her boots for slippers but still smelt of the open air and the cold. She gave out an unfocused friendliness, her fine dark eyes rather vaguely danced and twinkled, she was thinking of other things, satisfactions, plans. She tossed and patted her wavy dark hair, and had a little air of capable self-satisfaction which would have been pleasing, even reassuring, in a situation which admitted of hope. As it was there was something almost allegorically sad about her detachment from the misery that surrounded her. The Count stood aside to let her in, then raised a hand to Guy and departed. The door closed. Gertrude, who had not entered with the nurse, had already gone back to the drawing-room.

The Count, it should be explained, was not a real count. His life had been a conceptual muddle, a mistake. So had his father's life. Of remoter ancestors he knew nothing, except that his paternal grandfather, who was killed in the first war, had been a professional soldier. His parents and his elder brother Jozef, then a baby, had come to England from Poland before the second war. His father, his name was Bogdan Szczepanski, was a Marxist. His mother was a Catholic. (Her name was Maria.) The marriage was not a success.

The father's Marxism was of a peculiarly Polish variety. He grew to consciousness in a wrecked post-war Poland, drunk with independence and with having asserted its nationhood in the best possible way by smashing a Russian army outside

Warsaw in 1920. Bogdan was politically precocious, a follower of Dmowski, but an admirer of Pilsudski. His patriotism was intense, narrow and anti-semitic. He left his mother and a house full of sisters at an early age. He thought of becoming a lawyer, and was briefly a student at Warsaw University, but was soon involved in politics. (Possibly he worked as a clerk.) His hatred of Rosa Luxemburg was only second to his hatred of Bismarck. (He hated a great many people, past and present.) An early memory was of his mother saying that Rosa Luxemburg deserved to be murdered because she wanted to give Poland to the Russians. (His father, whom he could scarcely remember, had of course performed a first paternal duty by telling him that all Russians were devils.) Yet, though he never stopped hating Rosa Luxemburg (and was mildly cheered up when she eventually was murdered), some hard absolutist streak in his nature led him toward Marxism. He felt himself destined by fate to be the creator of a pure Polish Marxism. He had a cousin who was a member of the small illegal Polish Communist Party, and with whom he had fierce arguments. Although the party was not only pro-Russian but also full of beastly Jews, the youthful Bogdan was curiously drawn to it. There was an intensity, an absolute, in Marxism which attracted him. It was a 'short path'. It was idealistic, antimaterialistic, violent, and did not promise ease. Surely Poland demanded no less than such a total dedication. Yet, as he later told his son, his particular patriotism did not allow him to become a communist. He remained a furious isolated idiosyncratic Marxist, the only man who had really understood what Marxism meant to Poland.

He got married in 1936. Then Stalin intervened in his life. The Polish Communist Party had never been more than a puny inefficient instrument in the hands of the great Russian leader. Polish communists would be displeased by a Russo-German rapprochement. Besides, they were infected by the virus of patriotism, and could play no role in Stalin's plans for Poland which could not be better played by the Red Army. So, with that calm purposive clear-headed ruthlessness, so characteristic of his policies and of their success, Stalin quietly had the Polish Communist Party liquidated. Bogdan's cousin disappeared. Bogdan himself, a self-confessed maverick Marxist, an intellectual, a typical trouble-maker, was now in danger. In 1938 he arrived in England with his wife and son. In the summer of 1939 he decided to return to Poland. However events had moved too fast for him and he was incarcerated in England, to be the frenzied and miserable spectator of the subsequent fate of his country, and to be tormented ever after by the terrible guilt of not having fought on Polish soil.

The Count was born just before the war and his first awareness was that he had had a brother, but the brother was dead. The brother had been wonderful. The Count, though lesser, must be a comfort, a substitute for his exiled parents. With the dawn of consciousness the fact of exile came too. The Count's first perception was of a red and white flag. The wonderful brother had been killed in an air raid. Warsaw had been destroyed. These were the Count's first data, clearer to him almost than his parents were. Bogdan, cheated of his return home, and now, again quite illogically, an ardent admirer of Sikorski, had joined the Polish Air Force, now being formed in England under the aegis of the government-in-exile. He wanted to get into the Parachute Brigade, and dreamt of returning home from the sky as a liberator, soon to become a leading statesman in the independent post-war Poland. However he never left the ground, since a stupid training accident returned him early to civilian life. He took employment (again probably as a clerk) with the Polish government in London. Here he consumed his heart and his time in hatred of Russia (hatred of Germany was taken for granted, that was scarcely an occupation) and in vain attempts to penetrate the high-level scheming which obsessed his more powerful compatriots. He (of course) offered his services as a courier to the underground Home Army in Poland, but was refused. (The Count never doubted that his father was a very brave man who would eagerly have given his life in the service of his country.) He was able to follow in some detail (and later often rehearsed to the Count who as a child was maddeningly indifferent to the fate of the Pripet Marshes) the agonising diplomacy whereby, after Sikorski's death, Mikolajczyk attempted to please Britain by placating Stalin, without giving away Eastern Poland to Russia.

The Red Army had of course entered Poland in September 1939, as agreed with the Germans. The news that the Russians had then secretly murdered fifteen thousand Polish officers was

8

one of the shocks which Bogdan's consciousness had to with-
stand and his ability for hatred to digest in the earlier part of
the war. By this time too there were tales of how the Germans
were managing their part of Poland. In the words of the German
governor, 'the very concept *Polak* will be erased for centuries to
come, no form of Polish state will ever be reborn, Poland will
be a colony and Poles will be slaves in the German empire.'
Rage, hate, humiliation, passionate love, mortally wounded
pride so contended in Bogdan's soul that it sometimes seemed he
might die of sheer emotion. When young the Count (forced to
relive these horrors and determined not to be damaged by them)
marvelled at his father's lack of realism. Could he not see how
helpless and unimportant Poland was? How could Churchill
and Roosevelt have been expected to care about the Polish
frontier? Obviously history intended, and had always intended,
Poland to be subservient to Russia. In fact Poland had not
done too badly out of the war as far as territory was concerned.
Later, about all these things, the Count felt differently. Bogdan's
war, and in some ways perhaps his life, ended on October 3,
1944. The Warsaw Rising, the great insurrection for which all
Poles had been waiting, began on September 1, when the guns
of the Red Army were rattling the windows in the city. The Poles
in Warsaw began to fight the Germans. The Russian advance
paused. The Red Army did not cross the Vistula. The Russians
withdrew. The Soviet Air Force disappeared from the skies.
Unhindered German bombers skimmed the city roof tops.
Meagre supplies of arms were dropped by the British and
Americans. Desperate appeals for help, to Moscow, to London,
went unheeded. The Polish Underground Army fought the
Germans alone for nearly five weeks. Then they surrendered.
Two hundred thousand Poles were killed. The departing
Germans blew up what was left of Warsaw.

As a child the Count did not want to hear of these things. He
was early aware of himself as a disappointment and a substitute. He shrank away from his father's guilt and misery and
humiliated pride. He did not want to join in the endless

agonising post-mortem. (And Stalin said . . . and Churchill said . . . and Roosevelt said . . . and Eden said . . . and Sikorski said . . . and Mikolajczyk said . . . and Anders said . . . and Bor-Komorovsky said . . . and Bokszczanin said . . . and Sosnkowski said . . . and so on and so on.) While his father, who by this time had hardly anyone to talk to except his son, went on and on about the Curzon Line, the Count, whose ambition was to pass his exams and be an ordinary English Schoolboy, wrote carefully in his exercise book *Miles puellam amat. Puella militem amat.* He did not want to hear of those centuries of misery, of 'partitions' and betrayals and Teutonic Knights and what happened at Brest-Litovsk and what mistake Duke Conrad made in 1226. He would not worship Kosciuszko and Mickiewicz or even remember who they were. Worst of all, while his mother was stubbornly refusing to learn English, he was stubbornly refusing to learn Polish. (His brother Jozef had spoken excellent Polish of course.) After he went to school he uttered not another word of Polish, addressed in Polish he replied in English, then affected not to understand, then genuinely did not understand. His father gazed down at him with unspeakable pain and turned away. The tempest which raged in Bogdan's soul rarely expressed itself physically. The Count could remember a few terrible incomprehensible Polish rows, his father shouting, his mother weeping. Later his father withdrew from his wife and child and also from his London compatriots. He never spoke again of returning to Poland. His mother and sisters had disappeared during the Rising. He stayed on in England, a country whose self-interested perfidy he could not forgive. When the London Polish government (no longer the Polish government) was disbanded (some to choose exile, some to scramble back to Poland to try to gain some foothold in the new, as it soon became, Communist government), Bogdan took an office job in an English insurance firm. His idiosyncratic Marxism, unfed by any hope, had now dwindled and been succeeded by a fierce hatred of communism. He watched the events in eastern Europe with an almost spiteful pessimism. He now occupied himself with detesting Gomulka. He was momentarily cheered by the death of Stalin, but hoped nothing from the Poznan riots. He watched the Hungarian uprising and its fate with bitter envy, bitter anger. He died in

1969, having lived long enough to see Gomulka sending Polish troops to accompany the Russian tanks into Prague.

The Count passed his childhood in an ardent endeavour to be English, tormented by his father and unable to communicate with his mother. Some narrow despairing ambition took him to the London School of Economics, together with the help of a Polish Relief Fund with which his father had been connected. The Count's name was Wojciech Szczepanski. ('That's a dog's breakfast of a name,' one of his schoolteachers had kindly remarked earlier on.) The English amongst whom he lived had to put up with his surname (which was not hard to pronounce once one knew how) but refused to tolerate the bizarre consonants of his Christian name. At school he was simply called 'Big', since he was even then markedly tall. He was not unpopular, but made no friends. He was laughed at and regarded as rather picturesque. He was ashamed of his father's outlandish looks and funny accent, though a little consoled when someone said, 'Big's father is a brigand.' Of course (and to his relief) his parents never invited his school fellows home. At college someone made a joke about all Polish exiles being Counts, and thus the Count became known as 'the Count' and addressed as 'Count'. Later it emerged that he had another harmless first name, Piotr, and some few people took to calling him 'Peter' or 'Pierre', but it was then too late to unstick the familiar nickname. The Count was in fact not displeased by his honorary title; it was a little English jest which bound him to his surroundings and gave him a shred of identity. He did not even mind when strangers sometimes took him for a real count. In small ways he played the aristocrat or at least the gallant heel-clicking foreigner, never sure if this was a charade or not. For all his efforts to be English he had a slight foreign accent. And he increasingly felt, in every cell of his being, an alien. Yet his Polishness was no refuge. It was a private nightmare.

His mother died two years after his father. She pined away into an absolute solitude. How solitary she had always been the remorseful Count now began to measure when it was too late, and when she was almost dying he began to live in his love for her and her now incurably wistful love for him. He had acquired, in spite of his determination not to, some sense of the

Polish language, and now began to learn it in earnest, sitting with his grammar book beside his mother's bed and making her laugh with his pronunciation. Near the end she timidly asked if he would mind if she saw a priest. Hastening to find one the Count wept. His father had hated Christianity almost as much as he had hated Russia, and his mother had been used to creep off to mass alone. She had never taught her son any prayer, she would not have dared to. She had never suggested taking him to church, and the Count had never thought of going. Now when he would so gladly have gone with her she was bed-ridden, and when a black-clad Polish-speaking Lithuanian entered the house, he treated the Count, with a mixture of apology and pity, as an Englishman. After his mother died the Count used to sit in Roman Catholic churches and indulge an intense confused incoherent sorrow.

After the L.S.E., where he showed a considerable talent for symbolic logic and chess, ambition gave out. He took a job in market research and hated it, then drifted at a modest level into the Civil Service. His mother, now gone, had not failed to make clear how much she wanted him to get married. (The first word he remembered learning from his father was *powstanie*, insurrection. The word *dziewczyna*, girl, was later often upon his mother's lips.) But somehow the Count never seriously considered the married state. He had some scrappy luckless affairs at the L.S.E. He was too much of a puritan to enjoy promiscuity. He had, fortunately, the strength required to terminate unhappy entanglements. He made out that he preferred to be alone. He felt that he was hiding, not waiting but hiding. He had friendly acquaintances, a fairly interesting job, but he was chronically unhappy. His unhappiness was not desperate, just quiet and steady and deep. His London flat became a place of solitude, a citadel of loneliness, from which he began to assume he would never emerge.

By now it had fully dawned upon the Count how irredeemably Polish he was doomed to be. At last, sick with anticipation, indecision, fear, he went to Warsaw on a visit. He told no one of his journey. No one he knew ever wanted to talk about Poland anyway. He went as a solitary tourist. There was no family to seek for. By now Warsaw had been almost entirely rebuilt, the city centre an exact replica of what the Germans had destroyed. He was fortunate enough to be present, in a breathlessly passionately silent crowd, as the gilded dome was lifted at last into place upon the reconstructed royal palace. He stayed at a big impersonal hotel near the war memorial. He was alone, a shy eccentric Englishman with an appalling accent and a Polish name. The handsome rebuilt city was ghostly to him. (He had so often heard his father say that Warsaw had been so totally destroyed that it would have been easier to abandon the flattened ruins and build a new capital elsewhere.) And in the handsome rebuilt city he wandered like a ghost, a watchful tormented excluded ghost.

Meanwhile Gomulka had been succeeded by Gierek. (The Count's father would have hated him too.) The Polish government, which had previously regarded exiled Poles as traitors, now began sagely to woo its diaspora. The Count was amazed to receive communications with Polish stamps, periodicals in English and Polish, literary journals, questionnaires, propaganda, news. He was surprised and oddly gratified to find that they knew he existed. His father would have been alarmed, suspicious. (He felt less flattered later when he realised they could simply have searched the telephone book for Polish names.) He devoured these offerings but did not reply. There was, he felt, nothing for him at the other end, and nothing for them either. There was nothing he could do for Poland. The bureaucratic missives touched his heart, yet they were love letters sent to the wrong address. Like his father he had, in his own way, interiorised Poland, he was his own Poland, suffering alone. In spite of all his childhood resistance, his father had taught him a burning searing patriotism which flamed on, endlessly, vainly.

He spoke of this to no one, and received indeed little encouragement to do so. No one came close enough to him to suspect the intensity of this secret life. No one was really interested in his nationality or even in his nation. Was Poland invisible? He meditated often upon the *fact* that England had entered the war for the sake of Poland. (So, in a sense, had everyone. *Mourir pour Danzig?*) But in England this meant nothing now, was forgotten. It was, of course an accident of history at what point, in those terrible years, England and France decided to draw the line. Everyone seemed to think of Poland, if thinking of it at all, in a sort of mechanical diplomatic sense as part of some more general problem: as a constituent of the Austro-Hungarian empire, as one of the 'eastern democracies'. The eternal 'Polish question' was never, it appeared, really about Poland at all, but about some use to which Poland could be put or some hindrance which Poland represented in the larger designs of others. No one seemed to perceive or appreciate that unique burning flame of Polishness which though still dimmed by a ruthless neighbour continued to burn *as it had always done*.

Such reflections (and they were frequent) bred in the Count a sort of frustrated fantasy heroism, as of one cheated of his inheritance and awaiting a call to arms. He had a heroic role in the world, though he knew that it was an impossible one which he would never find. In reality, he was not a crusader. (He gave money to causes but never attended their meetings.) He felt now in a new way that he was alone with his father. Admiration and love and yearning reached out mournfully toward that shade. His father had been an exile and a thinker and a gentleman, a brave man and a patriot, a man lost, destroyed, disappointed, and laid in ruins. He had died with *finis poloniae* written upon his heart. The Count, measuring by that stature his own meagre being, soberly translated his 'heroism' into a sort of negative sense of honour. He would never die for Poland, as his father would have done if he could, gladly and without a second's hesitation. But he could avoid any baseness which might demean that memory, and could cultivate a narrow moral stiffness with which to resist the world. Such was his honour. He knew that his father had, all his life, seen himself as a soldier. The Count too saw himself as a soldier, but a very ordinary soldier with a soldier's dullness and circumscribed lot and extremely small chance of glory.

When the Count was over thirty he received a tardy promotion and moved from his obscure department to the Home Office, and here he met Guy Openshaw who was the head of his section. Guy won his heart by asking him questions. The Count was a phenomenon. Guy liked phenomena. Guy never asked quite the questions which the Count wanted, and the questioning never quite succeeded in making the Count talkative. But although it may be that Guy never entirely *saw* what was before him he did ask (which oddly enough no one, not even a woman, had done before) about the Count's childhood, his parents, his beliefs. And it was not just the precision of the questions which charmed the Count, it was the expectation of the answers, which had to be simple, direct, lucid, truthful, and uttered with a certain calm dignity. This method of questioning did elicit truth, but with an almost deliberate limitation, as if there were a definite periphery of things which Guy did *not* want to know. A less expert interrogator might, whether he liked it or not, have heard more. The Count played this game with Guy, and to some extent he played it with Gertrude, who had instinctively picked up, perhaps against her nature, some of Guy's affectionate quizzical precision. In fact the Count did tell them, just these two, some important things about himself, and thus eased his heart and was by these 'indiscretions' bound to both of them.

He had been a docile student, and an excellent examinee, and he readily fell with Guy into a relation of pupil to teacher, almost (although they were of an age) of son to father. In fact to many people in his acquaintance, Guy represented some kind of patriarch. He was a very good administrator destined (it had seemed) for the highest office. His dignity, his particular cleverness, his power were for the Count guarantees of stability, proofs of meaning. He enjoyed admiring Guy and looking up to him. He stopped playing chess with Guy because he hated (invariably) beating him. Guy did not mind, but the Count did. And so it was that he became a member of the Openshaw 'circle' and found for himself a sort of home in the big flat in Ebury Street, and through it communicated with English society, and as it sometimes seemed to him, with the cosmos.

The Count stood at attention before Gertrude Openshaw. She did not look at him. In her grief she avoided everyone's eyes, as if so much grief made her ashamed. A sort of terrible embarrassment united her and the Count. They did not display emotion to each other, there were no outbursts.

'It's snowing again, did you see?'

'Yes.'

'How was he?'

'In good form.'

'Did you have the white swan?'

'No.'

'Or "She sold the ring"?'

'Yes.'

'What's that?'

'I don't know—'

'Who—what ring—oh God. The upper side of the cube?'

'Yes.'

'What is this cube?'

'I don't know,' said the Count. 'It could be something in the presocratics.'

'Have you looked?'

'Yes. I'll look again.'

'Or about painting?'

'Could be.'

The Count, tracking Gertrude's mind, knew how appalled she was by her husband's ramblings, by the fact, which they had all had to face in the last weeks, that Guy was no longer himself. The Count, almost with cunning, had tried to console Gertrude by saying that there was something visionary and poetic in the strange things that Guy sometimes said, that they should be seen as beautiful utterances indicating some inner happiness or light. But Gertrude, who hated religion and anything 'mystical', found no ease in these conjectures. She saw Guy's irrationality as something terrifying and almost disgusting, a kind of mental incontinence. It was an additional unexpected horror. The Count soon gave up his attempts to comfort her by references to Blake. He did not really believe what he said in any case. He had come to see Guy's mild raving as something mechanical, the unpredictable failure of an electric circuit, a loose connection.

The Count, Wojciech Szczepanski, stood before Gertrude. He was tall, taller than Gertrude, taller even than Guy, and very thin. He had a pale thin face, very light blue eyes, and straight colourless fair hair. He had the hard keen Slav face of his race, so unlike the solider more sensual Russian face. He looked like a chess player, a symbolic logician, a breaker of codes. His mouth was thin and clever. Yet he had also a timid diffident look, always a little questioning, even bewildered. He still seemed boyish, although his dry pallid face often looked gaunt, tired, no longer young.

Gertrude (née McCluskie), in her late thirties, was a handsome woman. Age, which draws down curtains of skin about the eyes and pokes holes in the brow, had scarcely touched her yet. She was of medium height, a little inclined to plumpness, with fine radiantly clear brown eyes which gazed at the world with a kind of happy authority. Her olive-golden complexion was like a pleasant sun-tan, and her longish faintly curling hair, a dark rich ochre brown, fell about in a neat copious friendly disorder. She dressed intelligently, austerely rather than smartly, and to please her husband. Guy's 'formative influence' in their married love was discreetly admitted by Gertrude, while at the same time she announced herself as a woman not easily dominated. She was half Scottish half English. Both her parents had been school-teachers, and after a successful college career she entered the same profession. After her marriage (she met Guy, who was then in the Department of Education, at a conference) she continued teaching for several years. She and Guy were childless. There had been a miscarriage, then the doctors had told her she could not have children. It was at this time, and feeling that Guy needed her presence at home, that she gave up her work.

'Did he sleep well?' asked the Count. He always asked this. There were few questions left to be asked about Guy's health.

'Oh yes—yes—nothing in the night.'

There was a now-familiar sound in the hall which was the Night Nurse opening the bedroom door to indicate that Mrs. Openshaw might now come in and see her husband.

Gertrude said, 'Count, you will stay for Visiting Hour, won't you, for *les cousins et les tantes?*'

Guy had a strong sense of family (his father had been one of six children), reinforced perhaps by his frustrated paternal instincts. He was a natural *pater familias* and would have been a dedicated probably rather strict parent. As it was, it was his fancy to gather his family, including its remoter camp followers, together into a little band under his benevolent supervision. In this picture of his life, his friends too had to figure as family. Thus it was that the Count had become a sort of honorary cousin. This small heterogeneous group of 'connections' Guy treated with a mixture of responsible concern and casual superiority. He referred to them collectively, in French for some reason, as *les cousins et les tantes*. He was a thoroughly kind and generous man, but his 'superiority' was not unconnected with money. The Christianised Openshaws (perhaps originally Oppenheims or some such) were a banking family, and accustomed to play the responsible role of rich relations among poor relations.

'Of course I'll stay for Visiting Hour. I've brought a book.'

'Proust? Gibbon? Thucydides?' Gertrude knew his tastes.

'No, Carlyle.'

The Openshaws had kept, in the old-fashioned tradition, a 'day' for visitors, when their London friends and relations were expected to drop in for a drink on the way home from the office. These informal gatherings had come to be, for the Count, the most enjoyable part of his exiguous social world. This was indeed the first time in his life when he had known and been known in anything which resembled a family group. When Guy had first become ill, but not yet hopelessly ill, *les cousins et les tantes* had taken to calling in briefly on other days to ask how he was. As the cancer declared itself, the number of visitors diminished, and only an inner circle of intimates continued to call, a few dropping in every evening to say hello to the sick man. Guy had, it seemed, enjoyed these visits. Of late however he had lost interest in company. The nurses and the doctor (who was a real cousin) advised against 'tiring' him. And the Count suspected that Gertrude wanted to conceal her husband, not to exhibit him in his enfeebled state to the sympathetic but necessarily curious gaze of those who in their role as clients and clansmen had so long regarded him with reverence. But to discontinue the visits would have been to announce the end. The 'family' continued to turn up for Gertrude's sake, and though she kept them away from Guy and affected to regard them as a 'nuisance' she was really not ungrateful for this show of support.

In fact the only person whom Guy really still wanted to talk to was the Count. The Count became aware of his privileged status with mixed feelings. He would in many ways, since it had to be, have preferred to say an earlier easier farewell. This long sojourn with Guy in the ante-room of death was a dangerous matter. Something terrible, painful, eternally memorable could happen. Years ago, when he was first admitted by Guy into the charmed circle of friendship, he had been haunted by the fear that it was his fate to be scrutinised and dropped. There was, behind Guy's suave superiority, something demonic, something which could be cruel. Later the Count saw Guy more as one who could be cruel but never was. Demonic he might be, but he was also dutiful. A strong sense of duty, of the cast-iron necessity of decent behaviour, was a positive characteristic of both Guy and Gertrude, something which, when you knew them well, was as evident in them as the colour of their hair and eyes. Also, as time went by, the Count, for all his diffidence, came to believe in Guy's affection for him, although he knew too that this affection was mixed with a kind of intelligent pity. So now, as he found himself the last one left, the only person besides Gertrude herself who regularly talked to Guy, he felt a mixture of gratification and pain. Of course he prized this remarkable sign of trust. But it came too late. And he could not help feeling that Guy, and Gertrude too, tolerated him at or near the end because 'it did not matter what the Count thought or said'. He was in the dying man's room as his dog might be. The Count brooded on this. Sometimes he read it as contempt, sometimes as a vast compliment.

The evening visitors, the 'intimates' that is, although excluded from Guy, continued to turn up. Every evening now a small number of persons arrived, the same or varying slightly, to ask after Guy, to leave messages, books, flowers, and to talk to Gertrude and give her comfort and the assurance of being surrounded. They accepted drinks, talked in muted voices, did not stay long, but the little ceremony had its importance. The Count could not help noticing that some of them could almost be said to enjoy it.

'All right,' said Gertrude, 'I'll just go in now and see Guy.'

The Count sat down on an upright chair near to the fireplace, where a fire of wood and coalite was burning in honour of the snow. He knew this room very well, better almost than the featureless rooms of his own small flat where there was so little of formal significance to attract the eye or the mind. He felt *safe* in the Openshaws' drawing-room. It was large, glowing with colour, and, in the Count's judgement, perfect. There was nothing large or small which he could have desired to change, or to move by as much as a millimetre. And indeed in the years during which he had known it the fine room had not altered at all. The only item that changed was the flowers, and they were always in the same place on the marquetry table beside the drinks. The Count marvelled at Gertrude's will even now to arrange flowers. In a large green vase she had artfully deployed eucalyptus and beech leaves with some white chrysanthemums donated by Janet Openshaw. (There were other flower donations out in the hall: not in Guy's room. Guy thought flowers should be kept in their place.) Guy and Gertrude had, perhaps, worked hard to make a beautiful room, succeeded, and had been content. They were not collectors, and indeed not very seriously interested in the visual arts, but had, for these purposes, 'good taste'.

The Count stretched out his long legs, ruckling up a silky faded golden rug which was covered with a very minute geometrical design. He opened his book, Carlyle's life of Frederic the Great. He was reading about the ridiculous relation between Frederic and Voltaire. This amused him because he hated Voltaire, about whom he and Guy differed. The Count identified himself with Rousseau, although he would have been at a loss to say exactly why. Of course the Count hated Frederic too (his hatreds were abstract compared with those of his father), but there was something about Carlyle's view of the world which appealed to him all the same.

'Would you like anything?'

'No, thank you.'

'Tea, fruit juice?'

'No.'

'Nurse asked about supper. Do you want anything special?'

'Just soup.'

'You wouldn't like to see anyone tonight? Manfred?'

'No.'

'Would you like any of your books from next door?'

'I've got books here.'

'I wish I could do something, bring you something.'

'Don't worry, I'm fine.'

'It's snowing again.'

'So Peter said.'

Gertrude and Guy looked at each other, then looked away.

Gertrude had spoken to no one about the way in which her relationship with Guy had now simply broken down. This was as terrible to her as the event of his death which it remained for her to live through. It was, in a way, his death, its true beginning, his death to her, the breaking of the bond of consciousness. There was a nightmarish barrier between them through which neither of them could pass. Guy had ceased even to try. He gazed at her with remote brooding preoccupied eyes. He could talk to the Count, but not to her. When he did talk he often rambled and said the strange things which frightened her so: that fine clear mind in whose *light* she had lived become helplessly confused and darkened. Perhaps he was silent because he feared to affright her. Or perhaps abhorred this final loss of face before his wife, this unspeakable defeat at the hands of fate. Or would not feed a love which was so soon to be transmuted, he to sleep, she to mourn.

They had always been very close to each other, united by indistinguishably close bonds of love and intelligence. They had never ceased passionately to crave each other's company. They had never seriously quarrelled, never been parted, never doubted each other's complete honesty. A style of directness and truthfulness composed the particular gaiety of their lives. Their love had grown, nourished daily by the liveliness of their shared thoughts. They had grown together in mind and body and soul as it is sometimes blessedly given to two people to do. They could not be in the same room without touching each other. They constantly uttered even their most trivial thoughts. Their converse passed through wit. Jest and reflection had been the language of their love. I shall die without him, thought Gertrude, not suicide, but I shall just have no more life. I shall be a dead person walking about.

Certain subjects the instincts of their affections made taboo. They never spoke later of the lost child. And (this was somehow connected) they never had any pet animal, a dog or a cat. Certain sweet and touching things had to be avoided. It was as if the mesh of their tenderness must not be made too fine if they were to avoid agony. Though they were playfully and demonstrably loving together they kept a rein upon certain runs or courses of sentiment. Their language was chaste and there was a reticent dignity in their love.

Of course they had always been very frank with each other and had lived their marriage as a mutual transference. They confessed to each other and redeemed each other. They discussed their past adventures and their present thoughts, their faults, their mistakes, their sins, always tactfully, always wittily, without self-indulgent gloating. They preserved consciously between them a certain modesty and innocence, an awareness of their luck and a determination to be innocuously happy.

Both had been, in different ways, fortunate spoilt children. Guy was the doted-upon only child of wealthy clever parents. Gertrude, also an only child, the great beloved of her father, had been the late offspring of practical busy public-spirited school teachers. Gertrude's father had taught her that she was a princess in the world. He had also taught her to love books and work hard, and to enjoy the things of the intellect without worrying too much about being an 'intellectual'. Her parents died before her marriage, but had the pleasure of seeing their splendid daughter become a very able teacher. Guy's mother never knew Gertrude, but his father lived long enough to bless his son's marriage. He approved of Gertrude, though he would have preferred a Jewish girl, having secretly returned in his heart to the faith of his ancestors. (He never of course revealed this shocking frailty to Guy, who despised all religion.) He grieved bitterly over the lost grandchild. About further progeny he never asked. He died soon afterwards. Guy was frighteningly upset.

Gertrude and Guy took it for granted that they would always be useful and busy. They were versatile, still young, and constantly thought that they might do 'all sorts of things' in the future. There were books to be written, skills to be learnt, intellectual heights to be scaled. They travelled a little, but not very much because Guy wanted to use his holidays for studying. As the years passed he had never settled it with himself whether he were not a scholar rather than an administrator. He became determined at any rate to be a scholar too, and began work on a book about justice, punishment and the criminal law. Gertrude had studied history at Cambridge. Guy had studied classics and philosophy at Oxford and always felt a sort of lingering irritable interest in the latter subject. When she stopped teaching Gertrude had intended to write a novel, but was soon dissuaded by Guy, and of course she came to agree. Did the world need yet another mediocre novel? For a while she employed herself as Guy's research assistant. She learnt German. She considered going into politics (they were both left wing). Just lately she had begun to teach English to Asian immigrants. There was no worry, no anxiety. There was plenty to do. Time passed, but there was always plenty of time.

But now time had gone mad. Guy's illness seemed to be carrying him through the stages of life toward old age before her eyes. Gradually the dimension of the future disappeared from their converse with each other. Gertrude, at a certain stage, stopped saying, 'You'll feel better in the spring.' She had never said, 'There is no cure.' Nor had the doctor. When she asked him if he had told Guy, he said, 'He knows.' When did he begin to know? There had been some hopeful treatment. Their eyes rarely met now. And what was most terrible to Gertrude, the little rituals of tenderness were gone from their lives. She did not dare now to take his hand. When she massaged his terrible thin cramp-ridden aching legs she did so as a nurse. In her avoidance of any word, any gesture which might cause them to weep, Gertrude felt that she must seem to him at times almost cold, as if she just heartily wished it was all over; and there were times when she did wish it was all over and that his suffering had ceased, cleaned away by death. If only she could unavoidably break down; but no, she was strong and would not break down. There was nowhere for her tormented love to run to and no expression which it could find. Yet the discipline of their happy life together divided them now perhaps mercifully, and she hoped and prayed that Guy too understood that mercy. If they were to start to cry and wail over the unspeakable cruelty of it all they would run mad with pain.

And Gertrude did not too often cry. Later, in that other time, she felt that she would cry forever. Now when she shed tears in private she washed her face and powdered it well. It's like a concentration camp, she thought. You cannot show your suffering for fear that worse befall. It did indeed seem like a concentration camp to her, a condition of horror which could not have been anticipated and which the imagination could not conceive of enduring, and which yet was endured, there being no alternative. She saw the beloved head change, and already she was ceasing to compare the past with the present. She watched without screaming while his beauty was destroyed and the kind, just, witty radiance of his mind was quenched. Surely there was no logic left in the world any more if Guy could ramble and forget.

Perhaps he hates me, she thought, perhaps that's what it is, resentment, revenge. Sometimes he was so curt, so irritable, so impatient. How can the dying not hate the living, the survivors? There was no way now to find out what he felt, no question she could frame or ask which would not set something terrible quivering in the room. She could not ask him about the upper side of the cube or the white swan. She could not ask him about the pain. Sometimes the nurse gave him pain-killing injections during the night. She tried not to think about the pain, but it was there, huge, in the room, as death also was in the room, and the two moved above the figure in the bed like two black clouds, sometimes separate, sometimes merging.

Well, thought Gertrude, if he hates the universe, if he hates God, as well he may, let him hate God in me if it will ease his anguish. Her love spoke thus, but it too was rambling and lost in the dark.

Manfred put his head round the drawing-room door. 'Hello, Count, all alone?'

'Hello, Manfred,' said the Count jumping up, 'Gertrude is in with Guy.'

'I could do with a drink,' said Manfred, 'I've had an awful day, and my God it's cold outside.' He helped himself from the tray on the marquetry table. Manfred North (his parents had been devotees of Byron) worked in the family bank. He was a second cousin of Guy.

The Openshaw's drawing-room (where the Count felt so safe) was a long room with three tall windows giving onto Ebury Street. It was elegant and snug, with a variety of handsome but fairly comfortable chairs placed at certain distances from the fire-place and facing towards it. Upon the plain carpet, the colour of Gertrude's hair, there were two good rugs, one the silky-gold one with the minute mathematical pattern which the Count had been scuffing with his feet, the other a long beautiful thing covered with graceful animals and trees, which ran along below the windows making a sort of privileged promenade. The wide marble mantelshelf was an altar upon which stood, at each end, Bohemian glass vases, red and amber and in the centre a most ingenious orchestra of china monkeys, playing different instruments, ranged in a semi-circle. These, and other bibelots elsewhere in the room, were religiously dusted with a feather duster by Gertrude's char, Mrs Parfitt, but never moved. The Count once experienced holy fear and indignation when he saw a guest idly pick up the china drummer and actually hold him in his hand while making a point. Oil paintings, some of ancestors, adorned the walls. Over the fire-place in an oval frame was a pretty picture of Guy's paternal grandmother, a small dark woman, her eager attractive smiling face peering from under her dark hair, and charmingly shadowed by a white parasol. Her family were orthodox Jews and opposed her marriage to Guy's grandfather. They gave in at last since he was Jewish and though 'officially' Christian had fervently declared himself an atheist. She in turn had disapproved of Guy's father's marriage to a goy girl, even though the bride had money and played the violin. However when the adored grandson arrived she relented. Other pictures represented powerful gentlemen, houses, possessions, dogs. Unfortunately few of these pictures displayed much aesthetic merit. (The charming little Sargent was an exception.) The Openshaws were a musical family who had produced (though not in Guy) quite a lot of performing talent. Uncle Rudi, who played the 'cello, had also been an amateur composer of some note. Where painters were concerned however they had unerringly preferred the second-rate.

'How's the office?' said Manfred. He was a tall man, taller even than the Count (the Count was six foot one, Manfred six foot three) and sturdily built, a big animal. His large bland face, which always seemed to express some superior secret merriment, looked down upon the world. Manfred's parents had returned, not unaggressively to orthodox Judaism, but Manfred cared for none of these things. In his late thirties and still unmarried, he was rated a successful man. The Count liked him, but was intensely irritated by the way in which he made himself at home in the Openshaw's flat. The Count would have liked a drink too, but was certainly not going to take one until it was offered to him by Gertrude.

'The office—oh all right.' What could he say? The office was nothing. He missed Guy there, missed him intensely, but he was not going to say that to Manfred. Nothing personal had ever passed between them. But Manfred liked the Count, he was not an enemy.

'Won't you have a drink?' said Manfred. This was mischief on Manfred's part.

'No, thank you.'

Stanley Openshaw came in. (Gertrude always left the doors open at Visiting Hour so that no one had to ring.) Stanley was Guy's first cousin. He had also married a goy girl, but was deemed to have gone too far in positively embracing Anglican Christianity, the faith of his wife. (Gertrude, like Guy, held no religious belief, unless hatred of religion could count as one.) He was a Member of Parliament, of the right wing Labour persuasion. He was a diligent kindly man, loved by his constituents (he had a London seat) but never likely to reach Cabinet rank. His wife Janet, an economist, was thought to be cleverer. She sometimes visited at Ebury Street, but did not get on very well with Gertrude. (Janet was such a good cook that Gertrude had early decided not to compete. Fortunately Guy scarcely noticed what he ate.) In spite of having one eye rather larger than the other Stanley was handsome, with Guy's leonine head. There were three handsome children all doing well in their studies.

'Hello, Stanley. Not at the House this evening?'

'No, but I can't stay long, I've got a surgery.' On 'surgery' nights Stanley would sit on till the small hours hearing the woes of his constituents.

'You love trouble,' said Manfred.

'Any sort of trouble interests me,' said Stanley. 'It presents problems. I cannot claim any moral merit.'

'I should hope not!'

'I only hope my car will start again.'

'Ed Roper has put chains on his.'

'He would.' (Ed Roper, an 'honorary' cousin, was in the art business.) 'Any Guy news, Count?'

'Nothing new,' said the Count. 'Gertrude's with him now.'

'I wonder if Gertrude will sell the French house?' said Stanley, helping himself to a drink. 'I wouldn't mind buying it.'

The Count resented the perfunctory enquiries, the detachment, the casual almost 'party' atmosphere. And yet how could they behave? They paraded for Gertrude, they brought her a whiff of continuing ordinariness which perhaps helped her more than the Count's sombre gravity. Stanley at least lowered his voice. Manfred's loud tones were harder to muffle.

'Hello, Veronica.'

'It's snowing like anything.'

'Oddly enough, we noticed.'

'Well, you two came in your motor cars. I walked.'

'I'll give you a lift back.'

'Thanks, Manfred. I left my boots in the hall, I brought these slippers in my bag, like we used to at children's parties. Hello, Count, I suppose Gertrude is with Guy. Oh a drink, thank you, Stanley dear.'

Veronica Mount (née Ginzburg), a widow, belonged to the older generation. She was Jewish, connected with Guy's family by marriage, and had early set herself up as an 'Openshaw expert'. She knew the family tree for ever so far back, as to its remoter origins in Germany, Poland and Russia, and exactly how everyone was related to everyone else. Her husband, Joseph Mount, long dead, was something to do with violins. Mrs Mount was a cultivated woman who lived in modest gentility, some said in poverty, in nearby Pimlico.

The Count said good evening. He always felt that Mrs Mount was mocking him a little, but perhaps that was an illusion.

'And here's Tim.'

'Hello, Tim.'

Tim Reede, a weedy young man, had come into the family picture, no one could quite remember how, as a protégé of Uncle Rudi. He was said to be a painter or something. He helped himself to a drink.

'I suppose there'll be a spring election? You needn't worry, Stanley, your seat is forever.'

'Anything can happen these days. One has a deep fear of rejection.'

'Haven't we all,' said Mrs Mount.

'Talking of elections, I've got a spare ticket for *Turandot*, anyone like it, Veronica?'

'Manfred is so kind, as always.'

'I know the Count doesn't want it, he hates music.'

'I don't—'

'Did you see Gertrude?' said Mrs Mount to the Count. She always spoke softly and had no need to lower her voice. 'How is she standing the strain?'

'Yes, how is Gertrude?'

'Oh she's—wonderful,' said the Count.

'Yes, she is wonderful, isn't she.'

'She needs her friends, she will need her friends, such a tragic business.'

'She needs us as an audience to keep her up.'

'Why, Sylvia.'

Sylvia Wicks (née Oppenheim) was a remote cousin, only Mrs Mount knew how remote. Yet Sylvia, once very pretty, bore a strange resemblance to the dark-haired grandmother with the parasol. Sylvia in middle age looked dishevelled, her dark locks, through which she peered out at the world, hanging in untidy strings round her face. However she still dressed well.

'Long time no see, Sylvia,' said Manfred.

'Tim, give Sylvia a drink.'

'What a pretty dress. Are your feet soaked, dear?'

'What an awful night.'

A tempest was raging inside the head of Sylvia Wicks. She had always been unlucky, only now it was more like being doomed. Her parents died when she was a small child and she was brought up by a resentful aunt who gave her no education but did at least leave her a little money. With this Sylvia bought some good clothes and a house. She took a lodger. He was Oliver Wicks. They got married. They sold the house and bought another one in Oliver's name. Sylvia ended up with no money and no house and no husband, and a two year old child. She also had the clothes and had been wearing them ever since (she was a clever needlewoman). She was never quite sure how it all happened. She was so glad to get rid of Oliver that she never went into the matter, and she was too ashamed to tell the family of Oliver's crimes. Moses Greenberg, the family solicitor (he had married one of her cousins), found out however and was very angry with her. (He wanted to pursue the delinquent Wicks.) Sylvia, then living on National Assistance in cheap lodgings with her son Paul, was angry back. It was too much to be chided when she was so unfortunate. Moses told Guy, who summoned her. He did not lecture her about the past (which was by now an inextricable muddle best left alone) but urged her to learn a skill. Sylvia took a typing and shorthand course at Guy's expense. Guy also took a financial interest in Paul's education. Sylvia, who was in some respects no fool, found herself a series of quite well-paid secretarial jobs. She was saving up to buy a flat. Paul was now seventeen and she yearned for him to have a decent room where he could keep books. Guy, who kept in touch with Sylvia intermittently, lent her the money which she still needed. This had happened quite recently. However (it was almost incredible) before Sylvia had got round to buying the flat someone had swindled her out of all this money too, a woman 'friend' who persuaded her to invest it in a boutique. The money was gone, the woman was gone, and again

Sylvia could not make out how it had happened. Again she told no one. She dreaded an enquiry from Guy or from Gertrude about the purchase of the flat. And now Guy was dying. Did that mean she kept the money? Only there was no money. Her head was spinning. But as if all that were not enough she had just, three days ago, learnt that Paul had made a girl of sixteen pregnant. The girl's father, angry, frenzied, had been to see her. When she had spoken of an abortion the father, who was a Roman Catholic, had shouted did she want two young people to start their lives with a murder on their conscience? However the father did not know what to do any more than she did. He would not let her see the girl. She would not let him see Paul. Maddened by his shouts she hinted that the girl was a little minx who had seduced her son. The father became almost violent and threatened to have Paul put in prison. 'I'll ruin you, I'll ruin you!' he screamed distraught while Paul was listening in the next room. Paul had stopped going to school. She had stopped going to the office. Paul would miss his exams. She had lost her job. She decided the only thing to do was to tell everything to Guy, including the episode of the boutique which now seemed a minor matter. Guy would know what to do, Guy would know the law, he would know what people usually did in such cases, he would get her and Paul out of it somehow. She knew that Guy was very ill, but she thought that even a short talk with him would give her some key to the situation. She hoped too that Guy would tell her she need not repay the money. She could not repay it anyway. All her savings had gone together with his loan. Did Gertrude know about the loan? (In fact she did not, Guy had told no one.) What should she say to Gertrude? She was a bit afraid of Gertrude, some people were. Meanwhile Paul was sitting at home crying. She smiled, holding her glass, as she stood with Stanley and Manfred and Mrs Mount. What one can hide inside one's head and smile.

'Balintoy is ski-ing in Colorado,' said Mrs Mount, 'or shall we say après ski-ing.'

'While we toil,' said Manfred.

'I bet he's staying at the Brown Palace Hotel,' said Stanley. 'He is.'

'Where does he get the money?'

'Balintoy gives ski-ing bursaries to poor boys.'

'How kind of him.'

'Sylvia says how kind of him!'

'We'll be ski-ing here soon if this goes on.'

Balintoy was a Lord, a real one, not like the Count. 'Just a mouldy Irish peerage,' as Manfred put it. His mother, a relation of Janet Openshaw, still lived in a crumbling castle in County Mayo. Stanley and Guy had taken up young (now not so young) Balintoy. Guy and Gertrude had stayed at the castle once.

'He wrote to Gerald Pavitt.'

'I'm jealous.'

'How is Gerald these days?'

'Manic.'

The Count, leaning against the mantelpiece, was watching the door for Gertrude. He badly wanted a drink. And he wanted to see her return from Guy's room with a calm countenance.

'Tim, dear boy, could you get me another drink?'

'Certainly, Stanley, what's your poison?'

Gertrude came in. The Count saw across the room her mask of tired pain, the screwed-up eyes, the terrible *concentration*. Then came the calmness he needed to see. She was smiling at Sylvia and Mrs Mount. Everyone fell silent and moved towards her.

'Victor has just gone in,' she said.

Victor Schultz, bald and handsome, was Guy's doctor, also his cousin, a pleasant unambitious general practitioner with a passion for golf. He had married a famous beauty of pre-eminent silliness, and was now divorced.

'How is Guy?' said Manfred, his big face looking down, solemn and gentle. Someone had to ask this question. Manfred usually took it on.

'Oh—you know—the same— Count, you haven't got a drink, do take one.'

The Count hoped that his politeness did not go unnoticed.

Tim Reede, having brought Stanley his drink, said to Gertrude, 'I wonder if there are any of those cheese biscuits in the kitchen? I was painting all through lunch and I could do with a snack.'

'Oh, yes, Tim, do go and help yourself to anything.'

'I suppose Guy doesn't want to see me, no,' Manfred said wistfully half to himself.

Mrs Mount began to question Gertrude about the efficiency of the nurses and how much they cost.

Stanley asked Sylvia politely how Paul was getting on at school.

'Oh,' she said, 'fine, he's expected to do well in his exams.'

'That's splendid. You know William has just gone up to Balliol? And Ned is turning out to be quite a mathematical genius, he gets it from Janet of course.'

'And how is Rosalind? Still mad about ponies?'

'I'm afraid so, but her music is gaining ground. Do you know, I think that little girl is the cleverest of the lot!'

'Of course you used to play the flute, usen't you, Stanley?'

'I gave it up. What would Uncle Rudi say?'

Victor Schultz came in with a bright grave face. He patted Gertrude on the shoulder, using his professional manner. He accepted a drink. He had a cheerful temperament and, once rid of the famous beauty, had resumed his youthful insouciance. He was fond of Guy, but when he became a doctor had made a pact with himself to survive by rejoicing with others but grieving with them moderately. He was soon smiling.

Mrs Mount said, 'Victor, I've just been talking to Gertrude about the nurses. I wonder if you could advise me. A friend of mine has this aged parent—'

Stanley was saying that he really must get to his surgery.

Sylvia had managed to sidle up to Gertrude. 'Gertrude, I wonder if—'

'Veronica, do you want a lift?' said Manfred.

Gertrude said to Stanley, 'Thank you so much for coming. Give my love to Janet. Tell her how lovely her chrysanthemums are looking.'

Sylvia said, 'Gertrude, I wonder if I could possibly see Guy.'

There was a moment's silence then, embarrassed, the guests began to talk again among themselves.

Gertrude flushed. Then a look of strain, almost of anger, wrenched her face, her mouth and eyes. 'Well, no, he's very— He can't see anyone.'

'I'd only want to see him for a few minutes. I wanted to ask him something.'

'No, I'm sorry, you can't see Guy—he's very ill—he can't

see people—any more—' She put her hands to her eyes as if to prevent tears.

'Drat the girl,' said Stanley to Manfred at the doorway, 'has she no tact, no sense? Poor Gertrude—'

'I'd only need a few minutes with him,' said Sylvia, near to tears herself.

'No—'

'I must go,' said Stanley.

'I think we should all go,' said Mrs Mount. 'Manfred?'

'Who's got cars?' said Gertrude. 'It's such an awful night.'

'I have, and Stanley,' said Manfred.

'And me,' said Victor.

'Who goes which way? You're going with Manfred, Veronica?'

'I can take Sylvia,' said Stanley. 'Come along, Sylvia. I'll drop you at the tube.'

'I'm sorry—but please understand—' said Gertrude to Sylvia.

'I'll take the Count,' said Victor, 'he's on my way.'

'Thank you all for coming—you know it means a lot—to both of us—'

'And Tim,—where's Tim? You can go with Stanley too, that's right, isn't it?'

Shushed to silence by Stanley they went into the hall and tiptoed to find their coats. There was a smell of wet wool, and the melted snow had made a dark mark upon the carpet. Mrs Mount sat down to pull on her boots. They filed out of the front door one by one. Stanley and Mrs Mount kissed Gertrude.

The drawing-room was empty. Gertrude came in and closed the door. She went and pulled back the curtains a little at one of the windows. It was still snowing. She heard the cheerful voices below as her guests packed into the three cars.

The Count would have liked to stay on after the others and

talk to Gertrude alone, but he feared to displease her or to draw attention to himself. The Count had been in love with Gertrude for years. Of course no one knew this.

He allowed himself to be hustled out and into Victor's car, but he soon made an excuse and asked to be set down. He wanted to walk home by himself through the snow. He bought some chestnuts from a man with a brazier. The stand with the glowing coals looked like a little god in a shrine. The snow was still falling but more slowly. The pavements were white, the roads were moraines of dark tossed snow and slush where the cars hissed cautiously past. Guy had been right to say that the world sounded different. There was no wind, and the large flakes fell solemnly, purposively, as if just released from a huge hand held close above the light of the street lamps. Railings and the bowed-down branches of shrubs in gardens were piled high with glistening crystalline structures. The Count was wearing a woollen cap which Gertrude used to laugh at. He adjusted his scarf and turned up the collar of his overcoat, and as he strode along with his long legs he felt warm.

The Count lived in a featureless block of flats in the no-man's-land between the King's Road and the Fulham Road, and he had not very far to walk. He had eaten some of his chestnuts and carefully put the charred shells away in his pocket. He went up in the lift and along a corridor, past many silent doors, to reach his own flat. He knew his neighbours amicably but very slightly. He let himself in and turned on the light, his face glowing with the change of temperature. His flat had two small bedrooms and a living-room which could have been pleasant only the Count had no sense of the visual world, and no social obligation to exhibit 'good taste'. He very rarely invited any guest. Dark green metal bookshelves covered three walls. On the third wall there was, above a shiny modern sideboard, a print of Warsaw. The Count had very few mementos from his childhood home, and none of them on view. He had a misty brown photo of his parents when they were first married, two staring youthful almost childish faces. He also had a Polish flag, perhaps the one which had formed his first perception. He kept the flag rolled up at the bottom of a drawer. His hand, questing for something else, touched it sometimes. There had been other Polish things which his mother, in her last illness, had given

34

away to an old Polish lady who used to visit her. His mother did not think that her son would want 'that old stuff'. The Count remembered this with shame.

He turned on the radio. He hated television. He lived in a radio world. He listened to everything, news, talks, plays (especially thrillers), political discussions, philosophical discussions, nature programmes, proms, symphony concerts, opera, the Archers, Woman's Hour, A Hundred Best Tunes, Desert Island Discs, On Your Farm, Any Questions, Any Answers. At some times of year the steadily changing weekly copies of the *Radio Times* seemed the most evident movement of his life's clock. Manfred had teased him by saying that he hated music, it was not true. He would never have gone near a concert hall. (They had stopped offering him tickets.) But he loved music although he had little conception of what it was. (He had had to have it pointed out to him by Gerald that church bells rang changes, not a continuous simple scale.) Ignorant though he was, he listened and was, like Caliban, enchanted. The terrible slow tenderness of some classical music seemed to him like the flowing of his own consciousness. He had his favourite composers too, he liked Mozart and Beethoven and Bruckner. He also got it into his head that he liked Delius because his music sounded English. (He was unwise enough to say this once to Guy, who asked him sarcastically what on earth he meant. The Count could not say, but he went on thinking so all the same.) He liked songs too, rousing memorable ones like *The Road to Mandalay*, or else sentimental ones which brought tears to his eyes like *Oh That We Two Were Maying*. Often of course he read while the radio rambled on, read his beloved Proust and Thucydides and Condorcet and Gibbon and Saint-Simon and Rousseau's *Confessions*. He did not read much poetry but cherished a narrow affection for Horace, salvaged from the days of *miles puellam amat*. (This was a taste which he shared with Guy.) He liked a few novelists (he scarcely counted Proust as a novelist, that was more like reading memoirs): Balzac, Turgenev, Stendhal. He had a secret weakness for Trollope and also liked *War and Peace*. At intervals he obsessively read Conrad, looking for some Polish clue which always eluded him. (His father had hated Conrad whom he regarded as a frivolous renegade.) So, mostly, he spent his evenings until he was sent to bed by the final gale warnings. He thought then of the island on which he lived. He thought of the dark vast sea. He thought of lonely men elsewhere who were listening to these warnings, solitary wireless operators on tossing ships, farmers and their dogs sitting in kitchens in the stormy fens. Attention all shipping. Here is a gale warning. Clyde, Humber, Thames, South east gale force nine, increasing force ten, imminent. Imminent, imminent. Biscay, Trafalgar, Finisterre. Cromarty, Faroes, Fair Isle. Solway, Tyne, Dogger. Imminent.

There is a gulf fixed between those who can sleep and those who cannot. It is one of the great divisions of the human race. Sleep was a problem to the Count. He was well capable of being cheerful, but the possibility of great unhappiness travelled always with him. He never (as Gerald Pavitt did) actually feared madness, but he knew that if he did not tend himself he could fall into a pit of crippling misery. Sleeplessness and night terrors were then greatly to be feared. He wanted the darkness of death-like sleep, even the hurly-burly of bad dreams, any-thing rather than an active idle consciousness. He would not use pills for fear of addiction. Balintoy had suggested to him a somniferent method which he adopted sometimes, although it could prove a mixed blessing. The Count imagined himself upon a road, or in a garden, or inside a large house, and then began to move (it was not quite like walking) along the road, round the corner, through the garden to a gate where another garden opened, along a grass path to some trees, through the trees, across a field, from room to room, across a hall, up the stairs, along a gallery . . . and so to sleep. But what was happen-ing? The rooms had grown dark, they were full of frightened people, the walls were shuddering with shell-fire, there were no doors, only holes in the walls torn by dynamite, through which the fugitives escaped from house to house, from street to street, until now there is the night lit by bursting shells, a jump in the dark onto bricks and rubble, a wide avenue to be crossed raked with bullets, nowhere to go, no food, no water, the enemy ever nearer, nearer. . . . Sometimes he dreamed of calmer scenes, Warsaw empty, very beautiful, rebuilt or never harmed, a magic city, a city of palaces, sinister. He saw as a place of destiny, perhaps of doom, the pillared war memorial, the grave where the fire ever burns, the sentries at attention day and night, the echoing goose-step of the relieving guard. The Count stands in the dark, glances shyly at the expressionless faces of the soldiers, glimpses upon the pillars the list of Polish battle honours, Madrid, Guadalajara, Ebro. Westerplatte, Kutno, Tomaszov. Narvik, Tobruk, Monte Cassino, Arnhem. Bitwaoo Anglie. Lenino, Warszawa, Gdansk. Rothenburg, Drezno, Berlin. Or is he back in London, beside the eagle-crowned column at Northolt, remembering the Polish airmen who died for Poland, who died for England? His father's squadron 303 Kosciusko, best of all in the Polish air force. City of Lwow, city of Krakow, city of Warszawa. Battle of Britain, Battle of the Atlantic, Dieppe, Western Desert, Italy, France, Belgium, Holland, Germany. His father and his brother are putting on their helmets and their parachutes and climbing into their Spitfires. And the Count wants to go with them, only there are pillars and more pillars, broken pillars, shattered columns in a ruined city, and on each there is a list of battles, gallant battles, gallant defeats, and now he is seeing, stretching away into the distance, not the past but the future . . .

The Count was used to nightmares. He wooed them and they left little trace. It was the waking horrors that left him exhausted and afraid. It was as if, at such times, as he lay in his narrow bed in his small bedroom and gazed up at the darkened ceiling, his father's spirit came and stood beside him, eager to conduct the argument into which, while his parent lived, the Count had been so unwilling to enter. *What went wrong?* They were living in a dreamland. Eastern Poland ought to have been conceded to Stalin while there was still something to concede. They thought the Western troops would reach Warsaw first. The Count's father had many times described the hour when he realised that the Russians would arrive first. So they were to see off the Germans and then resist the Russians! Were they *mad*? What was the point of the Warsaw Rising anyway? To 'stir the conscience of the world'? To assert Polish independence by possessing Warsaw before the Russians came? What a nemesis. They wanted their fight and the Russians left them to it. Why did they not *wait* until the Red Army was bombarding the city? Accidents, accidents, mistakes, mistakes. The men in London bemused by years of agonising diplomacy, the men in Warsaw worn out by years of secret organisation and nerve-destroying terror. The crucial hours it took to decode messages. The vain hopes of Moscow diplomacy, of Anglo-American help, of German collapse. Two men who were late at a meeting. A false intelligence report. Desire, desire, desire for the longed-for end, the crown of so much scheming and suffering. The inability to wait. Then the catastrophe, humiliation worse than anything dreamt of in their wildest fear. The Count could think of nothing like it in history except the Sicilian Expedition. (The comparison was his father's.) It was a strange fact that his father had never talked to him about the Fight in the Warsaw Ghetto in 1943 when the Jews of the city had risen in inspired courageous hopeless rage against their tormentors. They fought without hope or calculation like rats in a trap and forced their enemies to tear them to pieces. Like rats in a trap; rats in other traps had not fought. His father's silence was not anti-semitism, it was envy. He envied the absolute simplicity of that fight, the purity of its heroism. There was no doubt where the unsmirched flag of Poland was flying in those days of 1943.

But why did the Red Army not cross the Vistula? The sleepless Count thus continued his argument with his father. Were the Russians really waiting cynically for the Germans to destroy their own prospective foes, the flower, the élite of a passionately independent Poland? When the Red Army entered Warsaw it was empty. Indeed it was scarcely there, the ruins were level with the ground. There was no sign of human habitation except for thousands and thousands of hasty new-made graves. His father had been unjust to the Russians, their lines of communication were stretched to breaking, it was an accident of war, the Count thought sometimes as he tossed sleeplessly to and fro. (Why had Hannibal not marched on Rome? For the same reason.) His father had been unjust to Gomulka. Those men were patriots who had tried, who still tried, to construct 'a Polish way to socialism'. What else could they do but play the precarious game which kept the Russian tanks from revisiting Warsaw? The Church still existed, a precious evidence of a freedom kept. Ought his father to have returned home? What was this 'ought' and this 'home'? The eternal 'what should have happened' of the human being in the face of morality and chance and the eternal malice of events. But then the Count returned to the horror of it all. What did it avail, the suffering of the virtuous, the death of the brave? Had any country ever been so malignantly vowed to destruction by its neighbours? The English had ruined Ireland, but casually, thoughtlessly. While History, like Bismarck, seemed dedicated to 'tear up Poland by the roots'.

The Count had, he felt, no illusions about the present state of his country, no sentimentality about what was in obvious ways a bad state. Fear of Russia had to be lived with, life under communism was another world where moral problems appeared with a difference. All states have a background which is partly evil. There the evil was evident, stronger. He saw the corruption, the hardened heart, the bureaucratic cruelty which could not be simply blamed on History or Russia. He constantly endeavoured to know who was in prison and why, who was trapped, who was intimidated, who was silenced. He could not have endured to live in Poland. But he could not help believing (perhaps this *was* sentimentality?) that his country had in spite of everything a spiritual destiny, an unquenched longing for freedom and spirit. There was some old unique indestructible entity over which the red and white flag could still proudly fly. (Often it appeared that that proud flag was being firmly held in the capable hands of the Roman church.) And he connected in his mind this ideal symbolic Poland with the sufferings of oppressed people everywhere, and the dogged dissenters who refused to compromise with tyranny, who wrote pamphlets and made speeches and carried posters until they were put away in prisons and labour camps where after their brief and apparently useless struggle for freedom and virtue they rotted quietly away into a slow anonymous death.

The Count went into the kitchen and put on some potatoes to boil. He liked potatoes. He opened a tin of ham, and when the potatoes were almost ready he made some soup out of a packet. At the table in his sitting-room he drank the soup out of a mug, ate the ham and potatoes, and finished up with a slice of ginger cake. He drank a little red wine mixed with water. He read some more of Carlyle's *Frederic the Great*. The slaughter-house of history, mediated by Carlyle's style, could be an object of contemplation. 'The war was over. Frederic was safe. His glory was beyond the reach of envy. If he had not made conquests as vast as those of Alexander, of Caesar and of Napoleon, if he had not, on fields of battle, enjoyed the constant success of Marlborough and Wellington, he had yet given an example unrivalled in history of what capacity and resolution can effect against the greatest superiority of power and the utmost spite of fortune. He entered Berlin in triumph. . . .' The radio was telling the Count what was going on in Cambodia. Then it told him about the life cycle of the fruit fly. Then there was a programme of Renaissance Music. Then there was a Labour Party political broadcast on race relations, the Count even knew the man who was speaking, an MP, a friend of Stanley Openshaw. After that there was a funny programme, then the news. The Count was apparently able to listen to the radio and to read Carlyle at the same time. He was also able to do all this while thinking throughout the whole evening about Gertrude.

Guy and Gertrude between them had performed some sort of miracle for the Count by introducing him to their 'set'. The very extension of their generosity made it seem less intense, less in need of definition. What was more natural than that Guy's discovery, his 'phenomenon', should be made welcome, even petted a little? He had not at first wondered, and they had perhaps never thought, just how they saw him: a silent man without a country and without a language, an awkward shy man who had to be jollied into the conversation, a thin pale tall man whose hair might be blond or might be white without anyone caring to determine which. 'Where did Guy dig up our Count?' 'Whatever was he doing before *we* discovered him?' These would be perfunctory enquiries. They were infinitely kind to him but they did take him a little too incuriously for granted. They might even take him for a calm man, a placid man! They had rescued him from nonentity, from a narrowing loneliness, and still he remained a shadow in their lives, a footless ghost. Yet all this, which the Count now frequently rehearsed, was unjust. Gertrude and Guy were undemonstrative English people, but they were also unconventional enough to take friendship very seriously. If he was often in their house it was because they often wanted to see him.

The Count was well aware of the crucial difference between loving someone and being in love. He had loved Guy and Gertrude out of gratitude, out of admiration, out of an amazed pleasure at the sudden welcoming ease of their company. He had now a house to visit, a warm bright significant place, people to see regularly, who were connected with each other and had readily, almost casually, bound him into their company. Then suddenly the absolute preciousness of Gertrude had come upon him in a dazzling transfiguring flash. She was absolutely precious, absolutely necessary. Hitherto his life had had a Polish meaning but no sense. Now Gertrude became the sense of his life, its secret centre. His impoverished soul turned in dumb wonderment to this sudden radiant source. The Count was changed, every particle of his being charged with magnetised emotion. His flesh glowed, his body waked from dull sleep and quivered. His love endowed his life, every day, every second, with thrilling purpose. It was a happy *activity*, a little crazed, deeply inherently painful, and yet, as happiness must be, steady, invulnerable, eternal. The situation was impossible, but at the same time it was absolutely secure, and the impossibility and the security and the secrecy were one. He could see Gertrude often, easily, in company. He did not even *want* to be alone with her. And when accidentally, when he had arrived early or stayed late, they were briefly alone together it was as if they were not alone. He could see Gertrude often, he could *go on* seeing her often, they were familiar affectionate friends, connected together forever; and yet the barrier between them was as absolute as if he had been her servant. And of course her servant, with joyful brooding pain, he saw himself eternally destined to be. It was moreover also part of the Count's impossible security that it was inconceivable that he should feel jealous of Guy. He felt no jot of jealousy, even of envy, so high above him was the whole concept of Gertrude's marriage. It was in a curious and precious sense a remote mystery which did not concern him. He revered Guy as Gertrude's consort, and continued to love and admire him on his own account. Having Guy as his office chief had transformed his work, his day. Guy, so clever, so cordial, so dotty, had touched and stirred up something in the Count which was becoming dull and selfish and old. And when the Count had stopped being afraid that his clever friend would suddenly drop him, Guy had become a stronghold. That stronghold remained, now become an inextricable part of the absolute secret safety of the Count's love for Guy's wife.

The Count had always known that he was not a gentleman volunteer in the army of the moral law. If ever a soul was conscripted he was. He intensely feared disgrace, loss of honour, loss of integrity. He stood, in his mind, as still and as expressionless as the soldiers at the Unknown Warrior's grave in Warsaw. Indeed he *could* do nothing wrong, since the situation held him in a merciful steely grip. Sometimes he imagined how he might one day defend Gertrude from attack, rescue her from danger, sleep across her doorway like a dog. Die for her. Indeed Gertrude was somehow to be there 'at the hour of his death' as he departed from her in gentleness with his secret intact. He had, in these flashes which were too swift and physical to be pictures, occasionally imagined a touch, an embrace, a kiss. But these were the involuntary lapses of a man attentive to the beloved in the whole of his dedicated watchful body. He never permitted any extended fantasy. It would have been wrong, it would also have been torture. He knew which way madness lay. Reason and duty commanded him to desist. So he had lived, happily enough, in the cast-iron safety of her marriage. It was a house that would surely last forever.

But now his life was about to change utterly. He felt grief, terror, and a more awful hope. He tried to banish hope, to banish the desire which breeds the illusion which breeds the hope; as the long long nourished desire to free Warsaw had fed the illusory hopes of those who fought and died in the ruined city. He must not think of . . . anything which he might want to have . . . as being in any sense . . . a possibility. Rather he must think of it as remote, as receding, as *lost*. He thought, my happiness was an oversight, a mistake made by fate, and is now over. Behind almost every misfortune there is a moral fault. I am like Poland, my history is and ought to be a disaster. I am guilty because my father fled, because my brother died, because my mother pined away in a cell of solitude. I can expect nothing now but to be returned to the grey loneliness from which

I came. Ah, how I have lived on illusions and fed myself with dreams! And I thought at least that my secret was harmless, to others of course, but also to me. Guy, it all depended on Guy, and soon Guy will be gone and my world will be a dead planet. Without Guy there was no way he could be near to Gertrude and safe, near to Gertrude and happy, near to her forever. No way . . . except one way . . . and of that. . . .

He tried now to think of Guy, to grieve for Guy, Guy propped up in bed with his gaunt old face and his unimaginable thoughts, reading the *Odyssey*. Guy had spoken of himself as Odysseus. But it was a different story now. Odysseus was setting sail upon his last journey and he would not return again to his house and his home. And Penelope. . . . Suddenly the Count saw it: Penelope and the suitors! The siege of Penelope by the suitors; but no master ever to return now to claim her as his true wife. She was to be the prey of lesser men. And they were all there . . . already . . . round about her. . . . The Count turned off the radio and buried his face in his hands.

While the Count was listening to the Renaissance music programme on the radio, Gertrude had already had her supper (soup and cheese) and had said good night to Guy. The Night Nurse was sitting reading in her bedroom which adjoined Guy's room. Gertrude could not read. No book could serve her now. She walked to and fro. She thought about cigarettes, but there were none in the house. (Victor had persuaded most of them to give up smoking.) She readjusted the chrysanthemums in the green vase. She looked out of the window. It had stopped snowing. She was sorry about that. She wanted extreme weather. She desired tempests, mountains of snow. She desired screaming winds and floods, a hurricane which would destroy the house with her and Guy in it. She wished that his death could be her death. How can I endure so much misery, she thought, without dying of it. She looked at her watch. It was still too dangerously early to go to bed.

The telephone rang.

She had muted the telephone so that it produced a faint buzz. She had asked her friends not to ring up in the late evening. Who could this be telephoning at ten o'clock? She lifted the receiver and uttered the number in the business-like way upon which Guy insisted.

'Hello. Gertrude?'

'Yes.'

'This is Anne.'

'What?' said Gertrude, not understanding.

'This is Anne. You know, Anne Cavidge.'

Gertrude tried to adjust her mind to this amazing information. She felt utterly confused, baffled. 'Anne?'

'Yes!'

'But—but surely you aren't allowed to use the telephone—'

There was a laugh at the other end. 'As a matter of fact I'm in a telephone box near Victoria Station.'

'Anne—you can't be—what's happened—?'

'I'm out.'

'You mean *out*—out for good—?'

'Yes.'

Anne, a member of an enclosed religious order, had been inside a convent for fifteen years.

'You mean you've left the Church, left the order, come back into the world?'

'Roughly yes.'

'What does roughly yes mean?'

'Look, Gertrude, I'm very sorry to ring you—'

'Anne, what am I saying, come round here *at once*. Have you money, can you get a taxi?'

'Yes, yes, but I must explain, I booked in a hotel, but they say they're full up, and I tried several others and—'

'Just *come round here*—'

'Yes. OK. Thanks. But I can't remember your number in the street.'

Gertrude gave the number and put the telephone down and

held her head. She had not reckoned with a surprise of this sort and she was not sure if she was pleased or not. Clever Anne Cavidge, her best friend at Cambridge, had shocked them all by becoming a Roman Catholic, after a series of wild love affairs, converted at Newnham before Gertrude's horrified eyes. And then, as if that was not enough, she had promptly become a nun. Gertrude fought her, mourned her. Anne was gone, her Anne existed no more. One cannot communicate with a nun. In the strange rare atmosphere which now divided them friendship could not live. Anne had become Mother something or other. Gertrude wrote to her occasionally, increasingly rarely, firmly addressing her communications to Miss Anne Cavidge. She received in reply brief hygienic communications written in Anne's familiar writing, but devoid of any sharpness of personality. Out of an awful curiosity she went to see her twice and talked to her through a wooden grille: beautiful clever Anne Cavidge dressed up as a nun. Anne was cheerful, talkative, glad to see her. Gertrude was touched, appalled. When she emerged she sat in a pub and shuddered and thought, thank God I'm not in that prison! She joked about it afterwards with Guy, who had never met Anne.

Gertrude now thought, oh if only things were different, if only they were, how glad I should be to see Anne, to *get Anne back*, to introduce her to Guy, how happy I should be, it would be a sort of triumph, a sort of renewal, the return of Anne from the dead.

She thought, I must open the downstairs door, she may not find the right bell and Guy mustn't be disturbed. She left the flat and went down to open the front door of the house, usually locked at this hour. Ebury Street, quiet now, glittered in the lamplight. The recent snow had covered the foot-prints on the pavement. The cold air bit Gertrude's face and hands and she gasped.

The taxi drew up and a woman got out and paid the driver. Two suit-cases were dumped on the pavement. Gertrude came down the steps, the snow engulfing her light slippers. 'Here, let me take this case.'

Anne followed her into the house. In the hall Gertrude said, 'Don't make any noise, Guy's asleep.' They went up the stairs and into the flat. Anne saw the Night Nurse who had emerged from her room and was watching curiously. Anne and the Night Nurse nodded. Anne followed Gertrude into the drawing-room. The door closed. The two women looked at each other.

'Oh — Anne — '

Anne slipped off her coat revealing a blue and white check woollen dress. She was thin, pale, taller than Gertrude. She now also looked older. Her hair, golden when she was a student, had faded, was still blond rather than grey, and clung, closely clipped, to her head. She held her coat a moment, then dropped it on the floor.

'I always meant to ask,' said Gertrude, 'whether you shaved your head under that ghastly head gear.'

'No, no, only cut the hair close. My dear, I'm awfully sorry to turn up like this, so late — '

'Oh shut up,' said Gertrude. She took Anne in her arms and they embraced silently, closing their eyes, and standing still, gripping each other in the middle of the room.

'You see,' said Anne, moving back, 'I didn't mean to — '

'Your feet are wet.'

'So are yours. I didn't mean to bother you — and you carried the case with the books in — '

'You mean you had *escaped* and you weren't going to tell me?'

'Well, "escaped" isn't quite the word, and I was of course going to tell you, but I didn't want to impose myself, you see I arrived by train and this hotel — '

'Yes, yes, yes — '

'I couldn't find anywhere to go and as you were so close I just thought — '

'Oh darling,' said Gertrude, 'darling, darling Anne, welcome back.'

Anne laughed a little strangled laugh and touched Gertrude's cheek. Then she sat down.

'Anne, you must be tired. Have a drink? Do you drink now? What about eating something, have you eaten? Oh I'm so glad to see you!'

'I won't have a drink. You have one. I won't eat I think, I can't — '

'But have you only just emerged, I mean sort of yesterday?'

'No, I'm doing it gradually. I spent a couple of weeks in the convent guest house. Oh it was so odd. I walked about in the

46

country. Then I spent some weeks in the village, I worked in the post office—and now I've just come to London—'

'Oh, but do relieve my mind. You are really out of that awful labour camp, you aren't going back? And you're really through with it all, with the whole thing?'

'I've left the order, yes.'

'But God, do tell me you've finished with God?'

'Well, it's a long story—'

'You must be so tired, I'll fix your room—'

'Who was that, the woman outside?'

'Oh that—that's the Night Nurse—'

'Nurse?'

'Guy's ill—he's—very ill—'

'I'm so sorry—'

'Anne, he's dying, he's dying of cancer, he'll be dead before Christmas—'

Gertrude sat down and let the sudden violent tears spurt from her eyes and drench the front of her dress. Anne got up and sat on the floor beside her, seizing her hands and kissing them.

It was the next morning. The Night Nurse had gone. The Day Nurse reigned in her stead. The Day Nurse was an elderly body, unmarried, wrinkled, wizened, but amiable, always with a little professional smile. She was a good nurse, one of the devoted people to whom it is hard to attribute a private life, personal aims, amazing dreams. She was quiet, untalkative, with a deft animal quickness in her movements. Guy had been got up, had breakfasted, was sitting in the chair beside his bed in his dressing gown. The Day Nurse shaved him. He kept saying that it really wasn't worth being shaved any more at this stage, but he could not make the decision to stop it, and Gertrude could not make it for him. Gertrude had told him of Anne's arrival, in which he had taken some interest. He even displayed an emotion which had apparently passed out of his life, surprise.

Now Anne and Gertrude were sitting in the drawing-room. Outside the sun was shining on the melting snow, smoothing it over, yellowing it and making it glow and sparkle upon unmarked roofs and untrodden square gardens. A strange mystical light pervaded London.

'What a nice flat.'

'It's odd you haven't been here—'

'What a lot of things you've got.'

'Are you chiding me?'

'Of course not! I'm just sort of not used to things, you know, ornaments and—'

'Wasn't your chapel full of beastly madonnas?'

'That was not—Gertrude, I'm sorry to have turned up so suddenly—'

'You've said that sixteen times. Where else should you come, but to this house? But why didn't you write to me before and tell me you were coming out?'

'I couldn't have explained it, I couldn't have written it down. It was all so strange and I was sort of frozen—'

'Well, you'll have to explain it now, won't you? We hardly talked at all last night.'

'I must go out soon and find a hotel—'

'A *what*? You're staying here!'

'But Gertrude, I can't, I mustn't—'

'Because of Guy? That's just why you must stay. I mean, I'd want you to stay anyway—oh God—Anne, you've *come*, you can't *go*, it's important—you understand—'

'OK. But—yes, I'll stay—if I can be useful—'

'Useful!'

'I have plans—I'm going to America—but, oh, everything can wait.'

'You are *not* going to America—but there's so much for you to tell me—and just looking at you is—oh marvellous, a sort of miracle.'

'I know, I feel it too. I'm so glad I had the sense to ring you up.'

'How lovely you look. But that dress isn't right.'

48

'I bought it in the village.'

'It looks like it! I'll help you dress, you've forgotten how, you never were much good at it.'

'I've got money, you know.'

'Oh never mind—'

'But I do mind. The order is going to support me for two years while I find a job, get some training perhaps.'

'What sort of job do you want?'

'What can I get? I don't know.'

'What did you do in *there*, I mean in the way of intellectual pursuits, or was it all prayer and fasting?'

'I taught some theology and Thomist philosophy, but it was so specialised and sort of simplified—I couldn't sell it outside. It wasn't a very intellectual order.'

'So you said at the start, and amazed me! You sacrificed your intellect to those charlatans!'

'I could teach Latin, French, Greek maybe—'

'You wasted all those years—You must start thinking again.' Anne was silent.

'Why not train to be a doctor? I'd help with money. Your father wanted you to be a doctor.'

'It's too late, and anyway I don't want to.'

'What were you intending to do in America before we decided you weren't going there?'

'Did we? There are courses run by Catholics for people like me, sort of retraining, for going into teaching or social work, and—'

'Aren't there courses like that in England? Or, is it that you want to run away? Some "fresh start" idea? I won't let you—we'll find you a job. I mean—I'll—find you a job.'

'We'll see,' said Anne. She looked at her friend with tired remote eyes and smoothed down her short fur of blonde hair.

'Anyway why do you want to go to a Catholic place, haven't you finished with them? You didn't answer my question last night.'

'I've left the order—'

'You said that!'

'Whether I've left Christianity, the Church, doesn't matter, I mean I don't know and it doesn't matter.'

'I should have thought it mattered. Your prying predatory clergy seem to think it matters!'

'It doesn't matter to me. Time will show—or it won't.'

'What's that you're wearing round your neck on a chain, I can see a chain.'

Anne pulled it out. A little golden cross.

'There you are! But, Anne, you must *know*, you must be *clear*—'

'All right, I've left, if that will please you!'

'You don't want to talk about it.'

'Not yet. Forgive me.'

'Forgive me. You know, you're *tired*, it has tired you, getting out of that cage. Do you still have those migraines?'

'Occasionally.'

'Well, you know what I think about the Roman Church, how much I hated your going in—you must allow me a little satisfaction when you come out.'

'Oh, any amount of it.'

'Funny, I thought you would have been a Lady Abbess by this time.'

'So did I!'

Suddenly they laughed together, an old familiar slightly crazy laugh, a special mutual intimate private laugh, signifying understanding, signifying superiority, signifying love.

'Would you have liked to be a priest?'

'Yes,' said Anne.

'I think there ought to be women priests.'

'If you disapprove of priests so much why do you want women to be priests?'

'Well, if there's anything going I think women should have it too if they want it.'

'Even if it's bad?'

'Yes.'

They laughed again. Gertrude thought, I shall cry in a minute. Perhaps Anne will cry. We mustn't. There will be time to cry later. She said, 'Do you remember how, at Newnham, we used to say: we will astound everybody?'

'I remember—'

'My God, those days—all the men were after you.'

'They were after *you*—'

'And then we said we would divide the world between us, you were to have God and I was to have Mammon?'

'I haven't done very well with my half.'

Gertrude thought, poor Anne, she has wasted her years, she has given away her youth for nothing. She is not a Saint, she is not even an Abbess! She has nothing to teach which anybody wants to learn. But I, what have I done? My husband is dying, and I have no children and no work. I am defeated by life. We are both defeated.

They looked at each other wide-eyed. The resumption of friendship had been so easy, they were both almost breathless, surprised at it, surprised at the existence of such a perfect understanding. They had been prize students together, clever Anne Cavidge, clever Gertrude McCluskie. They were two strong women who might have been rivals for the world. They had divided it between them. It occurred to Gertrude now, so strangely, that she had somehow rested in her resignation to Anne's withdrawal from life. She had not wanted it, she had vehemently opposed it, but once it had happened it seemed fated. It kept Anne safe somehow, and now her escape had changed the order of the world. Had she then wanted Anne to live behind bars and pray for her? Inconceivable. She had wanted Anne settled in some way, the problem of Anne settled. Now Anne was ambiguous, at large, and who knew what she would do with herself or what would become of her. The world would have to be divided between them once again.

'What are you thinking?' said Anne.

'I'm wondering if you prayed for me in the convent.'

'I did.'

Gertrude came to her friend and stroked the sleek blonde bird-head. They gazed at each other without smiling.

Anne Cavidge sat on the bed in Gertrude McCluskie's

handsome guest room, and looked at herself in the dressing table mirror. She looked straight into her narrow suspicious blue-green eyes. Her face already looked different, it was a looked-at face, looked at by strangers, looked at by herself. In the convent her hands had been her eyes, and she had needed no mirror to adjust to perfection the white wimple, the dark veil.

Anne had been with Gertrude for several days now. She had not seen Guy, but she had met *les cousins et les tantes*. She had been explained, a runaway nun. There had been mild friendly enquiries, even jokes. Of course she embarrassed them. Perhaps a certain awkwardness would travel with her for the rest of her life. She had irrevocably lost something worldly after all, a certain ease, a mode of growing up.

Gertrude wanted her to borrow her clothes, but Anne would not wear Gertrude's clothes, nor could she face going to the shops, feeling materials, looking at prices. She was still wearing the blue and white check dress, although she now agreed with Gertrude that it would 'not do'. When she had been accepted by the order the Abbess had told her to give up any bad habits such as smoking and drinking, any little accustomed vanities, well before she came in. Would she now be living the process in the reverse direction? She would have to learn to reinhabit her name. Her name in the convent had been different, she had begun to forget who Anne Cavidge was.

It was true that, as Gertrude said, getting out had exhausted her. Anne was more stunned, more dazed, more dazzled than she had at all conveyed to her friend. Walking in the country near to the convent she had felt calm. At Victoria when she could not find a hotel she had felt total panic. Surely people looked at her strangely. She felt like an escaped prisoner, a spy. No wonder since she had, against all that she could earlier have imagined, emerged from a place where she thought she would stay forever, in which she was certain that she would die: a place where she had solemnly vowed to remain for the rest of her life, within the same house, the same garden, giving up her will.

After the first surprise Gertrude now seemed to take her defection for granted, as if it were an obvious outcome, the end of a brief aberration. They had by tacit agreement not renewed any extended or searching conversation, it was no time for deep enquiries into the past and the future. That would come later. They talked now of immediate things, of arrangements, of cooking and catering, of books Anne might like to read (she must have a library ticket, a better reading lamp), of what the nurses did or did not do, of politics and the public world. Gertrude talked about the family, the visitors, sketching each one: Manfred worked in the family bank, Ed Roper imported art objects, the Count was a Pole but not a count, Stanley was an MP, Gerald was an astrophysicist, Victor was the doctor. Of Guy they did not speak.

Anne knew that Gertrude was very very glad that she was in the house. She scarcely wanted Anne to go outside the door. 'You'll go away into London and not come back.' Anne was allowed to do a little household shopping. Gertrude perfunctorily cooked. Now for the first time since her 'escape' Anne terribly missed the convent routine, the special silence in which activity took place, the blessed mechanism of the necessary. How could she deal with a day without a strict routine? She had to invent her own. She made herself useful. She sewed and mended. Gertrude hated sewing. The convent had made Anne a skilful and willing sempstress. She washed and tidied and dusted (Mrs Parfitt had 'flu). She could not yet, though vaguely exhorted to by Gertrude, settle down to any sort of serious study. She felt too blank about the future, too absolutely occupied by what was happening in the flat in Ebury Street. She intended to brush up her Greek to match her Latin, perhaps these were skills she could sell. She had taught a little New Testament Greek in the convent, but it was many years since she had read any classical Greek. But although Gertrude brought her Guy's Greek grammar and *The Oxford Book of Greek Verse* she did not open them.

Sometimes she sat in her room and read a novel. She had read none during her fifteen years 'inside' and she inspected them now with amazement. There was so much heterogeneous *stuff* in a novel. She had been interested in pictures once. (The practice of visual art in the convent had been limited to the creation of terrible Christmas cards and a little *art deco* religious sculpture.) One day she walked along the river as far as the Tate Gallery and looked at the Bonnards. They affected her rather as the novels did, marvellous, but too much. She went twice to Westminster Cathedral and sat in the huge darkness for a while. Gertrude sometimes went out briefly, she still saw one of her Indian pupils, perhaps other people. She did not always want to see Anne and there was that strange taboo upon their talk. She wanted to know that Anne was there, captive, waiting, in reserve. Sometimes they sat separately in the house for long times. There were special periods when Gertrude sat with Guy. Anne did not see Guy, did not even know whether he was aware of her presence in the house. Gertrude and Anne went to bed early. Anne missed the hooting of the owls at night which she had heard for so many years at the convent. She still always woke up at five.

It was afternoon, already dark. The Day Nurse had brought her some tea and smiled her lipless selfless smile. Anne felt an affinity with the Day Nurse and wondered if the nurse felt it too. Gertrude was with Guy. The flat was silent. The day had been yellow, a dark yellow London winter day, never really light at all. The snow had gone, succeeded by rain, now by this quiet murky pall. Anne had been reading *Little Dorrit*, it was amazing, it was so crammed and chaotic, and yet so touching, a kind of miracle, a strangely naked display of feeling, and full of profound ideas, yet one felt it was all true! How transmuted her life had been. She looked round the warm pleasant room at the 'things' on which she had commented to Gertrude. Gertrude wanted her to make the room her own, to colonise it, to adorn it with treasures from elsewhere in the flat, to let Gertrude buy this or buy that to make her more comfortable. Anne could not be interested, said the room was lovely as it was. The silky striped curtains had been smoothly pulled together by their strings. The mantelpiece had blue Chinese dogs, a snuff box. There was an embroidered fire screen representing a blackbird on a branch. An American patchwork counterpane which she was rumpling by sitting on. A mirror with a marble base upon the dressing table. Victorian family silhouettes upon the wall. A smell of furniture polish and continuity and well-being. Anne looked at her watch. In the dark cold chapel the nuns were singing like birds. And *I* am *here*, she thought, and *they* are *there*.

Anne's conversion had been a flight to innocence. Her Anglican Christianity though not deep, had come with her a long way. Later she remembered the unformed unmarked faces of girls at her boarding school, and kneeling on lisle-stockinged knees on a rough wooden floor for evening prayers. The day thou gavest, Lord, is ended. Now close thine eyes in peace and sleep secure. She apprehended the innocence of childhood, saw it almost as her teachers perpetually saw it. The idea of a clear conscience had affected her, even as a child, as a primary moral concept. She had a happy childhood, she loved her parents and her brother. Her father was a doctor, an upright diligent conscientious man. It had seemed to her that life was and ought to be simple. Terrible things happened when she was a sixthformer. Her mother died, her brother was killed in a climbing accident. It seemed that this affliction was setting a seal upon some deep resolve. Her father died later. He had hoped that she would be a doctor. He did not want her to become a nun, but he understood.

When Anne went up to Cambridge secrecy entered her life. Her open communication with her father came to an end. She went home for vacations, was talkative and cheerful, but never now spoke about what concerned her most. After the quietness of home and school, Cambridge had been for Anne a carnival, a maelstrom, a festival of popularity and personality and sex. She was astounded by her success. She worked hard and obtained a first class degree in history. But most of her time and energy and thought and feeling was devoted to love affairs, to an extent which she felt bound to conceal even from her women friends. There were so many jostling men, they impeded each other, offering so many dazzling choices, so many flattering vistas. Anne, offered everything, wanted everything. She became skilful at conducting two, even three, affairs at the same time, keeping the victims happy by lying. She did not quite feel that this was wrong, because everything was so provisional and moved so fast, and other people were behaving quite as wildly as she was. She felt that she was living at an accelerated speed through a whole era, a long period of time during which she was even growing old.

When the era came to an end and she saw her great choice looming ahead she felt it as determined by her earlier rather than by her later life. She had not (as some of her friends believed) half accidentally bundled herself into solitude from disgust at too much society. Rather that had been a teaching, a way laid down perhaps from the start. She felt no surprise at what she was, when the time came, bound to do. She had been shown the world, and what in the world she herself was. She did not later judge her sins therein too harshly. She felt no morbid guilt. Of the 'bad habits' which she duly dropped some considerable time (for it was not easy to get in) before she entered the order, relations with the other sex was by far the easiest to surrender. She had perceived a contrast and had chosen with knowledge what she had earlier valued by instinct.

When she was being converted she was already purposing to be a religious. Conversion could have, for her, no other outcome. Naively at the start, and later out of a deep personal reflection, she had thought of her goal, any goal which at that stage concerned her, in modest terms. She was giving her life for a quiet conscience. A fugitive and cloistered virtue was better than none. She would regain her innocence and keep it under lock and key. Innocence was then the form under which Good appeared to her. She wanted to be eternally possessed of a quiet mind, in a life of enclosed simplicity. She wanted to be independent of worldly thoughts, her own and those of others, to reach a certain level where she could float free. She did not, at the start, think clearly of 'goodness' or 'holiness' as a visible goal. She took to a fervent belief in a personal God, a personal Saviour, with an ease which took her friends' breath away. All these things, the flight, the inevitable refuge, the redemption, were mingled in her mind. She felt both the distance of God, and the reality of the magnetic bond that compelled her to Him. The idea of holiness, of becoming good in some more positive sense, naturally gained power in her mind in the earlier years in the convent. As Gertrude had said, her order was not one of the most intellectual, and as Gertrude had hinted, this had been a deliberate choice. Clever Anne Cavidge, in her desperate flight from the world, had shrewdly decided to make the sacrifice of the intellect as early and as irrevocably as possible. Of course there were 'studies'. She was marked out to be a teacher and became a highly respected one. But there were intellectual achievements in which she took care to be no longer interested. That was not for her the direction in which salvation lay. The Aristotelian philosophy she was required to teach was simplified and brittle, and in so far as she was ever tempted to enlarge it the atmosphere was against her, and the talents of her pupils not suited to metaphysical speculation. Holiness not cleverness was the path. But this path, some while after it became real to her as a sense of direction, began to fill Anne with strange doubts, doubts which were however not directly connected with her 'defection'. Her instincts and intuitions had begun quietly to point her back toward her earlier and simpler objectives, simplicity, innocence, a kind of negative humility which did not aspire to the name of goodness.

That the concept of a personal God began to seem to her more and more problematic did not too much dismay her. She lived as a member of a small mutually tacit 'intelligentsia' among those of simpler faith, a faith which she and her like refrained from disturbing. 'The clever ones' looked into each others' eyes and said, on the whole, little, certainly less than all, about the changes they perceived in themselves, and which, isolated as they were, they could not help connecting with the deep spiritually guided movement of a certain Time Ghost. Most of them kept calm, Anne not least. To visitors from outside whom, under their rule, they did not see often, and always saw briefly through bars, they remained though kind, attentive, humorous, yet aloof and enigmatic. The Abbess (a new Abbess, not the one who had received Anne) did not encourage either special friendships within the house or close relations with outsiders. Thus one could go on indefinitely; and Anne knew well that many who thought as she did remained, and would remain, inside, nor did she blame them; sometimes she felt more inclined to blame herself.

Gertrude had said it must be like getting out of prison. Well, how hard, how ardently, she had tried to get *into* that prison; and it was like a prison, there were cells, bars, high walls, locked doors. God had put her under house arrest, and with a glad and willing heart she identified herself as a prisoner. How did it all come, oh so gradually, to change? It was not, as Gertrude imagined, like an escape. Of course there was sadness and failure in the convent. No one spoke of this to outsiders. Ordinary relations with the outside world soon wilted, as her friendship with Gertrude had wilted, because of a certain bland reserve, an absence of familiar frank communication. Something was happening which could be variously described. Love itself altered, was constrained perhaps clarified. Some old deep anxious needful worm shrivelled, diminished. It was, within, very slow; but in the face turned to the outside the change seemed absolute. Communications of another sort took place of course, with certain seekers in certain contexts, those who gripped the bars, disciplined to receive admonitions which might seem impersonal or cool, but were perhaps nevertheless the purest form available to them of the love of God. Beyond this point 'the world' did not see; and even within the 'failures' were spoken of with restraint and only in a certain kind of language. No one spoke of 'nervous breakdowns'. There were nuns, though in Anne's experience not many, who became miserable or bored or mad. There were, but rarely, sudden unbridled emotions and wild tears. The characteristic calm brightness of the scene struck Anne rather, the special way nuns laughed, for they did often laugh in recreation and at times when there was no rule of silence.

The 'failures' sometimes found their way back into worldly life, clutching a doctor's certificate or a letter from a priest skilled in psychiatry. Anne's exit had not been like that, she was one of the strong ones. She had become steadily penetrated by a sense of being 'in the wrong place'. The enclosure itself did not irk her, she was able to love its austere beehive safety, and to make for herself a vast space inside its narrowness, which space was God. When she had entered she had spoken to her novice mistress about her conscience. She had been told to forget her conscience, to surrender it to the guiding power of divine love. To let go forever of selfish vain pettifogging moral anxiety. A cleansing sea of spirit would flow through to make her empty and clean and free. As years passed, years of confinement and prayer and teaching and manual work, these things made sense to Anne, and she released herself into that other Love whose reality, as she experienced it, she could not doubt. Not I but Christ. Worship and adoration became to her like breathing, and were sometimes a delight so intense as to seem almost sinful. Simplicity and innocence and the absence of worldly striving and concern were now her daily bread, and she was filled with a joy which was far beyond anything which she had been able to imagine beforehand, when she had first felt called to give her life thus absolutely to God. She became, in due time, novice mistress herself. She spoke with attentive wise concern to those who pressed their wrinkled branded faces to the bars. She envisaged being called by God to higher responsibilities within the order. But then, and somehow moving within her like the first tiny symptom of a serious illness or a vast physical change, she felt once again anxiety, conscience.

Of course there had been flaws, imperfections, irritants in that closely-crowded community of women. Anne had lived with these, conscious of them, letting them somehow drift as she had been taught to do, offering them to God. It was impossible to avoid the exercise of power. She did not always agree with the Abbess. There was one whom she loved more than the rest and could not change or sacrifice that love. There were reforms, alterations, plans which the Community was forced to consider. Anne's opinion was overruled by those whom she could not but judge to be less wise. These trials were not crucial, she gave them over daily to God, it was not thus that her conscience so strangely came back to her. She went on living calmly enough a stripped busy life of work and prayer, hearing (she could not sing), as a sort of pledge of the permanence of all about her, the beautiful thin constant plainsong of the nuns, so exquisitely disciplined, so frequent, so familiar, a chant of caged birds heard only by God.

The sacrifice of the intellect had not of course proved as easy as Anne had, with fantastic confidence, anticipated. But it was no hunger for other thoughts, for different books, no stormy crisis of intellectual doubt which had now driven her back into the world. She had lived a long time with the practice of prayer, not as a regular intermittent willed routine, but as a total mode of being. She had lived with the passion of Christ, with the mystery of that supreme pain within which He also judged the world. She had lived, with a sweet and natural ease, somehow inside the doctrine of the Trinity, surrounded by the spiritual stream which united Father, Son and Paraclete. Sometimes she wondered how much she had really changed; more often, turned towards her God, the question seemed idle. She was aware that within the continual force of that spiritual current her ideas were changing, the shape of her cosmos was changing, making what was far near, and what was near far. But what these so-natural changes did, and out of their fullness and their

59

sweetness, bring to her at last for her pain, was a profound urgent notion, felt increasingly as a *duty*, that she must now move away to *some other place*. Duty: a conception which she had somehow consigned to the past, together with her old narrow ideas of moral will and moral change. She had imagined that the way to death lay straight and clear ahead of her, a well illumined path, and that any changes lying there in wait were the concern of God alone. In the narrowing of her will, the widening of His, there could be trials, but no more problems, no more awful anxious wrenching choices. But now it was as if she was being required to abandon what had been 'achieved', and to start all over again.

She discussed her motives, apparent and possibly concealed, with the Abbess and with her confessor. She had no deep or emotional bond with either. (Anne had never needed a warning against the 'danger' of the confessional.) She had by now asked to be relieved of her teaching duties. The exercise of any sort of spiritual or doctrinal authority had become abhorrent to her. She already felt that she was beginning to lie. She asked herself, and the Abbess asked her whether there were not some deep unacknowledged reason for her strange desire to run. One motive in particular the Abbess wished her to acknowledge, but she would not. Nor was this exactly a crisis of faith. She admitted now, more frankly than ever before, to the Abbess, how her sense of the living God had, perhaps profoundly, changed. They looked at each other in silence. The Abbess looked away. Anne and the Abbess were not, in a worldly sense, framed to 'get on together'. They had dealt with that problem intelligently and faithfully. The Abbess, older than Anne, had joined the order in her later twenties. Out in the world she had been a titled lady and an heiress. She had been a brilliant student, then an administrator, and had turned away from a field of intellectual prowess and admired success. There were many things which Anne would have liked now to discuss with unfettered frankness with this highly intelligent woman, but it could not be. Their talk concerned only what Anne should do and why, and no hint of a shared bewilderment was allowed to soften the severity of the interrogation.

Anne did come to agree that her sense of being 'in the wrong place' was somehow connected with the changed perspectives of her faith, but she refused to regard this, as the Abbess at first pressed her to do, as the usual intermittent darkness, a *secheresse* which must be endured and expected to pass. She equally rejected a position which the Abbess adopted later on (for these discussions continued for some time) to the effect that this change was in some exalted sense the will of God. Yes, it was no doubt God's will, said Anne, but there was no great positive 'showing' here, no revelation of a new task. It was under a negative and agnostic sign that she must now proceed. To do what? asked the Abbess. Anne did not know, why should she know. But she was very determined to go, and to go with consent and if it might be with blessing, and the Abbess saw her determination. The Abbess, who had so often thwarted her, was now most unwilling to release her, but at last Anne began to have her way.

'So, where will you go, to *whom*?' 'I shall live alone,' said Anne. The Abbess, whose gentler face Anne had learnt, in these talks, to perceive, looked at her piercingly. 'Do not be too proudly confident that you can remain innocent when you are *there*. Think *now* what you are losing.' 'I am not proud or confident.' But one thing I know, thought Anne, I should be able to bear any pain except that of guilt. *That* I must at all costs avoid, and I think I know how. 'You will need help. Why not retain a connection with us? There are those who live as anchoresses in the world.' 'Perhaps I shall be an anchoress,' said Anne, 'but if I am I shall be so alone, and known only to God.' 'Then when you leave here,' said the Abbess, 'you leave totally and forever.' 'It is better thus,' said Anne.

In the end she departed ambiguously, quietly, by consent, but without farewells. Once outside, in the guest house, she was vanished from them forever. She saw only the three extern sisters, who treated her with quiet sympathy as if she were ill. And now, she thought, sitting drinking her tea and rumpling the beautiful counterpane, I am in London and, so strangely, I have a task which will for the time put off further choices. I must see Gertrude through this awful trial and there is no point now in looking further. I have been blessed with a task. I have been honoured with an order. Was that the way to see it? Yes, I am here, and they are there, she thought. But already the words were becoming empty, like a vain plea. The Convent was receding from her and was already transparent and dream-like. For two years there would be a little money in her bank. But no messages would come to her from that place ever again. It had been taken away into the invisible world.

Now she would live secretly, as a secret anchoress. This idea put, perhaps cleverly, into her head by the Abbess, pleased her, it seemed an illumination. She felt as if she were being sent back into the world to prove something. Or perhaps she would be more like a spy, one of God's spies, the spy of a non-existent God. What could be odder? But that was what she would now have to *work out*. Would that 'working out' be the return to 'thinking' which Gertrude had wished for her when she had spoken of the 'wasted years'? Had they been wasted, those years, had she spent them inventing a false Christianity and a false Christ? She could not think so. The Abbess, who suspected Anne of a concealed spiritual collapse, and seemed to expect her to fall rapidly into trouble (yet what did the Abbess think, perhaps she envied her?) had said, 'How can you live without the mass?' Anne had not said so, but she had in fact no intention of living without the mass. She would not go to confession, she might or might not under the still unrevealed rule of her secrecy, permit herself to receive the sacrament. (How precious in a new way was that familiar longed-for food.) But she would not henceforth live without the mass, any more than she would henceforth live without Christ. Christ belonged to her and would travel with her, her Christ, the only one that was really hers.

Can anyone who has once had it really give up the concept of God? The craving for God, once fully established, is perhaps incurable. She could not rid herself of the *experience* of God's love, and the sense that only through God could she reach the world. Could joy be sought elsewhere save at that true source? And would not lesser goods corrupt her shaken soul? She was soaked in Christianity and in Christ, sunk, saturated, stained indelibly all through. The cross was round her neck like a fetter, like a noose. Could she live now by the ontological proof alone? Can love, in its last extremity, create its object? Would there be still adoration and worship, could there be? Prayer remained with her, continual prayer like breathing, but what *was* it now? For the time, it was like the strange awful breathing of a body kept alive by doctors after the brain is dead. Would that body rise and live again? She did not think of this as happiness. Happiness was no part of her plan. That concept at least had been, she hoped, burnt out of her by fifteen years 'inside'. And the joy that had gone from her might never return. She knew that, through her part in Gertrude's trial, she was strangely blessed by an interim, had been granted, before what was to come, a kind of rest. A different suffering, waiting its hour, would surely follow. The dark night had not yet begun, but would begin, and she would weep. I must be alone, she thought, with no plan and no vision, homeless and invisible, a wanderer, a no-one. Otherwise, I shall prove the Abbess right and fall into the snares of the world.

'Oh Anne — Guy wants to talk to you.'

Anne who had been sewing in her room, patching a triangular tear in one of Gertrude's favourite blouses, jumped up, looking rather alarmed.

'He only likes to talk to strangers now. It's people he knows he can't stand.'

Gertrude was startled all the same. Guy had not mentioned Anne since the surprise he had expressed at her arrival. Now suddenly he wanted to see her.

Anne put her work aside and followed Gertrude out.

'Don't stay too long, will you — he gets so tired.'

'No, I won't.' Gertrude held the door open and Anne entered Guy's bedroom. The door closed.

The room was rather dark with one lamp alight beside Guy's bed. It was evening. He was lying propped up with pillows, and had been reading the *Odyssey* in the Loeb edition. He rose only for a little while in the morning, now, to provide some simulacrum of ordinary life by sitting in his bedside chair. His walk to the adjoining bathroom, helped by Gertrude or the nurse, made his longest journey.

Anne saw half his face illumined by the lamp, then more of it as his head rolled. He looked to her like an old man, or like pictures she had seen of gaunt staring men just released from prison camps. There was a great pale shiny bald brow, then a thin web of grey-streaked hair. His hair was tangled, he tangled it with restless fingers, however often the nurse combed it out. He was clean shaven but with a greyish shadow of beard visible. His nose was thin and sharp, hooked, and his eyes were dark and glittering, moving quickly to Anne, then searching the room as if expecting something. She particularly noticed his mouth, which was beautiful, long and shapely, tender, sensitive. His skinny arms were stretched out, and his long white, almost blueish, thin hands clutched the blanket, then released it, in a convulsive movement. Pity filled Anne, and she thought, but he is too ill to talk, why have I come? I will say a word or two and go away. Perhaps he will not be able to talk at all. He just wants to see what I look like. How thin and far away he is.

Guy said, 'Hello, Anne.'

'Hello, Guy.'

'I'm glad you've come.'

'I'm glad too.'

His voice was unexpectedly strong, a voice of authority. There was a silence. Guy was turning his head rhythmically to and fro, and bending and stretching his fingers. Anne wondered if he was in pain.

'Won't you sit down? Come nearer. I want to see you.'

Anne pulled a chair up beside the bed and sat down. She smiled at Guy.

He smiled with a strange quick spasm. He said, 'I'm so glad you've come, for Gertrude. You will stay till I go, and after too?'

'Yes, of course.'

'She loves you, I think.'

'Yes. I love her.'

There was silence again. Anne breathed quietly, praying blankly, feeling an immense tired quiet like a cloud rising up out of her. She did not feel able to make conversation, but there might be no need, perhaps it was all right just to sit there.

'Why did you leave the convent?' said Guy.

Anne was suddenly alert, electric with precision. 'I changed my views about religion. It would have been a lie to stay.'

'Maybe you should have hung on. Christian theology is changing so fast these days. The relieving troops would have arrived. You would have heard the sound of bagpipes.'

'No theologian could have rescued me!'

'Lost your faith — ?'

'That's not quite the phrase. Perhaps people don't all that often just *lose* their faith. I want to make a new kind of faith, privately for myself, and this can only be done out in the world.'

'Inside you had to say what you didn't believe, even if you said nothing?'

'Yes.'

'Do you still believe in a personal God?'

'Not in a personal God.'

'Then in some sort of mysterious world spirit? Zeus, whoever you are.'

'No, nothing of that sort. It's hard to explain. Perhaps I just can't make any more use of the word "God".'

'I've always hated God,' said Guy.

'You mean the Old Man?'

'Yes.'

'Did you ever have any Jewish religion? But of course your family were Christians.'

'Scarcely. We knew about the Jewish festivals. There was a kind of nostalgia. It was odd. I knew about holiness.'

'Isn't that religion?'

'What did you mean about a faith privately for yourself?'

'I suppose every faith is private. I just mean — it wouldn't have names and concepts, I would never describe it, but it would live and I would know it. I feel as if I've finished talking.'

'I've often felt that,' said Guy, 'but it was an illusion. What will you do?'

'I don't know, some sort of social work, I'm not thinking about it yet.'

'And Jesus, what about him?'

'What about him indeed.'

'Will he be part of your new faith?'

'Yes,' said Anne. 'I — I think so —'

'My uncle David Schultz once told me that if at the world's end it turned out that Jesus was the Messiah, he would accept him. It's interesting to speculate on the alternative.'

'Some of your family kept to the Jewish faith?'

'He was an uncle by marriage. But yes. You must ask Veronica Mount, she's the expert. I used to hate Jesus too.'

'However could you? I can imagine hating God, but not Jesus.'

'I mean the symbol not the man. One must pity the man. Judaism is a sober religion, teaching, prayer, no excesses. But Christianity is so soft, it's sentimental and magical, it denies death. It changes death into suffering, and suffering is always so interesting. There is pain, and then, hey presto, there is eternal life. That's what we all want, that our misery shall buy something, that we shall get something in return, something absolutely consoling. But it's a lie. There are final conclusions, one is shortly to be reached in this house. Eternal departures take place. Suffering has the shifting unreality of the human mind. A desire to suffer probably led you into that convent, perhaps it has led you out again. Death is real. But Christ doesn't really die. That can't be right.'

'Right or wrong, it's the point.'

'It's not *your* point.'

'No—' Anne wanted to think about what he was saying, though his strained utterance distressed her. 'I think—we want our vices to suffer—but not to go away.'

'Yes. Yes. We want . . . because of the suffering . . . to be able to keep . . . everything . . . to be forgiven.'

'That seems to you soft?'

'Yes.'

They were silent again. Anne thought, I can say anything to this man.

Guy said, 'You don't, I imagine, believe in the anti-religious idea of life after death?'

'No. I agree it's anti-religious. I mean—whatever it is—it's happening now and here.' That's what I couldn't tell them in the convent, she thought.

'I wish I believed in the hereafter,' said Guy. He had been looking away from her, twisting his hair with one restless hand, showing her his hawk-nosed profile. Now his eyes glittered at her. 'Not for any vulgar reason of course. Not just to be let off this thing that's going to happen in the next few weeks. But — it's something I've always felt — '

'What?'

'I would like to be judged.'

Anne reflected. 'I wonder if it's a coherent idea? It seems to me a little like what you didn't care for about Christianity.'

'I know exactly what you mean,' said Guy. She had pleased him. He smiled a sweeter smile which softened the taut face. 'It's romantic, sad-masochistic, a story-idea, not what it seems — indeed' —

'Do you mean judgment as estimation, a clear account, or as punishment?'

'Oh both. I think one *craves* for both. To look over the Recording Angel's shoulder. And to have consequences. Consequences would prove something.'

'What do you want proved? Gertrude said you were writing a book about punishment.'

Guy frowned. 'Did she? It's nothing yet. I mean — it's nothing, just a sketch.'

'Can you tell me anything about it?'

'It's an impossible subject. If a Home Office official writes a book on punishment it's bound to be — oh you know — about deterrence and rehabilitation.'

'And leaves out retribution, and that's what you want?'

'For myself, yes.'

'Don't you think others may need it, want it, too?'

'Oh may be, but I'm only interested in my own case. Like you.'

They both smiled. Anne sat tense, concentrated.

'Justice is such an odd thing,' Guy went on, 'it cuts across the other virtues, it's like brown, it's not in the spectrum, it's not in the moral spectrum.'

'I don't understand,' said Anne.

'It's a calculation.'

'What about mercy?'

'Something quite different. Anyway there can't *be* mercy.'

'Why not?'

'Because crimes are their own punishment.'

'If so why do you want an after-life?'

'Oh but one can't *see*. I would want to understand it all. I would want to have it exhibited, explained. That's why the idea of purgatory is so moving.'

'What about hell, is that moving too?'

'No. Incomprehensible really. But purgatory, suffering in the presence of the Good, what joy. Computerised suffering, suffering with a purpose, with a progress — no wonder the souls in Dante plunge joyfully back into the fire.'

'But purgatory is rehabilitation and you said — '

'Purgatory is magical rehabilitation, guaranteed to work. In real life punishment may produce any result, it's wild guess-work. And retribution is only important as a check, it's necessary for the sort of rough justice we hand out here below. I mean, the chap's got to have *done* something, and we must have a shot at saying how large or small it is — '

'Otherwise we might penalise people just to do them good.'

'Or to deter other people, yes.'

'I understand what you feel about purgatory,' said Anne.

'I once saw a Victorian picture called "Abject Prayer". I envied the man in the picture.'

'I know the picture. Oh — heavens — yes! It's all so unutterably consoling and as you said romantic, and yet — '

'Why shouldn't poor sinners be consoled?'

'Yes. But about retribution, when you say you want to be judged is that just a general idea, something "soft", to use your word, or do you relate it to things you've done, as it were — ?'

'Oh well — ' said Guy. He smiled again, sadly, his dark eyes fixed intently upon Anne. His eyes were moist and shining in his dry pale face where the skin was stretched so tight across the bones.

'I mean I'm not asking what you accuse yourself of, or just about how you think of it — '

'We specialise, don't you think?' said Guy. 'We are selectively decent, if we are decent at all. We each have one or two virtues which we cultivate, not much really. Or we pick a virtue which always seems to help, to mediate goodness somehow, as it might be resolution, or benevolence, or innocence, or temperance, or honour. Something not too large, not too impossibly hard that seems to suit us somehow — '

'What's yours?'

'My — ? Oh nothing high. Something like accuracy.'

68

'Isn't that the same as truth?'

'No. We are not really very versatile when it comes to being good, we are awfully limited creatures. How much scrutiny would the lives of the saints stand up to? Everybody is beastly to someone. Even your friend Jesus, what do we really know about him? He had the luck to be celebrated by five literary geniuses.'

'Luck? Well—'

'Our vices are general, dull, the ordinary rotten mud of human meanness and cowardice and cruelty and egoism, and even when they're extreme they're all the same. Only in our virtues are we original, because virtue is difficult, and we have to try, to invent, to work through our nature against our nature—'

'But doesn't every vice have its corresponding virtue. I mean aren't they defined in terms of each other?'

'Only apparently. For virtue is awfully odd. It's detached, something on its own.'

'You mean demonic?'

'That's another romantic idea. No, I won't pick it up. Just— original—idiosyncratic—odd—Vices are general, virtues are particular. They aren't in a continuum of general improvement.'

'I'm not sure,' said Anne. 'They must be related to each other in some sort of—'

'System? Hierarchy? That's metaphysics.'

'And virtue is often quiet and dull, I've seen it. I agree it's specialised. We are good in a small area that suits us. But you are thinking of virtue as being all interesting and original inside, and I don't see that. It's a sort of—conjecture.'

'I didn't say "interesting"—and it is a conjecture—But you asked me if . . . when I wanted punishment . . . I wanted it . . . for anything in particular. . . .'

Guy was staring at her intently. Anne was suddenly frightened and felt her face flushing. It had occurred to her that Guy might actually want to make some sort of confession. Suppose he were now to tell her something terrible, something that was on his mind, tormenting him? Was it for this that he had asked to see her? She thought, if I were a priest it would be my duty to hear it. But I am not a priest. With me it would be muddled and personal. I have no role here, no magic power to transform what might happen, no authority to touch his soul. I could say nothing good to him and he would regret it.

She said gently, 'I think I am tiring you. Gertrude said I mustn't stay long.'

Guy continued to stare at her. Then he sighed, smiled a little mocking smirking grimace, and turned his head away. He said, 'I frightened you just now, didn't I?'

'Yes.'

'I'm sorry, it was nothing. And it's—all right. Hey, hey, the white swan. Nurse will come in a minute anyway.'

'I must go.'

Guy turned back to look at her. Anne felt a surge of emotion which almost made her gasp. She trembled. She felt for a moment, *I can't go.*

Guy stretched out his hand towards her. Anne took hold of the thin papery hand, feather-light in her strong grasp, and leaned over and kissed it.

'Oh Anne—go now—we'll talk—another time—'

But Anne never saw Guy again.

≫ ≪

'Is that all you've got for our supper?'

'Yes.'

'Bloody Christ.'

'I suppose we can buy something.'

'Oh shit!'

Tim Reede and his girl Daisy Barrett were sitting drinking in the Prince of Denmark. Tim was drawing the Prince of Denmark cat. The cat, a slim black beast with a noble bony face and white paws, was cold and vain. It stared contemptuously at Tim out of its ice-green eyes, then stretched voluptuously and adopted another pose. Tim started again. That cat (its name was Perkins) had a larger repertoire of attitudes than any cat Tim had ever drawn, and he had drawn many a cat. The Prince of Denmark, a pub near Fitzroy Square, had also possessed a dog called Barkiss, an animal of infinite jest, recently kidnapped by a passing client. Tim and Daisy liked the place because it was quiet and unfashionable and seedy. There was a big mahogany bar with a superstructure or screen composed of little pivoting panels of Victorian engraved glass which looked like the east end of a Greek orthodox church. There was indeed an ecclesiastical atmosphere. The place was dimly lit and smoky and the customers talked in low voices. Little cubicles, like confessionals, lined one wall. Tim and Daisy were seated in one of these. There was no juke box.

The time was nine in the evening and the day was five days later than the day upon which, as narrated at the start, Manfred and the Count and Sylvia Wicks and Stanley Openshaw and Mrs Mount and Tim had gathered for Visiting Hour at Ebury Street. Since then Tim had been there, including the present evening, twice. He did not always ask Gertrude for food, it had to be done casually. He hoped she did not observe in any detail the results of his raids on her kitchen. If he took a little bit of a lot of things it would not show. Tim didn't want to acquire the reputation of a scrounger. What he had laid out now in front of Daisy upon the beer-stained table was as follows: two slices of bread roughly smeared with butter, two pieces of cheese, one cheddar, one stilton, two tomatoes, four oatmeal biscuits, a slice of cold roast lamb and a small bit of fruitcake.

'I don't think it's too bad,' said Tim.

'Weren't there any cold potatoes?'

'No.'

Tim's mackintosh, into the capacious pockets of which he had hastily stuffed the goodies, hung on the back of his chair, dripping. It was raining outside, and a cold east wind was making the rain run rippling across the streets of north Soho, which glittered like rivers under the street lamps. The brief snow was now gone and forgotten. Daisy had been waiting for Tim for some time.

'I think we're getting *too* poor. OK, we wanted to be poor, we chose to be poor, but this is ridiculous. How is it that everybody else has got money and we haven't? How is it that they can earn money and we can't? We have talents, why can't we sell them?'

Tim did not know the answer. Tim and Daisy had long made a joke of being penniless. They counted themselves as wanderers, misfits, flotsam and jetsam, orphans of the storm, babes in the wood, mendicant artists, destitute hedonists on a perpetual picnic. Tim had a one-day-a-week teaching job at a polytechnic in Willesden. Daisy, who used also to teach painting, was (Tim hoped temporarily) unemployed. Payment was by the hour, so there was no pay for holidays. The term was now near its end and (Tim had not yet told Daisy) he was not to be employed next term. They both, rather furtively and without telling each other, collected National Assistance. Only somehow, perhaps because they failed to fill in the forms properly, they never seemed to get as much as other people. Their rents had lately been raised (they lived separately now). They had discussed stealing but agreed that they were conditioned against it and would be terrified of the disgrace, it was nothing to do with morality. They could have lived more cheaply if they could have made up their minds to give up drink or to live together again, but they could not make either of these decisions. Spatial problems in cheap rooms had defeated them. Tim now ameliorated their plight (he had a more extensive social life than Daisy) by removing food from the houses to which he was invited (this surely was not stealing). Any sort of party was a bonus, especially a big reception where one could pocket sandwiches. He had laid in a store of nourishment at Jeremy Schultz's Bar Mitzvah. (Stale sandwiches are delicious fried.) The wedding of Moses Greenberg's niece to one of the Lebowitzim was now happily in prospect.

Tim and Daisy had been together now for a long time, and it was not easy, even for them, to define what their relation was. Earlier Tim would have married Daisy had it not been for her surprisingly ferocious hostility to the institution of marriage, which she connected with 'homes and gardens and hoovering the wall-to-wall carpet and generally becoming dead'. She had a special resentment against idle women who married so as not to work, and lived lives of bourgeois selfishness. The 'haves' with their husbands and their kiddies and their houses full of bloody furniture! Worthless people full of moral complacency and contempt for others! Daisy and Tim prided themselves on being free and having no possessions. They saw themselves as having deliberately and happily missed the bus. They had been young together. Now they were not so young together. Though still childish, they acknowledged the years, years which were fleeting by for both of them. They were comrades with a special relationship. It had long been established that they suited each other, and no one else seemed to suit either of them, and they had searched long enough. They were, for each other, the only ones they couldn't leave. They had lived, and lived still, by a light of romance, tracking each other across London and meeting in pubs and afternoon drinking clubs as they had done when they were students. These rendezvous, which took place daily, were more thrilling than dull old living together which they had tried and discarded. They envisaged life, they said, as soldiering on from one little festival to another, and for them almost anything counted as a festival. They conspired to be eternally youthful, and on that they restlessly rested.

They had both, as children, had unhappy homes, and this seemed to make them 'like brother and sister', two of a kind. Daisy had a French Canadian father; the family name was Barrault, but had been changed for some reason, by her eccentric father to Barrett. Her mother was a Bloomsbury lady, remotely related to Virginia Woolf, who had been a dim dilettante painter in a Euston Road style and a protégée of

Duncan Grant. The marriage broke up when Daisy (an only child) was four. The mother and child stayed in London, the father returned to Canada. He had been some sort of sculptor, according to Daisy, but turned more successfully to art business. Daisy's mother, who wanted to be 'in society', but was now very poor, resented Daisy who, she thought, somehow prevented her from marrying again. The mother died when Daisy was ten and she went to Canada to her father who, though fitfully affectionate, regarded the child as a confounded nuisance. In due course he took her back to England and dumped her at Roedean, while he increasingly lived in France. Holidays were spent scrappily in hotels. Daisy hated Roedean. Then noticing that she was becoming tall and handsome, her father fetched her to Paris to share a house with his latest mistress. Shortly after that be became bankrupt and returned to Montreal to drink himself to death, leaving Daisy in Neuilly-sur-Seine with a remote relation whom she knew as Tante Louise. Encouraged by some of her father's friends, Daisy began to study art. To escape from Tante Louise she came to London and lived there as an art student. Her father, while he lived, sent her an irregular but not ungenerous allowance. She had talent, and finally reached the Slade. It was here that she met Tim, who was two years her junior. She spoke perfect French but detested France.

Tim's history was different but equally unsatisfactory. His father, who was Irish but had always lived in England, had been a barrister and an amateur musician. Music not law was his real love and he finally gave up his law practice. He was a good pianist but never achieved excellence. He had dabbled in composition, but now devoted himself wholly to it, at first with some modest success. He was a big brilliant funny laughing red-haired man, a great success with women. He had a fine baritone voice and knew every song. He could play anything on the piano. He was a concert in himself, whether comic or serious. As a husband and father he had fewer talents. Tim's mother was also a musician. She had played the flute in the *Jeunesse Musicale*, later in the London Symphony Orchestra. She was a Welsh girl of modest background and delicate health (she had had TB as a child) and was briefly extremely beautiful. The two got married in haste and repented at leisure, at least Tim's mother repented. Tim's father, who departed soon after the birth of Tim and his sister Rita, showed no sign of uneasy feelings. He went to America, and though his musical career gradually foundered he apparently did not cease to enjoy himself. He married again, then divorced. He turned up in England at intervals to see the children of whom he was, when he saw them, demonstratively fond. Neither parent attempted to give Tim or Rita any musical education. The father was absent, the mother, whose flute was heard no more, had no will to urge her unruly children to practise the art which had brought her only sad memories.

The children adored their father. In the rather dreary and impecunious life which they were living with their mother in a London suburb he was a beam of brilliant light, a being from another world, a boisterous shining god. The children laughed and shouted with pleasure when the big handsome redheaded papa made his appearance and sat down at the piano. They mourned his departures and longed for his return and lived in a dream of going to join him in some paradise of wealth and freedom (they assumed of course he was vastly rich) on the other side of the Atlantic. Their frail nervous irritable disappointed impoverished money-grubbing mother excited their aversion. Their talk was always of when they would 'get away'. Their mother's departure came first however. When Tim was twelve and Rita was ten the unhappy woman reverted to her TB and died, and Tim and Rita were whisked off to Cardiff where they lived in the family of their maternal uncle, among cousins who resented their presence. Tim, who dreamed of protected children in warm nurseries, was tormented by a gaggle of disorderly little girls. When Tim was fourteen Rita died of anorexia nervosa, a disease at that time very little understood. After the mother's death the brilliant father never reappeared. He was killed fairly soon after in a motor accident.

However the god-like papa had in fact laid up one last useful little treat for his children and it was through this that Tim came in due course into contact with Ebury Street. His father had been in his London days, a friend of Rudi Openshaw, also a musical lawyer, who was one of Guy's uncles. Cornelius Reede (for that was the father's name) had left in his will some money in trust for his children, in the care of Rudi Openshaw and the 'family bank'. Rudi became in effect the children's guardian.

He was a bachelor, awkward with children, and saw his wards only once when he came to Cardiff to make some financial arrangements with Tim's uncle. These arrangements, though welcome to the uncle's family, did not improve Tim and Rita's lot in any way. Rita died. Rudi died; and the trust for Tim's benefit passed to Guy's father, and later to Guy, who became in this odd way *in loco parentis* to Tim.

Tim's desire was and had always been to get back to London. When he was seventeen, with Guy's father's consent and the blessing of his uncle, aunt and cousins, he travelled to the capital to become an art student. He suspected later that the idea of his studying art had arisen not through an analysis of his talents, but because this represented an easy inexpensive way of giving him a scrappy bit of further education. What Tim never knew was that the trust money had given out some time earlier and that Tim's quite lengthy student days were financed by Guy's father, later by Guy, out of their own pockets. Guy never told anyone, not even Gertrude, about this. Tim's tuition was paid for (later he obtained a government grant) and he received a modest allowance upon which he lived in a student hostel, then in digs. He began his studies in a suburban art school, after which, to his teachers' surprise and not least to his own, he scrambled into the Slade. When he had finished his final course Guy informed him that the trust money was nearly at an end and that the allowance could continue only for another six months. After all, thought Guy, the young fellow must learn to stand on his own feet. Whether Tim ever stood there was something which Tim himself often wondered. When Tim left the Slade he was twenty-three and Guy was thirty four.

Later on Tim began to feel differently about his mother. When he could no longer console and love her, his heart turned towards her. He dreamt about her, that he was searching for her in dark vague halls or upon endless stairs. When he was a child his father had represented freedom, his mother bondage; but how unjust it was, with the deep casual injustice of a rotten world. His father had been an egoistic irresponsible bastard. His mother had been solitary, impoverished, ill, even her children had turned against her. Of course, as she struggled unsupported with every sort of difficulty, she became tired and ill-tempered. She needed help and love, only now when there was love for her in Tim's heart it was too late. He had come round to loving his mother and hating his father when they were both ghosts. He longed vainly to make amends. He talked to Daisy about this guilt and this pain. Daisy said, 'Yes, our shitty parents let us down, but I suppose we have to be sorry for them. They were miserable and we're happy, so we win in the end.' Tim thought that his father wasn't miserable, and that he himself was not always happy, but he did not argue. Tim had a modest view of his rights and talents, and although he sometimes felt he had been unfortunate he had to admit that his adult life so far had been devoid of catastrophes, and he was prepared to settle for the contentment of 'the man who has no history'. He saw himself sometimes as a soldier of fortune, a raffish footloose fellow, a drinker, a wandering cadger, a happy-go-lucky figure in a shabby uniform (not of course an officer) who lived from day to day avoiding unpleasantness and procuring small fairly innocuous satisfactions. There was no ground-base of happiness in his life, but he was naturally merry. He had (and he counted it his nearest approach to virtue) a cheerful temperament. He often thought too about his sister Rita, only about her he did not talk to Daisy. (Daisy had also suffered from anorexia nervosa when she was a girl, as a protest against Roedean.) Tim and Rita had fought a lot but they had been very close, allies against the world; which would have been an *utterly different* world now had Rita lived. As it was Tim had nobody but Daisy.

When Tim had first met Daisy, when he was entering the Slade and she was leaving it, he had admired her from afar. She was, then, a striking figure. She was very thin and boyish, with short very dark hair and large dark brown eyes, a pale pure-complexioned well-shaped face and a long sensual mouth that drooped at the corners. She had a sharp pretty nose and a mole beside one nostril. The mole matched her woody-brown eyes like a droplet. She could move her scalp backwards and forwards in an amusing manner. She dressed outrageously and was regarded by persons of both sexes as a desirable object. Though rarely inclined to formulate consistent policies, she was also regarded as something of a leader. She preferred the other sex to her own, but had emotional friendships with women, especially (at the Slade) with a group of vociferous American

Women's Liberationists. Her own opinions were of the anarchistic extreme left variety, and when roused to controversy her dark brown eyes would become square with fury. She was a talented painter of whom much was expected. When, two years later, she took Tim for a lover he was extremely proud. He felt it was the beginning of a brilliant new era.

Now Tim was thirty-three and Daisy was thirty-five. She was still handsome and boyish and slim, and her fine painted eyes still had what Tim called their 'Etruscan look', but sometimes, he had to admit, she looked almost old. Her thin face had become prematurely haggard and her close-cropped hair showed streaks of grey. Rows of fine lines seamed her upper lip. Her face had become more emphatic and expressive so that she seemed to be grimacing as she talked. She had increasingly the rather dotty smile of a Goya peasant. It was harder than it used to be for her to communicate with people. Her voice, a curious mixture of a French accent and a Canadian accent, dominated by the Bloomsburian upper class voice of her mother, grew more strident. Her language, always lurid, grew more foul, and she laughed at Tim's shudders. Tim was old-fashioned enough to object to the words 'shit' and 'fuck' occurring constantly in the mouth of the woman he loved. Tim's appearance had of course changed too, but, he felt, not so much. At twenty-three he had had long curly blazing red hair. He now wore his hair shorter and it had lost its curl and faded, it might even almost be called 'ginger'. His pallid freckled face seemed unchanged however. He had a small nose which often wrinkled (he had an acute sense of smell) and his lips were ruddy. His eyes were azure, not a pale snake-blue like the Count's, but the full glowing blue of a summer sky. He could perhaps have been diagnosed as Irish by a compatriot because of a certain quirkiness about his mouth and a quick nervous vagueness about his eyes. (There is a fierce hard Irish face, and a soft gentle one, and Tim had the latter.) He was slight, shorter than Daisy. He was clean-shaven at present; when he wore a moustache he looked like a boy lieutenant in the first war.

Tim and Daisy had stayed together for a while, parted, and come together again. Both had had other love affairs, usually unsatisfactory and in Daisy's case very stormy. Daisy seemed to hate all her former lovers, whereas Tim was on quite good terms with the wayward Welsh girls of his past. (In this respect London had quite redeemed Cardiff.) Daisy was indeed full of hates. She hated the bourgeoisie, the capitalist state, marriage, religion, God, materialism, the establishment, anybody with money, anybody who had been to a university, all the political parties, and men, with the exception of Tim whom she said (and he was not sure if he was pleased or not) she did not count as a man. The tall noisy American women had departed to found some sort of women's community in California, but their ideas lived on in Daisy's turbulent bosom. Men were beasts, vile selfish egoistic bullies. 'Look at our bloody fathers!' Hetero-sexual male humans were the nastiest animals on the planet. Some of them drove themselves literally mad with egoism. Tim was occasionally depressed by her universal belittling malice, but more often he found it oddly invigorating. He recognised in her a deep generosity of spirit and a kind of innocence which disarmed her sharp opinions. Her left wing views had gradually composed themselves into a sort of passionate anarchism. She upset Tim most by professing a sympathy with terrorism. 'It's just an aesthetic reaction against materialism.' She sometimes said she would like to be a terrorist herself.

It was never very clear what happened to Daisy's career as a painter. She took a part-time teaching post in a well-known London art school, and produced some promising work, abstract of course, they were all abstract painters in those days. (This early work often consisted of tiny squares or tiny crosses of slightly varying colours with which she meticulously honey-combed enormous canvases.) Then suddenly she changed her style and one obsessive mood followed another. At one time she would paint nothing but piles of boxes (matchboxes, card-board boxes, crates), at another nothing but (extremely realistic) spiders, or window frames, or burning candles. She went into a half-satirical 'primitive' phase, and at this time sold a modest amount of work to people who found her paintings 'charming'. The experts had begun to shake their heads how-ever: she was not developing, there was a moody versatile cleverness but no depth. Daisy herself now began to declare that she was not seriously interested in painting and was not properly a painter at all. She announced her discovery that she was really a writer. She gave up her teaching job and wrote a novel and to everyone's amazement got it published. It had a little success but was not reprinted. She wrote another novel which was not published. Tim, with whom she was once again living, persuaded her to go back to art teaching. Jobs were now a good deal harder to find. She found a part-time post teaching art history, about which she knew little (but little was required). She became interested in screen-printing and textile design and thought she would set up on her own as a designer, but nothing came of this except that she left her job. She started on a third novel which was still intermittently in progress. She took another job and then lost it. Tim knew that she was, or had been, a better painter than he was. But he knew no magic by which he could persuade her to work.

Meanwhile Tim, more modest and more cunning, had managed to keep himself afloat and indeed increasingly to keep Daisy afloat too. He also had failed to improve, to 'develop', but he kept on painting assiduously, content to be a mediocre painter and enjoy it. He had no identity, no 'personal style', but he did not mind. (Guy once told Tim that it did not matter, having no identity.) He became a cubist, then a surrealist, then a *fauve*: a futurist, a constructivist, a suprematist. He adopted expressionism, post-expressionism, abstract expressionism. (But never minimal or conceptual or pop, these he despised.) He imitated everybody he admired, everybody fairly modern that is, he could not imitate Titian and Piero. (He would have done if he had known how to start.) He painted pseudo-Klees, pseudo-Picassos, pseudo-Magrittes, pseudo-Soutines. He would have done pseudo-Cezannes only that was beyond him. He attempted spotty interiors in the style of Vuillard, and breakfast tables in the style of Bonnard. One of his teachers had said to him, 'Tim, I think it is your destiny to become a great faker.' Alas Tim could not rise to this. Faking demands a patience and a knowledge of chemistry which Tim did not possess. It also demands a considerable talent as a painter. Tim did not possess this either.

Tim would not have agreed with the Shakespearean dictum that if all the year were playing holidays to sport would be as tedious as to work. He had occasional bouts of childish misery but they did not last long. His exiguous teaching was not arduous. When he tired of painting he went to the pub. He was not an industrious painter, he was indeed rarely systematic. He was not a reader of books. What he knew about the history of his art he picked up in an instinctive and random manner. He went to the picture galleries and remembered what he liked. He also, in a spirit of hedonism, haunted the British Museum. His interest in the exhibits was purely visual, he knew nothing of their history. Unencumbered by extraneous facts he taught himself to look at Greek vases and Etruscan tombs and Roman painting, and Assyrian reliefs, and vast Egyptian statues, and tiny jade objects from China and tiny ivory objects from Japan. All sorts of things took his fancy and pleased his magpie taste: elegant Roman letters, curled-up Celtic animals, jewels, clocks, coins. These aesthetic adventures rarely influenced his painting, and it never occurred to him that he might be inspired by what he could not copy.

He attempted to sell his paintings, but this was difficult since no one would exhibit them. Friends and acquaintances occasionally bought his work out of kindness (the prices were modest). The Count bought a painting (a pseudo-Klee), and Guy bought one and hid it. Tim, never very ambitious and now resigned, went on drawing and painting randomly, it was after all a natural function. He drew people, figures in pubs or on streets, whom he thought of as 'spectators at a crucifixion'. A man drinking beer watching a crucifixion, a man selling newspapers watching a crucifixion, a man on a passing bus watching a crucifixion. The crucifixion scene itself, however, never materialised. His drawings could appear impressive and he once obtained a lucrative commission to produce some carefully specified pornographic pictures; but he felt disgusted with himself afterward and never did it again. He sometimes did pretty-pretty representations of flowers or animals, of which he felt differently and mildly ashamed and which did at least sometimes sell for small sums. If he sold them through shops, the shops took a commission. He had a friend, a commercially minded painter and dealer called Jimmy Roland (whose sister Nancy was one of Tim's old flames), who exhibited at the Hyde Park railings on Sundays, and he sometimes put some of Tim's 'pretty-pretties' in with his work. Tim's most successful line was cats. In England a drawing of a cat will always sell if it is soppy enough. Tim studied soppiness. For a while he had a three-day-a-week job teaching drawing in a polytechnic in North London. Then the teaching was reduced to one day a week. The cats were a useful stand-by, but he was getting tired of them. He went on painting 'seriously' but without much hope of selling anything.

When he and Daisy joined forces for the second time, just before Daisy's 'literary phase', they lived together in a pleasant flat in Hampstead. This was a brief period of expansion and domesticity. They developed a sort of social life together. They went folk dancing; Tim was a good dancer, he had been a keen Morris man as a student. They learnt to play chess and had hilarious incompetent contests which ended with Daisy pushing the board onto the floor. Tim even learnt to cook a little; Daisy despised cooking. However by the time Daisy had finished her second novel they were living in a smaller nastier flat in Kilburn and coming to the conclusion that though they would stay together they could not live together. Close proximity brought on endless tiring quarrels which Tim felt were Daisy's fault and she said were his fault. Tim was obsessively tidy, Daisy wildly untidy, and it became necessary for him to get away so as not to live amid perpetual mess. He was appalled by her unwillingness to clean or embellish. He wearied of picking her clothes up off the floor and washing them. He needed more space in which to paint, while Daisy said his presence distracted her from writing. They both really feared proximity, lack of privacy; cohabitation was becoming altogether too exhausting.

Tim moved out and wondered if this was the end, but it was not. Their relation was revivified, rendered suddenly more romantic and exciting. Their love-making, which Daisy had announced was becoming 'bloody dull' was once more impetuous and unpredictable. When they decided to go home together, to Tim's place or Daisy's place, it was as if they were students again, creeping up the stairs and giggling. Sometimes one would say 'We're bad for each other' so that the other should say 'No'. Or 'We are just flitting through each other's lives, in one door and out the other.' Or Daisy would say to him 'Go and find yourself a dolly bird, I'm too old,' but she did not mean it. Really they felt that in their odd way (and they gloried in its oddity) they had settled down. Tim and Daisy loved all pubs the way some people love all dogs. The pubs were innocent places wherein they were innocent children. They returned to the Soho pubs which had been their original home, where they had spent every evening before returning to cheerless digs or hostels when they were young. This sort of urban life suited Tim, pub-crawling, wandering, looking in shop windows. He loved the charm of noisy messy changing London, pedestrian bridges and roads on stilts, the magic of Westway, of modern pubs beside noisy roundabouts. Soho in summer was his South of France.

Daisy moved out of the Kilburn flat, which had become too expensive, and for a time had a cheap room in Gerard Street where at first she rather enjoyed being molested, but then became frightened. Tim found her a little one-room-with-kitchenette place in the dusty confines of Hammersmith and Shepherd's Bush, with a shared bathroom, very cheap. She was now out of work and he had to help to support her. She had also begun to take more seriously to drink. Tim himself had been very lucky in finding a large room, a sort of loft, over a garage just off the Chiswick High Road. There was an outside lavatory with a wash basin, and he installed an electric ring for cooking and a paraffin stove for heating. Rent and rates were very low, as the room was not supposed to be a dwelling. Tim pretended he just used it as a studio. The garage man, called Brian, who saw Tim as a romantic Bohemian, winked at lights on late at night. Once, in order to save money, Daisy had let her flatlet to a tourist for a limited time and moved in with Tim. Once Tim moved in with Daisy and, in order to encourage her to let her flat, pretended he had let his. He did not really let it, however, since he feared inquiries, discovery, police, and a vast unpayable bill for arrears of rates. Tim was frightened of 'officials' of any kind. (This was perhaps why he never managed to get more than the most meagre amount of National Assistance.) Guy had once mentioned to him, in connection with some show of excessive anxiety on Tim's part, an expressive Greek verb, *lanthano*, which meant *I escape notice* doing something or other. Tim decided that his motto was *Lanthano*.

Tim was partly touched, partly exasperated by Daisy's assumption that he would support her. Sometimes, in the ebb and flow of their relations, the assumption seemed natural, sometimes not. There was always the possibility that he would get a better job, that she would decide to teach again, that her novel would make a fortune. They soldiered on, as the years fleeted by, still saying, 'Maybe we'd better part, give it up, we might be better off with someone else.' To which the answer was 'Who'd have us now?' and off to the pub. Daisy took to keeping flagons of wine in her flat and staying in bed till noon. They never really tested their relationship on a public scene. The very modest 'entertaining' of the Hampstead days was no more. Their old Slade friends had mostly drifted away. They had some pub friends. Daisy had women friends whom Tim hardly ever met, more 'Women's Libbers', and left wing toughies. Tim, who had no politics, had a few odd pals such as Jimmy Roland and one or two of his art school colleagues. And then there was the mob at Ebury Street.

Tim's relation with Ebury Street had, throughout recent years, remained steady without ever becoming deeper or more interesting. Tim, when he was a student, and after the demise of Rudi Openshaw, had been acquainted with Guy's father, a rather alarming figure who lived in a large house in Swiss Cottage to which Tim went at intervals to say how well he was getting on and to receive advice about how to live more economically. Guy, the son, was at that time a shadowy figure, lately married, who occasionally passed by in the background when Tim was visiting the father's house. On one visit Tim saw Gertrude, a younger slimmer Gertrude, all dressed up to go out to a party. When Guy's father died, Tim came instead, at rather rarer intervals, to report himself at Ebury Street. He was never then invited to any social function, though Guy, whom Tim regarded with nervous veneration, usually gave him a glass of sherry. When he finished his studies and his allowance ended Tim assumed that now Ebury Street would know him no more. Indeed his conception of Guy at this time was hazy, and of Gertrude vaguer still. None of the others had he ever met at all. However, as a result of some mysterious decree, his status, instead of sinking into nothing was, by the change, enhanced. The vanishing of money from the relationship had somehow rendered it social, unofficial. Tim was asked to drinks, he became a regular attender at the Ebury Street 'days'. Sometimes there were large parties. Once he took Daisy to one. It was not a success. She was impolitely silent, then left early. Tim stayed on, then had a row with her afterwards.

Daisy set herself up to detest these 'bourgeois grandees' who were, she professed to think, gradually swallowing Tim, digesting him into their horrible snobby world. At the same time, Daisy said, they despised him, mocked him, treated him with condescension and contempt. They were artificial unreal people, she hated them. She was of course, as Tim realized, jealous. However he did not intend to give up Ebury Street. He tried not to mention his visits there, only Daisy kept returning to the subject and needling him about his 'snobbery' and telling him he was being 'drugged by the odour of affluence'. Daisy's instinct was in a sense right. Tim was rather enchanted by the Ebury Street scene, not (he felt) by its whiff of affluence, but simply by its atmosphere of family. Tim had no family, no belongingness anywhere except with Daisy. The Ebury Street gatherings were familial, and it gave him pleasure to be a taken-for granted junior member of that circle of family and friends. Nor indeed was he indifferent, after the dirt and chaos of Daisy's flat and the frugal simplicity of his own, to occasional visits to a warm clean tidy house where sherry was served in handsome glasses. Altogether, and in a sense he never troubled to define, Ebury Street was for him an abode of value.

The person there with whom he got on best was the Count. (Tim knew he was not a real count.) The Count had been markedly kind to him from the start, and Tim had intuited something of the Count's particular loneliness and alienness. He was grateful to the Count for having bought his picture (it was entitled *Three Blackbirds in a Treacle Well*). He hoped the Count might invite him to his flat, but that never happened. Balintoy was also kind to Tim and petted him, but he could not understand Balintoy, and felt uneasy with his fellow Irishman. Once or twice Gerald Pavitt had asked Tim for drinks in a pub, but Gerald was very odd and self-absorbed and Tim found him difficult to talk to. Gerald knew nothing about painting, and Tim knew nothing about the stars (or whatever it was that Gerald did, he was not sure). Stanley Openshaw, also very kind to Tim, invited him to lunch once. He was not asked again, he suspected, because Janet did not like the look of him. With Guy and Gertrude his relations had always been cordial though formal. He was a little afraid of both of them. Guy had been quite prepared to play the heavy father, especially when once, in desperation and not long ago, Tim had asked him for a loan. He had lent Tim the money and given him a lecture too. This debt was on Tim's conscience and not repaid. He wondered if Gertrude knew about it.

Tim had greeted the news of Guy's fatal illness first with incredulity. How could anyone as strong and real as Guy propose to disappear from the world at the age of forty-four? Then he felt a fear which pierced into his entrails. In a respectful way, he loved Guy. But he felt a deeper emotion for himself. How on earth would he manage in the world without Guy? It was not just a question of money or of drinks or even of 'advice' which Guy might give him. Guy had taken over a parental role in Tim's life. There had for so long always 'been Guy' there, a safe stronghold, a final refuge. If 'everything crashed' (a vivid entirely unclear possibility which Tim constantly envisaged) Guy would somehow be there to pick up the pieces. Guy's background presence even in some way helped Tim to manage his life with Daisy. He was able to be calmer and more rational because of that (and not just financial) 'last resort'. There was wisdom, there was authority, there was calm truthful affection. Guy had always exacted from Tim, as he had usually managed to exact from everybody, a particular sort of directness. The mysterious urge to lie, even pointlessly, is not always understood. Tim was evasive by nature, even something of a casual habitual liar; but he had learnt early on to tell the truth to Guy. Would there now be no more truth?

There had perhaps been one case of *suppressio veri*. Tim had never told Guy about Daisy. Of course there had been no special occasion to do so. Guy did not question Tim about his 'private life' in general, nor had he asked about Daisy in particular, whom he had no doubt (at that unhappy party) scarcely noticed. Tim never, after the occasion of the party (now some years ago), spoke of Daisy at Ebury Street. It was clear that he could never take her there again even if she were willing to come. She had been so quietly bloody-minded, had exhibited so much 'dumb insolence', and he hoped that she had, in that quarter, been forgotten. Tim thought afterwards that, when he asked Guy for money, he ought to have mentioned Daisy in answer to some of Guy's questions. But he shrank from exposing the rackety life which he led with his dear one to the meticulous, though discreet and charitable, scrutiny of Guy Openshaw.

As Tim never looked ahead he did not explicitly say to himself, Daisy and I will be together forever, I will die in her arms or she in mine. But it was the atmosphere of their connection, although Daisy never spoke of it either. They were two of a kind. Tim drew them as birds, as foxes, as mice, as mates, as pairs of timid uniquely similar creatures escaping notice. *Lanthano.* They were Pappagena and Pappageno. He said this to Daisy who, although she hated opera, accepted the idea. Pappageno had had to go through an ordeal to win his true mate; and like him, Tim too would be saved at last in spite of himself. As he felt how inevitable and yet how imperfect was his relation with Daisy he wondered sometimes whether the ordeal which was to perfect it was yet to come.

By this time, back in the Prince of Denmark, Tim had eaten one piece of bread, the cheddar cheese, one oatmeal biscuit, a tomato, and half the cake. Daisy had eaten one piece of bread, the Stilton cheese, three oatmeal biscuits, a tomato, the cold roast lamb, and the other half of the cake. They had also bought and divided a ham sandwich. They decided they could not afford a Scotch egg.

'Who was there?' Daisy meant at Ebury Street that evening. Although she despised the 'ghastly crew', she sometimes made Tim call them over, and took a ghoulish interest in their doings. She had even picked up Guy's phrase *les cousins et les tantes.*

'Oh Stanley, the Count, Victor, Manfred, Mrs Mount—'

'Not Sylvia Wicks?'

'Yes—'

'She was the only one I liked in that infernal galère. Victimised by a bloody man.' On the occasion of the party, Daisy had elicited the tale of Sylvia's marriage.

'Here's a new beer mat. Would you like it?'

'Yes, thanks.' Daisy collected beer mats. 'Let's face it, men are beasts. Well, you're not. Thanks for the grub. Was it still raining when you came in?'

'Yes, a little.'

'Why there's Jimmy Roland with that fool Piglet, pissed again.'

'Daisy, there's something I haven't told you.'

'Something bloody awful? Are you ill?'

'No. I won't have any teaching next term.'

'You mean they've sacked you?'

'You might put it so.'

'Fucking hell fire. And there's something I haven't told you. They've raised my rent again. I think I'll have another double whisky.'

Tim went to fetch it. From the bar he looked back at Daisy, smiled at her. Sometimes she wore jeans and an old jersey. Sometimes she put on outrageous feminine fancy dress. (She could not give up a childish covetous habit of buying cheap clothes.) This evening she was wearing black fish-net tights, a voluminous skirt of a deeply saturated blue Indian cotton drawn in to her narrow waist, and an ill-fitting yellowish décolleté lace blouse, bought at an old clothes shop. A necklace of glass beads closely encircled her thin neck. Her dark streaky hair was sleeked away behind her ears, revealing the form of her narrow bony head. She had put on today a red mouth and red cheeks, and had encircled her large long eyes with dark blue. (Some days she wore no make-up.) A shaggy old woollen cardigan which she wore underneath her overcoat lay across her knees. Her skirt was well hitched up. There was something exotic, handsome, violent, raffish about her which touched his heart. And she was, for all her panache, so absolutely vulnerable. She smiled back at Tim.

Tim was wearing narrow grey tweed trousers, old but good (he never wore jeans) and a loose turquoise-coloured woollen jersey over an apple green shirt. He had fortunately, from better days, a supply of decent sensible clothes; woollen vests cost the earth now. He enjoyed mating colours and would often dye his garments with meticulous care.

'Thanks, Blue Eyes, you are good to me. What the hell are we going to do about money, fuck it? Cash is real, cash is earnest. We'll be reduced to drinking the left-overs in the pubs, like bloody Frog Catholics living on the Eucharist.'

'I wish you'd paint,' said Tim, 'I wish you'd *really* paint.' He said this at intervals just to keep the idea in her head.

'Fuck it, darling, I can't paint. I mean I won't paint. I know you think women can't paint because they have no sexual fantasies—'

'I don't,' said Tim.

'What's it to do with money anyway if I paint. I'm a writer. I'm writing my novel. You'd better do some more of those mogs. Everyone in this stupid little country has a picture of a cat and wants to buy another.'

'I'm drawing Perkins, I'll do another set, but they fetch precious little.' Tim knew that it would be spiritually impossible for Daisy to paint sentimental pictures of cats, and although this was a pity in a way, he treasured the fact as evidence of her tough invincible superiority to himself.

'God, if we could only get out of bloody London, I'm stir-crazy, I'm so tired of this Christ-awful old familiar scene, I'd like to get drunk somewhere else for a change.'

'Yeah.' This too was something which was regularly said.

'It would be great not to have to worry about money *all* the time.'

'I'll have to get another job, any job, and you must drink less, can't you just bloody try?'

'No, I just bloody can't. I gave up smoking to please you and that's it as far as abnegation is concerned. And don't pretend you're going to get a job washing up or something, you know you can't stand it, it ended in tears last time.'

That was true enough. 'Maybe we can manage on National Assistance.'

'Not with my rent we can't. And the drink, all right, but the drink is a fact of life. You drink too after all, and just imagine doing without it. I'm sorry I'm not a millionaire like your grand friends at Ebury Street. I bet everybody in this pub is on social security, and I bet they all squeeze more than we do out of the bloody Welfare State.'

'We're lazy, that's our trouble,' said Tim. Sometimes he thought this was a profound truth.

'We're hopeless,' said Daisy. 'I can't think how we stand each other. At least, I can't think how you stand me. You ought to find yourself a girl, there are plenty around the pubs who'd fancy you even if your hair *is* falling out.'

'It isn't falling out. And I've got a girl.'

'Yes, you've got yer old Daisy. We've been a long time in the love-me and leave-me game and here we still are. We're OK.'

'We're OK.'

'Except we're a bit stuck for what we shall eat and what we shall drink and what we shall put on. Hell's bells and buckets of blood, if only we could get out of London I could finish my novel. But meanwhile you'd better get on with the moggies. If only one of us could make a rich marriage and then support the other.'

'If you married a millionaire I could be the butler.'

'You'd be boozing in the pantry. And I'd be with you.'

'We're servants' hall types.'

'Speak for yourself, I'm not! Your wealthy friends put on airs but they're just *nouveaux riches*. My mother was really upper class.'

'Yeah.'

'Can't you borrow money from any of that lot, what else are they for *les cousins et les tantes*? Can't you get something more out of Guy before he kicks the bucket? Do you think he'll leave you anything in his will?'

'No. And no. I can't ask Guy for money now, it's too late.'

'What bugs me is the way you revere them, and they're all so fat.'

'They aren't.'

'And they treat you like a lackey.'

'Oh stow it—'

'The trouble is you've kept up appearances, we both have. You ought to look as poor as you are. But no, off you trot in your best suit. Nobody has the faintest idea how poor we are. I expect they think we've "got money of our own", that wonderful phrase! Jesus bloody Christ. What about Gertrude?'

'No.'

'Why not, you can ask her. You've got no *pluck*. God, she's a stuffy bastard, she sucks in all the oxygen so you can't breathe.'

'You only met her once.'

'Once was enough, dear boy. That *grande dame*! She was the get of two little Scottish dominies. I'm upper classer than her.'

'I can't ask Gertrude.'

'I don't see why not. And that orchestra of china monkeys.

God, *they're* an orchestra of china monkeys! What about his excellency the Count?'

It amused Tim to let Daisy think the Count was a real count. This fed her scorn and made her happy.

'The Count's not rich.'

'They don't have to be rich. What about Manfred, he really *is* rich.'

'No, he's too—'

'You're frightened of him.'

'Yes.'

'I think you're frightened of them all. You must ask someone or we won't eat. Maybe there's a good time coming but it's crisis now. What about Balintoy?'

'No.'

'You always look funny when I mention Balintoy. What is it?'

'Nothing.'

'You're a terrible liar, Tim. Some people are just liars like being red-haired.'

'He hasn't any money.'

'You said the noble lord was in Colorado. How do people with no money get to Colorado when we can't even get as far as Epping Forest? Mrs Mount?'

'No, she's poor.'

'She's a snake.'

'Well, she's a poor snake.'

'You're always around with your posh friends but you never seem to get anything out of them except a couple of tomatoes and a bit of stale cheese.'

'It wasn't stale.'

'Mine was. An orchestra of china monkeys! That's them exactly. Oh shit, what's the answer. I suppose there isn't one.'

'Daisy, we've got to manage *on our own.*'

'We keep saying that, but things get worse. What happens when one's destitute? Do you think I like taking your pennies when there's so little—I do notice! *Rien à faire,* one of us will have to marry for money.'

'Make a rich marriage and join the bourgeoisie?'

'Yes, well, at least we're free, we've stayed outside in freedom, in reality. We don't live artificial faked-up lives like your rich pals. You can't imagine *them* here, can you? Or living on frozen fish fingers like us. Pity our upbringing won't let us steal from supermarkets. Are you sure Guy won't leave you any money?'

'Pretty sure.'

'I bet he cheated you out of that trust money. You never saw any of the papers, did you? I bet there was a lot more cash than they pretended. You ought to have asked to see the documents.'

It was true that Tim had never seen any papers, it had not occurred to him to ask. The Openshaws could have cheated him, but he just knew that they had not. Sometimes Daisy's malice depressed him, her determined belittling of people he respected. Of course in a sense it wasn't serious, it was just a way of complaining about the world in general. Sometimes he found himself drawn into a tacit complicity of malice, it was easier than arguing.

'*Time, gentlemen, please.*'

'There are ladies present!' shouted Daisy, banging her glass on the table.

She shouted this every night at the Prince of Denmark. People sometimes walked along the road from the Fitzroy to hear her.

'I wish you had seen Guy earlier,' said Gertrude. 'He was so beautiful.'

She and Anne were sitting together in the drawing-room. It was late afternoon. Anne was sewing buttons onto one of Gertrude's mackintoshes. Gertrude was trying, following Anne's new enthusiasm, to read a novel, but the words of *Mansfield Park* kept jumbling themselves up into nonsense before her eyes.

'He's beautiful now,' said Anne. To please Gertrude she had bought another dress, a plain dark blue tweed dress with a leather belt. She smoothed back her straight silver-blonde fur and looked at Gertrude with a loving intentness which sometimes comforted and sometimes exasperated her friend. Gertrude had become, in the last days, somehow wilder and more desperate and she sensed Anne's sense of the change. Gertrude felt as if she were suddenly ageing. I am growing older and Anne is growing younger, she thought.

Gertrude had been amazed by the frightful jealousy which she had felt when Anne had talked so long and so ardently with Guy on the previous evening. She had even heard them laugh. She did not eavesdrop of course. Guy had had a sort of collapse afterwards and she had thought: he will die, and Anne, arriving out of the blue, will be the last person to have talked to him. Anne had emerged looking strained and exalted with tears in her eyes. Guy had rallied but he remained, with Gertrude, aloof, vaguely bitter, almost spiteful. Sometimes his eyes had that mad fishy look which made him seem another person, a breathing simulacrum of the loved one weirdly kept alive. He is not himself, she thought; but how terrible to die not oneself. She thought this, but could not yet really think 'die'. Guy had that morning decided not to be shaved any more. Already his face had changed with the dark outline of the stubble. He looked like a rabbi. She would never again see the face that she had known.

While Guy was talking to Anne the Count had arrived with Veronica Mount, and they had both spoken appreciatively of Gertrude's 'nun'. Victor was absent dealing with an epidemic of Asian 'flu. Manfred came, as he always did, and Stanley who brought Janet with him. She had just been giving a lecture. She brought more flowers and was sweet to Gertrude. Mrs Mount talked about a splendid exotic Jewish wedding she had attended in her deceased husband's family, with oriental music and dancing rabbis. She went on to criticise the arrangements at Jeremy Schultz's Bar Mitzvah. Stanley talked about 'the House'. Moses Greenberg, the family solicitor, a middle-aged widower who had married an Openshaw, arrived late. He talked about his niece who was to marry Akiba Lebowitz, the controversial psychiatrist. He also mentioned that Sylvia Wicks had come to consult him on a point of law on behalf of a friend. Sylvia had not reappeared since the night when she asked to see Guy. Gertrude felt she had been rude to Sylvia. Guy had not wanted to see the Count, and had been curt with Gertrude later in the evening. Gertrude had not asked Anne what she and Guy had talked about and Anne had not said.

Today it was foggy and neither of the women had been out. London was huddled under a damp freezing-cold pall of brownish air. The street lights had been on all day, and Gertrude had pulled the curtains at three o'clock. A fire was burning in the grate. Janet Openshaw's chrysanthemums were still quite fresh with the beech leaves and eucalyptus on the marquetry table. Gertrude had arranged Janet's new flowers, a mass of mauve and white anemones in a big oatmeal coloured Staffordshire mug, and put them on the mantelpiece, beside one of the Bohemian vases. (Flowers were never put in the Bohemian vases in case the water made a mark on the glass.) She felt a physical agony of restlessness, and a desire to cry out loudly. She dropped her book on the floor, aware of Anne's quiet gaze.

The nurse put her head round the door. 'Oh Mrs Openshaw, Mr Openshaw wants to see you.'

Gertrude leapt up. This was unusual. The days had fallen into such a steady pattern. This was still the time of Guy's rest. Then the nurse was with him. Then after that was Gertrude's time. Gertrude thought, this is it. But the nurse was smiling her dry professional smile as she held the door open.

Guy's door was ajar. Gertrude entered, breathless with fear. The single lamp was lighted by the bed. Guy was sitting propped up. His bearded face shocked her. Other things were different too. He held out a hand towards her.

Spellbound, Gertrude took the frail hand, sat in the bedside chair, was convulsed with a desire to sob. Guy was suddenly present to her, all present, with his whole tenderness, his whole love, his real being.

He said. 'Steady, my darling, my dear heart, my love, my own dear one, my dear —'

Gertrude cried quietly, leaning over, her tears dropping onto his hand, onto the sheet, onto the floor.

He said, 'You know how it is. We aren't parted. In a way we'll never be parted. Forgive me if I've seemed so sort of far away.'

'I know — I know —' said Gertrude. 'Oh Guy, how can I bear it —'

'Bear it you can, and if you can you must. I'm so full of

beastly drugs, that's partly the trouble. And—I don't want to weep my way to the tomb. It's better to be calm and dull. I don't want to see you distraught, I don't want you to be distraught. We know about our love and our life, how good it has been. We don't have to repeat it all now with weeping and wailing. You understand, dearest heart?'

'Yes, yes—'

'Well, weep less, there's something I want to say to you.' He shifted sighing, pulling at his hair for a moment with his other hand. 'I enjoyed talking to Anne.'

'I'm so glad.'

'It was a foretaste of heaven.'

'A—?'

'You recall some witty Frenchman said that his idea of heaven was *discuter les idées générales avec les femmes superieures*. But don't worry, I haven't been converted. "Heaven's morning breaks and earth's vain shadows flee!" Do you remember Uncle Rudi singing that?'

'He knew all the Anglican hymns.'

'One thing one does learn at an English Public School. A perfectly suitable song for a cantor. I'm glad Anne's with you.'

'So am I.'

'I wanted to—'

'To tell something?'

'Yes.'

'Are you all right, in pain—'

'I'm fine—'

'You suddenly seem so much better—oh God if only—'

'Gertrude, don't. Now listen my darling, my dear one—kiss me first.'

Gertrude kissed his strange bearded lips. She felt desire for him, which had been absent. She groaned and sat back, holding his hand and caressing it with a sudden passion.

'Good dear girl. Gertrude, I want you to be happy when I'm gone.'

'I can't be happy,' she said. 'I shall never be happy again, I can't be. I won't kill myself, it won't be necessary, I'll walk and talk but I'll be dead. I don't mean I'll go mad, but I won't be happy, it isn't possible. I can't be happy without you, it's a fact of nature. I wasn't happy till I met you.'

'An illusion,' said Guy, 'and anyway a quite different point. You will recover.'

'What does it mean to—'

'We've had a wonderful time.'

'Yes—'

'Listen, I must talk rationally while I can. I most intensely want you to be happy when I'm gone. They say "He would have wished" this or that has no sense, but it has. I am giving it sense now, for you, do you understand? Don't waste time being miserable. I want you to find happiness, to be ingenious and resolute to live, to survive. You are intelligent and strong. You are young. You can have a whole other lifetime after I am dead.'

'Guy, I can't. I shall be dead too—walking and talking and dead—Please don't try to—'

'You love me, but you won't grieve forever. I want you to seek joy and to seek it intelligently. I beg and pray you not to grieve. I know you can't imagine it now, but you will pass out of these shadows. I see a light beyond.'

'Not without you—'

'Now, Gertrude, stop. You must try, for my sake, to have the will *now* to please me in the future. In that future when I won't exist any more. There won't be any me any more and long grief will be stupid. People mourn because they think it does some good, it's a kind of tribute. But there's no recipient. "Many a one for him makes moan, but none shall know where he is gone!" Can you remember any more of it?'

'It's a Scottish ballad, but I can't remember—'

' "His lady's ta'en another mate"—'

'Oh—Guy—'

'Don't just be emotional, *think* and think *with me*. Be *with me* now, even if it's hard. Why shouldn't you marry again! You could have a whole new happiness with another person. I don't want you to be alone.'

'No. I am you.'

'So you feel. It will be different later. Life, nature, time will work upon you. I've thought about it and I want you to marry. You could marry Peter for instance. He is a good man and he loves you. He is pure in heart. You know that he loves you?'

96

Gertrude hesitated. She sort of knew. She had never worried about it. 'The Count, yes. It did sometimes seem — But I —'

'I'm just saying this to concentrate your mind. Heaven knows what will happen to you next year. It may be something entirely unexpected. But I so much . . . want you to be . . . safe . . . and happy . . . when I'm not around. . . .'

He sank back among the pillows. 'I want to die well . . . but how is it done?'

Just outside the partly open door the Count, who had arrived early and come quietly up the stairs, stood frozen upon the landing. The drawing-room door was shut, so was Anne's door. The nurse was in the kitchen. In silence and alone he overheard Guy's words concerning himself. He turned about and tiptoed away, out of the flat and down the stairs.

TWO

Time had passed and Guy Openshaw was dead. He lived longer than had been expected, but obliged the doctor's prediction by dying on Christmas Eve. His ashes had been scattered in an anonymous garden. It was now early April in the following year, and Gertrude Openshaw, *née* McCluskie, was looking out of a window at a cool cloudy sunlit scene. To her right, fairly close, was a small rocky headland where furry emerald grass was brushed down like a hat over a bulge of grey cliff, cluttered with tiny facets, which descended into the sea, it being now high tide. At low tide the rocks descended to a beach of stones below which was a little line of pale yellow sand. The stones were grey, oblong flattish, of a uniform size and shape, so that from a distance they looked like the scales of a fish. They had been clashed and beaten by the millennial sea into a terrible density and an absolute smoothness. Here and there only was one chipped or pitted or covered with little runic scratches. The faceted headland was quite easy to climb, and had been climbed by Anne Cavidge the day before. Ahead of Gertrude was the open sea, a cold dark blue sea with burly white clouds moving above it. The waves were breaking upon the semi-circle of stones which formed the little cove, with the house at its centre. Between the house and the stones there was a windswept garden, a sheep cropped lawn, and two low crumbling downward-reaching stone walls lined by tormented hawthorn trees, through which the frequent rain crept and dripped. At the foot of these trees, in densely crowded profusion, primroses were in flower. On Gertrude's left, where the land continued to slope gently to the sea, there was a pattern of little fields, surrounded by more stone walls, in rather better repair, which cast hard shadows when the intermittent sun shone upon them. Gertrude was staying alone with Anne in Stanley Openshaw's country cottage in Cumbria. Manfred had driven them north three weeks ago in his big car.

Guy never asked to see Anne again, he seemed to have forgotten her. He saw the Count once more briefly. He never talked to Gertrude again as he had done on the evening when he asked her to be happy when he was dead. The Day Nurse told Gertrude later that he must have been in great pain during that conversation because he had refused the pain-killing injections so that his mind should be clearer. After that evening Gertrude held no more 'Visiting Hours', and *les cousins et les tantes* retired to a distance, ceased almost to enquire, waiting for the event. Guy became aloof and dreamy, silent, gazing past Gertrude at what was to come. He asked to see Moses Greenberg, but they did not talk at length. All the legal arrangements had been made much earlier. Victor became evasive, had nothing to say. Toward the very end, Guy became suddenly confused, talkative, rambling to himself about 'the ring' and 'logical space' and 'the upper side of the cube' and 'the white swan'. He also talked about Heidegger and Wittgenstein. Then he asked anxiously for his father and for Uncle Rudi. In the end he died alone, in the night, probably in his sleep the Night Nurse said (yet how could she know). The nurse, not Gertrude, found him dead. Gertrude looked once on his dead face and turned away. There was a convulsion in her like an act of birth.

Gertrude attended the Cremation. She leaned on nobody's arm. She did not otherwise leave the house for several weeks. She lay in bed, and now took all the pills and drugs which Victor prescribed for her. She wept quietly or sobbed, her body racked by a choking breath and a droning wail. Drugged she slept, then woke to the renewed horror. Anne taking control, tended her. Gertrude heard dimly, sometimes, the muted voices, voices she recognized, Mrs Mount, Stanley, Manfred, Gerald, the Count, talking to Anne in the hall, anxious enquiring voices trying to develop solutions and plans. She saw no one except Anne, though at first she did not communicate even with her. Then one day in January she suddenly stopped sobbing and moaning and got up, though her eyes remained red and wet. She accepted from Anne speech, touch, love, the food of consolation, although at first she did it really more for Anne's sake than for her own.

Moses Greenberg came with a brief-case full of papers which he spread out on the dining-room table. Of course Guy had left everything in apple-pie order. His will was simple. He left everything of which he died possessed to his beloved wife Gertrude. There were no other legacies. Moses tried to explain something about investments to Gertrude, but, handkerchief to mouth, she did not understand. She had never thought about these matters of which Guy had never talked. She summoned Anne, who did understand. Anne and Moses Greenberg discussed problems about taxes and insurances and bank accounts. Moses Greenberg could not have been kinder.

In a fever of activity Gertrude began to change the flat. She sold the bed which Guy had died in, and the bed in which they had slept for all those years together. She would have liked to burn them in a ship at sea. She moved everything in the flat, made new bedrooms for herself and Anne, moved pictures and rugs and ornaments which had not been moved for years. Then, accompanied always by Anne, she set out as if dutifully upon a round of family visits. It was as if she wanted to 'show herself' in her widowhood to Guy's people. Many, even remote Schultzes, invited her to stay. She spent a few days, with Anne, at the Stanley Openshaws' London house. Then, on Janet's suggestion, they came north to the cottage in Cumbria. Some calmness came to Gertrude's misery, but it was a black black calm, and the old wild despair came back in gusts, and walking by herself beside the sea she wailed aloud.

Had she expected with death, some relief? Not to see the 'simulacrum', to imagine the grinding pain, to suffer the daily loss of the bond of consciousness, to see the eyes vague, mad, even hostile? But no, death, absence, utter absence was worse, the thing she had not imagined. The empty space, the nothingness of what had once lived and moved, the loss of that sense of his being *somewhere* which gave poles to the world. Guy was gone, and her heart questing for solace discovered only void. Even Guy alienated, suffering, had been a place of comfort to which she could come, for all the pain. Now she was alone. She thought, all those memories of me are gone, no one knows me any more at all; I too have left the world. All the things which he might have told her were gone, everything which they had known and loved together was taken absolutely away. No joy which she had had with Guy could be a joy to her ever again. Yes, absence, that was worst. She had therein a new kind of being composed of tears. She heard the birds singing in the misty English spring, but there would be no happiness in the world any more.

Yet very gradually the terrible mourning subsided, and the time passed when Gertrude felt that she must die literally of a broken heart. She could not imagine now how she could have survived without Anne Cavidge, and Anne's return to her now carried the significance of the world.

'I was possessed by a devil and you saved me.'

'Why by a devil?' said Anne.

They were walking at noon beside the sea, walking in stout brogues upon the flat grey stones which the sea had so battered into a dull beauty.

'Oh I don't know — I gave myself up to it. Like wanting to die in a bad way. Like fighting the world and wanting to hurt it.' Gertrude was thinking of how Guy had wanted her to be happy. She would never be happy, but there was a duty to resist despair.

'One must resist despair,' said Anne. 'That's one of the few rules that exist everywhere always. I think it's a duty even in the torture chamber, though there no one might ever know whether it had been obeyed or not.'

'Only God would see.'

'Only God would see.'

'Such a useful fiction.'

'Yes!'

Gertrude understood about duty. She thought, Guy would have enjoyed discussing this.

The light had changed and under a warm sun the sparkling sea was covered with mysterious trails of lighter blue.

Anne thought, it is Lent. What will happen to me at Easter? Easter had always seemed to her like a great slow explosion of dazzling light. She shifted her mind to thoughts of innocent unstained things. Children at Christmas, children at Easter. Children enacting the Christian story. Was innocence her good now, not that intolerable light? At first she had felt like one who has successfully committed a crime. Now she wanted shelter in the world, a refuge from sin.

Gertrude was thinking I want Anne to stay with me forever, I can't live without her now. The presence of Anne in the house is necessary to my continued survival. Gertrude had put off saying this clearly to Anne, though she had hinted it.

'I could not have survived without you, Anne. God sent you to me.'

'Another convenient fiction.'

'No, no, you know what I mean. You've come now when I need you. It means something.'

'It's superstition, my darling. But I'm glad—I'm glad—I've been of use.' Yes, superstition, thought Anne. Any idea of God's purpose in my life must henceforth be just that. And yet she wished that she could respond to Gertrude's idea.

'Anne, dear heart, stay with me—won't you—'

'You know I said I'd—'

'No, I mean always. *Forever*. You must. We'll be together, *deeply* together. Of course we'd go away and do different things, I wouldn't tie you, but we'd make our home together. Why not? It's so clear to me. You're *free*, Anne, you're *free*, and everything's different now. Choose this, please. I think you have chosen it. Stay with me always.'

Anne thought, Gertrude keeps telling me I'm free, but what does it mean? She did not yet want to think urgently about Gertrude's 'forever' though it moved her very much. She said, 'I'll never be far away, you know that—'

Gertrude thought, I won't say more for the moment. I think she will stay, she *must* stay.

'I want you to help me spend my money,' said Gertrude.

'Jet travel and champagne?'

'Well, that too, why not! I was thinking of good causes.'

'You know more about that than I do. What about all the work you've been doing with the Asian women?'

'I'm such a beginner at that. They're so beautiful and spiritual, they ought to be teaching me! Maybe I'll go back to school teaching, I don't know. But whatever I do I want you to do it with me. You're our nun now, the Count was saying that about you. You're our holy woman and we need you. A widow is a kind of nun, we'll be nuns together and do virtuous things! I don't see why Stanley's children should have all Guy's money. Let you and me spend it together.'

Guy had put nothing on paper, but it had been almost tacitly agreed between him and Gertrude that she should make at least an interim will in favour of William, Ned and Rosalind Openshaw. Gertrude, who had no close family, had always accepted Guy's family as her own. Now however she felt detached from them, almost resentful. Guy, the flower of them all, was gone, while they lived on.

'You may marry again,' said Anne.

'Never! And thank you, dear heart, for keeping *them* at bay. Without you they'd have eaten me alive.' By *them* Gertrude meant *les cousins et les tantes*. Anne had taken charge. *They* had not all been pleased.

'They love you.'

'Yes, yes—'

'Anyway, I'm glad you're learning Urdu.'

The two women had established in their time at the cottage, a routine of work. In the mornings they sat apart, studying, Gertrude in the little sitting-room and Anne in her bedroom. Gertrude worked on Urdu. Anne was polishing up her classical Greek. More even than her convent training, her own temperament forbade her to be idle. At least she could be attempting to learn a trade. Gertrude too was unwilling to be idle, though she was more restless than Anne and laid aside her books sooner. Anne now saw in her friend the restless lost middle-aged widow. She had lived through her husband. Now she had no children and no work and had lost her way. Well, had not Anne too lost her way? There was one once who had said to her, 'I am the Way.'

Before lunch they went down to the sea, then drank a glass of sherry, sitting outside on a bench beside the hawthorn trees, if there was even a gleam of sun. Anne had never learnt to cook, and made it clear that she would not start now, so Gertrude cooked lunch. (Gertrude was a modest cook, she had never learnt Jewish cookery as the other Gentile women had done. Janet Openshaw's *gefilte fisch* was famous.) After lunch they performed household tasks, then usually set off walking, along the coast or inland, following little winding lanes between stone walls where purple and white violets grew, and seeing further off the curving hills of gauzy green, spotted with white sheep, where the cloud shadows constantly passed. There was a small farm near the cottage, but the nearest village was a pleasant two miles walk away. The village shop closed and the village pub opened at the same evening hour, so when Anne and Gertrude came to shop they could imbibe the local cider before walking home to dinner and to lamplit reading. Anne was reading *The Heart of Midlothian.* She read very slowly, thoughtfully. Gertrude was reading *Sense and Sensibility.* Gertrude read with a sad quiet feeling of revisiting another period of her life and its forgotten pleasures. She had somehow, until Anne arrived, given up reading novels. (Guy only liked philosophy and history. Popular biography was his 'lightest' reading.) Anne read with continued amazement. What an extraordinary art form it was, it told you about everything! How informative, how exciting, how funny, how terribly sentimental, how full of moral judgements! Sometimes they argued about the novels. (They disagreed about Jeanie Deans.) They went to bed early.

'Hey hey the white swan.'

'Still can't do it,' said Anne. Gertrude had asked her about this white swan of Guy's. What did it mean? Anne did not know.

'I'll never find out now, or about that cube,' said Gertrude. Her eyes filled with tears.

Anne had been surprised by the fierceness of Gertrude's grief and its duration. But with a kind of professional detachment she knew that the violence of it would not last, even though the pain would never go.

'It will never go, the pain,' said Gertrude. Sometimes, it seemed to Anne, they picked the very words out of each other's heads, so close were they. 'I remember now he used to say it earlier sometimes when we saw a pub called the Swan. But I never asked him, I feel now I let him down, I ought to have asked. And then I somehow couldn't—perhaps it was something religious.'

'I don't know.' Anne added, 'You are without guilt here, don't invent it. That pain at least is spared you.'

'I'll sell the flat,' said Gertrude. 'We'll give up the world together. I can't do it on my own.'

Anne thought, I left the convent so as to be homeless. Foxes have holes, but the Son of Man hath not where to lay his head. I must go onward with my Christ, if I still have a Christ. If I stay with Gertrude I shall have a home forever. (She tried not to think: oh what happiness!) Gertrude's idea of giving up the world would be a little house in Chelsea.

Anne suddenly laughed, and Gertrude very nearly laughed too. It was an old laugh, that special mad complicit laugh which they had used to laugh together when they were at college, and this laugh Anne was teaching again to Gertrude, who had as yet no other.

'What are you laughing at, darling?'

'The idea of you giving up the world!'

'I wonder if you ever really gave it up?' asked Gertrude.

'It's a good question.' How pride supports me, thought Anne, how unbroken it is. Have I really changed at all, can people change? That death in life which she had attempted: to refuse false gods, to undo the self, a little every day, like picking off leaves or scales. . . . Was it not *imaginary*? Gertrude thought of Anne's religion as a prison from which she had emerged, an obsessive delusion of which she had been cured. How unlike this it really was. And yet how was it? Her prayer continued, not a 'let me out', but a deep insistent 'let me in'. Where would she and her Christ wander to now and what would become of them? She had left the convent in order to be truthful and lonely and harmless. If she were to find a cell where she could live as an anchoress in the world and retain her innocence, would that too be 'imaginary'? Or would she, like Kim's lama, settle down with Gertrude? How much could love and duty show her here? I could easily do it, thought Anne. That 'forever' was at times very very close to her heart.

'You tried to destroy yourself,' said Gertrude, 'but you failed.'

There was a sharp vehemence sometimes in what Gertrude said to her, almost an incoherent resentment, a desire to probe and needle.

Anne sat quiet in the mornings and the evenings. Sometimes, without thought, she knelt. Was this superstition? Did it matter so much, what was and was not superstition? Would she ever be able to talk to anyone about this? The early birds reminded her of the nuns singing.

'It's Sunday.' The distant sound of church bells, now renewed, had already brought this news to them over the gauzy sheepy hills. The church was in the village, beside the pub, a little grey sturdy building with thick Norman pillars and a narrow dog-toothed doorway. Anne had entered it, with Gertrude and alone. It had seemed to her a beautiful empty place. Whoever lived there had gone away long ago.

'Yes. The pub won't open till seven. We forgot last week.'

'I've thought of another reason why you must stay with me forever,' said Gertrude.

'What's that?'

'I need someone in my life who can drive a car.'

'I've forgotten,' said Anne.

'You were a demon driver once.'

Anne had indeed been a dedicated driver in those days. Now she really felt she had forgotten. Manfred had wanted her to drive his big car on a lonely stretch of road coming north, but Anne had refused.

'You wouldn't drive Manfred's car,' said Gertrude. 'You funked it.'

'I funked it. Manfred drives too fast.'

'You are censorious, I've been noticing it. Maybe it's the one thing you really took away from that gloomy convent. You will judge people. You told me last night I was drinking too much.'

'You were.'

'Yes, a judge, I see you as a judge, a holy judge in our lives. I'm not teasing, darling, I like it, we like it, we need it. You shall dispense justice.'

Am I censorious, Anne wondered. She certainly found it harder than she had expected to accept the *tempo* of worldly lives now she was among them. People irritated her, even Gertrude did. She disliked being marked off as 'holy' or 'a nun'. Yet did she not feel different, superior? Yes. A terrible admission.

'Who's "we"?' she said to Gertrude.

'Oh—I don't know—Sweetheart, stay with me. I love you, why can't I have you? Damn giving up the world. Guy wanted me to be happy.'

'He was right, it is for you.' But not for me, thought Anne. Happiness has no part in what drove me out and must drive me on.

'Of course we'll both work. You can teach. Or why not write a book about losing your faith? That could help a lot of people.'

'Oh *Lord*!' My Lord and my God, when will the real suffering start? Consoling Gertrude was a safe interim. Yet her love for Gertrude was the first reality she had encountered outside those gates.

If she had been a priest would she, inspired by some idea of obedience, have stayed inside? Would the priesthood have lifted her above some level where she felt at times that it did not matter what she thought or did, because she was a woman? She carried no precious cup from which the many fed. Anne was confused by speculation which often seemed to her positively diabolical. Better not to think. Yes, with Gertrude she was in safety. Yet it was exactly here that she must wait for the night to begin. It would begin.

Anne and Gertrude had, for their morning walk, gone to the end of the beach, near to where the hard many-surfaced cliff rose out of the breaking waves. The waves rose, leaping rampant up the cliff side, and the keen wind carried the spray. A strong sea was running. The two women turned back, walking on the grey stones near to the foam which was racing in bubbles to their feet. The wet stones were almost black. The dry stones were an absolute grey in which even the brightest sunshine could kindle no hint of any other colour. Anne picked up a stone. They were so similar, yet so dissimilar, like counters in a game played by some god. The shapes, very like, were never exactly the same. Each one, if carefully examined, revealed some tiny significant individuating mark, a shallow depression or chipped end, a short almost invisible line. Anne said to herself, what do my thoughts matter, what do their *details* matter, what does it matter whether Jesus Christ redeemed the world or not, it doesn't matter, our minds can't grasp such things, it's all too obscure, too vague, the whole matrix shifts and we shift with it. What does anything matter except helping one or two people who are nearby, doing what's obvious? We can see so little of the great game. Look at these stones. My Lord and my God. She said aloud, 'My God.'

'What?'

'Just look at these stones,' said Anne. She dropped the one she had been holding, then with a sort of animistic possessiveness turned to pick it up again, but she could not now discern which one it had been.

'Yes,' said Gertrude. 'There they are. What about them?'

'There they are.'

'It's hot,' said Gertrude. 'If the wind drops for a moment it's positively hot now the sun is shining. Hold these while I take my coat off.'

Anne took from her the little bunch of primroses and short-stemmed violets which she had picked here and there on the green turf edge and under the hawthorns as they descended to the beach.

Gertrude pulled off her coat. They were both dressed for cool weather, but the April sun was now suddenly warm, even hot. Tall Anne was wearing now, for out of doors, the blue and white check woollen dress which she had bought at the village shop in what seemed a remote previous existence. (She wore the dark blue tweed dress for evenings.) Round her neck she wore a long mauve Indian scarf which Gertrude had given her. She had refused to let Gertrude 'dress her'. She wore black knee-length woollen stockings with the stout convent walking shoes. Her hair had been growing, but she had decided to keep it cut fairly short. Gertrude liked it like that too. She recalled the big golden mane of Anne's student days, but this silver-blonde fur was now more precious. Walking, a little sun had browned Anne's thin face, but only lightly, pallidly. Her rather narrow blue-green eyes were, as Gertrude put it, shaded or hazed over, still puzzled by the world. Gertrude was wearing, under her coat, a brown almost summery light jersey dress, sprigged with yellow-brown flowers. Her face had changed a little, become perhaps permanently strained and older. So very much crying had worn it a little, as if it had been touched, like the stones, by a lightly pressing finger. Her bright clear brown eyes stared more from deeper sockets, her fine mouth drooped more, lengthened by two faint descending lines. Her hair, which she had only lately started to wash regularly again, was its old self however, knowing not of grief, profoundly and variously brown, longish, now wind-tangled flying upon the collar of her brown-sprigged dress. She had become slimmer, she was shorter than Anne but she walked as fast.

Sun had now taken charge of the whole landscape. Over the emerald turf of the headland an invisible lark was crazily singing.

'Oh — the sun — it's the first time —'

'Yes.'

'Oh Anne, look at the sea, it's all blue now, and flashing, like signals —'

'Yes. Almost ready for swimming.'

'You were a demon driver. You were a demon swimmer too.'

'I thought I'd never swim again.'

'What about a swim now, would you?'

'Are you daring me! Or do you think I'd funk it, like driving Manfred's car?'

'It's much too cold, of course, I was joking.'

'It's not all that cold. I think now you mention it I'll go in.'

'You mean now? Anne, don't be silly — it's *icy* cold! You aren't serious —'

'I am,' said Anne. 'It's a wonderful idea. If you want to see me swim, I'll swim!'

'I don't! Oh please, *please.*'

Anne had already kicked off her shoes and was pulling off her socks. The flat grey stones were smooth and chill under her bare feet. She undid the Indian scarf and the belt of her dress.

'Anne, don't be *crazy*, look at those waves — I wasn't daring you, we aren't nineteen!'

Anne was now in a sudden wild frenzy to get into the sea. A strange piercing sensation like sexual desire had sent a spear through her entrails. She dragged her half-unbuttoned dress violently over her head. A moment later, dressed only in the little golden cross upon its chain which hung close about her neck, she advanced into the running creamy foam. She went on quickly, stumbling a little upon the shifting stones, until the white water was above her knees.

'Anne — Anne — *stop* —'

The sea was intensely and beyond expectation cold. Wild mad exhilaration licked her naked body. The beach descended steeply, a wave met her breast-high and broke over her head. Gasping then yelping with the cold she lost her footing, then leapt into the following wave and was swimming, kicking, lifted up by the strong incoming rollers, her eyes blinking away the spray, seeing the blue-green white-flecked crests of the advancing waves and the brilliant light of the blue sky beyond. She cried out now in wild joy, feeling her limbs becoming warm in the fierce water as she swam out strongly from the shore and gave herself confidently to the huge movement of the sea.

Anne had been an athletic girl, a golfer, a swimmer, a tennis player. Physical strength and physical prowess had been taken for granted in her life, part of a calm sense of superiority which had never faltered until it had run to its destined fulfilment in an ecstatic submission to God. She was strong Anne Cavidge. She felt this now as she turned on her back and kicked the rhythm of the waves into a matted foam round about her. Enough now. She dolphin-leapt into the fast elegant crawl which she had not forgotten, any more than she had forgotten walking, and headed toward the land. The sea was indeed very cold.

As she now swam back she felt, like an unexpected blow, a sudden lassitude. What had happened to the strength in which a moment ago she had been exulting? Her arms no longer moved effortlessly, they were puny and aching, and her naked body was coated with a profound cold. The nuns had prided themselves on keeping fit. Garden walks were not enough. Anne had followed a regime of exercises. Perhaps it had become less strict as the years went by. The vigour of youth was gone. What's the matter with me, she thought. I'm weak, of course I haven't forgotten how to swim, but I'm weak, my limbs are strengthless. Anne gasped, swallowed salt water. She continued to swim toward the land, but now with a terrible exhausted slowness. Over the flecked jumping wave-crests she could see the figure of Gertrude upon the shore very far away, and beyond her the grey cube of the cottage. Perhaps there was a current taking her out to sea! It could not be just her own weakness which made the land seem to recede? She tried harder, spurred now by fear. Was she going to drown now, stupidly, *wickedly*, before Gertrude's eyes? Yesterday she had climbed the cliff to impress Gertrude. It had really been quite difficult.

Gertrude could see Anne swimming hard to get back against some force which seemed to be preventing her. Gertrude could see too the malignant violence of the breaking waves as they smashed down on to the stones. It was easier to leap out against those waves than to swim in with them. The sea seemed to have become greater and fiercer in the short interval since Anne had rushed into it. I dared her, thought Gertrude, it is my fault. Now, just when I have found her, she is going to die in front of me, to drown helplessly and disappear. Gertrude could scarcely swim. She had always feared the sea. She called 'Anne! Anne!' wringing her hands.

Anne, now nearer to the shore, had also begun to understand the strength of the waves, their great size and how violently they broke. Their deafening noise, which she did not apprehend as sound, but as some deadly terrifying vibration, was overwhelming. She looked behind her. The sun must be clouded as the high backs of the incoming rollers were now almost black. Her courage failed, and she began to swim to and fro parallel to the shore, unable to decide to attempt the ordeal of return. She felt in her body, mingled with the chaotic roaring of the broken water, the tremendous force of the oncoming waves, now sweeping her shorewards, so that she had to resist their power in order to stay where she was. She tried to swim out to sea again. She must not become conscious of the cold. She was the helpless plaything of great mechanical forces which could kill her in seconds. She tried to *think*.

The problem was this, that when she came in, carried by a wave into the area of the breakers, she would not have sufficient strength to scramble out quickly enough or stand up firmly enough not to be knocked down by the next wave which would then pass over her and draw her back in the undertow. She had not noticed in her former exultation, but she could see and feel now, how steeply the beach shelved, so that where the waves were actually breaking she might scarcely be able to touch the bottom. She could also now discern, amid that unbridled complex of forces, the terrifying clatter of the grey stones as the receding waves drew them down and back into the sea.

Oh my God, oh my God, help me, thought Anne. She thought, I have got to chance it, and now. Already in her weakness she was scarcely swimming but simply fighting with the sea, losing her breath and gasping and swallowing water in the attempt to keep her head up. She did the only intelligent thing open to her. She turned again to look at the huge black-backed waves that were coming in behind her, and chose one which was a little smaller than the others to carry her, now swimming furiously, right in toward the beach. She saw, close to her now, the slope of dark shifting stones and the spread of the creaming raging foam. As the wave with which she was travelling began to break she ceased swimming and tried to touch bottom. The foaming white water rushed past her and over her, then her feet touched, deep down the shifting sloping race of the stones, drawn by the force of the water which was already beginning to flow back. She could see, half-turned, the high just-curling crest of the next wave. She attempted to leap so as to keep her head above it, but it was impossible. She could not gain footing, the water was too deep and too fast as it retreated beneath the incoming roller which now leaned over Anne like a translucent black-green wall. She lost her balance, her strength was gone. The wave crashed down over her engulfing her completely. Her head was below the water, her breathless mouth was open.

Gertrude, paralysed with terror, had seen and understood her friend's dilemma. She too had estimated the mechanical forces of the waves, the point of breaking, the slope of stones, the sucking speed of the undertow, the impossibility of standing erect. She saw exactly what Anne was trying to do, and how difficult it was. She saw her friend's body, helpless, struggling, naked as the damned consigned to hell, about to perish utterly; and at the moment when Anne's head disappeared from view under the crushing curling descent of the second wave, Gertrude entered the water.

Anne, as she saw the vast size of the wave above her, and as she lost her footing and descended into a dim cave of swirling foam, and as the sea entered her mouth which had opened to gasp for breath, thought, I am drowned, this is the end Oh forgive me, forgive me. The next thing she knew was daylight and the sight of a human arm, and the brown material of Gertrude's dress, darkened by the water. Anne's feet were again upon the stones and she had taken another breath. She breathed, she took two stumbling agonising steps, gripping the arm, the brown material. The two women fell and the foam raced about them. Then they rose again and Gertrude pulled

Anne into the shallows and then up beyond the water on to the land.

They sat down on the stones, Anne choking, gasping, spitting, then breathing more quietly.

Gertrude said, 'Are you all right?'

'Yes. Are you?'

'Yes.'

'Thanks for rescuing me.'

'I thought you were a goner.'

'Me too. I'm very sorry.'

'You really are a prize idiot.'

'Yes. Yes. Yes.'

'Look, put my coat on. Can you walk?'

Anne put on Gertrude's coat and picked up her own clothes. Arm in arm, shuddering with cold, they climbed up on to the grass below the cottage. Then suddenly they stopped, holding on to each other and laughing, laughing their old laugh, but with a touch of hysteria.

'All the same,' said Gertrude, 'you looked rather lovely dressed in your cross.'

It was the day of Gertrude's return to London, and the Count was sitting in a refreshment buffet in Victoria Station. He had ordered a cup of coffee, but could not drink it. He had spilt a little upon the plastic surface of the table and now sat with glazed eyes moving the liquid about into various patterns with his finger. It was a quarter past five in the afternoon. The Count's heart was beating violently. The heart is a strong machine. The Count's was now like some terrifying thing in an iron foundry. He put his hand to his side, to still the pain and as if to prevent his frenzied heart from hurling itself out of his body in a sheer despair. For despair was what he felt now. Or was it hope? How could such fierce despair seem to be identical with such fierce hope? He was consumed by a vast emotion which had taken over every mental and physical cell of his being. He knew one of its names for certain. He was in love. He could not stop trembling. He watched his trembling hands with fascination.

Last night he had dreamt about his mother. He was with her in a big dark church. She was praying aloud and he wanted to pray with her but he could not understand the words. He thought, it isn't Polish, what is it, what language is it? His mother was wearing a dark veil over her head, embroidered with red and blue flowers, and he thought suddenly, how strange, I never realized it, she is Jewish. Then he thought, no, she is not Jewish, she is *dead*.

The area of the Warsaw Ghetto became smaller and smaller. People went away and never returned. But those who remained, except for a few, would not believe that those who went away were being murdered. Even when they half-believed it each one felt, it will be different for me. The Count had read in books that many Poles, in the midst of their own misery, still hated the Jews, pointed them out to the Germans, glad to have someone more wretched, more defeated, more in peril than themselves. Yet there were also Polish gentiles who helped the Jews, even died with them in the final battle when the false hopes ended in the frightful holy courage of despair. Troy is burning, Warsaw is burning, they have burnt the Ghetto and flooded the sewers. The Count knew that if he lived in Poland now he would be automatically transforming the past in his heart to make it bearable. Was this his past, *his* past? What was it to do with him? Sometimes it all seemed 'literary', as remote as an epic poem, as remote as Thucydides. What ought Bor-Komarovsky to have done when the Red Army reached the Vistula? What ought Nicias to have done after the defeat in the Great Harbor of Syracuse? Surely Justice must hover over the misery and humiliation of men to clarify and purify, not as vengeance but as truth. Sometimes this awful past which was his and yet not his was a subject about which he could almost calmly reflect. Sometimes it came upon him suddenly as a painful incomprehensible jumble against which he had no natural defence; it penetrated into his body, making him feel fear and remorse and shame, and mingled, as it did now, with some quite other anguish.

The period after Guy's death had been a dark time for the Count. He had given himself up with a kind of strange relief, almost gratitude, to mourning for Guy. He was more affected even than he had imagined beforehand by this death. He had got used to Guy's absence from the office. It was a different matter to get used to Guy's absence from the world. Guy had been not only a wise and benevolent companion but a figure of authority. Guy was one of those who inspired in those about him a confidence in morality, in continuity, not drawn from any theory but inferred somehow from Guy himself, as from something monumental. (The Count knew how Guy would have derided the notion of such an 'inference'.) With Guy gone, the Count felt, anything could happen. He had lost his best friend, the one with whom he could always talk, to whom he could always turn. Now the ghost of his own awful loneliness rose the taller, stalked the closer and now at times the Count saw a mark of madness upon the face of that ghost.

Mourning for Guy had mercifully postponed the other and more terrible frenzy. The Count tried not to think it, not to feel it, yet. He knew it would rage before long in all its force, it would prowl like a tiger unconfined. He tried in the interim to think of himself as a servant, Gertrude's servant, as it might be her footman or her groom. He was, indeed, serviceable. He helped in the funeral arrangements. He made a list of Guy's office friends who should be notified. He helped to move the furniture in the flat. He was continually, deferentially, available. But he was not, as it turned out, in proportion to his dreams of servitude, actually necessary. Other, more useful, helpers excluded him, and he had to admit himself to be, in Gertrude's extremity, of less value than they. Manfred and Manfred's big car were in Ebury Street every day. So after the funeral, was Moses Greenberg, attentive, important, laden with vital incomprehensible papers. And the place of chief consoler and chief confidant, which the Count had occasionally dared to hope might be his, had of course been taken by Anne Cavidge. It was true that Gertrude was 'safe' with Anne. The Count liked Anne very much and felt a sort of reverent admiration for her as an unworldly person; yet he could not help resenting the fact that Anne, appearing suddenly out of the blue, had stolen his role.

At times, sitting alone late at night and listening to the gale warnings, for Fastnet, Hebrides, Fair Isle, Faroes, the Count had sometimes upbraided himself for wanting so ardently to console his beloved. Did he then want her to suffer so that he could comfort her? He was indeed appalled by her grief, her awful *public* tears. He had his own tears too, strange Polish tears which he shed meagrely in those late nights, sitting beside his radio set or over his history book. (He could read Proust no more.) He had quaked before Gertrude's weeping, his whole body wrung by a violent response of sympathy, the more terrible in that he could express so little of it openly. He wanted to cry aloud and fall down and embrace her knees and kiss her feet, but all he could do was to stand awkwardly about, mumbling senseless words of consolation and feeling that he was in the way. He told himself many a story about false hopes, including some terrible ones. But he had not been able to stop himself from thinking: *my time will come.*

But in that 'later on' when he would perhaps be able more fully to play his part as Gertrude's sympathetic friend and helper, what else would be? Moses Greenberg's task would be done, Anne would go away, Manfred's big car would be less often seen in front of Gertrude's door. What then, between himself and Gertrude? The Count knew perfectly well that if he had not chanced to overhear those fateful words uttered by Guy, he would be feeling very different now. Of course he had been in love with Gertrude, *in love* with her, for years. But this love had been kept easily within bounds by reverence for her marriage, friendship with Guy, the impossibility of any change. It had been contained too by the Count's faith in its perfect secrecy. But they had both guessed! So even the past was now charged with a new and strange causality. Of course with Gertrude a widow he would have hoped, but it would have been a moderate and sober hope, wherein too he might more easily have calmed himself with the thought: of course, after Guy, she will never marry. But now, with Guy's words 'marry Peter' lodged in his soul forever, how could his hope not be uncontrollable, tigerish? And bitterly lacerating himself into a further frenzy he would think, after he had turned off his radio and lay in the darkness of his bed: she could marry any of them. He had never been jealous of Guy. But how could he bear it, how could he live, now, if she were to marry somebody else? He saw her as surrounded, besieged, by suitors, all of them interesting, attractive, possible. The line stretched out to the crack of doom. He thought, Guy told her to be happy. She will choose her happiness, why not? She could marry any of them. Gerald, Victor, Moses, Ed, Balintoy, Manfred.

The Count looked at his watch. Hours had passed but it seemed to be only five thirty. Gertrude had written to him from Cumbria to say that she would be back in London that afternoon. (Precious tiny kind uninformative letter, it was in the Count's breast pocket.) Would Anne be with her? The Count ardently hoped not. The Count had written (briefly, soberly) to say that he hoped he might see her for a moment that evening, and would ring up at six to ask if he might call. He had (impelled by that terrible hope) taken two days off from the office. He leapt up now in a sudden anxiety. He must find a telephone box, a box unoccupied and in working order. He could not wait till six. He had to see her, he had to be in her presence. What would he do with the evening if she would not receive him he did not consider. He would have to go to Ebury Street, even if it were only to walk up and down and look at her window. The merciful interval of her protected absence was over. He thought, I will wait a year and then ask her to marry me.

Dreadful seeds of insane happiness were stirring in him. He found a telephone box.

'It was the Count,' said Gertrude to Anne. 'He wants to drop in for a drink. I said OK. You don't mind do you?'

'No, of course not, I'd love to see him.'

'I've had such a nice letter from Rosalind Openshaw, you know, Stanley's daughter.'

'Darling, I'm so glad you want company. You must be so tired of seeing just me.'

'I don't want company. I don't want anyone but you. And I'm not—oh don't be silly—I can't argue with you, I'm too tired.'

'Manfred drove too fast.'

'He always does. And you said so before. And you still wouldn't drive.'

'I'm not used to a car that size.'

'Oh God, Anne, it's so strange to be back here. You aren't going away, are you, ever, you will stay always, always?'

'I'll never be far away, how could I be. Shall I cook my own dish for supper, just to show you I still remember it?'

'I'm sure you've forgotten it, I can't think why I bothered to teach you, you didn't want to learn. Hang cooking, let's go out for supper.'

'And the Count?'

'No. Just us. Now we've put our suitcases in through the door I just want to get out of this flat again.'

Gertrude looked about her. Putting the key in the door she had felt sick, ready to vomit, ready to faint. It was really beginning now, her life without Guy. The rest had been an interlude. She had, with quiet self-regarding prudence, changed the flat a good deal before she left for Cumbria. She did not want to come back to the exact scene which she had made and lived in with Guy. She did not want that terrible *absence* to spring upon her once again. But what struck her now was how unchanged it all was, and the absence, it was there: that special form of Guy dead which belonged in the flat and now appeared again, claiming its tribute of a grief renewed. The furniture had been shifted in the drawing-room. The marquetry table still supported the drinks, but now stood near the door instead of between the windows. The vase of flowers (fresh narcissus, Janet Openshaw must have been in) was perched upon a bamboo stool beside the fireplace. A Spanish rug from Anne's room had replaced the golden mathematical rug, which had replaced the long animal rug which was now out in the hall. But the orchestra of china monkeys had stood their ground upon the mantelpiece because Gertrude had not been able to think where else to put them. And the pictures, Guy had arranged them. Gertrude had not the will to touch them. They were so heavy, so confidently established in their positions. She looked at the ancestral faces. Guy's ancestors not hers. How alien and remote they seemed, as if only now they too had died.

To stop the wretched tears from rising she thought, the Count is coming, I shall be glad to see him. Gertrude had not forgotten Guy's words about Peter, but she had not, during the first mourning time, reflected on them. They were words, wrapped up, stowed away in her mind. She would not marry. She must not cry. The Count was coming and she would be glad to see him. The door bell rang.

'Oh hello Count, how nice to see you, do come in.' Gertrude led the way through the hall and into the drawing-room. The cold sunshine of the April evening had a dim clear light, faintly gilding the calm clever Jewish ancestral faces. The room smelt of narcissus and the uneasiness of spring. Gertrude had changed her dress and combed and patted back her thick curly brown hair in honour of her visitor. Now they turned to face each other, both in a state of extreme agitation, Gertrude suddenly so, the Count as the climax of a long and agonising expectation. The Count felt that he was face to face with the new, the possible Gertrude for the first time, and it was like meeting a strange woman, who was yet so dear, so familiar. He felt it would have been natural to take her in his arms. His pale snake-blue eyes glared down at Gertrude, his pale face was distorted into a mask of piteous intensity. His lips were wet, and he looked in his pain almost ferocious. He was visibly trembling. Gertrude felt, with the quick shock of his emotion, her own. Suddenly alone, she was confronted with a man who desired her, who loved her, and to whom she would have in some way to respond. Her heart accelerated and she put her hand to her throat.

Anne came in carrying a tray with glasses.

'You've changed the room,' said the Count. He knew this since he had helped Gertrude to move the furniture, but he needed something to say.

Anne, seeing the last seconds of the encounter, thought to herself, the Count in love, how odd, how *improper*! She had, she realized, thought of him as somehow, like herself, isolated, separated. And Gertrude is moved, yes, she is moved, she is blushing. Anne felt suddenly sad.

The Count greeted Anne and the three of them began to chat.

Tim Reede was mooching around in his studio over the garage off the Chiswick High Road. Below, as always during the day, there were sounds of voices, of engines. Smells of petrol and oil rose to Tim's sensitive nostrils and mingled with those of turps and paint. He liked all these smells. He looked at himself in his shaving mirror, over the sink, beside the electric ring. He was wearing a blue paint-stained overall, the uniform which he had worn ever since he had dreamed of saying to himself: I too am a painter. His eyes were as blue as ever but he had a little less hair, and his newly-shaven chin, which had once, with its myriad points of brilliant red, glowed like a barley field, now looked dark, even dirty. He wiped his face with a damp towel. Someone at the Prince of Denmark (that idiot Piglet, Jimmy Roland's friend) had said to him: You ought to worry more about Daisy. Tim had reflected on this cryptic remark. Well, perhaps it was not so cryptic. There were so many obvious worries in the Daisy area. But was Tim worrying *enough*? Sometimes he tried to worry more, but it was temperamentally difficult. Anyway, where would worrying get them? Daisy didn't worry. She complained ceaselessly, but she didn't worry. This was a part of her marvellous magnanimous strength, the strength upon which, Tim knew, he rested. He rested upon her strength, not she on his. She had a kind of deep electric energy which Tim absolutely lacked. He lived upon her energy. If people thought him irresponsible about her, they did not see that she was the strong one. Tim often let Daisy decide things, even if the decision seemed dotty, because he trusted her instincts and because if he decided anything and it went wrong she never stopped blaming him, even if she had agreed with the original idea.

Just now there were no very clear ideas. Daisy was behind with the rent. Tim could not yet face the prospect of having her with him at the garage. There would be one long row, the usual one-sided row with Tim saying nothing, but feeling bitter and sad. Once Daisy, in a rage, had thrust a rose which he had given her, long thorny stem and all, down the back of his shirt, and that sharp pricking pain all the way down his spine came back to him during those vituperative monologues. Besides, he *could* not have Daisy here. Brian the garage man vaguely knew that Tim lived in the loft and did not just use it as a studio. Daisy came to lunch there often enough, indeed she was coming today, and she had once stayed with him briefly when she let her room, but if she came permanently and started hanging her underwear out of the window or something (she was incapable of being inconspicuous) Brian might get fed up and point out that the loft was not residential accommodation. Then the 'local authority' would become involved (Tim hated authorities), and he would be questioned, fined, ejected, his name mentioned in the paper. All his horrors would descend on him. He would lose his last refuge. *Lanthano*, he thought, oh *lanthano*! So it was impossible to have Daisy living here, and indeed neither of them had yet suggested it, though both of them had thought of it.

Something, however, would have to be done. Tim smiled to himself as he reflected how many many times it had come to that; and, well, something always *had* been done and would doubtless be done now. He had had no teaching this past term and would probably have none next term, though there was the possibility of a two days a week job in September. That was certainly a light on the horizon. Daisy refused to look for a job. She was writing her novel. Tim had nearly had a commission to illustrate a comic cookery book, only then the firm decided not to publish it after all. He had a brief temporary job looking after someone's little art gallery, sitting at a table while a very occasional visitor dropped in to walk gloomily round the show. But the gallery, which was going bankrupt, could pay him very little and he had to find his fares to Hampstead.

The cats were going quite well. It was a matter of inventing strong attractive images. He had done several of, as it might be, Perkins sitting on a window ledge beside a vase of flowers (Tim liked painting flowers) with a landscape behind him. The flowers were Odilon Redon, the landscape Rowland Hilder, the cat (Tim hoped) Tim Reede. The result, he had to admit, was tame (not that that mattered from a commercial point of view). He was now developing a more interesting version of Perkins at his toilet, one leg raised vertically, staring impertinently at the spectator. The background was a problem, and somehow the cat's body refused to inhabit the space (not that that mattered either from a commercial point of view). But there was also the problem of whether there *was* a commercial point of view. Tim was painting now on wood rescued from rubbish tips. (The cats were no good in water colour.) He used acrylic paint which was expensive. Moreover, his destined clients liked fussy gilt frames which made the mogs look like 'real pictures', but Tim could not make such frames himself, and good frames were now hard to find in junk shops. If he bought suitable frames new the finished product was no longer profitable. If he used cheap plain frames the cats looked less like pretty gifts and more like bad paintings. And then, how to market the stuff? He had quarrelled with two gift shops because they wanted a commission which left him almost no profit. Galleries were out of the question. He could not draw attention to himself by exhibiting at the studio. Jimmy Roland, who sometimes helped him, was (according to Piglet) in Paris. Tim tried sometimes to sell his wares in pubs (not the Prince, where he would have felt ashamed). He tried the Chiswick pubs from the Tabard to the Barley Mow, and also the Irish pubs in Kilburn where he put on an Irish accent which he had stwed away somewhere in his unconscious. By this method, he occasionally sold a picture by reducing the price to almost nothing, or more often was told by the publican to clear off. Tim was made utterly miserable by aggressive rudeness. He had not the temperament of a salesman. But what else to do?

Ebury Street was no more. Gertrude had gone away to the north with her friend Anne Cavidge, so she had told him in a short note replying, after an interval of time, to his laboriously written letter of condolence, and although she might by now be back in London he felt that the links with Ebury Street were broken. Had he ever really thought of those people as his 'family'? He could think of no method of re-establishing the contact which had once seemed so natural, no pretext on which he could now re-enter that house. It had all depended on Guy. He was not needed or wanted there, and no one would henceforth give him a thought. He was not *real* like they were. Would Gertrude write to ask him how he was getting on? Inconceivable. He had once (in February) rather daringly rung up the Count at his office 'to say hello'. The Count *had* asked him how he was getting on and Tim had said fine. He then hoped the Count, whom he liked, might invite him round, but no. Probably the Count never invited anybody, and Tim had not quite had the nerve to suggest meeting the Count in a pub. The Stanley Openshaws were of course too grand, and anyway Janet disapproved of Tim. (He wished now he had taken the opportunity to make friends with William Openshaw.) He thought of ringing up Gerald Pavitt, but his number was not in the book, and Tim had accidentally discovered from a newspaper that Gerald was a world-famous physicist. This fact staggered him. He had vaguely connected Gerald with telescopes, but had never conceived that the rather shaggy nice individual with whom he had had a drink or two at the Wheatsheaf was a great man, considered for a Nobel prize. (They occasionally met by accident in Soho since Gerald, a serious eater, frequented a gourmet restaurant not far from the Prince of Denmark.) Tim felt now that he could not possibly expect Gerald to notice him any more. Balintoy was still away, and anyway Tim felt funny about Balintoy. Tim had not been invited to Moira Greenberg's wedding. He was well and truly out of the picture. He felt sad about it.

It was April. Down below in the garage the motors hummed,

eager to depart to country lanes. The sun gave a little warmth and Tim no longer wore woollen mittens for painting. The blue skylights revealed in utmost detail the grey lined pattern of the bare boards, the mattress upon which Tim slept and where he woke every morning to think: I'm free. (This meant no longer in Cardiff, a consolation which Tim would carry with him for the rest of his life.) The kitchen table was laid for lunch for two. In the angle made by the two sloping roofs and the floor were stores of wood and painting material, neatly stowed. Tim was a neat man. The two vertical end walls were whitewashed. A door painted green and blue by Tim, led to outdoor steps and the lavatory below and the forecourt of the garage. There was a radio but no television, which Tim could not have afforded and which he despised anyway as a crime against the visual world. Next to the door was a wooden dresser with plates prettily arranged, and an old trunk for storing clothes. Upon the wall opposite the door he had fixed a big piece of plywood on which he pinned his favourite drawings. These were some of his real drawings, his crucifixion figures, old men feeding pigeons, young men drinking beer, painted girls waiting. These drawings too were waiting.

Tim had lived now for a long time with himself as a painter. He had been ambitious and ceased to be, he had been disappointed and ceased to be. He knew he was absolutely, and would always be, a painter. What else was he? He was Daisy's lover, keeper, friend. That was enough for a life. He went on trying, though he never tried very hard. Any artist who is not a beginner faces the problem of enlarging into a working space the line that runs between 'just begun' and 'too late'. The hard work lies in the middle, when preliminaries are done, and the end is not yet enclosing the form. This is the space which longs to collapse, which the artist's strength must faithfully keep open. Tim was vaguely aware of this, but he was idle and lacked confidence. He was almost but not quite aware that he chose daily to remain mediocre. His efforts tended to be either 'sketches' or 'spoilt'. Yet he kept on drawing and in this activity something purely good, often mislaid, tended to come back. He knew nothing, he read nothing, but he kept on looking. Tim possessed by nature a gift yearned for by sages, he was able simply to *perceive*! (He did not realize that this was exceptional, he thought everybody could do it.) This gift does not of course ensure that its owner can paint well or indeed at all. In Tim's case it was almost a hindrance. He got so much pleasure from the external world, he thought sometimes why trouble to paint, it's all there, *there* in front of me, unless one's great, why bother, why not just live happily with Nature so long as one has eyes? Even Cézanne said he could not possibly create the wonderful colours that he saw.

Tim knew nothing. One of his teachers at the Slade (the one who had said he would make a great faker) had urged him to learn some mathematics, but Tim was lazy and just *knew* he would find it too hard. However, as for the swallow which flies from Africa back to the English barn where it was born, dark knowings were effective in Tim's mind. He picked up ideas about 'form' from his teachers and fellow students, yet it seemed that he never learnt anything which he had not always known. He had a 'feeling' about plants, how their parts connected. He instinctively understood how feathers had to grow to make a wing. His body told him about gravity, about weight, what falling was, what flowing was. He had shirked what might have been a valuable class on anatomy, but when he looked at Perkins or drew Daisy lying partly clothed upon the bed he knew what went on under the skin. He knew about light without looking into learned books. He painted a colour circle when he was five. Perhaps if he could have been persuaded to study geometry he would have learned much to profit and amaze him. Yet, untaught, it was as if in another life he had glimpsed some of the working drawings of God, and in this life had almost but not quite forgotten them.

When his companions at the Slade had laughed him out of the life class he took to abstract painting with an obsessive fanaticism. He lived in a sea of graph paper. His squares became dots, pinpricks, then something invisible. It was (as someone said at the time) like a not very gifted savage trying to invent mathematics. It was as if he wanted to decode the world. His paintings looked like elaborate diagrams yet what were they diagrams of? If he could only cover *everything* with a fine enough mesh. . . . If he could only *get it right*. Sometimes in dreams he thought that he had done so. No one liked these 'fanatical' paintings, and in the end for Tim they became a sort of sterile torment. Then one day (he could never explain how) it was as if the mesh began to bend and bulge and ever so quietly other forms came through it. When he returned to organic being it was as to something which had been vastly feeding in captivity. Everything now was plump, enlaced, tropical. Live existence which had been nowhere was now everywhere. Everything curved and undulated and swelled and swayed. He drew human fishes, human fruits, deep seas full of knowing embryos and jigging jelly. No one liked these paintings much either, they said they were derivative which they were. Of course this too was only a phase.

Someone (it was Jimmy Roland's sister Nancy) had once said to Tim, 'You painters must feel as if you are creating the world.' Tim never felt like that. He felt at his best working moments, a sense of total relaxation. Of course he was not creating the world, he was discovering it, not even that, he was just seeing it and letting it continue to manifest itself. He was not even sure, at these good moments, whether what he was doing was 'reproducing'. He was just there, active as a part of the world, a *transparent* part. Daisy, who hated music, had once said to denigrate that art, 'Music is like chess, it's all there beforehand, all you do is find it.' 'Yes,' said Tim. That was exactly what he felt about painting.

However by now the days of the 'mesh' and of the rediscovery of the world belonged to the far past, though he still occasionally did ink drawings of fat monsters smudged with water colour, or portrayed himself and Daisy as bulbs or sprouting seeds or fish. The 'good times' Tim had now were when he was drawing his crucifixion figures. Why did he, in order to care about them, have to think of them as uninvolved spectators of something frightful? He would never see or paint a crucifixion. The great drama and passion of the world had already passed him by; and it occurred to him that the ordeal by which he was to win his Pappagena would turn out to be simply this, that there was no ordeal, one simply soldiered on becoming older and balder and less talented. His army service was to grow old in the ranks without glory. Meanwhile there were the great consolations, drawing and Daisy and drink, and going to the National Gallery. The great pictures were Tim's heaven, where pain became beautiful and calm and wise. The dead Christ lies parchment-pale among the holy women, whose crystal tears shine like jewels upon the canvas.

But sometimes at night he had a dream of hell. He was in the National Gallery and the pictures were all gone, or all darkened so that the forms could scarcely be discerned. Or else, and this was worst of all, he suddenly saw that they were trivial, valueless, inane.

'Bloody baked beans again,' said Daisy.

Tim and Daisy were sitting down to their lunch. Lunch consisted of baked beans on toast, boiled cabbage, brown bread and golden syrup (a favourite of Daisy's) and a bottle of white wine.

'You said you were tired of spaghetti and potatoes and—'

'Spuds and spadgers fill you up at least. Never mind, this looks delicious. Fill my glass, dear boy.'

'Had a good morning?' said Tim. Daisy's arrival always gave him a feeling of festival. He dealt with her glass, then poured the beans onto the toast from a saucepan.

'Fucking awful. How are the pussies getting on?'

'OK. I've done four of these.'

'Not bad. I can't think how you manage to make them look all the same. Actually I like the sticks in-front attitude better.' Daisy meant Perkins's way of sitting upright with both back legs projecting rigidly forward along the ground.

Daisy had decided to look sexy again today. She was wearing a long Indian cotton robe of an intense greenish blue, with a design of stylised brown trees upon it. She had surrounded her eyes with a thick powdery make-up of a matching blue, her Etruscan look. Her dark short hair looked glossy, almost as if it were wet. Her haggard handsome thin face beamed with energy and discontent.

'Why don't you do some dogs? You did some good sketches of Barkiss and that door-mat animal in the park. Have you lost them?'

'I never lose anything.'

'You're as tidy as an old maid. Why don't you work them up? There are dog lovers too, you know.'

'Could do.'

'I wonder where old Barkiss is now? The Prince isn't the same without him. I bet that ghastly American actor took him away in his car. I don't love any creature except Barkiss and maybe you. Where is he now, that noble animal?'

'But it's not much good piling up the pix if I can't sell them.'

'Oh do stop binding. Think of something. How will we eat, where will we sleep?'

'Edward the Confessor slept underneath the dresser, when that began to pall he slept in the hall.'

'Yes, yes, yes, and don't stare so, I know I'm a messy eater, you eat like a cat, you'd bury your shit if you could.'

'Don't be so vulnerable and touchy.'

'I'm not vulnerable and touchy, do you want me to break something? OK, I'm vulnerable and touchy. Well, God will provide. And don't be so bloody mean with the wine, young Reede.'

'I told you that cookery book fell through.'

'Yes, twice. You're good at funny drawings—'

'So are you.'

'Don't start that, boy. You're good at funny drawings, you could illustrate a language book, you know, English for foreigners or something. Why don't you go round the publishers and show them some stuff? OK, you're too frightened. Somebody might be nasty to you. I think you're the most cowardly person I ever met. I may be a cow, but I'm not a coward.'

'Well, we are poor but we are honest.'

'Honest? You? You're the biggest liar in North Soho, I can't say stronger than that. I think you positively like lying, you do it selflessly for its own sake. God, to think that when I first saw those beautiful blue eyes I believed everything you said!'

'OK, OK, now have an idea.'

'I've got an idea, I had it yesterday but I forgot. Why don't you copy the animals in the National Gallery, just by themselves, and put them into glossy frames like the mogs? You're so good at copying. They could look awfully charming those animals.'

'You mean like the little dog in the Van Eyck and the big soppy dog in the Death of Procris and—'

'Yes, the place is stiff with beasties.'

'I'll try it—. Has your landlord been after you again about the rent?'

'Yes, but let's not think of that. Oh God, I feel so stir-crazy in April. I wish we could get out of London to anywhere, Market Harborough, Sutton Coldfield, Stoke-on-Trent, anywhere.'

'Yeah. Me too. Christ, we're nearly out of golden syrup.'

'Don't give it all to me, Blue Eyes, old Blue Eyes, you're almost as nice as Barkiss.'

'I'll go to the National Gallery tomorrow and look at those animals.'

'No, for God's sake stay here and paint cats, that's our only hope for my rent and more golden syrup. Jesus bloody Christ, can't you go back to that gift shop in Notting Hill? They'd take them. I know you say it's a mingy profit but beggars can't be choosers.'

'OK, OK.'

'And if you go to the Nat Gall you'll just moon around and waste time. I wish I hadn't suggested it.'

'I get inspiration there.'

'It's a total fallacy that painters inspire other painters. Either you paint or you don't, either you're good or you're not—It's like being able to wiggle your ears, or like moving your scalp, which I can do and no one else can that I ever met. Painting is just factual. It's nothing to do with charming emotions. I know what you're like in the National Gallery, you wander round in a fantasy world where everything's easy and pretty.'

'Beautiful, not pretty. And not easy.'

'Easy and pretty. Prettification, that's what your friends Titian and Veronese and Botticelli and Piero and Perugino and Ucello and all that famous old gang are on about. They take what's awful, dreadful, mean, grim, disgusting, vile, evil, nasty, horrid, creepy-crawly in the world and they turn it into something sweet and pretty and pseudo-noble. It's such a lie. Painting is a lie, or most of it is. No wonder Shakespeare never mentions a single painter.'

'Yes he does. Giulio Romano. Guy told me.'

'Guy would admire Giulio Romano!'

'He doesn't admire him, he just said—'

'You can tell some truths in a book. But nearly all painting is for sweetness, it's nice, it's like cake, look at Matisse, look at—'

'You don't like any painter unless he's sadistic like Goya.'

This was an old argument. Almost anything could start it up. Once it started they could not stop it from blundering on over the same ground to the same explosive conclusion.

'Sadistic! You mean truthful. Your Christian friends are the real sadists, with their crucifixions and flagellations and be-headings and frying chaps on gridirons. And Saint Sebastian showing off his figure and smirking at the audience. Well, we know what *that's* about. Never a sign of real pain in the whole *galère*.'

'If there's no pain then it's not sadistic.'

'It's never-never-land art. At least Goya *cares*. God, have we eaten everything already? Give me some more wine for Christ's sake. Your painting was always prettykins, or rather you chose such a weak soppy lot to copy, you never had any ideas of your own, at least you never thought it meant anything, you were right to give it up.'

'I haven't given it up!'

'I used to imagine you could draw, and to think I wanted you to do me as the madonna once for a lark!'

'You've really given it up. You might at least try, even just to earn us some cash.'

'Fuck painting. I'm a writer. You can say something that matters in a book.'

'Well, maybe you were right to give it up. There never have been any good women painters, and there never will be. No sex drive, no imagination. No women mathematicians, no women composers, no—'

'Oh stop rubbishing, you know you're only doing it to hurt me. Ever since the bloody world bloody started bloody men have been sitting down and being waited on by women, and even when women get some education they can't concentrate because they have to jump up whenever little mannie arrives—'

'Yah!'

'And who the hell are you, Tim Reede, you put on airs and a fancy smock and who do you think you're impressing? You can't do *anything*, you're less use to the world than the bloody man who picks up the bloody glasses in the bloody pub, you're a parasite, a scrounger, living out of other people's fridges, a toadie, a mean cadger, you've got the soul of a servant and a bloody useless dishonest one at that—'

'Daisy—darling—'

'Oh shit! Don't darling me, and don't start reminding me that you pay my rent.'

'I wasn't going to—'

'All right, go away, fuck off, if you're fed up, I'm not asking you to stay, go and find yourself a nice little typist, at least she could earn some money for you to live on. No more beans on toast. You could have a little house in Ealing and a dear little mortgage and a couple of bloody kids, just like everybody else, except that you'd be living on your wife. Oh you make me so mad, you're so bloody pleased with yourself—'

'I'm not—'

'You think you're not but you are. I've seen you when you thought no one was looking, with your perky little face so jaunty like a little bantam cock, and peeking at yourself in the mirror and prinking and smirking. You think you're a wonderful little man, *awfully* sweet and *rather* clever and thoroughly harmless and lovable and nice. Oh Jesus bloody Christ! Let's face it, we'd be better apart, we just torment each other, we drag each other down, with our pretences and with our lies, it's all lies, Tim, let's chuck it. . . . We're *bad* for each other, we meet just where we're most unreal. You want to go, why don't you say so, why do you mask it in these spiteful attacks? Leave me alone. You think I couldn't manage without you? I could manage bloody better. I'd pull myself together and *do* something if I hadn't got you fussing around and pretending to look after me.'

'Oh Daisy, stow it. We say these things, it means nothing. We're us, we're together, there isn't anything else. Let's love each other, what else can we do? Have some more wine.'

'Have some more wine seems to be the final solution every time. OK, you pay my rent, do you think I enjoy it?'

'I've got that job for September.'

'September!'

'We can manage if we drink less and don't buy clothes.'

'You mean if I drink less and don't buy clothes. Yes, this dress is new, at least it's new to me. I got it in a second hand shop. It cost—'

'Oh never mind! I say we'll *manage*.'

'I suppose we won't die. Sometimes I wish I could. Life with you is beastly. Another life might be better. I just can't arrange it. As you say we're poor old us and we'd better love each other. My novel will make some money. I know you don't think so! Only I can't write at present, I try every day but I'm blocked. We're a priceless pair. We're landed with each other all right. Oh fuck, the wine's finished. What are we going to do with ourselves?'

'You could move in here I suppose.'

'In this space we'd kill each other.'

'Daisy, we may have to try it.'

'The flat's cheap, OK nothing's cheap if you're penniless, but it's rent-controlled and I'd never get another one at that price.'

'You can let it, you did before.'

'The lodger's only got to say "it's mine" and it is.'

'Well, you could find a—'

'Oh yes, a rich American spending three weeks in London who wants to live in a stinking little room in Shepherds Bush and share a bathroom with a lot of smelly bastards!'

'You managed it before.'

'That was a bit of luck and it was the tourist season. Besides, you don't want me here, I don't want myself here, you couldn't work, I couldn't work.'

'You could sit in the public library.'

'Fuck the public library. You know it isn't on.'

'Well, what *shall* we do?'

'You could try Ebury Street.'

'I've told you, there isn't any Ebury Street any more. They've dropped me. Guy was the only one who bothered about me. Now I've vanished, they've forgotten me, they wouldn't remember my name!'

'Well, remind them. Ask the Count for a loan. It's not all that long till September.'

'Daisy, I *can't*—'

'Oh you're so spineless. Can't you do *something* for us? They're all rolling in money—'

'They aren't—'

'And we haven't any. It stands to reason. It's natural justice. God, if I had a gun I'd bloody go and *take* it off them!'

'I can't see it as justice,' said Tim, 'I mean expecting them to help us.'

'Well try, try to see it as justice!'

Tim tried. He almost could. After all, he had always been somehow like a child among them.

'I'm sure they swindled you out of that money, that trust fund money.'

'They didn't.'

'Oh, I'm so tired of these arguments. Can't you *do* something? Go and see Gertrude.'

'I can't.'

'Why not? You're frightened of her.'

'All right, I'm frightened of her.'

'I bet she was head girl of her school.'

'Anyway, she's a liberated woman, you ought to approve.'

'Gertrude, liberated! *Laissez-moi rire!* She's just a new style of slave. Is she still away?'

'She should be back by now. But I've never had any dealings with Gertrude. Guy was the one who cared for me. But he's dead and I can't go and bother Gertrude now, it's out of the question. I'm finished there, I'm past history, there's no connection any more.'

'You mean she'd show you the door?'

'No, but I just mustn't go there any more, not unless I'm invited, and I won't be.'

'So, for a social nicety, we starve!'

'Darling, don't exaggerate our sorrows, we shall survive!'

'I think you don't understand. I am asking you to do, for you and me, something which is *dead easy*. What have you got to lose? OK, she may just stare at you with her glassy eyes and change the subject, but *what have you got to lose*?'

'I don't want to be glassily stared at—and—oh I can't explain—it's to do with Guy.'

'With *Guy*? But he's *dead*!'

'Oh—Daisy—' Tim could indeed not explain, and scarcely to himself. It was something to do with his special relation with Guy, his respect and affection for Guy, his private farewell to Guy. These things concerned nobody but Guy and Tim. He could spoil all that now by going cap in hand to beg from the widow.

'You're afraid of that fat female.'

'She isn't fat.'

'She's podgy and stodgy.'

'In any case—'

'So you admit you're afraid?'

'No—Oh Daisy, do stop. Let's go to bed. There's always that.'

'There's always that! Oh *Jesus*!'

'You mean you're short of money?' said Gertrude.

'Well, yes—' said Tim. That did about sum it up.

Daisy had at last persuaded him. He hated it. He had put on a tie, and one of his suits from better days, the one he used to wear to those Ebury Street 'evenings' which now belonged to an ancient and vanished past. It was six in the evening and they were standing beside the fireplace in the drawing-room holding sherry glasses. Tim put down his glass and toyed with a china monkey flautist. He had hoped that cold Anne Cavidge would not be present. She had given him a very chilly look when she had found him, before Christmas, rifling Gertrude's fridge and stuffing things into his plastic bag. There was no sign of her at the moment, thank God.

Gertrude was silent, seeming embarrassed. Tim's heart was in his boots. It was going to be the glassy stare and the door after all. Of course Gertrude would be kind about it—

Gertrude could certainly not now be called 'fat'. She was thinner and looked older. In some ways this suited her. She was wearing a dark coat and skirt with a high-collared white blouse and a yellow and brown silk scarf tied in a bow. She wore brown patterned stockings, and a smart brown leather shoe tapped on the fender. She had small feet. Her copious slightly-curling hair had been cut and swept in closer to her head. Her brown-complexioned fine-nostrilled face had, with the faint anxiety, its fastidious look. The brown eyes frowned at the blue eyes, the blue eyes flinched and turned elsewhere.

I've spoilt it, thought Tim, I've spoilt the past, I've sinned against Guy, against what just for a moment seemed to be my family; and, in that belief, somehow they *were* my family. Why didn't I *wait*? Gertrude *might* have written to me, asked me to come. Now I've upset and annoyed her and ruined it all and she'll despise me. Even if she gives me a hundred pounds, it won't be worth it. I don't even want it. Why ever did I let Daisy persuade me? I'm a *creep*, and Gertrude must be seeing me as one.

Tim had laboured over a letter to Gertrude. Was it better to pretend he was proposing a social call, or should he at once strike the note of business? He tore up the letter, he could not write things. In the end he just rang up and said he would be near Victoria that evening and could he call in? Once there, and seeing Gertrude's smiles, he could not bear to pretend. He at once, awkwardly, bluntly, rudely, made clear that it was money he was after. Oh God!

'I see,' said Gertrude. She began to finger a china monkey violinist. 'But—well—if you don't mind—I'd like to under-stand—I thought—I imagined—you had a teaching job—and you sell your pictures—I suppose—'

'I should have explained,' said Tim, 'it's just a matter of getting through the summer. I shall have employment in the autumn. I haven't got a job at the moment—'

'Have you tried? I suppose you could get *some* sort of job?' said Gertrude.

Tim felt cold. Well, maybe he could. But what a world of experience separated him from Gertrude! Maybe Daisy was right about her after all! 'I might be able to,' said Tim, 'but I want to go on painting.' He realized at once that this was, in this room surrounded by the faces of hard-working Judao-Christian puritans, the very worst thing to say. Was he then asking Gertrude to support him in a life of unpractical self-indulgence? It certainly sounded like it.

'Then you can sell what you paint? Or can you?'

'No, not much,' said Tim. 'I mean, there's a time-lag you see—'

'But you have paintings stored up—I mean ones you could sell? I believe painters sometimes don't want to sell their work, they don't want to part with it, I can understand that.'

'I have some things,' said Tim, 'but I don't think they'd fetch much. I'm not a very fashionable painter.' That was one way of putting it.

Gertrude latched onto this. 'I'm glad you say that. Of course you mustn't try to be fashionable just to make money. What are you painting now?'

Tim wondered if he could explain to Gertrude about the cats. He decided he could not. He said, trying to be at least partially truthful, 'I'm drawing at present—drawing people, people I see in—in parks and places—and animals and—and things—'

'Drawing is like practising scales for a musician?'

'Oh yes, very like, just like that—'

'I expect you do it all the time while you're waiting for the next big thing that you do?'

'Oh—yes—'

'And what will that be?'

'I'm—I'm not sure—'

'But you don't want to leave off and do art teaching? You *were* doing some teaching, weren't you?'

'Yes,' said Tim patiently, 'I *was*, but that job has folded up. All the art schools are short of money and the part-time staff are the first to go. I can't get another teaching job at present, I've tried and tried, everyone is after these jobs. I'm unemployed until September unless I want to—er—'

'Take something very uncongenial?'

'Yes. And even that's hard to get now. It's just hard to get work. It's a bad scene.'

'I realize of course—' said Gertrude.

Tim thought, now I'm exposing my sores and accusing her of being a sort of Marie Antoinette! No wonder she looks annoyed. I've got *everything* wrong! He began to say, 'I'm sorry I—'

Gertrude said, 'I suppose you can apply for unemployment benefit?'

'I have, I do,' said Tim desperately. 'It's not much of course—but as you say—I'll go again and get some more—of course I *can* manage perfectly well—it's not as if I wanted to live in luxury—I'm sorry I bothered you, it's not important really.'

'Have you only yourself to support?' asked Gertrude.

Tim had no difficulty with that one. 'Oh yes—only me—no dependents.'

'Forgive me for asking. I really know so little about you.'

'Not at all—'

'And this job in September, it's part-time teaching? Is it certain or only possible?'

Tim hesitated. He was really not sure. He had told Daisy that it was certain, to cheer them both up. But with things as they were nothing was certain. 'Nothing is certain,' he said, 'but I hope—I mean I think—'

'Have you any money saved?' said Gertrude.

'No—well, scarcely—I mean—No.'

'It sounds a bad situation.'

'Oh, it's not so bad really,' said Tim, 'I rub along perfectly well, in fact I can't think what I'm complaining about—'

'Where do you live?'

'I have a little sort of studio flat, in Chiswick, it's cheap.'

'Forgive me for asking all these questions,' said Gertrude, 'It's just that if I'm going to help you, I've got to understand the situation, I've got to *see* it all.'

Tim felt his full dismay at the prospect of this relentless just scrutiny. Would Gertrude demand to see his studio, look at his pictures? Would it be a proper means test? Oh why why why had he come!

'These are the questions,' said Gertrude, 'which Guy would have asked you.'

The truth of this touched Tim. He put down the china monkey flautist. He had been looking at Gertrude's elegant brown foot. He raised his eyes now and met her intent worried gaze. He said, 'Guy was very good to me. I miss him very much. I'm sorry—' He wondered if he should now mention the fact that Guy had lent him money, but decided not to.

'I was going to write later to ask how you were,' said Gertrude. She put down the violinist with something of a clack. It sounded like a reproach. During the questioning she had been purposeful, business-like. Now she was embarrassed again, possibly annoyed.

'I'm sorry I didn't wait for your letter,' said Tim. This now sounded rude.

'I can't think why Guy didn't buy any of your pictures.'

Of course Guy had bought one, but he had evidently never shown it to Gertrude.

'Oh—they're not much good—'

'Have you had shows, exhibitions?'

'Good heavens no.'

'Sorry,' said Gertrude, 'it sounds as if I'm saying it would be an act of charity to buy your work and I don't mean that of course.'

This conversation is becoming terrible, thought Tim, and that ghastly Anne Cavidge will probably turn up in a minute and find me scrounging again. I'd better get out. He said, 'I'm sorry to have troubled you. It's done me good just to air my worries. Just talking about them has helped. In fact I now see that I can manage perfectly well. It's only till September. I just wanted to see you, really, say hello. I thought it would be nice to—to see you—to be in this room again. I've thought so much about Guy—and how awful it—you know—I simply wanted to drop in. Forgive me for chatting about my little bothers. They've all blown away now anyhow. Thanks for the drink—and now—dear me it's late—I must be off—'

'Tim, please, just stop *fussing* me,' said Gertrude. 'Look come and sit down here and let me get you another drink.'

Tim obediently moved to an upholstered upright chair just beyond the edge of the Spanish rug.

Gertrude said, 'I just want to *think*.'

Tim said to himself, she is trying to imagine what Guy would do now. He was right.

Gertrude gave him another dose of sherry in one of the cut-glass glasses which had so much excited Daisy's scorn. He accepted it gratefully. The first dose had been insufficient. Gertrude pulled another chair up opposite to him. It was like a small business meeting. It was not exactly a social scene.

'I could lend you some money,' said Gertrude.

'Oh no, no!' said Tim, confused (he had already gulped the sherry). Daisy had impressed on him, 'If possible don't let her *call* it a loan—we probably won't repay it, we can't, but if it's *called* a loan you'll fret, you won't raise a finger to pay it back but you'll fret.' Tim recognized the justice of this prognosis of his character. Then he thought, well, let it be called a loan, so long as it's money. But he had already cried 'No!'

Gertrude went on, 'But it would be much better if I could find some way for you to earn money. One must earn one's living. You want to—I must help you—'

I don't want to, thought Tim, I just want the money! But he said, vaguely wildly, 'Oh—yes—yes—!'

'If you were out of London, could you let your flat?'

'My—oh—yes—yes, I could.' I couldn't thought Tim, but what does it matter. Gertrude is losing her grip, I'm not going to get any money out of her, I must just get out of the house politely. And I mustn't accept another drink or I'll just sit here waiting for more alcohol.

'Would you mind being somewhere else? I mean, you could work anywhere, couldn't you?'

'Oh, yes—anywhere—'

'Supposing you went to live in our house in France?' said Gertrude.

'In—*where*?'

'In my house in France,' said Gertrude, correcting herself.

They were upright, facing each other, holding up their sherry glasses, as in some kind of contest.

'But—' said Tim, 'I—*what*?'

'I've been thinking,' said Gertrude, 'of something which you could do for us—for me—something like a job—where you could paint too—and if you could let your flat as well—'

'I'm afraid I don't understand,' said Tim.

'You see, there's this house in France, it's a cottage really, in some little hills, not quite in Provence, Guy and I bought it ages ago and did it up, and we used to go there, almost every year, and we let it sometimes—'

Tim had vaguely heard of 'the French house'. 'Yes,' he said.

'Well, I won't be going there again I think. I'll probably sell it. By the way, can you speak French?'

'Oh *yes*,' said Tim. He could scarcely speak French but his mind was racing.

'We—Now the tourist season's starting it's better to have someone there, like a caretaker sort of. And if I'm going to sell it, it would be just as well to see that everything's in working order, like the electricity and the water, and there's something with the roof I remember or a window. If you could just activate the builder and—Could you bear it? You'd be all alone though, perhaps you'd hate it?'

'*I'd love it,*' said Tim. Exerting all his will power he stared into Gertrude's eyes.

'You could stay for a while, as long as you like. Just live in the house and find out what's working and what isn't. There's water and electric light, no telephone I'm afraid, it's all very primitive. I'll tell you how to get in touch with the people in the village. It's a bit isolated but there's a bike. And there's food there, tins and stuff, you may as well eat up. But the village shop has most things. You wouldn't be lonely? I'd pay you of course for caretaking, and you could paint too, couldn't you?'

'Yes—yes—yes—'

'Do you paint landscapes?'

'Oh yes—I paint everything.'

'Well, Tim—you could do something which Guy always wanted, and we somehow never managed it—he wanted an artist to paint a picture of the house and of, you'll see, the hills, the view. It seems sad now, but I would so much like you to do it. I'd buy anything you managed to do of the place.'

'Gertrude, wait a minute,' said Tim. He got a grip of himself and leaned forward. He was about to tap her brown-stockinged knee, but refrained. 'Listen. *I am not a very good painter.* So if *that's* the point—'

'It isn't—I mean I'm sure you are, the scenery will inspire you—but I want you to be there—'

Tim swayed back again, 'Well, I'll do the best I can. And it'll be just me, no one else there? I'd *love* that.'

'Yes, just you. It's right out in the countryside, you understand, but you can meet the village people if you want to. Everybody loves a painter. You can stay for ages if you like, until September. It gets terribly hot of course. If I decide to sell the place it would be very useful to have someone speaking French and English on the spot to show it. In fact, now I come to think of it, it's a brilliant idea.'

'Gertrude, you're a *genius*!' said Tim. He thought, what a fantastic break for Daisy and me! She can let her flat, she says she can't but she can. And we can spend the whole summer in France! She speaks the lingo. Gertrude will pay me. Daisy and I will live on bread and wine and olives like blooming lotus-eaters! 'Oh thank you, Gertrude!' Tim cried. 'Thank you, thank you!'

The bell rang. Anne Cavidge pressed the button that released the street door, then opened the door of the flat. Manfred and the Count were coming up the stairs.

'We met at the door,' said Manfred, smiling. The Count's pale eyes glared unseeingly at Anne.

'Gertrude is talking to Tim Reede,' said Anne as they came in.

Gertrude opened the drawing-room door. 'Tim is just leaving,' she said.

Tim slithered out. He said, 'Thanks, Gertrude. Oh, hello, cheerio.' He went out, stumbled over the step, and fell down the stairs. He picked himself up, reiterated 'Cheerio' and ran off.

Anne Cavidge thought to herself, there's something about that young man that I don't trust. Her dislike of him was of course, as she knew, partly based upon a sense that he disliked her.

Manfred and the Count had entered the drawing-room. Anne went into her own room. She combed her hair and looked at her thin colourless head in the mirror. Had those years 'inside' really made her invisible? Was invisibility the gift she had been given by a discerning and just God, in lieu of the *great* gift which she had sought, the pearl of great price? Innocence, the lack of any power to hurt, even to touch, the innocence of an invisible strengthless spectator! Was what she now felt herself to be a permanent condition, or was it the anaesthetic numbness which preceded the ghastly suffering attendant upon a change of being? The soft creature which has lived and walked secretly upon soft feet curls up and sleeps, lying half buried in the damp earth, then wakes in an agony of pain and strife to find that it is becoming something quite else, a winged beast, entirely different, even living in a different element. In Anne's case the change was the other way round; she was destined to become wingless and weak and small. Only for now she was dead, pale, unseen and without significant images of her life.

What had so far helped her most perhaps was the way in

which Gertrude, dear Gertrude, had taken her arrival, her service, so absolutely for granted. Gertrude's questions about the convent had been uninstructed and perfunctory. *Obviously* Anne would come out (why had she delayed so long?) and *obviously* Anne would now, somehow, be with Gertrude always. And yes, thought Anne, somehow I suppose I will be, with her, or near her. If ever one was *sent* to another I was sent to her. But life changes, and how will I be, and how will this be a part of my mission, for it must be only a part? And indeed have I a mission, why do I think I have been *sent* back into the world! Is this idea not a blind consolation? Why do I retain the notion of obedience after I have rejected all authority? Had all that gilded panoply really departed, the cherubim and the seraphim and the Most High seated in the midst, a focus of unimaginable light? Anne looked into the mirror, looked into her narrow blue-green eyes and prayed: oh let it be well, let me *see*, let me *see*. How odd to pray looking into a mirror.

She turned away and patted her dress. She had several dresses now. Gertrude called this her Quaker dress since it was dove-grey with a white collar. She opened the door of her room and listened for a moment to the murmur of conversation in the drawing-room. She had noticed again, and been irritated by it, the Count's agitation, his annoyance at arriving with Manfred. So would her task be simply to escort Gertrude into the arms of her second husband? Well, why not. Anne trotted across the hall and joined the company.

'Hello, Anne, have a drink, you drink wine now, don't you?'

'Give her a little white wine mixed with soda water, she likes that.'

Manfred had risen politely, smiling. He was always solicitously courteous to Anne.

The Count, who had been sitting on a stool beside Gertrude's armchair, failed to rise, then staggered to his feet and sat down again.

'I hear you've passed your driving test, Anne,' said Manfred.

'Yes, I thought I should have a licence.'

'Well done.' Manfred attended to Anne's drink. He said to Gertrude, 'What did Tim Reede want?'

'He wanted money!' said Gertrude. They laughed.

'A preoccupation, I imagine, with that young man,' said Manfred.

'I am afraid I never imagined it,' said Gertrude.

'Did Guy support him?'

'Not that I know.'

Gertrude was thinking: how clumsy and stupid I was with Tim. Of course I had to try to understand the situation. That's what Guy would have done. But I did it so tactlessly, like a sort of inquisitive official. And he really was fond of Guy, that was so touching. And Guy was fond of him, he regarded him as a son. I must have hurt his feelings. He wanted kindness and really I gave him none. It was right to find a way of letting him earn the money. And it is a good idea he should stay at Les Grandes Saules. But I was too successful in making it look like something just devised for my benefit! Maybe I should have said at once: Tim, don't worry, you are a member of the family, I will help you, of course.

The Count was thinking: I must control my feelings. I must stop being *sick* with love. Yet how can I, I don't want to stop. I cannot endure to be in company with Gertrude, and yet if I am alone with her I risk horrifying her by some outrageous breakdown, I might seize hold of her, I am dangerous, I am *mad*. She is a woman afflicted, in deep mourning. She must not know that I am boiling with emotion. She smiles at Manfred, their fingers touch as he hands her a glass. I ought to go away but I can't, I won't. She must not know.

Anne was thinking: I must go into retreat soon. Not in a religious house of course. This has nothing to do with Easter. Perhaps I should ignore Easter, give it up as an irrelevant pleasure. I must be alone, I can't stand company, even Gertrude's. I haven't been properly alone since those long walks just after I came out of the convent. I must learn to pray in my new way, I must learn what it means. If there is anything to be found I can only find it alone. Gertrude is all right for now, she is surrounded by family, by friends, by suitors, I shall not be missed. I shall come back to her of course. But I must be away for a while and converse with my other self. Maybe I could go to the cottage in Cumbria or to Gertrude's house in France.

Gertrude was thinking: dear, dear Count, how he stares and

trembles. Manfred has noticed it and is amused. I wonder if I should give Guy's philosophy books to the Count? I am glad that he loves me. I cannot help being glad. And yet I feel so far away from him, so far away from everybody. I pretend, I pretend. They watch me for signs and they think I am better but I am not. Grief returns like the rain, like the night. I am all wound, all loss, though I smile. I am utterly maimed. Oh dearest husband, why have you left me? Oh Guy, Guy. I must not weep now.

What Manfred was thinking will be revealed later.

THREE

Tim Reede was alone in France. He was monarch of all he surveyed. He was mad with joy.

He was standing on the terrace of Les Grandes Saules and looking down into the little valley below him. Rough grass near the house, scythed no doubt the previous year (one could hardly call it a lawn), was covered with little blue flowers rather like grape hyacinths only smaller. Above these, like perpetual live confetti, flickered a mass of very small blue butterflies, even smaller brown moths, and innumerable bees. The sun shone, not yet hot, the heat of the day and the crackle of the cicadas still to come. Beyond the level of the cut grass the ground descended through an overgrown olive grove where the trees, set in trios, fell about in grotesque attitudes, splitting into huge semi-recumbent forms possessed of elongated faces and writhing bodies. Grass grew randomly upon the earth, which had at some time been ploughed, and crowded in clumps about the bases of the trees. Below the olives an invisible streamlet in the valley bottom nourished the big silver-grey willows which gave the house its name. They were not native to the area and had been planted there by Guy's predecessor. A winding line of green canes, already grown tall, marked the further course of the stream. At night the music of frogs arose from this dell. On the other side of the stream there was a grove of poplars set in rows with clean light paper-brown trunks and a high twinkle of leaves. Then there was a small steep vineyard, and then the brilliant rocks which could look white or blue or pink or grey, and which rose, interspersed with bushes and grassy ledges and rare umbrella pines, to a fairly low and not distant skyline.

The house of grey stone, once a small farm house, was handsome but not large. At one end its solid cubical form rose into a sort of tower. It was roofed with faded tubular red tiles and set upon a terrace of cracked paving stones which was partially shaded by a fig tree. Just below the terrace, and before the rough grass began, Gertrude had once made some confused efforts at a garden. Here rosemary and lavender and ramping geraniums survived, and a clump of radiant lyrical light-giving pink-white oleanders which made Tim positively shudder with colour-experience. The upper storey of the house had elegant square windows which retained their original stone lintels. The lower part once a barn and byre, had been altered by Guy. An archway, closed by a folding door, gave onto a domed summer-dining-room, and a big French window opened to the sitting-room. From the kitchen at the back another original square window looked out over a wilderness of brambles toward a garage made of pierced bricks with rambler roses planted beside it and (Guy's contribution) a eucalyptus tree. From here a short drive led to the little gravelly road. A bookish room beside the kitchen had clearly been Guy's study. Above there were three bedrooms and two bathrooms and the tower room, reached by a ladder, which contained nothing but a lot of shrivelled onions. Tim thought of hauling a mattress up there, but the novelty of not sleeping on the floor was too attractive and he chose the small corner bedroom whence he could see both the willow valley and, through a cleft in the rocks, a triangle of far-distant green hillside. No human habitation was in sight, and in spite of all the cultivation it was an entirely empty landscape.

Taking possession of the house had been an adventurous experience which appealed to Tim's sense of 'loot', a mixture of fear and weird burglarious triumph. He enjoyed the space, the quiet attentive pleasantly furnished rooms, all his now. He felt profoundly safe in the house, as he had felt in childhood when his father was staying with his mother. He slept, relaxed, lying on his back, always a good sign. It had been a bit eerie at the start, inserting the key which Gertrude had given him in far-off London, opening the door, and coming in to that significant silent interior. He could understand why Gertrude did not want to come there, to see the books lying on the table, a *Times* of last year, papers and a pen upon Guy's desk. There was also, for the benefit no doubt of tenants, a set of instructions in Guy's fine pedantic hand. The heating for the bathrooms turned on in the airing cupboard. Rubbish should be taken to the village tip, *never* burnt. In case of mistral put garden chairs away promptly. You are advised to read the note in the First Aid Box about what to do if someone is bitten by a viper. Crockery broken should be (reasonably) replaced. *Please* do not remove books or maps. Mindful of his charge, Tim had at once checked as far as he could the condition of the house. He was relieved to find that the water and electricity were in working order. The roof appeared to be sound, but had yet to be tested by rain. A pane of glass in the study room was cracked. A little vine-covered loggia upon the terrace just outside the archway room had partially collapsed, but Tim had managed to mend that already with some stout poles which he had found in the garage.

Tim had crossed France by train, then come by bus to the village which was seven kilometres from the house. From the village he walked, after purchasing bread and wine. His first concern on entering had been to inspect the larder. This storehouse exceeded his wildest dreams. Tin upon tin stretched away into endless recesses, jars of apricots, figs, plums, peaches marshalled themselves upon the upper shelves, immense jars of olive oil lurked in corners, wine bottles glistened in racks, virgin whiskies in cardboard boxes. Tim thought, I can live the whole summer off this, after all, Gertrude said I could eat anything I liked, and I can save the money she's given me in advance for my salary! The desert island life! I knew it would suit me down to the ground. I'm a solitary chap by nature, I've just never had a chance to be really alone. The garage revealed two bicycles, one male, one female, both in working order. Tim (it was now the fourth day on his desert island) had biked twice to the village for bread and milk, fruit, vegetables and the local wine (he felt he ought not to drink the serious stuff in the racks). He had already made friends Frenchlessly with the shop keepers. He had, in his solitude, a new and invigorating feeling of independence. He was entirely alone for the first time in years.

His solitude was not, however, going to last. Daisy was coming. Tim looked forward to her arrival, looked forward to showing her all the things and places he had made his own. (He felt he had lived here for months already.) Yet also he felt a bit sad. Daisy's restlessness would alter his perceptions; and he would have liked to be *really* alone in Gertrude's house, it would in a way have made him more honest. Of course he had not breathed a word about Daisy to Gertrude. Not that, he imagined Gertrude would have minded, said 'in that case, no' or anything. He was not quite sure why, but it was somehow clear that he could *not* ask Gertrude if he could take his girl friend along. It was an aesthetic matter really. He could never have explained Daisy. (He felt herein protective about her.) There would have been an embarrassment, a wrong impression, and somehow Gertrude's vast imaginative act of kindness would have been insulted and spoiled. Yet was he not insulting and spoiling it now by deceiving her? As often in his life, Tim felt he was in a slightly shady position which had become unobtrusively inevitable. Of course it was not very important. Gertrude need never know, and if later she did find out that a woman had been there, Tim could say that Daisy was travelling in France and had dropped in for a day or two. What made Tim sadder really than his little deception was the fact that now he did just intensely want to be, in this paradise, alone.

Gertrude had indeed been immensely kind. Before even he left her on the evening when he had broached the matter of being 'short of money' she had given him a sizeable cheque, payment in advance for some of his caretaking work and for some hypothetical pictures. Overcome, confused, Tim had offered to deliver, should she wish it, his entire present *oeuvre* to the flat in Ebury Street. Gertrude had laughingly agreed to accept 'a little drawing' as a gift. Long and earnestly, back at the garage, did Tim ponder upon what to give her. Looking at his work in the light of this question made him see, for a piercing moment, how bad most of it was. Cats were out of the question. Some of the crucifixion drawings had charm but were, he had to admit, slight. At last he uncovered one of his earlier works, a pastel sketch for a never-completed Leda and the Swan, a pretty piece that certainly looked like something, though without the title (which Tim did not append) it would have been difficult to say what. This he mounted and framed and wrapped and carried to Ebury Street, rather cravenly hoping that he would not have to have another interview with Gertrude, the last one having been so perfect. Fortunately she was out, and he handed the drawing over at the door into the keeping of cold censorious Anne Cavidge.

He had hastened at once of course to tell Daisy, had taken the Victoria Line to Warren Street and run all the way from there to the Prince of Denmark where Daisy was waiting to hear what had happened. Daisy had behaved exactly as he expected, saying 'fuck bloody France', 'bugger bloody Frogs', and declaring that she would never set foot on Gertrude's property, but falling in with the plan all the same and even becoming childishly excited about it. Already on the following day she was combing through her wardrobe wondering what clothes she would take with her. Tim told his usual lie about having let his studio to the niece of the garage man who wanted to spend a time in London. Daisy forgot her objections to letting her flat and immediately remembered a holidaying American girl who might be just the person to take it on for the summer. The girl however was away for a week and Daisy had remained behind to await her return and make the letting arrangements. Tim had cleaned Daisy's flatlet from end to end and made it look much more attractive and presentable. Then he had left for France. There was still a space of four days before Daisy's earliest arrival. Yes, he knew that once she had arrived he would enjoy her company. But now, looking upon the blue-grey shimmer of the rock walls he felt how much better and happier he would have been if he had really planned to be here alone. He had decided to leave the problem of the broken window until Daisy arrived with her perfect French. There was plenty of time, and the French word for 'window pane' eluded him, even, hang it, the word for 'glass'.

Out of a cloudless sky a sunflower sun blazed down upon an earth still cool from night. The shadows etched the rocks into silently changing forms. A vast silence possessed the little valley. Swallow-tail butterflies visited the white-pink oleander. Upon the low wall of the terrace panting lizards with spider feet lifted up their reptilian heads. From their nest beside the fig tree an army of ants crossed the flag stones in two close columns, one coming, one going. Tim breathed. Behind him the glass doors of the sitting-room stood open. Hairy centipedes, equally at home inside and outside the house, scuttled then paused, brown smudges upon warm grey stone or cool plastered wall. Huge dark moths, escorted by mosquitos, flittered into the darkness of the house. (Only the upper windows had mosquito netting.) Behind an open shutter a green toad sat thinking.

Tim had had his breakfast, consisting of fresh crusty village bread, pallid creamy village butter, and Keiller's orange marmalade from the larder, accompanied by milky coffee. He had prepared a picnic lunch consisting of bread and butter, some paté from a tin, cheese, a yellow apple and a bottle of wine. The goodies were in a basket, the painting gear in his rucksack. After reflection, he had brought with him to France only water colour, gouache, and wax crayon. He breathed, he looked. He picked up his things and set off, crossed the flowery 'lawn' and the olive grove, traversed the streamlet on a wooden bridge set in a density of willows and green canes, passed through the middle of the aligned poplars, went steeply up through the vineyard, and made for the rocks. Tim had not at first gone far afield, there was so much to enjoy near the house. He had drawn the fig tree, the spear-leaved willows, the old tortured glaring olive trees with their sweet veils of silver foliage. The poplars defeated him. Many an impressionist could have rendered those straight smooth densely textured stems, those high clouds of flickering communicating leaves; but Tim could not. Dutifully, he had at once attempted to draw the house, but this too was curiously hard. The interest of the house lay in the squareness of the upper windows, the odd way the tower grew out of the roof, the live faintly powdery colour of the well cut rectangular grey stones, the shallow tilt and faded look of the tiles. In Tim's sketches the house looked quaint and dreadfully English. He was in any case by now becoming obsessed by the rocks.

A little path which he was following hopped here and there among the vertical strivings of the rocks, mysteriously keeping its identity. Already the house was out of sight. The sun was hot on Tim's neck and a pleasant runnel of perspiration drew its light touch down his brow and crept onto his cheek. He was climbing. Down in the valley the cicadas were singing, but the rocks had their own silence disturbed only by his breath and the occasional scrape of his shoe. A distant bird chucked. But it was a sadly birdless land. The only wild things he had seen were some very early morning rabbits playing among the olives. What he had taken to be animal bones turned out to be pieces of stripped wood bleached white, very smooth and shapely. He had already collected some of these. Close to, the rocks were whitish grey, close-grained and extremely hard, covered with tiny black spots. They were ridgy with small undulations as if convenient to the hand. They rose out of each other in pillared segments, each tilted and recessed a little from the one below, so that there was an effect of steps, and up these steps, following intermittent lodgements of grass and earth, the path continued; and it *was* a path, a trodden way of pilgrimage although the landscape through which Tim moved was one of the emptiest he had ever seen. Despite the olive groves and apricot orchards and vineyards down below, there was absolutely no sign of human beings. The few houses he had seen, all closer to the village, turned out to be derelict, or else shuttered up like little fortresses, their owners far away in Paris or London. The village was populous enough, but outside it the population ceased. Once, upon the road, when he saw a man in the distance, his heart had fluttered with fear. Up among the rocks there was nobody, and yet there was a path.

Tim's objective was an amazing place which he had discovered the previous day, just as he was about to set off for home. Twilight sent him homeward promptly. He was frightened of that empty rock-lorded land at night, and indeed during the day too. He had been drawing an ash tree that hung over a small chasm. Then he had been attempting to draw a rock formation. As has been mentioned, the visual arts had been Tim's university, but his studies therein had been eclectic and eccentric. When quite young he had been immensely pleased and impressed by some drawings of rocks by Ruskin. He had thought that if he could ever draw one tenth (hundredth) as well as Ruskin he would be content with his life (he still thought this). Having (on the previous afternoon) found the grey spotty rocks curiously undrawable, he gave up, returned to the path, and began to climb higher, hoping to reach the crest, which seemed so near, and to look down (which he had not yet done) into another valley, another country. He was searching in fact for somewhere to swim. Tim loved swimming, it had been one of the few joys of his time in Wales, but in recent years it had almost entirely passed out of his life. The streamlet near the house was too small to swim in, but it boded other water, and Tim had climbed toward the crest hoping therefrom to see, perhaps, below him, a tree-shaded river, green pools. He did not reach the crest; the rocks he saw as the summit revealed beyond them another summit, and then another. But he found something else. The path had made one of its intermittent stops at a narrow square-cut rocky cleft, rather like a door. Tim hesitated, then decided that his way led through the cleft. Holding the two sides of the rock, he had to lever himself up onto a step-like platform within the 'doorway', and then to descend two or three smaller rock steps on the other side. Occupied with scrambling, he did not look about him until he had descended onto a level place beyond, where there was an unexpected stretch of grass. Then he looked up and saw *it*.

It was a rock, a rock face, and indeed in some unspecifiable way *like* a face, which some fifty or so yards away down an enclosed glade rose before him. Uneven rocky walls rising on either side shut out the declining sunlight and the place was dim. At the far end there was a sort of cliff, something quite unlike the endless tilted ridgy progressions of the open rocks. Part way up this cliff and in the uncertain light seeming almost to hang separated from it, was a conspicuous paler area which looked like marble. The stone here was smoother, as if polished, nearly circular, and pitted with shadowy marks. It glowed a little like an occluded mirror. The cliff above it was darker in colour, scored with vertical straight lines, very faint like pencil lines. The relation of the parts was unclear. Sometimes it looked as if the lower paler part was itself a face, or a head wearing a crown. Sometimes the whole large formation looked like an indecipherable awful countenance. At the top, how high Tim could not reckon, there was a dark irregular mark, probably a large crack containing vegetation. From somewhere above that, long strands of creeper were hanging down. Most amazing however to Tim's startled gaze as he advanced across the grass was something which had been invisible at first. At the base of the cliff below the 'marble' where the rock was recessed a little, there was a large circular pool of very clear water. The gleaming pool was so round, its rock edges so smooth, that Tim could scarcely believe it to be a work of nature. He looked upon it with awe. Then all of a sudden he was aware of the absolute silence, the absolute solitude, the darkening air. He turned and fled, scrambling through the door-like cleft and scuttling away down the winding path between the rocks, across the vineyard, through the poplars, over the murky bridge, between the twisted olive trees, up the meadowy lawn, over the terrace and into the house, where he turned on all the lights and closed and bolted the doors.

Today, in the bright morning light, a good deal braver, he was going to revisit the 'great face', perhaps even draw it. He had some difficulty in finding it since his path seemed to have developed since yesterday any number of tributaries and ambiguities in its upper reaches, and he kept discovering new and distracting marvels, such as rock-bound shelves where little pink and white tulips were growing upon miniature lawns. At last when he thought himself lost and about to reach the real summit of the endlessly receding piled-up rocks, he suddenly saw, some distance away, his narrow cleft gate, now below him, and began to clamber down towards it panting and streaming with sweat. He pulled himself onto the high step of the gate, and in a moment was standing once more upon the long stretch of grass in the enclosed presence of the 'great face'.

In the daylight the huge thing looked different but no less awe-inspiring. Tim could now see, far up, the V-shaped crack out of which some ferny vegetation was hanging. The pendent creepers came from farther above where the rock merged into leaves and shadows, he could not see the top of it. The descending cliff with the narrow 'pencil lines' was now seen to be marked by a yellowish moss which grew in the narrow shallower scoring of the lines, giving to the rock a soft glowing stripy look. The round area beneath was remarkable, slightly salient, without vegetation, shadowed still but glistening in the bright reflected light. It hung above Tim, its lowest part a little above the level of his head, and its diameter might have been about twenty feet. Below it the rock receded into a shadowy alcove. Coming nearer Tim saw that the whole circular surface, of a pallid creamy whiteness which contrasted with the surrounding rock, was gleaming with water which seemed to be somehow exuding from the round shallow pores with which it was lightly pitted. The water veiled the rock, yet did not drip into the pool below.

The stone basin, seen by day, was clearly a work of nature, though a surprising one. It was circular, roughly the same size as the pale sweating stone above it. The verge was formed of the grey spotted rock which here rose vertically out of the grass, surrounding the water with a sort of broad undulating frill, and joining the base of the cliff in the rocky 'alcove' which projected a little way over the pool. The water of the basin was, as

Tim had apprehended last night, particularly pure and clear, almost radiant with its own clarity. It was difficult to say how deep it was, perhaps eight or ten feet in the centre, toward which the sides gently and regularly sloped. The entire floor of the basin, including its sloping sides, was covered with small crystalline pebbles, some white, some creamy, as if little stony tears had dropped down from the face above. Gazing at the strange pool Tim saw, with a further thrill of surprise, that the whole body of contained translucent water was very very faintly, throughout its entire extent, shuddering or quivering but with so small a vibration that the transparency of the medium was unaffected, while being as it were shot through by swift invisible almost motionless lines. Nor was the tension of the surface disturbed at all. The basin was evidently a source, but where exactly the water rose from and where it departed to Tim was unable to determine. None spilled over the side, nor was any streamlet visible nearby. The beautiful radiant pool simply quivered in perpetual occult donation and as perpetual renewal.

Tim stood for a while gazing at the cliff and at the pool, and his heart was so filled with joy that at one moment he had to clutch at it with both hands. The great round white pitted rock now seemed to hang there like a vast heroic shield. It was (or did he imagine this?) faintly steaming in the hot air, although the sun was not shining, perhaps never shone, directly upon it. He began to look cautiously round about him, at the expanse of grass which was so fine and short as if cropped by sheep (only there were no sheep) and at the way in which the loop of grey rocks, composing a narrow amphitheatre, made the place so secret. At last his pulse slowed down and he walked back to the cleft where, at the base of the 'doorway', he had left his rucksack and his basket.

The idea of swimming in the pool had at once occurred to Tim, and been at once rejected. He could not sully that pure water with his sweat or with his gross splashing interrupt its sibylline vibration. He permitted himself only to break the surface with his fingers. It was extremely cold. Now Tim unpacked his little stool, his sketch book, his pencils, his crayons, his paint box and brushes, his handy water-pot, filled at the kitchen tap. He had that pure clean blessed beginning-again feeling. He was full of grace. He sat down, completely happy, and began to draw.

About four o'clock in the afternoon Tim was still there. He was exhausted. He had consumed his lunch. To do this he had retired outside the 'door' as it seemed to him improper to eat in the presence of the rock and the pool. He had eaten the bread and butter, the paté, the cheese, and the apple, but had drunk sparingly of the wine, since he feared to go to sleep in the place. By four o'clock he was on the whole pleased with what he had done. He had done a number of drawings of the rock face. The circular area with the strange straight lines above it was so odd, that he feared it would not, on paper, look like anything. However the subject somehow took charge of him and conveyed some of its grandeur into his vision. He did some larger water colour sketches, outlines in brown ink, of the whole cliff face, including the vegetation. Then perched in the 'amphitheatre' he had tried, with wax crayon on grey paper, to convey the radiant light-giving quality of the crystal basin. This was less successful. Now it was time to stop. He packed up his gear and retrieved his basket, gave one last hasty anxious look at the scene which was already darkening, then climbed through the cleft into the outer world. At once he felt giddy, as at a change of pressure. Outside it was brighter. An undulating glow was rising from the pale spotty sunlit rocks. He looked upward, shading his eyes, deeming it yet too early to return home, and decided to try once more to climb over the rocky skyline and see what lay beyond. The little path soon vanished, or he had lost it. Perhaps its only task had been to lead him to the Great Face.

He mounted the steep rocks, scrambling, holding onto the hard ridgy surfaces, digging into their crannies with his finger nails. The climb, never dangerous, became more difficult, and he was hampered by the basket until he decided to leave it under a little bushy fig tree which offered a rare landmark. Only when the rocks to which he clung actually ceased in front of his face did he realize that he had reached the top. He rose panting to his feet upon the very crest. He was indeed now gazing down into another land. Far off he could see a sunlit plain with fields, and beyond it mountains, real blue mountains much higher than his 'little hills'. Near to him the rocks frilled downward in a series of small valleys or gorges which were now in shadow. Directly below, however, Tim saw something which drew his gaze away from any further view. There, at the very foot of the rocks upon which he stood, and easily, as it seemed, accessible by a natural rocky stairway and a green grassy slope, was a flashing river. It was not wide but even from here Tim could see the joyful commotion of its copious waters. With an exclamation of pleasure he began to descend, and was soon rewarded by sound as well as by sight. The coursing of the water had become distinctly audible, together with a more distant drone of what might be a waterfall; and it occurred to Tim that this was, apart from the cicadas' song lower down among the trees and a very occasional bird cry like an exclamation of woe, the only sound which the hot quiet landscape had vouchsafed him throughout the whole day.

The climb was longer than he had expected, as he had to circumvent a gully filled with box and brambles, but at last, sweating again and panting with exertion he had crossed the grass and stood upon the very edge of the water. He saw at once that this flashing torrent was no river. It was a canal. Straight as a die, it made its way through the landscape, appearing from below some rocks a little distance off and disappearing further on into a haze of young pines. What a miracle that in this dry dry land all this precious water stayed together rejoicing in its own elemental being! Where he stood the bank was steepish smooth and grassy, the water opaque, a light chalky grey. It gurgled and curled and swirled as it went along producing quick vanishing circlets of foam. It was infinitely inviting to a hot tired man. There was of course no one in sight. Tim dropped his rucksack and tore off his clothes. He sat upon the sweet cool very green grassy verge and slid down into the moving stream.

Instantly he was seized by a water demon. It was as if two firm light grey hands had gripped his waist, lifted him and conveyed him firmly along, turning him over and ducking him in the process. The stream was very cold. As from a moving train he saw the grassy banks speeding by, he entered the sudden shade of the pines. Swimming was out of the question, no movement of that kind was possible even in embryo. The force of the water drove his arms towards his sides as if the water demon were making of him a mere stick to twist and twirl about. He tried to kick his legs to keep his head up but the speed of the current gave him no purchase. He could not touch bottom. Spewing water from his mouth, Tim collided with something, grasped it, and was abruptly dragged round and jerked against the steep bank by the combined forces of the rushing water and the drooping pine branch which he had managed to take hold of. The branch broke. But a moment later Tim had hold of a bushy thorny acacia, whose ferny leaves were sweeping the water. He was flattened horizontally against the bank, but he held on. He struggled, pressing his knees into underwater grasses. Gradually his limbs obeyed him and with immense relief his feet touched a stony bottom. He clung there, a little out of the force of the stream, panting and resting. Then he managed to pull himself up, holding onto the acacia, then onto the hanging clumps of stout grass. The bank was not quite sheer and there were scooped out sandy footholds. He got up onto the level ground and collapsed, exhausted, buffeted by the water, his hands bleeding from the acacia thorns, his feet bruised by the stones.

His body was water-cold, he could feel the hot blood on his hands; then gradually the sun warmed him, and he got up. He had seemed to be a long time in the water but he had travelled less than a hundred yards and could now see, through the tufted branches, his clothes and rucksack not far away, fortunately on the same side of the canal. He walked back, testing the wholeness of his body. The sun had dried him by the time he began to dress. He looked down with amazement at the headlong force of the grey curling water in its deep narrow bed. It looked to him now dangerous, terrible. Shouldering his gear he walked along a bit, past the pines to see what the dreadful thing did next. Here of a sudden the canal curved to the right and became narrower, now enclosed by beautiful walls of hard neatly cut grey stone, which gave a clean stony footway at the top. Tim walked on upon the stone edge, looking down. The water was becoming more turbulent, more noisy, swifter, rising up into a curling wave on the inside of the curve. Then Tim saw something which shocked him with cold fear, with that sense of the fragile mortality of his own body, which comes to most of us as rare reminders, too soon forgotten. The water was now racing downhill between its narrowed stony walls. Then, in an esctasy, it discharged itself, suddenly become glassy smooth, onto a long slope of slimy green stone. Down below, at the foot of the slope, it churned itself into a white chaos of contending foam and then entered the dark hole of a subterranean tunnel. The mouth of the tunnel was just under water and the stream had to stoop and crowd to force its way in. In this manner, with a roar and a rumbling clattering sound it descended into the earth and vanished totally from the sunny landscape. Tim shuddered. He now wanted very much and very quickly to get home.

It was twilight in Tim's valley when at last, and unexpectedly, he saw below him the curve of the concealed rivulet and the red tiled roof of the house. He had of course lost himself on the return journey. He forgot about the basket and the fig tree which could have been a guiding mark. The rocks in the setting sun looked flat, their cracks fading into a uniform surface like veined marble. It was difficult to make out formations or judge distances. Once he had to pass through an area of dense scrub oak which he had never seen before. He descended, then found himself having to climb again.

He felt tired, but, as soon as he was away from the canal, not unduly dismayed by his adventure. It was exciting to think that he had escaped death. If the water demon had carried him just a little further on he would have slid helplessly down that slippery glassy slope and been sucked into that dark turbulent hole. His body might never have been found, even his rucksack might not have been noticed for weeks. He imagined Daisy's arrival, her annoyance, her puzzlement, then her alarm. Well, that would have been the end of his troubles and possibly, he reflected, a blessing in disguise for Daisy too. No one else, he thought to himself now a little sadly, would care a fig. It would quite amuse the people at Ebury Street to learn that Tim Reede had mysteriously vanished somewhere in France.

Tim was relieved to see the valley. He began to descend from the rocks into the vineyard. As soon as he felt underfoot the soft turned soil after the hardness of the rocks he paused to rest. The house was now well in view below him and he looked down upon it. Then he became rigid with fear.

There appeared to be a person standing on the terrace. The uncertain light seemed to jump and flash before his strained tired eyes. He closed his eyes for a moment, then looked again. The shape had moved. It certainly looked like a human being. Tim had gorged his nervous apprehension with tales of roving thugs and tourists murdered in lonely houses. Such fears regularly returned with the dark. His impulse now was quite simply to hide. He moved cautiously behind a row of vines, crouching and staring down through the young leaves at the maddeningly shadowy and unclear scene below him. He kept blinking his eyes, trying to make out what refused to be clarified. He crept a little way downhill, then crouched back into the open again, the terrace still in view. From here, with puzzled surprise and a little relief, he perceived that the mysterious person was a woman.

But who on earth could it be? There were plenty of female terrorists after all, often worse than the men. Perhaps they used this usually-empty house as a hide-out? Could it be Daisy arriving early, having let her flat more quickly than she expected? The shadowy figure, now moving again, did not look at all like Daisy. It had however begun to look vaguely familiar. For a horrible moment Tim thought it looked like Anne Cavidge. Then he realized, with an almost equally dismaying shock, that the woman standing upon the terrace was Gertrude.

Gertrude too, as it grew darker and no one came, had been feeling frightened. The empty house, Tim's protracted absence, filled her with foreboding. And when at last, looking down the hill, she saw a man emerge from the willows and begin to mount the slope through the olive grove she felt sheer terror until she made out Tim's friendly wave and heard his voice calling to her.

Gertrude had been unable to settle down in London. The old misery awaited her at Ebury Street. And then Anne had said she wanted to go away for a time to be alone. Of course she would come back but for a short while she must be somewhere by herself, even if it was only in a hotel in Pimlico. Gertrude thought that Anne might expect her to offer Les Grandes Saules as a retreat house, but Gertrude said nothing to Anne about the house in France or about Tim's being there. In fact she had told nobody about her ingenious plan and felt rather shyly secretive about it. The others might think that Tim had 'imposed himself'. Perhaps it had been a bad idea after all. Gertrude telephoned Stanley and in the end Anne returned to the cottage in Cumbria. Gertrude then felt she must get out of London. Without Anne she could not endure the flat. There was no one whose presence she wanted there as a companion, though Janet proposed herself, then Rosalind. When Manfred suggested that Gertrude should join him and Mrs Mount on a drive across Europe she rather desperately accepted. The objective of the drive was Manfred's flat in Rome, but the idea was that they would go slowly and Gertrude should come as far as she pleased.

Gertrude did not particularly want to be alone with Manfred, of whom in an odd way she felt a little shy, but she found, after they had set off, the company of Mrs Mount rather irksome. Manfred was always very good to the old thing, but Gertrude could have wished for another (Manfred was so exquisitely tactful) chaperone. As soon as she was in France and driving south she began to want to go to Les Grandes Saules after all, to know the worst, to see the worst, to confront there in another place, where they had been so happy, the ghost of Guy. She wanted to get it over with and be ready to sell the house. She could not leave the arrangements for the sale to Tim, she would have to do it, sometime or other, herself. Tim's presence was, in the context of this sudden frantic urge, but a slight embarrassment. Tim was not someone who weighed in any way upon her soul, he was, to Gertrude, a harmless powerless figure. Anyway he would be away painting all day. He would not mind her or she him. She would linger a few days, possibly make arrangements locally about the sale, and then go home again. Once home it would not be so long till Anne was back, and meanwhile she could go and stay again with Stanley and Janet, they had asked her often enough and she was really quite fond of the children, especially Ned.

Gertrude said nothing about Tim to Manfred and Mrs Mount, and she did not allow them to come to the house. (She said she had the key, which she had not, but fortunately Tim had left the place unlocked.) She said she must go there alone, it would be better so. With protests they dropped her in the lane and she heard with relief the sound of the big car dying away.

Tim's first feeling on seeing Gertrude there upon the terrace had been: oh crumbs, Gertrude, that's torn it, she'll spoil everything, how mean of her to come after all! I wonder who's with her, I hope they aren't staying long. Then he thought, *God*! Daisy! She'll be here soon, unless I can put her off somehow.

He mounted the steps to the terrace.

'Oh Tim, I'm so glad to see you! I've been quite frightened here, it's stupid. I thought supposing you didn't come back, supposing something had happened to you—'

Gertrude really did seem glad to see him, Tim was amazed. He said, 'Something nearly did happen to me—'

Gertrude went on, 'I'm sorry to turn up without letting you know—'

'But that's all right—'

'I suddenly felt I had to come here and get it over—'

'Who's here, who brought you?'

They were both talking at once.

'Manfred and Mrs Mount dropped me off,' said Gertrude. 'They've gone on to Italy. I'm sorry to intrude.'

'But I'm delighted—'

'I won't stay long. I must see people in the village about selling the house. I won't interrupt your painting.'

'No—of course—'

'I hope you've done some. I hope you like it here.'

'I like it *very much*.'

'Let's go inside, it's getting cold. I'm so relieved you've come, I thought something might have happened to you.'

'It nearly did—'

Gertrude went in through the open doors of the sitting-room

and switched on a light. It had become quite dark outside while they talked. Tim followed her and closed and bolted the windows and pulled the curtains. It was another scene.

The sitting-room was large and square with two white plastered walls where the shaggy centipedes sat or scurried like little bits of mobile carpet and lizards sometimes came. The wall where the fireplace was showed the original stone of the farmhouse. The furniture was simple, mostly made of cane, with copious flowery cushions which Gertrude had lovingly made on long winter evenings in London. There was a fine wooden table, made locally and stained with linseed oil, and a matching sideboard upon which there had been a tray with an empty gin bottle and a glass. (Gertrude had removed these.) One picture hung on the wall, a reproduction of a Munch print of three startled girls on a bridge which Janet Openshaw (who quite liked pictures) had given to Guy and Gertrude many years ago at Christmas time.

Tim, who had hitherto eaten his meals in the kitchen, saw with surprise that a red cloth had been put upon the table and plates, cutlery and glasses laid out neatly for dinner for two. There were even table napkins. It was years since anyone had laid the table for him. It seemed like the work of fairies.

'Gertrude! You've laid the table!'

'I hope you don't mind the tablecloth. We—we always used it so as not to make wine rings on the table. Well, I suppose it—doesn't matter much now—'

Tim hoped Gertrude had not noticed the wine rings he had been vaguely aware of making upon the kitchen table where he also recalled he had left rather a mess behind when he set out in the morning.

'Tim, you've cut your hand!'

'Yes, I caught hold of a thorny bush, you see—'

'There's a first aid kit upstairs.'

'I know. I'll just tidy myself. I'll be with you in a moment.'

He slipped out, visited the kitchen where, as he feared, everything had been cleared up and the table scrubbed. (He was usually tidy and grieved over this blot on his reputation.) He ran upstairs, noting Gertrude's suitcase in the larger bedroom. What on earth was he going to do about Daisy? Could he be sure that Gertrude would go before Daisy arrived? An unexpected meeting between those two women would be a major catastrophe.

Gertrude called up, 'Did you have any lunch?'

'A little—'

'I'm cooking spaghetti, is that all right?'

'Marvellous!'

Tim washed his hands and face. His hands had started to bleed again and he put some plaster on. After some hesitation he changed his shirt. He put a jacket on. The evening was cool. He had brought no tie. He combed his hair. What a pickle! He came downstairs a little self-consciously.

Gertrude too seemed embarrassed. She had set out wine and a jug of water, also bread, butter, cheese and apples. She was just ladling out the spaghetti which was liberally dosed with olive oil and tomato sauce and basil. She had made a salad of green peppers (Tim had bought them in the village) to go with it.

The sight of the excellent food and wine sent Tim's spirits soaring up. He beamed, then had to remind himself how sad Gertrude must be feeling. He composed his features and, after waiting for Gertrude to be seated, sat down.

'May I give you some wine, Gertrude? When did you come?'

'Just after lunch. I got suddenly frightened. I've never been alone here before, I don't think, even for an hour. It's a strange countryside.'

'I think that too—I've found—oh such wonderful places—but of course you must know them.'

'We don't own the olives. Guy always worried because they weren't properly looked after. There are so many suckers—'

'But they're beautiful—and the rocks—'

'What have you found?'

Tim suddenly felt that he did not want to talk to Gertrude about the Great Face. He said, 'I found a canal going at a hundred miles an hour.'

'That's very dangerous.'

'Yes, it nearly drowned me!'

'You mean you were *in* it?'

'I thought I'd swim, I scarcely survived!'

'Tim, you mustn't go into that canal, promise.'

'Oh yes.'

'Several people have been drowned, stupid tourists of course.'

'Well, I'm a stupid tourist. But what a place!'

'I hope you've been painting.'

'Oh like anything. I'm inspired, but nothing to show yet, only sketches. I think this place is paradise. A sort of dangerous paradise, but maybe paradise would be dangerous.'

'I won't bother you, Tim. I'm glad it's paradise for you.'

Tim flushed and looked down. He realized how glad he had been to see Gertrude in the role of someone to whom he could 'tell his day'. He had once more forgotten how unhappy this sojourn must be for her, with the house itself about to die, a continuation of Guy's death. But he could not say this to Gertrude. He looked up at her with puzzled embarrassed apologetic eyes trying to think of some slightly formal sympathetic utterance. She had been looking at him but at once looked away.

Gertrude now clearly felt that she had obtruded her sorrow. She said brightly, 'Have you found the moss fountain?'

'The moss fountain — I don't think so.'

'You'd know it if you'd seen it. I'll show it to you tomorrow. At least — I'll tell you where to find it.'

'I'll — I'll like that —' said Tim. The conversation was becoming lame.

'It's cold,' said Gertrude. She got up and pulled on a cardigan.

How much older she has become, thought Tim, with his exasperated pity. Her wild brown hair had been trimmed and seemed a little grey in front. Her sensitive curling mouth now plunged markedly at the corners sketching lines which would become permanent. A little persisting frown was making a dint in her brow above one eye. The wrinkled area about the eyes seemed soiled, now a trifle reddened. She has been crying, thought Tim, crying here all alone when she was waiting for me. Tim felt upset, almost disappointed, a little alarmed. It was like finding one's mother crying. Well, how often he had found his mother crying and how little he had ever really tried to comfort her. He had simply felt let down by her tears, affronted, neglected, abandoned.

He said to Gertrude, 'If I can help in any way —'

'Oh no — thank you —'

164

'After all, I'm the caretaker! And—er—Gertrude—how long will you be staying, do you think?'

'Not long—two or three days, I expect—I won't disturb you.'

It's not worth risking, thought Tim. I must tell Daisy to wait. But how? I must give Gertrude the slip tomorrow and send off a telegram.

UNEXPECTED SNAG DO NOT REPEAT NOT COME YET LETTER FOLLOWING LOVE TIM.

Such was the telegram which Tim had sent to Daisy on the day after Gertrude's arrival. It was now the third day of her sojourn.

It had proved quite easy to send the telegram. Tim had bicycled into the village with Gertrude. It had been funny cycling together and quite nice. Then while she went to see the agent about the house, he had gone shopping and had dodged into the post office. He had also written and despatched his 'following letter'. The letter ran thus.

Dearest, what a sell, would you believe it, Gertrude and Manfred and Mrs Mount have turned up! I am utterly disgusted! And I was having such a nice time, apart from missing you! My dear, this is a heavenly place, you will love it, even though it is Frogland. One sees nobody, whom you've always wanted to see! And the house is crammed with grub and vino, and there's a nearby village with lots more and cheap too. But about the invasion, don't worry, Gertrude has just come to arrange about selling the house, and then they are off to Italy. She won't come back. She says she just wants to get rid of the place as it gives her no pleasure now, and she doesn't want to see it again. I'm to be in charge of all the selling business now, I've seen the agent and all, he speaks English. So as soon as they go you can come! I'll send you a

165

telegram when it's all clear, meanwhile hang on. I wonder if you've let the flat? I do hope you are eating properly, darling, how ever can you manage without me? *Don't* write in case the mob stays another day or two. I'll alert you. Much love to dear old Daisy from her blue-eyed boy,

T.

Tim, rarely separated from Daisy in recent years, had hardly ever written to her, and it occurred to him that he had no 'style' for doing so. He was not much of a letter-writer anyway. He found the letter, which he had written late on the previous evening, quite a labour, and thought it a bit stiff when he had finished it. Never mind. Daisy would soon be here. The lie about Manfred and Mrs Mount came so easily that Tim scarcely noticed it. (It was sort of nearly true, after all.) He did not want Daisy to think of him as being alone there with Gertrude, it might annoy her, so many things did.

Gertrude had, on the first morning, after Tim's post office exploit, introduced him to the agent, whose eager English saved Tim from exposing his French (a bad moment there). After that Tim no longer accompanied Gertrude to the village. He went out early, taking his lunch with him (Gertrude seemed to expect that) and returning at twilight to find, as on the first evening, Gertrude waiting for him on the terrace and the table laid in the sitting-room. He enjoyed his painting, but not quite so much as when he was alone. His mind was disturbed, his concentration lessened. However he soon found it easy to get on with Gertrude, partly no doubt because he did not see a great deal of her. Their meal times together were pleasant, each telling the other of trivial mishaps and adventures. Gertrude enquired 'how he had got on' but did not ask to see his work. She was abstracted, not uncheerful in manner, adopting her usual briskness with him. Whatever sorrow she felt she did not reveal, and her special renewed mourning remained something private. She showed even less emotion than at the start of their 'desert island' life together. Tim was relieved yet disappointed. Gertrude was determined to keep him at a distance, not to let him help her. Tim had no idea what sort of 'help' he could possibly be, in so extreme a situation, to someone he knew so little, but he felt somehow sorry not to be 'called upon'. Sitting up in bed at night, with his arms round his knees, he heard her stirring, once softly moaning.

It was now the morning of what was probably Gertrude's last day; she was talking of leaving tomorrow after a final talk with the agent. This morning was special, since Gertrude had said that she would walk with Tim toward his painting place and on the way would show him the 'moss fountain'. Since Gertrude's arrival Tim had not returned to the crystal basin or the 'great face'. He was reserving these for the time after her departure. Nor had he returned to the canal. That too he would do later. During Gertrude's stay Tim had taken another route, turning left after the wooden bridge, not passing through the poplars but following the stream upon rough ground until there was a way to climb up through a thicket of gorse and reddish box bushes to the rocks at a point quite distant from the region of his first discoveries. Here there were other marvels. In one place the rocks turned pink, as if stained by some spilt dye. There was a high grassy plateau, narrow, about half a mile long, entirely surrounded by smooth walls of serrated rock. Here tiny yellow marbled irises were growing, and Tim saw a praying mantis. Through a small high gap in the rocks he could see, quite close and below, grassy terraces, olives, a pink painted farmhouse, fields. Tim turned quickly back. The area of the rock kingdom, which seemed so endless, was really small, but he did not want to know. He settled his stool upon the plateau and tried to render in wax crayon the effect of the frilly grey-blue rock crests against the intensely brilliant sky.

Thither, upon this early sunny morning, he was ultimately bound, but first to walk with Gertrude to the 'moss fountain' which she said was quite close. They had crossed the brook and walked up through the poplars and the vineyard, and now Gertrude had led the way to the little path. Tim had rather hoped that the moss fountain was not that way. He did not want to pass with Gertrude anywhere near to the great face. But perhaps the moss fountain was not so far on. This proved to be so. Diverging from the path after a few minutes Gertrude led him by a short scramble to a little round tree-shaded hollow into which they descended by a smooth ramp, and where the grass was a vivid green and wet underfoot. Tim saw, at the end of the hollow before the rocks rose again, a small green pillar, like a monument. On coming close he saw that it was a solitary rock about three feet high entirely covered with beautiful thick flowery moss and wet as if water were oozing out of it. He put his hand gently upon it and felt the coolness of the soft damp moss, the hardness of the cold wet rock, and he turned in amazement to Gertrude.

'Where does the water come from?'

'I don't know, it seems to come out of the very top and run down.'

'If there's a spring at the foot, could the moss carry all that water *up*?'

Tim stood entranced, staring at the brilliant green pillar, then walking round it and stroking it gently.

'Your hills are full of marvels.'

'There are more wonderful things than that.'

Gertrude turned away and began to climb back up the ramp. She was wearing plimsolls and white socks and her plump calves, already a little tanned, looked girlish. Tim, following her, saw a white petticoat flashing under her blue dress. She was agile. She waited for him at the top of the ramp, then led the scramble back to the little path. Here, instead of turning back toward the house, she continued without a word to follow the path upward. At turnings he could see her profile and the sad intent abstracted look upon her face as if she imagined herself alone.

'What's that bird?'

'A blackcap. Guy knew all the birds.'

There was silence again. No, not silence. Down below the cicadas were hugely singing, filling the air with their dry ceaseless inaudible voice. It was becoming very hot. Perspiration trickled down Tim's cheeks. His shirt was wet between his back and his rucksack. He hoped that Gertrude was not going to the great face. He did not want to go there with Gertrude. But already she had reached the cleft and disappeared through the doorway. Tim followed.

When they were down on the grass, not yet near to the great rock but in sight of it, Gertrude turned to Tim. It was like a question.

He replied, 'Yes, I have been here.'

Gertrude turned away and looked along the glade at the cliff with a kind of lowering look. She pushed the sweat back into her hair. Tim wondered if she wanted him to go, but he did not like to speak again. He watched Gertrude.

'Guy loved this place.'

'Would you like me to go away?' said Tim.

'I have to visit his places to say goodbye. Please excuse me—'

'Would you like—?' Tim then realized he had misunderstood her last words. Gertrude was unlacing her plimsolls and stripping off her socks.

She went on, 'I'm going to swim.' She began to walk away barefoot across the grass in the direction of the pool carrying her shoes and socks.

Tim thought, my *God*, she's going to swim *there*! He said after her, 'Oh yes, well, I'll just wait outside, beyond the—'

Gertrude was nearing the pool as Tim scrambled back through the cleft door. He went a few steps down the path and found a place where the rocks made a sort of ridgy shelf, with little cracks full of moss and saxifrage. He took off his rucksack which seemed to have become extremely heavy.

Then he heard, in the cicada loaded silence, the distant sound of splashing. He thought, if she swims there she will become a goddess, or else give proof that she already is one.

He sat down on the rock. Then he stretched out full length and settled his rucksack behind his head. The rock was warm. The sun beat down. Then, in the most extraordinary way, he fell asleep.

When he awoke, Gertrude was sitting beside him lacing her shoes. She smiled a brief perfunctory smile, then combed her wet hair with her fingers, patting it back, and screwing up her eyes against the sun. The skirt of her dress clung to her still wet legs. She said, 'I'm not much of a swimmer, but it's not deep except in the middle.'

Tim sat up. He thought, the water will be all disturbed with little waves, moving about, gradually becoming still. Or is it already quiet, resuming its own mysterious rhythm and glowing like a mirror? He said, 'I was asleep, have I been asleep long?'

'No, I just came back.'

'I had a strange dream, but I can't remember it.' I had a

169

wonderful dream, he thought, but what was it? 'How stupid of me to doze off.'

'Let's go on,' said Gertrude. She did not suggest that Tim might like to swim too.

He donned his rucksack and followed her on up the path, and then when the path vanished, on over the rising rocks. Some sort of spell seemed to be broken now. They had both moved easily before. Now they slid about awkwardly and lost their footing and stumbled. Tim was thirsty. He had water and a sun hat in his rucksack but he could not stop. He blundered on after Gertrude, wiping the sweat out of his eyes. She was climbing now with a sort of frenzied haste. He could hear her panting, almost sobbing with exertion just ahead of him. Then she paused upon the summit, and as he joined her he saw below the flashing arrow of the racing canal.

Gertrude looked at him, then pointed down. More slowly now and still puffing she began to descend. Soon the soft roar of the water could be heard and then the deep drone of the waterfall. He caught her up as she reached the grass and they walked together down the slope to the canal bank.

Tim wanted to sit down. He tried to think of something to say. He felt afraid of the water. Suppose Gertrude were to fall in, suppose she were to throw herself in? Was it perhaps for that that she had hurried here? She had begun to walk along the bank, past the pines, and as Tim followed he could see the stone walls and the frothy curving stream racing between them. Gertrude was walking now upon the cut-stone footway that formed the top of the wall. One of the laces of her shoe was trailing over the edge. The canal sank lower, then changed abruptly into the green slope with its sliding sheet of water, then foamed a brilliant white and disappeared into the tunnel. Tim thought, what a horrible fearful place, and yet how beautiful, how strong, how utterly and splendidly *mechanical*. And how maddening it was to be so hot and not to be able to bathe in that lethal tantalizing water. He sat down on the stone coping a little short of the slope and dangled his legs.

'Be careful, Tim.'

'Where does it go to?'

'I don't know.'

'Gertrude, do come away from here.'

'Oh my *God*, what's that?' She was pointing upstream.

A human body, tossed and tumbled by the water, was being carried towards them, something limp and drowned, sodden, turning strangely over and over.

Tim scrambled up. Then at once they saw that it was not a human being, but a large black dog, very dead. Its pale bloated belly had looked for a moment like a human face. The pink skin caught the sunlight for a moment as the thing whirled past. Tim made a helpless gesture as if to save it. But it was certainly dead. The corpse hesitated for a moment at the top of the slimy water slope and they saw the pathetic black muzzle, the white teeth, a paw suddenly lifting. Then the dog turned over and tumbled down the slope, surfaced briefly in the whirlpool below and was engulfed in the tunnel.

Gertrude had turned away and covered her face with her hands. Tim was about to say something when he saw her shoulders hunched and shaking. She was crying desperately.

Tim said, 'Oh dear —' He did not know whether to approach her, to touch her. He felt disgusted, annoyed, frightened by these tears and by the horrible portent of the drowned dog.

Gertrude was now audibly sobbing. She knelt down, her face still covered, then lay face down in the grass. She removed one hand to adjust her skirt. Tim stood there helplessly, staring at the soles of her shoes. He said almost irritably, 'Oh, Gertrude, stop it, please. You upset me so much.'

Gertrude did seem to stop. Her shoulders stopped moving and she lay still. Then she said in a firm controlled voice, speaking into the grass, 'I'm sorry. Please go away. I'll go home soon. I must be alone now. Just go away from here, please.'

'Sorry. I'm off. I'll go and do my painting. I was going along this valley anyway.' But he said to himself, I'll pretend to go, but I won't leave her, I'll hide.

At the foot of the rocks where the little gulleys and crevasses were full of dry precarious vegetation there was plenty of cover. He tramped audibly away and then hastily crawled into a rocky hollow behind a screen of spiky broom. He eased off his rucksack and peered back at Gertrude. He thought, if she suddenly looks like throwing herself into the canal, what can I do? Probably nothing.

After a few minutes Gertrude sat and looked around to see

if Tim had gone. She sat for a while, gracelessly, rubbing her face with her hands. Then she got up slowly, laboriously, like an old arthritic person, shook out her dress, and stood immobile staring across the canal into the distance. After that, to Tim's relief, she turned and walked back towards the rocks. She passed quite close to him, but he crouched down, and did not see her face. She began to climb, not with the agility she had displayed earlier but grudgingly, wearily, leaning down and using her hands, almost crawling at times.

When she had disappeared over the crest Tim leapt up. He paused to drink from his water bottle, then scrambled along after her. From the summit he could see, intermittently, the blue patch of Gertrude's dress. He also saw, quite near, the bushy fig tree, and under it the basket which he had left there on the day when the canal nearly drowned him. He picked up the basket and followed Gertrude, who was walking very slowly. She did not look back. He watched from above as she went, with her slow desolate sometimes wavering step, through the vines, through the poplars, across the stream, through the olives, and at last right into the house. Then he turned back among the rocks.

He walked a little, then sat down. He looked at his watch. It was not yet eleven o'clock. He could not decently go back to the house until the late afternoon. Gertrude would hate him if he intruded on her grief. He wondered what to do. He did not want to go anywhere. He did not want to paint. He began to feel utterly miserable, and the misery was upon him like a sickness. His legs ached, his head ached. He had a dark iron feeling in his stomach. He got up laboriously, as Gertrude had done, and took a few steps, then stood aimlessly like a dog. He suddenly recalled how Gertrude had swum in the crystal pool, but he did not want to go there, he did not want to see the Great Face. He thought, perhaps I shall never go there again, perhaps I shall *forget the way.*

He thought, what's the matter with me? I feel terrible, useless, utterly sick of myself. Where am I going, what am I for? What has my life been, what will it be? I just live by lies, by deceiving myself. I can't paint, I can't earn money, I can't do anything. I'd better give up painting, I've tried long enough and it's clear I'm no good. Better to chuck it and admit I'm a fake, a bloody fake, nothing but that.

He took off his rucksack and threw it on the ground and kicked it. He recalled Gertrude's crying face and he wanted to cry himself but he couldn't. He thought tomorrow Gertrude will go. Then Daisy will come. I don't want to see Daisy, I don't want to see anyone. I'm no use to Daisy, she's no use to me. That's a bloody lie too.

And he thought, I won't show the Great Face to Daisy, I won't show her the canal. I don't want her here at all. I don't want myself here, or anywhere else either. I wish the whole bloody masquerade was over, I wish I was dead.

Lying on her bed Gertrude had started to cry again. She cried quietly, wearily, it was like a natural function. She lay limp, unable even to get up to find a dry handkerchief. The one with which she was fruitlessly mopping her face was so wet she could squeeze the tears out of it. Her face felt raw with weeping. She was sick and dizzy with grief.

Since Guy's death she had watched herself suffering, she had seen herself wanting to suffer, then very gradually wanting not to suffer, wanting to recover, wanting to want to live. Now, in this place, so full of Guy, full of his thoughts and his ways, his knowledge and his happiness, she had seemed to be surviving so well. She had even endured without too much pain seeing Tim Reede riding Guy's bike. And now all the little tissues and tendrils of her recovery had been clawed away. She was back in the old deadly misery. She thought, I'll never recover now, it's the proof.

She had not been worried about Tim Reede's presence, she had been on reflection glad that someone would be there, that she would not be alone at Les Grandes Saules. She had never been alone in that house. Guy had always been there. She had never, she thought, even walked alone, only with him. In fact, she realized now, she had always been afraid of those rocks, of that silent empty countryside. Guy had defended her from that fear, as he had defended her from all fears.

Tim was useful as someone before whom she had to keep up appearances. And there was, she thought, a further bonus, which arose from Tim's own perfect selfishness. Tim's tactless inability to be suitably solemn had had something of a cheering effect on Gertrude, his simple absorption in his own interests, the absence of any intrusive desire to console, to possess or probe. She was soothed by his detachment from her troubles, his unashamed ability to look eagerly elsewhere. This self-centred cheerfulness made a kind of space, a relief from being pitied and looked after. Only now, when she had escaped from it, did Gertrude feel how tired she was of the solicitous curiosity and busy sympathy of those who had surrounded her: a sympathy which, it occurred to her, was in many cases insincere. How much did Janet Openshaw or even Stanley really care about Guy's death? It merely put them in mind of the day when their children would inherit Guy's money from Gertrude. No wonder Rosalind Openshaw wrote her such splendid carefully worded sympathetic letters! Gertrude could measure now how much Guy's family was not really her family. Anyway, people always delight in the misfortunes and griefs of others unless they are positively wounded themselves. What did Mrs Mount care, or Gerald, or Victor, or (another splendid letter-writer) Balintoy? Sylvia Wicks had not even written at all. What did Manfred care? Sitting in a café while Manfred was parking the car, Mrs Mount idly chattering had revealed, what Gertrude had never suspected but Mrs Mount evidently assumed she knew, that Guy and Manfred had never got on very well, had always regarded each other with rivalry and suspicion. Gertrude now thought she could recall, especially after he became ill, a kind of irritation in Guy concerning Manfred. Manfred was probably secretly glad that Guy was gone. Guy had overshadowed them all. His evident superiority must have irked them. Why had Gertrude imagined that they loved and revered him so much? They had envied him and his evident distinction had made them feel inferior. Only the Count had truly loved Guy, and now truly missed him. And Anne, dear dear Anne, had truly sorrowed in Gertrude's sorrow, had truly cared for her and tended her. Yet even Anne, thought Gertrude—how could

Anne not be somehow pleased that just as she returned to the world there I was needing her so much? She must have been pleased, she must have found it so satisfying, so gratifying, to be able to cut all the others out and look after me!

Gertrude, her tears abating, pictured that dear head, the thin pale silvery furry head, the narrow clever blue-green eyes. Brilliant strong Anne Cavidge. What a long way they had come together since that night when Anne had rung up from Victoria Station. And she remembered Anne, naked Anne with the cross round her neck, entering the sea like a damned soul. And how she had seen Anne dashed by the waves, struck down, nearly killed before her eyes. And how she had rushed into the foam, suddenly buffeted herself by the huge waves, her dress clinging to her legs and impeding her. And this fierce water mingled in her vision with the deadly racing water of the canal and the bloated twisting corpse of the dog which had suddenly spurred her grief.

Gertrude became breathless and had to sit up, gasping and panting. She squeezed out her handkerchief and mopped her eyes. Anne was so necessary. But would she go away? What judgement would Anne make upon Gertrude's life? She had said she must be alone, she had encouraged Gertrude to go to Italy with Manfred and Mrs Mount. Would Anne end up by returning to the living death of her convent after all? She recalled something Anne had said, a medicine no doubt for Gertrude's desperation. 'One can always live by helping others, it's a consolation that is always to be had.' Could I live so, Gertrude wondered, if Anne were to leave me? Of course Anne won't leave me I know. But I can't exist just through Anne forever, it wouldn't be fair to her. She thought, I've helped Tim Reede, does that console me? Yes, a little. And how extremely easy it was! Who else could I help, who else could I make happy? Someone said Sylvia Wicks was in some sort of trouble, they didn't say what. I could help Sylvia. I could help Mrs Mount. I could help the Count. She pictured the Count, so thin, so straight, looking down at her with anguish in his pale, pale blue eyes.

Then in a flash she understood something. Why had Guy said to her, 'if you marry someone, marry Peter?' *Because he wanted to cut out Manfred*, to divert her from that terrible choice, the choice of his rival! That he should be dead and Gertrude in Manfred's arms; was this the nightmare which had tortured Guy, made him cry out at last, 'I want to die well, but how is it done?' He had not really wanted her to marry the Count. He had simply wanted her not to marry Manfred.

'I wish you had let me cook,' said Tim, 'I *can* cook.'

It was the evening of the black dog day, and they were sitting down to supper in the sitting-room.

Tim had taken his misery away among the rocks and found a shady place where he had had an early lunch, eating little but drinking up the wine in his rucksack and also the wine that remained in the basket. After that he fell asleep. He returned to the house at half past four and knocked on Gertrude's door offering to bring her some tea.

Gertrude had refused but had at last pulled herself together. She got up and washed. She took off her crumpled blue dress and put on a smarter *café-au-lait* shirt-dress with an open collar. She inspected her swollen face, put on make-up, combed out her hair which was matted and tangled from swimming and crying. She then drank a little whisky from the flask in her suitcase and sat for a while in an easy chair in her bedroom with her eyes closed. She thought, yes, Anne is right, I'll help people, at the very least I can give them money. I'll help Tim more. She thought of Tim, his diffidence, his particular egoism, his boyish animal self-satisfaction, his ignorance, his needs. She thought, Tim is so *easy* to help and she found herself smiling. At half past six she came downstairs and took another tot of whisky with her out onto the terrace. Here she found Tim watching the ants. Now they were at supper together.

Supper consisted of onion soup, black sausage with tomato salad, and a local cheese with herbs.

'I'm afraid it's very simple again,' said Gertrude. 'You'll be able to cook tomorrow when I'm gone. You must let me feed you. I can't do anything else. I can't paint.'

'Neither can I!' said Tim, but he said it cheerfully.

When Tim heard Gertrude stirring, and as the day went on toward supper time his equanimity returned to him. The strange misery-sickness went away and was succeeded by an almost elated cheeriness. The prospect of food and drink usually restored him. He was happy, and the soup smelt delicious.

'I'm hungry!'

'So am I,' said Gertrude. 'I hope you had a good day. Do you ever get bored in those long times painting?'

Tim thought of trying to explain what a painter's concentration was like, then just said 'No.' He added, 'I'm sorry you're going tomorrow. It's been fun—I mean—'

'I'm sorry too,' said Gertrude, 'but I must get back.' Why must I, she wondered.

Tim was looking brown and ruddy, he looked a little plumper too, a different man from the pallid weedy rather hang-dog young fellow who had come to Gertrude with apologetic hints about needing money. He seemed bigger, stronger. His lips glowed. His shaven beard shone like a barley field. Red hair curled on his chest in the unbuttoned front of his shirt. As he rolled up his sleeves ready for his supper his arms gleamed with points of light.

It was dark outside, but the landscape was not yet invisible. The feathery leaves of the twisted olives seemed to give out a silver glow, and the rocks retained a curious dark grey light which seemed to vibrate irregularly like a signal.

'It's getting awfully dark. Shall I turn on a lamp?'

'Not just yet. Can you see your soup, Tim? I want to look at the rocks.'

Tim thought, perhaps this is the last time Gertrude will look at those rocks. He said, 'I wish you weren't going. It's been nice just eating and drinking with you, coming home and finding the table laid— You've been kind to me, you've been a real sport—sorry, that's not a very graceful compliment!'

Gertrude laughed. She said, 'We've been good companions.'

They ate the soup in silence. Gertrude set out the black sausage and the salad and the cheese. She filled their glasses with the local red wine. Tim sat in a trance looking out of the window. He jumped as Gertrude turned on the lamp and the outward scene disappeared. He looked at her and could see the traces of tears. All the same her strong crinkly hair glittered heroically.

'It's silly,' said Gertrude, 'but I simply can't remember how you came into our lives. I mean, how we got to know you.'

'Through Uncle Rudi. He was a friend of my father's. Then he was sort of my guardian.'

'Oh yes. He was musical wasn't he, your father, he was a composer?'

'Sort of. I have no music in me.'

'Then Guy's father became your guardian when Uncle Rudi died?'

'Yes. Then Guy. Your family have been awfully good to me,' he added.

'And you're an only child like me, like Guy?'

'No—' Tim had to pause. I'm in an awfully emotional state this evening he thought. He saw Rita's face so clearly, first laughing, she had had blazing red hair which fell around in straggly coils, and blue eyes to match his own. Then he saw her pale, sad, thin, terribly thin, her eyes so frightened, asking to live but surrounded by a gathering dark. Her sudden death had surprised everybody. It seemed to him that he was the only person who had really noticed how little she ate, how thin and frail she was: and he had not understood. He said after a moment's silence, 'I had a sister. She died when I was fourteen. She died of anorexia nervosa.'

'Oh I'm sorry—' said Gertrude. 'Oh I'm—so sorry—' She turned her head away.

Tim helped himself liberally to some more wine.

'And your poor parents, they must have been—'

'Oh my parents—My father cleared off when we were small children. My mother died when I was twelve. We lived with my mother's brother in Cardiff. It was horrid. Oh never mind, don't let's talk of it, sorry—'

'Sorry, Tim—'

'No, no, forgive me, I do want to talk in a way. No one's ever asked me—I was so unkind to my mother, I see it now. She was musical too, you know—' He recalled suddenly the sound of her mother's flute, always such a sad sound, heard less and less as the years went by.

'She was unhappy?'

'She was anxious and bothered and children hate that. Children are *awful*. There wasn't much money. We loved our father because he wasn't involved in the mess of our lives.'

'And your father?'

'He vanished. Killed in a motor accident when we were in Cardiff. Later on of course I escaped and came to London, and became the property of your family!'

'Of Guy's family, yes. I have no family. I mean, I was an only child. My father left Scotland and lost touch, he was from Oban. My mother was from Taunton. They were both school-teachers and we lived a roving life, like being in the army. My parents weren't well off. It was all very simple and quiet.' Why do I say this now I wonder, Gertrude said to herself. I haven't thought anything like this for years. I've simply been absorbed into Guy's life, into his family, into his world, it's been a home. Now I have no home. I never thought I had a gloomy childhood, surely I was spoilt and happy, yet suddenly it looks like that.

'I always imagined you were rather rich and grand like Guy. Sorry, I keep saying the wrong thing tonight!'

'No, no, Tim, say what you like, it's good to talk! I think I'll close the doors, it's getting cool and the moths are coming in.' Gertrude closed the glass doors and the dark shiny mirror of the window suddenly enclosed them. Tim saw the table, the two figures sitting opposite each other, reflected in the glass.

'It's nice here,' said Tim. 'It's sad you're going, we're getting to know each other a bit, have some more wine.'

'Thanks. You mustn't disappear, Tim. You must come to Ebury Street like you used to. You said you were the property of—' Would Ebury Street go on, Gertrude wondered. She pictured herself entertaining *les cousins et les tantes* as the years went by. What value would they put upon her once the interest of her bereavement was over? Did she have then to be *assessed* by them? She looked at the red table cloth and the broken bread and the wine.

'Oh, yes, thanks. Are your parents still alive?'

'No. My father died when I was in my first job—you know I was a school-teacher too?'

'Oh yes, I know *that*!'

'Dear me. My mother died just before I got married. She met Guy. She got a sudden — thing — '

For a moment Tim thought Gertrude was going to cry again. She made a little gesture with two hands, the moment passed.

Gertrude thought, it was so terribly sad, Guy and my mother just missing each other like that. We could have made her so happy. I didn't do enough for her after Daddy died. Oh why am I thinking these things now? Everything is coming apart, it's coming *unsewn*. All my energy, all my youth, went to Guy, as if Guy invented my youth. I went to Guy like Anne went to the convent.

'Did you have a lot of lovers before Guy?' Tim asked. He thought, I must be drunk!

'No. I was never really in love, I was just muddled and unhappy, till I met Guy.' Then the certainty started. But has it gone now? Did not Guy make me? But am I permanent?

How handsome she is, thought Tim, an Arthurian girl, a heroic girl out of a romantic picture, with her fine face and her brave hair and her pure sincere brown eyes. Her complexion glowed and her eyes were bright with thought. Her mouth pouted a little reflectively, the lips had a gentle look. The gauntness Tim had seen earlier had left her face, as if some force inside her were moulding her, smoothing her in a new way. Her patterned mane shone in the lamplight as if each individual hair had a line and a colour all its own : browns and golds, some reds, some greys. Some locks fell round her neck and brushed the nervous brown hand with which she was adjusting the collar of her dress. The pale milky-coffee colour of the dress showed how much already she had been touched by the sunshine. He thought, she's so *alive*, so compact and genuine, how her hair glows and her eyes are such a wonderful pure brown, I've never seen such beautiful eyes in a woman. She's recovering. I'm so glad. He meant to say, You are recovering, I'm so glad. He said, 'You are beautiful, I'm so glad.'

Gertrude smiled, then looked at him intently, then looked away. She began to play, but less absently, with the bread crumbs on the table-cloth.

What is happening to me, thought Tim. A kind of thought, or was it a thought, what was it, had come to fill his whole mind, like a fast approaching comet which suddenly fills up the whole sky. In a moment there would be some kind of crash or cataclysm, the end of the world. The thought, or event, was that he had got to, he had simply *got to*, reach out his hand across the table and take hold of Gertrude's hand. Some vast cosmic force was compelling him. Its strength, present in him, made him feel that he was about to lose consciousness. He reached out his hand across the table and took hold of Gertrude's hand.

Breathing very deeply Tim looked down at the red cloth, at the fragments of bread just beyond his plate. Now that he had got hold of Gertrude's hand the terrible pressure had, for the moment, abated. He had done what he had to do, what the cosmos had to do, he was not even responsible. He had moved like a gentle automaton. He felt almost impersonal, like an engineer who, alone in a great engine room, has, as a matter of routine, pulled some vastly important lever.

Gertrude looked with surprise at her hand which lay like a small captive animal in Tim's firm grasp. She looked at the brilliant lively red hairs on the back of Tim's hand, and at a smear of blue paint on the unbuttoned cuff of his shirt. For a moment she could not think what to do. Then she drew her hand back and the two hands separated. Then Tim and Gertrude both sat up straight and stared at each other.

Tim clasped his hands together on his knee. His right hand which had held Gertrude's felt as if it was on fire. He contained it carefully within his left hand. He looked straight at Gertrude with an amazing calm. He felt as if his eyes had become enormous like great calm lamps. He had done what he had to do and now whatever happened nothing could touch him. His substance was changed, he had become something else. He felt his mouth relax, his whole body relax. His gentle complicit hands relaxed. He almost smiled. He stared at Gertrude.

Then in a remote detached way he began to think, but so slowly, so calmly, poor old Gertrude, she's *embarrassed*. But it had to happen and in a wonderful way it doesn't matter. I'm so happy. In a moment or two I'll have to start apologizing, saying I was drunk or something. But it doesn't matter.

Gertrude frowned and looked down. Her hand was at her neck again, fiddling with her collar. She looked flushed, almost frightened.

Tim said in a matter of fact tone, 'I'm most awfully sorry. I hope I didn't startle you. It came over me all of a sudden.'

'Not at all,' said Gertrude.

It will go away, thought Tim, it will get lost forever. At least, *it* won't go away, because *it* is eternal. But this long long moment will end. And then *I* shall be lost. 'I apologize,' he said.

'Please,' said Gertrude. 'I realize it was—' She shifted her chair slightly.

Tim groaned and put his hand to his eyes.

There was another moment's silence.

What is it, thought Gertrude, why do I feel in a state of shock? I feel cold and sick, I feel faint. Has there been an earthquake tremor? Something uncanny is happening. How blue his eyes are and how awfully he stares at me. I must do something, but what must I do?

'I am very stupid,' said Tim, 'and you must forgive me, but before you say goodnight I must just tell you that I think I've fallen in love with you. I mean it's not just drunkenness or anything. I really do apologize.' I had to say it, he thought. I had to say it like something one might die for saying but which has to be said, like a sort of bearing witness. But I *am* stupid and I *am* drunk and how terrible it is all going to be. The glory has passed already in a sort of atomic flash. It was brief enough. Now there's nothing left but the pain. I've fallen in love. Nothing could be more certain than that. He said, 'I think I'll go to bed now, Gertrude.'

'Don't go yet. Have some more wine.' Gertrude poured some wine into his glass. She held the bottle with both hands, even then some wine spilt onto the cloth.

Tim could not resist the sight of the full glass of wine. He drank. He thought, I'll just sit quietly for another minute or two, then I'll go. He moved his chair slightly back and looked down at the floor, examining the grain of the wood. He felt humble and wretched and proud and sad and solitary but with a sort of greatness.

Gertrude seemed to be struggling to say something. Twice he heard her intaken breath as for speech. At last she said, 'Tim— dear Tim—'

'Oh don't bother,' said Tim. 'I just love you. It doesn't matter. Please don't feel you have to discuss it. I'm going in a minute. Why shouldn't I love you? It's just a fact. It doesn't make anything else in the world different. It's quite harmless. It doesn't matter.'

Gertrude's chair scraped again. Tim, thinking she was going away, began to rise. Then he saw that she was coming round the table and he sat down again.

Gertrude took another chair and pulled it up near Tim's so that they were sitting rather awkwardly side by side.

'What's this about?' asked Tim casually, almost roughly.

Gertrude thought, I'm at the edge, I'm over the edge. I've got to come close to him, I've got to touch him. It is to do with the present moment and the necessity of it and how it's all complete, all here, all in *him*. Everything that is necessary is here, there is nothing left outside, and I have to act, I have to move. I must touch him, but how. I feel so giddy, so disjointed, so disconnected, as if my limbs have been taken off and put on the wrong way round. Without looking at Tim, she half turned towards him and with a gesture of abandonment, laid her hand on the table.

Tim seized her hand and began to kiss it. He kissed it humbly, gently, reverently, avidly, hungrily, as if he were eating some holy manna. He said, 'I love you.'

'I think I love you too,' said Gertrude.

Tim held her hand up against his eyes. He had again the sense of some inconceivable annihilating flash of light. Then he laid her hand down again upon the table and moved his chair a little away from her. He breathed open-mouthed, pulling at the neck of his shirt. He said, 'Dear Gertrude, you don't mean what I mean. You haven't understood. It doesn't matter. All right. You're drunk, I'm drunk. You've been under an awful strain here. Let's say goodnight now. And tomorrow we'll just wave each other goodbye. We've been good companions, as you said. I'm very grateful for that. Don't let my stupid declaration spoil it all. Yes, I do love you, sorry to have to keep saying it. But you don't have to do anything special, you don't have to be kind to me.'

'I'm not being kind to you, you fool,' said Gertrude. 'But maybe you're right and we should go to bed and to sleep and — sober up and —'

But they continued to sit there, entranced, terrified, breathing deeply, spellbound to their chairs. Their faces expressed the most terrible gravity, like people waiting for news of an execution. Yet at the same time it was as if each of them were deperately calculating. Tim poured out some more wine. He shifted his chair so that it was parallel to the table. He stared at Gertrude's profile.

Gertrude stared at the Munch print of the scared girls on the bridge. She thought I've got to kiss him, it's the end point of the world, I've got to. It was like a duty, she quaked and shook with it. She could feel her cheeks burning, she could feel Tim staring at her. She too turned her chair and moved to face him. Her knee overlapped his knee.

Tim clutched her clumsily, one arm round her waist and one round her shoulder, and pulled her toward him. He saw her close to, her glowing amazed eyes, her wet mouth. Then they both rose to their feet. Then it was simple. Their bodies locked together, their arms locked together, their eyes closed. So they stood for a time. Then Tim moved her a little, drew back a little and kissed her with one slow gentle kiss. Then he let go of her, she stepped back, and they stood for a moment in a strange quiet modesty. Gertrude smoothed down her dress.

'Tim—I'm going to bed now—I don't want to see you again tonight—stay here a while. We'll talk in the morning. Goodnight.'

Tim bowed to her, an odd bow such as he had never bowed before. Then she was gone. He sat down to finish his wine. He looked at the black shining uncurtained window and saw himself reflected there, a man sitting alone. He tucked in his shirt tails and buttoned up his shirt, and looked at himself. He thought, the old silent rocks have been looking in at us. All the gods and demons of the valley could have crowded round that window and watched us. Perhaps they did. He thought, she was drunk, poor thing, she will *hate* me in the morning. But the morning was still a long way off. He drank more wine. He was dizzy, floating, prolonging a not quite incomprehensible ecstasy. He could hear Gertrude moving about above. Then there was silence. At last he left the table and turned out the lamp and went quickly and quietly up the stairs.

Tim thought that he would now lie awake all night, but he found the quick sleep of one who has laboured hard and well.

He fell into a deep dreamless pit of dark joy. Gertrude too thought that she would not sleep, but she did. She slept soon and dreamed of Anne.

Tim Reede awoke. He was lying on his back. It was daylight and a bird was singing. He thought at first he was at home in his garage loft, where there were nearby trees in a little garden and birds came and sang. A deep thrilling stream of happiness flowed through him as he lay and listened to the bird. He noticed the happiness and that it was unusual, amazing. He wanted to sleep again. Then he thought, I'm in France. Then he thought, *Gertrude*.

He sat up and pushed his feet out of the bed. He listened. Silence. In desperate haste he got up and slithered tiptoe into the bathroom. Gertrude's room had its own separate bathroom so there was no danger of colliding with her. He washed and shaved and cleaned his teeth and glided back to his own room and dressed. The stream of happiness had turned into a stream of pure fear. He must find out, he must *know*. But oh Christ, Gertrude was probably still asleep. He listened again. Silence. He combed his hair. He felt sick to vomiting with anxiety and terror.

He went to the window. Gertrude, dressed in her pale *café-au-lait* dress, was standing in the little meadow among the blue flowers, looking away toward the rocks whose near side was still dark although the sun, shining from behind the crests, had filled the valley with colours.

Tim did not call. He ran, almost falling down the stairs, and out the quickest way through the dining-room archway and across the terrace. Gertrude had turned towards him. He stumbled into the flowery grass, then stood, not close, holding out his hands towards her.

'Gertrude—'

'Yes, yes, it's all right.'

'What's all right, what do you mean?'

'It's still there.'

'Oh my God—' said Tim. Then he said, 'But *what's* still there, what does *that* mean?'

They spent the morning in conference. 'Conference' best expressed the extraordinary intense careful colloquy which, under Gertrude's chairmanship, took place, during that morning. There was, by Gertrude's will, no kiss, no embrace, and this abstention contributed not a little to the thrilling calmness of their debate. They sat now, not in the sitting-room, but opposite to each other at the trestle table under the open dining-room archway, just in the shade. There had been no question of breakfast.

They talked with apparent clarity above a silent chaos of astounded fear. Both wanted to comfort, to reassure, to say 'It's all right'. At the same time, both were filled with a curious almost shame-faced caution, an anguished sense of timing, a desire not to go too fast, not to go too slow, not to say anything offensive or scandalous or tactless or improper. Vast metaphysical doubts assailed them about whether they had really understood what the other thought or wanted. There were moments when they stumbled and lost each other, terrible checks and silences when they gazed across the table in dismay. They had to work out what had happened, or not really to work it out, not yet to explain or clarify it, but simply to make it bearable by surrounding it with a net of ordinary words. And they *argued*, scarcely knowing what it was they were arguing about.

'It was a wonderful moment when you came striding through the twilight on that first day.'

'You think it was prophetic. But you didn't come here to see me.'

'And you didn't want me to come here.'

'That's ancient history. We've survived the night. Will we survive the day?'

'We must *think*—'

'I'd rather you didn't. This couldn't have happened at Ebury Street.'

'Don't keep saying so.'

'Suppose I hadn't taken your hand.'

'You said you had to.'

'But suppose I hadn't?'

'But you did.'

'It's because of here.'

'Because of here needn't mean just because of here.'

'You'll have a reaction, a revulsion, you'll suddenly see me as—'

'No—'

'You're suffering from shock, you've been under stress. People in stress situations get sick, they get a bit crazy, they could imagine that they fall in love. They have huge emotional illusions and make huge emotional mistakes.'

'We shall see.'

'Well, I'm *terrified.*'

Gertrude leaned across and touched the back of his hand with a kind of quick routine rap, like touching someone to keep him awake.

'All right,' said Tim. His mouth was dry. 'We shall see. But I feel that some god is playing a game with us.'

'You keep trying to make what has happened into something else.'

'But what has happened? You won't say—'

'Tim, I don't know what to say. But I'm sure—'

'I'm sorry, why should you commit yourself to anything. I just mean it's so-unsafe, so unreal. All this can unhappen. You can unhappen it just by saying we won't speak of it again, goodbye.'

'But I'm not saying that!'

'And I should be grateful, I *am* grateful. But, my dear, we're dreaming and we'll wake up. It's too good to be true.'

'Oh Tim, stop, we've been over this.'

'How extraordinary, I've just remembered.'

'What?'

'That day when you swam in the pool—it seems a hundred years ago—I fell asleep in such an odd way and I dreamed and I forgot the dream—and what I dreamt was that I was holding you in my arms. That proves it.'

'Proves what?'

'That it's just something to do with here, with this place, this landscape. We're under a spell. But when we go away it will fade. You'll see I'm just a dull fellow with ass's ears. Gertrude, you are deluded, you can't love me, I'm not educated, I'm not clever, I can't paint, I'm going bald —'

'Oh don't be so destructive. Something has happened to us. Can't you just be true to it long enough to see what it is?'

'You're so brave! I feel that if I lose this whatever it is now I shall die. I existed without it before, but now that it's here, *if* it's here —'

'Tim, I haven't asked this, perhaps there's no need but I just want to be sure, have you any ties — any girl — or anything like that — ?'

Tim's lies usually came to his lips so fast that he scarcely noticed they were lies. Now he hesitated for one second before replying, 'No. There's no one like that in my life.'

'I'm glad.'

Ought I to have told her about Daisy, Tim wondered. Better not, how could I possibly have explained about Daisy, it would have given the wrong impression straight away and somehow spoilt everything. I couldn't mention Daisy without it seeming important in a way that it's not. Really, Daisy and I gave each other up years ago, it's not like a real relation. Besides, all this with Gertrude may be a dream and there's no need to decide what to say just yet.

He said, 'Gertrude, I'm an awful liar —'

'You mean — ?'

'I said I could speak French and I can't.'

'I'm glad you told me. I'll teach you a bit of French —'

'You won't. We won't be here. We won't be at Ebury Street either. We haven't anywhere to go, we haven't anywhere to *be*, we're just impossible. We can't be together like real people are. Gertrude, I'm not real, don't rely on me.'

'I shall make you real. We must wait and see, meanwhile trust each other. What else can we do?'

'Oh Jesus Christ — but what do we *do* while we're waiting?'

Tim Reede awoke. Joy, contentment possessed his body. He was naked, covered in sweat. All was silent. He breathed deeply and breathing was joy. He thought, I feel so happy, like never before, ever in my life. I feel so pleased and heavy and warm and damp and limp. I really exist and it's so good.

He opened his eyes. He was lying in his bedroom, in his own narrow bed, and Gertrude was lying with him. She was asleep.

It was the afternoon nearing to evening, he could tell by the light. He eased himself off the bed and stood up and looked down at Gertrude. The quiet sleeping face looked like that of a stranger. A woman in his bed. He felt amazement, tenderness, fear that she would wake. The sleeping face having lost some characteristic expression, some cautious protective dignity, looked anonymous and defenceless and sweet. Gertrude's thick brown hair was everywhere, netted over her brow and over the pillow, crossing her face moved by her breath, streaked down into the perspiration on her neck. The salient collar bones glowed and shone with moisture. The large breasts were pale. Gertrude of Ebury Street, the goddess of the crystal pool, had changed again into this strange magic brown-haired girl with long heavy sleepy eye-lashes and limp open hands, and nestling feet.

Tim crept away as he had done in the morning, for it was the same amazing day. He sponged off the sweat and got dressed. He went quietly downstairs and stood on the terrace and watched the evening sun making the rocks move, making them breathe, very quietly expand and contract like some organism under the sea. He thought, well, something has happened *now* which can't unhappen. And yet at any moment—He did not want to think frightening thoughts. He felt a blank blinding empty happiness. He also felt extremely hungry. He wanted to dance. He went down onto the flowery lawn and executed a few Morris steps. Then with his hands on his hips he danced down as far as the olive grove. He stood there and gazed at the rocks. When he turned about he saw that Gertrude was standing on the terrace in a flimsy white garment which might have been a nightdress. He began to dance towards her across the flower-shadowed grass.

Gertrude, as if she could hear the same silent music, came down the steps and joined in the dance. Instinctively, hands on hips, they danced with the zigzag snakelike motion of a hay. It was as if other dancers were present to whom, as they passed, they turned their backs until, in the middle of the meadow, solemnly, unsmilingly, they passed each other, reached the extremities of the space and came weaving back. Gertrude's small bare feet flashed among the blue flowers and it was toward her swift feet that Tim looked each time as he approached her. At last the music ceased, the dance was done, they slowed down and in the centre of the meadow took hands and smiled.

They had had no lunch. Lunch too had proved impossible. But dinner now proposed itself as a feast. They drank white wine upon the terrace and considered what there was to eat. The bread was stale, but there was minced beef in the fridge, and tomatoes and onions. They were both hungry but there was no hurry. They watched the moon begin to glow, huge and yellow in the still-blue sky. There was a faint gulping of frogs in the bottom of the valley. At this time Tim and Gertrude said almost nothing to each other. They touched each other shyly and looked at each other with great eyes. They spoke of the moon and of the strange illumination of the rocks and how close they seemed at this time of day. They held their breaths and sipped the honey-joy which had been allotted to them in the magic circle of that day.

Then at a certain moment of darkness and coolness they went inside and Gertrude began to cook, and then, as they sat down hungrily to eat, the conference, as they both knew, had to begin all over again.

'You're a sweet lover, Tim.'

'So are you. Isn't it *amazing*, isn't it just *incredible* that *this* should have happened to *us*?'

'Yes—'

'I've never experienced anything like it. It's much more extreme—it's—it's mythological—'

Gertrude was silent.

Tim thought, but how *can* she? He felt almost shocked. He wondered, what is she thinking? When will she suddenly feel ashamed?

He said, answering his thought, 'All right, we'll wait and see. I won't be "destructive" like you said. Let's drink. Let's just let it go on for as long as it will, like that dance. I loved that dance.'

'So did I.'

'Perhaps we shall never dance again, but at least we have danced that dance among those blue flowers. And now the sky is dark and the moon is shining and I love you. Oh I'm so happy, even if I die tomorrow.'

Gertrude had taken off the white dress, perhaps it had been a nightdress after all, she had certainly had nothing on underneath it, as Tim had noticed in the meadow, and she had put on a dress which he had not seen before, a flimsy flowing yellow robe with a brown willow-leaf pattern. She had combed her many-patterned hair and patted it into shape. She looked handsome and remote and grave. In the flush of his sense of possession of her, Tim loved and worshipped that remoteness which reminded him now so incongruously of the dignified lady of Ebury Street.

'I don't want you to die tomorrow, Tim. I don't want to die tomorrow myself.'

'Well, who cares about tomorrow. Yes, it's amazing! Wouldn't they be surprised, the Ebury Street mob, if they knew you'd taken a lover and that the lover was *me*!'

Gertrude frowned.

'I'm sorry,' said Tim. It was a wrong tone, a wrong move. He saw now suddenly before him the face of Guy, puzzled, friendly, as it had so often been when turned upon Tim. He had not wanted to think of Guy, but somehow it had not been necessary to exclude him. Today Guy had simply been *absent*. But Guy still existed, representing, even in death, another place, an aspect of that *impossibility* concerning which Tim had cried out earlier. He did not wonder what Gertrude thought about this matter, Gertrude the widow. The weight of her widowhood would all too soon destroy the honey-magic.

'I haven't taken a lover,' said Gertrude.

'You mean we won't make love again. OK. I'll leave tomorrow. OK.'

'Oh Tim, be serious —'

'I am being serious. Deadly wretchedly serious. I don't understand you.'

'You must see, a love affair is impossible.'

'Yes, of course, all right, I *see*, that's what I'm saying. It's been magic, it's lasted a day, an eternal crystal-perfect day that I'll carry with me forever. And I'll be grateful to you for ever and ever and ever. But—Gertrude, I can't be less than I've been. I mean, things can't just suddenly be as they were. I wouldn't want to be here with you like that. I wouldn't want to be here at all any more. And of course we couldn't travel together, I mean I've only, I suppose . . . really understood it . . . this very moment. Oh my God, if we must stop, and we *must*, I'll go away tonight.'

'Tim, don't be a fool.'

'All right, I won't be tedious or dramatic. I'll go away tomorrow. And I'll go with—oh so much gratitude.'

'Oh stop. When I said a love affair was impossible I meant . . . if we are to love each other . . . we must get married.'

Tim gazed into the solemn brown eyes. Then he did up all the front buttons of his shirt. He pulled down his sleeves and buttoned his cuffs and put both hands on the table and stared at his wrists. He was trying to work something out. 'But we can't get married, so we can't love each other or have an affair.'

'Of course we can get married, it's *possible*,' said Gertrude impatiently. 'That's what we've got to wait and see about. I mean, we can go on, but only on that assumption, only with that idea, only with that in view. Otherwise it must be, with something as extreme as this, nothing.'

'You mean you would *consider* marrying me?'

'Yes! You dolt!' Gertrude got up and noisily piled some plates, then sat down again.

Tim continued to inspect his wrists. He unbuttoned his cuffs. Then he raised his eyes. 'Gertrude, will you marry me?'

'Oh Tim, Tim, dear—I love you—but we can't tell. It may be you're right that it's a momentary magic, a delusion we've both got. But if we go on together we can only do it if we hope to marry. We can't play with this thing, it would be horrible to do so, it would be a betrayal, it would be a crime. Are you willing to go on, for a time, and chance it, to stick with the hope?'

'And the risk,' said Tim. '*Yes*. But, oh Gertrude, the risk—it's so terrible—if we lose *now*.'

'The risk—think what I risk—think of the *moral* risk.' Tears started into Gertrude's eyes and she slowly wiped them away with one hand, still looking at him, now almost glaring.

Tim did not move. He was not quite sure what she meant. He said, 'My darling, if we go on—well there isn't any if, we must and will go on. *As* we go on, what do we do—about *them*?'

'I've thought,' said Gertrude, and now she sounded almost weary. 'We won't say anything yet, perhaps for some time.'

'You mean, keep it a secret?'

'Yes. I don't like secrets, but it's better so.'

'While we're waiting and seeing we won't want any spectators, will we.'

'No.' They looked at each other in silence.

Gertrude was sitting by the roadside. Her bicycle was propped against a steep brambly bank. The sun was hot. In her bicycle basket there was milk, eggs, coffee, tomatoes, cheese, olives, the day's bread.

She was sitting on a tuffet of grass, with her back against the bank, in the shade of an apricot tree. She was about half a mile from the house, upon the deserted silent road, and she was thinking. At this time of the morning Tim would be out painting, so she could have had solitude to think back at home, but she preferred to sit beside her bicycle in the road.

It was now three days since the day of the conferences and the dance and the love-making. There had been more love-making. It was indeed, as Tim had said, extreme. And as Tim had said, mythological, amazing.

Sometimes she said to herself, 'What a pickle I'm in,' as if by using such language she could somehow simplify the situation and make it more ordinary. Was she bewitched? The honey-magic had lasted, had grown even more intense and wonderful. She had looked at herself in the mirror and seen a different woman. She remembered something that Guy used to say, perhaps it was a quotation, about one's will changing the limits of the world, and how the world 'waxes and wanes as a whole'. Gertrude had changed her world and everything in it was different, not only shown in a different light, but different in its cells, in its atoms, in its deep core.

There was no doubt about the *fact* of her being in love with Tim, and Tim being in love with her. This was the real, the indubitable and authoritative Eros: that unmistakable seismic shock, that total concentration of everything into one necessary being, mysterious, uncanny, unique, one of the strangest phenomena in the world. This happening itself was something like a vow, and to this reality she was bound as to a new innocence. She was as if shriven. She had a new consciousness, her whole being hummed with a sacred love-awareness. She loved Tim with passion, with tenderness, with laughter and tears, with all the accumulated *intelligent* forces of her being;

although there were times when she was rational enough to ask herself, well, and what follows from *that*?

The odd thing was how pure and clear all that joy had remained in the midst of Gertrude's dark accompanying preoccupying consciousness of herself as bereaved, as widowed, as in mourning. How did these two things connect? Did they connect? Were they simply, accidentally juxtaposed? Or had one somehow *caused* the other? And if so, had it caused it in a good way or in a bad way? Tim had spoken of 'illusions' which arose out of 'shock' or 'stress'. Had she gone out of her mind with grief and rushed for solace to a wild fantasy? Had her grief *changed*? She was not sure. Or else, so accustomed to love somebody, had she fallen in love with the first man with whom, after Guy's death, she had been really alone? How quickly can the past lose its authority, what *is* its authority? What did it mean to count the weeks, the months, how did time enter here? The magic of the place, the heat, the rocks, presented perhaps a lesser enigma. Tim kept saying that it could not have happened in London SW1, and that no doubt was true. But any love may be prompted by some chance felicity. It was the connection with Guy that troubled Gertrude, and troubled her deeply, and not only because of something dark and awful which was a grief contaminated now by guilt.

She had come to France to mourn for Guy, to confront his shade, to sort out the poor sad remnants of his things, pieces of paper with his writing on which she had burnt in the fireplace one morning when Tim was absent, in what they now spoke of as 'prehistory'. She had burnt those remnants. Had she come then to mourn, but also in a sense to clear Guy away, not to have to fear these further confrontations with his relics? Had she, because the pain was too great, attempted to blot Guy out, and had she thus made a vacancy in her soul into which Tim had come? There were rat-runs of thought here into which Gertrude did not want to enter. She feared some terrible imprisonment of guilt and obsession which she knew would be bad. Guy was dead. Tim was alive. She must not, out of some sentimental self-destructive madness, make of this a machine to honour the dead simply by hurting the living. There was such a thing as *just* mourning. Guy would have understood these problems very well indeed.

He had said, 'I so intensely want you to be happy when I'm gone. . . . You will pass out of these shadows, I see a light beyond. . . . They say "he would have wished" has no sense, but it has. . . . Have the will now to please me in the future when I won't exist any more.' And Gertrude had said, 'I shall never be happy again. . . . I shall be dead too, walking and talking and dead.' And he had said, 'I would very much like you to marry again.' Guy, her husband, rational, strong, good, the man she had loved and worshipped. Tears came into her eyes, quiet deep tears out of deep wells. She had felt it impossible to live without him. Yet she was living. She had fallen in love with another man, a man as different from Guy as it was possible for one man to be from another.

Was there any sense in asking, what would Guy think? Gertrude had thought again about Guy and Manfred. She felt less sure now about her theory that Guy had put forward the Count as someone she might marry in order to divert her thoughts from Manfred. It was plausible. Yet would it not be out of character? Gertrude felt giddy for a moment. It was as if she didn't really know him, enough, any more. All Guy's wise good words were also compatible with his really not wanting her to marry anybody. There could be little doubt that he had reflected about 'the suitors' as he lay dying and reading the *Odyssey*. He must have passed them in review. Had Tim appeared upon that fateful list? No, Guy would never have thought of Tim. Would he, if he knew now, laugh and wish them luck? What would a shade do, and how can one imagine it as other than a mournful spectator?

One thing Guy would certainly have disapproved of was the secrecy, the (for that is what it would come to) lies. What would *they* think? What *will* they think? This was something which Tim almost maddeningly kept repeating and the reiteration distressed Gertrude because she had to admit that she was worried too. Both of them feared the emergence of their love into the public gaze. A sense of secrecy and conspiracy had grown up between them and influenced them both. They wanted to *hide*. That was not good. They had decided to stay on at Les Grandes Saules, at any rate they had made no plans for leaving. This seemed, for the present, sensible. They must be together, they must be alone, testing a reality which was already for both of them firmly established. There was no shadow of doubt in the clear looks which they gave each other. But other tests would come, and there would be strains and changes. Viewed in a certain light their situation was obscene — and was not that light the *general* light? Yes, their love would change. Ebury Street would change it. Marriage, if it came, would change it. Gertrude was blessed (and she was thankful for it) with a clear head on the main point. She could not 'play' with Tim. If she took him on at all it must be eternally and absolutely. 'I can't imagine marriage,' said Tim. 'Marriage is unimaginable,' said Gertrude. *This* marriage was indeed unimaginable.

The strength of the 'mob' had been shown by the fact that she and Tim, sitting over their wine (they were drinking a good deal) had discussed the whole lot of them one by one even down to the remoter figures such as Peggy Schultz, Rachel Lebowitz, the Ginzburg twins (one was the well-known actor, the nicer one was a lawyer, they were related to Mrs Mount). Of course Tim was afraid of them. What would Moses say? What would the Stanley Openshaws say? What would Manfred say? Gertrude was interested to learn that Gerald Pavitt had been kind to Tim and that Tim was fond of him in a respectful way. She was not surprised to learn that Tim was frightened of Manfred, and that the two he liked best were Balintoy and the Count. Especially the Count.

The pale thin tall snake-eyed heel-clicking figure of the Count now rose accusingly before Gertrude. His love had touched her, had pleased her, lately had comforted her. She had, before what had now happened, looked forward to seeing him again on her return home. Gertrude had said to Tim, 'we must keep this a secret,' and she had added afterwards, 'till Christmas.' She did not say, but of course Tim knew, that this was the anniversary. Piety, reason, shame, their private testing of each other seemed to suggest some such delay. To speak out now would be 'too soon'. And yet — at the end of the year, the Count would propose. Gertrude had already worked this out for herself. He too would be waiting, waiting and watching and hoping. Could she deceive the Count, let him hope vainly, building up dreams, which every smile of hers would add to? If there had been no Tim, would she have loved the Count? Gertrude thrust this useless question from her. Suppose she were to tell the Count about Tim and swear him to secrecy! No, that would be impossible. Or spend the whole of the waiting time with Tim here, or somewhere else, seeing no one? That would be impossible too.

And then there was Anne. Would she dare to lie to Anne? Tim had rather avoided the subject of Anne and Gertrude guessed that he was frightened of her as well. He could not but see her as an alien power in Gertrude's life. What would Anne think? Would she, Gertrude wondered, be dismayed, be *jealous*? That was possible. Had Gertrude encouraged Anne to envisage a shared life, herself and Gertrude living together, growing old together? Yes; and Gertrude had wanted this too, and ardently. She recalled their talks in Cumbria, their walks beside the sea, the rescue from the waves. Was she not bound to Anne? Surely there could be no question of her *losing* Anne? This idea was suddenly acutely painful and Gertrude put it away. Anne had come to her in a time of dereliction for them both. Anne had lost her convent 'family', had lost her God. Perhaps even now, led on by Gertrude, Anne was thinking how she and her old college friend would henceforth be inseparable. These speculations troubled Gertrude very much. But herein too she drew comfort from Anne herself. Anne Cavidge was rational and strong. She would do all things well. She would live her own life. She would stay near Gertrude forever. And she would learn to know Tim and to love him because he was Gertrude's husband.

'Husband': a great word, a dread word. Would she stay the course, would Tim? Was it not foolish to worry so intensely about the motives and results of what might after all never happen? *How* would it be? Gertrude had preached to him enough about how they could both work, he at his painting, she at her teaching. She might even now, she felt, go back to teaching in a school. 'We'll work.' 'I'll always be a bad painter.' 'I want you to become a good painter.' 'If you want that you mustn't marry me.' 'All right, you shall work as a bad painter!' They had already been practising this regime. Tim went out every day to paint, Gertrude did the house-keeping and looked at her Urdu grammar. She made no progress however, it was too difficult without a teacher. She lived with the event, the fact, the new being. She loved Tim, his childishness, his gaiety, his wry humility, his animal playfulness, his love for her, his talent (for she believed in this), his lack of pretension, or ambition, or affectation, or dignity. It was not (and she had asked herself this question too) just a profane love, the sudden lust of a lonely older woman for a younger man. It was a deep true love which could only envisage permanence as its outcome. Of course she could have a casual affair with Tim. Indeed Tim had expected it. But that was only out of his modesty, out of a feckless futureless aspect of him which she could not help loving too. Somehow life was easy with Tim.

Really no one else matters, she thought. I do not have to give an account of myself to *them*. They are not my family, I have no family, I am alone, Tim has made me realize this. Well, Anne matters, in a special separated sort of way. And I care for the Count, I really do. But in the end this is a matter between Tim and me — and Guy. And she thought, oh my dear Guy, my dear heart, my love. How will it be? Oh the risk, the risk of it. She was not sure what this was, but there was moral danger ahead, moral frightfulness, deep awful possibilities of torment and confusion and crime.

'Gertrude! Oh Gertrude!'

Gertrude was startled out of her reverie by Tim's voice.

He was running towards her along the white road, waving his arms and raising the dust with his pounding feet. He was panting, and as he came closer she saw that his face was streaked with blood.

'Oh Gertrude, help, something terrible has happened!'

About the time when Gertrude was propping her bike against the bank and settling down on the grass tuffet to think, Tim was returning toward the house. He had gone out early to paint but could not concentrate and began to feel too hot. He had not been back to the Great Face, he was not sure why, but he had done some drawings of the moss fountain. It was not easy to draw. He decided now to come back and make himself a cool drink and wait for Gertrude to come home from the village for lunch. Lunch was now of course an important festival. He liked being away from Gertrude, by himself and yet thinking of her at every second; working on something else, looking at other things, yet aware of her as if she were distributed in the air like pollen. Gertrude said that she felt the same. She liked the ordinariness of his going out to work, her going to shop, their quiet thrilling knowledge that they would be together again soon. Life was amazingly simple and already had its reassuring patterns as if this life between them had already lasted for a long time.

Of course Tim was anxious, but his anxiety was irrational and patchy, full of unconnected and incompatible ideas. He did not feel afraid that Gertrude would tire of him, though he knew that it was possible. About that he felt a kind of humble resignation which co-existed with his daily experience of being absolutely able to 'get on' with Gertrude, to amuse her, to delight her, to 'lark about' with her, to talk seriously with her about all sorts of different serious things, and of course to make love to her. That quiet 'of course' was important. There was nothing frenzied or wild about their love-making, no worry about 'performance' or 'success'. They were gentle and clumsy and tender together, and Tim found himself easily and naturally assuming power as if he were a hereditary prince in a peaceful happy feudal state. This gentle power often made him laugh for joy, and Gertrude, understanding, laughed too. They laughed often together, but they were grave together too, and Tim often guessed that Gertrude was thinking about Guy. He valued her magnanimity in allowing herself to be pleased with him. If she felt guilt she kept it to herself and did not feel compelled to become suddenly cold because she felt, in such circumstances, glad he existed. He did not speculate about her thoughts. Gertrude's mourning was her own affair, and so were any comparisons she might privately make between her husband and her lover. Of these matters he did not speak to Gertrude.

The 'serious things' which they discussed were largely personal. Of course, feeling for the moment at any rate in safety, they ran through all sorts of reasons why their relationship might be judged to be, might even be, precarious. Gertrude said she was a mother figure and that Tim could perfectly well marry a younger woman. Tim said could he be sure he was not after Gertrude's money? And did she not just love him because she could help him? Perhaps these discussions were not really so serious. They were pleasurable and reassuring. They both talked about their parents, their childhood, their education. Tim described the Slade and his early experiments in painting. Gertrude talked of her school-teaching days and how lonely she had felt when she was young. They did not speak of Guy. Tim avoided any discussion of Anne Cavidge. He did not like to recall those cold blue-green eyes and that accusing critical stare. And of course he said nothing about Daisy.

What worried Tim during this period, upon which he looked back with such amazement later, was partly a sort of tactical or technical problem. He could not imagine how he and Gertrude were going to exist once they moved out of exactly this place and exactly this way of passing the time. His fantasies of married life, and his scrappy experiences of cohabiting, had suggested to him that allotment of time and occupation, a difficulty for a single person, was doubly difficult for two. He did not doubt that he and Gertrude loved each other, but he could not see how this love was going to function, to have a rational working daily time-table, once they came away from France. He could not see himself living in the flat in Ebury Street and turning Guy's study into a studio. Would they give dinner parties? He could not *see* that future, and it was as if some angel had thereby revealed to him that it did not exist.

Of course a ubiquitous embarrassment in his imagination of the future was the question of Daisy. This problem however, which might have seemed to be a major one, did not trouble Tim unduly. He had always been good at dealing with profound and awful difficulties by a method which was no doubt connected (although Tim was unaware of this) with something which made him an indifferent painter. This method might be described as a systematic lack of thoroughness. As has been explained, Tim's work rushed blindly on from the stage where it was only a sketch to the stage where it was too late to bother. Similarly in moral matters, Tim felt it was not worth while to work out problems beforehand because after all one did not know what was going to happen and it might be that the threatened problem might not in fact materialize; then when events overtook him he was consoled by a fatalistic sense of helplessness.

In relation to Daisy this arrangement worked as follows, and here his inability to imagine the future was of discreet assistance. If Gertrude abandoned him there would have been no need to tell her about Daisy. Indeed all sorts of things, such as his own death, might intervene to make the revelation superfluous. And how could he, cut off here in France for what might turn out to be a long or a short period, know what it was best to do? He was suspended in a provisional interim. Decisions must wait. Gertrude sometimes spoke wistfully of their staying on in France until September, but he suspected that Gertrude's own anxiety would prevent that. In any case, there were too many unknown quantities about for it to be wise for him to confess about Daisy just yet. That Gertrude would immediately cashier him if he told her now he did not believe. Besides, there were all sorts of ways of telling which would render the information innocuous. He was more, and obscurely, troubled about how the revelation would affect his own state of mind. He was careful not to imagine what he would say if Gertrude eagerly pressed him. There would be psychological consequences and there was no point in starting up that train of consequences when he was so far away from London. Of course if all went well he would tell Gertrude something about Daisy later on, and when the time came he would know what to say.

Tim was aware that he was thinking here in a double way, but this seemed unavoidable. He made no attempt, amid all that was so amazingly happening to him, to reassess his feeling for Daisy, nor did he try at all to diminish it. It remained where it was, separate, in parenthesis, not in play. And this indeed was useful in a tactical sense since it gave him the motive power to go on behaving to Daisy just as he would have behaved if the amazing things had not happened and if what he was telling her had been actually true. He wrote another letter to her saying that Gertrude and Manfred and Mrs Mount were still maddeningly in occupation, and that he would let Daisy know when they had gone, which he hoped would be soon; and meanwhile she was to wait for news. This lie was, he felt, simply necessary and did not trouble him beyond the immediate difficulty of composing the letter. What did cause him some anguish was the purely mechanical problem of posting the letter. He could not entrust it to Gertrude, and he was supposed to paint while she shopped. He walked along the road in both directions without discovering a pillar box. He did not dare to walk to the village in his painting time in case he were to meet Gertrude there or be later given away by the villagers. He had been reduced, on the previous day, to saying that he felt like a bicycle ride, and would accompany her. Then, while she was in a shop, he slipped the letter into the box and experienced a liberating relief.

The human mind is full of compartments, sealed areas and dark areas and boxes. Tim had not thought about marrying Gertrude until the moment when she herself uttered the word, though also he had not thought about not marrying her either. That moment had wrought a profound change in him. There was something quite new in his mind and his heart, something which co-existed with his delights and his anxieties and his mechanical evasions and habitual lies. This new thing might be described as a kind of moral hope, a hope which, when he felt pain, caused him the deepest pain. Or was it simply a desire for security, a desire for a house and a home, a desire for a mother? Tim was a child and children want order. No, it was more than that. The desire which he felt now, and which he had never felt so clearly before, was for a life of simplicity, an open honourable life where the expression of love was natural and truthful and direct and easy: as somehow in his own experience it had never been.

Tim entered the house and dropped his kit in the sitting-room and went upstairs to cool his face and arms in the bathroom. He ran the cold water for some time, cooling his wrists luxuriously. Then he went back to his bedroom and stood a while looking out of the side window toward the far off rocky cleft wherein the more distant hillside made a segment of greeny-blue. He meditated for a time upon the colour while some of the thoughts recorded above jostled about uncomfortably inside his head. He longed now for Gertrude's return, for the absolute safety of her presence and the indubitable experience of her precious love.

In the cicada-hung silence nothing stirred. Then he moved quietly to the other window and gazed across the terrace, across the hillside and the valley to the rocks. It seemed to him that he had been looking at these rocks for years, that he had seen them long ago in his childhood. Their eternity irresistibly entered his eyes and his mind. The sun, which had risen behind them, was now striking them obliquely, filling them with holes and shadows, and making their exposed surfaces flicker with a dazzling grey. Tim gazed and his mouth relaxed and he forgot his troubles.

Then as he began to turn away he looked directly down onto the terrace. He stood rigid, breathless with fright. A figure was standing just below him upon the steps leading to the flowery meadow. It was a man, who was gazing away across the valley, looking, as Tim had been looking, at the rocks. The man was Manfred.

A hot ball of shame and terror rose up into Tim's throat. Total confusion overcame him. He tiptoed a step or two away from the window and stood still again, holding onto his shuddering breast. Had Manfred seen him? Surely not. Would Manfred come up the stairs and find him? Should Tim go down and speak to him, greet him in a natural way? Gertrude had said no one knew that Tim was here. How could he now explain his presence, how not look guilty, confused, found out? *What* was he to say? What would Gertrude *want* him to say? And if Manfred kept him talking how could he let Gertrude know what he *had* said? They had not envisaged this, they had planned no fiction, they had invented no cover story. Ought he to *hide*, *could* he hide, simply not appear at all? He must ask Gertrude, consult with Gertrude, but how? If only Manfred would go away. He leaned toward the window and peered. Manfred showed no sign of going away. He seemed to be enjoying himself there, gazing around upon the countryside.

If I could only get *out*, thought Tim, I could try to meet Gertrude and warn her, only I can't get out with him there, there isn't a back door. If only he'd go away, go for a walk or something, but of course he won't. He's more likely to come into the house. He's probably looked in already and decided there's no one there. Should I just stay here till Gertrude arrives? No, I must know what to say, and besides if she isn't warned she will give us away by sheer confusion. Then Tim thought, I could get out of the kitchen window, and I'd better try and do it *now* while he's still outside. I may meet him coming in, but it's worth trying. Then, even as he gazed, Manfred walked down the steps and into the meadow grass where he began to examine the flowers.

Tim glided to the door and down the stairs, and in a moment he was in the kitchen, climbing up on to the sink. The kitchen window, which was not usually opened, had no mosquito netting. Fortunately it opened easily and silently. Tim sat down awkwardly on the sill, thrusting his feet out. He was confronted by a vast extensive sea of brambles. He hesitated, then he thought he heard a step upon the terrace, and he dropped down close to the wall. The ground behind the house was lower than he had expected. A roof of leaves closed over his head.

He crouched against the wall, completely concealed, but also entirely unable to move, surrounded by a thick impenetrable enlacement of tough thorny branches. What a mindlessly idiotic thing he had done! His cheek had been torn in the fall, and he could feel several thorns quietly embedded in his arms and in his ankles, ready to tear him as soon as he stirred. His trousers, his shirt were gripped by scores of tiny brambly fingers. Oh fucking hell fire, why had he been so damnably stupid, what on earth was he to do! Even if he wanted to get back through the window now he could not, it was too high above him. It would have to end with his calling out ignominiously for help!

The crouching position became suddenly agonising and he moved, half kneeling, tearing his clothes, tearing his flesh. He could feel the blood coursing upon his arms, his legs, his face. And then, as if a god or a fairy-tale magician had touched his eyes, he saw an entirely new scene, a possible path to liberation. Just beyond the layer of brambles in which he was now entangled there was, roofed by a higher dome of branches, an open space; and beyond the space, near to the ground, there was a sort of shadowy archway. Oblivious now of the tiny spears which were clinging to him, scraping and scratching, he leaned forward through the leafy thorny screen and fell upon his elbows into the space, then gingerly drew his legs after him and kneeled in the green twilight.

Before him was a tunnel leading away through the bramble thicket, a clean clear tunnel with a floor of hard beaten earth. The tunnel resumed on the nearer side of the space, veering in toward the wall of the house. This was clearly a pathway made by some animals, foxes perhaps, and the domed space was perhaps their meeting hall, or playground, or dancing floor. Tim did not waste time in speculations about the fauna. He set off on hands and knees along the arched pathway which led away from the house. It was, for a man, distinctly low and narrow, but Tim was slim and lithe and he crawled and wriggled his way rapidly along it. He was now so mauled by the brambles that he was indifferent to further scars.

After what seemed a long way, but was probably no more than about five yards, Tim saw something white before him and guessed that this must be the whitewashed wall of the garage, and the exit from the bramble patch. He was right. Now he could see ahead of him the sun shining upon the peeling trunk of the eucalyptus tree. The brambles thinned and ended in a sort of ditch occupied by other plants which ran along the side of the garage wall. Tim slithered gratefully out into the ditch and was about to rise cautiously to his feet when he was aware in front of him of something unusual, something large and black. He peered out through the foliage. The large black phenomenon was Manfred's big car, which was parked on the gravel outside the garage. And there, leaning back against the bonnet, not more now than twenty feet away from Tim, was Mrs Mount.

Tim did not wonder if she had seen him. It was immediately evident that Mrs Mount thought that she was alone, she had the fussy, self-absorbed movements of a private animal. Frowning, she scratched the side of her nose, then examined her finger. Then she pulled up her skirt and began to hitch up her tights. She noticed a hole in the tights, upon the thigh, and she examined this, observing how the flesh rose very slightly in a little mound through the hole. She resumed hitching up her tights, then, still frowning, carefully pulled down her white petticoat and the skirt of her dress. She was wearing a smart silkish red and white dress and was clearly feeling rather hot. She thrust her hand in through the neck of her dress, loosening the petticoat and feeling her perspiration. She wiped her hand upon her neck and picked up her handbag which was lying beside her on the dusty bonnet of the car. She saw the dust, shook the bag and then shook out her dress and resumed her pose, opening the bag and taking out a powder compact. She examined her face in the mirror of the compact and as she did so a remarkable change came over her expression. The frown vanished and was succeeded by a look of angelic calm. For a moment Mrs Mount blew out her cheeks like a zephyr, and then positively smiled into the mirror, not a grin but a calm sweet reflective smile. She touched her forehead lightly with her fingers, smoothing away lines, and gently stroked the skin around her eyes. Then she very lightly powdered her face. She examined the results, maintaining the calm plumped-out expression which perhaps she had adopted long ago as a routine protection against wrinkles. And indeed she had none. Bronzed by the southern sun she looked, for the moment at any rate, younger, almost handsome. The bright light showed the clear dark blue of her clever nervous eyes. Only a slightly seamed upper lip and her fairish-grey hair made her look like 'an older woman'. She put her compact away, picked up her bag, shook out her skirt again, moved round the car and disappeared in the direction of the house. She seemed to be dragging one foot a little. Her footsteps on the gravel receded, then as she turned the corner to the terrace the sound ceased.

Tim sprang up like a terrier, dodged round the car and ran lightly down toward the road whose trees soon screened him. He began to run along the road in the direction of the village, soon slowing down, panting and holding his side. Sweat poured, mingling with the drying blood. At least he knew he could not have missed Gertrude, she was bound to come back this way. After a little time he saw her, not bicycling but sitting by the roadside. He ran toward her crying out.

'Oh Gertrude, help, something terrible has happened!'

'Tim, what is it, are you all right? My God, you're covered in blood!'

'Oh that's nothing, I crawled through some brambles — but, darling, the worst has happened. Manfred and Mrs Mount have turned up!'

'Oh Lord! What did you say?'

'They didn't see me. I got out of the kitchen window —'

'Oh — poor Tim — look, quick hide the bike, we'll get into

this field. They might decide to drive to the village to look for me. Thank God they came the other way.'

There was nowhere to hide the bike except by lifting it over the bank. This they did, dropping the eggs in the process, which smashed in the road. Then they climbed into the field, which was ploughed and full of fruit trees, probably apricots, and sat down with their back to the grassy bank on the other side, invisible from the road.

'Now let's think—oh Tim, you're all scratched, like you were that first evening, remember!'

They sat holding each other's arms like hidden half-frightened children.

'Perhaps they'll go away if no one turns up.'

'No they won't, not they, they'll stay and make themselves at home!' said Gertrude. 'Besides it's obvious I'm there.'

'Oh God—I'd better hide. I'll stay here, you go back and get them to leave, then you can come and fetch me.'

'It's not so easy, they may want to stay the night, and besides—'

'Oh crumbs, oh Christ, I left all my painting kit at the sitting-room door, that rucksack with my name on it—we're blown!'

Gertrude in her willow pattern robe, sitting on the little bit of bumpy grass at the foot of the bank, hitched up her skirt over her brown legs. She now held onto the wheel of the bicycle with one hand and onto Tim's shirt with the other and she thought.

'Oh my darling, whatever shall we do?' said Tim.

'We can't conceal you. We must go and see them.'

'But not tell them?'

'No. Tim, listen, I *hate* this—but perhaps it's providence that we have to start it so soon—'

'Start what?'

'Lying. But I can't see any other way. Listen, I'll go back now and find them, and I'll tell them that you're on a painting tour of France and you turned up unexpectedly yesterday and that you're out painting somewhere—'

'Better say walking somewhere, in case they see I haven't got my stuff.'

'All right. And I'll arrange to go back home with them at once—'

208

'*Go back home with them — ?*'

'Yes, Tim, *think*. We can't be there in that house with those two watching us. And we can't let them leave us alone together, that might sort of interest them.'

'I could pretend to leave, then come back again when the coast's clear.'

'It's too risky. Even if they say when they're going they may change their minds, or they may hang around in the neighbourhood and come back. It's much better if I go off with them, as soon as possible, this afternoon. We might make some blunder, they might notice something.'

'And what do I do?'

'You say you're going on with your tour. Don't forget, you're travelling, you're on a tour. I'll tell you to lock up and leave the keys at the village hotel, only don't do that, bring them with you, and —'

'But won't you come back?'

'No. You must make your own way home and we'll meet in London.'

'Oh Gertrude, no, please not — And they might take you to Rome or something —'

'Do you think I like this? I hate it! But now they've come we mustn't mess around with the situation. I can't suddenly rush back to France or disappear. I'll get back to London, if they're going on they can drop me. Please Tim, you must do as I say. We won't be parted for long.'

Tim knelt beside her, pulling her towards him until she knelt too, letting go of the bicycle and they faced each other with the high splintering sun narrowing their eyes.

'Gertrude, if we part suddenly like this we won't find each other again. We haven't had long enough. I'll turn up at Ebury Street and you'll be a different person, you'll have forgotten me. Don't go away with those two, they'll take you over, Mrs Mount will marry you to Manfred.'

'Tim, please, we're bound to each other, you know that, I love you —'

'And you'll marry me — sorry, I mustn't ask —'

'I love you. I hope — Oh don't torment me now. Please be sensible — it's best — anything else will turn into some kind of awful muddle.'

'But then when I get back, I mean how will I find you, what—'

'Just ring up. I'll be at Ebury Street.'

'But I'll not say—no, of course—and I won't come round, I'll ring—I'll be discreet—I'll do whatever you say—oh what *hell* this is, why did those bloody people have to turn up and spoil it all!'

'We would have had to go back soon anyway. Our reality lies there, Tim, over in London, and we've got to go and find it there. Now help me with the bike.'

'Wait, I'm all confused. I'm to stay here a bit and then come back and pretend I've been out painting, I mean walking—'

'Yes, and don't forget to be surprised, and don't forget you arrived *yesterday*. Oh you're so dirty and covered in scratches—poor dear Tim, poor sweet love—'

'I'll say I fell in a bramble bush.'

'You'd better give me half an hour or so, don't leave it too long. I'll keep them to lunch and then we'll go.'

They got the bicycle back onto the road and Gertrude mounted. She seemed now in a frenzy to get away.

'Gertrude, wait, you will remember me, won't you—'

'Tim, don't be a *fool*.'

In a moment she was away, pedalling hard, speeding along the narrow tarmac road, her dress fluttering on either side.

Tim gazed down at the mess of broken eggs and touched it with his foot. He groaned and looked at his watch and stood there miserably. All his scratches were searing hot and his head ached.

'So Tim Reede just arrived and foisted himself?' said Mrs Mount. 'Poor old you.'

'Well, he only came yesterday,' said Gertrude, 'I've hardly seen him. He's just passing by, you know. He's been out sketching or walking this morning, I don't know where he is. I went to the village to shop. I imagine he'll be back for lunch.'

'And it's OK if we whisk you off?' said Manfred.

'Oh absolutely, you're heaven-sent. I was wanting to get away. I've done what I came to do. But are you sure you don't want to go on to Italy?'

'No, we changed that plan.'

'We couldn't stop worrying about you,' said Mrs Mount.

They were sitting on the terrace on wooden chairs in the shade of the fig tree drinking white wine.

'Why there he is,' said Gertrude.

Tim had appeared in the valley near the stream and was now coming up through the olive grove as he had done on the first day. There was a moment's silence as they watched the approaching figure.

'*He* won't want to come with us, will he?' said Mrs Mount.

'Oh, I don't think so.'

'I'll ask him,' said Manfred.

Tim crossed the meadow, his shirt sleeves rolled up, swinging his arms. His face looked very red against the white shirt. He glared at the assembled company.

'Why, what a surprise!'

'Hello Tim.'

Gertrude noticed that he must have washed himself in the stream and the bramble scratches were less evident, though his shirt was stained with blood.

'I fell in a bramble bush.'

'What people suffer for art!' said Mrs Mount. 'Why, he's as red as a lobster! Give him a drink, Manfred.'

'Manfred and Mrs Mount are very kindly taking me back,' said Gertrude. 'We'll be leaving after lunch. You can stay on a bit if you like, leave the key at the village hotel when you go.'

'Oh, OK, thanks. I might stay a day or two.'

'I liked your drawing of that rock,' said Manfred.

'What rock?' Tim glared at him.

'That big rock over the pool. I was looking at your sketch book, I hope you don't mind. Is it for sale?'

'How do you know about that rock?'

'Manfred has often been our guest here,' said Gertrude. 'Now you all stay. I'll just quickly put some lunch together.'

'Can I help?' said Mrs Mount.
'No, no, stay here.'
'Is it for sale?'
'No. Sorry.'

What's happened? thought Gertrude, giddy and frightened as
she laid the table in the shadow of the archway. I've suddenly
told a lot of lies, I'm involved in a whole lying situation, yet
what was the alternative, and I suppose it's sensible to go off
with them at once, but it's so awful and I won't have a chance
to speak to Tim again, and we simply mustn't make a mistake.
Tim and I could have found it so hard to decide to leave.
Perhaps it's just as well Manfred has decided it for us. But this
deception is absolutely hateful.

She looked out at the three people sitting in the sun. How
small Tim looked, compared with Manfred, how red and
agitated. He's so thin, she thought; and she thought suddenly,
that's what it's going to be like, in the future. He has such thin
arms. He's not an impressive figure. Now Tim was leaning
forward tilting his chair, staring into his glass, scratching his
ankle. Manfred dressed in a dark lightweight suit and wearing
a tie in spite of the heat, had stretched out his long legs and was
telling some motor car story. Mrs Mount, looking unusually
smart in a red and white dress, was laughing at Manfred's story.
Gertrude was visited by a very precise desire to comfort Tim by
touching his cheek, by stroking his rough glowing cheek very
gently.

A ghost scene from the past breathed upon her. The two men
were Guy and Stanley, the woman Janet. That was the last
time she had looked out in just this way through the arch.

'Goodbye!'
'Goodbye!'
'Have a nice paint!'
'Bon voyage!'
'Goodbye, Tim!'

They had gone. After an argument, Gertrude had insisted on getting into the back of the car. He saw her tousled hair and bright smile.

He returned to the empty terrace. Manfred had stepped on the line of journeying ants.

Tim carried the plates to the kitchen and washed them up. He had already decided to leave at once. He did not want to spend the night with any ghosts which might have been enlivened by recent events. There was also the very physical ghost of Gertrude to be reckoned with.

He went upstairs and packed his bag. He locked the bicycles up in the garage. He ran round the house closing the windows and fastening the shutters and turning off all the things he had turned on when he arrived. That was nine days ago. My God!

He was now in a frenzy to leave. Manfred and Mrs Mount had been maddeningly unhurried and it was now late in the afternoon. Tim decided he would spend the night at the village hotel and leave for England early in the morning. Lunch had been torture, although Tim had been amazed to find how well he and Gertrude managed. Given a background of habit, the human capacity to dissemble is almost limitless. It had been unnervingly easy to pretend to be strangers. The merry discussion had ranged easily over the local landscape, French and Italian politics, motor cars, the weather at home, whether a stop in Paris was feasible, what Balintoy was up to in Colorado, what Rosalind Openshaw would study at the university. It occurred to Tim that he had never seen Gertrude in just this sort of social scene before. How young and attractive she was, how much she laughed at Manfred's stories. Tim laughed too.

He secured the sitting-room door and then in the shuttered dark found his rucksack and suitcase and went out by the archway door, closing and locking it behind him. In his hasty tidying up he had noticed the cracked window pane in Guy's study. Neither he nor Gertrude had got around to having it mended. Now without looking back he walked along the terrace, down the gravel path to the garage, past the ditch from which he had observed Mrs Mount powdering her face, down the little bumpy driveway to the road, and then on toward the village. The afternoon heat was already over and the coolness and vivid light of evening was rising as if from the earth.

Something beside the road caught his attention. It was the brown paper bag and scattered remains of the dozen eggs, which had tilted out of Gertrude's basket that morning as they were hastily bundling the bicycle over the bank. Tim paused to contemplate the viscous mess already much explored by insects. It looked strange and in an odd way exciting, wet and slimy and iridescent, a kind of alien emergence from the dry land. He thought, you can't make an omelette without breaking eggs. Then he thought, well, here are broken eggs, but no omelette! He went on to the village.

Here he was surprised to find, on arriving at the little hotel to book his room, that he was already a well-known, even a popular figure. Who was it who had said to him, long long ago, that 'everybody loves a painter'? Why, it was Gertrude! Although he had seen no one, it appeared that many people had seen him, as he set up his stool here and there upon the rocks or among the olives, and *le peintre anglais* had been voted quite a picturesque addition to the local scene. The welcome at the hotel, the pretty bedroom with the view of the *château*, the glasses of *Kir* which he consumed in the cafe before dinner, the money in his pocket: all these things ought to have been ingredients of happiness, and he distractedly apprehended them as such without feeling happy. What an idiotic wretched parting. He and Gertrude had scarcely looked at each other during lunch. He had not managed to see her alone, had not dared to try to. Seeing her in Manfred's big car was like seeing her abducted, kidnapped, lost. What would Gertrude think when after a journey with Manfred and Mrs Mount (they might even stay in Paris) she got back to Ebury Street? What could she think but that she had been temporarily mad?

Tim had dinner in the hotel. The dinner was *extremely good*. The excellent wine assisted Tim's ability to hope. Perhaps all would be well. Gertrude would save him, as good women have always saved sinful men in stories. He thought again about the 'open and honourable life', and the 'new innocence and the fresh start'. And even when he considered the question of whether these things were not, in the last analysis, a function of *money*, he was not, for that evening at any rate, depressed.

FOUR

'Well, and how is yez?' said Daisy. 'You've come back to your old Daisy. I thought that French caper was too good to be true.'

'So did I,' said Tim.

'I didn't manage to let my flat after all, it fell through.'

'So did mine.'

'Just as well, as things have turned out. So big Gertie's installed for the summer with manly Manfred and the Snake of Pimlico. No wonder you sneaked off. Rather mean of her, though, after she promised you.'

'She may come back soon, I don't know — I just — thought I would — come back, I mean.'

Tim's hopefulness had disappeared with the effects of the hotel dinner. The next morning he had woken to misery and frenzy. He got himself back to London by the quickest way, by train and 'plane, and rang the Ebury Street number from Heathrow. There was no answer. Of course Gertrude had not yet arrived. Tim went back to his garage studio. The studio was damp and cold. The London skies were grey. He sat on his bed on the floor and moaned with anxiety. He ran out and telephoned. He telephoned again and again. No answer. Was Gertrude sitting there and listening to the 'phone ring?

The next morning (still no answer) he decided to go and see Daisy. Neither of them had telephones, so he just turned up about noon and found Daisy still in bed, drinking wine.

Daisy's flatlet consisted of one room, with a sink and a gas stove behind a lattice partition. The bathroom next door was shared with other tenants. The room was quite large, with a dirty window looking out onto a tree and a wall and a narrow strip of sky. The walls were painted pale blue and Daisy had at different times stuck posters on them with sellotape. Some of the posters regularly came unstuck and hung out like flags. On the mantelpiece and on the window ledge, surrounded by dirty glasses and cosmetics and dust, stood Daisy's potted plants, donated mostly by friends who were leaving London. No nameless sprout (which had flowered once and never would again) was ever turned away. Tim, usually an ally of green things, disliked these ailing growths. He felt a spot of euthanasia would do them a lot of good. The room was let 'furnished' but there was not much furniture. Some open shelves contained Daisy's books, mostly novels but some on occult or mystical subjects. She had once read, but did so no longer. There was also a mahogany chest of drawers, quite handsome but extremely marked and battered, a cheap deal wardrobe, some crippled kitchen chairs, a monstrous armchair, a solid table covered by a cloth beside the window where Daisy wrote her novel (she used a typewriter) and the divan bed where Daisy now lay propped up, the two litre bottle of wine and a glass upon the floor beside her. She had pinned a gay pattern of beer mats onto the lattice partition.

As soon as he came in Tim had started, as he always did, to tidy up. He picked up Daisy's clothes off the floor and folded them and put some in the armchair, others into drawers. He picked up plates and glasses from various surfaces and took them through to the sink and put them in a basin to soak. The sink smelt of sour milk. The room smelt of alcohol and dirty clothes. There was no hot water.

Daisy was dressed in a shirt and a housecoat. She had, before Tim's unheralded arrival, made up her face, accentuating her dark brows and reddening her drooping mouth and making blue rings and black lines round her eyes. She looked, though grotesque, rather pretty. She had combed her shorty shiny dark hair, there was not much grey in it. Her eyes sparkled. She was glad to see Tim.

And in spite of everything, in spite of heaven and hell, Tim was glad to see her. A habit of speech is a deep matter. Years and years and years of talking to Daisy lay behind him. He could not help feeling, separately in the midst of everything else, a familiar reassuring sense of return. He had come back to tell Daisy his adventures, as he had always done after an absence. But oh *Christ* he thought, whatever shall I do! He had made no plan. He had intended to put off seeing Daisy until after he had seen Gertrude. Supposing Gertrude sacked him? Then he need never tell Daisy anything. Everything would be as before. Or would it be, could it be? In any case it would be wise not to tell Daisy anything now. Who knew what the future held? He had come to Daisy stupidly, weakly, just out of misery, just to have a drink with her, just because he was in London and London meant Daisy. Just because the way to her door was a known magnetic way.

'You're fatter,' said Daisy, 'it suits you. I mean, you're still like a little bean pole but you've lost that gaunt undernourished look. And, my, you're brown, I've never seen so many freckles, you're like a spotty dog! What was the weather like?'

'Pretty good.'

'It's been foul here, fucking awful as usual. Can't stop raining and it looks as if it's doing it again, God's blood! Oh shit, I've knocked the blasted glass over. Fill me up again, there's a dear boy, and give yourself another. I've missed you. Have you missed me?'

'Yes—'

'I wish it had worked out. Fuck France, but all the same, I could do with a bit of sunshine and we could have had some fun, bit of a change from trudging along to the Prince of Denmark.'

'Any news of Barkiss?'

'No. Your feline friend is lording it. Well, it's back to the mogs, isn't it? Jesus, how are we going to last the summer on no money? Back to square one. Seems like we live at square one!'

'Seen Jimmy Roland?'

'No. He's in America, according to that blithering idiot piglet. Or Australia. Could we get an assisted passage to Australia? After all we're white. Trouble is I suppose we're hooked on London.'

'Yes—'

'Oh do stop tidying, don't bother with all that stuff, what a fusspot you are!'

'What did you get up to when I was away? Were you OK?'

'What did I get up to? Nothing. Was I OK? No. What damn silly questions you ask. It was so bloody cold I had to stay in bed.'

'How's the novel?'

'Stuck. Writing's harder than painting, I can tell you.'

'I expect it is.'

'Painters can just look. They don't need minds. A writer has to have a mind.'

'I'll never be a writer.'

'What's the matter with you, Blue Eyes? You seem awfully in the dumps. Not that I blame you, coming back to this sodding island.'

'Daisy—'

'Wait a mo, just pass me my slippers, I must go to the loo, then we can go down to the old Prince.'

Tim passed the slippers and Daisy got out of bed and flip-flopped out of the room. Was he going to tell her?

When she came back and was reaching for her jeans, he said, 'Daisy, I must tell you something.'

'What? Dear old thing, don't look like that!'

'I'm going to marry Gertrude.'

'Gertrude who?'

'Gertrude Openshaw.'

'Sorry, I'm making a joke. You made a joke, so I thought I must too. Two bad jokes. Christ, these jeans are splitting.'

'But I am. Daisy, I am going to marry her.'

Tim thought, I can't lie to Daisy, so why did I come here? Perhaps for that reason. I've got to tell her. It's something I've got to do for Gertrude, or *to* Gertrude. I'm making Gertrude true by telling Daisy. Oh let it be true. But oh Christ, how *awful* all this is. And how real and true Daisy is somehow.

'Get along wid ya. Is it raining outside?'

'No.'

'Why are you saying this about Gertrude, is it part of some game? Jesus fucking Christ, haven't I enough troubles? Don't irritate me with your nonsense.'

'I am going to marry her. I proposed. She accepted. At least she sort of accepted, because it's too soon. No one knows yet, it's a secret, and—'

'Sit down, Tim.'

He sat on one of the upright chairs. Daisy, in shirt and jeans, sat on another.

'Now just what is this bloody rubbish, are you drunk already?'

'Daisy, it's *real*, it's *happened*, please *believe* me—'

'Tim, you must have gone off your chump, or else you've been taking drugs or something. Just stop it, will you? I know we said that one or other of us must make a rich marriage but that wasn't serious, at least I thought it wasn't. Dear boy, I know you haven't much in the upper story, but if you're developing this fantasy for my sake—'

'I'm not—'

'If you want to ditch me, dear fellow, you don't have to make a funny story about it.'

'I don't—I mean—'

'I should just think not! But you mustn't get all mixed up about Gertrude. Gertrude's a fiction, she's nothing to do with us at all. Being in France must have disturbed your mind! Do you really imagine we can live on Gertrude's money? What would she think? Or have you told her?'

'No—'

'Look, you're sillier than I thought, and that's saying a lot. I know we *said* that one of us must make a rich marriage and support the other, OK? But that was just being funny, OK? It was a joke, you know what a joke is, for God's sake. If dear old Gertrude would give you the money for your birthday or obligingly die and leave you a fortune, that's great. But you can't get it for me by marrying the old cow, though I must say I'm touched by the lengths you suggest going to, would you really do this for me? I know it's all in your mind, but really— look, are you drunk or am I?'

'Daisy, I'm serious.'

'You're pottikins. Come on, let's go to the pub.'

'I am going to marry Gertrude.'

'And we live on the proceeds, fine! Except that you're not and we won't. Do stop raving, dear old thing.'

'Daisy, will you *listen*—'

'No I won't, not while you go drivelling on like some poor old loony repeating the same crazy bit of nonsense over and over again. Dear boy, we cannot live on Gertrude's money, not even if you marry her, well, especially not if you marry her, I know we said it would be a good idea, we even said it several times over, or *I* said it, I suppose it was my fault, I thought it was funny, I didn't know this dotty notion would lodge in your idiotic little pinhead. I think this is the pottiest conversation I ever heard, I must be sozzled to be engaging in it!'

'I am not suggesting we live on Gertrude's money!'

'OK, so what are you talking about, fuck you!'

'Something happened in France, I fell in love, I fell in love with Gertrude, Gertrude fell in love with me.'

'Oh go jump in the Thames. And Manfred will be best man and the Snake will be bridesmaid.'

'They weren't there. I told you a lie. They just dropped Gertrude and went off. Gertrude and I were alone together and we fell in love.'

'And swooned in each other's arms.'

'Yes—'

'Oh tell me another. You're such a liar, Tim Reede. You live in a fantasy world. I ought to be used to it by now. What I just can't see is why you're telling me *this* lie. I thought you were serious about our living on Gertrude's money—'

'I'm not, I never said a word about it, it was you—'

'Good—but then why this tale of romance? If you want to plague me and make me jealous why not invent something more probable?'

'I know it's improbable. It just happens to be true!'

Daisy stared at him. Tim felt frightened of the stare but he gave it back. He felt the deep foundations of his life moving, moving gently as if on ball-bearings, shifting as if by chance, and yet also somehow in the darkness propelled by his will. In those amazing hours with Gertrude he had never felt like this. He had felt then the trance-like power of the inevitable. He felt now that he was acting, crushing something, breaking something, bringing about a different future, different futures, deliberately, irrevocably, altering his own being, and Daisy's. In fear, he reached out a hand. The hand happened to be holding a wine glass. Daisy hit the glass and it fell and broke upon the floor.

She said, 'I can just, *just*, understand that silly bitch imagining she was in love with you. She's not very intelligent and she's suffering from shock, though I should have thought she could have found a better man in her extensive entourage. But that you should imagine you're in love with her—is just—impossible —unless you really are after her money. Are you?'

'No.' Tim rolled up his sleeves, shaking the wine off his wrist.

'What are those scratches on your arm? The clutch of love, or were you fighting?'

'I fell in a bramble bush.'

'You would. Poor little boy, poor little blue eyes, he looks ready to weep. He fell in a bramble bush, and he's so sorry for himself. I'd push you in another if there was one handy. Let's have some more wine. Here's another glass. Fucking arseholes, we've finished the bottle. I hope I've got another. Yes, I have.' Daisy opened the bottle and poured the wine and they resumed staring at each other.

Tim thought, it's like falling in love again, only it isn't love, it's death, it's love in reverse. But it *is* love. Oh God, I can't be losing Daisy, that can't be what's happening. I *can't* lose Daisy, can I? After all the years and years. He gulped some wine, hoping to feel drunk. He felt drunk.

'Tim, just start again and try to tell me what this thing is about you and Gertrude.'

'We fell in love in France.'

'And made love?'

'Yes.'

'Where is she now?'

'I don't know—'

'Why not?'

'She'll be here soon. We left separately. It's a secret—'

'*What's* a secret?'

'That we love each other. That we plan to marry. But of course it's too soon—and I don't know if it will happen at all— I don't know what will happen—I don't know—'

'You don't know much it seems. That's better. OK, something happened in France, but it's over now. And you expect me to forgive you. I'll think about it.'

'It isn't over—'

'If I thought you were really capable of marrying that stuffed partridge I'd pitch you out of the window.'

'Daisy, it's a secret, and—'

'Oh don't bother me with your secrets! As far as I'm concerned it's so secret it doesn't exist! I was rather touched at the idea that you'd marry the bitch so that we could live on the proceeds. Now you boast you had her in France—'

'I'm not boasting, and please don't—'

'And you rave about marrying her. Well, don't rave here. Good Christ, are you really that keen on her money, has it come to that?'

'It's not the money!'

'Of course it's the money! What else is there to her? What else made you hang around Ebury Street with all those fucking awful bourgeois creeps? Of course money's nice. And Gertrude *is* money, she and her money are one, she looks money, she smells money—'

'*It's not the money!*'

'Don't shout at me, *tu veux une gifle?* Did you tell her about us? Silly question. Of course you didn't. Poor little orphan boy wants a rich mummy and a nice house!'

'There's nothing wrong with wanting a wife and a house—'

'I shall be sick! Well, what's stopping you? Are you blaming *me* now because you hadn't the guts to leave me years ago and find yourself a little bourgeois wifie! God, you're *feeble.* And you whine *now*! I used to think it was nice that you weren't a big bullying strapping male, but to be as wet as this—'

'Daisy, let us stop, let us be quiet—'

'And you made love to that fat old bitch! I'm surprised she didn't kill you by rolling on you, the old sow!'

'Daisy—'

'Let me know when the wedding is. I love a good laugh— we'll have an outing from the Prince of Denmark!'

'It isn't going to happen—'

'You've had her and you won't marry her? Isn't that just like a man!'

'It won't happen—it was a dream—I mean we did make love—but that was just in France—'

'Oh we know what happens in France!'

'She won't remember, she won't want to—'

'When she gets back home? I daresay she won't. But I'm not interested in this story any more. I'm not interested in you any more. Go to your rich widow, and if she won't have you find another one!'

'Daisy, please don't be angry, please talk to me quietly, I can't bear this—'

'Oh fuck off, you horrible little man, and don't come back, get out, *get out*!'

Daisy's brown eyes were rectangular with rage. She leapt up and Tim sprang back knocking over his chair. A glass flew past his head and smashed against the wall. Daisy ran round the lattice into the kitchenette. Tim made for the door. A plate crashed on the floor around his feet. A cup struck him on the hand. As he crossed the landing he heard the sound of more smashing crockery and then a loud splintering noise as Daisy reeled back against the wooden partition. He raced down the stairs.

Once in the street he kept on running until he was out of breath. He slowed to a walk, glanced round, and walked on briskly until he reached the Brook Green Hotel. Here he entered and ordered a double whisky. His pockets were full of money. He thought instinctively, I ought to have remembered to give Daisy some. He was extremely upset, but he thought, that's not the end of Daisy. That was not how the end of Daisy would come, if it ever did come. When he saw Gertrude, if he saw Gertrude, would he at once tell her about Daisy? Well, not at once. He must be able to speak of Daisy as something belonging to the past, and so he had better wait until she *was* past, or rather more past than she was now. But when was this pastness going to begin? Oh God what a bloody mess!

As he sat over his drink he pictured Daisy and was filled with a deep protective love-pain. Compared with sleek well-cared for Gertrude, Daisy was a shaggy ill-fed beast who wintered in the open. Well, did not he himself belong 'in the open'? He did not want to be a guilty secret at Ebury Street. Would that, in the end, prove to be the best that he could hope for from Gertrude? Not the 'new start' but a messy dwindling clandestine love affair. He thought these things, but at the same time he felt himself helpless. He knew that the categorical imperative of Eros lay upon his love for Gertrude.

There was a telephone in the pub. He went to it and dialled the Ebury Street number. Anne Cavidge answered. He put the receiver down.

'We're the official reception committee,' said Anne. 'We've kept all the others out!'

She and the Count, standing in the drawing-room, were looking down at Gertrude with bright loving eyes. Gertrude, still with her coat on, lay sprawled in an armchair. It was six o'clock in the evening.

'I left Manfred and Mrs Mount in Paris,' said Gertrude. 'I wanted so much to get home.'

'Oh—I'm so—it's so—happy that you're back!' said the Count.

'We've worked so hard,' said Anne. 'Haven't we? Ever since we got your telegram. Of course Mrs Parfitt has been in, but we wanted the place to look perfect. The Count took a day's leave and we've polished and tidied everything and shopped for you and done the flowers—I hope you like the flowers—I used to do the flowers in chapel sometimes.'

'It's wonderful,' said Gertrude, 'wonderful.' She thought, Oh God, I don't even know Tim's London address!

Gertrude had arrived at Ebury Street to find Anne and the Count in charge. The Count had carried up her suitcase and put it in her bedroom. Faced with their glowing eyes, their love, their concern, their welcome, she felt weak and almost excluded as if the flat no longer belonged to her. It did not feel like a home-coming, which was odd since that was just what those two dear ones were so devotedly organizing for her. Anne had put an arrangement of foliage and irises on the mantelpiece and a lovely vase of red and white tulips upon the marquetry table.

The Count thought, Gertrude looks tired and worried. Why does she sprawl so? She doesn't usually sit like that. How touching and helpless she seems. She looks like a refugee. How beautiful her hair is, all brown and gleaming and untidy. How much I should like to touch it. He looked down at her, beaming with love. The precise desire to touch, together with the impossibility thereof, filled him with a tender excitement. The Count had been curiously happy and unworried during Gertrude's absence. He did not even mind her being with

224

Manfred. Nothing, as yet, could happen to her. He felt her to be safe, sacred, reserved, and he had been able to give himself up, as never before, to dreaming about her and loving her and looking forward to her return. Such unthreatened looking forward is perhaps one of the happiest of all human occupations.

'We've been longing for you,' said Anne.

'*Oh* it's good to see you!' said the Count. 'But you must be tired. Aren't you tired?'

'She does look tired,' said Anne. 'Would you like to lie down a bit?'

'No, no, I'm fine.'

Gertrude thought to herself, Anne has been encouraging the Count to love me. She has somehow licensed and released his love. Perhaps he has been pouring it all out to her, and it has become that much more public and official. He is more confident, more open. With Anne as an ally he feels he can express his feelings. They are cornering me. It is a conspiracy, they are cornering me with love! But of course it's all happened naturally, maybe they haven't exchanged a word, they both just love me perfectly! Oh God, am I not lucky?

Looking at them she felt exasperation, pleasure, gratitude. And she thought, how handsome the Count has become. Hope suits him.

'Take your coat off, darling,' said Anne.

'I'll hang it up,' said the Count.

'I feel I'm the guest!' said Gertrude.

'Well, you are, just for this evening!'

Gertrude pulled off her coat. The telephone rang. Anne lifted the receiver and spoke the number, then put the 'phone down puzzled. 'That's odd, the same thing happened this morning, someone rang and as soon as I answered they rang off. Do you think it's burglars ringing to see if anyone's at home?'

'No, just a wrong number.' Gertrude thought, he'll ring tomorrow morning and I must have Anne out of the house.

The telephone rang again. 'I'll take it,' said Gertrude. She hopped up. Then she thought, but what'll I say? It was Janet Openshaw.

'Yes, Janet dear, I just got back. Dinner tomorrow would be lovely — yes, yes — I'll so much look forward —'

'They're all after you,' said Anne. 'We just reserved you for tonight. You'll be out for every lunch and dinner for the next month, it's a bombardment! There's a long list of people you must ring beside the telephone.'

'I can't face it,' said Gertrude. 'Look, let's go out now, the three of us. You're free, aren't you, Count? I feel I want to get out of the house. Let's go and have a drink somewhere and then have dinner out.' She thought, if Tim rings again I shall burst into tears.

Anne and the Count looked at each other in dismay. 'Oh, I've got you such a lovely dinner to have here,' said Anne, 'it is something I can cook, I've been practising since you went away—'

'Oh well of course, let's stay, how lovely, how kind—only do you mind if we don't answer the telephone? Let's go and sit in the dining-room straightaway.'

'I'm sure you'd like a drink?' said Anne.

'*Yes.*'

The drinks were no longer on the marquetry table. Anne had put them away in the kitchen.

During dinner, through two closed doors, the telephone bell sounded several times. Anne's masterpiece, a *coq au vin*, was much praised. Everyone asked questions. There was an atmosphere of happy excitement, of celebration.

'So you were all alone in France?'

'Not all the time. Manfred and Mrs Mount were there at the start, and for the last bit. Just the last evening Tim Reede turned up and wanted a bed for the night. He was on a painting tour of France.'

'Tim?' said the Count. 'I'm so glad he's got away on a holiday.'

'Are his paintings any good?' said Anne.

The Count laughed. 'I bought one once, just to help him. It was called *Three Blackbirds in a Treacle Well*! I couldn't make head or tail of it.'

'I quite enjoyed the drive back,' said Gertrude, 'only Manfred drove slowly for once, and would stop at cathedrals! Now tell me how you two are?'

'Anne has toothache,' said the Count.

'Not now—' said Anne.

226

'You poor thing, have you got a dentist? You must go to ours, Samuel Orpen, he's very good, he's a sort of cousin of Guy's. How did your retreat go? You know Anne's been in solitary retreat in Cumbria? I can't remember when Easter was. Were you there for Easter?'

'Yes.'

'Did you go to that little church?'

'No.'

Gertrude looked at Anne. Anne was wearing a black dress which Gertrude had not seen before. She looked thin and bird-like, no less beautiful but as if she had been fasting. Perhaps she had been fasting. How mysterious religious people were.

'I wish I had had a religious upbringing,' said the Count. 'Easter is a great time in Poland, people rejoice. The religious life is so necessary. Religious people do something for us.'

Anne said, 'I think the Count is romantic about religion because he's Polish!'

'Yes, I suppose the Poles are really rather like the Irish and the Spaniards,' said Gertrude.

'Not at all!' said the Count. 'The Irish are deficient in dignity, and the Spaniards lack the patriotic principle.'

'I think your patriotic principle is a kind of mysticism,' said Gertrude. 'I always feel the Poles are other-worldly unrealistic people.'

'Pilsudski wanted to invade Germany in 1933. Wasn't that realism?'

'He didn't want to do it alone?' said Anne.

'No, with Britain and France, only they wouldn't.'

'They were too realistic!' said Anne.

'The Poles always discuss their history,' said Gertrude, 'they are like the Irish. We shall be back in 1241 before we know where we are!'

'Do you often go there?' said Anne.

'No—but I have been—'

'Are you going to Poland this summer, Count?' said Gertrude.

'No—that is—I have no plans yet—for this summer—'

'One would like to visit a country where Lodz is pronounced Wudge. Anne dear, could you find us another bottle?'

The Count thought, wouldn't it be wonderful if Gertrude would come with me to Poland! Might she, would she? It would not be impossible to ask her, only I would have to do it light-heartedly sort of, not solemnly as if it would be a great decision. Of course I mustn't yet say anything about *that*—but I could just ask her to come with me on a short visit. Why ever not? She sounds interested. Oh my God, I'd show her the war memorial and the memorial in the Ghetto and where the Pawiak prison was and those rooms in the old Gestapo building and. . . . Then he thought, but these are all sad or awful places, which I think of first. Would they make her sad? The image of Gertrude shone in sad Warsaw like the image of Christ in Limbo. The Count thought, is that somehow *the answer* which I have been waiting for and which has never come? The answer, the event, the blinding light. Suddenly all the terribly terribly sad things will come together with the wonderful things, the happy things. There will be a great act of salvation. Christ will have risen.

He smiled at Gertrude and his pale straw-like hair shone in the lamp light and his pale face was smooth and clear as ivory and his pale pale blue eyes shone with a lucid light of pure love and joy. Anne smiled at Gertrude too, turning to her a full calm face of reassurance and welcome.

Gertrude thought, I expect it's the wine, but I suddenly feel that everything is going to be all right. She thought of Tim. And she thought of the Count and Anne. And she thought, somehow or other all will be well.

She said, 'All will be well.'

The Count said, 'All will be well.'

And Anne said, 'And all manner of things shall be well,' and she laughed, and the other two laughed with her.

Tim and Gertrude stood facing each other in Tim's studio. A soft rain was pattering or pawing on the skylight, and the light in the room was gentle, pearly-grey. They looked at each other with huge saucer-eyes as if each one were seeing an apparition. Then they moved forward and with the greatest slow care gathered each other into an embrace, clinging now and closing their eyes, not yet kissing.

Tim had telephoned that morning at nine o'clock. He would have telephoned earlier only he could not find a telephone box in working order. Gertrude had been sitting with Anne in Anne's room, persuading her friend to try on some jewellery. She wanted to have Anne fixed there when the telephone rang. She was just wondering what she would do with her life and her mind if it simply did not ring, when it rang. Gertrude went to the telephone closing both doors behind her, and when she heard Tim's voice she just said, 'Where are you, I'll come at once.' Tim gave an address and Gertrude rang off. She told Anne she had to see a social worker about an urgent problem, and ran from the house and into a taxi.

Now they were together. A space enclosed them. Walls surrounded them. They could breathe each other's presence, look and touch and feel the time measured by each other's heart-beats. There was a sweet luxury in the silence and the slowness of their meeting; and the strange almost cunning way they half-smiled at each other were proofs that they had indeed not been dreaming.

'So it *did* happen?' said Tim at last, detaching Gertrude so that he could stare at her again.

'Yes. It happened. I've been worrying so terribly —'

'So have I !'

'But it's all right now.'

'I thought you might have forgotten me.'

'I remember you. You're Tim. Let me look at your arms.' She undid his cuffs and rolled up his shirt sleeves. There were the bony wrists covered with red down, the thin arms still scarred with bramble scratches. She undid his shirt at the neck and gently stroked the hair within.

Tim now regarded her with a kind of crazy sardonic joy. 'Yes. And I remember you. Dear girl. Take your mac off. Give it to me. Why, it's all wet.' He hung it over a chair.

'The taximan couldn't find the place, and then —'

'I love you.'

'Yes—yes—'

'Come, let's sit here. I want to look at you. I want to worship you quietly.'

He sat her in an upright chair opposite to him, and they sat with their knees touching, overlapping, as they had sat on that first night in the sitting-room at Les Grandes Saules. He undid the buttons of her mousy-brown dress, touched her breasts, then pulled the dress together again. They both sighed and leaned forward, holding each other's arms at the elbows.

Tim said, 'I want you very much, but this place is hopeless. Brian, that's the garage man, tends to come up. And I sort of share the place with another chap. He's not here much, but he could arrive.'

Tim was thinking of course that Daisy could arrive. It was most unlikely that Daisy would turn up here. She was not in the habit of 'dropping in'. She was almost certain to remain fuming at her own flat, or else simply expect Tim at the Prince of Denmark. But it was just conceivable that now, out of contrariness, she might take it into her head to come round and bang on the door. And the idea of him in bed with Gertrude, and Daisy at the door made Tim feel sick with terror. In fact he had decided, because of the Daisy risk, not to let Gertrude come to the studio at all, only when on the telephone she had suddenly asked for the address he had in his agitated flurry given it to her, unable to think of anything else to say. They must not stay long in this dangerous place. But where in the world else could they go?

Gertrude said, 'I'm glad that I love you and that I can't help it.'

'I'm glad too. But I don't quite see what we're going to do. Just wait, I suppose. What do you think we'll do, girl, darling, Gertrude queen?'

'I can't—predict,' said Gertrude. As she uttered the helpless word quiet tears came into her eyes.

'We haven't thought it out, have we?' said Tim. 'We had to part rather suddenly, didn't we, beside all those broken eggs. We didn't have time to think it out. Don't cry, sweet one.'

Gertrude took Tim's hand and wiped her tears away with the back of it. 'At any rate,' she said, with something of her old 'conference' manner, 'the essential things are clear.'

'Are they?'

'Aren't they?'

'What are they?'

'Well, we love each other—'

'Yes, yes, yes,' said Tim. 'We keep saying it, and it's true. But . . . so . . . ?' Tim was thinking, we do love each other, there's no doubt about that thank God, but now she's back in London she may decide she just wants a love affair. He said, 'Maybe you've decided you just want a love affair, and not the other thing, the long eternal thing. If you just want an affair— do say—tell me now—'

'Do you just want a love affair?'

'No.'

'Neither do I. I want the long eternal thing.'

'Good. I want it too. You were right about that in France. Either this is nothing or it's everything. But, Gertrude, darling, I—'

'What?'

'I can see the goal but I can't see the way. I feel now that I can't bear to be separated from you, even for a moment. I wish we hadn't started to conceal it. Maybe we should have faced Manfred and Mrs Mount straightaway in France—'

'We couldn't—'

'I'm frightened of this concealment. I'm so terrified of losing you. I'd like to marry you at once. Can't we get married tomorrow, next week?'

'Tim, we can't—'

They moved a little apart, staring at each other, concentrating.

Tim thought, I must *secure* her, but how's it to be done? She could change her mind, or have it changed for her. Nothing is really safe here. 'We could get married and keep it a secret.'

'Tim, no.'

Tim was thinking, Christ, we must get out of this place, I keep thinking I hear Daisy on the stairs. But where the hell else can we even hold hands? I shall go mad. Shall I tell her about Daisy? No, not yet, not just when we've met again like this, we've got enough problems. Let it recede a bit, then I'll tell her gradually. I must rethink Daisy, see her more in perspective (Tim meant diminish her a little) before I say anything to Gertrude, I must be able to be casual or she'll think there's more than there is. It's all so precarious, I must get some sort of firm way of life with Gertrude, and maybe she'll settle for a love affair after all. Oh God! If she leaves me now I'll die.

Gertrude was thinking, I love him so much, but what can I say? I suppose he understands, but I can't even think how to ask. I can't marry so soon after Guy's death, it's unthinkable. I can't even conceive it myself, and what would the others say? I'm in mourning, and I *am* in mourning, there's a whole me that doesn't know of anything else. I've got to be that person, I've got to wear my loyalty to Guy, my unending love for Guy, in the midst of this new reality, and it is a reality and I didn't choose it or seek it, it happened. God must forgive me, Guy must forgive me. I can't marry Tim, or let anything be known yet, for a long time, we will just have to wait. Oh, will he understand? I don't want him to be hurt or have doubts. He might have so many doubts that he ran away. Will he think that I'm just afraid of the 'mob'? And she thought of Tim's crude words, 'How surprised they'd be if they knew you had taken a lover.' She could not appear to them like that, she, Gertrude. But it wasn't just idle pride, it was deeper. How could she explain?

Tim was thinking, she minds so much what the others think. Well, what will they think, what will they *do*, could they separate us, crush me, drive me out? He said, 'I'm not much of a catch, Gertrude. They'll say, why did she take up with that rat?'

'Tim, don't—'

'That liar, that scrounger. Did you know that I used to steal food from your fridge? Not very romantic is it, to take up with a chap that used to steal food from your fridge.'

'You were so hungry? Poor Tim.'

'Poor Tim. That may be the best light I'll ever appear in, to them.'

'Never mind about them. It isn't them.'

'I know. It's Guy.'

'Yes.'

'I understand.' Tim thought, and Guy—why shouldn't Guy separate us, crush me, drive me out? When the romance calms down a bit she'll get to thinking, Guy was like that, Tim is like this. And she'll be amazed at herself.

'I'm glad you understand,' said Gertrude, 'we must wait.'

'OK. I'll go mad. But never mind. I've been nearly mad since we parted. I've been ringing up, no answer, then I got that Anne, then nothing. I thought you'd changed your mind! When did you get back? Where were you last night? I know nothing. Did Manfred and Mrs Mount bring you back to London? God, I felt so jealous of Manfred taking you off in that car. He's so big and so handsome and he's got such a large car—'

'Oh don't worry about Manfred. I got the 'plane from Paris and they went on to the ferry. It didn't really save time, but I just wanted to get away from them. Last night I was at the flat with Anne and the Count.'

'And you didn't answer the phone! I was frantic!'

'I'm sorry—I couldn't get rid of them—and with both of them there I felt I couldn't talk to you, I'd have started to cry—'

'And you had dinner with those two. Well, tonight you'll have dinner with me!'

'Tim, I can't, I've got to dine with Stanley and Janet.'

'Oh hell—why did you have to—oh *damn*. They'll get you in the end. There's so many of them and only one of me.'

'What did you do after I left?'

'I spent the night at the hotel. I cleared out of the house in half an hour. Then I got the bus and the train and a flight to London Airport and started telephoning you.'

'And this is where you live. I haven't even looked round.'

'It's not mine really, I'm a tenant, I'll have to leave soon, it belongs to a man called Jimmy Roland—'

Gertrude was walking round now. Tim had had time to hide the cat pictures. He had put out some of his best work, old stuff, disposing it casually here and there. He tried to see the studio through Gertrude's eyes. It looked romantic. But there would be no romance here. He must soon tell Gertrude that he had had to leave it. One day, Daisy would come. Would Gertrude set him up in a flat? Where would he be this evening? At the Prince of Denmark? Life was losing its order, losing its sense. And now for the first time Tim Reede saw how much order and sense his apparently dotty life had really had.

'I like that,' said Gertrude, pointing to a drawing of a boy pouring wine from a bottle. 'And that.' That was a rather messy

Ernst-style bird with a pretty blue background of horizontal brush strokes. 'And that.' That was one of the cats which had got overlooked in the tidy-up.

'Oh, that's nothing.' Tim hastily turned it to the wall.

'No, I *do* like it. You're a very good artist.'

'Darling Gertrude, you know nothing about it!'

'You will go on painting, won't you, on and on?'

'When I'm — Oh Gertrude, you are wrecking my life, you are destroying it. I don't mind, I'm glad. It needed to be wrecked and destroyed. But I'll have to start again from the beginning.' Yes, that was what I felt about innocence, thought Tim. I am to be broken and made again, I will make myself again, with her. Oh let it be.

Gertrude was undismayed by his language, and Tim loved her coolness. 'But you will start again as a painter, that won't be gone?'

'That won't be gone. Oh Gertrude, it's so strange and wonderful seeing you here, like a miracle.' He stared at her. It was amazing to see her against the background of his studio, like a piece of bold collage. There she was, sleek brown Gertrude, with her plain mouse-brown dress revealing a high-necked blue silk blouse and a round gold brooch. He looked at her smart quiet expensive shoes and her discreet leather handbag. Was this his girl?

'Are you my girl?'

'Yes, Tim.'

'I hope you're right. But I mean it, about everything being gone—all my habits, all my time—you've broken in like a tornado, it's all flattened—everything is different, everything will be so different, when we're—Look, let's get out of here. It's stopped raining. What's the time? They're open. Let's go to a pub. You must get used to sitting in pubs when you're—' Would they sit in pubs? How would they *pass their time*? Marriage was indeed unimaginable.

'To a pub? Now? It's so early.'

'Why not? What else is there to do? Come on, put your coat on.'

Gertrude obeyed.

So she does what I say, he thought, she does what I tell her. What were the limits of this power? The idea of dominating

Gertrude was new to Tim. It seemed almost funny. A new thought came to him. 'And afterwards—do you know what I want to do? I want to go to Ebury Street. I want to be there, in that flat, with you. I mean just *be* there, stand there. Do you mind? It's important.'

'I know it's important,' said Gertrude, 'and I understand about the destruction. I'm—my life is being destroyed too.'

'Darling—I'm sorry—I—'

'No, no, it must be. But we can't go to Ebury Street, Anne's there.'

'Why is that a reason for not going?'

'I thought you wouldn't like it.'

'I'm afraid of Anne. I feel she'll persuade you to give me up. But I'll have to meet her around the place. I mustn't be too much of a surprise for *them*! They must begin to realize that we're sort of friends now!'

He's right, thought Gertrude. He must appear somehow, sort of casually. But how will they not guess? And Anne—I can't ask her to move out. And there's Stanley and Janet tonight. And oh, my whole way of life doesn't make sense any more, my time, my day, is all gone wild. Can this be right and good? What a destroyer love is.

'Let's go to Ebury Street,' said Tim. 'Let's go *now*. We'll have our drink there. With Anne.'

'It's Mary Magdalen in reverse!' Gertrude had said to Anne, as she poured out her jewel box onto Anne's bed; and they had both laughed crazily, laughing their old laugh, the memento of their youth, the symbol of their lives, bound together forever.

'Darling, you can't wear that black dress without jewellery,' Gertrude had said, as she sorted the gew-gaws out into two piles. One pile, Anne guessed, were the pieces which Guy had given her. Among the others Gertrude rootled, picking out this

235

and that which she thought might suit Anne. 'You must keep
them, no, no, you must, I've got such a lot, as you can see.'

Anne had put on the black dress again, at Gertrude's insistence. Gertrude had now gone out to see her social worker,
and Anne was sitting looking at herself in the mirror. She was
wearing round the neck of the black dress a dark amber necklace with a long amber pendant which glowed with a magical
reddish light. The dress had a high small collar which concealed
within Anne's tiny golden cross upon its chain. The glowing
pendant hung down between her breasts. It did look nice.

Anne looked at her thin face and at her narrow eyes. Looking
in the mirror was becoming a kind of meditation. Gertrude
had agreed that her smooth close-grained faintly shiny complexion required no make-up. Her shrewd pale mouth showed
a very faint colour. Her dull faded blonde hair was clipped and
shaped to her long head. This gave her a boyish look which did
not displease her. Her brow was unmarked and smooth, and so
was her thin elongated neck. The close-fitting well cut black
dress suited her; and Gertrude was right, it asked for a necklace.

Anne sat calm, relaxed, her hands limps, her mouth at peace.
Her mind was not calm, but as she gazed she felt her body
lithe and still about her. It was as if her body had some secret
ease of which her mind knew nothing. She looked at her head
and imagined it as it had so long been, with the white wimple
and the black veil which she had so deftly adjusted every day in
her little bedroom, hurriedly dressing before the dawn. She
looked at her watch. She knew exactly what they were all
doing now back there in the precious holy repetition of their
worship of God. 'You have put on Christ like a garment.'
Garments can be taken off and laid aside. Had she thrown away
the essential, kept the inessential, given herself over to an
ineluctable corruption? It was very possible.

She thought, Mary Magdalen in reverse! A very apt idea.
Her vanity had awakened, she could feel it twist and turn and
peer about. She could feel old appetites stirring. She had
regained the concept of herself as a good-looking woman, still
young. It was for her an unnecessary, even a bad concept.

The retreat had been profitless. A routine was needful, some
deep repetitive rhythm of the soul. Alone at the cottage she had
invented and imposed routine, but it had seemed arbitary and

superficial and in the end startlingly irksome. Yet no novelty pleased her either. Old prayers that came to her unbidden seemed like demons. She gazed with horror upon the wet grey stones, and the solitude she had craved for served her not. When Easter came, the period between Good Friday and Easter Sunday seemed interminable. She had so often followed Christ's journey, the suffering illuminated by the light of a cosmic triumph. Now, even to put it to herself that at last she *felt* that he had suffered hideously and simply died was a kind of hollow intellectual comfort. What she experienced was worse than that, something beyond words, a sickness with the whole of being intensified at this time by some old senseless spiritual chemistry. She felt for the first time in her life afraid of her mind, afraid of some independent cancerous life of its own which it seemed to be developing. Strong Anne had never conceived of herself as likely to have a 'breakdown'. The Abbess had warned her, and she had warned herself, of a black time to come, a dark night, a night of fruitlessness. Of course I shall become depressed, she thought. She had not conceived of a dry despair wherein, as with a trick of vision, odd and awful things flickered at her. She began to have strange fears at night. She returned to London sooner than she had intended. Here she walked the streets daily until she was thoughtless with weariness. She went into a shop and bought the black dress. She began to feel a little better and found herself intensely looking forward to Gertrude's return.

The telephone rang. Anne jumped up and went into the drawing-room. She spoke the number, in Gertrude's manner, which was Guy's manner.

'Oh—is that Anne?'

'Yes. Hello, Count. Good morning.'

'Anne—is—is Gertrude there?'

'No. She's gone to see some social work people. Can I give her a message?'

'No. It's you I want to see. Look, I'm at Victoria. May I drop round for a moment? There's something I want to tell you.'

'Yes, come at once.'

Anne put the receiver down and stood breathless in the room, her hand upon the amber pendant. The Count had sounded so agitated. Or had she mistaken his tone? Perhaps it was nothing, a triviality, some little present with which he wanted to surprise Gertrude or something of the sort.

Within minutes the bell rang, she pressed the button to release the street door, then heard the Count's feet upon the stairs. She opened the door of the flat. 'Come in, what is it, you look bothered, tell me, what is it?'

The Count went on into the drawing-room. He took off his black mackintosh which was lightly spotted with rain, held it a moment, then dropped it on the floor. Anne did not pick it up. She looked intently at his troubled face. Then, looking down at her, he changed his expression, smiled in a gentle apologetic way. 'Anne, I'm sorry. Forgive me for alarming you.'

'You are alarming me. Whatever is it?'

'I don't know what to think,' said the Count, 'and perhaps I oughtn't to worry you, but I must just ask you something. I have allowed myself to become — I ought to be at the office —'

'Count, tell me. Let me *help* you.'

'You are so good — and because you are somehow — I've always felt — as it were detached, so wise —'

'Tell me!'

'And you are so fond of Gertrude, and you know her so well. I think she relies on you more than on anyone.'

'Is it about Gertrude?'

'Yes.'

Anne sat down. She thought, Gertrude has cancer and nobody told me. A blackness surrounded her. She said, 'Is it that Gertrude's ill, very ill?'

'No, no, no, nothing like that.'

'Sit down, please, Count, and explain.'

The Count would not sit down. He walked to the window and looked out at the rain falling quietly onto Ebury Street. Then he walked back and looked down at Anne.

'Perhaps I shouldn't. Perhaps one should ignore such things. But I can't ignore this, I can't —'

'*What*, for heavens sake?'

'I have received an anonymous letter — about Gertrude —'

'But — what does it say?'

'Look.' He drew a piece of paper from his pocket and handed it to Anne.

238

She unfolded it. The message, typewritten and unsigned, simply read: *Gertrude is having a love affair with Tim Reede.*

Anne felt a shock like a blow, then a hot flame and flash of emotion. She put her hand to her face. She recovered herself. 'It's impossible. It's a lie. A horrible joke. It *can't* be true.'

'I'm glad you say so,' said the Count gravely. 'I wanted to hear you say so. That was my immediate thought. But then—if it's a lie, why this lie, if it's a joke it's an odd joke. You haven't yourself—forgive me—Gertrude has said nothing to you?'

'No, of course not! It's inconceivable! When did you get this?'

'This morning. It was posted last night in central London. There's the envelope.'

'How eerie,' said Anne, 'who ever would have sent it? How *horrid.*'

'Yes, it's—unclean. I felt I ought to tear it up and try to *forget* it, wash it right out of my mind—but I couldn't, I became upset, then I felt I had to come and ask you if you knew—'

Gertrude had been wrong in imagining that the Count had poured out the story of his love to Anne. He had said nothing to Anne of his love for Gertrude. But of course Anne had perceived this love some time ago, when the Count had been to see them, after they came back from the north, when he had stood and trembled and gazed helplessly at Gertrude. And she had seen it again just lately, more confident and stronger, after her own return and before Gertrude's when the Count had rung up for news, then come round to join her in welcoming Gertrude home. He had been so happy then. Anne did not need to be told how deeply and how tenderly the Count loved her friend.

'Oh my dear Anne,' said the Count, 'can it be true?'

'I don't know,' said Anne, 'but I'll find out and let you know.'

Her practical tone seemed to alarm the Count even more. Perhaps he felt it sounded crude, as if he had run round to recruit a spy. 'No, I didn't want—I just wanted to ask you in case you knew—much better not to say anything—I feel one ought simply to ignore anonymous letters, destroy them, obliterate them, I'll tear it up—'

'No, don't do that, keep it.'

'But if you think it's sure not to be true—Gertrude would be so hurt to think that we seriously — I mean we *can't* believe that she would — so soon after — do that — and with —'

'Don't worry, Count. Let me deal with this. You're right, we can't ignore it, it must be cleared up. Don't worry. It's probably some weird piece of pure spite, something we may never understand at all, or else —'

'You feel certain it isn't true?'

'Yes. But I'll find out for sure, and much better to do so at once.'

'You won't tell her about the letter or that I came round —?'

'Leave it to me. You'd better go back to the office. Off you go.'

The Count was reluctant to go. He wanted to stay and be comforted, told that this horror was impossible. But Anne picked up his coat, opened the door of the room and the door of the flat.

'Will you telephone me at the office? I'll write down the number.'

'I don't promise to,' said Anne. 'Oh well yes I will. Just stop worrying, go and do your work. Go, go.'

The Count departed.

Anne went back into the drawing-room. What an amazing possibility. She thought of Tim Reede as she had seen him with one hand inside Gertrude's fridge, the other holding the bag with the stolen goodies. Their eyes had met. He had stopped with his mouth open, the picture of guilt. She had frowned and turned away. Her majestic Gertrude and that petty man? *No.*

Anne went to her bedroom. She took off the amber necklace and put it on the dressing-table with the other things which Gertrude had wanted to give her. Then she took off the black dress and put on her dove-grey dress with the white collar. She put her hand to her face, realizing that she had tooth ache. She must make an appointment with Samuel Orpen. She recalled the gloomy convent dentist who had told her, while doing intricate bridge-work, that he had lost his faith. She looked at her books which were piled against the wall. There were not many, devotional works, Latin authors. She had left most of them behind. The convent had been vague about ownership of books. Gertrude had offered her a bookcase but she preferred to keep the books in an unordered pile. She picked up her Greek grammar and laid it down again. She was no longer in love with novel reading. She had never finished *The Heart of Midlothian*. During her brief retreat she had read nothing. The absence of organized work from her life was bad. Many things were, now, bad. She seemed to be living in a fever of subdued excitement and fear, perhaps in expectation of the darkness which was monstrously playing with her. The devil was alive in her life and seemed to have taken over some of the functions of God. She thought about the horrible letter. This too was part of the excitement and the badness.

Anne left her bedroom and began to walk about the flat. She went into the room where Guy had lain when he was ill and where he had died. Gertrude had sent the bed away, sold it no doubt. The small room was characterless now, a clean neat room with oddments of furniture, including the empty bookcase which Gertrude wanted to move into Anne's room. Gertrude had dispersed Guy's books, given some of them to the Count. She had removed, for it caused her too much pain, Guy's 'look' from the flat. Anne recalled her conversation with Guy, his hawk-face and glittering eyes, and how he had wanted the precision of judgement and purgatory. Vice is natural and general, virtue is particular, original, unnatural, hard. Guy would have understood about her devil, her monster. Guy too had wanted to keep out of the mess of life. His virtue was accuracy. That was his kind of truth. His desire for justice was his very private substitute for holiness. He worked for other men, he served his family, he was kind and generous and decent, but would have given himself no credit for that. His need for things to be precise and clean was a part of his secret judgement upon himself. Her idea that he had wanted to confess something to her now seemed like a piece of romanticism. Perhaps he had simply wanted to say certain words aloud to somebody: justice, purgatory, suffering, death. He had wanted to feel that their precise *meaning* was there somewhere, kept safe by someone, even just at one moment existent in thought. He lay there in the small last light of his mind, calculating, trying to get something clear, to get something right. Then one day it was over, the feverish humming electricity had ceased, the spark was gone, the room was empty, and Gertrude was crying out like a wild beast.

Anne heard a step on the stair, the sound of the key touching the flat door, and she came quickly and guiltily out of the room. Gertrude came in, but she was not alone, a man was with her. It was Tim Reede.

Tim and Gertrude were both rather red, nervously smiling. 'I met Tim. I've brought him for a drink.'

'Is it still raining?' said Anne.

'No, it's stopped.'

'You go in. I'll bring the drinks.'

They left their mackintoshes in the hall. Anne fetched glasses and sherry, vermouth and gin.

'I think we might leave the bottles on the marquetry table like we used to,' said Gertrude. 'There's no need to take them away every time.'

'I'll try to remember. And whisky too. Would you like some now?'

'No, sherry's fine. Sherry, Tim? Won't you have anything, Anne?'

'No I don't feel like it.'

'You don't drink much?' said Tim, smiling.

'No, not really.'

'Anne mopped up the local cider when we were in the north.'

'You can get good cider in London,' said Tim. 'I know a place in the Harrow Road.'

'Aren't the flowers lovely? Anne did them.'

'Lovely.'

'She used to do the flowers at the convent.'

'I was one of many people who did,' said Anne.

'They're lovely,' said Tim. He smiled at Anne, then turned back toward Gertrude. Gertrude moved slightly away, touching the mantelpiece with a feigning gesture, avoiding Tim's eye. Then she looked quickly at Tim and looked away again.

It's true, thought Anne; and a feeling of the horribleness and dangerousness of life overcame her like a sudden nausea. This was the warmth, the mess, which she had fled from to the convent and which Guy had wanted so much to exorcise by the precise working of his own private justice.

'You didn't want him to stay to lunch?' said Anne. 'I was trying to intuit what you wanted.'

Tim had gone. They had chatted for twenty minutes.

'No, no, just a drink. He's nice, isn't he? Have we any lunch, by the way?'

'Yes, there's some of yesterday's stuff left.'

'Your masterpiece! It should be delicious cold. Or shall we heat it up?'

'You stay and finish your drink. I'll do everything.'

'You're an angel.'

Anne had already decided not to say anything to Gertrude about the anonymous letter. She was even angry with the Count for showing it to her. Such filth should not circulate. Surely the Count could have said simply that he had 'heard a rumour'? But that reflective evasion, that discreet lie, was not in the Count's character. Anne's head buzzed with angry crazy unhappy thoughts, and she found herself banging the plates about in miserable exasperation. Meanwhile the Count was sitting in his office, in torment, waiting for her telephone call. Well, perhaps her intuition had been wrong. She could only hope that now Gertrude would tell her of her own accord. But if she did not?

'What's the matter, Anne, you seem bothered?' said Gertrude, holding her glass, standing in the doorway.

There was something the slightest bit cold and detached about Gertrude's tone and the way she stood. We are being separated, thought Anne. She is beginning to treat me like a servant, she thought. Then this seemed mad. Then am I not a servant? Whatever else should I be between now and the end of the world?

'I think I'll have a drink after all,' said Anne. 'Lunch can wait a bit. There's nothing to do anyway.'

They both went back to the drawing-room and Anne poured herself a glass of sherry. Gertrude took another one.

They stood there, at opposite ends of the mantelpiece, drinking; each of them, out of a deep old knowledge and with a sensitive probing intelligence, was trying to read the mind of the other. Anne was looking at the monkey orchestra, Gertrude at Anne's arrangement of blue and white irises with sprays of dark green box.

Gertrude said, in a conciliatory tone, for she had understood Anne's reaction to her last remark, 'I hope you really liked the necklaces and things. It would give me such joy to see you wearing them.'

'Oh yes — yes — I do like them — thank you — '

'I mean keep them, they're yours now.'

'Oh not all those — '

'I like that dress too,' said Gertrude, 'though you ought to iron it, its getting creased. I'll iron it for you. But you need some proper summer dresses. I suppose we will have some summer, after all it's May, we might go shopping tomorrow, would you like?'

Gertrude's manner was conversational, chatty, though with a little edge of deliberate gentleness. Anne thought, she just wanted Tim to show his face here. Now she wants to blur the effect, to change the subject.

Anne said, 'I must work, I must find regular work, I am becoming demoralized. Perhaps your social worker friends would help me. How did this morning go, by the way?' Not till that moment did Anne realize that of course the 'social worker' was a fiction. Gertrude had spent the morning with Tim Reede. She looked at Gertrude, who was blushing.

'Oh, OK. I'll introduce you to those people if you like.'

'Gertrude — ' said Anne.

'Yes?'

'There's some sort of thing between you and Tim Reede.'

Gertrude looked at Anne. 'What makes you think that?'

'Intuition. It's true, isn't it?'

'Yes.'

'OK, none of my business. I'll get lunch now.'

'Anne, don't be a fool. Stay here *please.*'

Anne suddenly did not know what to do with herself. She regretted having forced Gertrude to tell her. Now, she did not want a discussion. But Gertrude would feel bound to talk, explain. Anne pulled a chair up near the window and sat looking out into Ebury Street. It was raining again.

Gertrude said, 'Oh God — '

Anne said, 'Sorry, I shouldn't have asked you.'

'Is it so obvious?'

'Well—'

'Did anyone say anything to you?'

Anne hesitated. 'No.'

Gertrude thought, I told no one. Has Tim told anyone?

Anne thought, without the anonymous letter would I have noticed anything, thought anything? No. 'I assume it's a secret,' she said. 'Don't worry, I won't mention it.'

'I'm not worrying! Do as you like.'

'I won't mention it.'

'I wonder what you're thinking, Anne.'

'I'm not thinking anything. It's up to you. Nothing to do with me.'

'That's a rotten reply and you know it.'

'I'm sorry, but what am I to say? I don't understand and I'm not asking you to tell me—'

'You're angry. Why? Are you jealous?'

'*Jealous?* You mean because you've got a man and I haven't? Gertrude, we've never conversed at this level of stupidity.'

'No, you fool. I mean—sorry, it was an idiotic way to put it.'

'It was.'

'You know what I mean. I feel possessive about you. Why shouldn't you feel possessive about me?'

Oddly enough this aspect of the matter had not really occurred to Anne since the first awful shock of seeing the letter. The aspect existed. She said thoughtfully, 'I suppose I do feel possessive, but not in any way which would make me resent a—'

'A what?'

'If later on you wanted seriously to marry somebody, somebody good—I rather hoped that one day you would recover and get married—I think I said so—And if you were happy like that I'd be very glad. I love you and I want your well-being, and maybe I'm conceited and optimistic enough to think that our friendship is indestructible.'

'It is indestructible, let's regard that as fixed. But still you're angry.'

'Not angry. Startled, sort of shocked.'

'Because it's so soon?'

'Yes. And because it's—who it is. Are you actually having a love affair?'

'Yes.'

'I'm surprised.'

'We fell in love in France. It was a *coup de foudre*.'

'Does anyone else know?'

'Not yet.'

'Just as well. I suppose — well, it will pass, won't it? Anyway — I'm sorry I seemed bothered. Let's have lunch now.'

'It won't pass,' said Gertrude. 'I'm going to marry Tim.'

'I should wait a while, if I were you, and reflect a bit. Let's have lunch.'

'I will wait. I am reflecting. I am going to marry Tim. Why are you so cold and beastly?'

'How long does a *coup de foudre* take?'

'About four seconds. That's how long it can take two human beings to change the world.'

'You're pleased with yourself. But it isn't true. I don't believe in *coups de foudre* and "falling in love". Loving people is a serious matter but falling in love is just a temporary form of madness.'

'Maybe you found it so. You think I should just have a secret love affair and pass on?'

'Yes. I think it's all a pity, but if it's started I suppose it'll go on. People in love can't restrain themselves, so it's said. That is why they are traditionally forgiven.'

'Now I come to think of it, in the old days you never said you were in love, you said you were involved.'

'Oh never mind about the old days, my darling, we were children, we were fools.'

'You think I'm still a fool. You've been cloistered a long time.'

'Let's stop this.'

'You said it wasn't just because it was too soon — and it is too soon and I'm amazed at myself — but because it was who it was. But what have you got against Tim? You don't know him, you don't know anything about him. If it's because you saw him stealing food he told me and it was because he was hungry and poor and I suppose that's not a crime —'

'No, no, that was just embarrassing. I haven't anything against him. Or well — only —'

'Only what?'

246

'He isn't up to you, darling, he's a small man, you're so much more than he is. You could choose a far better person. He seems to me flimsy and not sort of solid enough to be really trust-worthy. And he's lazy and too anxious to please—I'm sorry, I may be quite wrong. But you asked me for my impression and that's it.'

'I didn't ask you for your impression, actually. I asked what you had against him. It seems that what you have against him is that you dislike him.'

'I don't dislike him, I just don't see the point of him. But don't let's talk like this, Gertrude. It's my fault. This sounds like an argument but it isn't. We're both taking up simple crude positions and uttering simple crude statements. This is not the way you and I usually talk to each other. This isn't communication. I admit I'm upset, you are quite right, and there may be an element of what you called "jealousy" in it. But I'm mainly upset because I think you're running straight into an act of folly which you will regret. It being "so soon" isn't very important except in a sort of pietistic way. Time is a pretty unreal business after all. Why shouldn't you love again now you're alone? But it's obvious that now isn't a good moment to make a great decision, when your life and your mind are still so confused. This might have been a good reason for not starting an affair, but maybe the affair doesn't matter too much either. In a way it's just a symptom of the shock and muddle you're in. I'm just advising you not to let words like "marriage" get into your head at all at present. Don't promise anything to anyone. You're not in a position to commit your future self. Say firmly that you can't see the future, because you *can't*. I don't know how seriously you meant this about marrying, but if it was serious that's what I think. And quite a separate point, I don't see him as right for you. He's not good enough. I may be wrong about his character. Maybe he wouldn't let you down. But I'm sure he'd bore you.'

Gertrude, who had sat down on the other side of the room, was silent. Then she said with a little sad laugh, 'Well, if *you* think that, the *others* will think it with knobs on !'

'Who cares what the others think?'

'Oh I don't care. Yes, I do care. It just makes me feel so alone in this business. And you are making me feel more alone.'

Anne said, 'I'm sorry. It wasn't to make you feel more alone that I came back to you.'

Anne was thinking, I must leave here, I must move out. If she's having a love affair she'll want the flat! I should have thought of that and said nothing! Yet how could I? Oh why did the Count have to show me that hateful letter! And oh my God, I must go and telephone him, he'll be waiting and I'll bring him such terrible news. Perhaps he could bear not to win her, but to lose her *like this*, how can he bear it?

Gertrude was thinking, why does Anne have to say these dreadful clear definite things? Why does she always judge? She's right that this is not the way to talk. Why does she talk then? And I'm sure she'll go now, she'll go away so as to 'leave me to it' and she'll grow cold and disappear. I shall lose her. I don't understand anything any more. I don't understand her or myself or Tim. And it was all so clear. I ought not to have brought Tim here, I should have seen it was dangerous to him, but he wanted to come and it seemed right. I shouldn't have let him make love to me in that horrible studio. It was a flimsy place, flimsy like Anne said Tim was, it was like lying out on a scaffolding with the wind blowing. In fact Tim and Gertrude had been unable to leave the studio without lying down together, but it had been an unhappy perfunctory love-making, Tim fretting and worrying in case somebody came.

As tears gathered in Gertrude's eyes and as she looked away across the room toward the door, a ghost of a feeling visited her, a shadow sensation out of the past, a little mislaid mental cluster which still hung somewhere there amid the furniture in its accustomed place: she thought, surely it will be all right, I shall tell Guy about it, he will help me, he will know what to do.

The Count was sitting beside his radio set which he had just switched off. It was late at night. He had listened to a symphony concert, a talk on archaeology, Kaleidoscope, the news, a political discussion, a poetry reading, the book at bedtime, the Financial World Tonight, more news, some prayers with jazz music, the weather forecast for the ships. Now all was silent. Fulham and Chelsea were quiet, except for the occasional distant lonely sound of a car or a rumbling lorry. The music and voices which had kept the Count company throughout the evening were still. They had been soft voices, at the end barely audible, for he feared to disturb his neighbours and had been upset for a long time when once, years ago, a man had banged on his door to tell him to switch off. Tonight indeed he had scarcely listened to what was passing. His simple lonely pleasure in those friendly sounds was quite gone.

He had eaten nothing. He had drunk a little whisky. Anne had rung him up about three and told him that, yes, Tim and Gertrude were having a love affair. Gertrude said they were in love with each other and planned to get married. They were keeping it secret at the moment. Anne added that she had not told Gertrude about the Count's visit or the anonymous letter. She had simply asked a question and Gertrude had told her everything. So the Count must not only tell no one, but not reveal to Gertrude that he knew. Anne said Gertrude would be hurt if she thought the Count knew before the moment when Gertrude decided to tell him or to announce it to the world. Anne hoped the Count understood. Anne added that she thought it possible that the whole thing would prove ephemeral and fall through, but it was idle to speculate and she only told him what she knew.

The Count of course did not entertain hope, it was not in his nature. He had imagined he knew what suffering was. He was well acquainted with sorrow, disappointment, loneliness, the remorse of one who has no real conception of his life, the homesickness of one who has no home. He had been used to saying to melancholy, even to grief, come in my friend, let us be quietly together. In this way over a long time the Count had come to think himself invulnerable. He had never been in a concentration camp or a torture chamber; but in the wear and tear of ordinary life he thought that he had tasted bitterness and accepted the diet. He had not achieved or wanted much in life; so how could he, living in between Fulham and Chelsea and travelling to Whitehall every day, be touched by any pain with which he was unfamiliar? He had been wrong. He now saw his melancholy as a bed of soft comfort and his bitterness as wine, and he wished for death.

He thought of the night when his brother had died. This was a story not a memory, since the Count had been a small child at the time. It was just before Christmas. His father who by then had left the Air Force, was absent, probably spending the night, as he often did at the Polish government headquarters in Bayswater. The mother with the two boys was living in Croydon. There had been an argument between his mother and another Polish woman who was lodging with them. The woman, who was very fond of the Count's brother Jozef, wanted to take him to the church to see the Christ Child in His stable with the ox and the ass. The Count's mother was afraid, she wanted her sons close beside her. Jozef had cried, wanting to go to the Christ Child. The father was absent. The mother relented. The church was hit by a bomb, the boy and the lodger were killed. I wish I had died then, he thought, I wish I had gone to the church with Jozef, or instead of him. He thought of himself living on as Jozef. He would have been a strong man.

The Count had lived almost happily with his cloistered love for Gertrude. He had lived by little anticipations and little rewards. She had, he felt, amidst all the others, a special smile, a special voice, for him. How quiet, how happy they had all been together. Thus people can pass a lifetime in silent unspoken trust, and live in peace without possessing their heart's desire; and those who let themselves be loved can of their bounty extend, even unconsciously, a harmless radiance of affection for the salvation of the solitary. Gertrude's marriage had made her unattainable and holy, but also *safe*, as if Guy were actually keeping her *for* the Count, the secure eternal closeted object of his secret love. Indeed upon her quietness, her immobility, the peace of his love had rested.

With Guy's death came the awful restlessness of hope, the cloistered passion released to wander. But the Count had never let himself hope much, and an absolute piety, the time of mourning and bereavement, had made it easy for him to inhibit, at least to delay, certain thoughts. And he had looked at Gertrude with eyes wherein he hoped that she could read his sadness for Guy, his compassion for her, his absolute joy at her existence. *Now* he wanted her to need, retrospectively, his love, and slowly, unstartled, to be comforted by it. All this, passing through the shock of Guy's death, was one with his life as he had lived it since he first met her. Since Anne's telephone call, only hours away in the past, the destruction had been total. It was as if a flame had licked backward through the continuum of his being annihilating all its structures. He could have endured not to possess Gertrude if she had remained his friend unmarried. He had indeed fully imagined and envisaged, even taught himself to expect, just this. To lose her to another was a different matter, although he had dutifully, and for the farther future, attempted to school himself to the possibility. But to lose her now and to this man goaded him into a frenzy of grief and misery and rage which made the continuation of ordinary life seem impossible.

An almost cynical remorse was part of his suffering. So, she had gone so fast. If he had dreamed that she wanted a man, wanted declarations of love and passion, would he not have given them to her, and not only on his knees? Could woman be like that, could *that* woman be? How stupidly, it now seemed to him, he had concealed his love! Yet, with a lover's double-think had he not often imagined that she must know how much he loved her? How can one think all the time about someone without their somehow knowing? Or had she, *could* she have, mistaken his tact, his gentlemanly honour and decorum, for a cool and rational affection? Some cruder clutching had attracted her attention when she was in the mood for being held. That she should have turned to *Tim Reede*. The Count had always liked Tim, but he measured now how much contempt his liking had contained. A patronizing attitude had somehow constituted and facilitated the liking. There was nothing of the rival about Tim, nothing of the equal. Nothing of the rival, he had thought. And *now* — tormented imagination animated a Gertrude how alienated, how changed, how irrevocably spoilt and lost.

The Count suddenly leapt up from his quiet radio set and

ran out into the kitchen. He took down from the wall Tim's picture entitled *Three Blackbirds in a Treacle Wall*. He stared at it. It was a horrible picture. He was about to smash it into the rubbish bin when some unseen hand prevented this exhibition of blind rage. His heart was beating violently. He went into his bedroom and opening a deep drawer thrust the picture away into the bottom of it. As he did so his hand came into contact with a soft roll of stuff which he recognized as being the Polish flag which was one of the few mementos he had carried away from his childhood home. Ready to weep, he prepared himself for bed. He would not sleep. Tonight was the first night of his absolute loneliness, the first night upon the dark road which led now straight on to death.

The Count did sleep, however, and had a nightmare which it seemed to him (only he was not sure) that he had had many times before. He dreamt that he was a Jew in the Warsaw Ghetto. It is wartime and the Germans are occupying Warsaw. The Ghetto is closed. Every day more Jews arrive, from other parts of the city, from other parts of the country. Every day the area of the ghetto grows smaller and smaller. The Jews fight like overcrowded rats for diminishing space, for diminishing food. Affliction does not make men brothers. Yet gradually too, after the first shock, there is comfort, comfort of order, comfort of survival. The Jews are together now without Gentiles, together in their own place. Inside the ghetto they are enclosed and safe, they can look after each other in peace. Their Jewishness is purified, justified. There is music, theatre, literature, a way of life. If only they can be left alone how well they will manage, how quiet and orderly they will be, each one knowing in his heart that he will survive. After all, there is enough food. There is work to do, work it is true for the Germans, but is not this work itself a guarantee of survival? The Count has found himself a corner in a room. Others are kind to him and he has his place. He has learnt what to do. If only people will be kind and orderly everyone will survive. What miracles of patience and endurance the Jewish people can achieve. Through such endurance they have survived and will survive. Against so much provocation, so great a tolerance and fortitude. Never hit back. Avoid the occasion of offence. Be invisible. Be silent. Wait. The Count feels safe. No one threatens him, no one sees him. The ghetto is at peace. Has it not its own Jewish authorities? Safety lies in order, in coming back to the corner in the room and living in amity and helping the sick and the weak. So few Germans can control so many Jews because the Jews are sensible and wise. They are a rational people who have seen much trouble. Be still my people, it is your destiny to suffer quietly. Sometimes Jews go away. There is a farmland at Treblinka where they go to work. The life is good there, there is more food. Someone has seen a postcard sent by someone's friend. There are rumours from Wilno but no one will believe them. Someone has said the Germans will kill all the Jews, but no one believes this. It would be madness to believe such a tale. The Jews are quiet, the Jews are useful, the Germans are a civilized people. Someone has told a story about gas chambers, about death by gas, but this is an invention, it is science fiction. Is it true that no one has returned from Treblinka. But people have seen letters, the food is good there, the work is not too hard. The Count feels fear in his heart. He banishes hatred as if it were a fatal disease. He banishes anger and the desire for revenge because he knows that these things mean death, and he wants so much to live, that he should survive it all and tell it later as a story. He does not want to die in the ghetto. He does not want to hear of any heroic legend. He does not want to be told what happened at Masada. But now he has seen young men with guns in their hands and insane red flames of rage darting from their eyes. Mad criminal young men who will be the death of us all. Oh let this pass. They are shooting in the ghetto. He has seen a dead German lying in the roadway, a *dead German*. The Count tries to hide, only where is there to hide? Now everywhere there is a sound of gunfire. Which way to go? A man in uniform appears, holding a gun and carrying a Polish flag. He waves to the Count and seizes him by the hand and shouts to him to follow. It is Jozef who did not die after all. Shells are bursting and in their light the Count sees Jozef's face, so beautiful, so like his father's face. Over a pile of rubble Jozef disappears into a cloud of smoke. A shell bursts. The Count does not follow, he runs away. But there is nowhere to hide. The sewers are full of gas. The ghetto is in flames. People are screaming and crying and jumping from windows. In some place high up two flags are flying together, the red and white Polish flag, the blue and white Jewish flag. Beside them there is a machine gun, the only one in the ghetto. The machine gun speaks. The ghetto burns. The Count runs. The machine gun is silent. A voice is speaking in Hebrew. 'Behold, happy is the man whom God correcteth: therefore despise not thou the chastening of the Almighty.' But it is too late for such wisdom, and there is nobody left to hear it. The gunfire ends, the flames subside. There is silence. The ghetto does not exist any more. They have taken the Count and put him onto the train for Treblinka, Warsaw is *Judenrein*.

>> <<

'You mean you want to call it off?' said Tim.

'No!' said Gertrude.

'What then? I haven't understood you.'

'I don't understand myself. I've been invaded by misery. I feel half mad.'

'*Please* don't feel like that.'

'I think we should wait.'

'We've already agreed to wait.'

'Yes, but wait—more—differently.'

'How, differently?'

'Put it in cold storage.'

'Cancel our vows? And don't say we haven't made any vows.'

'Tim, please help me, don't be hostile.'

'Gertrude, I love you, I'm hostile to what you're saying because it's killing me.'

'I don't know what I'm saying. I love you. But I just—I just can't live myself at present. I've never felt like this. My mind, my being, has become impossible. I can't exist as I am. I've got to change.'

'But what must change and why? And can we not change together? Gertrude darling, you're frightening me to death, I'm terrified. Please put this madness away, just rest with me, let me make you quiet and keep you safe.'

'You can't, you're part of the trouble. I've got to be alone for a while. We must undo it.'

'You want me to go away and never return?'

'No! But we must postpone—undo—our engagement.'

'Engagement! We've never been "engaged". Oh Gertrude, you can't even talk to me properly any more, you're—you're alienated—you're taken over. You're ashamed of me.'

'Tim, don't talk offensive rubbish.'

'That's what it comes to. You can't acknowledge me in front of *them*, you shudder at the thought. You feel you'll lose face. I don't blame you. I daresay they've guessed, someone's been getting at you, someone's been saying—Oh I can imagine what they've been saying! Oh Gertrude, everything's spoilt—I was so afraid of this—'

'Tim, wait—please don't say things—'

'You're saying things! You say you want to cancel the "engagement", send back the ring, only there's never been a ring! I just love you, I want to marry you like you said, that was the most wonderful thing anyone ever said to me, I want us to be husband and wife and live in the open. We've been special to each other, you know that, *no one* could understand what we are to each other or see into it at all. Can't you be brave enough to be true to what we *know*, we two, just us—?'

'Darling, dear heart, please don't just cry out at me, I'm in such pain. We must have a space, I must have anyway. Tim, love me enough to give me this time, this interval. I don't know myself. It isn't the others.'

'It is.'

'Or if it's anyone it's Guy.'

'Oh well,' said Tim, 'Oh Christ—I can't fight with Guy. I do understand. I'll go away.'

'No, no, don't go—'

'It's better, Gertrude. You've made a mistake.'

'No, I just need time—'

'Oh God, if only we could *sleep* for six months!'

'Tim, please—'

' "Let's just be friends for a while".'

'Yes, yes—'

'I was making a joke. We can't be friends.'

'Tim, be sane, be rational, let's *think*. The secrecy, and living like this, it's impossible. We're in a jungle of lies. I must be alone and suffer alone, or I'm unclean. I must just go away for a while and be by myself. Let's both be—separate—like in retreat—still loving each other—and meet again later—'

'How much later, months later, years later? Don't pretend Gertrude, it's all finished, you've simply changed your mind, why not? I knew this would happen. I knew it in France. As soon as you see me *here* you realize you've been temporarily insane! Let me go now, my heart, my queen, don't maul me, I can go, I can walk, I'll live, we'll both live. Don't make a tragedy of it, don't make a bloody slaughterhouse. Oh don't cry so. God, this is breaking my heart!'

'I don't know what to do!'

'Neither do I. Your friend Anne has ruined it all. I knew she would. I'm sure *she's* guessed.'

'It was your idea to meet her.'

'I wanted to meet people with you, I wanted to stop being a guilty secret! You say we're in a jungle of lies. We can just come out of it hand in hand. Only you don't want to. It was stupid of me to move in here, obviously you can't stand seeing me here. I'll go. Let's forgive each other and—I'll—go—'

Gertrude had said to Anne that she had been possessed by devils. But the real devils had come now. She felt incapable of managing her mind. It was as if her mind were drunk, reeling about, lurching to and fro in crazy sudden movements which made her physically sick. Anne had moved out, Anne was in a *hotel*. That fact alone, Gertrude felt, was enough to craze her. Tim was living with her at Ebury Street, they were living a secret life, not answering the telephone. Gertrude had told Janet Openshaw she was going away, none of this made any sense.

'Nobody knows that he lies there but his hawk and his hound and his lady fair. His hound is to the hunting gone, his hawk to fetch the wild fowl home, his lady's ta'en another mate. . . . Many a one for him makes moan, but none shall know where he is gone. Over his bones when they are bare the wind shall blow forever more.' Yielding to what seemed almost like a vicious temptation, Gertrude had looked up the ballad which Guy had quoted. Guy had quoted it when he was telling her to be happy after he was dead. But what a bitter terrible poem it was, and how could it have been other than bitter in the mouth, in the heart, of a dying man. Guy, noble, brave, and good had said to Gertrude what he felt he ought to say, and had refused the pain-killing injection so as to be able to say it when he was most himself. But those heroic words masked, and masked even for Guy, though only for a moment, the black hateful solitude of death. No wonder Guy had become a stranger in the land of the living, withdrawn, and speaking a different tongue. His warm and loving wife could comfort him no more, nothing could comfort him any more.

Gertrude had become possessed, as if a cloud-demon had swept her up, by a terrible pity for Guy. Death, which defeats the earthly Eros, had made her vulnerable and mad. Her love for Guy invaded her, it raced through her veins like a fierce drug, she was sick with this hopeless love. She dreamed of Guy every night. She stretched out her arms toward his ambiguous and elusive shade. She wanted to be alone so as to indulge this terrible love, yet also she feared to be alone. And she was not alone, Tim was there like some extraordinary *accident*. She looked at him with amazement, she saw him with a new clear vision, a slight man with ginger hair and nervous timid apologetic blue eyes. Tim, like a lodger, like a student, like a sort of helpless dependent, like a child. And she pitied Tim too, and she had not stopped loving him.

They made love, like addicts, but afterwards wanted metamorphosis and flight: to sleep, or else to rise quickly and dress and look at each other in a good light with puzzled frightened tender looks, and to drink. They were both drinking a good deal. Gertrude felt how provisional, how precarious it all was. It was no better than that hasty horrible love-making in Tim's studio, lying 'as if on a scaffolding' and listening for feet on the stairs. Here, they listened for the door bell, which they breathlessly ignored, or for the telephone whose buzz they could not entirely silence even though they had pushed several screws of paper in to jam the bell. Leaving the house separately, they vanished into London every day. They had a festival lunch and a festival dinner. They showed each other things. They went to the museums and art galleries which Gertrude admitted she scarcely knew. The idea of simply visiting these places had never occurred to her. Tim took her to funny out-of-the-way pubs. They explored obscure seedy places along the river. They were not pretending to enjoy themselves, they actually did, by some miracle, enjoy themselves, although hell was loose in Gertrude's mind, and she sometimes thought in Tim's too. His head, his face had a particular puzzled vulnerable touchingness when he was naked, he looked so different then, and she pitied him with a deep possessive erotic pity and took refuge in the seekingness of his fierce embrace where she rested in an unexpected strength. They hid their eyes in each other's shoulders and neither yet dared to speak plainly of the future. Their Eros had not left them, but at times it seemed a crazed doomed Eros. The sense of something provisional and clandestine was in the air that they breathed. But although their 'new life' had lasted only days, they told each other that they felt that they had lived together for a long long time.

Anne's departure had shocked Gertrude, although it was quite clear that Anne would and must depart. Anne had been very kind to Gertrude, as kind as gentle loving clever Anne knew how to be. She had spoken of the indestructibility of their love. She had said she would be always available, always near. They had not again discussed Tim. Anne packed her bags and departed to a small hotel in the Paddington area. She spoke of getting a flat. They said goodbye as for a longish parting and had not communicated since.

Gertrude had been shaken by Anne's reaction, by her attack on Tim, by her 'marry somebody good'. Of course Anne mattered more than *them*, but it was a foretaste of a public response to which she found herself not looking forward: she was not 'ashamed of Tim', it was not like that. But she felt, in relation to Anne, oddly and miserably ashamed of herself. And everything seemed both inevitable and wrongly done. Of course Tim had to come to Ebury Street. His studio lacked privacy and they wanted to be together. Of course they had agreed not to tell anyone yet. But this meant they were living like criminals.

All these thoughts made up a poisonous witches' brew in Gertrude's mind. Rising from dreams of Guy her instinct to ask for his *help* was stronger than her reluctant ability to compose a waking world. And now a separate and quite peculiar torment was making itself felt. It concerned the Count. Gertrude had vaguely told Janet Openshaw that she was probably going to be away for a bit, and assumed that she would send the news around. She had even said, with the instinctive talent for lying which even truthful people can quickly develop when they find themselves in a false situation, that she was going to see an old school friend in Hereford. (This person, called Margaret Paley, actually existed.) After this however she had felt a kind of odd special compunction about the Count. He was indeed special, and needed a special treatment, a special place, he was not just one of those who were to gather by a rumour that she had left

London. She thought of telephoning him, but then on impulse sent him a note asking him round for a drink. She would then inform him that she was perhaps going away. She told all this to Tim, and it was agreed that Tim was to be present, then to leave, and this would contribute to the vague notion of their being, after all, pals. This was what Tim wanted; and Gertrude had not told him how disastrously this idea had worked out in Anne's case. The Count was another matter. He would suspect nothing and ask nothing.

The Count replied by letter that unfortunately he was engaged on that evening. He wrote in his usual slightly formal but friendly style. Gertrude had never received many letters from him. But it was no oddity of style which now made her suddenly mad with a new and unforeseen anxiety. It was simply the fact that he did not come. Gertrude had always assumed in her heart that if ever she summoned the Count he would turn up, whatever else he might have to cancel in order to do so. Whatever the obstacle he would overcome it. His not appearing could surely only mean one thing. He knew. And if he knew perhaps everybody knew. Had Tim told anyone? He swore he had not. Had Anne? Impossible. But not even the thought of their 'knowing' worried her so much as the sudden appalling feeling that the Count condemned her, that he was terribly hurt, upset, alienated, shocked. That things would never be the same again ever between her and the Count. She began to feel that nothing in the world mattered so much as that the Count should have a good opinion of her. She had a violent desire to run round in the evening to his flat where she had never been. She wanted to see him, to see his gentle pale eyes, and to receive the reassurance of his esteem, his love. It was as if she had fallen in love with the Count! She who was already in love with Guy, and with Tim.

The poles and pillars of her world had been removed. Guy was dead, Anne was gone, the Count no longer loved her and — she increasingly realized that she could not either go on living this crazy criminal life with Tim, or announce him to the world as her love and her husband. She could not. She wanted things to be somehow as they had been, or as they had never quite been but might have been, or might be if only things were different which could not be different. She wanted to be the old Gertrude, Guy's Gertrude, the centre of a loving admiring circle, she wanted Anne and the Count – and Tim too and all the love that had come with them out of France. But she could not be an outcast with Tim, a wanderer, a vagabond. She saw him now as a gipsy who would take her away out of her life into his. Only he had no life, he had no place. She asked him about his friends. He had no friends. He had come to her for a life and a place. It was nothing to do with money (that she never thought). But she increasingly saw Tim as a waif. He had no background, no belongings, no world. And she would be a waif too, unless she drew back, unless she somehow *solved* the absolutely insoluble problem.

'News, news, Gertrude has taken a lover!' 'No! Who is he?' 'Tim Reede!' 'You mean the little painter chap? You're joking!' Did they know? If she stopped it now it would never be more than a vague rumour which would fade away and be forgotten. No one would be certain; after all it was so very improbable. But what was she now thinking? There was so much in the balance against poor Tim. There was Guy and Anne and the Count. And now some hideous mean pride which she hated but which was profoundly a part of her as well. It had seemed so sensible to keep it dark, not to admit so soon to another attachment. Now it was beginning to seem impossibly hard to admit it at all. Yet the idea of parting from Tim, really parting, was unthinkable. Gertrude's mind dodged this way and that like a poor hunted hare. There seemed only one issue, muddled and temporary, but which left, for the time, all the essentials unharmed. She must ask Tim for a moratorium, an interval, a time for reflection, or rather a sort of non-time when everything stood still.

Gertrude had thought this yet had not thought it. She had run to Tim's arms away from thought. She had wanted Tim to *prove* his inevitability. The crucial, the revealing conversation started really by accident. They had finished one of their long festival dinners. How easy they found it to talk, they got on so well together, they talked about anything! This was one of the ever-fresh miracles of their love which Gertrude had noticed with surprise. (Anne had said, 'He'll bore you.' She could not have been more wrong.) Gertrude felt, in her detached separated way which made her like a spy able to divide her mind, calm and loving. They were sitting in the dining-room, in the lamp-light, at the strewn table, drinking wine. Gertrude had suddenly said, 'We can't go on like this,' and Tim had said, 'My God, I know!' and then they had set off on this disastrous argument. They looked at each other in horror and misery but could not stop saying the things which would divide them forever.

'Gertrude, this is the truth. You just want it to end. You want it to end before anyone finds out. You want it never to have been at all. You want me to vanish. All right, I'll vanish.'

'I *don't* want that—'

'Yes, you do, you want me to be kind and do it myself so that you won't have to feel afterwards that you did it. You're right, our love will simply be spoilt if we go on. Better to stop now while it's still pure. We shall end up hating each other, or rather you'll hate me, I'll just be a bloody millstone. Of course it was too good to be true. It's been wonderful and I'm grateful and I'm not angry or hostile, but oh God I'm so unhappy—'

'Tim, I'm so unhappy too, I'm wretched and frightened, yet half an hour ago I was happy with you. This is madness. Oh Tim, why can't we make happiness for each other?'

'Because you don't love me enough, my darling. It's no surprise, no accident, that we're here.'

'Where's here?'

'The parting of the ways.'

'No, no, no. Tim, dear, we *can't* part. Let's stop talking, let's go to bed. We've said too much.'

'OK. You go. I'll follow. I want to finish the wine.'

Tim rose almost formally as Gertrude got up. She came and leaned against him, clinging to his white flapping shirt. His skin was moist.

'Go to bed, darling.'

'All right, Tim. Come soon.'

Gertrude had fallen asleep. She had kicked her shoes off and lain down on the bed. Now she woke, listened. The light in the bedroom had been turned off. She felt sure the flat was empty. She leapt up and ran from room to room calling his name. There was no one there. Then she noticed that his rucksack and his old suitcase which had been in the hall were gone.

Gertrude went into the drawing-room and turned on all the lights. There was a letter on the table.

My darling, you want me to go and I've gone. You are right, we should just quietly undo it. I've felt, being with you like this, that it's just not possible. You don't really want to marry me, and we can't be together any other way, it's too serious, and I don't want to be driven mad. I can't be a secret lover. Don't look for me at the studio, I won't be there, I won't be anywhere where we might meet. If we see each other it'll all start again. You must go back into your real world with your real friends. You'll soon feel happier. You'll feel relieved. Oh my darling, I'm sorry it didn't work. My love for you is in so much pain.

T.

Gertrude unbuttoned her dress and tore at it. She grasped her hair and pulled. Her mouth opened in a grin of pain and rage, tears like thunder-drops rained from her eyes. She sat down and remained absolutely still for nearly half an hour.

Then she got up and poured herself some whisky. She wanted Tim so much that her body seemed to be falling apart, moving away into separate pieces. She could scarcely prevent herself from scuttling about like a mad animal. She had never really said to herself, 'It's just physical, it's lust, shock-lust, a flight from grief', and she did not say it now. But she felt her physical longing for Tim as something detached and strange, as a sort of emanation, a second body, her longing for his thin red-haired hands and his smooth sweet skin and his kisses that solved all problems and answered all questions.

Gertrude drank the whisky and called upon her reason, with quiet deliberation as one might call a servant. Tim had said 'it's no accident'. It was no accident that just that conversation had started, though just when it came seemed random, a matter of chance. It had to come. They had been on the brink of that conversation for days, almost ever since Tim moved to Ebury Street. She felt that they had both rehearsed it, had both had their statements ready. 'It's true,' she said aloud. 'I can't marry him.' She had tried hard to bind Tim into her life, but he was alien tissue and the saving blood would not flow from her being into his. In the end she rejected him. She did not try to think why. There were many many reasons. She ought to have fallen in love with someone else, but she had fallen in love with Tim by mistake. About Tim's state of mind she endeavoured not to think, and indeed it was obscure to her.

She looked at her watch and was amazed to find that she was wondering if it was too late to ring the Count. Of course it was. It was nearly two o'clock. She got up and pulled back the curtains and looked out into empty silent Ebury Street. There was nothing to conceal now. And just in that gesture of pulling back the curtains she felt relief. The lying, the concealment had poisoned them. Their love had been something amazing and wonderful, but not strong, not sane. I suppose it's my fault, thought Gertrude, but the idea of fault doesn't really apply. I must simply recover, people do recover. I'll see my friends, I'll gather them about me, that's how I'll live from now on forever, with my friends. I'll bring Anne back here, and tomorrow I'll see the Count, I'll have lunch with him and see his happy eyes. That's the real world. And I'll have a little party and invite Manfred and Gerald and Victor and Ed and Moses and Janet and Stanley and Mrs Mount. And I'll ask Sylvia Wicks round for a drink separately because someone said she was unhappy. And I'll take Rosalind Openshaw on a jaunt somewhere, to Athens or Rome, and Anne will come too. We'll have fun, and I'll be kind to people and find out how they are. And everything will be good and simple and open and innocent again. Tim has been kind to me. He has been wise and brave. It is better to finish like this.

And no one will know, she thought. It will be all sealed away. Even if there was a rumour, no one will believe it if I go about as usual. This will preserve it, in a way, our love. It will stay perfect, safe in the past. It won't have been spoilt by quarrels and hate and by the stupid vulgarity of people who would despise it. No one could have understood it ever except Tim and me. Now it's taken away and safe. It's better so.

There was a pale dawn light over Ebury Street, descending from above over the dim street lamps like a pearly mist. Soon it would be June and midsummer. The houses were still, as if held in a grip of judgement.

Gertrude turned away to go to bed. The courage of the whisky had gone from her. Her head was aching. She undressed and took some aspirins. As she sat down on the bed the great thunder-tears began to roll again. I'm alone, she thought. I hoped I wouldn't be, but I am. I've lost him, my love, my playboy. And o'er his bones when they are bare the wind shall blow forever more.

'So yer back,' said Daisy. 'I thought you'd come slinking back.'

'Did you?' said Tim. 'I didn't. Give me some of that wine, for Christ's sake.'

'There ain't much. I hope you've got money, I haven't.'

'Plenty.'

'So at least you've come back with money in your pocket.'

Tim had wondered whether he should send the money back to Gertrude. He decided not to.

Tim sat down on one of the swaying rickety chairs. Sun shone into the stuffy dusty room. Daisy, sitting on the bed, propped with pillows and with her knees up, was dressed to kill today. She had been putting the finishing touches to her make-up when Tim arrived unannounced. Daisy was wearing a black and white striped silky skirt pulled into a black shiny belt, and a black and white sprigged blouse with a floppy collar tied by a black and orange scarf. Her long legs were in black tights, her shoes were black patent leather with big metal buckles and extremely high thin heels. She had a blue and white clown face on.

'How's the novel?'

'Fine. It just raced ahead while you were absent without leave.'

'Good.'

'So you ratted on Gertrude?'

'We ratted mutually. It was a short excursion into total insanity.'

'I said so. Did I not say so?'

'You did. Who are you dolled up for?'

'You.'

'You didn't know I was coming.'

'I expected you daily.'

'How touching.'

'Of course it wasn't for you. I was just going down the old Prince for lunch.'

'Have you found someone else in my absence?'

266

'No. But it wasn't for want of trying. I haven't forgiven you, you know.'

'But you will.'

'Well, it doesn't matter, it's all states of mind. I missed you! That's a state of mind too. Did you miss me?'

'I think so,' said Tim.

'I think so! That's a fine Tim Reedeish remark! So it's over?'

'Yes.'

'It had better be. What was it like? I'm expecting an amusing blow by blow account.'

'I can't, Daisy. Let's forget it. Forgive and forget. It's gone, it's undone, like a knot is undone, and the string is straight again.'

'Very picturesque. I've often thought that our life together was like a piece of string, a dirty old piece of string all unravelling at the ends.'

'You didn't try to get in touch with me?' said Tim. He had returned to the studio, but there was no letter. After a day and a night alone at the studio he had run to Daisy. He feared Gertrude's arrival and he could not stand the solitude. And he suddenly absolutely needed to talk to Daisy.

'Why the hell should I, fuck you? You cleared off saying you were going to get married. Did you expect me to run after you? Good bloody riddance, thought I.'

'But you're glad I'm back?'

'I suppose so. I've been in and out of an alcoholic haze, actually. I'm used to you, dear boy. I can talk to you. I think you're a mean selfish lying bastard, like most men. I just hate the others more.'

'Daisy—'

'Will you get us some more wine, or shall we go to the Prince? Jimmy Roland's back, by the way.'

'Oh good—'

'He says America's empty, like being inside a clean white cardboard box.'

'Daisy, do you mind if I stay here just for the moment?'

'You mean live here, share my bed?'

'Yes, just not for long—'

'OK. "And there's always that," as you so romantically say

when you want to make love. No wonder all the girls are after you. What's up at the studio?'

'They're turning me out.' This was untrue, but Tim did not want to continue the pain of wondering if Gertrude would come.

'Really! I wonder if that's true. Not that it matters much. I have no more curiosity about your truthfulness. You can't bring your bloody paintings here.'

'The garage man will store them. Thanks, darling.'

'You'd better bustle round quick and find a flat. You know how we two get if we're shut up together like rats. We'd be OK in a palace. Money would do a lot for our characters.'

'I'll bustle. Shall I get some wine or shall we go to the Prince of Denmark?'

'Oh get some wine, and some grub too while you're about it. I don't want to go to the Prince, it's too far at lunch time. Jimmy Roland will be there laughing at his own jokes and I can't stand that asinine bray, and poor Piglet squeaking. Don't go yet. Come and sit beside me and make up to me in a humble penitent manner.'

Tim sat beside her and looked into her large dark woody-brown eyes outlined in blue between their spiky black lashes. He touched the little brown mole beside her nose. 'Old pal.'

'Don't do it again, Tim Reede. I mightn't forgive you next time. Funny, I did think at first that you were doing it for us, to get her money, you're crazy enough. I was quite touched. I wonder if she'd have put up with it in the long run, you could always tell some fib about seeing your old friends at the Slade, you're such an expert liar. Did you tell her about me?'

'No.'

'Promise? Not a word?'

'Not a word.'

'Good. I bet you told her lies about how lonesome you were. I think you smell of her. You're a disgusting brute.'

'Take your shoes off,' said Tim. 'They're like bloody spears.'

'You take them off. I can't get at them. You're in the way. Do you love me?'

'Yes.'

'You don't sound very enthusiastic, where's all that warm bright Irish talk you used to be so famous for? I've never seen a man more like a beaten dog. And your hair's going grey.'

'*Is it?*'

'I'm only kidding. Wait, you're messing my collar, I'll take the scarf off. Christ, it's hot.'

'Oh Daisy, I've been so unhappy, it's been so awful.'

'Do you want me to console you because Gertie saw what a little rat you were? Poor little Timmie. Put your head there then. Women are for consolation, they're always the safe house. You come back to the woman you left and ask her to console you because your caper went wrong. God, we're fools. I wish I could find a better man.'

'I wish I was a better man.'

'Poor Tim, poor sinner. There, put your arms around me. Don't grieve, you're safe here.'

Everything began to go wrong, Tim thought afterwards, from the moment of the perfunctory lovemaking in the studio. His excessive anxiety about being disturbed annoyed Gertrude and made her insecure. She was jumpy and uneasy. She resented his inability to protect her. Then the meeting with Anne (his idea) had not been a success, he had been unable to think of anything intelligent to say, and Anne had stared with her cold eyes as if she were reading his thoughts. He felt sure that she had made Gertrude tell her the truth (though Gertrude denied this) and had told Gertrude to stop it! At the first public test, Gertrude had given way. Looking through the eyes of a third party, she had seen the absurdity of her proceeding. It was just as well he had never breathed a word about Daisy. If he had, and Gertrude had *then* left him, he would have imagined that the cause, and would have had the extra torment of reproaching himself for imprudence. He could picture how he would have worked at it, thinking of how, without that fatal revelation, he could have kept his love. As it was, he had at least this consolation: Gertrude had left him, not because of some slip or accident, but because of the deep unworkable structure of the situation. She was ashamed of him, that was what it came to. Tim felt no resentment or surprise. He was ashamed of himself; only under normal conditions this did not matter and he scarcely noticed it.

It had seemed easy enough in France to say, we'll keep it secret for a while. It had seemed prudent and simple. But the tactics of secrecy had turned out to be intolerable. If Tim had had a secure dwelling it might have been easier, and here indeed the fact of his relation with Daisy was injurious. Anne's prompt departure (Gertrude *must* have told her) to visit an old school friend in Hereford (Gertrude was becoming as good a liar as Tim was) opened Ebury Street to them; but Ebury Street was not secure either. Polite well-trained cousins and aunts did not 'drop in', but their presence pressed upon the horizon. Gertrude was not independent of these people, though she pretended that she was. There remained the vast pleasure-palace of London and fitfully, wandering there together like people on holiday, they had felt happy. Tim had showed her pictures, objects, places. Gertrude really knew remarkably little about London. They frequented the British Museum. (There was a secluded seat in the Etruscan room where they could kiss each other.) Tim took her to pubs, far removed from the Prince of Denmark and from the Ebury Arms, pubs in Chiswick, and some which he remembered in North London (not Hampstead, which was full of aunts and cousins). They went to a shabby cider house in the Harrow Road, she liked that. They were like student lovers, or a caricature of happy children.

They had walked, got drunk, made love. It had all the marks of a secret affair. Indeed it *was* a secret affair. The strange passion which had come to them in France with such sudden urgent wing-beats was still there, that intense inexplicable mutual attraction of carnal beings. The indubitable Eros had not failed or fled. They made love more frenziedly, with closed eyes, groaning against each other. Then leaping apart almost with suspicion and dressing hastily as if to make an escape. Tim was now surprised by Gertrude's passion, which in France he had somehow, under the sign of that amazing change, taken for granted. In Ebury Street it was something very odd, and he felt that she must feel it so. Besides, the flat at Ebury Street was terrible to Tim, full of accusing memories, and must be far more so to her. Neither of them spoke of this.

In spite of his policy of *lanthano* and his cheerful ability to say what was not the case, Tim had never before concealed his relationship with a woman. He could not cope with the secrecy, which they did not discuss or make a jest of. It filled him with terrible doubts. Yes, one day, sometime, gradually, he would be introduced into the circle of Gertrude's acquaintance as a friend, then as a special friend, then as a fiancé. They had agreed that they could not love except in the prospect of marriage, only that vista would save their great love from despair and corruption. But he had felt the vista closing. They had begun to live in the present, as doomed lovers do. Unhappiness rose steadily about them like a sea.

In all this, Tim never said to himself that they had made a commonplace mistake, that of taking a trivial lustful fancy for a great love. He still believed in the great love. It was just that not every great love can make itself a place and a way in the world. He often thought, in this connection, of the rocks near Les Grandes Saules and of the crystal pool and the 'great face'. Somehow it had all started there; and herein he made a distinction. The great face had lasted in his mind as a reality, he connected it with his work, with his being as an artist. He recalled its strange configuration, the pale round rock with its wet pitted surface, the mossy 'pencil lines' rising up like pillars, the dark cleft above with hanging ferns and creepers blurring the further ascent of the cliff into places unknown. The numinous power of the rock shook him, even now in memory (he could see it with the utmost distinctness in his mind's eye), with a reverence which was a kind of love. There had been as it were an announcement of truth, and he felt still a magnetic tension as of a persisting bond between himself and the rock. He could believe that the rock existed now, continued to be, quiet and alone, shadowed and gleaming in the sun, darkened in the warm night. About the crystal pool he felt differently. His fear of the great face was an awe inseparable from reverence. His fear of the pool, for he feared it, was different, sharper, a fear of what was magical, dangerous. He found it hard to imagine that the pool was there at this moment, and that perhaps a bird was drinking from it, a snake swimming in it.

271

Trying to make sense of what had happened in the later days of his despair he had sometimes thought: we were simply bewitched, after Gertrude swam in that pool. It was like a drug, a love-elixir. Something that was there bewitched us, perhaps quite casually, we have been temporarily deranged, and now the effects are wearing off. This would have been one way of looking at the matter. But in his deepest heart Tim rejected it. That danger had not touched them. It had not been like magic, it was not magic, although it was in the ordinary sense magical, enchanting. There was absolute truth in the thing, something of wholeness and goodness which called to him from outside the dark tangle of himself. He loved Gertrude with a love that was better than himself. There was a self-authenticating ring about it all, a certainty which he had not felt before. This expressed itself in him as joy; and he felt it even as late as the time when he and Gertrude were getting drunk together in the Harrow Road.

But what is true and good can be bodily destroyed, leaving its truth and its goodness as a pure fine aura in the world of concepts. He and Gertrude could not support their love, could not live it out. She wavered, he despaired. If only, he kept thinking, it were a little longer after Guy's death, another few months and I might have been saved. Yet, another few months and Gertrude would have been a different woman, her shaken soul not tuned to that precise key wherein it vibrated with Tim's. That it should have been accidental did not dismay him. He was wise enough to know that mutual love depends on accidents, and this fact alone does not make it fragile. But he felt sad, almost bitter, to think that perhaps the sheer proximity of Guy, that strange commanding absence, had exercised the fatal power.

They had both, in their feverish 'holiday', foreseen the end. They had their lines ready. Tim could not have begun that conversation. Gertrude began it. But once she did so he knew what he had to say. Looking back it seemed to Tim that he had displayed courage. Yet what was the alternative? He could have wept and begged. That would have put the end off for a while, but only for a while. He had seen irritation and annoyance in Gertrude's eyes. He dreaded like the pains of hell the sight of hatred there. He saw how Gertrude was caught. She could take him as a lover but not as a husband. She wanted now to return to her old pattern of life, to her old and dear friends, to what was after all her family. If he overstayed his welcome he would become a hated encumbrance. And he had been told, as clearly as Gertrude could bear to tell him, to go.

He thought, I shall never now be as I once was, simply happy, like a dog. I never really believed she would endure, he thought. And he believed two incompatible things, that Gertrude had loved him wholly and perfectly, and that she had not loved him enough.

Lying naked in Daisy's arms in a warmth of sweat upon which the cool airs played from the evening window Tim said to himself, if we could die now we could be conveyed to hell just as we are, packaged and ready. Oh how I wish we could die now.

'What are you thinking, Blue Eyes?'

'About death and hell.'

'You're a merry fellow.'

'You remember about Pappagena and Pappageno?'

'Yes.'

'I think we've had our ordeal.'

'Sez you. You'll be off again at the next flicker of skirt. Gertie just got you started.'

'You've been very kind, very sweet.'

'Ha ha. I'm just so fed up with men I don't care.'

'I'm hungry.'

'Me too.'

'Let's go to the Prince of Denmark.'

'Yes, let's. The old Prince is lovely on a summer evening like this.'

FIVE

It was done. Gertrude McCluskie, who had become Gertrude Openshaw was now Gertrude Reede. Tim and his wife stared at each other in amazement, dismay, joy, embarrassment, terror. The marriage took place at a registry office. The witnesses were Anne, Gerald, the Count, Mrs Mount, Janet and Stanley, and Moses Greenberg. They asked Manfred, but he had to be in Brussels on business.

The marriage was in July. It was now early August. The resolution taken by Tim and Gertrude to make an end of their love had proved a weak one. As they a hundred times said later, they came together again because they could not keep away from each other, could not do without each other. The illness was too extreme, the affinity too deep, the need too violent, the destiny too relentless: they employed many such words smiling at each other and holding hands. Tim had only managed to depart on that night, and Gertrude to tolerate, to survive his departure, because a secret voice in each of them said: this is not the end. The parting was a drama which they 'had' to enact. It was a necessary strategy of the Eros who held them in bond and to which they knew in secret from themselves that they had to be true. They had to *prove* how essential each one was to the other, had to try to do without and to find it impossible. It was an ordeal, they said, through which they had passed with flying colours, and the idea of banners held aloft appealed here to both of them. Tim drew for her many pictures of himself and Gertrude meeting each other with flags as upon a battlefield, or dancing together among the blue flowers.

The operation had of course taken some time. Neither of them could resist behaving like a lovelorn swain. Tim walked along Ebury Street late at night and looked up at the lighted windows. He did not intend to call or even to meet Gertrude by accident. He just had to torment his pained heart in this way. He had said heroically that he would 'do it', he would perform the act of departure so as to take the moral burden of it away from her. Later he terribly regretted this and saw his rash action as a sort of inexplicable conceited initiative. If only he had waited everything would have been quite different on the next day. Gertrude was only testing him, prompting him to tell her firmly that everything was perfectly all right. He ought to have taken charge of her faith and her hope. Gertrude too thought, why did I say all those things, I didn't even think them, it was a sort of mechanical tirade. I drove him away and now I've lost him and the light and joy of life, an innocent good happiness which I might have achieved, has gone away with him forever. And she said in her heart to Guy, you told me to be happy, but you see I can't be. And this thought was sometimes a sort of consolation.

Anne did not come back to the flat, though they met there and Gertrude told Anne that Tim had gone and it was over. They did not discuss the matter. Though Gertrude begged her to return, Anne stayed on in her hotel. She was negotiating for a little two-room flat in St John's Wood. Moses Greenberg dealt with the contract. Gertrude inspected the flat. She saw Anne each day. They discussed furniture, curtains. Their friendship was in a sort of 'air pocket' which they knew would soon pass. The Count was another matter. Gertrude had, as she had intended to, seen him on the day after Tim's flight. She had rung him up at the office and they had lunch together. The Count knew from her voice what had happened. And when they were together it was plain to Gertrude that the Count must have known about Tim. And the Count knew that she knew of this knowledge: of course neither of them mentioned Tim's name, and the only cloud in the Count's smiling eyes was (Gertrude guessed) the shadow of a guilt he felt for not having accepted her precious invitation. He blamed himself for having acted less than perfectly, for not having done what a Polish gentleman ought to have done: to have obeyed his lady's call, even though it be to view his rival. The Count, as it turned out, had ample chances later on to display his qualities as a Polish gentleman, but at this stage neither he nor Gertrude knew what a reversal the future held. Gertrude felt a little glad that she could so easily make him be happy. They went to a small Italian restaurant off Wardour Street, drank a good deal (neither could eat much) and talked about politics, Poland, London, their childhoods, the Count's work, Gerald's theories,

Anne's flat. The Count told Gertrude the story of his brother's death in the war. He had never told this as a story to anybody. It was the first time he had been alone with Gertrude, other than briefly, since Guy died. It was indeed the first time that they had talked to each other for so long, so easily and openly and with so frank a warmth of affection. The Count went back late to the office in a daze of joy.

However Gertrude's feeling of return to the natural world of her dear friends did not last her long. Tim had sown within her some special seed of discontent. She could not be as she once was. Tim had opened a vista of a kind of pleasure, a vista of *youth*, which was new to her. He had been a wonderful *foreigner* in her life. And passion tormented her, she could not have expected or imagined such a violent revival of physical passion. She did the sensible things which she had planned, she restored her existence to its old rational pattern. She invited *les cousins et les tantes* and they seemed as usual, throning her in their esteem, loving, merry, unsurprised and blessedly familiar. Yet the things which she had told herself she so much needed were not enough for her and soon seemed empty. She had felt unable to go on without the approval of the Count and Anne. The Count's approval, now that she had it back, seemed less than totally essential. And about Anne she had, especially after Anne had refused to return to the flat, larger views. She and Anne would always be riding together in that indestructible chariot. Only since it was so indestructible there was perhaps no need to let it run over her dreams. The fact was that she still wanted, and went on wanting, that slim young blue-eyed red-head, and nothing else in the world would do.

The pattern of Tim's adventures was similar but different. He stayed two days with Daisy, during which time they were continually drunk. Then they began to quarrel as usual. Daisy's room became intolerable to him. It was desperately hot and stuffy (the hot weather was continuing) and smelt of sweaty clothes and cheap wine. Tim had not the heart to clean or tidy. Finally he left saying he was returning to the studio (which he didn't have to leave after all) and that he would see Daisy in the Prince of Denmark. He did not go back to the studio. He went to stay in a cheap hotel in Praed Street (not very far in fact from where Anne was staying, only they never met). Staying in the hotel, he had money for once, gave him a crazy detached anonymous feeling which seemed at first to soothe his grief. But soon the idleness and homelessness began to make him feel blackly miserable and mad. He wandered about London and drank in pubs. In the evenings he went to the Prince of Denmark and sat with Daisy and got drunk. Daisy made jokes and cursed the world. She seemed to be talking to herself, uninterested in whether Tim was there or not. Jimmy Roland joined them on two evenings. On the second evening Tim's old flame Nancy, Jimmy's sister, turned up and was insulted by Daisy. Then Jimmy disappeared to Paris on art business taking Nancy and Piglet with him.

Both Tim and Gertrude were now looking for each other, only neither could quite acknowledge that this was what was happening. Gertrude was almost ready to say to herself: I have tested the craving and it has survived so why not have what I want? As they both kept returning compulsively to places where they had been together they were likely to meet. Once they visited the same pub in Chiswick on the same day but at different times. Chance could have ordained a prolonged separation however. What they would *then* have done, they often discussed later, always concluding that they would soon have broken down and communicated by the letters or telephone calls or abject knockings on doors which they were always rehearsing in their minds. As it was their search did not last unendurably long. They met finally in the British Museum, when Tim found Gertrude one morning sitting on a seat near the Rosetta Stone.

The joy of that meeting was, for both a final proof. In a second all the black misery, the anxiety, the fear vanished as at a celestial trumpet call. The sad old world was folded up, a golden heaven unrolled spotty with suns and stars. There was no need of words. They took each other's hands, unaware of people passing, and were indeed perhaps invisible in the curious and majestic darkness which pervades this part of the museum and perhaps emanates from the Egyptian antiquities. They caressed each other's hands and wrists, and looked into each other's eyes.

Gertrude's final difficulty, as she put it to herself, had now nothing to do with Anne or the Count or with what would be thought by *les cousins et les tantes*. It had to do with Guy. She found that her relation with Guy so far from having ceased or been frozen or consigned to memory was alive and changing. Her feelings now about the trio Tim, Guy and herself, were quite different from what they had been in France and different from what they had been on her return to Ebury Street and different again from what they had been when she told Tim that it was all 'impossible'. On the last occasion she had felt quite simply accused by Guy's bitter shade. Guy himself had said, though he had said it to comfort her, that 'what he would have wished her to do' would still make sense after he was dead. He had said he wanted her to be happy, and had spoken of marriage and the Count. Gertrude had worked it out that whether or not Guy had commended the Count so as to protect her from Manfred, and whether or not he had really wanted her to marry the Count or to marry at all, he certainly 'would not have wished' her to marry Tim! This thought was not a direct cause of her rejection of Tim, it appeared rather as a strong spontaneous element in the state of mind which pictured Tim as 'impossible', and was part of her sense that she was falling in love with Guy all over again.

Now with Tim lost and found Gertrude had changed again. She felt that she had reached a position whence she could judge the previous changes and understand them. Her strange love for absent Guy had not diminished, it had even perhaps increased, but it was purged of much of the painful anxiety and bitter speculation which had made it earlier almost like a hostile calculating love, a love relation in which he was angry and she resentfully compliant. There had been, she felt, a kind of madness in that relation, it was almost like a haunting. Now she felt more gently and naturally separated from Guy, more able to look towards him quietly and tenderly; and she rested in the certainty that her connection with him would remain alive and subject to change as all living things are, as long as she herself existed. It was not that she felt that she now carried Guy in her or with her or 'lived' him. They were separated. But it was now as if she said to him across that space: I love you, put up with me, it's just me, I have to go on living and making decisions without you, and I expect I shall do all sorts of things which you think are stupid, but that's how it is.

And Gertrude felt the pain of her loss now as a purer cleaner pain, like a cleaned and disinfected wound.

After a while she was even able to talk about some of this to Tim, and about how her mourning had to go on inside her marriage. She was not worried any more about the 'time scheme', or about what in this connection 'the others' would think. Guy had died in December, Gertrude was to wed in July, with mirth in funeral and dirge in marriage. Well, so be it. Guy had often said to her that time was unreal. The question of time-lapse now seemed to her superficial and mechanical, something subject to her own judgement upon her own history, her own sense of what was proper and what was real. She no longer anxiously reckoned the weeks and the months of her widowhood. She would decide what to do about Tim in the light of her relation with Guy, and about Guy in the light of her relation with Tim. Love itself would here be her light. These calm thoughts helped Gertrude not to worry too obsessively (though she did worry) about what Guy's family thought of her or about how madly their tongues were wagging. They were of course, to her, infinitely polite, considerate, intelligent, amiable. She knew that among themselves they would be talking of nothing else, and she imagined vaguely, not in detail the degrees of shock, amazement, malice and moral disapproval which would spice these conversations which they would all enjoy so much. Positive encouragement had come to her from Gerald (who seemed genuinely fond of Tim), Moses Greenberg (who adopted a fatherly role) and rather surprisingly from Mrs Mount who went out of her way to be pleasant. Manfred of course behaved perfectly, but Gertrude had, as usual, little idea of what he was thinking. (It appeared that his absence on the wedding day was unavoidable. There had been rather short notice of the event.) Gertrude was not, at present at any rate, too worried about them. Perhaps she had been a cause of scandal. But, in this quarter, her sense of duty did not torment and puzzle her.

Anne and the Count, those two 'noble souls' as Gertrude thought of them, were another matter. Tim and Gertrude had 'lain low' during the fairly brief interval between their reunion and the amazing announcement. They lived at Ebury Street, but without their previous obsession with secrecy. They said nothing, but anyone might have seen them together. Gertrude once more feigned to be 'probably' away, at least she said this to the Count and Anne (the others did not matter) without knowing whether they believed her, and a little hoping that they might not. It would perhaps be better, now, if they were to work it out for themselves. Just before she told 'the family' Gertrude wrote brief affectionate letters to them both telling them of her intention to marry. Of course they congratulated her, and the Count wrote a warm letter to Tim. Gertrude invited them to drinks with Moses, Manfred, Gerald, Victor and Mrs Mount, and they both came and the little party even achieved a plausible appearance of merriment. Tim seemed happy after the party, he said 'they've accepted us'. Gertrude was not so sure. She talked a little to Tim about the Count. Tim had been vaguely aware that the Count cared for Gertrude, but he had never known how much, and Gertrude did not now inform him. Anne's behaviour was impressive. As soon as Gertrude told Anne that she was definitely going to marry Tim, Anne expressed no more opposition and whole-heartedly set about being pleased with the situation. The Count could not be pleased, doubtless could not even try to be. He behaved well, but was, though in general very cordial (it was now a point of honour to accept her invitations), a little remote and aloof. Gertrude measured in detail these movements of detachment and retreat. Now that she was determined to marry Tim she did not feel quite the same anguish about losing the Count's good opinion which she had felt earlier when her liaison had seemed, even to her, like a messy doomed 'affair'. But she guessed how much he was suffering. There were rare moments when his eyes could not resist the quick flicker of pain. And she thought to herself, very sadly, well, I have lost the Count, I suppose. He will slowly recede and go away. He cannot do otherwise. I can't expect to have everything, can I.

During this period Tim gave himself over to a sort of orgy of pleasure. He entered a time of festival from which anxiety was to be banished. He did this the more conscientiously as he felt that his enthusiasm must carry Gertrude who had her own burdens of sadness. Not that he doubted, this time round, her whole-hearted assent to their love. But he knew, because she told him, of her thoughts about Guy, and, because he guessed, of her worries about Anne and the Count. As a part of the festivities, Tim attempted during this time to change his persona, to make himself look different, younger, more picturesque. He trimmed his hair carefully and washed it more often. He shaved his barley-field beard down to invisible pin-points, but developed curly side whiskers. He still had his 'caretaker's salary' to spend (he and Gertrude laughed about that) and dressed himself up like an artist in an opera with floppy coloured shirts and subtly contrasting cravats. He did his best at least to amuse Gertrude's friends. He played the painter heartily for their benefit, and hoped that, after the first shock, they found the act intelligible and reassuring.

Of course Tim could not really banish care. He thought about Daisy, though not obsessively. He thought about her at intervals for certain periods of time and then stopped thinking. He worked out certain things which would have to be done and which would be done, and then, for the moment, ceased to fret. He felt a deep sad tenderness about Daisy but no desire to see her. He felt that she was receding from him. In a certain positive way he was glad to have got away from her, it was something which, in a way, he had long wanted to do, but which without Gertrude's help he could not have done. He welcomed and cherished this thought. He made certain good resolutions, one of which was that he would tell Gertrude all about Daisy, but not yet. He wondered whether he ought not to tell her at once, but decided on reflection not to. The revelation would hurt her, and she was suffering at present enough pain on his behalf. Moreover to explain Daisy would not be easy, Gertrude might very well misunderstand. Supposing, through some silly impulse of frankness, he were now to lose Gertrude after having so miraculously found her again? To risk this would be a gross ingratitude to the gods. Tim did not exactly put it so to himself, but he really needed time to rethink his relation with Daisy and remove it to a position of comparative unimportance in his autobiography. If only he had not run back to Daisy after Gertrude's 'rejection', if only he had *then* had more faith in their love, this rewriting of his history would now be considerably easier, he would be much nearer to being 'in the clear'! He must wait. Later, in the midst of a fortified and perfected married love, he could tell this tale less painfully and more safely. And by then it really would be something that belonged to the far past.

With this settled in his mind, Tim planned the sad necessary steps of the severance. He had of course ceased to appear at the Prince of Denmark. He sent Daisy a short letter saying that he was again with Gertrude and would marry her. He had composed a longer letter with penitential paragraphs, but he tore this up. Daisy's apt gibes occurred to him as his own thoughts. There was no point in 'saying sorry'. The facts spoke clearly enough. It would be an insult to Daisy to surround them with the vaguely self-justifying emotional rubble of his mind. His mind was indeed full of rubble. He had a very long habit of loving Daisy, and among the shifting mental debris there was an odd idea; suppose he were to tell Gertrude about Daisy and say that he could not altogether give Daisy up but needed to continue to see her as a dear friend? Suppose he were to assume confidently that Gertrude would understand? He entertained this idea as a soothing compromise but of course recognized it as nonsense. It would shock Gertrude, and Daisy would spit upon it. He was, in the midst of his happiness, so complex and versatile is the human mind, thoroughly unhappy at times about Daisy. He did not expect her to reply to his letter, and she did not. Was she waiting for Gertrude to be finished and for Tim to return? Or had she finally consigned Tim to the devil? Should he write again, explain more fully? Every letter was a new bond. Yet he must, he felt, have *some* sign of dismissal from Daisy, some indication that she knew, that she had taken it all in. He could not bear her not to know. Suppose the first letter had gone astray? There were mad lodgers in Daisy's house who might steal letters. He really did need, for his peace of mind, her forgiveness, but for this he could not formally ask. Daisy's forgiveness in any case would have its characteristic expression. At last, and after he was married Tim sent a letter containing a stamped envelope addressed to the studio, with a blank card inside it. His letter said, *My dear, I am married. Pardon me and say goodbye*. The envelope came back. Daisy had written *Fuck off* on the card. This was his pardon and he was deeply grateful for it. He recalled Daisy's saying that without him she would pull herself together and *do* something. He hoped and half believed that this was true, and gradually he began to worry less about her.

'When you leave the studio where will you store your pictures? We could have them here—'

'No need, I can leave them at Jimmy Roland's place.'

'Isn't he the chap you share the studio with?'

'Yes, but he's got another place.'

Tim was painting at Ebury Street now. The studio was still 'dangerous', a moody Daisy might come there one day, though this was unlikely. He imagined Daisy breaking in and slashing his canvases. It was an exciting scene, but out of character. He did not actually want to part with the studio just yet. Moving the stuff would be a lot of trouble, and the reference to Jimmy Roland was an instinctive fiction. He decided to let the matter drift for a while.

Tim and Gertrude were sitting over a long lunch in the dining-room at Ebury Street. Guy had been a fast eater. Tim was a slow eater. Although they were both working, the festival atmosphere still prevailed. On some mornings Gertrude taught English to her Asian women. She had only just started to teach these women when Guy fell ill, and she felt she was still a beginner. Her pupils, often patently intelligent, come of a resourceful and clever race, were diffident and timid. They would not come (with or without their husbands) to the flat and had not yet invited Gertrude to their homes. Lessons took place in a school room atmosphere at the community centre. The language barrier was paralysing. A little Urdu or Hindi would have helped, but Gertrude was no linguist. She took her pupils singly, and confronting those dark handsome thoughtful anxious women, dressed in the most beautiful clothes in the world, she sometimes felt that she herself was being transported far away. Sometimes, speechless, she reached across the table for a frail brown hand, and pupil and teacher communicated, almost with strange pleasant tears or else with helpless laughter. She tried to describe all this to Tim, but without meeting the women he could not understand.

Meanwhile in the mornings Tim worked at painting. He liked to be alone then, with the safety of Gertrude in his mind, but alone. That was necessary. He had taken over Anne's room as a studio, the light was good, and had transported there by taxi the larger and more picturesque elements of his craft together with some of his more presentable pictures. He had also brought a supply of his rubbish-tip wood for painting on, though he scarcely needed this since Gertrude had bought him a number of fine new expensive canvases: or he had bought them with Gertrude's money, or with his own money since their worldly goods were now mutually endowed. This would take a bit of getting used to, and he maintained his thrifty habits. He had not yet touched any of these beautiful white rectangles even with his thought. He had fiddled with some of the sketches made in France (not the drawings of the Great Face, those he left alone). He did two unsuccessful water colours of flowers at Gertrude's request; and on some days when she went out teachign, he went to the park and drew trees. They travelled a little way together on the Underground, they liked that. Tim had to admit that he could not yet really settle down to his work.

The afternoons were various. Sometimes Gertrude went back to her community centre to make arrangements or to attend meetings, and Tim returned to his new studio. He also liked cleaning and tidying and mending things. The excellent char, Mrs Parfitt, still came twice a week but Tim discovered plenty of tasks for himself. Sometimes after lunch he and Gertrude would go shopping together for food and household goods like a young ménage, they enjoyed buying mops and brushes and cake tins and tea towels and other items which were usually unnecessary as the flat was well equipped. They encouraged each other to buy clothes, but their expenditure was tacitly modest. Occasionally they invited people for evening drinks. More often they went out for London walks ending in pubs. They frequented the Ebury Arms. They had not yet invited anyone to dinner, their evenings together were too precious.

Gertrude and Tim constantly commented to each other on

how amazingly well they got along. Both of them had, though without imagining in detail, expected disagreements, blockages, periods of non-communication. But these painful episodes did not occur. There were all sorts of little unforeseen concessions which they had to make to each other, but love and good sense enabled them to make them promptly. A vast scheme of small quick adjustments was no doubt taking effect the whole time. They looked at each other with a kind of wide-eyed benevolent generosity which took in each other's deepest failings with a quick 'Oh!' followed by the ingenious accommodations of married love. Gertrude came to realize how far her life had depended upon Guy's absolute efficiency, his reliability, his meticulous omniscience, his rational grasp upon the world, his effortless power over builders, plumbers, waiters, taxmen, motor cars, people on telephones, people in offices, people in shops. When she mentioned her income tax problems to Tim he said smilingly that he knew nothing about tax, he had never paid any. Tim was meticulously tidy and could clean and cook and wash clothes, but he lacked the concept of paying bills, or even keeping them. He could not write a business letter or conduct an impersonal telephone conversation. She was also shocked at the way he seemed to be able to live without reading.

Tim on the other hand was amazed at how little Gertrude knew about painting and how little visual sense she possessed. She did not seem to know much about any art except literature. She professed to enjoy music but (rather to Tim's relief) did not suggest concert-going. Thus each of them felt, in a new way, a little superior to the other, while quickly transforming the superiority into a kind of protective tenderness. Gertrude saw that Tim was inefficient, inaccurate, even lazy. Tim realized that Gertrude was (unlike Guy) not a polymath, and, in spite of her swim in the crystal pool, not a goddess. But each continued to find the other utterly charming and quite sufficiently clever. Tim found in his wife the absolute security for which he had always craved. He perceived her virtue and rested upon it. She had rescued him from his demons and renewed his innocence.

Gertrude did gasp to herself sometimes to think that she had perfectly loved Guy, and now perfectly loved Tim, although the two men were so totally different. Sometimes she thought how *can* I be happy with someone so unlike Guy? She underwent in holy secrecy the pains and shocks of her mourning which continued their due ritual unaware of Tim. She had altered the flat as much as she could, but could not avoid seeing Tim's shaving tackle in the bathroom where Guy's had been; and there were many many 'frames' of her life where she still instinctively expected Guy and found Tim. She shed strange secret tears. She was even able in her inmost heart to grasp the idea that Tim was morally inferior to Guy. But her lively versatile love managed its new economy with self-regarding wisdom, and she found Tim not only adorable but very amusing. She often gazed at him, when he was intent on doing something (drawing, shaving, looking out of the window) and thought to herself: this absurd funny strange enchanting animal is *my* animal! She was aware of him as younger and of herself as travelling to join him in the land of his youth. She knew that she knew of death and he did not.

'When we get a new flat you'll have a better studio.' They talked of finding a new place, but although both of them wanted to neither felt it was urgent. It was as if they did not yet want any new project, even this one, to disturb the magical continuity of their days. Life was still a honeymoon. They had not gone away after the wedding. Simply being together was their holiday. 'You say the light's good in Anne's room. But it isn't big enough.'

Tim wished Gertrude would stop calling it 'Anne's room'. It was his studio now. Sometimes he still wondered how much, in the amalgam, he was marrying for security, for his art, so as to be able to spoil expensive canvases with experiments. Was there a grain of that in it all? He trusted his love enough to know that it didn't matter.

'The room is fine,' said Tim.

'Anne wants us to go for a drink at her new flat.'

'Oh of course she's in. Where is it, I forget?'

'Camden. She says it's cheap'

'When does she want us to go?'

'Six o'clock tomorrow.'

'We were going to do the Battersea walk to the Old Swan.'

'We can do that next day, there are lots of days.'

'May it be so! I keep thinking you'll die or I'll die.'

'We'll try not to. You know, I meant to tell you something—

286

I feel I must tell you everything like in transference.'

'What? Not anything awful?'

'No, no, just odd. You know when—when we were just back from France and we got into that funny state—'

'You did!'

'Well, someone sent an anonymous letter to the Count saying we were having an affair.'

'Oh God,' said Tim. He flushed scarlet. 'Who?'

'I've no idea.'

'What did the Count say, what did he think—?'

'I haven't discussed it with the Count,' said Gertrude. She was blushing too.

'But how did you know?'

'The Count told Anne. Anne then asked me.'

'Asked if we were having an affair?'

'Yes.'

'And you told her we were?'

'Yes.'

'Christ—'

'But she didn't tell me then about the letter, she pretended she'd guessed.'

'Then she told you later?'

'She told me when I saw her yesterday. I meant to tell you but I simply forgot—which shows how little it worried me!'

'It worries me,' said Tim. 'Did she show you the letter, was it typed?'

'I don't know, I didn't see it.'

'Has she told the Count she'd told you?'

'I didn't ask, it all just came up as I was leaving.'

'But *who* could have written him a letter?'

'I simply can't imagine. Could Manfred have guessed? Surely not. Anyway Manfred would *never* write an anonymous letter. You didn't ever tell anyone, well of course you didn't, or sort of let anyone perhaps guess?'

'No.' Could Daisy write an anonymous letter, Tim wondered. If so she was capable of a degree of vindictiveness which he would never have expected. Could she threaten his love, his happiness?

287

Jesus Christ came to Anne Cavidge in a vision. The visitation
began in a dream, but then gained a very undreamlike reality.
And, later, Anne remembered it as one remembers real events,
not as one remembers dreams.

The dream part opened in a beautiful garden, a rose garden
with the roses in flower and the sun shining. It was not a place
that Anne knew. The garden was upon a slight slope and above
where Anne was standing, upon a higher level, there was a
stone balustrade with a criss-cross diamond pattern. Some way
beyond this there was a large stone-built eighteenth-century
house. Anne began to walk slowly up the slope in the direction
of the house. She felt lazy and happy. She mounted some stone
steps to the level of the balustrade. Here the ground was flat
and a close-clipped lawn stretched away toward a gravelled
terrace which surrounded the house. To her right, a large
copper beech tree threw its shadow upon the grass. To her
left, where she did not look, she was aware of a tennis court
enclosed by wires, and beyond it some flowering bushes and a
wall with a door in it, perhaps surrounding a walled garden.
There were two eighteenth-century-style statues upon pedestals,
one at either end of the terrace.

As Anne walked on across the lawn she became aware of
something very strange. The two statues, which represented
angels, appeared to be gaudily painted. Then she realized that
the statues were alive, they really *were* angels, very tall angels
with splendid huge golden-feathered wings and wearing
elaborate and brilliantly coloured silk robes. When Anne saw
the tall angels she began to feel frightened. She wanted to run
away, but she knew that she must continue to advance, and she
went on across the grass, but more slowly and cautiously as if
she were stalking some rare and interesting birds; and the
angels did behave as if they were wild birds, for, being aware of
Anne's approach, they quite quietly came down from their
pedestals and began to walk away along the gravel of the
terrace, past the windows, in the direction of the corner of the
façade. When she saw them moving away, Anne was filled with

a terrible anguish, as if the most wonderful thing she had ever possessed was being taken from her. She did not run, but she hastened now toward the terrace and mounted the step which separated it from the lawn. By now the angels, walking with dignity, had reached the corner of the house and were about to round it. Anne called after them, 'Tell me, is there a God?' One of the angels, turning back to her rather casually, said 'Yes.' Then the two great bird-like figures vanished round the corner. Anne now ran after them along the terrace and reached the corner where she could see another similar terrace stretching along the side of the house. The scene was empty. The two angels had disappeared. Filled with a kind of elated sadness Anne began to walk slowly on. When she was about half way along the terrace whence the angels had vanished she heard a sound behind her. She could distinctly hear the crunch of footsteps upon the gravel. She *knew* that the person following her was Jesus Christ. She did not turn, but fell straight forward onto her face in a dead faint.

It was at this point that her dream changed into a veridical vision. She woke up in her little bedroom in her new flat and at once remembered the dream. She sat up quickly in bed, filled with a vivid sense of the beauty of the dream and its significance. Then again she became aware, she *knew*, that there was somebody in the next room, somebody standing in her kitchen in the bright light of the early summer morning. And she knew that that person was Jesus.

Anne got out of bed and put on her dressing-gown and slippers. She felt extreme fear. Then she quietly opened the bedroom door. The kitchen was opposite, across a little landing, and the door was ajar. She pushed open the kitchen door.

Jesus was standing beside the table, with one hand resting upon it. Not daring yet to raise her eyes to his face, she saw his hand pressed upon the scrubbed grainy wood of the table. His hand was pale and bony, the skin rough as if chapped. Then he said her name, 'Anne', and she raised her eyes and simultaneously fell on her knees on the floor.

Jesus was leaning with one hand upon the table and gazing down at her. He had a strangely elongated head and a strange pallor, the pallor of something which had been long deprived of light, a shadowed leaf, a deep sea fish, a grub inside a fruit. He was beardless, with wispy blond hair, not very long, and he was thin and of medium height, dressed in shapeless yellowish-white trousers and a shirt of similar colour, open at the neck, with rolled-up sleeves. He wore plimsolls upon his feet with no socks. Though the shape of the head seemed almost grotesque, the face was beautiful. It did not resemble any painting which Anne had ever seen. The mouth was thoughtful and tender and the eyes large and remarkably luminous. Anne did not notice all these details at once, but she remembered them well later, except that she could not recall the colour of the eyes. It was a brilliant darkish colour, a sort of blackish or reddish blue she felt inclined to call it later.

Anne felt very afraid and yet filled with a thrilling passionate joyful feeling that passed through her like an electric current while making her absolutely still.

He said again, 'Anne—'

'Sir—' Anne had never used this mode of address before in her life. Why do I not call him 'Lord', she wondered, or 'Master'?

'Who am I?'

'You are the Christ,' she said, 'The Son of the living God.'

He said, 'Get up.'

Anne rose and moved slightly forward, facing him across the table. As soon as her knees lost contact with the floor she began to feel different, more vulnerable and terrified. She trembled. She looked into his face, and whereas before she had seemed to see only the luminous eyes and the tender mouth, she now saw his expression which was quizzical, almost humorous.

'How do you know?'

Anne said, 'Who else could you be, Sir? Unless you are the Other One.' This seemed a terribly rude thing to say—she lowered her eyes, unable to sustain his gaze. She looked at the white hand which rested on the table. It was unscarred.

She said, 'Your wounds, Sir—'

'I have no wounds. My wounds are imaginary.'

'But indeed you were wounded, Sir,' said Anne, raising her eyes. 'Indeed you were. They pierced your hands and feet with nails and your side with a spear. They shot your kneecaps off,

290

they drove a red-hot needle into your liver, they blinded you with ammonia and gave you electric shocks—'

'You are getting mixed up, Anne. And they did not pierce my hands. They drove the nails through my wrists. The flesh of the hands would have torn away.'

Anne looked at the wrist. The wrist was unscarred too.

'You do not need to see my wounds. If there were wounds they have healed. If there was suffering it has gone and is nothing.'

'But your pain—is not that—'

'The point? No, though it has proved so interesting to you all!'

'But then—what was it—' said Anne. She could not find words for the terrible pressure of her questions, she thought, I have such a chance to ask but I cannot find the right thing to say.

He went on, 'Of course the way to Jerusalem was not a state progress. Only the women didn't run, they loved me for myself. The rest were ashamed, they felt degraded and let down. Yes, pain is a scandal and a task, but it is a shadow that passes! Death is a teaching. Indeed it is one of my names.'

'But there is pain,' said Anne. 'Animals suffer—' She was not sure why she said this.

'I had a pleasant life until the end. The Sea of Galilee is one of the most beautiful places in the world. Have you been there?'

'Thou knowest, Sir,' said Anne, 'that I have not visited Israel.'

He smiled. 'Do not fear, I know who you are, all that concerns your salvation I know.' He removed his hand from the table and tossed back some strands of the wispy straight blond hair. His hair was just long enough to touch the collar of his open shirt. He now put both hands behind his back and stared at Anne with his dark brilliant eyes, his mouth whimsical as if he was teasing her.

'So there is salvation?' said Anne.

'Oh yes,' but he said it almost carelessly.

'Sir, what shall I do to be saved?' Anne had now put her hands on the table and was leaning forward. She had turned up the cuffs of her blue dressing-gown.

He looked at her for a moment. 'You must do it all yourself, you know.'

'What do you *mean?*' said Anne. She said it almost crossly. Then she said, 'I can't.' Then she said, 'Oh my dear, my dear.' She thought he is here, *he* is here; and she was suddenly shaken with a great shock of love so that she quaked and had to hold onto the edge of the table to stop herself from falling. She was filled with urgent desire almost as if she would seduce him. She wanted to touch him. She said, 'Do not go away from me, how could I live without you now that you have come. If you are going to leave me, let me die now.'

'Come, come, Anne, you will die soon enough.' He spoke briskly. 'As for salvation, anything you can think about it is as imaginary as my wounds. I am not a magician, I never was. You know what to do. Do right, refrain from wrong.'

Anne gave a groan and closed her eyes for a moment.

'What am I holding in my hand?'

Anne opened her eyes and saw that he was holding his right hand, closed, up against his shirt.

She thought, then said with confidence, 'A hazel nut, Sir.'

'No.' He opened his hand and put something down on the table. Anne saw that it was an elliptical grey stone, a little chipped at the end. It was, or was very like, one of the seaside stones which had so much appalled her upon the beach in Cumbria. She had brought one or two back with her as souvenirs, but she could not make out whether this stone was one of the ones she had brought or not.

Still holding hard to the edge of the table, Anne stared at the stone. Then she said slowly, 'Is it so small?'

'Yes, Anne.'

'Everything that is, so little—'

'Yes.'

'But, sir— how can it not perish, how can it be? How can *I* not perish, how can I be, if all this—'

'Ah, my dear child, you want some wonderful answer, don't you.'

Yes, thought Anne, I do.

'Have you not been shown enough?'

'No, no, I want more,' said Anne, 'more, more. Tell me— what are you—where are you—'

'Where do I live? I live nowhere. Have you not heard it said that birds have nests and foxes have holes but I have no home?'

'Oh Sir, you have a home!' said Anne.

'You mean—'

'Love is my meaning,' said Anne.

He laughed. 'You are witty, my child. *You* have given the wonderful answer. Is *that* not enough?'

'No, not without you,' she said, 'not without *you*.'

'You are spoiling your gift already.'

'But what am I to believe,' said Anne, 'you are so real, you are here, you are the most real, most undoubtable of all things — you are the *proof*, there is no other.'

'I prove nothing, Anne. You have answered your own question. What more do you want? A miracle?'

'*Yes*,' she said.

'You must be the miracle-worker, little one. You must be the proof. The work is yours.'

'No, no,' she said fiercely, leaning forward and staring at the long pale elongated head and the eyes, full of a bright darkness, which now looked grave, almost sad. 'It is *I* who need *you*. Oh give me words. I am deep in sin, I live and breathe the horror of it. Help me. I want to be made good.'

'Oh, I'm afraid that's impossible,' he said, looking at her sadly.

'No, no, please understand, please — I mean — I want — I want to be made clean like you promised, I want to be made innocent, I want to be washed whiter than snow—'

'Go then,' he said, 'and wash.' He pointed toward the sink.

Anne could hardly walk. She moved, holding onto the table, then onto a chair. She turned the tap on and found the soap. The sun had risen and was now shining brightly into the room. She began to wash her hands under the tap. She looked at her hands. Then she dropped the soap and turned the tap off. She could not find the towel because her eyes were blinded with tears. She said, 'It's — no good — it — won't work—'

'All right, why are you surprised? Don't cry. Are you really so sentimental? Art thou well paid that ever suffered I passion for thee? If I could have suffered more, I would have suffered more.'

'Don't, *don't*—' cried Anne, and her eyes were all tears, blurring her sight. 'I can't bear it, I can't *bear* it!' She reached out her dripping hands towards him.

He said gently, 'Love me if you must, my dear, but don't touch me.'

Anne thought, is he real, is this real flesh? Oh I love him so much, I must touch him, I must kneel and embrace his knees, lie and kiss his feet. But she did not kneel. She took a staggering step forward and tried to touch his arm with her right hand. He moved back and one of her fingers just brushed the rolled-up sleeve of his shirt, she felt the texture of the rough material. Then she felt a searing pain in her hand and her eyes closed and she fell to her knees and then flat to the ground in a sudden faint.

Anne woke up in her bed. She recalled the scene in the kitchen and how, when she had become conscious again, she had found the room empty, and how, weak with exhaustion and still giddy, she had come back to her bed and instantly fallen asleep. She leapt quickly out of bed. She was still wearing her blue dressing-gown with the cuffs turned back. She went into the kitchen, but of course there was no one there. She dried her hands on the towel and then thought, my hands are still damp, so he cannot have been long gone. She sat down heavily on a chair beside the table. Then she saw upon the table the elliptical grey stone with the chipped end which he had put there to show her. She picked it up. Was this one of her stones, or another one? She was not sure. She turned it over. It was just an ordinary grey stone, and she put it down again. Then she noticed that one of the fingers of her right hand was raw, the skin abrased, as if it had been burnt. She gazed at it. Then she began to cry and cry as if her heart would break.

'How is your toothache?' said the Count.

294

'Oh, better,' said Anne, 'I keep taking aspirins. I've got an appointment with Mr Orpen.'

'You've hurt your hand.'

'It's nothing, I burnt it.'

'Oh Anne, Anne—' The Count was thinking of his own pain.

It was seven o'clock in the evening and they were drinking sherry in Anne's little sitting-room. The sun, blazing through the window made the room seem dusty and cramped and gaunt. The kitchen received the morning sun, the sitting-room the evening sun.

Anne's flat was very small, the whole area of it was no larger than the drawing-room at Ebury Street. It consisted of the kitchen and bathroom, the sitting-room and Anne's bedroom which was almost a cupboard. The scanty furniture was Gertrude's, which she had got out of store for Anne. There were trees outside the window. The early morning birds reminded Anne of plainsong.

The Count was sitting hunched on a tiny sofa, his long legs bent, his knees sticking up towards his chin. He had asked Anne's permission to take his jacket off. His immaculate office shirt, white with a thin blue stripe, was tucked neatly into the belt at his narrow waist and a skinny dark blue tie hung from his tightly buttoned collar. His colourless blond hair flopped in a heavy curve over his brow and he blinked helplessly into the sunlight. He was perspiring and plucked now and then nervously at his shirt. Anne wondered if she should tell him to take his tie off, or whether this would distress him.

'Are you all right, Peter? Is the sun bothering you? Shall I pull the curtain?'

'No, no, I'm fine, thank you, thank you.'

Anne was sitting on an upright chair on the other side of the tiny fireplace where a gas fire had been fitted in front of a black cast iron grate. On the mantelpiece above there was a blue and gold Worcester cup, a present from Gertrude.

It was two days since Anne's Visitation, and she was living her ordinary life again; except that her ordinary life was so extraordinary. She had thought to herself, *he* never mentioned *this*; I suppose because he thinks its irrelevant, like his not remembering I had never seen the Sea of Galilee. Sometimes she felt that she was going mad.

Something terrible had happened to Anne. It had happened some time ago and it was going on happening. She had fallen terribly terribly in love with the Count. Of course she had told no one of this dreadful love.

Sitting alone, walking alone, for she shunned company and was often by herself, she had with meticulous care recalled and examined every minute, every moment, which she had spent in Peter's company since she had first met him (introduced by Manfred) at an evening gathering at Ebury Street just after her arrival there. She had thought him tall and strange, oddly foreign. But he was invisible to her. Her mind had been filled with Gertrude's sorrow. The first time, she thought, that she had really *seen* Peter was when, in the spring, on her return with Gertrude from Cumbria, she had noticed that he was in love with her friend, and had felt an instant pang of irritation. She had attributed this feeling to the old aboriginal possessive love which she felt for Gertrude and upon which the Count had seemed for a moment to be an intruder. However, reinterpreting the past, Anne now saw this little pang as the first symptom of the terrible illness, the first onset of the terrible pain, that now entirely occupied and composed her heart and darkened her heaven with a lurid cloud. Of course she did feel possessive about Gertrude. But what she had felt then had really been: and must she be loved by *him* as well?

Anne began to see the Count in a new way. True love gallops, it flies, it is the swiftest of all modes of thought, swifter even than hate and fear. Anne grasped, like someone at last grasping a vast theorem, Peter's absolute charm. She worshipped him in her thought from head to foot, she embraced him in the soft beating of her passionate wings. And all this time, in the outer world, she stirred no finger and blinked no eyelid. She watched him intently, she watched Gertrude intently too, and she crushed down the hope in her heart. But she could not now control her love. Her huge love demanded life, and to have it more abundantly. She measured *now* how far the concept of happiness had not been burnt out of her. (On the occasion when Peter rang her from Victoria to ask to see her about the anonymous letter she had been unable to check the idea that he was coming to say he loved her.) She longed to be with him, to feed upon his presence and his looks: the pallid floppy hair which she longed to touch, the thin clever melancholy mouth which she wished, so slowly and carefully, to kiss, the very pale blue eyes whose sadness she could now so well decipher, the handsome anxiety of his intent face, the way he would stand at attention and throw back his head. She thought, he has kept his innocence and is pure in heart. He was so tall, so thin, so gentle, so alien, and so lost. She felt she was discovering, almost *creating*, this obscure silent being whom everyone else had so stupidly overlooked. No one had ever so *concentrated* upon the Count; and Anne could not but think of him as responding unconsciously to that strong secret attention. Anne could not control her love, though she crushed down her hunger and her hope and clearly formed in her mind the prediction that sooner or later Peter would marry Gertrude.

The advent of Tim Reede had been a vast explosion like the explosion of a volcano which sets free a red-hot catastrophic outpouring. Anne had thought she loved Peter to all the limits of her being. But now permitted hope brought its message to every part and her love swelled and multiplied, celebrated and sang out in wild joy. Anne lay upon her bed, sometimes weeping, sometimes *laughing*, with the unexpectedness of the rescue. She laughed, not hysterically but with a deep quiet vibration which went on and on, as if she were laughing into the deep earth and making the tilting planet shudder. Of course she was outwardly sober. Still she did not move a finger or flicker an eyelid; and with a discipline which was a last rein upon her passion she told herself that Gertrude would soon tire of Tim, would never marry him. And, with a pain which brought her some consolation, she set about what she felt to be her absolute duty. She did her best to persuade Gertrude not to marry Tim. She did this partly because she believed what she said to Gertrude, that Tim was inferior, a flimsy unreliable thing, a man of straw. But also she felt the deep, perverse need to work against her own interests, to purify herself by exerting no influence (prompted by who could know what deep motive) to make her friend do what would, or would conceivably or perhaps or somehow or sometime, benefit Anne. Later, she could not have courted the Count if by the least hint or gesture she had encouraged Gertrude to turn from him. Also perhaps she too much feared the anguish of an open field and the horror *there* of defeat. When

Gertrude said she had given Tim up, Anne felt that she had worked but too well, and her laughter turned to tears and she enjoyed her perfected honour with an awful bitterness. Then came the joyful day, when she stood with Peter in the little dark room of the registry office and saw Gertrude Openshaw become, before her very eyes, Gertrude Reede. Anne's eyes shone, her face blazed with private joy, and she laughed in her heart her shuddering cosmic laugh. Then as Tim put the ring onto Gertrude's finger Anne turned to look at Peter. She wished she had not; his face was calm and benign, but she knew of his bitter pain and that he was totally and absolutely unaware of her.

With an open field the problem was different, the pain perhaps worse. Hope, gone mad, screamed like a tornado, tormented love to make love mad too. Anne tried to think of it as a *problem*, something which could at least be reached by reason, measured by reason's outstretched touch. In the depth of the problem lay the terrible fact that Peter still saw her as a nun. 'Once a nun always a nun.' He had intuited her status as 'anchoress in the world'; and he took her now evident concern for him as natural in one so selfless. She was for him, as Gertrude had said, 'a phenomenon', into which there entered perhaps some Polish romanticism about the Roman Catholic Church. Everyone will always see me as a failed nun, thought Anne, Gertrude's many speculations about Anne's future had not included the idea of marriage. Peter was consoled by the invisible religious 'habit' which Anne still wore. Anne had for him a priestly function which she could not prevent herself from constantly fulfilling, being for him just as he wanted her, although this instinctive service seemed now to estrange and separate her more and more from the Peter whom she loved and wanted. He saw her as a holy woman, innocent, calm, untouchable, and chaste. At times Anne longed to destroy this imprisoning image, to cast it down violently at his feet and trample on it. Gertrude had said it could take four seconds to change the world. Anne could do it in two, she had only to *cross* the space (three feet, as she talked to him now) which divided them and everything in the universe would be different. But suppose she were thus to *change* before his eyes and he were to recoil in horror, disgust—pity? This thought too travelled with her. And in a natural response to the gentle strong pressure of his need she went on playing her part. And she thought, of course it is not a part, it is not something false, I am that, I am what he sees, as well as that other thing, that mad desperate desiring crying thing. If I were a priest and if I had even a little faith left, I would let myself die of being torn apart rather than destroy the cool innocent icon which is perhaps a unique consolation to him in his present travail. No, I could not destroy it, I must endure. But she said to herself too, for a time, for the present.

Anne had felt it her duty to dissuade Gertrude from an unworthy marriage. Now she felt it her duty to observe Peter's sufferings, to understand their quality, their width and depth. And with a discreet tenderness whose exercise was anguish to her, had made it easy for him to find the relief of speaking. In fact the change from reserve to speech had come with an ease which she took to herself for comfort. While he told her at last of his distress, Anne kept her heart within a steel band. Although she could not prevent herself from speculating about the duration of his gloom, she tried not to keep looking for encouraging signs. She did not want the details of his pain to feed her hope. She wanted to be, for him, all servant. She must wait, she must learn the metaphysics of waiting. And she was prudent and she was afraid.

Not that Peter had ever raved or groaned. He spoke to her as he always did with a kind of calm quiet precision. As he spoke to her now, when he said, 'I don't think I can stand it—I shall have to go away.'

Oh let me come with you, my darling, she thought. Let us indeed *go* together. She said, 'Where to, Peter?'

'I thought of going to America.'

'What would you do there?'

'That's the question. I'd never get a job. What can I do? Nothing really. I'm trained as a British civil servant, an administrator. But I could never get a job outside this country. I can leave London though. I'm going to apply for a transfer to the north or the west. Don't mention it to anyone yet—'

'I won't.'

'I can't stay here like a sort of embarrassing death's head.'

'You could stay and—'

'Learn to smile?'

'Yes.'

'Anne, I can't.'

'Don't decide in a hurry.'

'I could retire early and live in Spain on my pension.'

'Don't be silly.'

'You must think I'm mad to go on being so stupidly in love, it's utterly improper. I know I've got to pull out of it somehow, but I can't without going away. Anne, I really must stop boring you with this selfish rubbish.'

'You don't bore me.'

'You're so kind, so calm, so sort of out of it all.'

She thought, Peter can do nothing now but meditate on his own emotions. And she thought, what else am I doing all the time? It is, as he says, utterly improper, but how does one stop? I mustn't let him talk to me like this, it makes him worse. And I mustn't have him here so close to me in this little room, it's torture. Suppose I were to kneel down now and take hold of his hand and weep? Oh how terribly I want to. But it would be a mistake, he's so obsessed, he's so full of *her*, he's half crazy. I must be patient, I must wait until he's recovered a bit, then I'll surprise him.

Anne said, 'Tim and Gertrude were here yesterday, they came round for a drink.'

Peter was silent for a moment, sobered. He said, 'Somehow I can't see them as a married couple. Tim's such a child.'

'We'll get used to seeing them as a married couple, we'd better try to anyway, there they are!'

'Did they seem — all right?'

'You mean did they seem happy? Yes, they seemed very happy.' This was perfectly true and Anne felt she had spent long enough sparing Peter's feelings.

'You are right,' he said, 'to make me look at it. I must look at it justly, honestly, with clear eyes, I must *know* it's happened and not try to imagine it away. I'm sorry. Everything about me now seems such — awfully bad form. I shock myself. I oughtn't to talk, I oughtn't to *think*. I must go away. I'll stay a while, then I'll very quietly clear out of London, no one will notice.'

'Oh stop being so sorry for yourself, Peter,' said Anne sharply, 'and as for your saying no one will notice, that's nonsense, I shall notice.'

'You're good to me,' he said, 'you're good *for* me. Yes, I am stupid. They say Poles want everything or nothing.'

'I suggest you try wanting something that you can have.'

'I'm so selfish and self-centred, I haven't even asked you about the teaching job you applied for.'

'I didn't get it. I'm too old and I haven't the right experience.'

'Oh I'm sorry—but you *will* get a job, don't worry.'

Anne had in fact applied for four school teaching jobs, to teach Latin, Greek, or French. One school did not even acknowledge her application, two others turned her down without interviewing her, and the fourth wanted her to teach German, which she could not. She read in the newspapers about increasing unemployment among teachers. Supposing she simply *could not* get a job?

'She's asked me round on Friday,' said the Count. He had forgotten Anne's plight already. 'I shall go of course. It isn't that I dislike Tim. I've always liked him. I just can't change my view of him. I feel he's too—It's all so *impossible*. Whatever would Guy think? I've known Gertrude such a long time, years and years—'

'Peter, I must watch the time—' Anne had invented a fictitious engagement so as to put a term upon her ration of Peter's company. She could not stand too long a time of talking about Gertrude, and she feared that she might break down. If Peter were *now* to realize her condition and, ever so kindly, to reject her she would run mad. She wanted to send him away and to think about him.

'Oh I'm sorry. Have I made you late? You're so kind to let me come. You are the only person I can talk to.'

He stood up and pulled on his jacket. Anne rose too and opened the door into the hall. She felt tugged at, as if large invisible forces were streaming past her, plucking at her flesh. Oh if she could only *break through* to the Count, what an absolute torrent of love might come to her from that deprived man! He looked down at her. 'I'll ring up, may I, Anne? Or will you ring me? I'm sorry to be like a sort of invalid needing a nurse.'

'I'll be away for a day or two. I'll ring you at the office.'

'Goodbye and thank you. I hope you'll find a job.' As he was going out of the door he said absently, 'I hope the fine weather will last.' He had picked up some English mannerisms.

Anne closed the door behind him and leaned against it. Tears spouted from her eyes. Then she went back into the little sitting-room and attacked the room. She overturned the chairs and hurled the cushions about. She kicked the rug and the wainscot and beat her hands against the wall. She kicked the gas fire and broke one of its panels. She threw her books violently onto the floor. She tugged at her dress and dragged off a button. She tore her hair and drummed on her brow. The only thing she did not attack was Gertrude's blue and gold Worcester cup. At last, sobbing and groaning, she stood still, and then gradually became silent, wet-eyed, wet-mouthed, staring blankly before her. At last she went into her bedroom and lay down.

What is happening to me, thought Anne, am I given over to devils? Is this the beginning of the darkness? Is this madness of being in love just a symptom of a breakdown which has been coming upon me for a long time? Was leaving the convent part of it too? They warned me that it would be worse, that I would collapse later. Is the dark night beginning? Am I collapsing now, will I need help, will I, *I*, have to confess that I can no longer manage my life?

She had decreed for herself a solitude, and the solitude was terrible, it made a vast dark space in which demons flitted to and fro. She refused all invitations. Mrs Mount had invited her, so had Moses Greenberg and Manfred and Janet Openshaw. Various well-intentioned religious persons, alerted perhaps by the Abbess, had tried to get in touch with her, including a learned Jesuit with whom she had corresponded when she was 'inside'. She wanted to be alone, to gorge herself upon the spectacle of Tim and Gertrude and Peter. And sometimes she thought, if it weren't for Tim and Peter, I could live so happily with Gertrude! And she thought, I am back in the hell of the personal, the very place I ran away from to God, back in the rotten criminal mess I got myself out of when I thought I would seek and find innocence and stay with it forever. I am mad, I am a danger to myself and others.

And what really happened on that morning in the kitchen,

302

she wondered. Was that amazing 'psychic experience' simply another symptom, a sign of some vast 'depression' or mental breakdown which was about to take charge of her life and perhaps deprive her of her sanity forever? Or had she actually been visited by the *Other One* in person? She felt herself surrounded by irresponsible spiritual forces. Several nights ago she had seen something very strange upon the stairs, when she had come home from one of her lonely night walks. There was no light upon Anne's flight of stairs. She saw it dimly, crouching in a corner, near to her door, something like a dwarf, entirely black. She had felt afraid to pass it. Then she had said to it, 'Strange creature, what are you doing here, you are frightening me, please go away in peace'; and she had gone quickly past it and into her flat in a sweat of terror. Later she had thought, perhaps it was a large dog, a sick dog, I ought to look to see. She had taken a torch and opened the door, but there was nothing there.

She had left the convent to come out into loneliness and a sort of renewed innocence and a sort of peace. Perhaps she could never have been empty and clean like an amoeba carried by the sea. But she had thought of her new life and her new solitude as a sort of simple austerity, and perhaps in her heart she had really seen herself as God's spy, a secret anchoress hidden in the world. She had felt this in her rediscovery of Gertrude, she had felt it when she talked to Guy. Her life 'inside' had, after all, a continuity with her life 'outside'. Perhaps the God whom she had lost had spoilt her for the world, but she would live as she could in the world, as a silent invisible crippled serviceable being. What had happened to these brave thoughts which had been, she knew now that they were gone, such a splendid consolation? Had she not been warned of the snares of the world, and had she not fallen straight into one? The religious life involves the total transformation of the idea of hope. And she had thought that she could only love God. But now it seemed as if all the old fantasies and illusions were back as if they had never been away. Not silence now, but blaring cacophony filled her head, foul self-stuff filled her soul, frenzied self-will and terrible possessive energy. Only now the rage of it was worse because she was older. This was the pain of hell, envy, jealousy, resentment, anger, remorse, desire, the pain that leads to terrorism. She had thought, if I cannot have what I desire I shall die. Now, in more despair, she thought, if I cannot have what I desire I shall have to live on with some new unredeemable horror of being myself.

Was God playing a game with her? After all he had played games with Job. What game would it be here? Chess? Hide and seek? Cat and mouse? Anne could not believe in a game-playing God. She had wondered earlier whether belief in God would ever return, sweep over her one day like a great warm wet cloud. Now she felt more absolutely godless than she had ever felt in her life. Her good was her own, her evil was her own. Yet *he*, her early morning visitor, was he not something? Perhaps indeed it was he, with his luminous eyes and his enigmatic witty talk that had shaken her and shaken the last remnant of faith out of her soul. Had she understood? A little. Who was he? She felt that he had truly come from a distant place. And it came to her that he was real, that he was unique. She was an atom of the universe and he was *her own* Christ, the Christ that belonged only to her, laser-beamed to her alone from infinitely far away. At least she had seen him once; and now perhaps the grace of prayer would return to her. Would it return now, a new and different kind of prayer? Yet how can it, she thought, since I love not Christ but Peter?

Anne got up from the bed. There was no ease. She decided she would go out and walk. She walked so much now, especially at night, especially along the river. Late dusky summer evening filled the little flat with dusty floating shadows. She turned the lights on. She went into the sitting-room. She looked at it with amazement. Chairs, lamps were overturned, books and cushions strewed the floor. She thought, did I do that, I, calm rational Anne Cavidge? The effect of the aspirin had worn off and her toothache had come back. She began slowly to pick up the debris. She found herself holding a stone. It was the chipped grey stone which *he* had given her and which, she remembered now, she had laid on top of some books: the stone in which he had shown her the cosmos, all that exists, and how small it is. She held it against her torn dress. Her tooth was aching, her burnt finger was hurting. She began to cry again quietly. She had cried so much in these last days. Yet she had left the convent almost without tears, left even forever that most beloved one. 'Goodbye,' Anne had said, and she 'God bless you,' passing in a garden, on an evening in autumn, not yet a year ago.

'Well, I think they're ideally suited!'
'Veronica!'
'Yes, I do,' said Mrs Mount.

It was drinks night at Manfred's. This ceremony had succeeded to the old Ebury Street gatherings, which now seemed to everyone present to belong to the remote past. Of course Tim and Gertrude were invited, but so far had not turned up.

'It's a foolish marriage,' said Janet Openshaw. 'Why couldn't she just have an affair?'

'Why didn't you stop her from marrying the fellow, Manfred?'

'My dear Ed, I can do nothing with Gertrude.'

'She was wearing her mourning like a nun's veil, and now this!'

Stanley Openshaw said, 'Gertrude couldn't have an affair, she's too serious and moral.'

'Is it serious and moral to get married to —'

'She loves him. That's the explanation.'

'Stanley! Guy died in December.'

'Or e'er those shoes were old. . . .'

'I mean, Gertrude couldn't do anything frivolous, so she must be deeply in love.'

'Just what I think,' said Mrs Mount. 'They both are.'

'I see Gertrude as a rather virginal person,' said Manfred, 'sort of chaste and solemn. I agree with Stanley.'

'Guy cornered her early in life.'

'Then it's a late case of wild oats.'

'Put it this way, Gertrude is the sort of woman who has got to love somebody.'

'Well, it won't last. He's such a lightweight. She'll regret it.'

'I don't think I agree,' said Gerald. 'I like Tim.'

'He's an adventurer, he's just after her money.'

'You're a cynic, Janet,' said Manfred. 'Romance is a complicated business.'

'Romance!'

'I think we'd better go,' said Stanley. 'I must anyway. I've got to get back to the House.'

'The House isn't sitting.'

'I am though! I've got to see a man about a tax.'

'Tim Reede has never had a thought for anybody but himself.'

'Which of us has any other thought, Janet dear? Mother love doesn't count.'

'I think they'll be happy,' said Gerald. 'I'm prepared to bet on it.'

'Gerald is starry-eyed.'

'What do you think, Moses?'

'I would view the situation with caution,' said Moses.

'Moses would view the situation with caution!'

'I think they're both in love and I think Tim is capable of loyalty.'

'My dear Veronica, no one's suggested he's a rotter,' said Ed Roper.

'I think he's capable of loyalty and seriousness.'

'She'll keep him up to the mark,' said Manfred.

'We'll keep them up to the mark. Gertrude needs us as a chorus.'

'Gertrude would hate to lose face. She'll do her damnedest to make it work.'

'Well, Gertrude is high-principled and he's timid, so their chances are good.'

'They'll keep each other up to the mark, up to different marks. They're so unlike, they'll expand each other's worlds. Tim has an instinct for happiness.'

'Moses says Tim has an instinct for happiness!'

'But really—Tim after Guy!'

'Happiness is not to be despised.'

'No one here despises it, I assure you.'

'Janet—'

'Yes, yes, Stanley.'

'Gertrude has an instinct for happiness too,' said Mrs Mount. 'She has an instinct for getting herself into the right place, like a cat. She was jolly lucky to get Guy. We all thought so at the time, well I did anyway, and then everyone got used to it. I think none of you see how clever she's been. You say "Tim after Guy". Precisely. Gertrude had an older man when she needed one, now she has a younger man when she needs one. She married her father, now she's married her son.'

'The result is certainly rejuvenating,' said Gerald. 'Gertrude looks much younger.'

'Janet will say "mutton dressed as lamb"!'

'Don't be beastly, Veronica. I just hope she'll be all right. If that man lets her down—'

'It's certainly a change,' said Moses Greenberg, 'and why not? She married the man who had everything. Now she's married the man who has nothing.'

'Materially or spiritually?'

'I see Veronica's point.'

'Janet—'

'Yes, yes, yes, Stanley, I'm coming.'

'You can stay, but I must take the car.'

'I'll come—you can drop me off. I've got to entertain Rosalind's string quartet.'

'How are the boys?'

'Ned's in California, William's digging in Greece.'

'Your children are so talented.'

'Gerald, I must have a talk with you about Ned. I'm so afraid he'll become religious. You must tell him mathematics is the road to freedom. Well, we must go.'

'Goodbye—'

'Oh hello, Victor, we're just going. Here's Victor.'

'Hello, doc. Goodbye Janet, goodbye Stanley.'

'Janet has just been deploring the married pair.'

'Which married pair?'

'Don't be silly, Victor.'

'Janet is fed up *à cause des chères têtes blondes*.'

'What on earth is Veronica talking about?'

'Naturally Janet's cross about the money.'

'The money?'

'The Openshaw children were to have Guy's money.'

'So Janet thought, anyway.'

'Nothing on paper.'

'Now Tim will gamble it all away, after all he's Irish.'

'Bound to.'

'He'll get rid of it in two years.'

'Gertrude won't let him.'

'That young fellow has more sense than you think.'

'Janet was so sure Gertrude would never marry again.'

'Janet thinks it's damned unsporting of Gertrude to marry.'

'Guy ought to have divided the spoil up a bit.'

'She might have married someone who could treble the cash.'

'Someone not a hundred yards from here could have done it, if I may say so.'

'Don't let's keep discussing Gertrude,' said Manfred.

'I agree,' said Mrs Mount. 'Let's wish them well and help them in any way we can.'

'No Count today.'

'No Count at all.'

'He's moping.'

'We wouldn't talk like this if the Count were here,' said Gerald.

'You're right,' said Manfred. 'Someone give Victor a drink, he's fainting.'

'Thanks, I've had an awful day. Hello, Ed, how's your you-know-what?'

'What's Ed's you-know-what?'

'Never you mind.'

'It's better, but please don't talk about it.'

'What's happened to the nun?' said Moses Greenberg. 'I can't remember her name.'

'Anne Cavidge, Gertrude's old school pal.'

'Anyone seen her? You ought to invite her, Manfred.'

'Oh I have, but she doesn't come.'

'Desperately shy, poor thing.'

'They never recover.'

'Well, I must be off.'

'Goodnight, Moses dear.'

'Moses is so censorious.'

'Do you see him as disappointed?'

'About Gertrude? No.'

'Perhaps he had his dreams, who knows.'

'Well, I *love* Moses,' said Mrs Mount.

'Any Balintoy news? Has Gerald been favoured with a letter?'

'Yes, he's in Hawaii.'

'Gerald's the favourite as usual.'

'Where on earth does he get the money?'

'No holiday for me this year.'

'I hope to get to Eastbourne,' said Mrs Mount.

'I suppose Manfred's jaunting off on business to Zurich as usual.'

'My business doesn't take me any farther than Fulham.'

'And Ed's off to Paris.'

'I *work* in Paris,' said Ed.

'There's no business like art business.'

'I suppose Gerald's going to a jolly conference in Sydney or Chicago or somewhere?'

'No, no farther than Jodrell Bank.'

'Made any discoveries lately, Gerald?'

'Well – yes –'

'Gerald's made a discovery, quiet everybody.'

Gerald, burly and sweating, put down his glass. 'I – I couldn't – explain it –'

'There's probably only two people on the planet who'd understand.'

'That's about it,' said Gerald.

'Gerald seems quite upset.'

'So am I. Is anything going to *happen*, Gerald?'

'Well – it could do –'

'Gerald says something's going to happen.'

'Does he mean a cosmic disaster?'

'This is a morbid conversation,' said Mrs Mount. 'Give me another drink, please.'

'Moira Lebowitz was here last week, she's become so beautiful.'

' "Women are trained everywhere to please, so any party is dull without them".'

'Who said that?'

'Guy, oddly enough.'

'I am here!'

'Sorry, Veronica. Have a cigarette?'

'Have a *what*?'

'Victor says he's going to make us all jog round the park every day.'

'Is he hell.'

'By the way, I've got a spare ticket for *Aida*. Anybody? Veronica?'

'I *hate Aida*.'

'You were talking about Gertrude and Tim,' said Victor. 'Any news?'

'I had a drink with them,' said Manfred.

'Anyone else there?'

'No.'

'It's funny,' said Victor, 'but Tim Reede doesn't seem to have any friends.'

'He doesn't want Gertrude to meet his boozy drinking companions, now he's joined the bourgeoisie.'

'After all *we* never met any of his friends.'

'We didn't try very hard to,' said Gerald.

'I asked Gertrude about that,' said Manfred. 'She said he mentioned a chap called Jimmy Roland. Gertrude hasn't met him—'

'Jimmy Roland?' said Ed Roper. 'I used to know a Jimmy Roland. He used to sell brass ornaments to pubs, things like that.'

'Talking of girls, anyone seen Sylvia Wicks?' said Victor.

'She seems to have sunk without trace. Manfred says he invited her.'

'She's probably invented an illness for herself, leukemia or something.'

'Oh shut up, Victor, I know you've had a bad day—'

'All right, Veronica, to return to Tim and Gertrude—'

'We can't—Manfred won't let us—he thinks it's in bad taste.'

'Oh I don't mind,' said Manfred. 'I just wanted an interval.'

'Well, I think that pair is unpredictable.'

'That's what makes them so endlessly interesting.'

'Anne — I have just heard something extraordinary — and terrible.'

So spoke the Count.

Two weeks had passed since the visit of Jesus Christ, two weeks in which Anne had been intensely busy in her mind. She had during this period seen the Count twice, once on the occasion of her attack on her sitting-room and once, uneventfully, a week later. She had also seen Tim and Gertrude once, and Gertrude alone once. She had seen no one else except for Mr Orpen the dentist. She had sat alone in her flat and walked immensely in the streets of London.

Mr Orpen had filled her tooth which ached no more. She had almost enjoyed talking to him. He was a cool man and, though a cousin, pointedly detached from the Ebury Street set. Anne intuited that he regarded them as snobbish. It emerged that he was a Roman Catholic. He knew of Anne's defection. He said, 'You're famous.' Anne did not pursue the matter. They discussed some Vatican politics of which Mr Orpen knew a surprising amount.

With Tim and Gertrude Anne had been merry, this was now quite easy. Tim exerted himself to please her and she found him quite amusing, though she was constantly irritated by the warm loving glances which Gertrude darted to and fro between her husband and her friend. Alone with Gertrude it was harder. Both of them knew that at some deep level all was well between them, but ordinary communication was destroyed in ways which neither could fully grasp. Gertrude half wanted and half did not want a heart to heart talk with Anne. Anne could see Gertrude, almost from minute to minute, calculating her moves. Gertrude was wondering whether it was too early, too soon after the recent shocks, to draw Anne close to her. She was estimating Anne's attitude to Tim and whether it was changing and how fast. Meanwhile a sort of wry formality reigned between them over which, so obvious was it, they could almost at times smile at each other.

Anne was wrapped in her terrible secret. She too was busy

calculating. Her mind had never felt more like a computer, a computer conscious of time limits and of possible deep mechanical faults. A number of things had become clear to her in the last fortnight. If her enterprise with Peter failed, Gertrude must never know. Part of the hell of the personal into which Anne had fallen back was this: that she felt that if Gertrude knew that Anne had loved Peter in vain, Anne's relation to Gertrude would become intolerable. Perhaps, for the sake of something, the intolerable could be tolerated, the unendurable endured, but Anne could not see that far. Nor could she see what Gertrude would feel or do should Anne's enterprise succeed; but about this she remained agnostic and worried less. That outcome was concealed in a blaze of light, and if Peter could love her all else would fall into place.

Meanwhile Anne watched Peter lynx-eyed, considering him in her soul, meditating upon him and bending her will upon him. She invited him, for the present, with a studied rarity. He did not invite her, but then he invited no one. She felt that, at their last meeting, she had discovered some slight change. He seemed a little less obsessed, a little less unhappy and she allowed herself to think in her dark secret heart, *he is recovering*. But she did not yet dare to stretch out towards him the hand that would change the world.

She meditated too, of course, upon her other visitor. She inclined now to think that she had received some kind of 'genuine' visitation. That is, she had not been dreaming or having some kind of chemically-induced hallucination. The source of the thing was a spiritual source. This however left much unclear. Anne was experienced enough (after all she had spent many years as a 'professional') to be willing to let the nature of her revelation declare itself slowly. The way it had lasted, even strengthened, in her mind and her heart made her feel a kind of faithful patience concerning its reality. This did not indeed exclude the possibility that her visitor was, or represented, the Other, or some ambiguous spiritual intermediary, some detached and wondering quasi-magical figment. Anne knew how terribly close, for human beings, all things spiritual lie to the deep fires of the demonic. Concerning this, she waited, she cultivated still the metaphysics of waiting. And she *noticed* in herself, like the slow growth of an innocent indifferent plant, a renewed impulse toward worship and toward some kind of prayer. What kind of prayer this new prayer would turn out to be she did not yet know. Sometimes, alone in her room, she knelt down, remaining quiet, wordless and blank. She was grateful to her visitor. And in some way, whatever his identity, she asked his pardon for the violent preoccupations and fierce desires which carried her continually away from a calm and humble attention. *That* must be settled *first*, she kept saying to herself and to anything which lay beyond. Sometimes she felt so unhappy that she wanted to die in some holocaust of doomed endeavour. Sometimes, when she felt quieter and calmer, she reflected that this calm was simply a disguised form of a wicked fantasy hope that pictured her safe at last in Peter's arms. There can be no compromise, no muddle. He will, when the time comes, hold me entirely, or else I will automatically be thrust away into empty space. Would there then be any home for her in that emptiness?

The Count had spent the interim in great misery. What Anne had interpreted as signs of recovery were better perhaps described as impulses of rational despair. He had applied for a transfer to the north, but had as yet told no one. He now wanted intensely to leave London, he pictured himself alone in some quite other scene, in some other little secretive flat with his books and his radio set. Although warmly invited by them, he kept clear of the 'Ebury Street mob' who now met at Manfred's flat. For the first time, he felt his nickname as a mockery, as a mark of genial contempt. It was time to go away and be among people who knew it not. In the north he would be 'Peter' from the start. He was, for them all here, a figure of fun. Any invitation offered by Gertrude he felt bound to accept. These invitations amounted to a drink with her and Tim every five days or so. The Count too could see Gertrude calculating, and he too was irritated, indeed maddened, by the way her affectionate gaze moved from him to Tim and back, and by the incoherent shy appeal which her looks expressed. Gertrude wanted him to do the impossible: to accept her marriage to Tim and to go on loving her all the same.

He struggled, or rather he did not struggle, he lived, with black demons of jealousy and resentment and remorse, with

313

sins which were new and alien to him. He would not have believed that he could be so bitter. His quiet cloistered love had been turned by a brief hope into a possessive rage. Endlessly he rehearsed it all in his mind to see what he had done wrong. If he had only tried harder, if he had only been more positive, more aggressive, put his love more on display, been less discreet, less highminded, less honourable. As it was the woman he loved had been taken by a simpler and less scrupulous man. The Count smiled blandly and chatted courteously with Tim and Gertrude, while a black veil covered his eyes. He had faith that the wicked bitterness would pass. But the pain, that would not pass.

He looked back upon the luncheon which he had had with Gertrude in the little Italian restaurant off Wardour Street on the day after Gertrude's resolve to wed had failed her. She did not tell the Count then that she had dismissed Tim, but he knew it and rejoiced. And, set free, she had come at once to him. That *tête-à-tête* was probably the happiest time in the Count's whole life, and, as he saw it now, his last happy time, the end of all his happiness.

It was evening, about seven o'clock. A warm thundery day had ended in a light silver rain which was now gently, steadily falling. Anne had closed the windows. She was writing an application for a job when Peter suddenly rang her bell. She had put her name down for 'supply teaching' and had received a notice of a temporary post to teach French at a school in Edmonton, not however to start until January. Anne could not interpret his evident agitation, but this time she did not imagine that it betokened a declaration of love.

'Something terrible? What, Peter? Oh what is it, what's the matter?'

He walked to the window and stood for a moment with his back to her, as if to compose himself. His hair was darkened by the rain and adhered in long dark streaks to the white collar of his shirt at the back. He had dropped his wet mackintosh on the floor in the hall. The stormy light in the room was dark yet vivid, and as he turned towards her his face had a kind of lurid radiance, almost as if he were not appalled, but stunned by

314

some revivifying amazement. He leaned back against the window.

'Something — extraordinary. But it can't be true.'

'Peter, what? You're upsetting me so much, you're frightening me.'

'Oh, don't be frightened.' He looked at her for a moment with that look of pale lucid gentleness which she now knew so well and which made her long simply to run to him. Then the lurid mask returned and he grimaced with a concealed emotion.

'*What?*'

'Listen,' he said, 'it's so *odd* — and I don't know what to do — It's — yesterday evening, quite late, Manfred rang up and asked me to go round to see him, and I went round because — it sounded as if he had something important to tell me.'

'Yes — go on — ' Anne had sat down on the upright chair, staring at him.

'Well, he told me this. Ed Roper has been in Paris. When he was there he met in a bar a man called Jimmy Roland, who is a friend of Tim Reede — '

'Yes?'

'And this man Roland told Ed that — that — Oh it's scarcely credible — '

'Go on!'

'That Tim has got a mistress, someone he never told Gertrude about at all, and whom he still sees — and that — that he and the mistress had made a — a sort of plot that Tim should make a rich marriage and go on keeping this girl as his mistress — '

Anne waited. Peter, after his utterance, reeled back against the window pane, almost cracking it. Behind him the sun was trying to shine through the rain.

'Is that all?' said Anne, after a moment's silence.

'*Is that all?*'

'I mean,' she said, 'if this is simply a story told by a man in a bar it's obviously false. It's a fabrication or a misunderstanding. I am surprised at — at Ed Roper even repeating it — or Manfred taking it so solemnly — or — '

'How can they not repeat it and consider it? Of course it may be false, but — '

'Yes,' said Anne slowly, 'of course one can't — not — go into it somehow.'

315

Anne now understood the wild lurid look upon Peter's face. However much he condemned himself for doing so, how could he not delight in this horror? If this was the end of Tim and Gertrude.

'But has anybody gone into it?' she said. 'Does anyone know who this secret mistress is? Has anyone told Gertrude this story?'

'No, *of course* not. Ed Roper was absolutely stunned, and he just told Manfred, and Manfred just told me. Manfred felt he ought to do something, but he couldn't think what to do. He suggested I should come and see you.'

'But you haven't said, are there any facts? It's all so impossible, so crazy. Where is this man Roland now, is he—'

'Well, he's disappeared, that's part of the trouble. Apparently he's a sort of roving chap, a bit shady, no fixed address.'

'Well then! Does Ed know him well?'

'No, I don't think so. But Ed believed the story, he didn't think Roland had made it up, and after all why should he make it up, he could have no motive to.'

'How do we know? Is he a friend of Tim's?'

'Yes, but Ed thought more like a sort of pub acquaintance. He knows both Tim and the girl.'

'The girl—who is she?'

'She's a girl called Daisy Barrett, she's a painter. Apparently she and Tim have been living together for years and years.'

'And he never told Gertrude this?'

'Manfred is pretty sure he didn't, but of course we can't be certain, and anyway he can't have told her about—about the plot—'

'And he's been back with this girl since he's been with Gertrude?'

'Yes. So it's said.'

Anne thought, if Tim had told Gertrude of a long-standing liaison Gertrude would certainly, out of a self-defensive prudence, have said something about it at some point to Anne, especially since she was so sensitive about Anne's sceptical view of Tim. She would have said, 'Of course Tim has had a girl friend for some time, but that was over before he began to love me.' Since Gertrude had said nothing of this kind it was quite probable that Gertrude did not know of any such girl.

'It's pretty shadowy,' said Anne. But already her swift mind had set it out. Tim and Daisy, Gertrude and Peter. No wonder Peter looked so guiltily excited.

He came now abruptly away from the window and sat down on the sofa, almost disappearing behind his knees.

'Anne, could I have a drink, please? I feel so shocked.'

Anne moved slowly to the cupboard and poured out sherry. She gave him the glass, their hands not touching. She was always careful not to touch him. She said, 'It's very possible that he's had a long-standing mistress and kept quiet about it. But I can't believe he's been with her since his marriage, and as for this idea of a plot to have a rich wife so as to keep his mistress, that's *impossible*; that would be wicked, and Tim's not wicked. I think he's a — I've never said this to you before —'

'What?' The Count looked at her eagerly.

Oh he's so *pleased*, she thought in despair. 'Only impressions — I think Tim's just a sort of natural liar, he wants everything to be easy and nice and he wouldn't tell any unpleasant truth unless he had to — he'd always have some way of convincing himself that it didn't matter. Of course I may be quite wrong —'

Peter, more soberly said, 'I've always liked Tim and I've never — made any *estimate* of him — morally. Why should I? It's not for me to judge —'

Anne watched his scrupulous gentle puzzled look and groaned to herself. 'Only now perhaps one has to. But what on earth can we do? It's just a wild story. We'll have to ignore it. It really isn't our business.' But already Anne could see before her the absolute necessity of pursuing the matter, of sifting it, of finding out the truth — the truth which could be her ruin. And to which she must *run* as if to her beloved.

'You mean leave it and forget it — and let it blow over?'

Anne could see in Peter's face, could read clearly in his mind, the counterpart of her own scrupulous calculation. Peter would not pursue his own advantage any more than she could pursue hers. Now that, after the first excitement, he saw the situation and where he stood, how to gain and how to lose, he would have to say: leave it, do not disturb them, do not do anything, anything in the world, that might divide those two. The sharp necessity of action rested with Anne.

The light had died out of Peter's eyes. 'You are right, Anne.

We have no business to do anything. I'll tell Manfred. As you say, it's so shadowy.'

'But as you say, how can we not consider it and go into it?'

'Yes, but I—now that I think about it—I see that it's not proper. A wild story, it's not evidence—We can't possibly interfere—'

'We ought at least to make some sort of discreet enquiry if we can, try to find out if—if it's even partly true.'

'Yes, but I see now that it can't be true.'

'What does Manfred think that we ought to do?'

'He doesn't know. He'd like to consult with you. He thought that maybe we could find out a little more.'

'Has Manfred told anyone else?'

'No. But he couldn't see how we could find out without—and it would be so awful if—'

'The Roland man has disappeared, but what about the girl, Daisy Barrett? Does anyone know where she is?'

'No—at least there's some pub where she and Tim used to go and it was in that pub that Jimmy Roland heard them making this plan—'

'Oh *no*, it's too disgusting, Peter, I can't believe it.'

'Neither can I. I wish I hadn't told you. Let's leave it alone.'

'We *can't*. Where's this pub?'

'Its called the Prince of Denmark, near Fitzroy Square.'

Anne rang the bell.

'Hello,' said a voice from the speaker beside the door.

'Is that Miss Barrett?'

'Yes. What do you want?'

'I'm a friend of Tim Reede, can I come in for a moment?'

318

There was a pause. 'Are you female?'

'Yes.'

There was a buzz and the door opened. Anne went in.

The hall was dark and smelly. Miss Barrett's name was in the slot marked *Second Floor*. Anne mounted the stairs and knocked.

'Come in.'

Daisy had not been difficult to find. Anne herself had gone to the Prince of Denmark. When it had become so dreadfully clear to her that she must uncover the truth, however awful, she was possessed of a ferocious urgent energy. The task was hers and hers alone. Manfred was full of scrupulous worries and doubts. He asked Anne, via the Count whom she saw again on the day following his disclosure, to come and discuss the matter, but she said this was unnecessary. It appeared that, in spite of vows of discretion, Ed Roper had already told the rumour to some of his friends, and that Moses Greenberg had heard it somehow, and had telephoned Manfred. It seemed clear, at any rate Anne announced that it was clear, that someone should investigate, that she would do it, and at once. She explained her plan to the Count. It was the simplest possible. She would find and talk to Daisy Barrett; and if she decided there was 'nothing in it' would depart without revealing her purpose. She decided against inventing any elaborate falsehood. She felt sure that she would soon discover what was necessary, and that it was better to speak impromptu and without any previous scheming. The Count was understandably paralysed. He said in his quaint old-fashioned way that surely he should escort Anne to the pub. Anne replied with unusual brusqueness, 'Peter, I am not a nun.'

In fact she had felt shy and nervous when, at six o'clock the previous evening, she entered the Prince of Denmark. She particularly dreaded an immediate public confrontation with Daisy Barrett, the necessity of requesting a private talk. And suppose Tim were actually there with her. . . ? She wanted to find out where Daisy lived. Suppose people questioned her, asked her why, told her to mind her own business? No such difficulties arose. She asked the publican who asked a man sitting at the counter who asked someone else (who happened to be Piglet) who produced the address.

'Friend of Daisy's?' 'Yes, I've just come to London.' 'She

may be in later.' 'Thanks.' Anne had postponed her visit till the next morning.

It was about midday. It had been raining earlier. Now the sun shone upon wet roofs and pavements, bringing out a blue glare. Daisy's little room was bright with reflected light and Anne blinked as she entered. Although the window was open the room smelt of alcohol.

At first there seemed to be no one there. Then, behind a lattice screen in a corner to her right, she saw a tall thin woman in jeans and a khaki shirt, fiddling at a gas stove.

'Just making lunch,' said Daisy Barrett. 'Who the hell are you?'

'My name's Anne Cavidge. Please forgive me—'

Anne had deliberately arrived without an idea in her head. Now she felt suddenly at a loss, as if she were making an embarrassing social call; and indeed in a way that was just what she was doing.

'Have a drink,' said Daisy.

She emerged from behind the screen and Anne saw her more clearly. She was tall, a little taller than Anne, and very thin and gaunt. Her hair, a greyish-darkish mixture, was rather tangled, cut short and swept back behind her ears. Her face was weary. It was not markedly wrinkled but was moulded by anxiety and exasperation, eaten by time, although she looked still young, even handsome. Remnants of bright powdery-blue make-up surrounded the large dark brown eyes, and dry faded flaky lipstick spotted the long mouth whose corners drooped into long pencil-thin lines. Anne felt sudden pity, and at the same time a sense of something formidable in this shabby unkempt figure. Daisy was not at all what she had expected; and she realized now how naive she had been to imagine that 'the mistress' would turn out to be something small and pert and fluffy.

Anne was about to refuse the drink but then thought she had better accept it. 'Thanks.'

Daisy gave her a large glass of *vin rosé* from a flagon and sat down at the table and poured out one for herself. 'Cheers.'

'Cheers.'

'Is it raining?'

'No.'

'Well, I suppose it can't be, that stuff looks like sunshine out there. What did you say your name was?'

'Anne Cavidge.'

'Never heard of you. Do you paint?'

'No.'

'I can't make head or tail of you then. Heigh ho. Would you like some lunch? There's nothing but beans today. Today, I say, as if there was fillet steak other days. Are you a vegetarian?'

'No.'

'You look like a vegetarian.'

'I won't have any lunch, thanks,' said Anne.

'Just as well, there ain't enough for two, I wasn't serious anyway. Drink up. You haven't said what you want. How did you find me anyway?'

'I asked at the Prince of Denmark.'

'I've never seen you at the Prince. How did you know I knew Tim? Silly question, everybody knows.'

'Of course I knew about you and Tim,' said Anne. 'I know you've been together for years and —'

'OK, OK. You're a funny piece. How do you know Tim, were you at infant school together? Are you looking for a long-lost friend?'

'No —'

'What's it in aid of then? Are you from the police? You could be a policewoman now I come to think of it.'

'No. What makes you think of the police?'

'I'm always thinking of the police. And Tim is *capable de tout*. He's not in trouble, well he's always in trouble, he's not in any special trouble is he?'

'No.'

'We don't seem to be getting anywhere. Let's not talk about Tim, I'm not in the mood. Let's talk about you. How old are you?'

Anne blushed at the direct question. 'Thirty-eight.'

'What do you do for a living? Your mac is quite expensive, though not new. Do take it off by the way and sit down.'

Anne took off her black convent mackintosh and sat down on a rickety kitchen chair. She was wearing a white Liberty summer dress closely covered with a pink cherry-blossom design, a present from Gertrude. She nervously tucked in the skirt behind her knees. She sipped her wine.

'I seem to be making all the conversation. Don't look so frightened. I'm not going to eat you. I'm glad of a mystery visitor, I don't have many visitors, mystery or otherwise. I like the way you do your hair, it's like mine. Are you married?'

'No.'

'Gay?'

'What?'

'Queer?'

'No.'

'What do you get up to then? Are you a writer?'

'No.'

'I am. Have another drink. You're not drinking up.'

'I thought you were a painter,' said Anne.

'No—used to paint—gave it up—I'm a novelist. Writing's hell though. But what do you do if you're not a writer or a painter or a homosexual or a housewife?'

'Until lately I've been a nun,' said Anne. The conversation which was not going at all as she had intended, was confusing her and she could not invent a lie. Nor did she want to. She found herself unable to help rather liking Daisy. But it was time to take control of the interrogation and find out exactly what she needed to know. There might be no other chance. In fact a vague acquaintance leading to another meeting was unthinkably out of the question.

'A *nun*? Oh *Jesus*! Not the kind that's all shut up and looked at through bars?'

'Yes, that kind.'

'It must be awful. There's something rather attractive about it though, sort of exciting. You ought to write a novel about it, could be a best seller. It's the sort of morbid stuff people want to know about. I wish I had your experience, it might get my stuff moving. Why not write a novel? Nun tells all. I bet there were goings-on in your convent, weren't there?'

'No.'

'You're blushing! Why did you leave, chucked out?'

'No, I lost my faith.'

'RC I suppose? I went to a ghastly convent school in France

until I ran away. I never had any faith. Shitty sort of childhood. What are you doing now?'

'I'm trying to get a teaching job, but—'

'No luck? Unemployed like me. It's a lousy society for creative people. Where do you live?'

'Camden.'

'What's your local? I mean your local pub, God can't you understand English?'

'I haven't got one.'

'Haven't got one? Oh well, it's understandable. I'll find you one. What's your poison? Sorry, I mean what do you drink? I mean, like some people only drink Young's beer or something.'

'I drink wine—'

'Ah, a wino! I love winos. Wine bars, I know hundreds. We might go on a wine crawl sometimes. Anyway since you go to the Prince of Denmark we could meet there.'

'I don't go actually—'

'Well, yer better make a start, hadden yer? We're all on social security these days, got to stick together. Why not let's meet at the old Prince this evening and I'll take you to a dinkum wine bar in Hanway Street?'

'I'm sorry—'

'Of course I still don't know why you're here. I take things as they come. I've learnt to do that. The things that come are usually kicks in the teeth. At least you aren't one as far as I can see, or are you?'

Anne was blushing again and felt a slight impulse to cry. She said, 'I really came to ask you some rather tiresome questions.' She had given up all hope of discreet indirect discovery. She could not tactfully elicit her information. She would have to bang it out. She felt unhappy and ashamed of her role. All the ferocious necessitous energy was gone from her.

'Of course, why didn't I think of it at once, Christ, I'm slow, you're from the Social Service, you're a do-gooder! Well, carry on, dear, there's plenty of good you can do around here! Do you know, I still haven't discovered how to get Supplementary Benefit?'

'I'm afraid I'm not from the Social Service,' said Anne.

'Then I give up. Have some more wine. Have a bean.'

'It's about Tim—'

'Oh him. What about Tim? You're not an old flame of his by any chance? He had a lot of dotty Welsh girls. Are you Welsh?'

'No. And I'm not—'

'You don't seem to be anything.'

'I know you lived with Tim for years and years.'

'Oh yes, forever.'

'And you're still living with him.'

'Oh yes, oh sure! What's your game, nun?'

'Forgive me, I *will explain*. But please answer the question.'

'Why don't I throw you downstairs? I must be drunk.'

Anne moved her chair a little backward and put her mackintosh on her knee. She checked the position of the door. Daisy was still sitting at the table. She had been liberally refilling her glass.

'You made a plan, didn't you,' said Anne, 'that Tim should marry a rich woman and that you should go on living together on the money.'

'Oh *God*!' said Daisy. She drank off her glass and then stared calmly at Anne with her huge Etruscan eyes.

'I'm sorry,' said Anne, 'I'm very sorry, but I must find out. Is it true or not?'

'Why shouldn't it be true?' said Daisy with a cunning look.

'Because it's—impossible, it's—'

'Why do you ask then? God, you seem to have been here for hours. Life is full of impossible things, or didn't they tell you that in your convent? If you ever were in a convent. Are you a private detective?'

'No.'

'I don't think I like you after all.'

'Do you deny it then?'

'Do I deny it? I deny nothing! We made such a plan, yes.'

'You—did—And you're carrying it out, you're still together?'

'Just tell me one thing, mystery girl, why are you here? And answer me truly or I'll clout you.' Daisy got up quickly. Anne got up too and moved back behind her chair.

'I'll tell you the truth,' said Anne. 'I'm an old friend of Gertrude, Tim's wife. I heard a rumour that you and Tim had made this—and you were still—and I wanted to find out if it was true— I didn't know what to believe—'

'Oh believe what you please! Yes, of course we're living it up on Gertie's money! So you're an old friend of Gertrude's, I *see*. Now I've got it. The intrusive old girl friend. You're in love with Gertrude! That's why you're so filled with spite and envy, coming round here and insinuating things and asking questions! Tell bloody Gertrude to ask her own bloody questions! Get out! Jesus bloody Christ, as if I hadn't enough trouble without being persecuted by jealous nuns suffering from sexual deprivation! Oh *get out*! And don't show your mean little face in the Prince of Denmark or I'll put a mark on it. Clear off, *run*!'

Anne ran. She half fell down the stairs, fumbled wildly with the door, and ran away panting down the street. It began to rain. Anne began to cry.

'Have you been to Samuel Orpen yet,' said Gertrude, 'I forgot to ask.'

'Yes, thanks,' said Anne. 'He filled the tooth. It's quite all right now.'

'He's nice, isn't he? Did you discover he was a Roman Catholic? I meant to tell you. A convert. Guy's father was furious.'

'I thought Guy's father was sort of Christian.'

'An Anglican atheist, hated God, but a bit sentimental about the old faith.'

'Yes, I found out Mr Orpen was a Catholic. We talked about the Vatican.'

'I wish a friend of mine was Pope. It would be such fun for him to emerge from behind the arras and say, "My dear, I've had an awful day, give me a drink at once!"'

'Yes—' said Anne, 'Yes.'

'What have you done to your hand?'

'It's nothing.'

'Do you like your cherry dress? It's very Japanese. You look marvellous. You're getting brown at last, well, pale biscuit. It suits your eyes.'

Anne was at Ebury Street. It was the next morning. Tim was away, he was on a shopping spree, buying paints and things, Gertrude said. Anne wondered if he was with Daisy. It would be so easy to be away a lot.

Anne had returned straight from Daisy to her flat and had found the Count, who knew of her errand, waiting outside the door. As she led him upstairs she felt what an ironically sad occasion it was for this urgent desire to see her. The Count was in a state of excitement, his usual dignity precariously at risk.

'So you think it's true?'

'I think it may be trueish. There's something.'

'If there's *anything*, then it's a catastrophe.'

'I agree. It's the end.'

Anne said what she believed. She thought it possible that there had been some sort of vague conspiracy, and likely that Tim was still seeing Daisy. She had been impressed by a casual air of *owning* Tim which she thought that Daisy had somehow worn. Yes, there was something. And the Count was right, that was enough, the details did not matter. It was enough to be the end of Tim, the smash of her own hopes, the return of joy and light into Peter's life. She thought, looking at him, if I loved him perfectly, would I not rejoice to see his face so changed.

The Count went to see Manfred. Anne did not go. She did not want to see Peter, Manfred, probably Moses, all excited and elated at what had occurred. Tim's fall would grieve no one.

Anne felt private and grim. She wanted events to hurry now, she wanted the crash to be over. Of course, the evidence was ambiguous, not clear; but Anne's impression was strong and she did not permit hope. In any case the matter had to be opened to Gertrude, the rumours were enough reason for that. She did not feel sorry for Gertrude. Whatever happened Gertrude would be blessed, she was under a lucky star. She did not feel sorry for Tim, her mind shied away from him, it looked like a messy nasty business. She felt a curious, confused sorrow about Daisy. The conspiracy, if there was one, must have been Tim's idea. All the same, they were an ill pair.

Manfred talked with the Count, also with Moses Greenberg. They agreed that Anne should say something to Gertrude. They left it to Anne to decide how.

It was a sunny morning. London was hot and dusty, full of tired smells, perhaps the smells of Londoners' dreams of the countryside. The Thames stank. Some sort of railway strike was on. Victoria Station was full of anxious ill-tempered travellers.

The drawing-room at Ebury Street smelt of tiger lilies, which Gertrude had been arranging. Gertrude had put the flowers on the marquetry table beside the drinks which had been reinstated there.

'Aren't they lovely? They always remind me of Alice.'

'Yes.'

'Is it too early for a drink?'

'I won't have a drink,' said Anne. 'I think I'm going to give it up again.'

'Oh no!'

'I think you all drink too much.'

'Oh darling, don't be so strict! Moses was here yesterday telling me to spend less money!'

'I suppose Tim spends it,' said Anne.

'Oh stop knocking Tim! You always find something to say against the poor chap. Stop it! I'm feeling cheerful this morning and I won't let you criticise anything or anybody. Do you know, we're going to Greece! Tim's never been there.'

With her hair cut shorter, now a chaotic brown mop, Gertrude looked very young. She had put on weight again, and kept looking at the sunburn upon her plump arm, bare from the elbow. The sun had cast a faint damson glow over her smooth brown-complexioned face. She was wearing a new smart much-pleated green and brown striped cotton dress. There was no doubt that she was spending money too.

'Have you been to Greece, Anne, I forget?'

'No.'

There was a slight pause while both women apprehended and passed by the thought that the natural: oh do come with us! could not follow.

Gertrude said randomly, 'Would you like to come and see Tim's latest paintings? He's painting again now, I'm so glad, he paints every day.'

'In a minute,' said Anne.

They had been standing together by the mantelpiece, as they often stood when they talked in that room. Anne turned and went to the window. She looked down at the sunny street through sudden tears.

'What's the matter, darling?' said Gertrude, with fear in her voice.

Anne touched the tears with her hand and turned. She felt grief for her awful role, almost that of an accuser or a judge, and for her own loss and because of an impending blank loneliness which had suddenly begun to swirl about her like a white mist. Would coming events deprive her of Gertrude too?

'Anne!' Gertrude would have come to her and embraced her, only Anne stayed her with a gesture.

'It's about Tim.'

'Is he ill, hurt, has something happened and no one told me—?'

'No, he's fine, he's all right, nothing like that. Listen, Gertrude, there may be nothing in this, nothing at all, but Manfred and Moses and the Count think I should tell you something, well, perhaps you know it or some of it—'

'What?' Gertrude's face had become stiff, wrinkled, almost ugly.

'Let's sit down,' said Anne. She sat down on the sofa and Gertrude drew up a chair.

'*Quick*, tell me, what—?'

'Well—Tim had a regular mistress for years, I expect you know about her, Daisy Barrett.'

Gertrude hesitated. She was wondering whether she should say, Oh, Daisy, yes, of course! But sheer cold fear and the awful expression of doom upon Anne's face compelled the truth. 'No.'

Anne let out a sigh. 'Well, what I tell you now is a rumour, and there is some evidence for it. It is said that—Tim still has relations with this woman, or has had until fairly recently, and —the story is that they made a plan that he should marry a rich woman and that they should go on living together on her money.'

Gertrude glared at Anne. Then her face relaxed a little. She looked sternly. 'I thought you had something serious to tell me.'

'Isn't this serious?'

'No. You speak of a rumour, a story. What is this story? It cannot possibly be true, it's just raving lunacy.'

'I thought that at first, but it seems —'

'Tim loves me, we're together all the time.'

'You're not together now.'

'Are you suggesting — ? *Anne*, what you say is awful, *vile*. Where on earth did you pick up this rubbish, this *filth*?'

'As follows,' said Anne. She felt calm now, cold, not tearful. 'Have you heard of a man called Jimmy Roland?'

'Yes, Tim mentioned him, they shared a studio, I never met him.'

'Ed Roper met this man in Paris and he said that Tim had been living with this girl Daisy Barrett for years, up to and including the time when he was supposed to be falling in love with you, and that their idea was that Tim should make a rich marriage and that their liaison should continue after it.'

'It's not true, Anne, I *know* it isn't true. You say "supposed to be falling in love with me". He *did* fall in love, he *is* in love, one can be perfectly certain about something like that! Tim may have had some long love affair years ago — I mean obviously he had affairs, he's told me a lot of things — there's some muddle here. Does this woman exist, has anyone seen her?'

'Yes,' said Anne, 'I saw her yesterday.'

'My God — and — ?'

'She *said* there had been this plan *and* that she was still seeing Tim. Of course —'

'Anne, Anne, you've been too long in the convent, you don't know that people tell lies. Why ever believe this woman who may be hysterical, jealous, vindictive, anything? It's all a nonsense. But what is all this that you've been doing behind my back — I resent it very much —'

'I'm sorry,' said Anne, 'and of course people tell lies. But what were we to do? We couldn't just ignore it when —'

'*We* — how many of you have been labouring on this rumour, discussing it all together? You said Manfred and the Count — Oh I'm so *upset*, so *shocked* —' Gertrude leapt up and ran to the window as Anne had done. She stared desperately out as if seeking help in a world that knew nothing of her trouble. She tugged her fingers through her hair and rubbed her burning face, then came back and stood at the mantelpiece, glaring down at her friend. She picked up the china monkey cellist and held him unconsciously in her hand.

'And Moses,' said Anne. 'We had to do something. They suggested I should tell you, simply tell you. And Ed Roper knows, of course, and it seems he's told one or two others. Moses heard it from someone else.'

'*Damn* Ed Roper. So *anyone* might know—And it's a *lie*, a *foul lie*—Anne, how *can* you—'

Anne sustained Gertrude's burning angry gaze. She thought, almost to calm her own feelings, Gertrude hates this, she hates the loss of face, she isn't yet believing it, she's just furious that other people might.

'It's not my fault,' said Anne. 'I'm just a messenger. If there's this unpleasant rumour you would be bound to hear of it in the end from someone, and isn't it better that you should hear it at the start from me? Please don't be so cross, my dear.'

'I'm not "cross"! I'm—it's unspeakable! And so *silly*—You and the Count are incredibly naive—but I'm surprised at Manfred—Anyway I still don't understand. You say you *saw* this woman? What's her name?'

'Daisy Barrett. Ed heard this story from Jimmy Roland who you say is Tim's friend. Roland said Tim and this woman—'

'Yes, yes, yes, don't keep repeating it, had arranged that Tim should marry me to keep them in comfort! Anne, Anne, just *think*!'

'I know it sounds insane,' said Anne, immobile and looking up. 'I'm not saying it's true! But something must have started the story. The bit I was able to check seemed to fit in—'

'How did you find the woman?'

'I got her address from a pub she goes to, Roland mentioned the pub to Ed. She said she'd been Tim's mistress for years, she implied she still was, she said there had been such a plan—Of course she may have been lying on all these points. My impression of her was that some of it was true. But hadn't you better ask Tim? If the whole thing's a malicious invention, it had better be scotched straightaway.'

' "Scotched", odd word,' said Gertrude. She could not, even at a moment of extreme emotion, resist a habit, caught from Guy, of commenting on words. She seemed a trifle calmer. 'Yes, OK, I know it's not your fault. What's she like?'

'Shabby, mannish, thin, rather haggard. Seemed educated. Is supposed to be a painter but says she's a novelist. Lives in a very nasty flatlet near Shepherd's Bush. Drinks a lot.'

Gertrude was thoughtful. 'Of course she's lying. She may be someone Tim knew years ago. Perhaps she heard of his marriage and invented all this so as to get money out of us – though I can't for the life of me see how she thinks it's to be done.'

'I can't either,' said Anne, 'and somehow she didn't strike me as the sort of person who would invent something to black-mail people. I rather liked her.'

'You *liked* her?'

'Yes, why not, one gets involuntary impressions of people.'

'You say she's a drunk?'

'I thought so. She may be irresponsible, a bit dotty, I mean sort of wild – she's certainly an eccentric – '

'You *liked* someone who is maligning my husband in the most repulsive way imaginable?'

'No, well, I shouldn't have said that. I just mean I don't see her as an obvious paranoid or a vindictive liar. Gertrude, I don't know what to think. I've said all I have to say.'

'You're enjoying this. You've always been against Tim, you've always hated him and worked to denigrate him and diminish him – '

'I'm not enjoying it!' Oh if you only knew how little, thought Anne. If you only knew with what diligent thoroughness I am working against my own interests!

'You despise Tim.'

'I don't. I only thought, and think, that he's not good enough for you.'

'You know nothing about him, you don't understand him, you're just *jealous*, meanly *jealous* – '

'At least I'm not after your money,' said Anne.

The china monkey cellist descended to the floor and smashed to pieces. Anne stood up. The two women looked down at the fragments upon the green tiles of the fireplace.

Anne's eyes filled with tears. 'Darling, I'm very sorry.'

'I'm sorry too,' said Gertrude, moving away. 'I'm suffering from shock. I feel attacked. I don't blame you. But you produce this awful crazy story – with a sort of glee – or perhaps I'm imagining it – I know you don't *want* to hurt me. I suppose if people are talking, someone had to tell me. I just wish it hadn't been you. I wish it had been the Count.'

'The Count—yes—oh if only you had married *him*.'

There was a sound outside which made them both stand frozen, then turn to each other staring and quickly dashing away traces of tears. The sound was that of a key inserted in the front door lock.

Tim entered humming, then came on into the drawing-room, carrying his packages.

'It's me. Oh hello, Anne.' He stood looking from one to the other. 'What's up?'

'I'll go,' said Anne quickly.

'No, Anne, don't go. I want you to hear Tim deny all this filthy nonsense.'

'What is it?' said Tim. He looked alarmed, then terrified.

'Tim,' said Gertrude, 'have you had a long love affair with a woman called Daisy Barrett and have you been with her since —since France—and did you make a plan together that you should marry a rich woman?' Her eyes were red, her lips were moist, but Gertrude spoke sternly and coolly.

The effect on Tim was violent and instantaneous. He dropped his parcels on the floor, and a blaze of scarlet flowed up into his neck, into his face and brow. His mouth opened and he gazed at his wife with appalled wretched eyes, the very image of guilt and speechless terror.

Anne ran past him and out of the room. She ran through the hall picking up her black convent mackintosh. She let herself out and raced down the stairs and ran away along the road as fast as she had run yesterday to escape from Daisy Barrett.

'Oh Tim—' said Gertrude and her eyes overflowed with tears. Her words sounded like some hollow echo of a final doom.

'So you know about Daisy—' said Tim. Confusion, stupidity, misery, and a sort of vindictive rage against fate, against himself, muffled his mind.

'So it's true,' said Gertrude. Her desperate word spoken, she was now again cool, stern, frightful. She searched for a handkerchief in her pocket, then turning from him, in her handbag. She mopped her eyes, then began to pick up the pieces of the china monkey and arrange them on the mantelpiece.

'Well, yes,' said Tim, 'I mean, I don't know what you're asking me. I ought to have told you ages ago, I was going to tell you. I know I've been very stupid but I think I haven't been bad, well, I suppose I have been bad, but you see—'

'You were going to tell me that you had been cold-bloodedly deceiving me?'

'I ought to have said, only I didn't think it would matter, I thought I'd wait, it wasn't like deceiving you, well, I suppose it was—'

'You've been living for years with this woman?'

'Yes, but—'

'And you're still with her, she's your mistress?'

'No!'

'You've been with her since we—fell in love—?'

Like many instinctive uncalculating liars Tim was too lazy to think out his lies with care, and faced with exposure tended perhaps as a token gesture to his conscience, to tell the literal truth. 'Yes,' he said.

'Then it's all over, isn't it,' said Gertrude. 'All over between you and me. All finished.'

'You don't understand,' said Tim. 'I *did* leave her, I did really leave her, and then I saw her again, but it was, it wasn't—'

'And you planned with her that you should marry a rich woman to keep you and your mistress in comfort.'

'We *talked* of it,' said Tim, 'but it was simply a joke, it was a *joke* between us, we never—'

'A joke between you,' said Gertrude. 'A joke which you have carried rather far. So you joked about marrying me!'

'No. You haven't understood,' he said. He was trying now to remember what he had said in the last few minutes. 'It's true that I saw Daisy after you—'

'And made love to her?'

'Yes. After you sort of dismissed me, after you said it—it wasn't on—I went back to her—'

'You went home to her, you'd never left her at all.'

'I had!'

'I never said it wasn't on,' said Gertrude. 'I mean I—I was

discouraged and unhappy and — and *bereaved* — it was a bad time — I needed you most of all just then — and you ran off and — '

'But it's all over, it's *over*, I haven't seen Daisy — '

'Where have you been this morning?'

'Gertrude! I've been at the shops buying — Oh God — buying paints and crayons — and I got a little — a little present for you — Gertrude, you *can't* think that I would do — you know I wouldn't — '

He was holding out his hands towards her but she would not look at him. She stared at the china pieces and pushed them about.

'I've lost my faith in you,' she said wearily. 'I think you're a liar. At any rate you've told me some very important — and damaging — lies — You've been deceiving me, perhaps you still are. Everyone said you were a liar and a worthless man — '

'Gertrude, darling, my love, don't talk to me like that — '

'You'd better go back to Daisy. From what Anne says about her she should suit you better than I do.'

'*Anne?* What's Anne got to do with this? It's all Anne's doing, she hates me — ' For the first time Tim began to wonder how it had all happened to him. *Why* had the world suddenly collapsed on him now, so dreadfully, so unfairly, like this?

'Anne went to see your Daisy Barrett and your Daisy Barrett said it was all true. I didn't believe it. Now I do.'

'But it isn't true!'

'You said it was just now.'

'Yes, but not like that — and I *have* left her — oh it's all such a jumble — '

'So it seems. I dislike jumbles.'

'But *Anne* — seeing *Daisy* — how could it be?'

'Your friend Jimmy Roland met Ed Roper in Paris and told him all about it. That's how we heard. Then Anne found out where your mistress lived and visited her. It's quite simple.'

'But Gertrude,' said Tim, 'have you known about this for a long time — ?'

'No, of course not! I'm not an actor and a liar like you. Could I have been with you — as I have been — if I'd known of this — foul deception? Anne told me this morning. Apparently everybody knows. I'm just the last to be told. At any rate they'll all have the satisfaction of saying "I told you so".'

334

Terror was depriving Tim of his wits. 'But, Gertrude, surely it doesn't matter all that much, my not telling you about Daisy, I know I ought to have—'

'Not matter that my husband is using my money to keep a mistress?'

'But I'm not, I'm *not*, I'm NOT—'

'I can't trust you, Tim,' said Gertrude. 'I don't know what you planned or half planned or intended or half intended. You just aren't mine any more.'

'I *am*! Oh damn the money—'

'Why damn it? Didn't you marry me for it?'

'No. *I love* you. You *know* that—'

'Maybe. But it seems that you love her more.'

'I don't, I *don't*—'

'Shouting won't help. We're finished, Tim.'

'But it was all ages ago—I mean not very long ago but—'

'Yesterday perhaps or this morning. It's a bit late to cashier her now, just because you've been found out. Besides it isn't fair to her. Don't you think she has rights? How many years have you been with her?'

Tim was silent. Then he said, 'Many years.'

'Well, then—' said Gertrude. She looked at him at last, and for a moment they were both silent.

The telephone rang. Gertrude picked it up. 'Hello, Manfred.... Yes.... Yes, Anne told me. I'd like to see you, now if possible. ... No, I'll come to your place.... Yes, lunch, but I don't exactly feel like eating. And do you think you could get hold of the Count and Moses? ... Yes, I shall be needing Moses' advice. Thank you for ringing. I'll be with you in about half an hour.' She put the 'phone down.

'But, Gertrude, we're having lunch here, you and me, I've been looking forward to it all the morning. I've got some plums and Caerphilly cheese and I want to show you your present—' For a moment Tim seemed to have forgotten what had happened.

'No. Poor Tim,' said Gertrude in her weary voice. She crossed the room, making a detour to avoid him. She went into the bedroom. Tim followed her and stood at the door. She was packing a suitcase.

'Darling! Don't be *mad*, don't leave me, don't go to *them*!'

'You've left me.'

'I haven't! I can't think what we've been talking about, a lot of different things got mixed up together, you've got the wrong idea, don't go away now in this awful way, I can explain, I haven't been bad, I haven't, I swear—'

'Oh never mind how bad you've been,' said Gertrude. 'You've been bad enough. If I was a different sort of person it mightn't matter. But I'm not that different person. I'm me. I can't sort of share you, on any terms, with a mistress you've had for years and years. I can't just say OK and go on—even if you say you'll leave this woman.'

'I've left her!'

'I can't necessarily believe you. I can't live wondering all the time where you are and what you're doing. I gave you all of myself. I don't want just a part of you.'

'You haven't got just a part! Gertrude, I haven't told you lies—I mean, I just didn't tell you the truth soon enough, and it's *not* all the things you said—won't you *listen*, and then forgive what needs to be forgiven?'

'You haven't understood,' said Gertrude. 'There isn't any question of forgiving or not forgiving. This thing between us is broken, it's not there any more.'

'But I can *explain*—Oh don't stop loving me or I shall die.'

'Don't appeal to me like that,' she said, doing up her suitcase. 'It's just emotion. Do you think I don't feel emotions too? I loved you and I married you against the advice of everyone I trusted. And when I was still in mourning. How do you think I feel now? If we were to weep and fall into each other's arms it would all just be to do again.'

'But, Gertrude, where are you going, when will you be back? You must let me defend myself, you've got it all wrong, or partly wrong anyway, it's *different* from what you think, and—'

'I'm going to stay away for a while with someone somewhere, I don't know who, but where you can't find me and please don't try. Tim, honestly, it's better to do it quickly like this—we shall both die of pain otherwise. I know you love me, sort of, but it's no good, it's no good to me, you're not good enough, like everybody said.'

'But my darling, my wife, what am I to do? You mustn't go away, you mustn't leave me—tell Manfred you're not coming—stay and let me—'

'You can stay here—Well, not, I'd rather you didn't. I won't be back for some time and I want you to be gone when I return. I'd rather you went away as soon as you conveniently can, and take your stuff. Go to her. Only please don't bring her here, that's all I ask.'

'Gertrude, you're killing me, you're *mad*, there isn't anything like what you're saying, I'm yours, I'm not anyone else's—please, please, please don't go, don't leave me, my darling, my darling—'

'Tim, *don't*, just *don't*—be kind to me, and don't. I know you're sorry, you're miserable at being found out, but you'll soon feel better.'

'You can't just go—'

'We are not as we were— Oh how I wish we could be but we're not—it's all changed, all spoilt. Get out of my way, please.'

'I won't let you go.'

'Don't touch me. *Please*.'

Gertrude's tears were flowing now. She picked up the suitcase and moved to the bedroom door. Tim tried to hold her arm but she evaded him and walked quickly across the hall.

'Don't follow me. I don't want a scene in the street.' She slipped out of the door and slammed it.

Tim wrenched the door open. 'Gertrude!'

The street door slammed below. He ran down a few stairs then came slowly back. He went into the flat, into the drawing-room. He lay down on the floor amidst the scattered packages and howled.

SIX

'What a bore you are, dear,' said Daisy. 'Now we see you, now we don't. I thought I'd got rid of you. I am just starting to celebrate this fact when you turn up again, surprise, surprise! And you aren't even cheerful about it.'

Tim was sitting on Daisy's bed staring straight in front of him. He was motionless, his face was blank, only his eyes blinked and rarely.

'Come on, Blue Eyes, cheer up, show some sign of life. I've never seen you like this. Usually you're frigging around like a water beetle, never still a moment. Now you sit for hours like a bloody statue. What am I supposed to do, perch on your head?'

'I'm sorry,' said Tim. The words came out in a whisper. He remained perfectly still, staring at the window.

'OK, so it's over,' said Daisy. 'It was hopeless from the start, you said so yourself. Anyone could see it was a mad idea. You're still suffering from shock. You'll soon feel wild, joyful relief. Damn it, you're *free*! Have a drink for Christ's bloody sake.'

Tim shook his head.

'Are you bewitched or something? Deep depression, electric shocks?'

Tim said nothing.

'It's a lovely evening, let's go to the Prince of Denmark. We'll walk there if you like, like you used to want to and I never would. That would please you, wouldn't it? A walk would do you good.'

'You go,' murmured Tim.

'Oh Christ! What can I do with you? Why don't you lie down properly and rest if you feel so damned frail—instead of sitting there like a waxwork? You're giving me the creeps. Take some pills, if you won't have decent alcohol. I've got some sleeping pills somewhere, at least I think they're sleeping pills. I'm going to take you to the doctor if you're like this tomorrow.'

'No, no—no doctor.'

'Speak up, can't you. Why do you whisper all the time, what's happened to your vocal cords? Are you sick or what? Don't be such a booby. You arrive here and expect me to welcome you back with open arms, then you instantly become a kind of ghost. Where's your spirit, where's your pluck? Try to behave like a man, even if it's only for my sake.'

'I'm sorry, Daisy.'

'So you know who I am. I've been wondering if you even recognized me. I'm yer old Daisy, remember. Old Daisy's Hotel, always open, turn up any time, always a welcome at Daisy's Hotel!'

'You've been very kind to me,' said Tim.

'Oh good, at least you can move your eyes, now we're getting somewhere!'

Tim had arrived at Daisy's flat that morning. The previous night he had spent alone at Ebury Street.

Tim had despaired very fast. There seemed to be refuge only in despair. Hope was too agonizing, too searching, too full of awful light. He had to conclude quickly that it was the end.

After Gertrude left he had sat for a while on the floor among his precious packages, crying in an awful way, not exactly with tears but with a wet mouth and a crumpled child's face. Then he sat still for a longer time trying to think what had happened. What had he said, what had Gertrude said? He tried to remember the conversation, but already a mist had descended over it. He had run straight into some final absolute catastrophe and he knew it was entirely his own fault, but he could not see quite how and why it had come about.

Tim knew at once that something terrible and irrevocable had happened to him. Like someone apprised of a fatal illness, he knew that he had moved into an entirely new state of being and that he would never be as he once was. He had lost Gertrude, his wife whom he loved. That was the centre of it. But the attendant horror was in the shocking manner of the loss, and the being, himself, that was left behind by this cosmic change. Tim sensed himself as sick, sick forever with a kind of moral sickness which he had never known before. He had ruined himself, utterly disappointed Gertrude and utterly lost her, because of some dreadful, unspeakable moral failure. Tim had not been used to think in these terms, they were alien to him. He had never had a high opinion of himself, but he had felt that he was harmless, innocent, kind, an ordinary decent weak man. It shocked him utterly, it scarred his soul, to think that he had done something terribly immoral and thereby destroyed his happiness and lost the precious wife whom, beyond his deserts, he had so amazingly achieved. As often happens, Tim measured the magnitude of the crime by the magnitude of the punishment. Before the axe fell he had felt little guilt, a puny guilt easily dismissed. Now, though vaguely, he felt how terribly he must have erred. How could he have had the *moral* folly to aspire to Gertrude? The sense of the loss crept into his heart as he sat there on the floor, tearlessly weeping, unable to stop the tattered remnants of his former being from expecting the continual treats of a happy married life. Gertrude would return, he would show her his new acrylic paints (she loved to see his paints) he would give her a funny necklace he had bought for her (her jewellery was so conventional, they always laughed about that), then there would be lunch with plums and Caerphilly cheese, then he would work, conscious every moment of her presence in his life, then there would be drinks, dinner, talk, laughter, plans. They were going to Greece. Then he would lie with her in bed, mouth to mouth, kissing her asleep, sleeping himself away into a deep sea of absolute safety and bliss.

Only now it was not so any more. Gertrude had gone. Tim had been revealed as a liar and a cheat, some sort of traitor. He had wantonly destroyed the innocent happiness of two people and made a desert of horrors round about him. Only, of course, his own happiness had not been innocent. Tim accepted the general force of the charge against him fully and at once, although he still could not work out its details or reconstruct exactly what had happened in that terrible conversation. Gertrude had not understood, he was not as guilty as she thought, but what did it matter now about degrees of guilt? Of course he had never planned to live with Daisy after his marriage; but he had concealed Daisy and her vast importance in his life, he had concealed a bond and a responsibility which, had Gertrude known about it, might have made her, at the crucial moment, hesitate. Gertrude had spoken of her 'mourning'. Anything, then, might have tilted the balance against him. And in the strange chemistry of his moral confusion, Tim's crimes against Daisy added to his guilt before Gertrude. Tim now measured how far he really was bound to Daisy, bound as if she were part of him, his sister, his mother. He had had to rewrite his history so as to obliterate Daisy from it. But without Daisy it was a false history, and this false history he had tried to live with Gertrude. He realized now, as he sat motionless, paralysed, on Daisy's bed, how much he was after all Daisy's property. He felt it with a despair which went beyond any bitterness even against fate.

After he had got up from the drawing-room floor and tried to *think*, he had, as his first action, telephoned Manfred's number. There was no answer. Evening was approaching and Tim had eaten nothing. He drank some whisky, taking the bottle from the familiar tray upon the marquetry table and pouring the whisky into a heavy Waterford glass, a ritual of pleasure now grown hideous and ominous. He looked with horror at the tiger lilies. Then he went back to the telephone. He rang the Count's office number, but he had already left. He rang his home number but there was no answer. He drank some more whisky. He rang Manfred again, nothing. He rang Gerald Pavitt, but then remembered he was still at Jodrell Bank. He rang Victor Schultz. Victor answered. Tim said thickly, 'Do you know where Gertrude is?' Victor replied to this strange request by saying, sorry, he was just off to the hospital. Obviously Victor already knew. Manfred must have swiftly sent the news around and the ranks were already closed against him. He rang Moses Greenberg, but Moses, as soon as he heard Tim's voice, put the 'phone down. He did not ring the Stanley Openshaws, as he knew that Janet Openshaw detested him. He did not ring Mrs Mount. She had made special efforts to be kind to him and Gertrude at the start, but by now must all the more regard him with abhorrence. He finished the bottle of whisky and went to bed and cried and slept.

The next morning was a terrible awakening. He woke, his body and his mind sleepily reaching out to Gertrude. She has gone. He remembered. He got up and hurried round the flat looking for he knew not what, Gertrude perhaps returned while he slept. He felt sick, his head ached violently. His body was possessed by misery. He considered eating something but could not. He started to make some tea but could not bear the sight of the kettle. He rang Manfred and the Count but got no answer. He sat in the drawing-room and tried, on Gertrude's expensive cream-headed paper, to compose a letter. But Tim was not a writer and the attempt to set down his defence only seemed to prove to him that he had none. He tore up his efforts. He *would* write a letter, but not now. He felt he had to act, to 'do something about it', since inaction was torment. Yet what could he do? He thought of running round to Manfred's flat. But no one would let him in, no one would answer the bell. In any case Gertrude would not be there, had doubtless already gone away to some secret place where he would never find her. Was there, anyway, any point in trying to find her? To see her again, to be rejected again, might add to his pain in ways he could not even imagine. Had he ever *really believed* that he was married to Gertrude? His crazed mind wondered even this. He could not stay on at Ebury Street. He thought that he re-membered that she had asked him not to. And the flat had become terrible to him, a place of torture and punishment, full of happy, unconscious memories of a lost paradise.

At about ten thirty he ate a piece of bread and butter. He drank some milk from a bottle. He put the butter and milk back in the fridge as Gertrude had taught him to do. He considered shaving and decided not to. What was the point? He packed up his painting gear. He packed his clothes in his old suitcase. Only now he had many more clothes. He thought of leaving them behind, the clothes that Gertrude had bought him, but this seemed improper. She would not want to see those shirts, those ties again. He collected his things from the bathroom. He thrust clothes, paints, sketch books higgledy-piggledy into plastic bags, and stacked up his canvases beside the door. He went out into the awful brightness of Ebury Street and found a taxi. The taxi man helped him to load the stuff, drove him to Chiswick, and helped him to unload it. Tim pushed it all through the door into the desolate damp emptiness of the studio. He closed the door. He had been thinking. The taxi took him back to Victoria, to a bank, where he drew a sum of money out of his and Gertrude's joint account. He then continued his ride as far as Shepherds Bush Green. From here he walked to

Daisy's flat. During this walk he pulled the golden wedding ring, which Gertrude had given him, off his finger and put it in his pocket.

As he was about to ring Daisy's bell he saw something terrible, obscenely terrible, which renewed his premonition that even greater, more awful unimagined pains awaited him in the future. The screw was turning. He saw standing at the corner of the street, watching Daisy's door, a familiar figure in a black mackintosh. Cold, cruel Anne Cavidge had come to witness the final act, to collect the final proof, of his absolute faithlessness. Her case was now complete. This, together with his drawing of the money, marked the end, the point from which he could not return. And as he mounted the stairs to Daisy's flat he knew that he himself had willed the end. Since he was rejected he would prove himself well worthy of it.

He had indeed come to Daisy not only with this logic in mind. He simply could not think what else to do, where else to go. What could he *be* now, how employ his continued existence? Should he go and live in a hotel in Paddington on Gertrude's money trying to compose convincing letters, explaining, asking for forgiveness? The idea of explaining seemed already far away in a lost past. He thought, I have run away from the land of morality. No doubt he would explain sometime. But, as he now dimly and with anguish began to see, he would be doing his explaining to Moses Greenberg during the proceedings for divorce. The scandal and the shame, everything that was happening now, would have to be lived through again in terrible detail. How he took the money, how he was seen on a certain morning, by policewoman Anne. . . .

Daisy behaved exactly as he expected. Daisy's absolute predictability was still a pillar of the world, a place almost, of absolute virtue which Tim recognized, though it gave him now no pleasure and brought him no consolation. Even in a perverse way he might have been briefly venomously glad if Daisy had turned him away with a curse. She had been making her lunch when he arrived. He refused to eat. After lunch she went out shopping and he lay on her bed in a phantasmagoria of misery. When she came back he sat up, paralysed and staring. The long day was passing.

'Tim, stop looking as if you've had a stroke. Move, walk, come to the Prince of Denmark.'

'We can't go there.' It was true. Tim was beginning to realize that he too must hide.

'Why not, fuck you?'

'We must leave here,' said Tim. 'We must live somewhere else. I've got money. We must go somewhere else.'

'Why? I like it here and it's cheap and your bloody money won't last forever, and who's "we" anyway?'

'We must go, we must hide.'

'You can hide, I'm damned if I will. I'm not a criminal!'

'I am,' said Tim. He continued to sit and stare out of the window. After a while Daisy went out slamming the door. The window began to grow dark at last.

'He took money out of my bank account,' said Gertrude.

Anne was silent.

Gertrude was back at Ebury Street. So was Anne. Anne had moved back into her old room, though she had not given up her flat.

It was late evening. Anne, in her blue dressing-gown had just been going to bed when Gertrude came in carrying a glass of whisky. Anne sat on the bed, Gertrude on the chair beside the dressing table. Gertrude had been out to dinner with Stanley and Janet Openshaw. She was wearing an amber-coloured silk dress.

'And he went straight to that woman,' said Gertrude.

Anne was not proud of her detective work. She had felt it necessary, some old academic sense of thoroughness, a desire for certainty, had led her to watch Daisy's flat. She had watched it on the evening of Gertrude's flight (she had telephoned the

Count to discover what had happened) and on the next morning. In the morning she saw with a curious mixture of pain and relief and shame, Tim's arrival. And she saw Tim turn and see her. It was a hateful role; but Anne wanted to be sure that she had not ruined Tim, and herself, for nothing. She resolved that she would not tell Gertrude. There was enough evidence without this horrible hurtful detail. At any rate she would keep this item in reserve, in case Gertrude weakened later. It might indeed never be necessary. However, she had been unable to restrain herself from making the Count happy by telling him of Tim's prompt return to his mistress. She also now felt the need to liquidate her own remaining hopes as quickly as possible. She wanted the new phase of the world, whatever it might prove to be, to begin. The Count then, after saying he would not, had been unable to restrain himself from telling Gertrude.

'Yes,' said Anne. 'I don't think you need go on fretting about having been unjust to him.'

'I wish it hadn't happened so quickly.'

'Better so. If he had had anything to say for himself he would have written or rung up.'

'He rang Victor and Moses. I expect he tried to ring Manfred, only Manfred silenced the 'phone.'

'Yes, but that was all on that day. He hasn't given any sign of life since then.'

'He could have found me, I didn't even leave London, he could have guessed I was staying with Stanley and Janet.'

'Why doesn't he write if he isn't totally guilty? He could ring up now if he wanted to.'

'I know. I—when the 'phone rings—I feel so—'

'Shall we go away, darling? Let's go to the country, to Stanley's cottage or—oh, somewhere else, anywhere out of London.' Anne here expressed her own wish to flee. She almost suggested going to Greece.

'No. I must stay here. I've got to—just in case of anything—and I must see Moses—about the arrangements—and the Count is such a support—and Manfred—'

Anne was silent. She was trying to read Gertrude's state of mind. It was not easy.

Nearly two weeks had passed since the terrible parting, and there had been no communication of any sort from Tim. Anne, as the days passed in silence, lived with her own anguish, watched Gertrude inevitably turning to Peter for comfort, watched the quiet cautious growth of Peter's sober hope. The Count visited Ebury Street, not too frequently. He had regained, with his hope, his dignity, his reserve. He was punctilious, heel-clicking, restrained; but now Anne could read him like a book. She saw the service of his love and could not but acknowledge it to be perfect. She could not but love him the more in seeing how wonderfully he loved her friend.

'I can't believe he actually planned to marry me for my money and support her—No, I can't believe he intended that.'

'I don't suppose he knew himself what he intended,' said Anne. 'He's a sort of moral imbecile.'

'Yes—'

Anne did her part, day by day, hour by hour, in helping to complete Gertrude's disillusion. It was a proper part, though such a painful one. Better that Gertrude should harden her heart quickly. Better for Gertrude, and better in a way for Anne. She did not want the scene at which she would have to assist, the events which she would have to witness, to last too long.

Gertrude's state of mind was in fact much more complex than Anne imagined, for Gertrude was now obsessed not only with Tim but with Guy. Her relation with Guy had taken another turn. A strong latent sense of guilt about her hasty marriage was now released and raged within her. It was as if Guy too were saying, 'I told you so!' Why did I marry so quickly, so foolishly, she thought to herself; and to Guy's shade she was constantly saying, I am sorry, I am so sorry. Yet she was not at peace with Guy. Rather, the peace which she had seemed to attain now seemed to her spurious, a tranquillized illusion necessary to the pursuit of her folly. She could not think of Guy gently, tenderly, sadly. She felt once more as if she were haunted by him, as if he came to her positively as a ghost; and with this haunting she felt the revival, with guilt and bitterness added to it, of her first awful grief. She had been formed and toughened by Guy's hatred of the sentimental, the vulgar, the self-indulgent, the false. How much she had loved that clean sternness. How much she had betrayed it. It seemed to her now that she had weakly withdrawn her total love from Guy as he became cut off, abstracted, unkind, untender, doomed. This withdrawal had been the start of her betrayal, her moral fall. She recalled Guy's saying once, we have individual virtues but general vices. No one is good all through, in all relations, for all purposes. As virtuous agents we specialize, we have to, because vice is natural and virtue is not. How quickly, without Guy, she had reverted to the natural level. How narrow, how artificial, it now seemed, her own 'specialization', which had somehow given her the illusion of being virtuous. And she said to him, why are you a ghost, why are you not with me really as my dear husband, as my support and guide. Your promises made me, and now you are gone. And she reached out into the void toward what she knew was now a figment of her own distressed and tormented mind.

About Tim she did not know what to think, except that he too was gone. She felt for him, thought of him at this time quite as if she were endowed with two minds and two hearts. She missed his presence with a detailed yearning. *Les cousins et les tantes*, eager, as Anne was, to obliterate her error, came sometimes near to hinting to her that it was 'purely physical', and thus momentary, or else a 'mental aberration' resulting from shock, a hysterical symptom, and thus also momentary. Gertrude knew that neither of these explanations was true. She had really loved Tim, and still did, with a love which would have to fade and wither. She comforted herself bitterly with a resentment against him, not only for his unspeakable treachery, but also because his awkward unnecessary existence and her own stupidity in sending him to France, had brought about that hasty and improper marriage, so offensive to the shade of Guy, and about which she now felt so painfully guilty and ashamed. She saw herself with the eyes of others and hung her head.

About the unspeakable treachery neither her head nor her conscience was entirely clear. She too, like Tim, had tried again and again to remember what exactly had been said in that awful nightmarish conversation. What exactly had she charged him with and what had he admitted and what had he denied? Was he always lying or only sometimes? Did it matter how much of the indictment was true, and what indeed *was* the indictment? She had at first tried to discuss this with Anne and the Count, even with Manfred, but all three were reluctant to hazard any views except rather general ones, and she herself soon felt such discussion to be improper. This meant that she was locked up alone with important, perhaps crucial problems. In fact Gertrude did not think that, in relation to her own decisions, the details could matter too much. Her sad foolish marriage was over. Tim was sufficiently guilty; and this appeared the more relentlessly clear as the days passed into weeks, without a word of any kind from her vanished husband.

Gertrude was also suffering from an ailment which had never acutely troubled her before, jealousy. The thought 'it is over' did not in any way alleviate this frightful degrading pain. Sometimes her jealousy seemed at the very heart and centre of the whole miserable situation. It was connected with her general sense of shame, her loss of moral dignity, her unwonted loss of face. She had always been the spoilt child of fortune, how could this happen to *her*, how could she be so woundingly insulted by fate? But it was more than this, deeper, more metaphysically awful. Tim had not just gone, he had gone to another woman, to whom he gave the physical love, the jests and sweetness and animal charm which Gertrude had so foolishly thought that she owned exclusively. She had learnt how death defeats love, at any rate defeats sex and tenderness. Now her tenderness was frustrated, embittered, but her desire raged. Tim had turned the light of his countenance elsewhere, and she would never know why or see that light again. Jealously she missed him, with anger and frenzy and bitter spiteful rage, and about this she could speak to no one.

'All the same,' said Gertrude to Anne, 'we ought to—I ought to—give him a chance to—explain. I mean, I don't want to see him—but he was so incoherent and—'

'Presumably he is silent because there is no explanation except a damning one.'

'I know. It's just that I want it to be all settled, finished. I want to settle down to it, do you see? I want to know that he has had a chance to defend himself and has refused it. I need to *know* that. Then I'll feel—better—'

'You are generous,' said Anne.

'Oh *Anne*—don't talk to me like that—I feel you're acting a part—sorry, I know you love me, I know you sympathize—'

How acute she is, thought Anne. I am acting a part. Oh such a dry desolate part. She said, 'I'm sorry, darling—'

'I'm not generous. I'm destructive and spiteful. I want to get out of the mess I've made. I want to see Tim as impossible, to know he's had a chance and rejected it. I can't explain. Sometimes we need a scapegoat. I want to save myself. It isn't generosity, and you don't think so. You can *see* what a miserable muddle I'm in.'

'Forgive me,' said Anne. 'I can't find the right words. I am trying.' She looked at Gertrude's dusky warm cheeks and handsome strong profile in the dressing table mirror. Gertrude had dressed carefully, chosen a bracelet, a necklace.

Gertrude came and sat beside her on the bed. She took Anne's hands and looked into her eyes. 'Your hands are cold. And look, that burn hasn't healed. You ought to let Victor look at it.'

'Maybe.'

'How lovely you look in your blue dressing-gown, it's like an evening dress. Blue suits you. Wasn't I clever to choose it for you?'

'Yes, very—'

'Anne, happiness has gone away. You first made me feel it was possible again. But I grasped a fake happiness, a wrong happiness—'

'You will find the possibility, the reality.'

'Guy said he wanted me to be happy—'

'Yes, yes—'

'Now I feel it would be a crime—Oh Anne, I know you have your troubles, I know you haven't been able to get a job, but don't worry about that. I want all your attention. I'm selfish enough and ruthless enough for that. We'll get you a job later, you'll see.'

'I'm not worrying about jobs.'

'It is *all right*, isn't it, darling Anne?'

'Yes, whatever it is!'

'I mean you and me, forever, the old alliance?'

'Yes, of course!'

'You'll stay with me always won't you, I can't exist without you.'

'Yes.'

'Yes, you'll stay?'

'Yes—Gertrude, I'm sorry, I wish I were better—' Tears sprang into Anne's eyes.

'Better! You're perfect. It's me that's all wrong. That terrible terrible mistake, upsetting everything and everybody. I feel I shall never get over it. Don't cry, my heart.'

'You'll recover,' said Anne, dashing away the tears. 'We all love you.'

'Yes, I'm very lucky. Everyone has rallied round, of course, they've proved right, but they're so affectionate, so kind. I've been such a nuisance to you, to Manfred, to the Count.'

'Nonsense. Did you have a nice evening with Stanley and Janet?'

'Yes. The Count was there. He's a wonderful being. You know, there's a lot to discover in that man.'

'Yes.' Anne released her hands. For a moment she stroked her friend's shining brown hair. 'Did you talk to him at all about what you've been saying to me, about settling down and being sure that Tim has had a chance—?'

'Yes. We talked when he came here that day—'

'Oh yes, when I had to go out.'

'The Count is so scrupulous. He was positively arguing on Tim's side. In fact he made me feel it all the more my duty.'

He would! thought Anne. 'Then you must do it.'

'Yes, but how? Anne, dear, would you—would you mind going back to that place, to that flat?'

'I'd rather not,' said Anne. 'Can't you write?'

'Oh *God*,' said Gertrude. She moved back onto her chair and started fingering her bracelet, turning it round and round. 'I suppose I could write. But I would want to be sure that he got the letter—he, and not someone else—Oh how *awful* everything is—'

'All right,' said Anne. 'I'll, if you like, deliver a letter and be sure he gets it.'

'Put it into his hands?'

'Yes.'

'Oh Anne, I'm so wretched, so stupid, so blind, so selfish, so *miserable*—'

Anne drew her friend back onto the bed and put her arms round her. She locked her hands behind Gertrude's silky back, where the long zip was already a little undone. She pressed her cheek against Gertrude's, suddenly seeing their two heads in the mirror, the silver-gold head and the chestnut brown one, their hair mingling. 'Darling, I do want you to be happy, I do want to *make* you happy.'

'Do you think you can do it by will-power?'

'I'll try my damnedest!'

'You'll have to put some sense into my head then. Oh what a mess, what a vile horrid idiotic mess!'

'I don't like the thought of you going there,' said the Count. 'That woman might attack you.'

'Oh she'd be quite capable of it!' said Anne. 'She might attack *you*!'

The Count looked worried. He said, 'I quite understand Gertrude wanting to be sure he gets the letter. After all the woman might destroy it, mightn't she?'

'She might.'

'One would have to try to see Tim alone.'

'One would.'

'You think she's an alcoholic?'

'I don't know. It's a bad scene.'

'Gertrude said you liked her.'

'I feel sorry for her. I think she lives in some awful rotten sort of twilight world full of illusions and half-truths and beastly muddle. I could smell it all in that room.'

'I'll take the letter,' said the Count.

'Oh all right,' said Anne. She was tired of the discussion. She thought, we're caught. Peter can't fight against Tim, and I can't fight for him. So I suppose in a way it cancels out. Except that I've got so much more sense and cunning than Peter has!

'I think Gertrude ought to see Manfred and talk it over,' said the Count.

Anne knew that Gertrude was having dinner with Manfred

that very evening. Evidently she had not mentioned this to the Count. She wondered how much he worried about Manfred.

'After all, he is the head of the family, I suppose, now that Guy is gone.' The Count said this with an air of lunatic solemnity which made Anne want to shake him.

'Oh the family!' she said with exasperation. 'There is no family, it's an invention.'

'An invention?'

'It's a trick, it's a game they play. They don't care about Gertrude. They enjoy her unhappiness.'

'Anne, that's unjust.'

'All right, Peter, it's unjust, yes, it is. They are good strong decent people. But it's not like a real close family all the same. I know some of them care for her. But she doesn't belong all that much. She married Tim to get away from them.'

'Do you really think so?' The Count looked worried again. The lines reappeared upon the white brow, brushed by the pallid wispy strawy hair. His pale blue snake-eyes gazed far away.

He is wondering, and how does that affect *my* chances, thought Anne. They were in Anne's flat. It was evening. The tired late August sun already showed crisp brown autumnal borders upon the plane tree leaves outside the window. Gertrude had said perhaps Anne would not mind discussing the matter with the Count. Anne had boldly telephoned the Count's office and suggested a meeting at his flat. He had replied no, he would call on her. Anne still visited her own flat on various pretexts. She wanted to keep her connection with it open and public. She did not know when she might not suddenly have to fly from Ebury Street. It seemed that the Count had not yet invited Gertrude to his flat, Gertrude would surely have mentioned it. He was playing a game as meticulous as Anne's.

'No, I don't really think so,' she said. 'I don't know what I think.'

Peter was silent for a while, and then said suddenly and with feeling, 'Poor Tim.'

Anne felt such a rush of love, she even made a slight movement as if to grasp his hand. She said, 'Won't you have a drink?'

'No, thanks. Everyone's against him.'

'He's against himself. But, yes. We like to have a sinner whom we can cast out and drive away into the wilderness. We pass on our pain by thinking of other people as evil.'

'Yes, it's like that isn't it. People enjoy the misfortunes and sins of others. He has carried all the blame.'

Anne wondered if they should now go on to assess Gertrude's share. They both decided not to.

'Of course he needs help too,' said Anne. 'I dare say he ought to leave that woman. If he stays with her he'll just drift off into a haze of idleness and drink. He'll probably become an alcoholic himself.'

The Count had not taken his jacket off this time. He was sitting on an upright chair beside the open window with his long thin hands on his knees. His thin bony wrists protruded from his clean stiff shirt cuffs. His hands were blanched, almond colour. The continued sunshine had made no difference to Peter, except for bringing out a very faint pinkish glow in his smooth cheeks. He kept hunching and twisting his shoulders as if his jacket irked him, and little transient frowns made pockets in his brow above his eyes. Oh Peter, Peter, I love you, I adore you, I want you, thought Anne. God, how people can deceive each other!

'Peter, do take your jacket off.'

'No, no, I'm fine.'

The Count, after his first outburst of confidence, perhaps ashamed of it, had ceased to talk to Anne of his love, though she knew that his pensive silence assumed her constant knowledge and sympathy. Oh suppose and suppose—suppose she were *now* to take his hand. But Peter was receding, changed, stiffened, alienated by hope. And the distance between them seemed to grow as he fed his hope and, for all her resolves, she could not stifle hers. Perhaps Tim would return and Gertrude would forgive him. Perhaps Gertrude would simply not want Peter after all. Perhaps she would marry Manfred. Or Moses or Gerald or somebody quite else whom she had once secretly loved. All these thoughts were so familiar to Anne from sleepless nights that they were before her like a physical place, a labyrinth with paths, a city with streets.

As time passed, as it was endured, and Anne went on with her patient efforts to see to it that Gertrude had every chance to recover from her infatuation with the redhead, Anne had also begun to reflect upon the restoration of her own sanity. She too wanted to 'settle down', to have some final proof that Tim was gone forever. Gradually, as hope faded, would not peace come? The peace even of a permanent commitment to the conjoined happiness of Gertrude and Peter. It was not easy. She was terribly alone. She saw only, precisely, Gertrude and Peter. The desire for other company was gone from her, though sometimes she felt she ought to seek it, as a sick person might attempt reluctantly to eat. She could see the learned Jesuit (he had asked her to lunch), she could go to one of Manfred's 'evenings', Janet Openshaw had asked her to coffee, an ecumenical group (how did they know she existed?) had asked her to give a lecture. But it was impossible for her to face the world. She *wanted* to stay in her corner with her demons.

She had attempted to turn her thoughts to her other visitor and to feed somehow upon his reality. Since his visit she had regained an occasional capacity for quietness, a stillness of the body which banished the restless aching in her bones. She felt something flow inside her head, as if a blank peace like white fog were flowing silently in. Sometimes she tried to speak to her visitor wordlessly. He still seemed to her at times like a sprite, a fairy thing, a lost vagrant spiritual being. Perhaps he was in some sense local, a little god left behind by a lost cult which even he had forgotten. Or was not his 'locality' determined rather by the whole universe beaming its radiance in upon the monad soul? She remained persuaded that he was *her* Christ, hers alone. He's all I've got, she thought. Somehow it was a true showing. Looking now at Peter's hands, she thought of *his* hands, his unscarred hands. 'I have no wounds.'

As Anne puzzled about the identity of her visitor she had, of course, not failed to recall a departed friend, the old traditional public Christ, the religious figure whom she had known so well ever since her childhood. She was amazed to find her imagination flinching from his sufferings upon the cross as from an abominable hardly conceivable torture. It was now like something she had read about in the newspapers, terrible things which gangsters or terrorists did to their victims. Many dedicated religious people accepted the traditional practice of deep continued meditation upon the passion of Christ. Her own order had not encouraged this (an enthusiastic nun who

354

developed the stigmata was treated as a medical case), and Anne herself had felt it unnecessary, even during a long time when the image of the crucified one almost never left her waking thoughts. She knew of the sufferings but she saw beyond them, as in familiar pictures where the suffering Christ is seen upon the cross attended by angels or gazed upon from above by God the Father. Now there were no angels, no Father, only a man hanging up in an unspeakable bleeding anguish, of which for the first time she was able to grasp the details. She felt appalled and sick; and with the loss of that old safety, morally tainted and astray. Innocence and clarity had left her. She had gained pleasure from thinking of Tim and Daisy as corrupt and evil, Peter, not she, had thought to pity Tim. It was from here that she returned to her own Christ, to gain the respite of his blank white foggy calm. Surely he had suffered. 'They drove the nails through my wrists.' But he spoke not of suffering but of death. Suffering is a task. Death is a showing. Sitting with Peter so close to her in the room, and looking at his hands, Anne was suddenly so persuaded of another, a supernatural presence, that she actually stood up with the intention of going into the kitchen to see if he were there again. At the same time, she uttered, half aloud, the word 'death'.

Peter looked at her. For a moment his thin hard clever face concentrated upon her, as if it had become pointed like the face of a fox. 'Anne?'

'Sorry —'

'I didn't hear what you said.'

'Oh nothing — Peter, if you see Tim will you talk to him, or just give him the letter?'

Peter's face lost its keenness and became again boyish and worried. 'Should I talk to him?'

'He needs help too. As you said, everyone blames him and he must feel driven out. Well, I know you'll be kind to him. Perhaps he should be encouraged to leave that woman. It might even help both of them. He must feel so awfully guilty, and if he just drifts on —' Peter's 'poor Tim' had touched Anne with a finger of sympathy and remorse. She had said enough to Gertrude about Tim's sins. Perhaps she had said too much.

'Gertrude would certainly be pleased if she knew he had left the mistress.'

355

'That's true,' said Anne. Of course Peter immediately saw it in terms of easing Gertrude's pain. His own jealous mind had perceived her jealousy.

'If he left the mistress—would he try to come back to Gertrude?'

'I don't know.' What am I saying, thought Anne, am I suddenly trying to push it all back the other way, back *my* way, before it's too late? She said, 'No, Gertrude would never take him back.'

Anne and the Count looked at each other. How muddled and strange emotion is, thought Anne. I love Peter, Peter pities Tim, I start imagining Tim—oh how I wish all the secrecy and muddle could be swept away and that all hearts could be opened and cleansed.

'You're right, he ought to leave her,' said the Count.

'There's so much pain in the world, Peter, but one can love pain if nothing's lost. It's the endings that are so terrible. That one can lose someone forever. That one has to decide. There are eternal partings, Peter, nothing could be more important than that. We live with death. Oh with pain, yes—but really—with death.'

For a second Anne saw a gentle beautiful prison face encased in white. Goodbye, God bless you.

The Count looked distressed, embarrassed. He said, 'Yes, poor Gertrude.' And then, 'I'll take the letter.'

Dear Tim,

I have heard nothing from you and I am told that you are living with your mistress. These facts perhaps speak for themselves. I do not ask to see you, but I am willing to hear from you by letter. Our last conversation was confused. You may wish to defend yourself on points where defence is possible, and I would wish to hear anything that you want

356

to say. We have both made mistakes. I am sorry for mine. I will shortly be in touch with Moses Greenberg about the future of our unfortunate relationship. If I do not hear from you very soon I will assume you have nothing to say to me.

Gertrude.

With this letter in his pocket the Count had set off to search for Tim.

The letter had cost Gertrude some trouble and much misery. It was, she realized, the first letter she had ever written to Tim. The first and the last. She wrote a number of drafts. In some she was angry and vindictive, in some gentle and accusing. Some were very long indeed. In none did she suggest a meeting or hint at a pardon. She eventually decided on a short business-like unemotional missive. She showed her final version to Anne and the Count, not to Manfred.

It did not prove too easy to find the recipient. The Count, very nervous, arrived at the house in Shepherds Bush where Daisy lived, found the street door open, climbed the stairs and, after discreetly listening, knocked. He feared viragos. No answer. Another tenant then appeared from a room opposite and informed the Count that Daisy Barrett and her redheaded young man had gone away, no one knew where to. The Count, relieved, nonplussed, went out, and telephoned Anne from a telephone box. It was noon, a grey cool day, and he had taken leave from the office. Anne was at Ebury Street holding the fort (what else had she to do). Gertrude, now very upset about her project, had gone off to teach clever sari-clad women what to say in shops. Anne told the Count to go to the Prince of Denmark before it closed, then to Tim's studio, whose address Gertrude had managed to recall. Tim had told Gertrude he had given up the studio, but this could be untrue.

The Count went, very reluctantly, to the Prince of Denmark, and sat there until closing time. He ate a sandwich. A black and white cat jumped on his knee. He sat nervously watching the door, expecting Tim, or Daisy (whom Anne had described) or Jimmy Roland (whom Ed Roper had described). Attempts by Ed and Manfred to discover Jimmy Roland's address, or anything further about him, had so far failed. At a suitably quiet moment, and with heavy nonchalance, the Count mentioned the three names to the barman, who gave him a suspicious look and no information. When the pub closed for the afternoon the Count emerged with relief and set off at once for the studio. He even took a taxi (it had started to rain), a thing which he rarely did.

He reached the garage and climbed the rickety wooden steps to a green door and, fearfully, knocked. There was a sound inside, then silence. He knocked again. Then he called out, 'Tim, it's me, the Count, just me.' Tim opened the door.

The shock of the sudden meeting made them both for a moment breathless. Tim blushed violently. The Count, who never blushed, grew paler. The pale blue eyes stared at the azure eyes. The Count felt pity, a sudden rush of affection.

'Come in,' said Tim.

It was a remarkable piece of luck, of chance anyway, that the Count should have found Tim at the studio. Tim and Daisy were not living there. Tim had simply run over to fetch a woollen jersey as the weather had grown colder.

The Count entered, quickly observing the scene and noting that there seemed to be no one else present. The long room, lit by skylights, felt cold and damp. The space contained a senseless chaos of pictures, frames, paints, pieces of wood, old newspapers, bulging plastic bags, open suitcases and scattered clothes. A mattress on the floor was piled with higgledy-piggledy blankets. There was a smell of petrol and oil and turpentine and paint and neglected clothes. A little rain had begun to fall, it pattered on the skylights. Down below motor cars roared softly.

'Oh Tim—' said the Count.

'I'm sorry there's such a mess,' said Tim. 'I'm not living here, you see. In fact I'm just moving out. Would you like a drink? There may be some beer.'

'No, thanks.'

Tim stood staring at the floor with his hands in the pockets of his unbuttoned mackintosh. He was unshaven. His gingery hair was unkempt, his ruddy lips drooped.

'Did you want anything special?' he said to the Count.

The Count had momentarily forgotten about the letter. He was overwhelmed by Tim's presence, by the reality of the whole business, its awful detail. Time had passed, Tim had been elsewhere, Tim had lived through time.

358

'Oh Tim—I'm so sorry—how can it have happened—what a nightmare—'

'I suppose you know all about it.'

'Yes.'

'You know more than I know then. Do you mind if I have a beer?'

'I looked for you at Shepherd's Bush and at the Prince of Denmark.'

'We've left those places.'

' "We"—'

'Daisy Barrett and me. My mistress, you know. Since you know so much.'

'You're—still together then?'

'Yes.'

The Count only now began to feel relief, noticed that he was able to, even permitted to. Had he expected that Tim would cry, take me to Gertrude? He had tried not to expect anything. He turned away from Tim and began to examine drawings of some rocks which were scattered on the floor, then a painting of a black cat with white paws. He said suddenly, 'I've seen that cat.'

'Yes, it's the moggie at the Prince of Denmark.'

The Count looked at the painting for a moment with pleasure, and his wrinkled brow relaxed as it had done in the pub when the cat jumped on his knee. Then he remembered the letter and rigidified himself. He stood at attention. All his fears returned together with his sympathy. 'Oh—I've got a letter for you from Gertrude. Here it is. She wanted me to put it into your hands.' He gave Tim the letter.

Tim uttered a little 'Ach!' and took it. He retreated, kicking a pile of clothes violently out of the way. He looked at the Count with an unhappy hostile face, his mouth crumpled with exasperation.

'You could read it now,' said the Count. 'It's quite short.'

'So you've seen it?'

'Well—yes—' said the Count remorsefully, more rigid than ever.

Tim hardened his mouth, now almost sneering, and tore the envelope violently, crumpling the letter. He read it quickly and held it out toward the Count. 'Thanks.'

'But it's yours,' said the Count. He reached forward, stepping into a pile of shirts. The letter fell to the ground between them and he picked it up.

'I don't want it,' said Tim. 'Do you imagine I want to put it in my wallet? It appears to be public property in any case. Sorry, this is stupid, stupid, stupid, *stupid*. Do you mind if I have a beer?' He went to the dresser and found a tin of beer. He dragged it open explosively and began to gulp it from the tin, his back turned to his visitor.

The Count looked at the hostile hunched-up back. Tim seemed to have grown smaller. The Count put the letter in his pocket. 'Tim, won't you come back to Gertrude?'

Tim turned, still drinking. He said in a moment, 'You read the letter. I'm not asked to.'

Rain was now falling steadily and running in a flickering stream down the glass of the skylights. Somewhere inside the room there was a sound of dripping.

'I'm sure she would take you back.'

' "Take me back". How I detest those words!'

'Well, what words can I use—'

'It's not on. It's *impossible.*'

'Why? Do you really love this other woman more?'

Tim gave a sort of sneering laugh and tossed the empty beer tin into the sink. 'Count, you're a clever man and you've read a lot of books, but you don't seem to understand the world at all.'

'But why?'

'It's not like that. One doesn't just look and choose and see where one might go, one's sunk in one's life up to the neck, or I am. You can't swim about in a swamp or a quicksand. It's when things happen to me that I know what I evidently wanted, not before! I can see when there's no way back. It's a muddle, I don't even understand it myself. But some things are clear, I've had it, I'm over. Gertrude should never have married me. I've made such a bloody mess of it all. I had this other involvement and I never told her. I just tried to imagine it didn't exist or it didn't matter and I could just step out of it and forget it. Well, I *did* step out of it, but when—Oh hell, I can't explain. Then somehow it all took me over again—No wonder Gertrude booted me out.'

'She didn't.'

'She did.'

'I think she feels you ran away. And that looked bad. You didn't talk, you just disappeared. Why did you? You didn't have to go. Gertrude would have changed her mind.'

'You say these beautiful simple things and they're just bloody horrible! Don't torture me with what might have happened and didn't.'

'I mean, she may still change her mind, I'm sure you should try. Anyway, you'll answer the letter?'

'No, what's the point? How can I? What is there to say? It's all *happened* and I can't unhappen it now. I've gone back where I belong. It's like magnetism or the force of gravity. I was never at home in your sort of world, well not yours, theirs, hers. I was in the wrong place. I can't write letters anyway and she doesn't trust me any more, and she doesn't love me any more or she wouldn't write me a sort of public business letter like that. I expect she hates me, why shouldn't she, she must be as sore as hell. I can imagine how the rich relations are crowing. She only loved me by mistake, because of the sun and the rocks and the water. She was under a spell, and it's broken now. She made a *mistake*, that's all.'

'Tim, please write to her, explain anything you can, say you're sorry. I'm sure it wasn't all like she thought.'

'She said I'd made a plot to marry her and keep Daisy on the proceeds! At least I think she said that. That wasn't true. And I did leave Daisy—'

'Well, there you are. You have things to say—'

'It's no good, it's not just accidents or things one could remove or explain. It's my whole life, it's me, that's the trouble. Like I said, I live in a swamp. She comes from a different world where everything's just so and people know where they begin and end and what's the case and what isn't and what's right and what's wrong and all that. It's not my world. I made a mistake too.'

'But you loved Gertrude, you love her.'

'You're trying to make up some noble speech to recite at Ebury Street! No. Anyway she won't be interested. You're trying to invent a sort of case for me—because—because you're you—and don't think I don't—appreciate it, Count. But it can't connect with her any more, it can't touch her. She's finished with me and I've finished with her. Oh leave me *alone*! Don't meddle with me, I don't want your kindness and your sympathy and your attempts to understand! Just clear off, let it go, let it pass, forget it, don't think about me any more, I don't want to be understood, just let me go to the devil in my own way.'

The Count was silent, stiff, his hands at his sides, his face now calm, unwrinkled, hard. He said after a moment, 'I think you ought to leave that woman. I don't mean this as anything against her, I don't know her. I just think you ought to be alone and to organize your life and your work and not just drift along. You might become an alcoholic—'

'Who put that idea into your head?'

'It is possible to leave people.'

'I know, I'm doing it. Christ, it's cold in here. Are you sure you won't have a drink?'

'You ought to be alone for a while and then you'll be able to—'

'No! No way, Count. Don't make that calculation. And will you for Jesus bloody sake, leave my private life alone, it's all I've got. As you say, you don't know anything about Daisy, or about how we live. I've known Daisy ever since we were students, practically children, she's my family. I know what all this is in aid of. It's that vile evil woman Anne Cavidge. I hate her, why doesn't she go back to her convent. She doesn't understand anything, and she goes round judging people as if she were God. She behaved like a bloody policewoman. And she's been turning Gertrude against me, I *know* she has—'

The Count could not deny this. He had heard Anne speaking her mind to Gertrude. He said, 'Tim, I'm so sorry about it all.'

'So am I, but there's nothing to be done, the party's over. Gertrude can arrange the divorce any way she likes, I'll do anything, sign anything. I took some money out of her account. I'll pay it back later, I can't now, I'm living on it, *we're* living on it. Oh Jesus!'

'I could lend you some money,' said the Count.

'Count, dear—' said Tim. He came forward and put his hands on the Count's arms for a moment, gripping his arms and looking up into the face of the tall thin man who stood rigid

as if at attention before him. Then he moved toward the door.
'You must go.'

'All right. But think it over.'

'Goodbye, Count. Thanks for coming. Sorry it's raining so
hard. You've been kind, very especially kind. And you've never
said a word of—well, you wouldn't. Entirely in character if I
may say so. Goodbye. I hope that Gertrude—may find a better
husband—'

'Oh Tim—Tim—'

Tim opened the door. The Count went carefully down the
rickety wooden steps, now slippery with the rain. He had no
hat. The water turned his straight colourless hair into dark
dripping rats' tails. He thrust Gertrude's crumpled letter, which
he had been holding in his hand, into his pocket. He walked
hurriedly away along the road. Then he began to smile. He put
his head back and smiled up into the rain.

'Well, who wrote that anonymous letter if you didn't?' said
Tim to Daisy.

'How the hell do I know? And what the hell does it matter
now?'

'I wish I'd taken it. I could have done. Then I'd have seen if
it was your typewriter.'

'Don't you believe me?'

'Oh—hell—'

'Are you setting up a police state here? You'd bloody better
not. You're as bad as that Anne Cavidge female, you're two of
a kind, you'd better set up together as private eyes, Reede and
Cavidge, Dirty Work.'

'I loathe that woman.'

'I rather liked her.'

'You're just saying that to annoy me.'

'You're easily annoyed.'

'We've done nothing but quarrel since we came here.'

'We've done nothing but quarrel since we first met, and that's a good many years ago now. Whatever that proves, maybe just that we're dead stupid.'

'Daisy, you did write that letter, didn't you, that letter to the Count, saying that Gertrude and I were having an affair?'

'NO I DIDN'T! Why the hell should I? I don't care who you have affairs with, you can walk out of this door any time and have an affair with anyone and marry them too, especially if they're rich—'

'Oh stop—'

'*You* stop! Do I seem to you like somebody who writes anonymous letters? I ask you! Anonymous! I'm not afraid of those buggers. If I'd wanted to give them a piece of my mind I'd have written a plain honest letter and signed it. Christ Jesus, do you know me so little after so long?'

'Well, somebody wrote it, and—'

'God, if you could only see your mean fussy little face! Shall I find you a mirror? You look like a nasty ferrety little police clerk. What the bloody hell does it matter who wrote the shitty letter? Are you writing your autobiography or something?'

'You were in a very vindictive state—'

' "A very vindictive state"! What words you dredge up! I wasn't vindictive, I was angry, fed up to the bloody teeth. If I'd wanted to put the boot in I wouldn't have done it in a mean secretive roundabout way—'

'Oh all right, maybe you didn't write the letter, but you must have told all those lies to foul Anne Cavidge.'

'What lies?'

'Oh about us having planned that I should marry a rich woman and so on and about our having been together after I got married and—'

'I didn't! Bloody Jimmy Roland started all that up according to you!'

'She said Jimmy Roland started it, God knows why—'

(What Tim did not know was that Jimmy Roland had never forgiven Tim for, as Jimmy saw it, jilting his sister Nancy. The news of Tim's fine marriage had come as an unpleasing reminder. Jimmy also disliked Daisy for mocking Piglet. The drunken 'disclosure' to Ed Roper had been a piece of impromptu random spite.)

'Who's this "she" you keep talking about?'

'Of course Jimmy might have heard us drivelling away in the Prince of Denmark any time. But Gertrude would never have believed it if you hadn't said it was true.'

'Said what was true?'

'Oh fuck, all that that I said! Gertrude said you told Anne Cavidge it was all true!'

'God knows what I said to that bitch. I may have said "oh yes!" to some insulting rot. Can't she recognize sarcasm? I just wanted to get her out of the door. I thought it was a bit much being persecuted by your wife's best friend. You know why she came of course?'

'Why?'

'Because she's in love with Gertrude.'

'Oh don't be stupid!' The idea was new to Tim. He thrust it away. It simply added to the ghastly jumble. 'You think everybody's queer.'

'You think nobody is.'

'You agreed to everything she said because you wanted to smash up my marriage.'

'I didn't want to smash up your bloody marriage! I wanted to be left alone at last! I wasn't interested in your marriage. Do you think I'd have raised a finger to get you away from your precious fatty? Anyway you don't seem to have needed any assistance. You seem to have smashed it all up pretty effectively yourself!'

'You must have made her think we'd been together after—'

'Oh hells bloody bells, do stop raking it over! Leave all that muck behind you. You're here, you came running back to me with your tail between your legs. We've even moved house because you're so frightened of that unspeakable mob. Isn't that enough? Do I have to listen to your endless reminiscences as well?'

'They're not reminiscences. I'd like to know the truth.'

'Truth! That's a funny word coming from you! You don't know what it means. You're all soft in the middle, Tim Reede, your soul's full of nasty squelchy pulp.'

'Why are you so unkind to me when you know I'm so unhappy—'

'Go back to darling Gertie, then.'

'You know I shall never do that.'

'Well I don't care what you do. Go and hang yourself.'

'If you weren't drunk half the time we wouldn't quarrel. Oh I'm so tired of it!'

'Who drove me to drink? You haven't any occupation except the bottle. Let me tell you something. I didn't miss you when you were away. I drank less, I worked more, I got on quite well with my novel. I haven't written a word since you so graciously came back.'

'Well, we've been moving house.'

'To suit you!'

'You said you liked it here.'

'It's a bit sleeker than my place, but we'll come down to earth with a bump when Mrs Reede's cash runs out. I haven't seen *you* earning much money lately.'

'You know I can't—'

'Because you're so mopy and sulky and whiny, yes!'

'Oh, I *will* earn money—You're destroying me, you're eating me, you destroy my substance, I feel I'm being gradually consumed when I'm with you. Just don't needle me the whole time.'

'You're doing the needling. I'd prefer to ignore you. If it wasn't for you I'd have a trade and a life of my own.'

'You keep saying that.'

'It's true.'

'Let's go to the pub.'

'It's always "let's go to the pub", and then you accuse me of drinking! You've demoralized me with your idle feckless ways and now you hate the sight of what you've done! And I hate the sight of you, you're a creepy-crawly. All right, go back to law and order and marriage and money!'

'I'd have married you long ago you know that, only you hated the idea of marriage, you hated the very word!'

'Do you imagine we'd have been different married?'

'I don't know. I'm sorry. It's worse than ever. I feel I'm in hell.'

'This is what hell is like, where we live, where we've always lived. No money, rows, and off to the pub. Christ, why did I ever get mixed up with bloody men?'

'Oh let's stop fighting. I apologize.'

'He apologizes! *Laissez moi rire!*'

'Let's try and be as we were.'

'We shall never be as we were.'

'Not that that was up to much.'

'You're spoilt, you're not my old Tim any more. You smell of that woman.'

'Don't say that, Daisy darling. Don't hurt me. OK, we two have made our hell, but can't we unmake it by mutual consent?'

'Are you suggesting a suicide pact?'

'Or at least be quietly together and not hurt each other.'

'In the municipal graveyard under the mown grass.'

'Oh be serious —'

' "Be serious" he says. Do you think I'm in a joking mood about this — this — Oh you unspeakable cad!'

'Daisy, I know you're jealous, or you were jealous —'

'*Jealous?* You stupid shit —'

'Yes, I am stupid, forgive me my stupidity and all the rest too. If you won't forgive me, no one will, so you've got to forgive me.'

'I don't see why. I hope you burn. If you aren't careful I'll put you in my novel. That's the worst punishment I can think of for anyone.'

'Dear Daisy, you will be kind to me, you are kind to me —'

'Oh you — I was going to say "rat" — you — guinea pig! You're a male chauvinist guinea pig. Except that guinea pigs don't whine.'

'I'm not whining.'

'You make me sick. The sight of your stupid pulpy face makes me sick. OK then, let's got to the pub. Let's get sozzled while the money lasts.'

Tim and Daisy were living in a furnished flat near Finchley Road Station. The flat had been let to them at a modest rent by one of Daisy's mysterious female friends who was temporarily in America. It was a pleasant quiet flat mainly furnished with bamboo chairs and tables and very large brown cushions which lay upon the floor. There was plenty of room for Daisy's ailing potted plants. Tim had felt a frenzied need to get right away from anywhere where *they* could ever find him. (Some of them lived in Hampstead, but not near Finchley Road.) The idea of seeing any of them again, Anne, the Count, Manfred, Stanley, Gerald, made him feel sick with horror. He did not consider seeing Gertrude, he did not touch this idea even with the finest remotest tentacles of his imagination. He was, in spite of Daisy's battering, in spite of their ambiguous addictive quarrels, trying to settle down to his new life which was also in such a strange way his old life.

Of course they were not as they were. Tim now looked back upon the old days, when he was painting cats and Daisy was writing her novel and they were having picnic lunches together and meeting every evening at the Prince of Denmark and occasionally making love, as a period of aboriginal innocence. They had been as children. Now he had spoilt all that. He was not Daisy's old Tim any more. The occasion of the loss caused him such misery that he did not come to work out whether he regretted the loss itself. No doubt the old world had been illusory, not as it seemed. Lies seemed to be everywhere in his life. He could see, still, the worth of Daisy, her courage, her extraordinary tolerant kindness to him. At the same time he saw even more clearly the impossibility of their relationship, an impossibility which they had lived with so long: the rows, the drink, the drift into chaos, the particular way in which they laboured at mutual destruction. Yet even all this could still seem innocent because, out of a kind hopelessness, they still forgave each other.

Tim was in extreme pain, a greater pain than he had ever felt before. When Gertrude had rejected him, when she had broken off their so improbable engagement and he had run back to Daisy on the previous occasion, he had suffered extremely. He had felt the misery of rejection and deprivation. He had loved Gertrude with wild erotic joy and deep attentive tenderness; and when she had said, 'I cannot', Tim had felt his grief as the most extreme that he had ever known. But it had been more bearable, not only because he had then, much as he loved his fiancée, loved her less than he had later loved his wife, but also because the miserable loss had not been his fault. He had run back to his hiding place thinking, I have always been unlucky, it was too good to be true; and he had thought this severance and this disappointment to be the worst thing that he could suffer.

His thought, winding ingeniously and endlessly in and out of the past, dwelt occasionally upon the fact that at that earlier time too he had been deceiving Gertrude upon a material point. Yet, she did not know it, which made him, because innocent in her eyes, more somehow innocent. And who was to say how soon he might not have told Gertrude everything if he had been left with her in his first happy state? The shock of her rejection, his loss of confidence, had, he told himself, tended toward the fatal delay in the confession later. There was also the *fact* that he had gone straight back to Daisy and to Daisy's bed. How important was that? He was not then to know that he would win Gertrude back. Sometimes he wondered, what exactly is it that I am accused of which makes me feel so cripplingly guilty and gives me this awful *new* pain with which I can scarcely live? Had he deliberately pulled some filth of sinfulness over himself like a cover? He had been prompt to take Gertrude's money out of the bank, and no small sum. He had once more run to Daisy, and if he was not yet in Daisy's bed this was no doubt a temporary accident of their mutual unhappiness and congenital irritation with each other. What have I done, he thought, what does it *amount* to? Sometimes he felt that his punishment was the main evidence against him.

It remained that his frightful loss tormented him in a mode of intense guilty remorse. He felt himself permanently stained and damaged by what had happened. He recalled what Gertrude had once said about 'a moral danger, a moral frightfulness'. What did she know of such perils? He had fallen into a trap of sin like someone falling into a deep pit and although he still did not quite understand why, he took the full consequences as something unavoidable and even just. He had messed around too long, juggled too much, tried to have everything every way and nothing properly, told too many easy and convenient lies. And if he now felt wretchedly miserable because he had been found out and punished, he did not thereby excuse himself. He fiddled around with the problem of what exactly Gertrude thought, what exactly she had said. But he knew that he had cheated. The phenomenon of Daisy was large in his life, it stretched far back into his earliest youth, it was, and perhaps would finally be, the main sense and enterprise of his existence. He could not magic it away out of his past or his present. When he thought of this phenomenon he sometimes hated Daisy; but this too was not for the first time.

The old Daisy problems were back. They could not live together, they could not live apart. They managed to share the flat for the moment because it was fairly large and they could get away from each other. They slept in separate rooms. Tim in the small bedroom slept with crossed arms, curled into a ball, or lay awake with his hands over his eyes, as the street lamps blazed through the thin curtains all night. During the day Daisy worked on her novel, or tried to and complained that she could not, but at least she stayed in her room. They went to various local pubs in the evenings and got drunk. Tim went out most of the day, occasionally he returned for lunch. Sometimes Daisy was out. They did not 'tell their day' any more. They irked each other with abrasive restless presences and itinerant unexplained absences. Doors banged. Tim had given up keeping the kitchen clean. The originally pleasant flat was beginning to resemble Daisy's place in Shepherd's Bush. He knew he would have to find somewhere else to live. They would have to return to the old method of meeting which had once (how touching!) seemed to them romantic. The problem of how they were to live was returning (as Gertrude's money ran out) towards its old basis in lack of cash. Tim could not work and did not attempt to. He supposed that after a certain lapse of time it would be safe for Daisy to return to Shepherd's Bush, for him to go back to the studio, but he could not bear to envisage it at present. *Lanthano*.

When Tim had said to Daisy that he was 'in hell' he had indeed meant something that was 'worse', worse than ever before. Nightmares thronged his days and nights. He had frightful recurrent dreams. In one dream a soft floppy effigy, which he was watching with horror, and who was also himself, was being tossed in a blanket by a sinister circle of maliciously smiling girls. Similar effigies, in the form of half-animated demons, followed him slowly but relentlessly in dreams, like soft life-size dolls which came pushing up against him, and when he

370

thrust them away came quietly back again. He was pursued by a stone head which rolled after him, groaning terribly as it went. He dreamed too of a hanged man whom, again, he saw but in some way was. The man, dead and yet also living and suffering horribly, was hanging from a long railing which looked like a stairhead. His eyes and mouth were open in frightful expressive pain, yet he was motionless, his hands and feet hanging limp, his head fallen on one side, a dreadful image of defeated punished guilt.

During the day Tim walked, he walked down the Finchley Road, through Maida Vale along the Edgware Road to Hyde Park, or else through St John's Wood to Regent's Park. Sometimes he went to Kilburn or to his old haunts in the Harrow Road. More often he made for central London, always on foot, and walked in the parks or as far as Whitehall and the Embankment. Walking now was his task. (It was Anne Cavidge's task too, and they nearly met head-on once in St James's Park, only Anne stayed by the lake to watch the pelicans and Tim turned off the path and crossed the grass to the Mall. Thus they passed unknowingly within two hundred yards of each other.) Sometimes Tim went into the picture galleries. The galleries attracted him because of terrible things which he experienced there and which he had to keep morbidly returning to. He no longer dreamed at night that the National Gallery was dim and senseless. The dream had become true, he experienced it walking, in broad daylight. The pictures were all dull and stupid, trivial, incoherent, mean. The colours were filmed over as if he had become colour-blind, or else they were suddenly gaudy, garish like sweet papers, like drifting idle trash. He *hated* the pictures, their pretentiousness, their pompous sentimentality, their pretence of solemn meaning, their essential emptiness.

Tim began to think about death. He felt tired of the stupid suffering which he was beginning to realize was like a virus, the very essence of his invaded being. No one inflicted the suffering, he was it and it would not go. It could not be removed or run from. When he had said to Daisy that hell might cease she had spoken of death. Well, Daisy could please herself, but he at least could go. He watched the big red friendly London buses rolling slowly along upon their great wheels. He imagined how he would move, slowly too, into the road, kneel, and then lie down carefully beneath one of those merciful moving wheels. It would be over in a second. The image consoled him. He knew indeed that he would not do this today or tomorrow, but it was good to know that it was so simple and he might do it some day.

He did not dare to think much about Gertrude, it was too agonizing. Sometimes he tried to exorcise her by doubting his love: he had, after all, married her for money. He was no longer young, he had married her for security and ease. He had married her so that he could at last paint as he pleased. He feigned to persuade himself, while yet he knew that his strong terrible love for her survived like a hidden beast, a rabid dog that would have to be pulled from its cupboard one day and killed, or else would take a long long time to starve to death. He wished sometimes, rather abstractly, that he could tell Gertrude that it had not been all lies, that it was not all bad, that the bad bit could be simply cut away and leave the rest. But what now was 'the rest'? He himself had erased it. He never considered writing to her. He did not dream of her. He dreamed more often of his mother. He felt broken, and words like 'integrity' and 'honour' occurred to him as names of what he had lost: words which were new to him and which he resented. Where had he picked them up? Had he acquired them somehow from the Count? Had the words got out of the Count's head and into his without being uttered? Could words do that?

As time went by he thought less about the painful conundrum of his last conversation with Gertrude, and thought more about his last conversation with the Count. The Count had said nightmarish things like 'I'm sure she would take you back'. Tim was not sure why those words were so repulsive. Perhaps because they reminded him of childhood, of his mother, of grudging untender pardons, of something on a scale which had nothing to do with him and Gertrude. The Count's persuasions, his 'simple ideas', had been really insults and proofs of his failure to understand. Of course the Count was doing his duty, and being the Count had done it conscientiously. His rival could hardly expect of him perfect sensibility and inspired eloquence as well. But other things which the Count had said had made sense for Tim, had touched live nerves, and remained with him as somehow uncontaminated thoughts. You ought to be alone, you ought to think and work. Oh yes, thought Tim, one can leave someone forever, it's possible and I should know.

If I were alone would it be better, he wondered, could I ever get back those things which I have lost, could I get back at least some scraps of some old innocence? If I were alone could I achieve a *clean* despair, a *clean* pain at last? Then I could deal with the beast in the cupboard. Then I could deal with the demons. Yes, when Gertrude and I danced that hay among the blue flowers it was with demons that we danced it.

He thought, I ought to be alone, and not for any purpose except to be alone. He thought, will I leave Daisy in the end? But he knew that, like kneeling down in front of the merciful red bus, this would not happen today or tomorrow.

SEVEN

'The rocks come closer at this time in the evening,' said Anne. It was almost twilight, darkening but bright.

They had pulled the table out of the archway onto the terrace and were sitting drinking white wine. The September evenings were very warm.

'Yes,' said Gertrude, 'they become sort of unfocused, I can't describe it exactly —'

'I know,' said Anne, 'I can't get them into focus either, they sort of jump at one.'

'What colour would you say they were now?' said the Count.

'Pink? No. Grey? No. They're certainly not white, yet they're whitish.'

'Spotty,' said Gertrude. 'Well, spotty isn't a colour. Now I can scarcely see them at all, they're dancing.'

'In Polish,' said the Count, 'colour words are verbs too.'

'How do you mean?' said Gertrude.

'One doesn't just say, "it is red", one can say "it reds".'

'That's good,' said Anne. 'So one feels the colour as sort of radiating actively from the thing, not just sitting passively in it.'

'Exactly.'

'The rocks are certainly pinking!' said Gertrude. 'You see they've changed — now they've gone fuzzy again. My God, how still it is.'

They listened for a moment.

'The cicadas have stopped.'

'It's so quiet and so clear, not a leaf stirring.'

'Nothing stirring but the rocks!'

'Look at the leaves of the willows and the olives — they're sort of fixed, outlined in silver.'

'It's like a painting,' said Anne.

'Have some more wine?' said the Count.

'Count is wine steward,' said Gertrude.

'I must go shopping tomorrow,' said Anne.

'You're always going shopping,' said Gertrude.

374

'Well, the driver must shop. I must go to the garage about the exhaust and fill up with petrol.'

'We'll come too,' said Gertrude.

'No, no, you two must do that walk.'

Anne had driven Gertrude and the Count to Les Grandes Saules in Guy's Rover. The car had been laid up after Guy's death, but it had proved quite easy to put on the road again. Guy, a careful meticulous driver, had kept it in excellent condition. Anne, with her brand new driving licence, had felt nervous at first, but the handsome car had eventually decided to drive itself.

The idea of the three of them going to France had come up in rather a confused way. Gertrude had declared that Anne needed a holiday. After all, Anne had not been out of England for fifteen years, Anne ought to see France, Italy, again. Anne had responded that she thought Gertrude needed a holiday and if Gertrude wanted to go abroad she would go with her. Immediately after this exchange the Count, now a regular visitor at Ebury Street, had arrived for a drink and joined in. Certainly Gertrude needed a holiday. They discussed where Gertrude and Anne should go. Greece was not mentioned. It was Gertrude herself who suggested that they should go to Les Grandes Saules, why not. Anne guessed that Gertrude wanted to confront and finish with her embarrassing memories of the episode there with Tim. Guy's ghost, now Tim's. By this time it had begun to seem natural, polite, inevitable that Gertrude should ask the Count to come with them. Had he not some leave which he could conveniently take? Why not come and stay at least a little while? After all, he surely needed a holiday too. It was the Count's idea that Anne should drive them. (The Count *of course* had never learned to drive.) He became quite insistent. Anne was sadly strangely touched and her heart stirred within her. So the Count wanted to be driven by her. Driving and being driven is a significant relationship. Then she realized that the Count's purpose was to cut out Manfred. The Count was becoming more confident, more positively Machiavellian.

They had been there now for three days. The weather was steadily goldenly bright and hot. Anne could see as in a glass, how happy she would have been to be here with Gertrude if only her heart were not in the process of being broken. It was as if the natural world, from which she had been exiled for so long, had come back to her, posing like a dancer and holding out its hands. No, that was not the image. It lounged rather before her like a lovely animal, it quietly purred and displayed itself. Anne had never liked the convent garden. It had seemed to her skimpy and formal and mean. She had taken her turn at working in it but it had inspired no interest and given no joy. The convent had been for her an indoor place, a hiding place: her little cell, the chapel, the dark corridors smelling of bread. The valley was, as Gertrude said, amazingly still and brilliant with detail. The little meadow where Tim and Gertrude had danced so long ago among the blue flowers was yellow now, the dry prickly grass smoothed and silkened in the evening light. A scattering of little mauve globe thistles had replaced the wild muscari of the spring. The old hunched-up olive trees stretched out their speary silvery foliage like the arrested hands of metamorphosed beings. Even the restless willows of the brook were still. Only the rocks moved, mysteriously mobile in the uncertain light. This was their hour. At other times of day they were starkly blindingly motionless.

The holidaymakers had so far been unambitious. The sheer shock of finding themselves thus alone together had been considerable. The journey, rather unspontaneously hilarious, had been easier. Now suddenly, in this established given space, they had to sort themselves, move about, warily, in relation to each other. Gertrude of course allotted the rooms. She took the large bedroom which had been hers and Guy's. Anne had the small corner room with the view two ways, over the valley and toward the cleft in the rocks. The Count was given the divan downstairs in Guy's study, with the cloakroom beside it. In other matters, Anne took charge, and indeed the leadership of the trio seemed naturally to belong to her. The other two were lazy, laughingly compliant. Anne did the shopping and organized their cuisine. They had decided to live simply on bread and cheese and salads with olives and wine and the plentiful fruits of the season, figs and melons and warm golden furry apricots. Oddments from the village deep freeze might be called upon to vary this diet. Anne, with her self-appointed tasks, found it easy to leave Gertrude and the Count together.

She also began to plead headaches. This was no fiction. She was being visited by an old enemy, migraine, brought on perhaps by looking so much at those enigmatic spotty unfocusable rocks.

Since their arrival they had sufficiently amused themselves by walking about in the valley and climbing the nearer rocks. They had all had lunch in the village yesterday at the little hotel restaurant, and Anne had invented one or two pretexts to go shopping. There had been a lot of sitting about and drinking. In the evening they played cards, three-handed bridge, at which the Count was so good that he had to make deliberate mistakes to render the game viable. The other two laughed a lot and threw away their advantages. No one concentrated much. Gertrude, taught by Guy, was in fact not a bad player. Anne, who had not played for many years, was at first ambitious, anxious to regain her skill and win, but she soon stopped trying, especially after she realized that Peter was cheating. It became a game of chance.

'Are you warm enough, darling?' said Anne to Gertrude. 'Shall I fetch your shawl?'

'I'm fine.'

'Shall we eat? I mean, there's nothing to eat but shall we eat it?'

'Anne always says there's nothing, and there's a feast!'

'Like the loaves and fishes.'

'I'll come and help,' said the Count.

'No, no —' Anne never called him Peter in front of Gertrude. 'Anne's Martha and I'm Mary!'

'Dear me, then who am I?' said the Count.

They laughed, as they always did at each other's silly jokes.

In spite of a certain quiet tension there was a holiday atmosphere. Gertrude had bought two new dresses, one of which she was wearing, a light yellow robe with wide sleeves, with a little necklace of blue Venetian beads close around her neck. Anne was wearing the cherry-blossom dress which Gertrude had given her. She had resolutely refused to let Gertrude give her any more clothes. The Count had, Anne suspected, invested in a whole new outfit. He wore light-weight flared trousers with a minute blue and white stripe, and a loose blue short-sleeved tunic shirt, open at the neck. His thin bony feet were on display in smart conspicuously unsmirched sandals. It was the first time

Anne had seen him informally dressed. She was not sure if it suited him. She watched him now as he lounged, his long legs extended, his knuckles beating a noiseless rhythm on the table-cloth as he looked tenderly, smilingly, at Gertrude. His pale snake-blue eyes, which looked cold when he was sad, were sparkling now, narrowed between little folds of laughter-wrinkles. The sun had touched his cheek with a pinkness which looked almost like rouge. But his thin arms, emerging rather gawkily from the short shirt-sleeves, were white, covered with long drooping black hairs. Anne looked at the thin hairy arms and longed to stroke them very gently.

'The only thing I miss in our diet is English cheese.'

'Why don't the French import it, they care so much about food?'

'Chauvinism is stronger.'

'When will the crickets begin to chant?'

'Soon.'

'I vote we eat now.'

Anne rose to go to the kitchen.

'Darling, would you bring my shawl after all?' said Gertrude.

The Count jumped up. 'I know where it is.' He ran in through the open glass doors of the sitting-room and brought out the shawl which be began to drape carefully over Gertrude's shoulders.

Anne retired quickly. It occurred to her that in preparation for what was to come she was trying to give up her love for Peter as she had given up smoking before it was time for her to enter the convent. Sex had not been difficult to give up. Giving up smoking had been harder. To stop loving Peter was impossible. She found herself, when alone, always stupidly close to tears.

Anne knew how grateful the other two were to her, how necessary she was and how no one else could possibly, for both of them, have played this necessary part. The atmosphere of a well-suited holiday trio was not a fiction. She could imagine the pleasant things which, complicitly, they said about her when she was not there. Complicitly, looking into each other's eyes. 'Anne is marvellous, isn't she?' 'Yes, a perfect dear.' 'I'm so fond of her.' 'So am I.' Anne wonderfully enabled Gertrude and the Count to be together in a kind of loving peace without

378

urgent problems, without dangerous decisions. Anne made continued speech between them possible and easy. Of course there was the tension in the air, a kind of high humming sound which they all heard, as of some vital time machine which was running its course. But Anne created, as if with her outstretched hands, a space for them, an interim wherein they did not have to consider either strategy or tactics.

Anne did not think that anything would, during this holy time, 'happen'. She was sorry about this. Being without hope, she wished that the matter could be hurried on to a conclusion. She even wondered whether anything which she could do would hustle them a little. She thought about Peter and Gertrude with the minute care of someone studying a mathematical or philosophical problem. She decided that Peter would do nothing (unless positively prompted to by his beloved) until after the anniversary of Guy's death. Probably he would wait until next spring. He might indeed go on delaying out of sheer fear of a refusal. At present, enclosed in the space which Anne held sturdily open for him, he was happy. He could look at Gertrude as much as he liked, knowing that he was not yet expected to do anything else. And Gertrude too was grateful to relax, to *rest*, tended and adored by two devoted beings, held in the warm beam of their concerted love. She sighed now and then, with a sigh as of sad or bitter thoughts, yet at the same time stretching her limbs as if she were positively basking in the comfort of that focused attention.

Would Gertrude say yes? In the end Anne thought she would. The presence of the Count in France was itself an indication. And in any case, whatever arrangement Peter and Gertrude came to, provided she did not marry someone else, if he were to become her happy *cavaliere servente*, there would be nothing there for hungry Anne. Of course, Anne had given some thought to Manfred. Gertrude had seen quite a lot of Manfred after the publication of Tim's shame. But she concluded that nothing was to be hoped for in that quarter. Manfred was a selfish young bachelor (he was younger than Gertrude) with a secret life. No doubt he was fond of Gertrude, she was fond of him. But probably Manfred, if he wanted a partner, already had some convenient one stashed away somewhere. In any case, if he wanted Gertrude he was quite confident and self-assertive enough to set about getting her, and Anne, observing him closely when she could, had seen no signs of this. He was in a good position to put himself forward as Gertrude's natural protector. As he had not done so presumably he did not want to. The Count had a clear field.

Anne was making her own plans. She did not want, very much did not want, to hurt Gertrude. Nor, of course, did she want the merest, slightest hint of her own state of mind to reach the other two. They must never know. Their never knowing would be, in the time to come, an important part of Anne's consolation. She would conduct them, like a priest, toward their nuptials. Then she would go. She loved Gertrude dearly, and could spare a little separate bitterness to think that she had found her friend only to lose her again in this particularly painful way. Meanwhile she must behave perfectly, watch with the eyes of love and speed with the feet of a servant. Thus Anne, as she watched that pair, the sight of whom was such a scandal to her heart, moved between a bitter almost cynical chagrin and a would-be selfless love which she felt belonged somehow to her future.

That future, she thought, would lie in America. Nothing less than another continent would be necessary when those two were united. She had already drafted, though not yet sent, a letter to the Poor Clares in Chicago. She had decided to write to them simply because theirs was the only American address which she knew. It would be a starting point. Something would happen to her in America. She would find work to do.

Oh but it is so sad, thought Anne, as she poured the greenish strongly smelling olive oil onto the salad. There is so much love in me which I used to give to God; and I shall have to abandon the two people to whom I most want to give it now.

'Anne darling.' It was Gertrude. They never stayed too long together. One or other of them always came to look for Anne. 'Can I do anything?'

'No,' said Anne, 'just be.' Maybe I should stay, she thought. Not go to America after all. Just stay and help them to be happy.

'So this is it,' said Daisy.

'Yes.'

'I'm glad. I wish you'd decided earlier. Perhaps I should have decided. I suppose I thought you'd drift off.'

'Did you want me to drift off?' said Tim.

'Yes, no—you know how it is, how it was. We're coming along to the past tense now, aren't we.'

'Oh God—'

'Don't be emotional, dear, dear Tim. I'm so grateful to you.'

'I'm grateful to you.'

'We're stupid really, a pair of duffers.'

'Yes.'

'We loved each other but we could never make any sense of our love.'

'Do you forgive me?'

'Oh don't be silly, Tim, that's your old silliness, making everything emotional, or romantic or something. We're like two bits of wood in a river. We've floated along together for a while. One bit of wood doesn't ask another bit of wood to forgive it.'

'But you don't feel—sorry, I can't find any words that won't annoy you.'

'You can't annoy me any more again ever.'

'Unless I go back on what I've said.'

'It's too late for that.'

'You mean—?'

'If you unsay it, I shall say it. Just for once we have agreed. We're in conjunction. It's a sort of cosmic moment. We see what's right and we see it together.'

'Darling, I—I do admire you—'

'Don't make me laugh, it would be too painful.'

'I'm so glad about what you said about getting on better with the novel when I was away.'

'Oh I just said that. I'm going to chuck the novel.'

'I'm sorry. What will you do?'

'That won't concern you—any more—ever again.'

'Oh—Daisy—'

'Don't weaken, oh my dear, don't weaken. You've been so splendidly brave.'

'Yes—very—brave—'

'You won't come running back this time, will you?'

'No.'

'Anyway I won't be here—or at Shepherd's Bush.'

'Which of us is to have the Prince of Denmark?'

'You can. I'm going to vanish. I think I shall leave London. I hate London, I've been trying to leave it for years.'

'Daisy, will you be all right for money?'

'That's another thing that won't concern you.'

'But really—'

'Yes, yes, I have rich friends, same like you.'

'I have no friends.'

'Well go and find some.'

'I could let you have—'

'No. I've got friends, for Christ's sake, they aren't all that rich actually, but I won't starve. I'll be absolutely somewhere else.'

'I never sort of thought—'

'Of course not. You pass your life in never sort of thinking. When you weren't with me you imagined I didn't exist. I have a whole world of people you know nothing of.'

'Oh.'

'Well, don't mope about it now, poor old Blue Eyes.'

'It's been a crazy relationship, hasn't it.'

'It's a crazy world.'

'We haven't been any good for each other.'

'We haven't been very bad either. We're people in limbo. Other folks settled down to making sense of their lives, making compromises and definitions and projects and that. We've remained children, we've retarded each other.'

'It felt like innocence.'

'Fuck innocence, we're ghosts.'

'Compromises and definitions, yes. Anyway—Daisy, you know I'm not doing this for Gertrude. This has nothing to do with Gertrude. It's something you and I are doing.'

'Our last action. Fuck Gertrude. I don't care why you're doing it, so long as you really are doing it.'

'No, but it's important.'

'Let him go, let him tarry, let him sink or let him swim, he doesn't care for me and I don't care for him—'

'Daisy, it's not for Gertrude, Gertrude's finished. I *couldn't do it* for that sort of reason. It's because it's — absolute — and clean — and—'

'Oh yes yes yes.'

'But you do understand? This is just us.'

'Yes. Yes, all right.'

'I feel—I feel I love you more perfectly now than I've ever loved you before.'

'It's the effect of parting. It will pass and you will feel relief.'

'Oh Daisy, you are so beautiful—'

It was true. They were in the sitting-room, facing each other, perched upon bamboo chairs amid an archipelago of cushions and potted plants. Daisy was in jeans and a clean shirt. She had 'done' her eyes with immense circles of powdery blue, but her lips were unpainted. Tim feared to see them tremble. But Daisy was strong, she was magnificent. He was strong and magnificent himself. They were like divine beings together. They seemed too like a new pair of people meeting each other for the first time.

'I think I'm falling in love with you,' said Tim.

'I know, I feel a bit like that—'

'My God, perhaps this is our only moment of real love, our *first* moment of real love.'

'No, it's an illusion, a sentimental by-product of our courage. It means nothing. It certainly doesn't mean that. We are in the presence of death. Death is love they say, but not our sort.'

'Suppose we were to start again, now. You're—you're transfigured.'

A lazy sun was making the room dusty, full of slowly moving particles. Daisy, sitting very straight, her hands on the arms of her chair, her short hair combed flat to her narrow head, her eyes huge, her face austere and hard, looked like a goddess. Tim had never seen that face before and it ravished him with love.

'No, my dear Tim, we shall not meet again in the world. This is it. This is the end.'

'But how's it done?' said Tim. 'It is like death, isn't it.'

Something weakened in Daisy's face, but only for a moment. 'And please, if ever in the future you're tempted to look for me, don't—for my sake, don't—'

'Daisy, I—'

'You say you've removed all your stuff?'

'Yes. I removed it . . . yesterday . . . when you were out. . . .'

'That was sensible. There's nothing left in your room?'

'No.'

'Would you like to go and make sure?'

'No.'

'Then there's nothing left to do but to go out of the door.'

'Daisy . . . I can't. . . .'

'You are asking the executioner for one more minute of life.'

'Yes—But—Daisy, I can't do it—we can't do it—We'll both be in the Prince of Denmark tomorrow.'

'No, Tim, be true to me here. We must give the *coup de grâce*. You've shown such pluck. This is the best thing you've ever done for me. Don't spoil it now. You've amazed me, you've done what I could never have, I think, and I believe you're not doing it for Gertrude, you're just doing it, and if you could see yourself now you'd see a god, I've never seen you more beautiful. But that has no connection with the future. We have no future. Be true to me, be good to me, brave dear Tim.'

'We've suddenly become—so much better—we've sort of—redeemed—so why can't we—'

'Oh don't make me laugh. We're stiff, we're strong, we're even *sober* because we are about to kill each other. It is like a suicide pact. But if we called it off we'd just become those two old zombies once more, quarrelling and boozing and being miserable and *stupid*. You know that.'

'Yes—I suppose so—'

'Go then.'

'I can't.'

'*Go.*'

Tim got up and made for the door. He remembered that he had put his shaving things in a plastic bag beside his chair, and he returned and picked it up, not looking at Daisy. Tears had now come into his eyes. He returned to the door, went out, crossed the hall, let himself out of the flat door, closed it quietly and began to descend the stairs. He thought, it's not real, so I don't have to have this terrible suffering. I can always go back, I can *always* go back. She can't vanish like she said.

He came out into the street and began to walk slowly toward Finchley Road Station. He felt estranged from his body, giddy, awkward as if he were learning to walk. How odd a procedure, to put one foot down, then lift the other and swing it forward, then put it down and change balance and lift the other. . . . He felt he might fall down at any moment. When someone came towards him on the pavement it seemed like a dark blur and he had to stop moving to let it pass. He walked along slowly with his mouth open. The hot tears in his eyes burnt him but refused to fall. He felt sick with a vast black iron sickness.

He could not determine the exact moment when he had decided to leave Daisy. It had been 'coming on' for some time. It had been like a huge mass of material bearing down on him and which he had seen out of the corner of his eye as he waited paralysed with fear. He had at last, gasping with emotion, acknowledged the reality of his intention. He had during the last few days, scarcely seen Daisy at all. She stayed in bed in the mornings, often till midday, and he left the house without seeing her. He returned late at night, and drank a glass of whisky with her if she was visible, then retired quickly to bed. Daisy was, during this time, drunker than usual.

During the day he walked London. He did not go to the galleries any more for fear of what he would see there. He sat in pubs. When they closed he sat on park benches. The weather was golden, London was dazzlingly beautiful. The huge long-armed plane trees were dreaming of autumn, already dropping big green and brown leaves here and there. Leaves sailed slowly down and laid themselves quietly at Tim's feet. He felt as if he were being transmitted into some other spiritual state. Sometimes he doubted whether he was still visible. He found that he was able to sit entirely immobile for an hour on end. He sat, and did not exactly think, but let things happen in his mind. The external world disappeared and he existed in the midst of some pale whitish void. Sometimes the void gleamed like the sea, turning silver. It hummed or throbbed quietly. Tim breathed.

He wondered if he were really changing, going mad perhaps. Was the onset of madness like this? He felt extremely quiet, but absolutely stretched as if space were bending and he were bending with it. Everything seemed to vanish including his own personality. He was a tiny scrap of being, a particle, and yet also he was the surrounding area which seemed infinite. He was an atom, an electron, a proton, a point in empty space. He was transparent. It was this transparency which made him feel invisible. He was empty, he was clean, he was nothing. Yet at the same time he was refined energy, pure activity, pure being. The experience was not in itself painful, though frightful pain somehow existed too, nearby, half hidden, sometimes like a black hole, sometimes like a dense mass of indestructible matter. The sense of emptiness was occasionally almost pleasurable. It was always awful. It's a condition of pure freedom, it's like being an angel, he thought once. In the later stages he did not even go to pubs any more. He ate very little. He sat quietly on benches in Regent's Park, in Hyde Park, in Kensington Gardens, and existed. If someone came and sat near him he quietly rose and moved slowly to another bench and his feet did not touch the ground.

The 'form' of his experience was, he supposed, his resolution to leave Daisy. And he said to himself, it's like the *Magic Flute* after all, except that something has gone wrong and the music is being played differently and Pappagena and Pappageno are not to be saved after all, they have lost each other in the darkness of their ordeal and are never to be reunited ever in any paradise by any god. Yet he knew too that his experience was more than this 'form', that it was absolute, some kind of ultimate phenomenon, some kind of truth, not as it were God, but the cosmos itself, gentle, terrible, final. It was also a vision of death. He breathed, amazed at breathing, as if he had just realized that all his life he had been counting his breaths. He was appalled by what was happening, terrified of himself as he had now become, yet he wanted too to prolong the experience. He could not see *how* to return to ordinary life, and he knew the return would be agony. He gradually formed his terrible resolution, or rather it was formed for him, but he was not then living in the ordinary world of time and space where resolutions are carried out and situations change irrevocably and forever; and only in this way could he have decided.

One morning at about noon he went into a telephone box at Baker Street Station and called the flat. There was no answer. He stood with the telephone in his hand and his heart beating so painfully it was like having a ferret in his breast. He left the box and stopped a taxi. He kept the taxi at the flat while he collected his belongings. He went on in the taxi to the studio and carried the stuff up the steps. He looked with amazement at the studio, immobile in its own quietness in spite of the surrounding sound, oblivious of history. Its peaceful chaos was just as it had been when he had stood there talking to the Count. No one had been in, nothing had happened. He returned that night to the flat at Finchley Road, and during the next day he went out as usual and walked and sat and walked and sat. But he knew that he had set off a terrible avalanche of events. The white separated time was coming to an end.

On the following day he did not go out early. He shaved and put all his remaining things into a plastic bag. He sat on his bed waiting for Daisy to wake and stir, and now he felt the pain, the black rending pain which had travelled with him and found its moment. He sat with closed eyes and doubled himself up over the pain, until at last he heard Daisy coughing, padding to the bathroom, at last fiddling in the kitchen; and he picked up the plastic bag and came out.

It was true that it had nothing to do with Gertrude. It *could not* have. In the white cold fire where he had been living there was no such thing as Gertrude. It was as if thoughts and feelings and judgments stretching away into the remote past had been collected and perfected in that blankness. The fabric of the resolution was made of old old things, ancient things that knew not of Gertrude. His whole life was collected, recollected, in what with dreadful inevitability was happening now. And the strange thing was that Daisy knew at once, knew as soon as she saw his face. It was like taking partners for a dance. She understood everything. She was perfect.

Yet was not that perfection his final ordeal? How *could* he leave such a woman? Was not this, which had happened, some sort of purification or consummation or redemption of their love, like, at last, a *marriage*? How could he *leave* and *forever* the person with whom he had shared, after so long a pilgrimage, that final experience of absolute truth? He loved Daisy more than he had ever loved her before. In the darkness of that final unimagined pain his perfection and her perfection met to negotiate the severance.

He felt that he needed to be in an open space, and he took a taxi to Marble Arch. The taxi dropped him off at Speakers' Corner and he walked away under the tree; and something which had been going very fast, perhaps his heart, began gradually to slow down. The white light seemed to be with him again but it was different now. It had become pearly, dove-grey, attentive, still. He found that he could see through it. He could see the trees, the huge quiet planes, with their immense friendly peeling trunks and the vast dangling swing of their downward reaching branches covered with feathery leaves. He walked on over the grass which was dry and warm and bleached to a faded gold, and it made a soft springy sound under his feet. He could see in the distance the line of the lake and the Serpentine bridge. Then suddenly his knees gave way, he knelt down and lay prone upon the grass. Like an orgasm, like a birth, something wrenched his body and then left it, leaving him utterly limp. A warm wave had broken over him and now flowed on and on. A wave of pure thoughtless happiness which made him, with his face in the dry grass, moan and moan with joy.

On the fifth morning the mistral began to blow. They had nevertheless not abandoned their plan of going into the village. Gertrude and the Count sat in the café while Anne shopped. Anne was also to discover someone to mend the cracked pane in the study. After that they intended to drive some way to leave a message with the electrician who usually at this time of year serviced the electric pump which brought the water up from the well. Then the idea was to have lunch somewhere on the way home.

The *terrasse* of the café was deserted and the doors were closed. Gertrude and the Count sat inside and drank cognac. The *patron*, usually their friend, was ill-tempered. The place was cold. Whenever anyone came in the door had to be gripped hard to prevent its crashing back against the wall outside. It was impossible not to bang the door when closing it. The *patron* shouted angrily. Pieces of newspaper and leaves swept in onto the floor. Gertrude and the Count sat hunched up over their cognac wishing they had brought their coats. Anne arrived. She had been unable to find a glazier. She remembered that she had forgotten to buy butter. Gertrude said it didn't matter, the Count said he would get it on the way to the car. They agreed not to go to the electrician or out to lunch but go straight home. When they were getting into the Rover one of the car doors doubled itself back with such violence that the hinges were damaged and it was extremely difficult to shut. Once shut, they decided it had better stay shut. However the Count, forgetting this, opened it again when they got back to the house and it took even longer to get it shut again. They had also forgotten the butter. Gertrude said the wind would probably blow for three days and then stop.

They went round the house securing the shutters, which they had failed to do before they left. Then they sat for a while in the sitting-room drinking more cognac and saying how exciting it all was. Eventually they had a lunch of fruit and cheese. Anne had also forgotten to buy bread, but yesterday's stale bread was not too bad. Anne ate practically nothing and eventually admitted she was feeling sick. It felt like a migraine coming on. She retired upstairs. Gertrude began a long querulous search for a book to read. *Colloquial Urdu*, at which she had thought she might have another go, was unopened. Guy had stocked the house with 'classics' and Anne and Gertrude had been able, jesting about this, to continue with the novels they had left unfinished in Cumbria, *The Heart of Midlothian* and *Sense and Sensibility*. But in the wind-racked house Gertrude felt unable to read Jane Austen. She found a detective story by Freeman Wills Crofts, which had been left behind by Stanley, and also retired upstairs. The Count had brought Proust with him, unnecessarily as the whole work, in French and English, was already in Guy's study. But the Count felt alienated from Swann. He did not want to read about the pains of jealousy. He went through Guy's books to find something about Poland and failed. Guy's books here (and indeed in London too) knew not of Poland. The Count felt a little chagrin. He did not quite feel, as his compatriots were sometimes said to feel, that really 'everyone is more or less of Polish origin'. But he did feel that every intelligent person must be interested in Poland. He thought he might go for a walk, and stood outside for a while in the wind, then came in again feeling as if he had been scalped. He sat on his bed worrying about Gertrude. Anne had been quite right in her conjecture that the Count had resolved to wait until after Christmas to propose to Gertrude. But now this resolution was weakening. Yesterday Gertrude had received a letter from Manfred. (The post was left in a box in the garage by an invisible postman.) The Count recognized Manfred's affected Italianate script upon the envelope as Gertrude carried it away upstairs. He felt that he could not wait much longer to know his fate.

The mistral had begun to blow suddenly at about ten o'clock out of a blue sky. Now the sky had become grey, but not in the usual manner by the arrival of perceptible clouds. It was rather as if each grain of blue had quietly, and without changing its position, faded into a grain of grey. It would indeed have been hard to be sure that the sky was clouded at all were it not that the sun was invisible. Yet perhaps it had already sunk behind the rocks? The Count, whose watch had stopped, could not now make out what time it was. He had lain down on his bed for a moment. Had he fallen asleep? He went out into the sitting-room. There was no one about. The wind blew, not as other winds blew in waves or moody gusts, but steadily, as if the air, set into some regular swift motion, were simply flowing past like a river. The wind-river, flowing parallel to the ground, carried with it, as the Count watched it from the sitting-room window, willow leaves, vine leaves, olive leaves, twigs and other items of debris kept aloft by the steady lines of force, as if the earth itself were being quietly disintegrated into a stream of particles. There was a monotonous machine-like roar, not very loud or piercing, but pitched so as to set every nerve jangling.

Gertrude came down complaining that she had been unable to rest. She made some tea which neither of them wanted. The house had become very cold. After some searching Gertrude found a small electric fire in a cupboard and plugged it in in the sitting-room and they sat beside it trying to be amused by the wind. Gertrude recited some of the usual folklore about it. A steady draught, a mini-mistral, was coursing through the room and up the chimney. The Count suggested that, if there was any fuel, they might light a fire that evening (well it was evening by now, wasn't it?) in the big stone fireplace. Gertrude applauded this. She was unwilling to go out as her coat was so thin, but she told the Count where the wood store was, in a wooden lean-to shed beside the garage. He went out and came back saying he had been unable to find it. Gertrude went out irritably hugging her flimsy coat. The shed was empty, the wood had been stolen. They came back and Gertrude began a fruitless search for hot water bottles which she said they would certainly need that night. When the mistral blew, the beds in some mysterious way immediately became damp.

Anne Cavidge lay in bed, propped up with pillows. She had covered herself over with all available blankets, with her coat, even with a mat off the floor, but she still felt cold. She had felt sick that morning in the village and had forgotten the bread and butter, which she much regretted. She had a terrible migraine, which was taking an unusual though not altogether unfamiliar form. She had entirely lost the centre of her field of vision. The centre was occupied by a large greyish round hole into which she seemed to stare, round the edge of which was a fringe of boiling particles not unlike porridge. Outside this the edges of the field of vision, what is seen 'out of the corner of the eye', appeared as usual. She had no ordinary headache, but a much worse sensation of extreme giddiness and sea-sickness, a spinning head and a dull heavy iron-grey desire to vomit. She had put some newspaper and a chamber pot on the floor beside her. She could not stand, sit, or lie flat. The propped-up position was the most endurable. She could not keep her body still but had to keep moving it about for relief, writhing her legs and

shifting her shoulders and rolling her head. She lay listening to
the monotonous roaring of the wind and the rattling of the
captive shutters. That morning in the village she had posted her
letter to Chicago.

Gertrude knocked, then came in.

When Anne heard her coming up the stairs she quickly
leaned over and pushed the newspaper and the chamber pot
under the bed.

'How are you, my dear? Do you mind if I look in your cupboard? There are some hot water bottles somewhere.'

'Yes, do.'

Gertrude rootled in the cupboard. 'There's one, but it looks
pretty ancient. How dark it is. Do you mind if I put the light on?'

Gertrude turned on the light. Anne covered her eyes.

'Here's another, that's something. Sorry, I'm dazzling you.'
She turned the light off again. 'How are you, Anne, dear heart?'

'OK.'

'Have you been reading Scott?'

'No.'

'I couldn't read either. I'm sorry about the hellish wind. It
will stop. Are you warm enough?'

'Yes.'

'Let me feel your feet.' Gertrude thrust her hand under the
blankets and felt Anne's restless feet. 'You're frozen. And your
feet are bare, you silly dolt. Haven't you any socks or anything
with you?'

'Well—oh, yes—in that suitcase—it doesn't matter—'

Gertrude found a pair of socks, pulled back the bed clothes
and pulled the socks on. Anne lay rigid for a moment, feeling
Gertrude's warm hand, then as Gertrude restored the blankets,
resumed her writhing.

'I'll give you a bottle,' said Gertrude, 'if either of these holds
water. How do you feel, really?'

'It'll pass.'

'Your dress is all crumpled. Wouldn't it be a good thing to
undress?'

'Will later.'

'You must see Victor when you get back.'

'Better other doctor, stranger.'

392

'You saw Orpen.'

'Dentist different.'

'Have you taken aspirins?'

'Yes.'

'Couldn't they do anything about this vile migraine at your stupid convent?'

'It's psychological.'

'You're a masochist.'

'No.'

'Would you like a little consommé?'

'No thanks.'

'You can't keep still. Would a sleeping pill help?'

'Later, thanks.'

'I don't know what to do with you. Brandy?'

'No thanks.'

'Oh dear, and the Count's like a cat on hot bricks. We're all unhinged today.'

'Sorry. I'm sorry I forgot the bread—'

'Oh *darling*—!'

Gertrude was wearing, over her dress, a brown dressing-gown which looked as if it might have been Guy's. She sat down on the bed and gently stroked her friend's covered form. Anne twitched with irritation. The room had got darker. Gertrude could not see Anne's face properly as Anne was rolling her head about so much. Anne could not see Gertrude at all, except as a blur in the corner of her eye. As the room got darker, the atom-fringed hole in the centre of her vision seemed to get brighter. In order to distract herself from the sickness and from a new localized pain in the back of her head, she concentrated upon the empty brightening circle. She wondered if something would suddenly appear inside that lurid hole, Jesus Christ perhaps. She wished Gertrude would go away.

'Anne, you won't ever leave me, will you?'

'No.'

'I mean—whatever happens—'

'What's likely to happen?' said Anne.

'I don't know. Anything might happen to anybody.'

'If you're in a wheelchair I'll push it.'

'I want us to grow old together.'

'Great.'

'All right, my dear, I'm going. I love you.'

'Ditto.'

Gertrude went out carrying the hot water bottles. When she had receded down the stairs Anne pulled herself up, dragged herself to the bathroom and tried to vomit. She could not.

'How's Anne?' said the Count.

'She's got a terrible headache,' said Gertrude. She put the bottles down and forgot them.

'Can I—can I get you a drink, Gertrude?'

'I'll help myself.' Gertrude poured herself out some whisky. 'You?'

'Yes—I think—some whisky—just today—'

'You're becoming quite a toper, Count.'

'Shall we turn on the light?'

'No, let's look out.'

They took their glasses to the window. The rocks had continued, even on this evening, to muster up some light, a kind of grey light which paled them slightly against a darker sky. They had abandoned their usual spotty flickering and seemed to be moving slowly up and down in vertical grooves. Below the rocks the valley was visible in a murky sulky sub-aqueous twilight, the stretched-out tugged-at branches of the olives and willows could be seen streaming in the wind, streaming as it seemed noiselessly since the wind took up the sound into its own monotonous roar.

'What a terrible noise.'

'Look at those poor trees.'

'And look at the terrace.'

The terrace was covered in a shallow stream of moving leaves, and was also covered with a less mobile deposit of twigs and branches and what appeared to be stones. Several chairs seemed to have disappeared. Beyond, the wind was passing like a moving wall between the house and the rocks.

'I hope those aren't slates off the roof.'

'We'd have heard them fall.'

'Not in this row.'

'My God, what's that?'

There was a crashing sound and something banged and bumped violently against the wall of the house.

'I'll go and see,' said the Count.

'Don't go out of the glass doors! Better go by the archway. I'll come with you. Wait, I'll hold the door!'

They negotiated the door, got out and shut it, then made their way along the terrace keeping close to the house. The wooden loggia (which Tim had mended) had come down and lay scattered in a mass of criss-crossing poles and vine branches.

'Oh dear, oh *dear*, the vine is broken!'

'Only one branch I think—yes, just this branch—shall we—shall we bring the grapes in?'

'Better bring the whole thing—oh *damn*—'

Moving against the wind they carried the broken branch between them, slipped in through the folding door which behaved like a wild thing as soon as it was unlatched, and brought the long trailing trophy into the sitting-room. They laid it along the narrow sideboard under the Munch print of the startled girls. Gertrude turned on the light.

'Oh what a shame!'

'How beautiful it is!'

The broken undulating stem had already arranged itself into a graceful form. The sudden light showed the brilliant emerald green of the veined leaves, with casually here and there a hint of purplish furry underside. The green unripe grapes gleamed, faintly transparent, like little pyramids of precious stones, punctuating the posed classic immobility of the serrated leaves.

'It looks like an eighteenth-century decoration.'

'Or something by Fabergé!'

'But the grapes aren't ripe,' said Gertrude.

'Wouldn't they be now?'

'Not quite. Anyway one couldn't eat anything so exquisite. I'll put this end in water so it'll last. Oh I am stupid, I should have brought the chairs in this morning.'

'They haven't blown away?'

'Yes, they have. Didn't you see, they're all gone!'

'Shall I go—?'

'No, no, they're just somewhere down the hillside, it's not the first time.'

'At least it's not raining—'

'What's *that*, oh *no*!'

They ran to the study. The tinkling crash betokened the

smashing of the cracked window pane. Through a jagged gaping hole the wicked wind was streaming in.

'What can we—what can we mend it with?'

'We can't mend it,' said Gertrude. 'Come on, we'll just shut the door. Oh God, I hate this, I *hate* it!'

She slammed the door and they returned to the sitting-room.

'Would you like some supper, Gertrude? Can I—?'

'No, you have some, make yourself some soup. Don't stand there shivering, put on a jersey, I can lend you one of Guy's.'

'Oh no—'

'Oh Count, you look so cold and so *thin*! Wrap yourself in something, even if it's only a blanket!'

'I'm all right.'

The Count had put on a light jacket over his blue open-necked summer shirt. He stood with lifted shoulders, wrinkling his brow, and his long hands and bony wrists protruded stiffly as if they were made of wood. He could not resolve to sit down or to go away, he could do nothing with himself. He dangled awkwardly like a marionette, in the now so comfortless brightly lit room, reflected in the black shiny window panes, unable to fit himself into space or time. He looked helplessly at his stopped watch. Gertrude regarded him with exasperation. She turned her back on him and pulled the curtains. The valley and the rocks had disappeared. Then she opened a drawer in the sideboard and took out a chess board and chessmen. She sat down and opened out the board and began to set out the chessmen to see that they were all there. The Count watched her uneasily.

He had still not been able to tell Gertrude the story of the letter and of his conversation with Tim, and he felt that he ought to do this. She had asked no questions, and twice when he had tried to say something about the letter she had shut him up. 'All right, all right, no more.' She clearly assumed the letter had been delivered and there was no reply. However the Count felt that he ought to tell her at least one of the things that Tim had said, and that he ought to insist upon this if necessary.

'Gertrude, I must tell you—it won't take a moment and then I won't mention the matter again—about Tim and your letter—I *must* tell you—'

'Oh, all right,' said Gertrude expressionlessly, still setting out the chessmen. She had turned up the collar of the dressing-gown

396

and its too-long sleeves. The Count watched her hands which had been browned by the sun.

'There's not much to tell. I found Tim at his studio. Just him —there—he said he was giving the place up. I gave him the letter and I saw him read it and he didn't say anything about a reply—'

'It's all clear,' said Gertrude, 'why labour the point?'

'I'm not labouring the point,' said the Count almost angrily. 'What I wanted to say was this, that he said he had never plotted against you to use your money for his mistress.'

'He's still with her—'

'Yes.'

'Finished?'

'You mean have I finished what I had to say? Yes. I won't mention it again.' The Count thought, it sounds as if I just wanted to say something against Tim, not something for him. Perhaps I should go on and try to convey—but no, it's no good.

'Let's play chess,' said Gertrude. She motioned the Count to sit at the table opposite to her. He automatically sat down. Gertrude began to study the board.

'Can you play chess?' he said.

'Would I suggest this if I couldn't?' said Gertrude, still looking at the board. 'I used to play with Guy. I'm not asking you to teach me!'

The Count knew that it was absolutely impossible that he should play chess with Gertrude. 'Gertrude, my dear, I can't play with you.' It was the first endearment he had ever uttered to her.

'Why not? You're rather good at chess, aren't you?'

'Yes.'

'Well, you can't have forgotten it!' Gertrude moved a pawn.

'It's impossible,' said the Count.

She looked at him now and they stared at each other intently across the board. Gertrude's brown eyes expressed irritability and aggression. The Count's pale eyes spoke abjection, desperation, love.

'Why? You play bridge with me, why won't you play chess with me?'

'Chess is different,' said the Count.

'How, different?'

'Gertrude, it's impossible that we should play chess because I am so much better at it than you are that we would be playing different games.'

Gertrude stared at him and her eyes grew quiet. They continued to look at each other. And suddenly, in the vast starry cosmos of the emotions, Gertrude and the Count were very close indeed, closer than they had ever been before. Then she said, 'Oh, all right.'

The Count wanted to say, I love you, Oh I love you, I love you with all my heart and I want you to be my dear wife. But he could not say it. He was afraid to.

After a moment Gertrude got up, jolting the table and upsetting the chessmen. She said, 'I'd better go and see how Anne is. Oh damn, I forgot her hot water bottle. What a bloody nuisance it is about that window pane.'

How exactly what happened to Tim next happened, he was not able in retrospect quite to determine.

The weird amazing joy he had experienced in Hyde Park ebbed from him in the days, indeed in the hours, that followed. It seemed to him later to have been something freakish, almost shameful. It left behind it an empty exhausted state of mind. There was an emptiness as if a lot of demons who had for long supported him had gone away leaving him weak and vacant. No hanged men or floppy ghosts now in his dreams: he scarcely seemed to dream at all. The parting from Daisy was something epoch-making, shattering. He never let himself doubt that it was final. He was surprised to find himself regarding it as the end of his youth, as if so conventional an idea could find lodgement upon such an abysmal precipice. The difference between this parting and the other was as great as the difference between the two women. The loss of Gertrude was bedevilled by a muddled guilt, the pain of which at times drove him almost mad. The loss of Daisy had this curious (he could only think of it so) *white* character, as if he had died and found himself entirely wrapped in cloud, aware of absolute and irreversible change. This was terrible pain too but being devoid of guilt it provided the energy which would at last be its cure.

He went back to the studio and tidied it up. He did not go again to the Prince of Denmark. He went to his local pubs, the Tabard, the Pack Horse, the Emperor, the Barley Mow, or else roamed, as he used to do, in northern London. He still had some of Gertrude's money. He thought how he would pay it all back one day, he would send a cheque to Moses Greenberg. He even composed in his mind a dignified letter to accompany the cheque, while terrible savage yearnings for Gertrude prowled on the edges of his thought. This misery, felt as remorse, utter loss, banishment from paradise, coexisted with that energy, gradually recognized as a new sense of freedom, which he derived from his decision to leave Daisy. The eternal question remained, how on earth was he to earn money. In answer to this he had two strokes of luck straightaway, as if the patient gods were sending him an approving signal. He took three of the cat pictures to a local pub and sold them at once (for a miserable sum it is true) to an Irishman who was starting a shop in Acton. On the same day Brian the garage man (who thought what Tim did little short of miraculous, but rarely expressed his appreciation by a purchase) bought another of the cats. Term was just beginning at the art schools and all jobs would have been filled long ago, but Tim went along on the offchance to the polytechnic at Willesden where he used to teach. The shadowy precious two-day job which had so beckoned in the spring was of course gone, since Tim, otherwise engaged during the summer, had failed to nurse it along. However he was offered a one-day-a-week post until half term because someone was ill. This was not great, but it was a good deal better than a slap in the face with a wet fish. It gave him a sense of mastery over time which helped to allay the prowling misery.

The next events formed, later, a sort of pattern in his mind. They all seemed to contribute something to the outcome, and without all of them, perhaps, nothing of what did happen would have happened. At the time, however, it was all a jumble. It was partly the leaves. Tim had always liked leaves, knew indeed quite a lot about trees, and had never ceased to draw and paint them. This autumn promised to provide an exceptionally good leaf season. London had been hot and sunny, then had become cold and windy. Frost was forecast. Then the weather partially recovered. Whatever the chemistry of hot and cold exactly was, it was beginning to produce, still in September, a superb collection of early autumn leaves. These little works of art lay about in gardens, stuck to damp pavements, or were collected into little treasure-trove piles by leisurely men in squares and parks. Sometimes they hovered in the air like butterflies in front of Tim's dreamily out-stretched hand. He collected them, at first picking up so many that he had to crush them by stuffing them into his pockets. He could not resist these master-pieces which were lying about free of charge: handsome plane leaves, green and brown or the purest yellow, maple leaves which turned tawny and vivid green or sometimes radiant red, and were often covered with the most elegant spots, curvy oak leaves, palest ochre and gold, beech leaves, brownest of absolute browns, and the more exotic joys of rhus cotinus, orange and blazing red with blotchy veins and streaks of the palest green, dark crimson of many-pointed liquidambar, and huge limp pallid flags of catalpa. Tim soon stopped pocketing these marvels, but carried with him in a large bag a portfolio with many sheets of blotting paper, into which, with increasing discrimination, he carefully put the leafy donations. At home, he pressed them, treated them discreetly with a glyceriny varnish, and then, inspired, began to make them into collages in the Victorian manner. For this purpose, and to show off the larger leaves, he used the parks as his wild countryside and collected bramble sprays and wild rose and old man's beard. He made his collections early in the morning when no one was about, when the low white mist hung over the steamy surface of the Serpentine. He watched the fishing heron. Once he met a fox.

When he had made a number of collages he framed them in

simple black frames, with plastic instead of glass, and showed them to the Irishman in the Barley Mow. The Irishman, called Pat Cameron, a sentimental soul, pronounced them the darlingest things and voted to buy the lot to sell in his shop. Tim made a cannier bargain this time, then ran home to make some more. He also painted several larger and more ambitious cat pictures from the drawings of Perkins which he had in stock. The next thing was that Pat Cameron asked him to come and help decorate his church for harvest festival. Tim agreed, assuming that Pat was a Catholic, and expecting to be ushered into some dark vaulted place full of saints and candles. Not so, Pat was a Protestant, a member of a very exclusive sect who met in a bright corrugated iron shed in Richmond, where there was no cross or altar, only a blue and white banner saying *Jesus pardons, Jesus saves*. Here the faithful had brought a lot of apples and pumpkins, and loaves of bread and a remarkable number of powerful roses, but had little idea of how to arrange these offerings. Tim took charge. He introduced quantities of Virginia creeper and yellow-fruited ivy and drooping hawthrown berries and red fans of cotoneaster, and produced in the end such a sumptuous series of tableaux that some of the faithful thought it positively Romish. Several people wanted Tim to stay to be pardoned and saved, but he gratefully declined.

During this 'time of the leaves', as he later thought of it, Tim was in a strange mixed-up unstable frame of mind. Often he felt weary and empty, and that was not bad. Sometimes he felt practical and busy, and that was not bad either. He was glad to have, for the moment, a sort of job, and to be able to sell something to somebody. He had enjoyed *Jesus pardons, Jesus saves*, but that was over now. He was curiously lonely, but he did not mind that, he felt that he had always been lonely. His parents, Daisy, had, and not accidentally, made him into a solitary man. He felt that he was reverting to a form of life that was natural to him. It was his proper destiny to be sad and disappointed and alone. Daisy had prevented him from making friends, while at the same time preventing him from having any proper relation with her. Perhaps he had, and not accidentally, performed a similar service for Daisy. He stayed at home a lot. He rearranged the studio and cleaned the skylights and scrubbed the dresser and even the floor. He washed his summer clothes and put them away. He went through all his paintings and drawings and destroyed some and sorted the rest into groups and wrapped them in cellophane and stored them neatly in the angles of the room. He ate frugally and 'like a cat' as Daisy had said. He went to pubs, new pubs, and made some casual acquaintances (no girls). He went to the White Hart at Barnes and the London Apprentice at Isleworth and the Orange Tree at Richmond. He became rather fond of Pat Cameron, who regarded Tim with a gratifying kind of awe because he was 'a real artist'.

And throughout this period he was at the same time, in the deeper part of his mind, very miserable indeed. He scarcely for a moment ceased thinking about Daisy and Gertrude. Every evening he imagined Daisy sitting in the Prince of Denmark, wearing her blue eye make-up, with Perkins on her knee. He thought that she had probably returned to her flat in Shepherd's Bush. He pictured her there, lying in bed till noon with no one to pick her clothes up off the floor. Or else he wondered whether she had actually left London, as she said she would. Perhaps she was already living with someone else. Her mysterious friends were, Tim conjectured, probably women. He really knew very little about Daisy. As he thought these various thoughts, he watched himself, watched for signs of frenzy and desperate need, desires, doubts, indecisions, intentions and hopes. There were none. There was a steady mourning and a bitter grief as for one dead. But there was no real wish to turn the clock back. Instead there was, together with sorrow, a melancholy sense of solitude and freedom. He awoke every day to a blank quiet relief that he had laid down the burden of Daisy forever, and done it cleanly and decently and honourably and with her consent. He recalled her words, her voice, begging him, for her sake, never to repent of their parting or try to undo it. He treasured his admiration for her and could think wistfully of her many qualities and sadly of the duration and the failure of their life together.

His thoughts about Gertrude were darker and more agonizingly and tightly knotted and more deeply and awfully frightening. He did, and did not want to think about Gertrude, he often tried not to, dodging the terrible thoughts like blows. He dreaded the letter that he would one day receive from Moses Greenberg. He had sent Moses his address on a postcard. Remorse and guilt remained with him, lived in him, grew in him he sometimes felt, increasing without rational proportion. And he could not stop himself from thinking about Gertrude sometimes in a live way which had constantly to be prevented from becoming mindlessly hopeful, as if he momentarily *forgot* all that had so irrevocably happened. He noticed, almost in passing, how he had always *got on* with Gertrude, and never with Daisy. He did his best with himself in his new life, at least he sometimes noticed himself trying to be sensible. He was able to be busy, with his old rather useless impecunious practicality. He cooked and tidied. He did not go mad. He produced no 'real art' but he made some little pleasing oddments. He had a tiny job until November. He could *see* the autumn leaves, though he was still afraid to go back to the National Gallery. But underneath it all the old dark stream went swirling on and when he woke in the night he remembered his last conversation with Gertrude and ran through it over and over and over again. It will pass, he thought, it will all pass, it must pass. I am *alone* and I am now hurting no one, and that is the *essential thing*. Oh if only Moses Greenberg would write that letter and the last grisly necessities could be done with.

A letter did come one morning, but it was not from Moses. Tim, who usually received only bills through the post, looked at the envelope with surprise, shock. He had been unable to cure himself of an idea, which he constantly suppressed, that Gertrude might one day write to him. This was not Gertrude's writing. It was an unfamiliar educated hand. He quickly opened it. It ran as follows.

Dear Tim,
    Please forgive me for writing to you, but I feel I ought to. I really know so little about you and about what you may be feeling now that it is perhaps an impertinence. But I must tell you my impression that Gertrude still loves you, needs you, and wants you to come back. She has not said this, but I believe it to be so. She is at present at the house in France, alone as far as I know. You may however by now be

developing quite other plans. Excuse this letter, the fruit of a well-wishing affection for you both.

Yours sincerely,
Veronica Mount.

Tim received this letter on the morning of Tuesday, his teaching day at the art school. He put it in his pocket and went to teach as usual. The next day he went to France.

'*Marie, Marie, c'est le peintre!*'

Tim's inconvenient popularity had caused him to be recognized on the bus before he even arrived at the village. Now he had been unable to avoid being hustled into the café to *prendre une verre* and be effusively welcomed by the *patron* and his wife. Several people were anxious to give him information, most of which he was unable to understand. He gathered that there had been a wicked mistral last week. But now all was quiet. The evening sun shone with benign calm upon the warm stones of the square and the motionless leaves of the pollarded plane trees in the little street.

When Tim had gone to his teaching on the day before he had been determined to ignore the baneful letter. He read it again during his short lunch hour and then tore it up. He felt that it must be untrue, and that in any case he ought to think it untrue. It was a bad letter because it disturbed, and if he was not careful could destroy something that was good, his ability to function in a fairly ordinary way. He did not want to be mad again, he did not want to suffer horribly again. He wanted to preserve the rational self-regard which would help him to survive, ultimately to recover. He tried to crush down savagely in his heart what was so terribly rising there. He said to himself, you are alone, you are in luck, you have at last made conditions for peace in your life. You may not be happy, but at least you can quietly hide. *Lanthano.* Do not go where you will simply be slaughtered, more terribly, a second time. Consider how, in all these horrors, you have got off more easily than you might have done. He did not trust Mrs Mount's judgment, he regarded her as a gossipy busybody, though it was true that she had been very kind to him and Gertrude, and he could not work out any motive she might have for lying now. Perhaps she actually did wish him well, perhaps she actually *liked* him, some people did. But could she be right? She admitted it was a conjecture. Her letter was probably a whim, born of an idle, though possibly well-intentioned, desire to meddle. The risk was too great. How *could* he approach Gertrude again? A failure now would really drive him mad.

But in the afternoon, during the drawing class, as he brooded wretchedly upon these things, he knew that he was done for. The image of the house and of Gertrude alone in it was honey-sweet. He had to go where that sweetness was even if he died of it. He had at least to go and look, and let the gods decide. He did not, he told himself, yet really intend to see Gertrude. He only intended to go to France. After all, Gertrude might not be there at all. But he had to go to that place to which every path and every thought now led. His precious solitude, his simple life, was now completely ruined. It had not lasted long. Perhaps really it had been a fiction, an illusion. It was spoilt by Mrs Mount's careless whim, and by the demons in his mind which had simply been waiting for a cue; and really, many chance events might have provided that cue. Moses Greenberg's letter might have done it. Why did he for a second imagine he had 'escaped'? Perhaps the real torment was only starting. He could not now inhibit or deny the desires and cravings which twisted so deep, the mindless hopes, the sweet hopes which were worst of all. He had achieved nothing. Well, he had achieved one thing. He knew that if he were still living with Daisy he would not have decided to go to France.

Sick with urgent terror he excused himself from the café. Absolute fear in the form of sexual desire made him almost faint. He went into the hotel next door to avoid his well-wishers. He left his mac and his jacket and his small bag, and vaguely indicating that he would return, left by the back door and set off walking along the road toward Les Grandes Saules.

It was now well into the evening. He had hoped to arrive earlier, but the aeroplane had been delayed. The sun was still over the horizon and the air was very warm and still. The little road was darkened by the strong shadow of the hedge of brambles and scrub oak. Blackberry bushes which he had seen in shrivelled flower now displayed the shrivelled remnant of their fruit. Below them, exulting in dryness, grew in long lines the ochre-coloured sage. Here and there some spiky broom, invisible earlier, still carried flowers of purest yellow. The air was warm and heavy and smelt of pines. After a while he left the road and walked through apricot orchards along a track, a short cut which he had discovered during his painting rambles. The track led to a farm. After that a path fringed with fennel and wild lavender led to some beehives. After that the rocks began. Tim stepped onto the familiar rocks and his hands touching them now and then as he climbed, remembered so much. He mounted slowly, carefully, for about five minutes. The light though still bright was uncertain, distances hard to judge, the rocks seeming to jump and shift before him. He had to keep pausing and blinking his eyes as if to expel some foreign matter. The rocks were yellow now, a hard brilliant whitish yellow in the last of the sunlight, with darkening blue-grey shadows marking their folds and lines of ascent, and all hazed over with a vision-defeating fuzziness as if millions of tiny bees were flying over them, or as if their own spots had risen up in an undulating swarm. They were warm and hard, dense, the densest stuff that Tim had ever touched.

He came by a way that he knew to a point that he knew, and now he looked down into the valley and saw the house. The valley that had been so verdant was bleached now, only the vineyard and the course of the streamlet carried a darkening green in the fading light. Tim, gazing at the house, saw that the loggia which he had mended had fallen down and the vine was prostrate on the terrace. There was something in the olive grove which looked like one of the outdoor chairs lying on its side. The place had a derelict neglected air. He thought he could see where tiles had come off the roof. If he had approached by the road he would have seen the Rover, but from where he stood the car was invisible. He was beginning to wonder whether Gertrude was there at all when a light suddenly came on in the sitting-room.

Tim had made no plan. He had simply come to 'look'. He felt that he would be in the hands of the gods. Of course it was now impossible not to go on to the house. It was more absolutely familiar to him than Ebury Street; and the idea of Gertrude there alone was absolutely irresistible. Of course, as Tim really knew, in coming to France he had decided to see Gertrude. It was just that the decision was so awful that it had to be taken in two halves, one conscious, one unconscious. He remembered how touching, how enchanting she had been on that first evening when she had stood upon the terrace and waited for him to come in the twilight through the vineyard and the poplars and across the stream and up through the olive grove, wondering a little if it was indeed he, so sweetly glad to see him when he came. He stood, wondering if she would again come out onto the terrace so that the scene could be magically re-enacted. But no one came out and he went on a little further and climbed down until he found the path at the foot of the rocks which joined the path across the vineyard.

Here again he waited. Indeed he sat down on the grass, looking across the valley at the one lighted window. His desire for her *presence* was intense, it was burning up his whole body. But his fear was intense too, his cowardice which made him simply want now to wait, to breathe, to continue to live. He so feared Gertrude's anger, her contempt, her terrible terrible rejection of him which he remembered with such intense and continued vividness. He felt that he had only sustained it last time because of sheer surprise and sheer stupidity. The parting had been fast and merciful. He had been like the victim of a catastrophic crippling accident whose pain is checked by a paralysis of the nerve centres. Now he was fully conscious, fully collected and prepared for torment. So much had happened, he had returned to Daisy, not least he had *thought* about the whole business, he had diligently, hopelessly, *made* himself into the intolerable guilty being whom she had rejected. Suppose now he were confronted with spitting anger, with hatred—he could do nothing, only run away, run into a mental desolation worse than any he had known before. That would be the final condemnation that would brand him forever as unpardonably guilty and lost. It was not the crime, it was the punishment that seared the mind, it was the shame. He had thought himself damaged, but he could be much worse hurt now. How could he face Gertrude, what could he say, what could he *explain* to her? Would she listen patiently while he rambled on telling how he hadn't been with Daisy like she thought, except that of course he had been with Daisy, and that, yes, he had gone straight back to Daisy, only now he had left Daisy again, and—Would Gertrude be interested? Could he tell her about the harvest festival and the leaves? He had felt he must look at the house. Could he just go home now to the quiet life of aloneness which had been graciously vouchsafed him? He was tempting a fate that had not crushed him entirely. But now he was here; and he knew that of course he had to cross the valley. He got up and started to walk down the path through the vineyard.

The poplar grove was full of fallen leaves, blanched yellow on one side and furry silvery white on the other. Motionless, appearing suddenly under foot, Tim could not at first think what they were, they seemed in the odd light like a pavement. When he got to the bridge he found it obstructed by a large willow branch. He was too impatient to pull it away. The stream was small, but too wide to jump, so he simply walked through it. It was very cold and deeper than he had expected. His trousers clung to his calves. He cursed, he felt frightened, he felt suddenly hungry, he felt ready to weep. Why on earth had he come here at night in this stupid way, he was a stupid man, doomed and ruined by stupidity.

When he was just below the terrace he had to stop because he could hardly breathe for the fear and the longing that was in him. He stood like a helpless animal, with his mouth open and his feet apart, gasping. When he was able to control his breathing he climbed up the dry slippery parched grass to the terrace steps. He thought, I'll simply look in, I'll simply look, and then I'll rest again. Nothing has happened yet, nothing need happen at all. He moved with caution, keeping away from the square of light that fell onto the stones. The valley behind him seemed dark already. He stepped carefully over the wreckage of the loggia. He reached the wall of the house and felt the warm squarely cut stones with his hand. Holding to the wall by the lines between the stones he edged towards the window. The first thing he saw was an amazing streak of brilliant green which he made out to be a long branch of the vine which had been laid out along the sideboard underneath the lamp. The second thing he saw was Gertrude and the Count, sitting opposite to each other and holding hands across the table.

As Tim gazed at the unconscious pair within, whose voices he could now vaguely hear though he could not discern their words, someone else was watching Tim, or had been watching him until a moment earlier when he had passed out of sight by coming up to the house. Anne's migraine was better, but now she pretended illness. Three nights she had left the other two together and listened to their voices murmuring down below as she endeavoured to fall asleep. She had thought the Count would wait. Now she thought he would not wait. She felt like somebody waiting for a loved one to die. Oh why can it not *happen*, she thought, twisting her head and her limbs as she had done when the migraine tormented her. The evenings were long. She drove Gertrude away. She lay on her bed or sat by one of the windows trying to read Scott, or looking out at the willow valley and the rocks, or at the cleft which showed the line of distant yellow hill upon which the sun rested longer. She gave herself up to a jealous pain which she knew was, in its present quality, temporary, but which she felt it pointless as well as impossible to evade.

This evening she had sat long at the window, not turning on her light though it was now too dark to read, gazing across the valley and trying to interpret the tone of the voices below. Everything was so still outside. When the mistral was there it was impossible to imagine its absence. Now it was impossible to think there could be anything but this particular quiet against which the significant sound of the voices rose up like a distant chant. Then she saw a man upon the rocks. She was thinking how unusual this was when she realized with a violent shock who the man was. She stood up. She covered her mouth. She observed his slow approach with a fierce wild almost cruel joy. But steadfast Anne was silent. She did not move or cry out or run loudly down the stairs. She simply watched Tim to see what he would do. She saw him creep up to the terrace, step over the loggia, and move toward the window. A moment later she saw him step back, carefully make his way to the terrace steps and begin to walk and then to run away down the slope into the gathering dark. Anne could imagine what it was that he had seen through the window. The pair below were silent now. Anne sat down in her chair, still holding *The Heart of Midlothian*.

Tim might as well have flown back across the valley for all he could afterwards remember of his escape. He must have run back instinctively the way he came, in order to return to the village. When he became conscious of where he was he was already lost.

The mental pain was so great that he had to try deliberately not to think. As it was, a cramp in his stomach made him bow down as he ran, now climbed, away from that hateful scene. As the silent rocks had looked in at him and Gertrude holding hands, he had himself been *doomed* to look in and see the identical tender scene, with the Count now playing his part. Perhaps those two chairs were enchanted. If he could have heard of it all in some other way, heard some rumour—but to *see it enacted* like a tableau before his very eyes. . . . And he thought, she told Mrs Mount she would be alone, and secretly she was with *him*. Of course Tim had reckoned on the Count, even tried to think conventional generous thoughts about 'the best man winning' and so on. These were unreal figments, wisps, clouds, illusions, in the awful presence of the reality to which he was now condemned. I shall think of it forever, I shall *see* it forever, he said to himself as his fingers crooked over the ridges of the hard hard rocks. He recalled the wonderful miracle of his holding hands with Gertrude on that night in the spring. When their hands joined a shock wave passed out through all the galaxy. And yet it was so quiet, so tender, a matter for gentle tears and humble prostrated joyful gratitude. Now even the past was desecrated, blackened, burnt. He and Gertrude had sat in a black shell constructed by demons.

He thought, I have been *betrayed*. He had been insulted, lied to, grossly and horribly mocked and rejected. His worst fearful dreams of what it would be like *now* to fail, to face Gertrude's anger and dismissal, had never included anything as frightful as this. Was it conceivable that it had been arranged on purpose? Had it all been planned by Mrs Mount? Had someone from the village alerted Gertrude? She had finally cast him into outer darkness, sealing his departure with a doom of jealous hate. Oh how well off he had been before when he was alone and hated nobody! Now he hated Gertrude, he hated the Count, and all the loathsome irresistible machinery of jealousy had been installed within him. How *could* they have been so *cruel*. Oh why had he come on this vile fatal journey! Had he not *known* it was a terrible mistake; had he not *known* that he risked his very sanity in coming? He had parted from Gertrude in some kind of dreadful moral muddle, but he had managed to accept the parting as final and even to try to put his life in order. He had left Daisy, he had *sacrificed* Daisy, who loved him, and had been with him forever. Why? It now seemed to him that he had given up this love, this last remaining comfort, simply to placate Gertrude! To appease, without gain to himself, her accusing lingering shadow. He had got rid of his guilt by leaving Daisy. Or rather he had tried to, he could never get rid of his guilt, it was a disease. And now, as a complication of this self-same disease, had come this horrible fever of jealousy and hate. Gertrude and the Count were black devils in his mind, and he could foresee a long long future time during which those devils would perform their appointed task of tormenting him. Oh, they would draw his blood! And where were they at this moment, what were they doing, just those two, together? He felt as if he would vomit, spewing out a black stream of loathing and hatred and shame.

These thoughts, after a while, were slightly checked by the realization that he had lost his way. He had, he supposed, been returning to the village. He had been clambering for some time and ought by now to have reached the place where the rocks came gently down to a slope of grass which led to the level place where the beehives were. But there was no sign of the easy descent to the grass. Instead he was constantly forced to climb higher to avoid little thickets of red-leaved wind-scorched box into a region which he could not recognize where the rocks rose in a series of curious mounds to an unfamiliar skyline. Moreover it had now suddenly grown much darker. When Tim stopped and lifted his head he realized that there was still a lot of brightness in the sky, but saw at the same time how indistinguishably hazy the dangerous rocks had become underfoot. Behind him a huge almost full moon had come into view, but still a cheesy yellow and giving little light. One or two stars were visible. The rock mounds, rising in lines above, seemed like forms in some oriental temple, vast heads of gods perhaps. He felt that he was now higher up among the rocks than he had ever been before, and that he had quite lost his sense of direction. He cursed miserably, hating himself, hating everything. Now *this* wretched stupidity of being lost.

He began to go back the way he had come, moving more slowly, often testing his steps with a cautious prodding foot. The rocks looked quite different, larger, set in greater more monumental masses, their innumerable edges and wrinkles blurred and erased. At the same time there was more debris, little slippery piles of broken rock which by daylight he would instinctively have avoided. Once he slipped upon one of these short screes and came down heavily on his side. He sat rubbing his ankle and decided he had better wait until the moon had risen further and gained light. It would be a suitable crazy finale to break a limb in this wilderness, where no one would ever find him, and die slowly shrieking with pain. He sat there and contemplated, fixed and clear in his mind as a brilliant icon, the image of Gertrude and the Count holding hands across the table.

After a while the chipped moon did what Tim expected of it, it rose higher and became smaller, more silvery and very very bright. It hung like a brilliant heavy stone in the sky. More stars appeared and sparkled. The rocks gradually emerged again, their details revealed in a new way by the odd creepy brown light. They exuded now, a positive tense stillness. They were piled round about him, great leaning monumental shafts, wherein the moonlight suggested little steps and ledges and even, close at hand, their spotty crinkly texture. The rocks rose up in tense quietness, like a symphony of frozen inaudible sound. Tim got up, feeling stiff. He felt awkward and cold and noticed that his trousers were still damp from crossing the stream. He was frightened of the rocks and even more horrified to think that he had still not *got away* from that accursed proximity. As it was he would have to spend the night in the village. He began to walk, as he guessed, back in the direction of the house, hoping at every few steps to see down into open country on his left, to see the white tops of the beehives, or perhaps the meandering dark course of the streamlet. The stream, he knew, led to the village, passing at several points close to the road. He scrambled cautiously, using his hands, and sometimes sitting down to place his feet carefully on a lower level. There was very little vegetation now, except for dark dry patches of what his fingers told him was moss. Sometimes as he clawed them, little cubes of rock came away neatly in his hand, as if the hillside were giving him a mocking present. Occasionally there were level ways that looked like paths, but they always ceased after a few paces. He hoped to find himself steadily descending, but little cliffs and shafts of rock continually barred his way, and when he had contrived to discover and crawl through gaps between them, he often seemed to be upon yet higher ground. In fact the light made it difficult to determine whether on the whole he was going up or down. He was tired and hungry and beginning to feel cold again in spite of his exertions. He cursed with anger and misery and a baffled frenzied desire to escape from the rocks which seemed with perverse intent to be keeping him in the one place where he had least wish to be. Scrambling through a defile he scraped his hand painfully on a rocky projection, and pausing to look at his knuckles found them covered with a brown shade which when he touched it felt wet. Then he could feel the warm blood running through onto his palm. He moaned aloud and raised his eyes and saw before him, now brightly illuminated by the moon, the rising series of rocky mounds, the heads of gods, which he had left behind just after darkness fell.

Panic overcame Tim now and he turned and began to try to run away across the rocks. It was in fact impossible to run, but it was possible in a nightmarish way to try to. With frenzied exertion he moved slowly, aware of the moonlight, aware of what was behind him, and somehow able to avoid a serious fall. He slithered recklessly into a steeply descending cleft which turned out to be full of little stone cubes like the ones with which he had been presented earlier on. He sat down and descended, half-sliding, and became aware of moisture; the cleft was the abode of a spring. The stones were now wet and cold and very slippery. Trying to get his footing he began to tilt forward and lose his balance, about to trip and fall headfirst downwards. He stumbled and slipped sideways, but not onto rock. He was lying on grass.

Scraped and bruised he got up and looked around, wildly hoping that he had at last got out of the rocks. He had not. They rose up, blocking the sky on every side, now concealing the moon. But at least he stood on grass, and the grass was not a solitary isolated patch but led away like a rivulet in both directions. There was something familiar about the profile of

414

the rock wall, sharp and black against the lighted sky. He had no idea which way it was best to go, but instinct told him to go to the left. Moreover the path that way led downhill. The grass was precious, firm, friendly underfoot. He walked a little, following the grassway round in a curve, and came suddenly to a space between two rocks where there was a step and the moonlit effect of a door. He set his foot upon the step and pulled himself through between the smooth pillar-like rocks, and saw directly before him and above him the moon shining upon the high round moist surface of the Great Face.

Tim went forward and tripped over something which tangled round his foot. It was a long strand of the hanging creeper which grew upon the high place above, which perhaps the wind had torn off. He stepped over the creeper and then paused looking up. He did not want to come too close. He did not want to see the moon reflected in the pool. From where he stood he could see the rocky rim of the pool, but not the water. He looked up at the pale pitted surface high above him. It gleamed in the moonlight, luminous, phosphorescent, as if glowing from within. It might have been a huge alabaster window of some lighted hall. The creepers hung down from above, motionless, shadowing the thing a little. Above it the rocks receded into a blurred shade which merged into the moonlight sky. The moisture gleamed and crept upon the pallid glowing surface.

For a moment Tim forgot everything except the marvel that was before him. Then he recalled, with added pain, not his long traverse of the rocks, but the scene at the house and the miserable end of his stupid fruitless journey. He thought he would go and he turned away toward the rock door. But suddenly utter exhaustion gripped him, and he had to sit down on the grass. His legs were useless now. He could go no further. The grassy place within the rocky shell was sheltered here, seemed gentler, warmer. He thought he would rest a while. Then he put his head down onto the grass and instantly fell into a deep sleep.

When Tim woke up there was a dawn light. He saw, first of

all, as if it were a separate thing, the light, very grey, very cold. Then he saw the grass, and the nearest rock, and the rock was grey and as hard as the light. Close at hand it looked like pitted cement. Just raising his head he meditated for a while on the light and the grass and the rock, not yet conscious of himself. Then, appalled, he sat up. The great face was still there, but extinguished, chill. He had never, in all the time he had spent looking at it, seen it so austere. The moisture upon it was invisible. It looked now like a round grey grille with a very fine mesh. Tim only then remembered Gertrude, and with this came consciousness of his body, aching and stiff and cold. He got up slowly and moved toward the middle of the glade.

A cloud of mist or steam hung over the pool. The grooved rock above the face looked brown and furred, perhaps because the moss fronds had withered. The grey light of the unrisen sun revealed a terrible immobility, the creepers looked like stalactites, even the mist was motionless. Walking stiffly, Tim approached the pool. He noticed that his right hand was covered with dried blood and he had an impulse to wash it, but then realized that this was out of the question.

The crystal circle of the water surface was totally visible beneath the level of the mist which hung like a halo a foot or two above it. Tim noticed that, although the surface was completely smooth, glossy, almost hard as if it were a sheet of transparent polished steel, the pool was more agitated than it had been when he last saw it. Perhaps it had been stirred by the mistral, from which some impulse still remained. The faint quivering pulses or rays which seemed to be passing through it, though without ruffling its surface, were more marked and had a different more urgent rhythm. It was unclear to Tim exactly how these pulses made themselves visible, and as he stared he half thought that he imagined them. Perhaps there was only an illusion of movement. Or, perhaps, the scarcely perceptible lines of force in the water were represented by bubbles which were so tiny that the eye could not grasp them. The water was not in any way obscured by these impulsions, it was very clear and seemed to have gathered light into itself. Tim could see the wide gently curving bed of pearly and white pebbles gleaming below, at some distance which he could not estimate, each pebble clearly discernible. Rounded, of uniform size, arranged

416

as if on display, the crystalline stones looked so precious, so desirable, that Tim felt a sudden urge to seize a handful of them: only they were undoubtedly out of reach and he could not bring himself to break the surface. At that moment he became conscious that he was *extremely thirsty*. Hunger was with him, he knew, but hunger could wait. Thirst could not. Again he leaned toward the water as if actually to touch the shining surface with his lips. But again it was impossible, and he thought *no*, I won't drink *this* water, not *this* water, no, no.

He turned round quickly. It was as if there was a presence in the glade. He decided he had better go. Without looking back he hurried to the stone gate and climbed out onto the grass path outside. Here everything was immediately familiar, his sense of direction was with him again, and he knew exactly how to find his way. To the left the path led down, toward the valley and the house, and adjoined the rockway toward the beehives. To the right the path went upward and stopped near to the crest beyond which lay the descent toward the canal. The sun had still not risen and there was no point in hurrying to the village. Tim did not want to return in the direction of the house. His thirst was agonizing, increased by the sight of the forbidden water. He decided to turn to the right and go to the canal.

As he went along the path he soon came to the steep slope of little cubical stones down which he had slithered in the dark. The lower part was overhung by gorse bushes and in his previous wanderings he had never noticed it. It was indeed a watercourse, the stones were damp and gleaming, though no water could be seen to flow. Already a cloud of wasps had assembled there to drink. Peering upward here Tim could even see, far above, one of the humpy stone 'domes' which had so much frightened him in the night. This region must be just above the great face. In fact the area he had covered during the night, when he had so totally lost his way, was probably quite small and he had simply wandered to and fro within it.

He followed the path until, a little further on, it came to an end where massive rocky 'steps' led up to the skyline. As he reached the top the sun was rising. He could now see the plain, squared out by lines of poplars into different greens with here and there the gleaming polythene arches of the tomato pavilions; and beyond the plain were the shapely blue mountains. The

417

rocks close to him, extending on his right, were a very light creamy blue in the sunshine, merging into an almost colourless yet bright sky which seemed so like the grey which it had seemed before that one could have believed oneself mistaken in calling it grey then, when it was so patently blue now. Below, the rocks were scooped out into little thickety valleys, and dotted with young pines, radiantly green, upon which green cones were perched at awkward angles like ornaments upon Christmas trees. Then there was the yellow grassy slope to the canal, the darting line of water flashing with its motionless speed. Tim stood a moment looking. A single bird was singing sweetly, sounding almost like an English blackbird. He began to descend quickly, avoiding the bramble gulley which had delayed him on the first occasion, and soon he was running across the grass toward the water. When he got there he nearly tumbled in in his impatience. He hurled himself down on the bank, levering himself down head first through the steep thick grass of the verge until, holding on with one hand, he was able to scoop up some of the icy cold water and hurl it towards his mouth. Long did he lie there, imbibing the water slowly and with exquisite relief. When at last he wanted to get back onto the top of the bank he found it quite difficult to do so. His head was so low, his feet were so high, he seemed able to do no more than to hold onto the grass to prevent himself from slipping forward. However, by snake-like writhings, he managed slowly to edge himself backward until the greater part of his weight was at the top of the bank, and he was able to twist back into a sitting position. He was exhausted, and now that the urgency of the thirst was gone, he felt hungry and aching and totally miserable.

He now became aware of the nearby weir, and also of the different softer noise of the stream as it passed him by. He sat looking at the racing jumbled olive-grey water whose little tossed-up crests were flashing in the sun. The sun-baked meadow behind him was prickly, covered with small mauve and yellow thistles and sharp pale wisps of dried-up grass. But the long lush green grasses beside the water were full of flowers, blue vetch and scabious and starry flowers like big golden pimpernels. Tim thought about Gertrude and the Count and how inevitable that conjunction was, how fated that vision of them which, as in a crystal ball, he had been vouchsafed. He felt no hatred now. How could he hate either of them? They were the blessed ones, the happy ones, the people of the other race. But he felt awful cancerous jealousy and envy and a dull anger with himself for having always muddled and messed up his chances of happiness. Would the village people tell Gertrude that *le peintre* had been here, and what would she make of it? Did the village people know that he was her husband? He would never know and it did not matter. He wondered what would happen to him now and whether he would ever now live a simple life and be cheerful about innocent things. He felt that he had betrayed the purity of his aloneness. As he miserably worked it out, what he had gained from losing Daisy, he had now totally lost by this disastrous expedition. No doubt he would have learnt later on of Gertrude's relation with the Count. Had he not himself predicted it, even feigned to imagine that it was in some way appropriate and right? But the impetuous foolish journey, carefully timed to culminate in actually *seeing* them together: that was real ingenuity on the part of the malicious imp that ran his life. *Now* it was so clear that he ought never to have come. He ought to have stayed quietly with his little bit of safety, his little bit of peace. It was all gone, smashed, his little achievement; and as he looked into the torment ahead he thought that he would like to die.

He turned and looked up at the etched folded rocks. Against the bluer sky they looked like Egyptian silver. Why do I suddenly think that, he wondered. It must be some sudden memory of his mother who had had a bracelet made of Egyptian silver, as she must have told him. He had not thought of that since he was a child. He was so unkind to his mother. He got up and began to walk along the edge of the canal. He passed the grove of pines and gazed, without any pleasure, at the clean edges of the hard cut stone which now enclosed the canal as it curved to the right. The sparkling raging water rushed faster now, darkening the walls as far as the wavelets reached. At the outside of the curve the water rose into a white foaming tidal wave and then where the bed of the canal evidently descended toward the weir, humped itself into tossed swooping billows. The noise increased as it surged toward the check of the waterfall, over which it leapt to glide down the slope into the whirlpool below; after which the whole canal vanished, stooping to enter the tunnel, filling it to the brim.

Tim stood beside the weir, watching the extraordinary transformation as the wild flickering waters sprang onto the top of the rock wall of the weir and ran with smooth docility down the vivid green slope and entered the white churning frenzy below before crowding themselves into the tunnel. He felt himself as mad, as self-destructive as that water, as wild and unpredictable as its atoms; and the substance of his madness was misery and remorse. And, oh he felt so tired. It was time to climb the rocks and return to the village and go back to England.

He retraced his steps along the curving stone verge to where the long green grasses and the thorny acacia bushes leaned down over the racing stream. A jay cried and passed, then posed momentarily in the acacia. Blue dragonflies zoomed over the water. The sun was already hot and a warm wind was blowing. A grasshopper took flight, opening rose madder wings. Brown butterflies swarmed near the pine trees. All these things which could have given pleasure were metamorphosed into things of sadness because the world was cursed. Tim looked upstream at the long vista of the turbulent grey cool water between its abundant banks of green. He looked, then suddenly he saw that there was a bulky dark object, tossed about in the current, approaching him fast. Immediately Tim was terrified. Was it a body, a drowned man, what should he do? It was a darkish and palish thing, turning over and over in the speeding foam. He stared, then recognized it as a dog. He saw the shape of the doggy head and the wet muzzle lifting. It was a large black and white dog which was being bundled along by the canal. Tim grimaced at the miserable portent, for he took it to be another bloated corpse, like the one which he had seen with Gertrude.

Then he saw, as the thing came near, that the animal was not dead but very much alive. It was a black and white beast, not unlike an English collie, and it was struggling desperately, making evident hopeless efforts to check its progress and get some hold on the steep grassy banks. Tim saw the helpless white paws reach up and touch the overhanging grass. In a moment the animal would be swept past him, would whirl round the corner between the stone verges, and over the weir to drown in the tunnel.

Tim's body had already identified itself with that drenched form, that desperate lifted muzzle, those white clutching paws. He threw himself down, as he had done when he wanted to drink, and slithered down the bank until one hand was in the water while the other hand held onto the grass. As the dog approached Tim reached out to grip it as it passed. His hand touched the long drenched fur and touched the warm slippery body (he felt its warmth). A paw brushed his wrist (he saw the claws). Then the dog, wrenched round by the water in an eddying whirl, moved out of his reach and passed him by. Tim slipped head first into the stream.

The translation, the cold, the shock deprived him of sense for a second. Then he found himself trying to swim. His instinct still was to rescue the dog. He could see the beast struggling only a yard or two ahead of him. With his utmost strength Tim contested with the swift water, to gain on it, to reach the dog and pull it to the shore. But the stream, not his efforts, determined their relative velocity.

At the next moment Tim had stopped thinking about the dog, he was thinking about himself. He tried to grasp the bushes and the trailing grasses which were fleeting by, but the stream jerked them from his grasp. He was breathless with swallowing cold water and wearied with his brief strenuous attempt to swim. He kept clutching at the banks and trying to veer off the main stream and arrest himself in their shelter, but against the flow he could not control his limbs or alter the direction in which he was being hustled along. His leg struck violently upon an underwater obstruction. Then his clutching hand touched smooth wet stone and he was being whirled round the curve of the canal.

Tim had by now pictured what was to come and had already made a plan. There was a precious crucial moment when the water paused at the top of the weir, when it checked and paused and hopped itself over the stone lip before it went streaming down the smooth green slide into the whirlpool. Tim felt that if he could only hang onto the stone at the top of the slope where the torrent became docile for a moment, or spreadeagle his body against the vertical wall below, he could gain enough control to cling there, to steady himself, then to edge along to the side of the canal and, rising to his feet upon the head of the weir, to climb out onto the brink.

He tried to straighten himself so that he could look ahead. This proved very difficult. If the stream had been straight it would have been possible to assemble his limbs for the operation. As it was, however, he was pinned against the outside wall of the curve by the centrifugal force of the water, and whisked along half choking by the high wave of foam. He was by now mainly concerned with keeping his head above the surface. He caught a sideways glimpse of the sudden glossy smooth line of the checked stream, and beyond it the stone wall above the tunnel mouth. He had a quick vision of the black and white dog appearing for a moment on the edge of the fall, then tumbling over and vanishing. Tim tried to prepare himself for the impact with the vertical edge, the near side of the weir. Then one of his knees banged against something very hard below him. He realized too late that there was an underwater stone ramp leading up to the head of the water slide. If he had been prepared for it, this ramp could have helped him to slow himself down in the shallower water against the tearing rush of the stream; but now the unexpected obstruction and the sudden knock simply confused him further and destroyed what was left of his intent to clasp the high point of the fall and stay there. He retracted his hurt knee, pushed his hands instinctively against the rising stones, turned sideways in the water, found his shoulder already upon the smooth lip of the weir, grasped helplessly at a green slimy surface, took the urgent current like a blow in the back, then found himself rolling over and over down the slope into the whirlpool.

When Tim's head rose above the surface of the raging foam he was already close to the tunnel. He could see the waters contending, boiling, stooping as they constrained themselves into the tunnel whose entrance was below the surface. The smooth stone walls of the canal now rose high above on either side, cutting out the light of the sky. Tim thought, oh why did I have to drink this water and not the other? And he thought, oh Gertrude, Gertrude — He was fully conscious that he was about to die. He took a last gasping breath and instinctively ducked his head into the foam as he was sucked down under the submerged centre of the stone arch.

Tim had taken another breath. He was aware of the breath as a miracle, a precious amazing event. Then something hit him very hard on the head. He swallowed water, choking. He was in total darkness, at any rate if his eyes were open, which he was not sure about. With the realization that he was still alive came an instantaneous absolute death-fear identical with hope. The roof of the tunnel was at this point and for the moment and only a little way, clear of the water. Tim took another breath. All the time he was, in some sort, swimming, that is he was agitating his limbs instinctively so as to keep his head above the surface. This was difficult since his legs seemed to have been swept below his head rather than behind it and the strong water in the narrower space had somehow imprisoned his arms. His dabbing feet could touch no bottom below. He made a schematic effort to float on his back with his nose and mouth toward the roof, but this failed, and he received in the process a hard bang on the brow. He had already grasped the problem, which was to keep his face above water while not being stunned and rendered unconscious by a blow from the roof. His body rather than his mind informed him that it was no use. In a moment the roof would descend to the level of the water or below it, or else the whole torrent would plunge headlong into some deep hole. He would die indeed like a rat, and perhaps no one would ever know what had happened to him. No one would know and no one would care. Oh let me live! he prayed. A little while ago he had seemed to want death, but now he desired so passionately to live. He thought, I must live, I must, I must!

The roof seemed to be descending, more and more often and more and more violently it struck him as he opened his mouth to breathe. He had by now established a rhythm, not just instinctively gasping, but taking a deep breath and holding it with his head ducked down in the water, then taking another. He even tried with one hand to gauge the height of the roof before he lifted his head to breathe. This was no help however since the darkness had deprived him of all sense of space and touch and it was difficult to manoeuvre his arms. Moreover his head was spinning with repeated blows and he was swallowing more water. Each time he took a breath he thought this may be the last. He thought this fear, this darkness, *is* death, this is what it's like. But oh I so much want to live, please let me live, any life is better than death, oh let me only live. . . .

Suddenly and with no warning, perhaps his eyes were closed after all, Tim emerged into brilliant sunlight. There was nothing now above him except the bright blue morning sky. He gasped, taking another wonderful breath. As he did so he saw ahead of him, with a clarity which remained with him forever after, the sparkling canal, looking so peaceful and beautiful between its grassy banks, running a little to the left and leaving behind it on the outside of the curve a little yellow stony beach. And upon the beach Tim saw the black and white dog climbing out of the water.

Instinct moved his wearied limbs and somehow it seemed at that moment that the canal actually helped him. It deposited him gently on the beach and hurried on. It had finished with him. Tim crawled on hands and knees out of the water. Looking up he saw the dog again. It was shaking itself. After a good shake it began to sniff a nearby tuft of grass. It lifted its leg against the grass, and then trotted off with a preoccupied air.

Tim blessed the dog, he blessed the open sky and the sun, he even blessed the canal. He crawled up the slope of stones until he reached the grass and lay there spitting. He felt that his body was full of water, it had entered his mouth and his nose and his ears, it had soaked into his flesh. He sat for a while and concentrated on breathing, that wonderful wonderful operation, now suddenly so easy. The sweet air, smelling of dry grass rushed gladly into his lungs. He breathed, not looking round him, letting the light dazzle his eyes.

Then he found that he was taking his shoes off. He was surprised to find that they were still on his feet. He recalled now how awkward they had felt in the first moments of his immersion. His feet seemed to have swollen inside them. When he had pulled them off he rested, lying flat. The sun was hot. Then he sat up, and with more difficulty took off his shirt and trousers and socks, and wrang the water out of them and spread them upon the grass. Then he rested again. Then he sat up and stared about.

He was in an unfamiliar valley, in a large flat meadow of yellow grass. There was no habitation, no person. On the other side of the canal (he noticed the canal with a kind of surprise as if he had forgotten it) there was a well-tended vineyard protected by three dense rows of cypress trees. Beyond the cypresses, far far away across the flat land, he could see the blue mountains. Behind him, on his own side of the canal, were the familiar rocks, rising up quite close to him out of dense dark green prickly undergrowth. He was glad that the stream had deposited him on the same side as the village. He would have been very reluctant to enter that water again.

Still sitting, he pulled his shirt and trousers on. They were still damp. He was aware of pains in his body. He had received a blow on the cheek bone and one on the brow and several on the top of his head. He felt these places carefully. He had a headache and felt giddy. The sun hurt his eyes and the landscape jumped about before him and became covered in dots. His hand was hurting and had started bleeding again. There was a nasty graze on his knee. He began to stop being glad to be alive, and to start feeling very ill and wretched. He felt very tired and very hungry. He tried to get up and failed, feeling too giddy. He got up at last and stood holding his shoes and socks in his hand and wondering which way to go.

He saw the wall of smooth stones out of which the canal was bubbling up like a spring, the opening being under water. Beyond it stretched the unbroken meadow, bordered by distant poplars and umbrella pines. He looked up at the rocks, trying to recognize something in their formation. Blinking hard, he thought he could descry at the skyline two of the humpy dome-shaped rocks which had been a feature of his night-wanderings, which now seemed so long ago. He could not estimate the length of time he had been in the tunnel or how far away the other end of it was. In any case he wanted to get away from the canal. He decided to see what the rocks looked like at the nearest point. He began to walk barefoot across the meadow, but the sharp dry grass hurt his feet. He sat down to put on his shoes and socks. The shoes would hardly go on, his feet seemed miles

425

away, and he felt so dizzy and fatigued he could hardly get up again. At the least exertion lights flashed before his face. One of his eyes seemed to be closing up.

The foot of the rocks, when he got there, proved to be defended by a mass of scrub oak and box and gorse and brambles, trailed over by the local version of old man's beard, which had woven itself into a barrier so impenetrable that one could not even introduce a foot, let alone dream of pushing one's way through. However after walking a little way he came upon a narrow path which had been cut through the thicket by one of those invisible persons who used the rocks for their own purposes. The path led up to an easy ascent and he thought that he could recognize the profile of the summit. He climbed wearily and slowly; and only at this point did he suddenly and urgently ask himself, *where am I going*? He had, he supposed, been making his way back to the village. What a fuss they would make at the hotel when he turned up looking like this. Would they insist on his seeing a doctor? Where was his wallet, where was his passport? Had the canal taken them away? As he began to search he remembered that he had left the wallet and passport in his jacket at the hotel. His questing hand found found something however in his trouser pocket. It was his wedding ring which he had put there on the day when he went from the bank to Daisy's flat at Shepherd's Bush. He slipped the ring onto his finger. He thought, I won't go to the village. I'm so tired and so hurt and so miserable. I'll go to Gertrude. After all, she is my wife.

Vigilant Anne Cavidge was once more the first to see him. She watched him descending slowly through the vineyard on the other side of the valley. Anne was in a different mood this morning. After a night of suffering she was feeling considerably less resigned and heroic. To let Tim go a second time would really be too much. She kicked her suitcase out from under the bed.

Tim could hardly walk now but his will and his intent had grown stronger with every step. He came very slowly through the despoiled poplar grove, treading on the gold and silver leaves. At the bridge he did not walk impatiently into the water, his impatience was over now, but laboriously pulled and pushed the big willow branch out of the way and crossed the bridge. He had no anxiety, no calculation. He wanted simply to reach Gertrude.

He mounted the hill panting loudly. It was hard to make the climb over the ploughed earth of the olive grove, but now he did not pause to rest. Nor did he look up at the house. He looked, trudging, bent forward, at the earth at his feet. He crossed the dry grass of the little meadow full of mauve thistles and wispy scabious, and climbed the last short slope to the terrace. He saw his feet planted upon the mossy terrace steps, upon the scattering of yellow fig leaves, then he stood upon the terrace straightening himself up and looking about him, still panting.

Gertrude came out of the sitting-room doors. She saw Tim and came towards him. 'Oh — Tim — darling — darling — thank God — ' And she took him in her arms.

'Come on, hurry,' said Anne to the Count. 'Pack your case, it can come later with the car. Just put a few things to take with you in a bag, here, take this bag.'

The Count was completely dazed. 'But I told Gertrude I'd help her to mend the loggia this morning — '

'Never mind the loggia, Tim will deal with that. Oh hurry, hurry, we've got to *go*!'

'But, Anne, what's happened?'

'I told you, Tim's back, he's *back*!'

'Yes, I saw, but — '

'We're off! We'll take the bikes. But be *quick, please*.'

427

The Count confusedly put his shaving things and a shirt picked up at random into the shopping bag that Anne had given him while she hastily stuffed the rest of his belongings into his suitcase. She had packed her own case in the four minutes that followed after Gertrude had put her arms round Tim.

'But, Anne, we can't just go like that—neither of them can drive, and—'

'Manfred can fetch them or fetch the car or whatever. He's made for fetching and carrying.'

'But Tim coming like this—it may not be—'

'It is. He's back. Anyway it's not for us to speculate. Don't you *see*?'

'Yes, but—we must talk to Gertrude, ask her—'

'We'll tell her, we won't ask, we'll leave a note. She's not concerned with us now. She's forgotten we exist. She's talking to Tim. We *must* leave them alone, we can't stay, we *can't*! Better to go without conversations or explanations. After all, what have we got to say to those two? Nothing.'

'Oh Anne—I don't know what to do—'

'Do what I tell you! No, leave the suitcase here with mine, we can't carry suitcases on the bikes. Have you got all you want in that bag? And your passport and money?'

'Yes—oh what a *muddle*—'

'You just check your stuff. I'll write a note to Gertrude.'

On a large piece of writing paper Anne wrote in capital letters, DARLING, I'M SO GLAD! WE HAVE GONE. WE THOUGHT IT BEST. MUCH LOVE. ANNE. PS Our luggage is packed up in our rooms. We'll leave the bikes at the hotel.

'Now come along, come *along*!' She pulled the Count out of his bedroom and down the stairs. She left the note in a conspicuous position in the hall, and taking the Count's sleeve firmly in her hand, led him out of the archway and down the drive to the garage. There were two bicycles, one male, one female. Anne felt the tyres. They were hard. She stowed the bags in the two baskets and gave the Count his machine. She even had to put his two hands on the handlebars. 'Come on, Peter, you're mine now,' she said, but he did not hear her, he was too upset and unhappy.

In the sitting-room Tim and Gertrude, deep in talk, vaguely heard a strange distant sound. It was Anne Cavidge laughing.

'But you're hurt,' said Gertrude. 'You've been fighting—'

'Have I got a black eye? It feels like it.'

'Yes—'

'I have been fighting, sort of, I'll tell you about it. I'll tell you *everything*.'

'Oh darling sweet precious Tim, darling heart. I'm so glad you've come back—'

'Are you? Oh *good*. Gertrude, this is OK isn't it, I mean I'm back, it's real, you won't tell me to go away again?'

'No, no, you're here forever, I can't think how I ever let you go.'

'Oh, I've been such a perfect fool, my darling—but I'll tell you, I'll *explain*—'

'No need to explain, I mean all right, but you don't have to, you're so absolutely here and that's everything.'

'But I must explain, I have to, you must *see* it all, you didn't *see* it before—'

'You didn't give me much chance to, you just ran off—'

'You told me to go—'

'Yes, but I—'

'I was so stupid and frightened, and I felt awful because I hadn't told you—'

'About that woman, what about her, I mean what about her now?'

'I've left her.'

'You're bleeding—'

'Oh I expect so. Gertrude, I *have* left her—'

'Yes, I know, I'm sure. Sit down and let me look. There's an awful bruise on your forehead—'

'I got banged on the head—I say, how pretty that vine branch is.'

'There's blood in your hair?'

'I nearly passed out—'

'Let me feel—'

'Is my skull fractured?'

'I shouldn't think so. Does that hurt?'

'Yes, but it would, wouldn't it?'

'But what *happened*?'

'I was fighting with the canal—or rather—I got swept into that tunnel—'

'But why ever—?'

'I know I promised you I wouldn't, but I didn't mean to go in, there was this dog—'

'Keep still—your hand's bleeding—'

'Yes, and I've got a cut on my leg, and here on my knee, look—'

'You went into the *tunnel*, however—'

'I didn't want to, there was this—'

'But how did you—'

'I went all the way through the tunnel and—'

'I can't think how you're still alive—'

'Nor can I—'

'Come to the kitchen, I must put something on those cuts.'

'I feel terrible, actually, and I'm awfully hungry—'

Gertrude put her arm through Tim's and led him. He leaned against her shoulder smiling a broad exhausted crazy sleepy smile. Gertrude saw the note in the hall. 'They've gone!'

'Who?'

'Anne and the Count. Never mind. Now let me wash those cuts and disinfect them. What a state your clothes are in.'

'I told you, I fell in, there was this dog—'

'Better take your clothes off and put on my coat, no, stay there, I'll get some hot water and—'

'I'm making the towel filthy—'

'Do keep still—'

'Oh, Gertrude, that hurts—'

'I don't think it's a deep cut—'

'Perhaps I've got concussion?'

'Perhaps you have, but don't frig about so.'

'I'm so hungry—'

'In a minute—'

'I haven't eaten anything since yesterday in the aeroplane, I came on this 'plane and—'

'I haven't any steak for your poor eye, we ate it last night—'

'I wish there was some. What is there to eat?'

'There's a chicken casserole, I made it, I decided I would—'

'You decided you would! Oh wonderful Gertrude, I do like your dress and those blue beads, I love you so much. Do you love me?'

'Yes.'

'And you forgive me?'

'Yes.'

'And you'll hold onto me for ever, and ever?'

'Yes.'

'We're married, and—'

'Yes, yes.'

'Look, I'm wearing my ring—'

'Yes, I see. I think I'd better put some plaster—'

'Oh don't bother. Oh Gertrude, do stop playing at first aid.'

'You thought you'd got a fractured skull and concussion.'

'I don't now.'

'I wonder if you should see a doctor—'

'No, I'm fine. Gertrude, I must have some of that chicken casserole or I shall go mad.'

Robed in Gertrude's coat, Tim sat at the kitchen table confronting the chicken casserole. He ate a little. Then he said, 'Darling, I'm sorry—I think—what I want now is just—to go to sleep. Do you mind?'

'Dearest heart, of course you must sleep. Come now. Come.'

He leaned again on Gertrude's arm as she helped him upstairs and led him to her bed.

'Will you be warm enough, would you like—'

'No, I'm all right—'

'I'll close the shutters—'

'God, I do want to sleep—'

'Sleep, my darling—'

'You won't go away while I'm asleep?'

'I won't go away.'

'Oh Gertrude, I feel so happy—it's like—going to sleep—
when I was a boy—after passing an exam—'

'Don't worry. You've passed your exam.'

'Oh Gertrude, you're so good to me.'

'Go to sleep, darling.'

Tim was already asleep. Gertrude closed the shutters. She
sat in the darkened room beside the bed watching Tim sleeping,
and her heart was full of an incoherent tender joy.

'You're telling it all topsy-turvy,' said Gertrude.

'There's so much to tell.'

It was evening. The sun, just behind the rocks, was bleaching
the pale blue sky with light. The tall folded rocks lifted their
majestic cliff faces, streaked with blue and creamy white. The
cicadas were busily rapidly finishing their last song in the
motionless pines.

Tim had slept for several hours and woken as into paradise.
His body had a limp feeling which might have been either
physical exhaustion or pure joy.

The evening was planned to move slowly. They both had a
sense of arrested time. Feeding his hunger now with a happy
temperance Tim had eaten a lot of bread and butter and paté
and olives. Eating, existing, had become a long musical slow
movement. The chicken casserole was still to come.

They were talking and drinking. Tim was trying to tell the
whole story, but there were so many interconnecting parts to
the story and so many parts that did not connect at all, so many
events which were over-determined, so many that were purely
accidental, he kept darting about and breaking off and starting
again, to present it all as a coherent picture was beyond his
talents as a narrator, and they were both so pleased with each
other's company that they could not concentrate.

'I think I was influenced by Anne,' said Gertrude.

'She disapproves of me.'

'She'll come round.'

432

'Will she?'

'She'll have to, I'll make her. Besides she's rational and good and she'll *see*.'

'Oh course she's right to disapprove, I mean, she isn't right really, but—'

'She's a bit jealous.'

'Wasn't it funny their both clearing off on bikes!'

'Well, thank heavens. We're not in a hurry to go anywhere.'

'Gertrude, I must be back by Tuesday, I'm teaching.'

'I'm so glad about your job.'

'Oh my dear, to be able to tell you everything, it's like being in the presence of God.'

'That gives us nearly a week here.'

'What about the car?'

'Someone can fetch it later, Manfred can.'

'Oh—Manfred—'

'You're not worrying about Manfred now?'

'Gertrude, I'm so frightened. I'm frightened of everybody, I feel that I shook your love for me so much that it must be sort of cracked.'

'It isn't cracked. It's entire. One knows.'

'Oh if only I hadn't seen you and the Count, it was like the end of the world.'

'Tim, I've told you—'

'I know, but I'll keep seeing it in my mind forever, perhaps it's a sort of punishment.'

'He suddenly thrust out his hand and I took it.'

'But that's just what I did—'

'Yes, but this was totally different. You know he's always been a bit soft about me—'

'Did he make some declaration, the scoundrel?'

'No, he said nothing. Then he said, "I'm sorry." It was all over in a moment.'

'How do you mean all over? You stopped holding hands and—'

'I said something like "all right" and he recovered and we went on talking about something else.'

'Like the situation in Poland or—'

'Something ordinary, I—'

'You shut him up.'

'He shut himself up. Tim, he's my friend, he was Guy's friend—'

'Oh—yes—yes—'

'There wasn't any sentimental conversation, there was just a funny moment—'

'I hate funny moments, they're dangerous.'

'He's an admirable man and an exceptional man. You're not going to go against him?'

'No, one couldn't. Besides, oh dear—oh dear—'

'But, Tim—'

'You're going to say who am I to talk.'

'No, I'm going to say I love you and no one else matters tuppence.'

'That's good. And you don't mind him and Anne clearing off?'

'I'm delighted! How ruthless love makes one. I never took them to our places.'

'I'm glad of that. Oh my God, oh my darling—Gertrude, I feel so bossy, do you mind?'

'I feel bossy too, it's just love.'

'But I must tell you how it was—'

'You've told me.'

'Not properly. I must tell you everything. I want to very much. I hardly understand it myself.'

'I'm sorry I was so awful, I made up my mind so quickly, at least it wasn't like making up my mind, it was as if the whole world had changed and I could do nothing—'

'And then, of course, other people rather took you over.'

'No, they didn't. Well, perhaps they did a bit. I was so *hurt*—'

'I know, I know, forgive me.'

'I started on a course and had to keep on just so as to keep sane.'

'I'm sorry, I didn't mean other people took you over—'

'If it hadn't all become so public at once one could have had second thoughts—'

'Yes, I know, I'm so bloody terrified of that lot—'

'But it wasn't just that—it was a kind of hardness, inner pride. As if I had to have a destructive occupation to cure the misery. Do you understand?'

'I think so.'

'And that terrible mixed up conversation—I felt I had to rush to a conclusion or die of pain—'

'Oh my dear heart—I've gone over and over and over that conversation trying to see what it meant.'

'So have I.'

'It all happened so fast.'

'We both became entirely irrational so quickly, like falling down a steep slope—'

'But the point is, listen Gertrude, how it happened, and I felt so guilty that made me instantly stupid—'

'I should have *waited* and let you *talk*—'

'No, do listen, you see there were a lot of different things, separate things really, well not quite separate but—oh hell, do you think I've got concussion?'

'Would you like to lie down?'

'No, I'm all right. I'm not sure what concussion is, actually. Anyway, there were those things. I suppose the main thing, the *awful* thing, was that I didn't tell you about Daisy at the start.'

'You should have done, you should have done it instantly, at moment one.'

'I was so dazed at moment one. Just remember what it was like.'

'At moment two then.'

'That's just it—I kept putting it off.'

'It would have been right, and it would have been easy.'

'You say that now, you mean you would have swallowed anything?'

'What a way to put it!'

'I was so bloody frightened, I thought I'd lose you if I told. I felt I just couldn't *explain* Daisy without our thing collapsing, you'd think it was *fatal*.'

'It was wrong not to tell, and you should have trusted me, trusted our love, surely you could see how much I loved you.'

'Yes. I believed and yet I didn't believe. I kept thinking how *can* she love me. Oh God. These things are separate, aren't they? I want to keep everything separate, there are so many sort of *items*. Anyway, I didn't tell, I wanted to and meant to but I kept putting it off, and as I did that I—I rethought it—'

'Rethought what?'

435

'About Daisy and me. I changed it in thought. I made it not important. I wanted it to shrivel up and go away into the past. I didn't want to tell you about it until it was tiny and meaningless.'

'Is it tiny and meaningless now?'

'No.'

'Go on.'

'Well, that was one thing, and another thing was that when you chucked me out on the first occasion—'

'I didn't—'

'When you chucked me out on the first occasion I ran straight back to Daisy.'

'And made love?'

'Well—maybe—yes—'

'I don't like that.'

'OK, but listen to it. I was so smashed up, just imagine, I suppose I needed comfort. I couldn't think where else to go—'

'I might start feeling sorry for her, only I don't want to think about her. I don't want to touch her with my thought at all.'

'Later on, of course, I saw how awful this was—'

'Yes, you just ran away.'

'I couldn't be with you as less than I had been. But perhaps I should have waited and argued and—hoped and—'

'Yes—'

'Well, later I felt I'd failed, given up, betrayed *that*, our love, that *fact*—'

'Yes, I failed too.'

'If only I'd stayed by myself, if only I hadn't gone to Daisy then, but I did, I fell right back into the—the old—routine—'

'Routine—'

'Well—anyway then I found you again, and that was so wonderful—'

'You could have told me then.'

'Then I thought I'd wait till we were married.'

'When *would* you have told me?'

'I don't know. I thought that if I waited it would get easier to tell you, but then I realized it was getting harder not easier.'

'Then it's just as well you were unmasked.'

'Yes. You see—my God, I do want to *understand* what happened. You see, I only went back to Daisy when I thought

I'd lost you, so I wasn't in *that* sense deceiving you, but then I was in the *other* sense and the things got mixed in my mind and I felt *hopelessly* guilty—'

'I understand—'

'And then when you suddenly went for me about that stuff you got from Jimmy Roland—'

'I'd just heard it, I was so confused, so shocked—'

'You see, Daisy and I did discuss how we'd marry rich people and support each other but of course it was just a silly joke. And I suppose Jimmy Roland overheard this drivel—'

'In that pub.'

'Yes. I can't understand how he can have been so beastly though—anyway—'

'That was another thing. I think I see what you mean about separating out the items.'

'Yes, and I felt *suddenly* so guilty, so much *more* guilty, when you accused me—'

'You added it all up in a muddled way—'

'Yes, and I couldn't help acting as if I might have done *anything*, and the fact I'd never mentioned Daisy's existence was so terribly important—'

'Yes—And Daisy's *existence* was important, something you so absolutely couldn't deny.'

'Yes. I couldn't have invented *any* lie then, I couldn't *then* have denied her. Oh God in heaven—'

'The truth got hold of you at last.'

'Yes, it got hold of *me*, but I wouldn't explain it to *you*. And not having had the faith and the courage to keep away from Daisy was like a kind of infidelity—'

'Was perhaps a kind of infidelity. But I understand—'

'And then of course when I ran back to Daisy for the second time, that really seemed to finish everything. I felt as if I were being compelled to act as if any awful thing that you imagined of me was true. And, oh God, I took that money out of the bank—'

'It doesn't matter—'

'I was going to repay it, I *am* going to repay it—'

'Oh Tim—'

'I think I did it to sort of ruin myself, to make return impossible, it was too painful to hope for.'

'I never believed you'd planned to live with Daisy on my money.'

'I think you believed it for a second.'

'It was such a terrible shock, the sense of being deceived by someone one loved and trusted absolutely—'

'My darling—'

'And I was so consumed by jealousy, I was *enraged* by jealousy—'

'Yes, you were terrible, you terrified me and I became utterly stupid—'

'It all suddenly burst over both of us like a storm, and there was a lot of deep awful vanity. I felt so damnably insulted—'

'Please don't start again—'

'In a way I wanted to think you were a traitor so as to ease the pain.'

'To feel you'd married beneath you and were well served!'

'Yes!'

'Gertrude—all this—all my fault—it hasn't *damaged* us, has it?'

'No, I don't think so. This, your coming back—it's all part of the sort of—logic—of our love. It's made everything more—I can't think of the word—detailed—There's so much more of us now.'

'Logic, yes. I couldn't discriminate. I had to learn how the lies were separable from the rest and from each other. Do you remember, I said I wasn't real and you mustn't rely on me, and you said you'd make me real? I think you've done it.'

'But, Tim. How about Daisy? How about her *now*? You say you've left her.'

'I've left her.'

'Have you really? Don't you still want somehow to have her in your life? She's been there so long.'

'I have really left her and I don't want to have her in my life.'

'That's really true?'

'Yes.'

'After all those years together?'

'Yes. It's finished.'

'But don't you love her still? You must do.'

The cicadas had stopped suddenly. Already the night crickets had begun their high miauw. An *hibou* made a low coughing *hibou* noise, quite unlike an English owl.

438

Tim was silent, thinking. He said, 'It's odd about stopping loving somebody. It's odd in a way that it can happen, but it obviously does. I could imagine stopping suddenly because I realized I hated them, my love was hate, though that's never happened to me. But like with me and Daisy I suppose it dematerializes, it fades away.'

'So you do still love her? Oh Tim, don't be frightened, I'm not trying to do hurt or damage, tell me the truth.'

'I'm trying to. I feel it's not important, it's metaphysical, it's over, it's already been taken away to a vast distance. I love you and only you and you are everything.'

'Yes, but answer the question.'

Tim thought about the years and years and years of Daisy, his whole adult life, really. He saw her narrow head and cropped hair and big painted eyes, and something happened in his heart.

'I can't help feeling something about her—'

'You pity her?'

'No. I think she's all right.'

'Better off without you?'

'Yes. She's got a strength of being which I never touched or knew. It's that I can't undo Daisy. I did love her and that period of time is still close. It's over though. I couldn't have come *here* if it hadn't been over. I thought I was leaving her so as to be alone, and I *was* alone, like I told you—'

'The festival of the leaves.'

'Yes, and *Jesus pardons, Jesus saves*. But maybe underneath it all I was simply going through a sort of procedure, like a sort of ritual or ordeal, so as to get back to you. It was all *about* you.'

'I wonder. Maybe it had to happen. Yet it was all so awfully accidental too.'

'I had to purify myself, to regain my innocence in order to return, it made me able to hope. In an odd way the Count helped me, he said I ought to leave Daisy.'

'The Count—?'

'Yes, and then there was Mrs Mount's letter—'

'Fancy Veronica writing to you! People think she's a cynic but she's a soft old thing really. She may even be sentimental about you!'

'And she said you were alone—'

'She probably just heard I was going and didn't know about the Count and Anne, I didn't tell anybody.'

'And then I arrived and saw you and the Count—'

'And then you ran away again, and had to be nearly drowned to teach you to come back!'

'Yes. At the other end of that tunnel there was a new world. I'm so glad the dog was all right.'

'So am I.'

'But about Daisy. It's really finished. It's more like as if she were dead.'

'Yes.' And Gertrude thought about Guy, and she thought to herself, isn't it strange, all those many years I deeply and faithfully loved Guy, and now I deeply and faithfully love Tim, who could not be more different. I shall become, well I shall partly become, a different person. But that is a movement of life that I can't and won't deny. It is so, like the stones and the leaves.

'I wish I could think of everything,' said Tim. 'I still haven't, it's still not all fitted together, there are dark bits and fuzzy bits and I so want you to see it—'

'Probably it can't all be seen. You've given it to me now, with the dark bits and the fuzzy bits, I've got it all. Yes, yes, I've got you, all of you.'

'Gertrude, I know you're thinking about Guy.'

'Yes.'

'I'm such a—by contrast—such a—mouldy old husband!'

'I love you.'

'Gertrude—'

'I love you, I love you.'

'Do you think we could have that chicken casserole?'

EIGHT

Anne was following the Count as a hunter follows his prey, as a disciple follows his half-crazed master, as a child follows its parent, as a policeman follows a wanted criminal, as a tracker follows a traveller who is lost in the bush.

She was literally following him now along the Chelsea Embankment, while the brown leaves were falling steadily quietly onto the pavement and into the river. There had been a little rain and then a little sunshine. It was Sunday and London was full of church bells. Anne and the Count walked and walked, usually in silence. Sometimes Anne walked behind him, holding his lean awkward figure in the intense tentacles of her attention. He did not seem to mind this method of companioning. Anne liked to watch him, to see his back and his pale limp hair shifting in the wind. She felt that she had him upon a lead. Sometimes she almost danced round him. He seemed not to see her, but she knew that he fed upon her presence, and this feeding gave her deep joy. Anne was so much in love that she could not believe that Peter did not see the world altering before him. Her love must surely change his world, would change it, in the end, completely. She felt as she walked this silent watchful walking a kind of happiness that was like her best days in the convent. She was fully occupied with what ought to occupy her, and she was in the right place in the cosmos, the place to which every atom pointed and every ray tended.

Anne's grip upon her beloved had not loosened since she had so promptly and skilfully removed him from Gertrude's house after Tim's arrival. As it turned out, they had to walk most of the way to the village pushing their bikes, since the Count, after falling off three times, admitted that he could not ride a bicycle, or at any rate if he had ever known he had forgotten. How Anne had enjoyed that walk indulging a pure sweet egoistic joy which entirely precluded, for the moment, any sympathy with her companion's pain. Anointed with perspiration, she lifted her face to the blazing presence of the

441

sun and continued inaudibly to laugh. How much she enjoyed her lunch upon the train! The Count let her organize their journey home. She led him along, holding him firmly by the sleeve of his coat. She longed to kiss the sleeve of his coat, which her fingers ever so gently palpated and caressed.

Once home, anxiety returned, terrible fear of loss. What had really happened? Was Tim forgiven, reinstated? Or had that momentous embrace been but a prelude to a quarrel and another parting? Would that couple *never* settle down? Of course Anne immediately removed all her things from Ebury Street back to her flat. She kept on telephoning until Gertrude's joyful voice filled her with equal joy. She flew round to see her friend. Gertrude was radiant. She at once asked if Anne had seen the Count, hoped he was all right, said she would invite him. She thanked Anne for her prompt tactful departure. She laughed at Anne's account of the ride to the village. Tim, slinking in and out, smiled with sly satisfaction. Anne still could not like Tim, but she had to admit that it looked like a case of two people in love. They were embarrassingly childish together, and it was plain that Gertrude was physically, totally, enamoured. Tim's presence, her *possession* of him, made her babble with pleasure. She looked years younger. Anne was content.

And she continued her silent vigil, watching over Peter with an intense silent tenderness. As far as she could see, he had not been to Ebury Street since Gertrude's return. She assumed that he had been, in some terms, invited. Gertrude had invited Anne with a casual 'come any time'. But Anne had so far not been to see her friend again. She wanted to feed longer upon that vision of Gertrude's happiness and she needed all her time and energy to concentrate upon Peter. She had, during this period, no other occupation. She had given up looking for a job. She had had a perfect letter from the Poor Clares in Chicago, the sort of letter which gave her a moment of nostalgia for the dedicated life of religious people. But the moment for Poor Clares had passed now. She politely refused such invitations as she received from Janet, Moses, Manfred, Sylvia Wicks (with whom she had become acquainted), Roman clerics, societies and causes, an Anglican bishop. When she was not with Peter she walked alone, or else sat at home reading novels.

She had finished *The Heart of Midlothian* which she had brought back with her from France. She was now reading *War and Peace*.

Anne waited. She felt like a player who has many advantages and is master of his game, but knows that he will need the utmost concentration to win. She played her game from day to day, wondering each morning whether it would be today that she would declare her love. But prudently she delayed. She felt that she could lose nothing by delay, whereas to speak too soon might startle or offend her quarry. Besides, she wanted to see Peter turn to her, seek her of his own accord. He had already come to her in that he took her interest in him for granted. She did not think that he saw, apart from office colleagues, anyone else. She was, however, still careful not to appear too often. They had walked on two evenings, now on a Sunday, they had sat in a pub, she had even been once to pick him up at his flat, he had come to drinks at her place. Gertrude was not mentioned.

One thing which made Anne feel that she must not put any pressure on him or startle him in any way was his intense gloom. This gloom was at times so extreme that Anne wondered whether he were not receding into some sort of clinical 'depression'. However, just when she was feeling really frightened for him, he would smile at her with so much gratitude that she would feel relief and even gladness that he could be so sad, and yet touched, reached, by her alone. The mourning would pass.

One day he spoke to her more directly.

'Anne, you are *too* kind. You really must stop acting nursemaid.'

'I do it because I care for you.'

'No, you are too kind.'

They were in Anne's flat. October rain was beating on the window. It was dusk. The Count had come from the office, passing by for his evening 'drink'. Anne did not try to detain him. These visitations had a kind of easy perfection.

'I am such a fool,' he said. He was standing at the window with his glass, looking out at a sky already tainted by distant yellow lamplight.

'Maybe,' said Anne. She wished that she could knit. She intuited that Peter would be pleased to see her knitting. As a next best she was sewing buttons onto a blouse.

'To want so much what one cannot have is stupid and immoral.'

'You should try wanting what you can have,' said Anne.

'You know that—well, you don't know—but when Gertrude got married I felt I must leave London, and I applied for a transfer to the north of England. Then I cancelled it when—'

'Yes? And now?' Anne thought, we'll go to the north of England together. We'll live in Yorkshire when we're married, or perhaps in Scotland. And we will become young again.

'Not now—' he said.

'So—what—now?'

'Anne, will you think me very stupid if I tell you something?'

Oh tell me that, tell me *that*, thought Anne. 'You know you can tell me anything, Peter.'

'I do admire and value you so much.'

'I'm glad—'

'What I want to say sounds awful—I think I am going to kill myself.'

Anne stopped sewing. She looked at the little pearl button on the blue blouse, at her sharp needle. She felt absolute terror. She said calmly, 'It's immoral,' and went on sewing.

'I have never been able to see why,' said Peter. 'I cannot be a guest or a spectator, you understand. Politeness? Impossible. I thought I would renew my application to leave London.'

'Isn't that more sensible than suicide?' said Anne.

'Then I saw it just wouldn't do, it was pointless. You know, all my life I have felt I was moving on towards some time of absolute disaster, a sort of permanent entry into hell, or as it were a black wall and I were in a ship moving towards it, or a black iceberg. And I resolved that when that time came I would end my life. Now, I go to the office but I cannot work, I go to bed but I cannot sleep—'

'Go to the doctor.'

'I have pills, pills cannot help me, except to quit this scene for good.'

'I think you are showing a contemptible lack of courage and a most irrational inability to predict. All right, you can't have what you want, and you say you can't go round there and be polite either. So give it up! In six months time you will feel quite different.'

'Anne, it's not just that. I've lived on illusions for so long. I've lived in an *imagined* love.'

Anne, still sewing, wondered what to say to this. 'But you did love, it wasn't a fake love.'

'No—but so full of illusions and dreams. We dream that we are loved because otherwise we would die.'

'Peter, you *are* loved,' said Anne. She threw her sewing on the floor.

'I lived upon that love, my love for her, for so many years, and it gave me dignity and purpose, partly because it was a sort of—a sort of channel—along which an imagined love came back to me. But really I was doing it all.'

'Doing it all?'

'I enacted it, I enacted both sides of the relation, and this was easy because she was inaccessible, because of Guy, because of all the people who surrounded her. While really—they all— and she too—regarded me with—saw me as just—as a figure of fun—'

'Peter, stop it,' said Anne. 'I've never heard such feeble contemptible rubbish in my life! Human beings are fearfully imperfect and care for each other in fearfully imperfect ways, but they do care. You must be humble enough to accept imperfect love.'

'Now that the whole thing has collapsed,' said Peter, 'I see there's nothing to live for. I had an escape route, it's closed, a technique of illusion, it's gone. I don't want to be melodramatic about this. I feel quite cold and factual about it. Maybe it's all to do with being Polish. My country has had nothing but persecution and misery and the destruction of every hope, it's been kicked to pieces by history. I am an exile. I disliked my father and I could not communicate with my mother. They would both have been glad if I had died instead of my brother. I don't fit into English society. I played at fitting in with all those people, it was play-acting. I have never made any real friends, I have no talents and my work does not interest me. I am a limited, perhaps fundamentally rather unintelligent man, at whom people laugh. Tell me why suicide is immoral.'

'Because it's usually stupid and it's immoral to do a stupid thing which is so important and so irrevocable. Your state of mind will change and *ought* to change. Why terminate your ability to be good and to do good? Suicide affects other people, for instance it's infectious. Your act could make another person despair. And it hurts those who depend on you and care for you.'

'But nobody does.'

'I do.'

'You are too kind.'

'Please, don't use that form of words, I'm tired of it. And suicide is so often an act of revenge, it certainly would be in this case, and revenge is wrong.'

'Revenge?'

'Yes, spite, violence, terrorism, an act of hate, directed against Gertrude, a mean contemptible expression of envy and jealousy.'

'I don't think that is so,' he said, 'in this case. That would be a foolish calculation. I don't think anyone would mind much. They would find it rather—invigorating.'

'It's a rotten act. Why perform a rotten act?'

'It's a unique act. Something irreversible has happened to me, some last lingering necessary conception of myself has gone. I had an illusion of honour, of a sort of soldierly being. Not a gentleman volunteer, as Guy used to say—'

'What would Guy think now?'

'He'd understand. We often discussed suicide. You must see, I have lost my mode of being and when that is lost one ceases to be able to exist. There's a knack, an illusion which I haven't got any more—'

'Stop talking about illusions. Try thinking about truth. This talk of suicide is escapist fantasy, it's just the idea that pain can cease. Think of something *better*, you can. Look at the better thing even if it doesn't seem to connect with you.'

'I lived by a sort of dignity which I now see as absurd. I used to think there would be a time of heroism—'

'Peter, it's now.'

'I can't work or sleep, I see nothing ahead. I cannot see any reason for going on, I don't believe in God—'

'Your life doesn't belong to you,' said Anne. 'Who can tell where his life ends? Our being spreads out far beyond us and mingles with the being of others. We live in other people's thoughts, in their plans, in their dreams. This is as if there were God. We have an infinite responsibility.'

'Why God, why not the devil? We walk as evil things in the minds of others, we are devils to them, we torture them by what we are and do.'

'*You* torture *nobody*,' said Anne.

'Because I am nobody and nothing.'

Anne laughed. She got up and came to him at the window. She took hold of the sleeve of his jacket as she had done when they were coming back from France. She said, 'Peter, this is what Polish heroism is for, to be nobody and nothing and try after all to enjoy it. Let me try to teach you how.'

The telephone rang.

Anne left him and picked it up.

'Anne—' it was Gertrude's voice.

'Yes.'

'It's me. Anne, can you come to a party tomorrow? Manfred has just brought the car back from France, and it's absolutely *full* of champagne—'

Gertrude's voice was clearly audible in the room. Peter had picked up his coat and was making for the door. He waved to Anne and disappeared.

'I'll try to get along,' said Anne. She wondered, shall I put the phone down and run after him?

'Don't try, succeed. Darling, you haven't come, I've wanted you so much and you haven't come. It isn't because—? I mean, don't feel that we want to—exclude anybody, least of all you. I want to see your blessed face. I dreamt about you last night. You do love me, don't you?'

'Yes, you idiot.'

'Then tomorrow about six.'

'Yes—tomorrow then.'

Anne replaced the 'phone. Would Peter commit suicide? Would he commit suicide *tonight*?

She got up and walked to and fro. She did not believe he was really contemplating suicide, he was just externalizing his gloom. He was soothing his pain with the idea of nothingness. She went into the kitchen and began to try to prepare herself some supper. It was impossible.

After a while she put her coat on and went out into the street. It was still raining. She found a taxi which took her to Chelsea and dropped her near the big ugly block of flats where Peter lived. She walked along the wet shining pavement looking up at the light in his window. It was not the first time that she had done this. She imagined herself ringing the bell, running up to his room, enfolding him in her arms.

She saw a lighted telephone box and went to it and dialled his number.

'Hello.'

'Peter, it's Anne.'

'Oh—' He sounded surprised. 'Anne—hello—'

'Peter, I want you to promise me something. Will you solemnly promise me that you will not commit suicide?'

'Oh—Anne—I—I can't just like that—it—who knows—'

'All right, when you're eighty-eight with cancer, but I want you to promise me that you won't commit suicide *now* because of your troubles *now*.'

There was silence. He said, 'All right—'

'Swear it. Swear it by the precious lifeblood of Poland.'

He said, 'I swear by the precious lifeblood of Poland that I will not commit suicide now because of my troubles now.'

'This year or next year.'

'This year or next year.'

'Good. That's all then. Goodnight, dear Peter.'

'Goodnight, dear Anne.'

She came out into the rain. It was a solemn moment. She imagined Peter's grave face as he sat beside the telephone. It was a moment which made a new bond between them. They had moved a step nearer to each other, perhaps the crucial step. I shall tell him everything soon, she thought, very soon. She stood watching in the rain until his light went out.

The Count lay sleepless. Ahead of him lay seven hours of moving his body from one comfortless position to another, closing his eyes, opening them again, gazing at the ceiling. Thinking. Picturing. The curtains did not keep out the diffused lamplight from the street below.

Earlier in the evening he had tried to distract himself by reading Horace. But the elegant frivolous fierce sublime poet seemed to be talking only of Gertrude, whether in memories of happier days, or in bitterness of loss and premonitions of age and death. The old beloved tags expressed and needled his sorrow. *Eheu fugaces . . . Quis desiderio. . . .* Then digging deeper into the Latin like a mad surgeon the Count, oblivious now of the poetry, found many a gobbet to match the increasing savagery of his mood. Not only *linquenda tellus et domus,* but also *mox iuniores quaerit adulteros,* and best of all: *quae tibi virginum sponso necato barbara serviet?* By the time he went to bed the Count had become Frederic the Great.

Longing for Gertrude, for her sweet presence, consumed him as he writhed. He imagined being with her, being held in her bright warm attention, holding her hand. He saw again the room in France where he had started to tell her of his love, at least he had stammered something, and she had held his hand so tenderly, saying little, but not saying no. What joy he had felt that night, with what joy and peace in his heart he had gone to sleep. Peace, Gertrude had always somehow given him that in the past, when she was married to Guy, and when he could live securely close to her, loving her, but not tortured by these intolerable desires and hopes.

The apparition of Tim, bruised and bleeding, in torn dishevelled clothes, had seemed to the Count pure nightmare, a sort of guy or faked-up devil, unreal and yet fateful, terrible. The Count had entered the sitting-room just after Gertrude had emerged onto the terrace. He had, like Anne, witnessed the embrace, but had not so quickly taken in what had *happened.* He could not clearly remember the journey back. He had felt all the time as if he were calculating, and as if by some calculation he could slip himself and Gertrude back into the slot in time before Tim's return. Had it been simply *nullified,* that tender moment? Was it not something sovereign, absolute? Could something which *had a future* be made not to by something else quite (as the Count felt) fortuitous? Surely there were some moments which *determine* the future and keep it safe? He was owed Gertrude's love. Tim was a traitor, a renegade, a cruel faithless villain. Tim was imprisoned, *fixed* in his own world, the world he had chosen and returned to: that world of drink and idleness which Anne Cavidge had cursed. The Count had done his best, and how nobly he had done had made the result seem all the surer. He had tried to persuade Tim to return. Tim had replied, 'I live in a swamp,' and he had said, 'Perhaps Gertrude will find a better husband.' Hadn't that finished the matter, was not Tim over and done with? How could he then appear like a bloodstained dummy, and so *easily* become Gertrude's husband once again? For the Count had no doubt now about the situation. He had received a letter from Gertrude saying that she and Tim would love to see him. She had also telephoned briefly in the same style. The Count had answered evasively.

And now what would be? He could not stay in London having dinner with the Reedes once a month. He could not live among new strangers in Harrogate or Edinburgh, working in his office all day and listening to his radio at night, he could not live so. The absolute loss of Gertrude had made him realize what a desert his life was. Little simple things which had pleased him before were now seen as trivial and dry. Herein, in describing his impressions, he had not exaggerated to Anne. On the other hand, and herein Anne was right, he did not really intend suicide, or at least not now. He was sorry, however, that he had promised good dear Anne that he would not kill himself. He had promised because he was startled by her sudden urgent voice and could not think how to refuse. He had not been intending to seek death, but the near presence of it had immensely consoled him. To die, to rest. He said to himself that he was a spineless coward, but these words no longer bit. The concept was flabby for him. What can morality, what can philosophy achieve, against the volatile faithlessness of the human mind? He wondered if, later, even the concept of a solemn promise might not become meaningless and flabby and soft. Even now he could not inspire himself with the idea of honour. His whining to Anne had been contemptible. It was even more contemptible that he really did not care what he had said.

Wide-eyed and tense he twisted and turned. The horrors, the horrors ahead. Why did the Red Army not cross the Vistula? Why did Hannibal not march on Rome? He closed his eyes and tried to go through one of his sleeping routines. He imagined he was on a country road, a grassy track, approaching a five-barred gate. Only Gertrude, dressed in that light yellow robe, with the blue beads round her sun-blazed neck, was leaning on the gate. He tried a garden, a big lawn with a distant huge tree, a great copper beech, which he was slowly approaching. But Gertrude was standing under the tree, with a little white sun hat on, and reaching up to touch the spread-out transparent leaves, then turning to him with a smile. He tried moving through the rooms of a house, but his heart beat violently because he knew that somewhere in that series of rooms she was waiting. He was in a park, she was there, in a wood, she was there. The birds were singing and the sun was shining. *Oh that we two were maying.*

Where can I go, he thought, where in the end can I go? I don't want to go to America, I don't want to go to Poland, I couldn't live in Poland, it would be impossible. Then he thought, I'll go to Belfast. Ireland is a bit like Poland after all, a miserable stupid mixed-up country betrayed by history and never able to recover from the consequences. I'll get myself transferred to a government office in Belfast. And when I am there perhaps some merciful terrorist bomb will kill me. And I shall be dead and I won't have broken my promise to Anne.

Tim was standing, Gertrude was sitting, and he was holding her hands. They had been making the preparations for the party. His dear wife was wearing a new dress which they had chosen together, a lovely light wool dress with a pattern of cream and brown leaves, with fine smocking, which she wore loosely over a high-necked white silk blouse. He stooped and kissed her hands again and again, then released her and stood back. Yes, she was all there, body and soul. He said, 'Whatever you want, angel, darling, my love.'

'Yes, but—You do see? You don't mind?'

'I do see. I don't mind.'

'It would make me perfectly happy.'

'Aren't you perfectly happy, damn it?'

'Yes. That's not the way to put it. It's more like a duty, a task undone, a flaw.'

'A flaw?'

'Not exactly that either. I just can't stop thinking. I've always looked after people, Guy and I always did.'

'I'm not so good at looking after people as Guy was,' said Tim. 'I had my work cut out looking after myself.' He was feeling very happy and this kept distracting him from the conversation.

'*We'll* look after people. I'd like that.'

'OK, so long as they don't always have to be coming to dinner. Can't we do it by post?'

Gertrude laughed. 'Oh darling! Here, come and sit beside me. I want to hold onto you. You're my Tim.'

'Yes, yes.' He sat, pulling up a chair close. 'Oh heavens I do love you.'

'We mustn't be selfish, Tim.'

'Why not? I want to be happy and selfish. I've been unhappy and selfish for long enough.'

'No, but you know what I mean. And you like him too, after all, very much you once said.'

'Yes,' said Tim, trying to concentrate. 'I like him. And I don't want him to be unhappy.'

'He's a poor exile. And like poor exiles he can live on very little.'

'That's what you'll give him?'

'It will be for him, a lot. I just mean—well, you know what I mean.'

'Oh, I'm not worrying about *us*,' said Tim, 'we're cosmic. I'm worrying about him. Won't it bother him?'

'No. Because he'll understand. It'll be like before only a little better.'

Tim recalled the scene in France, the icon which he had thought would kill him with pain, of Gertrude holding the Count's hand. The vision was painless. 'But doesn't he already know that he's not sort of out of it, not on the rubbish dump I mean?'

'No, on the rubbish dump is just exactly where he thinks he is. And, Tim, very little is able here to change very much.'

'Such is your power.'

'Such is my power.'

'Proceed then, queen and empress. So long as you think he won't be more unhappy sort of seeing you occasionally like—'

'I'm sure.'

'Then I'll leave you. I've got the shopping list. Do you really think they'll eat all those biscuits and pies and stuff?'

'Yes. They are insatiable.'

'Perhaps they'll bring plastic bags with them, perhaps they'll even raid the fridge, the blighters.'

'Tim, I want you to paint.'

'You mean now? I'm going shopping.'

'No, not now, I mean later. Forever.'

'All right. I'll paint forever.'

The Count came into the drawing-room. He had left his overcoat and his ridiculous woolly cap in the hall. Gertrude was alone. She had telephoned to say that she and Tim were giving a party and *please* would he come a little earlier before the others? Something in her voice had made him come.

'Oh Count—sit down—have a drink. Your usual, white wine?'

The Count clicked his heels and bowed. He accepted the drink. He waited till Gertrude had sat down, then took a distant chair and waited.

'Count—may I call you Peter?'

'Yes, of course.'

'Don't be angry with me.'

'I am not, Gertrude.'

'Yes you are. But stop it, we must be at peace.'

'We are at peace, so far as I know.'

'You are planning to go away, I'm sure you are, you are going to Africa to hunt lions.'

'I have no plan to go to Africa,' said the Count.

'Sorry, that was figurative.'

'Figurative?'

'I mean, you're planning to go away to forget. Where are you planning to go?'

'To Ireland,' said the Count.

'To *Ireland*? Peter, what rubbish is this? Anyway, I asked you to come because I have to tell you you don't have to go anywhere.'

'What do you mean, Gertrude?' said the Count. He spoke stiffly, formally. Gertrude's suggestion that he was angry was indeed not far from the truth. He was angry with Gertrude for making him come, and with himself for coming.

'Listen, Peter, dear, let's talk plainly. When we were in France, and you reached out your hand to me across the table—you—'

'I'm sorry. That was a mistake.'

'No, it was not a *mistake*. And I wanted to say that of course you didn't tell me anything then that I didn't know already.'

'When I say a mistake I mean it was improper, a *faux pas*. I ought not to have expressed—'

'Your feelings. But your feelings existed—and exist.'

'They are my own concern. Gertrude, I am sure you mean well, but I do not want to discuss this matter.'

454

Gertrude was silent. She was in fact intimidated by Peter's stiff bearing, by his grim stern face. For a moment she felt that she had made a mistake, a *faux pas*. She looked away, confused, not knowing what to say next.

Her silence did its work upon the Count. Terrible emotions clawed about inside the steel of his demeanour. He leaned forward slightly and said, 'Forgive me.'

'Forgive *me*. Peter, listen, you may want to go away and not see me any more. I must even—myself—understand that it might be wiser. It's hard to say this—I feel—oh so much—I'm sorry—'

'Don't worry,' he said, 'It's only me.'

'Oh Peter, you darling. Listen. Let me put it just awfully clearly. I love Tim and we are married and that is an eternal fact.'

The Count nodded, bowing his head formally.

'But I care for you and you are an old friend. Well, you are an old friend and I *love* you. Why should love be classified and constrained and denied and destroyed all the time? People can love each other honestly and truthfully in all sorts of situations and all sorts of ways. Of course I'm selfish. I'm not really thinking about your welfare. I'm thinking about mine. I've talked this over with Tim of course. Oh don't be hurt. I don't want to waste your love, I don't want to lose your love, I don't want you to go away into some desert in Ireland or somewhere and just feel rejected. You *aren't* rejected. Why should you go off miserably instead of staying here and giving and receiving affection and being happy? Why? It's as simple as that. Oh it is so simple. I love you, I have love for you, it's not rationed. Tim likes you very much, I'm sure you know that. But I'm talking now about you and me. Let us be sometimes together in truth and in love. I don't mean anything wrong or crazy. I mean just to talk, to *be* with each other and for each other. Let your love for me go on existing, and we'll go on through life not losing each other, but knowing each other. Sorry, I'm not explaining it very well—'

'I think you are,' said the Count, 'explaining it very well.'

'We have known each other a long time, Peter, and in a way we have known each other well, but there has always been a barrier between us. I don't mean the barrier of marriage, that of course, I mean the one that distinguishes a friend from a close friend, you understand. I want that barrier to go. I want us to meet and talk together as we have not done before, just us two, to love each other and give happiness to each other and be without reserve. Peter, I *want* this, I *ask* for it.'

What could the poor Count do? He said, but still stiffly, 'I cannot deny you what you ask.'

'That's all right then,' said Gertrude. She had been more moved than she expected. It had not occurred to her to fear a rejection, but now her heart beat with a strange alarm.

They were silent, looking at each other, she flushed and wide-eyed, he glaring with a stern cold intensity.

'Gertrude, some things must be laid down, I mean under-stood—' So he was now dictating conditions. He went on, 'What you suggest might be regarded as—a recipe for folly and mad-ness suggested by a woman's vanity.' He paused. 'But because you are you—'

'And because *you* are *you*—'

'I think—'

'That it will be all right, possible?'

'I know that you will not play with me. I love you—very much—you know that—'

'Yes.'

'But there will be no drama or chat about love or even— continuation of this conversation. You have said something and I have understood it, that and no more.'

'Yes. But—the *difference* will be there. So you *agree*?'

He stared at her, then he said almost helplessly, 'You have made a move which I cannot counter.'

Gertrude's eyes had already begun to laugh at him. She got up and came to him and he rose and took her hand and kissed it.

'I *must love you*,' she said. 'You must be my friend forever. Will you swear to me not to run away and vanish?'

'I swear—by—by the precious lifeblood of Poland.'

'Then that's clear. That's all I want. So you needn't stop loving me and you needn't be unhappy any more. I love you and need you. Will you promise not to be unhappy any more?'

'Ah—Gertrude—I cannot promise that—I shall always be—'

'In pain? Try not to be. Or let it become—a different sweeter pain. Unhappiness is stupid. There are such a lot of things in

456

the world, dear Count, dear Peter. I should be glad if, because of me, you could enjoy so many *other* things more, things which have nothing whatever to do with me. We're both upset now, but we'll grow calm and survey the world together and live in security and safety and peace. Is that not good?'

'Yes, yes. But, oh Gertrude, how will it be?'

'Perfectly ordinary, you'll see. We'll have such ordinary talk. But deeper and — permanent. Permanence, that's what one wants in life, and that's happiness too.'

'And Tim —'

'I've told him that you must be my dear friend, and our dear friend. He knows I'm saying just that to you. Tim is wise, you know he's wise.'

'I wish I was wise. But — oh Gertrude, my dear — perhaps it *is* possible to be happy after all!'

'Possible — easy — you've made the great discovery! Oh I'm so glad, so relieved. There now, we've said enough, and we won't endlessly discuss it, you're right. We'll talk of other things and we'll be calm then. And now enough. Good heavens, I'd forgotten all about the party, they'll be arriving any moment, you'll stay, won't you? You must. Why, you're looking quite a different person already!'

'Anne, my dear, have some champagne!'

Anne had telephoned the Count at the office in the afternoon, but he had already left. She telephoned his flat, but there was no answer. She waited a while in case he came, but she did not expect him as nothing had been arranged. Then she set off for the party wondering if she would see him there.

With the quick awareness of love she took in the already crowded room, seeing his tall figure with his back to her, near the mantelpiece. He was talking to Tim, stooping a little.

Janet Openshaw was giving her some champagne. 'Anne, we haven't seen you for ages. You've been in retreat.'

'Yes—sort of—'

'Do you know everyone here?'

'No, not everyone—'

'This tall handsome boy is my younger son Ned. He's just back from California where he's been into Buddhism.'

'Oh really—'

'Ned says he wants to empty his mind. When I was his age I was trying to fill mine. But you're really a mathematician, aren't you, Ned?'

'Well—'

'This is Anne Cavidge. She used to be a nun. You don't mind my saying that do you? I'll leave you together. I must circulate the eats.'

'Were you a nun? What kind? Anglican, Catholic, enclosed?'

'Catholic. Enclosed.'

'How awfully interesting! I'm awfully interested in religion. Why did you leave? Did you lose your faith? Do you believe in a personal God?'

'No, I don't think so,' said Anne, 'do you?'

'No, I think it's the most anti-religious idea you can imagine. Religion is to do with the destruction of the personality. Would you agree?'

'In a way, but it depends—'

'What method of meditation did you use? Do you still meditate? I say, do you think we could have a talk some time? No one here is interested in religion, it's amazing how un-interested they are, and after all it is the most important subject isn't it? I never got any real religion as a child, you know my father's Jewish and my mother's Gentile and they play at being Anglicans but they never even taught me to pray, and as for my school, I'm at St Pauls you know—'

'Hello, Anne, hello, Ned—'

It was Gerald Pavitt, bearish, big, odoriferous, untidy.

'Oh Gerald, Anne was a nun. You don't mind if I call you Anne? You know Gerald, of course you do, he knows about quasars and black holes and things and time and space coming to an end and—'

'How are your maths getting on, Ned?'

'Ma put you up to asking that!'

Taking her opportunity Anne began to move away. She wanted to get across the room to Peter.

Ned called after her, 'I'll ring you up, can I, about that talk.'

Tim Reede had had his necessary conversation with the Count. Of course they merely exchanged pleasantries, but much was understood. There was a little embarrassment but this quickly vanished. It was suddenly 'as it used to be', and yet also of course different. Tim was surprised and touched to find in himself a renewed and stronger flow of affection for the Polish exile. It did not occur to Tim to feel patronizing, such an attitude would have been impossible to him. But he found himself feeling, within his own happiness, a special lively affectionate pleasure. He sensed in the Count a corresponding feeling, quite unmixed with any embarrassing 'gratitude'. The Count looked amazingly conspicuously happy. They smiled at each other and parted. Now Tim was paying marked attentions to Mrs Mount, he had even begun to call her 'Veronica'. The idea that she felt 'sentimental' about him had quite changed his view of the 'old creature'.

Rosalind Openshaw was trying to decide which of the men in the room was the most attractive, apart that is from her brother William with whom she was rather in love. She was quite keen on Tim, she could perceive the 'nice animal' aspect of him which so much appealed to Gertrude, but she found his lack of dignity a serious drawback. Manfred had dignity, but was too conventionally handsome and too tall. Victor Schultz was beautiful but bald, and there was something of the 'playboy' about him which repelled Rosalind. Akiba Lebowitz was yummy of course but just married. Ed Roper (who looked like a toad, quite a nice one) had brought along a French writer called Armand something whom Rosalind liked the look of, and at any rate he was a novelty. He was very dark and skinny and wicked-looking. Rosalind liked his clever little slit-eyes. She had always found Gerald Pavitt attractive, though this idea seemed to occur to no one else. She was moved by his burly fatness and by a curious benevolent cunning in his much-folded face and by his smell. A friend of William's, one David Idleston (now talking to Moira Lebowitz), was generally rated a stunner, but of course he was too young. Rosalind could not be attracted by any young man, other than her brother. Her fine intelligent gaze rested on the Count. He was tall, it was true, but not too tall. His absolute pallor, his gentle mien, his straight floppy colourless hair, and those sad pale blue eyes made her heart turn over and over. She turned and began to make her way in the direction of the Frenchman.

Anne detached herself from the politeness of Stanley and from the boisterous familiarity of Ed Roper who had now suddenly decided that she was his dearest pal. She edged round the back of a lawyer called Ginzberg (twin brother of the actor), an old friend of Guy's, lately returned from The Hague, and now she had the Count in full view. He was talking to Gertrude. Anne felt an extreme awful shock before she quite knew what it was that she had perceived or thought. The Count was radiant. The terrible gaunt mask of despair and gloom was gone. It was a quite different Peter, one whom Anne had never seen before, who was now leaning towards his hostess, laughing, his face almost zanily wrinkled up with amusement and pleasure. Anne thought, is he *drunk*? Then she saw Gertrude's face. And Gertrude was holding the cuff of the Count's jacket and pulling at it playfully. The Count had stopped laughing, and was saying something to Gertrude. His face was tender, calm, joyful, at peace.

Quick, perceptive Anne had, in another second, understood it all. Gertrude had made a love-treaty with the Count. He was not to be miserable or to go away. He was to stay forever as her courtier, within the light of her countenance. Tim would not mind. It was, for Gertrude, easy. She had fielded him casually, as if in passing. She had only to stretch out her hand, she had only to whistle ever so softly. The little which she would give Peter would be enough for him, would be much. He would humbly accept whatever, with a loving will, she spared him. Perhaps all that he required was the sense that she needed him, he could live on that. Intelligent warm-hearted Gertrude had magicked him into happiness. And Anne could guess that this was not just a benevolent act. Gertrude needed his esteem to support her. She had always valued his love and saw no reason why she should not go on enjoying it forever.

Anne turned away. They had not seen her. She concentrated on preventing tears from rising into her eyes. She would quietly slip away and go home. No one would notice.

She found herself face to face with Manfred.

'Hello, Anne. More champers? Where's your glass?'

'Thanks, but I have to go.'

'Oh don't go. Are you all right? You look a little—'

'I've got a slight migraine, that's all. I'm going to go home and lie down.'

'Do you suffer from migraine? So do I. Only I've got some marvellous pills—'

'I must go.'

'Anne, let me drive you home. You don't look at all well.'

'I'm OK. Thank you so much. I think a walk will do me good.'

She got as far as the door.

Gertrude caught her up. 'Manfred says you've got a migraine, don't go, you must lie down here.'

'No thanks, my dear. I just need some fresh air.'

'I wanted to talk to you, only we can't now. Could you come round for lunch tomorrow? Just us two?'

'Yes, I'll come. I'll be all right tomorrow.'

'Bless you, dear dear girl. Do you know, you've made a conquest? Ned Openshaw says he's fallen in love with you! Oh hello, Moses, I'm so glad you managed to get here.'

'I say, Gertrude, have you heard the news?'

'What news?'

'About the new Pope! He's a *Pole*!'

'What's that? The new Pope?'

'Listen, Moses says the new pope is *Polish*!'

'It's not possible!'

'Quick, quick, tell the Count!'

'Where's the Count? The new Pope is a POLE!'

'Count, Count, listen, the new Pope—'

'Hooray, the new Pope is Polish!'

'How absolutely marvellous! Count, have you heard?'

'Hooray for the Count, the Count for Pope!'

'A toast to the Count!'

'Oh, just look at his face!'

'Hooray for Poland, hooray for the Count!'

'Three cheers—'

"*For he's a jolly good fellow,*
  for he's a jolly good fellow,

for he's a jolly good fe-el-low
AND so say ALL OF US!'

'Were you there when they were singing "For he's a jolly good fellow"?'

'Yes,' said Anne. She had heard the song break out as she was going down the stairs.

'Peter was just crazed with joy.'

'Was he?' said Anne. She was sitting over lunch with Gertrude in the dining-room at Ebury Street.

'I call him "Peter" now,' said Gertrude. 'I'm trying to get used to it. I'll gradually teach the rest of you to say it. I think it's time he was Peter to us. I rather wonder whether he ever liked being called "Count". More cheese?'

'No thanks.'

'Anne, you've eaten *nothing*. Are you sure that migraine has gone?'

'Yes, thanks.'

'Manfred says he has some super pills.'

'I've got some super pills too. I'm OK. Thanks.'

'And you've still got that burn on your hand.'

'No, it's a different one.'

'You careless clumsy girl.'

'I'm all right.'

'You can't be if you keep saying so. Funny, you're wearing that blue and white dress again, the one you wore when you came here from the convent. What a lot has happened since then.'

'Yes.'

'It's marvellous about the new Pope. I'm so pleased. It's a good omen, it's a breath of hope. Don't you think so?'

'Yes.'

'Stanley was saying, oh never mind what Stanley was saying.

And the Count—he's a changed man. I'm so delighted that the news came through on just that day, and at the party.'

'Yes, it was nice. And everybody cheered him.'

'Yes. Oh I feel so complete. God bless Peter, God bless Poland, God bless Anne. Drink up.'

'I'm drinking.'

'You aren't. Do eat some cheese or a divine Cox's Orange Pippin.'

'No, thanks.'

'I must tell you something about the Count, about Peter.'

'Yes?'

'By the way, thank you so much for looking after him for me. He says you gave him a talking to about not despairing. He says you held his hand like a priest.'

'I didn't hold his hand.'

'Well, figuratively. He's immensely grateful for the holy woman act, it kept him going.'

'It was no trouble.'

'We're both so grateful. I should have done something about him earlier, only—'

'You were so busy.'

'Yes, an awful lot has been happening. But I must tell you. I wouldn't tell this to anyone else, except Tim of course. I felt I couldn't leave the Count all lonely and sad. Tim agreed we had to draw him in.'

'Into the family circle.'

'More than that. You know, well, it's no secret, everyone knows, Guy knew, the Count is very much in love with me.'

'Yes, indeed.'

'I must call him Peter. Peter was, is, very much in love with me. But, in the past, we never talked about it, it was just understood between us.'

'Quite.'

'And of course when I was a widow how could he not hope?'

'How indeed.'

'And then Tim was there.'

'And then Tim wasn't there—'

'Yes. And I know Peter suffered very much and hoped and suffered and couldn't bear it any more, and he decided he would go away to Ireland.'

'To *Ireland*?' said Anne. 'He never told me that.'

'He's very secretive. He hardly ever talks to anyone. He told me he was going to go to Belfast and he hoped he might be killed by a terrorist!'

'He told you—?'

'Yes, after the party, of course he'd changed his mind by then! Anyway I couldn't just let him drift off. Where could he go, to *whom* could he go, that would make any sense for him? I, and *we*, are his people. Only he was so hurt and so proud and so silent and so *Polish*. I think he really wanted to go away and pine away and die. And I couldn't let him do that, could I?'

'No.'

'He's a strange man, ridiculously hard to communicate with. You know how one can be close to someone yet not, perhaps never, get the knack of direct communication—'

'Yes.'

'I might not have been able to get through to him without his having first broken down the barrier.'

'And did he?'

'Yes, in France. You know, when you were feeling so rotten I saw quite a lot of Peter alone—and one evening he held my hand for a moment—what an achievement that was! And he sort of murmured that he loved me. It was only an isolated moment, but it changed things.'

'As you said once, you can change the world in four seconds.'

'Yes. He thought that that moment was nullified by what happened after, but it wasn't. It made a sort of opening through which I could talk to him.'

'Through which you could beckon him and draw him.'

'Yes. Well, I probably could have done it anyway, it just needed time for me to think about it.'

'So now?'

'Now—well, did you see him last night? Even before the Polish Pope news! His cup is full and running over. I have told him that I care for him, I love him and he doesn't have to stop loving me. He is perfectly happy.'

'Isn't that splendid. And you think it will last?'

'Yes, I think I can *guarantee* that.'

'Tim won't be uneasy?'

'No, of course not. That's what makes it all possible. Tim

and me — I can hardly explain, it's so *deep* — and it's been tested enough as you know. I could only have married Tim — I could never have married Peter — I see that now. Tim knows he's absolutely secure, and he rather loves Peter on his own account. Peter was always very kind to Tim in the old days.'

'So everyone should be able to be happy, under your guarantee.'

'I don't see why not! When one is secure in marriage one is free to love people and be loved by them. I'm much less buttoned up about that than I used to be, much more free, in a way Tim has helped me to be emotionally more free.'

'And you thought why shouldn't you have Peter too.'

'Yes. Not loving Peter and his being so unhappy was the only flaw in my happiness, and I thought why ever shouldn't I be completely happy and make him happy. And I do care about what he thinks —'

'What he thinks about you?'

'Yes, and —'

'You didn't want his mind to get away, I can understand that. In the end he might have judged you.'

'I don't think he would ever have recovered enough to do that!'

'Even if he had gone right away —'

'I had to save him from despair, to hold him, to rescue him. Why should he be miserable when I can so easily make him happy just by *attending* to him? Unhappiness is stupid. He's an intelligent man —'

'He's heroic,' said Anne.

'Heroic?'

'To be content with little.'

'You call it little to be loved by ME?'

'Oh Gertrude, I adore you!' said Anne, and she laughed in spite of herself.

'He wants to go on loving. Loving is an activity, you know, it's like an employment. He will be happy in his love if he knows that I know of it and value it.'

'I understand.'

'So — well, you saw. I've got the Count forever. He promised he wouldn't go away. He swore it by the precious lifeblood of Poland.'

465

'By *what*?'

'By the precious lifeblood of Poland. Isn't he a perfect romantic?'

'Whatever would Guy think of it all!' said Anne. This was unkind, but she needed the distraction from her own pain.

Gertrude was able to deal with this. 'You think it odd that I can talk of happiness when I've lost Guy—'

'I wasn't suggesting—'

'It is odd. Do you think my grief for Guy isn't still there? It is there, it lives, it moves. But the human mind is so large. It co-exists.'

'I know.'

'All right, I said not having Peter was the only flaw. I meant, among things that could be different. In most lives, perhaps in any life, there are terrible things which cannot be different, and which the mind stores and deals with in the process of surviving. You don't have to remind me.'

'I'm sorry, I—'

'No, no—and as for what he would think, I've been wondering myself. He would understand about the Count. Though, with Guy it couldn't have happened like that. Guy would have felt it was—bad form.'

'Yes, I can imagine.'

'And with Guy alive the Count was OK, he could manage.'

'Yes—'

'As for Tim, of course Guy would be astounded! But in a way, the question what would Guy think is empty. It's another world now. If Guy had lived I would never have loved anyone else, never have looked at another man. Guy made me the person I was and still am. But I've changed too. In order to survive a terrible loss one has to become another person. It may seem cruel. Survival itself is cruel, it means leading one's thoughts away from the one who is gone.'

'Yes.'

'I didn't plan Tim. I didn't expect or want any such thing. But it has happened. And one must live joy, as one lives grief, if it comes.'

'Yes.'

'Hey, hey, the white swan—did I ask you about the white swan?'

466

'Yes.'

'All the mystery of Guy is gone, his particular greatness and sweetness, his being can't be questioned any more. And "she sold the ring" —'

'Was that something he used to say?'

'Yes, there were these funny things he used to say, like charms, like the cube, and "she sold the ring", or "she oughtn't to have sold the ring".'

'That's Jessica of course,' said Anne. 'In *The Merchant of Venice*. She sold the ring which her mother gave to her father.'

'Good heavens you're right. Why didn't I think of that? Guy often said he identified with Shylock. I do wish you'd met Guy.'

'I had that one talk with him.'

'Yes, I remember. Well, how strange and inexplicable and terrible life is.'

'Yes.'

'Oh Anne, I'm glad you're here. Your coming to me like that when Guy was ill was so wonderful, so heaven-sent. You've helped me through everything, you've made it possible for me to recover. You've made me able to marry Tim and to hold onto Peter — you've done it all really!'

'I'm glad.'

'I thought I would never be happy again, never even *want* happiness again. You did it all.'

'I didn't, but thanks.'

'And now here we are. Oh I'm so pleased about the Count, about Peter. It sort of completes the picture. I couldn't have let him stray away and be lost in the void.'

'Of course not.'

'It's like a sheepfold with the sheep gathered in.'

'Or a playpen with the children in it.'

'Yes! I'm childless, so everyone is my child. I've realized it's so simple to love everyone and be loved by them.'

'Good.'

'And now what about you, I'm not at all up-to-date. You know, since — since France — I've been living in a sort of over-lifesized world. Everything has been amazing. But I'll calm down. We'll calm down. Tell me how you've been getting on.'

'Oh fine.'

'What about jobs?'

'No luck.'

'Do you *want* a job? You know, darling, there's an awful lot of money. You won't ever worry about money, will you? What would you *like* to do? I feel so benevolent, I want to give everybody exactly what they want! Well, not everybody, but certainly you. You *must* have what you want, and I will *get* it for you.'

'Oh I must have a job.'

'Yes, I suppose so. Let's think what we can do—'

'I'm going away, actually,' said Anne.

'Oh? Where to?'

'To America.'

'To America? How long for?'

'For ever.'

'Don't be silly, Anne.'

'I'm going to live and work over there. I know some people who will find me a job of some sort.'

'Anne, what *is* this? What job, where, I won't let you!'

'In Chicago, there's a community of Poor Clares—'

'Anne! You're not going back inside? Oh God—'

'No, I'm not going back inside. I shall be a camp follower. That's a way of life too.'

'You're mad, I thought you'd got over all that—What do you imagine you'll do—?'

'Oh some sort of social work, anyway that's where I'm going. I've decided to settle over there.'

'Anne, you *can't!*' Gertrude held the edge of the table, lifted it an inch and let it fall. The glasses rocked. 'You can't, you won't, you shan't!'

'Sorry, my dear. I've made up my mind.'

'You are not to go away. I can't do without you. *You are not to go.*'

'Sorry—'

'But why? Is it because of Tim?'

'Tim? No.'

'You imagine you don't like him, but you will like him, you'll learn to—'

'Yes, I—'

'Or do you still think I married a worthless man?' Gertrude's

468

eyes flashed with anger, with exasperation, with her old eternal will to have her own way.

'Gertrude, it's not Tim, I like Tim already, I don't have to learn.'

'I've thought so much about the four of us, why can't we all be a happy family? I thought how good it would be at Christmas, with you and me and Tim and the Count. It would have been such a special consolation. I cannot and will not accept that you and Tim can't get on together. You already like Peter and he likes you—'

'At Christmas. How touching. How sad.'

'*What's* sad? What *is* it? Oh Anne, Anne—is it that you want me?'

'Oh—you—'

'You want to have me all to yourself? You can't share me with Tim? Is that it?'

'No, I assure you, it isn't that—'

'I think it is. You're jealous. You're going off in a huff.'

'I'm not going off in a huff!' said Anne, angry now herself.

'Anne, be generous. It's a failure of generosity, a failure of magnanimity. That's not like you.'

'I'm not in the least—'

'Anne, you're not being *noble*, like what's-his-name, going off into the snow? What sort of silly idea has got into your head? Are you feeling cross at losing me? You haven't lost me. Do you imagine you won't be able to be nice to us all any more—?'

'Gertrude—please—'

'Why go away? It's lunatic. Is it some sort of spite? Peter off to Ireland, you to America, has everyone gone mad? You'll hate America. Anyway, you're not to go. I can't do without you. You're to stay here, that's that.'

'Oh my darling, my dear heart—'

'You promised you'd stay—you said you'd never be far away—'

'America isn't far away nowadays.'

'Oh that's unworthy of you! You *wicked* girl! You're breaking your word and you know it! I felt so safe. I felt so secure, I thought you would be with me forever.'

'I've got to go,' said Anne. 'I'm sorry.'

'But *why*? You *can't*. I love you, we all love you. You're at home here, you belong to us. Why are you running away, what are you afraid of? You'll find a job in London. You know how we said we'd do virtuous things. If you want to do social work I can find you a job myself with the Asian people. There's hundreds of necessary things to do here. Why go away?'

'Because I am given to the religious life,' said Anne, 'and I have got to be alone.'

Gertrude was silent. Then she said, 'I was afraid of that.'

'I am in a sense still a nun.'

'You're still wearing that bloody cross around your neck. I hate the sight of that chain.'

'You have all seen me as a nun.'

'Yes, but you're *our* nun. We need you—'

'I have got to go,' said Anne. 'I have thought about it. I must go. Forgive me.'

'Anne—*I must have you too—please—*'

Tears had brimmed over Gertrude's eyes, and her cheeks in a moment were flushed and wet.

Anne got up and moved her chair next to her friend. They embraced silently. Anne, weeping too, gripped Gertrude's shoulder, drew the dear head close, their tears mingled. She seemed to see, beyond the blurred outlines of the room, an abomination of desolation. She wept out of an irresistible sympathy with Gertrude's cry, and she wept for herself and for the loneliness to come.

Quickly they recovered, moved apart, dried their tears.

'You'll change your mind,' said Gertrude.

'No. No.'

'Oh *damn* you.'

'I'm sorry—'

'So—after all—we are to divide the world between us once again. I am to have the old world, and you the new.'

'We'll meet,' said Anne.

And already she saw it ahead of her, how it would be. The exchange of witty letters, fewer as time went on. The meetings, once in three years perhaps, without the men. They would sit in a bar in New York or Chicago or San Francisco, and talk about old times. And they would laugh their old sad mad

470

laugh, as they had done years ago when Anne was going into the convent.

And as she had said then, at that earlier parting, Anne said now, 'It's not goodbye.'

But it was goodbye, and they both knew it.

NINE

'Why did Anne decide to go?' said Tim.

He and Gertrude were sitting on over dinner at Ebury Street with a bottle of *Beaujolais nouveau*.

'I don't know. She's a deep girl. I think when she came to me straight out of the convent and I depended on her so much she built up some sort of picture of our being together forever. I think I had some such picture myself. Then she felt she couldn't share me with someone else. She was always rather possessive about me, even at college.'

'It isn't her disliking me?'

'No, I don't think so.'

'I'd be very sorry to think you sort of lost her because of me—'

'No, no, it would have been the same whoever I married, she wanted to have me to herself.'

'She always frightened me rather. But I did try.'

'I know, my darling, you did. She said something about being given over to the religious life and having to be alone.'

'I thought she'd given up all that stuff.'

'So did I. But she hasn't. With someone like her it's an addiction. And really she's a puritan, a masochist.'

Gertrude did not reveal to Tim how very deeply she had been wounded by Anne's defection. How could she leave me, she thought again and again, how *could* she, when I needed her and loved her so much? Oh why can I not have everything, all that was given to me after Guy went. Anne was such a necessary being. This was another great grief to carry, one that would so very slowly diminish. The indestructible chariot in which she and Anne were to ride on through life had turned out to be an illusory vehicle after all.

At Tim's suggestion they had abandoned the dining room and ate their meals on a little table in the drawing room where a fire was burning every evening now that the weather had turned frosty. Tim had already cleared the plates away, and the chess board had been set out between the wine glasses. They usually played an incompetent game of chess before retiring. They had found out that they were quite evenly matched. They had decided not to tell the Count.

'You're lunching with Peter tomorrow?'

'Yes, it's your teaching day.'

'Don't forget Pat Cameron and Ed are coming to drinks.'

'*And* Mr and Mrs Singh. That's a triumph! I do hope your thing with Ed will work.'

'He's not doing it just to oblige me?'

'No, it's business.'

Ed Roper had lately launched out into ceramics, and had suggested that some of Tim's cats might appear on some of his mugs. Tim had also suggested to Ed a scheme for designing match boxes. Every tourist will buy a match box.

'I never saw myself much in commercial art, but now I rather fancy the notion. Perhaps I shall become obsessed with making money. What did Manfred say, by the way?'

'He thinks it's a great idea.'

'I was afraid he would think it was a joke.'

'Manfred never laughs at money.'

'No, but he laughs at me.'

'He likes you.'

'I like him. I'd like to have him for a pet. I'd love to make a fortune just to impress Manfred. He's an odd bird, isn't he.'

'Yes,' said Gertrude, 'he's very secretive.'

'Queer?'

'I don't know. He's a very kind man, he keeps an eye on people. He's very sweet to Veronica Mount, and I know he used to send money to Sylvia Wicks, and I keep meeting people he's helped.'

'Will you give Manfred a picture?'

'I'll offer him one.'

'Not the one of grandma.'

'The one that looks like Sylvia, no, I know you like that one.'

Since they were going to leave Ebury Street Gertrude had decided to distribute some of the family portraits.

'We have too many possessions,' said Tim.

'We can spare a few of them.'

'I love thinking about our new place. You're sure you don't

473

mind Hammersmith? I always wanted to live in Hammersmith somehow.'

'You shall have your studio with the rivery light.'

'It's a sort of sacred area, between Hammersmith Bridge and Chiswick Mall, and there are such lovely pubs.'

'We shall frequent them all.'

'Oh Gertrude —'

'What is it, my darling?'

'I'm so happy, would it be awful to open that other bottle of Beaujolais?'

Their days had fallen back into the pattern which they had been achieving in the little peaceful time after their marriage, and yet the texture of their life was different in many ways. Tim was busier, he still had his teaching which promised to continue, and he was involved with Ed Roper and the ceramics factory, learning a new craft. Gertrude continued her work with the Asian community and was hoping to return to part-time school teaching next year. She was sorting out her library and almost every day she bought books. The idea of studying again, studying with a purpose, pleased her. And of course the new house, whose purchase was now almost complete, obsessed them both. They were quite giddy with looking at wallpapers.

Tim had resumed his solitary London walks. These were necessary. Sometimes he walked all the way from Ebury Street to Ed's little factory in Hoxton. Sometimes he walked in the parks where the frost-rimmed brown leaves were fallen, and men were gathering them into mounds and making fires whose smoke rose straight up into the cold still air. Sometimes he went back to the picture galleries. The pictures had changed again. They had resumed their beauty and their deep meaning. They were more beautiful and more significant than they had ever been before. Tim did not always stay long. He looked at the pictures and smiled.

Of course he was often afraid, afraid that he was being too lucky. He did not deserve his happiness and might soon lose it. He did not ever think that Gertrude might tire of him or leave him. But he thought she might be mugged or run over or become ill and die. He worried about her safety when she was not with him. Sometimes he thought about Daisy and felt sad. Of course he never went to the Prince of Denmark, but he did not now imagine that Daisy was sitting there with Perkins on her knee. He felt sure that she had gone, she had left London, perhaps left England. He knew that he would never see her again, and he mourned quietly for her as for one dead. He did not avoid speaking of her to Gertrude. Gertrude occasionally asked questions, such as what he and Daisy used to do at Christmas time, but she showed no deep interest in Daisy, or at any rate did not interrogate him. Sometimes he wondered whether, if he had told Gertrude the truth at once, he could somehow have retained Daisy as a friend, as Gertrude had so cleverly retained the Count. But the cases were after all so different. Daisy and her time were over. It was possible to leave someone forever. And it seemed to him in retrospect that he and Daisy had been good friends and had in the end brought about a clean and honourable parting, for which they should be eternally grateful to each other.

Tim was pleased with his new role as a commercial artist who might actually one day earn some money. He was so far from being the spendthrift which the family feared, that his old careful economical habits were hard to break. But, as he dreamed dreams about the new studio with the 'rivery light', he found himself returning to old preoccupations. He spent a lot of time drawing funny animals and strange half-creatures which amused Gertrude, sometimes frightened her, and which she regarded as jokes. But for Tim it was as if these beings were coming to him out of a faintly discernible background of relentless form which he could apprehend as taking shape behind them. Sometimes he filled in mathematical patterns of which his 'animals' were part. He had reverted to painting on wood, and to his old habits of roving round the rubbish tips. He had painted on big wooden panels with bright acrylic paint some purely abstract 'network' pictures which did not displease him. But then how did these networks connect with the organic forms which also so spontaneously appeared? His thoughts about this were nonsense, and he never spoke of these deep things to Gertrude, but he lived calmly and patiently with the nonsense in expectation of, if not clarification, at least change. He began, drawing them out on graph paper, a series of compositions of Leda and the swan. The battling struggling bodies, Leda's thighs, her breasts, her head bent forward or thrown wildly back, the swan's slim curving neck, his beating wings and powerful feet, these forms in prolific developing patterns emerged out of a background which he began more and more to think of as determined, and he worked at them in a kind of furious obedience.

He often thought about what had happened in France and pictured vividly in his mind the 'great face' and the crystal pool, the flashing water of the canal, the terrible entry to the tunnel. He saw too the yellow beach of stones and the black and white dog climbing out of the water and shaking itself. He looked once or twice at his drawings of the rocks, and thought them good, and hid them away again. Something in his life had begun there, something which tied deeply and mysteriously together Gertrude and his art, or so at any rate he wished to believe. He felt this bond but did not reflect much upon it. He supposed that he and Gertrude would be together again in those holy places, but he did not imagine this pilgrimage and neither he nor she had yet suggested it. He felt a little frightened of going back, but he knew that when Gertrude casually raised the subject it would be easy to envisage.

Sometimes he thought, thank heavens I went to Gertrude on that day when I had been nearly drowned in the tunnel. Suppose I had not? Suppose I had gone home and weeks and months had passed? It would have become more and more impossible to return, and this was terrible to imagine. The murderous waters of the canal and the blackness of the tunnel had beaten and baptised him back to life. Had he then returned to Gertrude purged and punished? This was romanticism. He had returned to her as a hurt child to its mother. He had come back because he was bruised and bleeding and half drowned. It was all a lucky accident. Why had he ever gone away from her anyway and what had he been guilty of? This became, as time went on, vaguer in Tim's mind. The idea remained that he had committed some great act of treachery for which he had been miraculously forgiven, though sometimes he felt that he had exaggerated it all and that it was simply being caught out that had made him feel so stained and awful. He knew one thing, that he ought to have remained true to his original revelation, the decree of Eros which had been so indubitable when it was first made plain to him and Gertrude on that May evening in

476

France. He ought to have trusted it throughout as he trusted it now when every day was bringing him a further proof of Gertrude's love. But did I *also* marry her for her money, he sometimes quizzically wondered? Was it *somehow* for the sake of a haven, for a place to draw and paint in, something desired instinctively, as birds migrate and eels return to the Sargasso Sea? He did not tarry with such suppositions. Love was what mattered, and the *work* of love in his absolute marriage with Gertrude, which would not always be free from care.

He said to her now, voicing a part of his thoughts, and prompting a reassurance which he knew he would receive. 'It isn't different is it, it's not spoilt in any way because of what happened, what I did?'

And Gertrude, understanding him perfectly and smiling, replied, 'No, it's not hurt or spoilt, but we are different because we've been shipwrecked and survived, so it's better really.'

'You are so good to me. But I often think, who am I, what am I? I am not like Guy. You must sometimes think—'

Gertrude's face changed in a way that he knew. It was not the first time that she had heard such words and she did not pick up his comparison. 'You know the odd things that Guy used sometimes to say, like spells or charms, and he said them a lot at the end when he was ill and they upset me so much because I couldn't understand them and I'd never asked—. He used to talk about a ring, "she sold the ring, she should have kept the ring". Anne interpreted that for me. Of course it's out of *The Merchant of Venice*. You remember the ring which Shylock's wife gave him and which Jessica took when she ran away—'

'And what happened to it?'

'She exchanged it for a monkey.'

'I wonder why Guy—'

'He identified with Shylock. He said to me that he always felt that one day he would have to drop everything and run. I suppose it's a deep Jewish feeling. It was as if he always had a bag packed.'

'He seemed to me like a monument of security. And there was that other thing he said about the white swan—'

'Yes, I can't make that out, and the cube—'

'What was the cube?'

'He talked about the upper side of the cube. Touching or reaching "the upper side of the cube".'

'Striking the upper side of the cube. I can do that for you.'

'What?'

'How strange. You probably don't remember, but years and years ago when Guy used to play tennis at Queen's Club —'

'He was so good —'

'He invited me to play with him a few times out of sheer kindness, I was hopeless. He tried to coach me, and he repeated something which his coach used to say to him, "When you serve, imagine that the ball is a cube of which you are going to hit the upper side".'

'Good heavens,' said Gertrude, 'I thought it was presocratic philosophy, and it turns out to be tennis! That would amuse Guy.'

'You know, Gertrude, I loved Guy, I loved him. I was frightened of him, but he was like a father to me. He was a good man.'

'Yes. Yes. Yes.'

They were silent.

Tim thought, isn't it strange, as the months turn and the dark days come, in the years that lie ahead, we shall make the pilgrimage through the anniversary of the day when we fell in love and then when we lost each other and then when we met again in the British Museum and our wedding day, and the awful time when we were apart again, and the festival of the leaves, and when we came together in France, and then moving into our new house, and then finally on toward the anniversary of Guy's death. Every year, as we celebrate Christmas, we shall be remembering that anniversary. Oh my God, what will the first one be like? What will it be like as Gertrude approaches that day? What darkness must gather in her mind? Already each morning she must be thinking: today a year ago. Yet she loves me and seems able to mourn and also to have joy. Will she suddenly break down? Am I *mad* to think she will go on loving me?

And Gertrude was thinking, have I run to a haven because my grief would otherwise have been too great? Am I only now beginning to mourn when I have a safe place in which to mourn? I know now that I shall survive. Yet I said to Guy that

I would die with him and I believed it. I said I would be dead too, walking and talking and dead. And I'm not dead. All sorts of amazing incredible things have happened to me and I am alive. And I have found Anne and lost her again, and I thought that she was to be the priest of my mourning and that we two would walk on together so slowly into the future, but all has turned out otherwise. I have evaded the stretched-out hand of death, and I cannot think it was wrong to do so. Am I the same person, what has become of me? Yes, I will mourn in my safety, I shall shed tears, and Tim will be silent and he will comfort me, as I weep he will stroke my hair and kiss my hand.

And Gertrude thought, it was about a year ago that Guy said to me, if you marry, marry the Count. And I worked it out that this meant, don't marry Manfred. I don't believe that any more. I think Guy simply wanted me to be safe and happy. He *begged* me to be happy. But what would he think now?

She no longer felt haunted by Guy but neither, as Christmas Eve came nearer, did she feel at peace with him. And she thought, it is impossible to make any final peace with the dead, unless indifference and oblivion be peace. They cannot condemn us but neither can they forgive. They have no knowledge and no strength or power. They can exist only as questions and as burdens and as pains and as strange objects of love. I shall always love Guy and mourn for him and miss him and feel pain, and the question and the burden of it will travel with me for the rest of my life.

And Tim thought, she is thinking about Guy. Oh the sadness of it, the sadness inside the miracle. And he thought, I will be faithful to her and serve her loyally and lovingly all the days of our lives. And I will never tell lies any more. Never. *Never*. Never? Well, hardly ever.

Gertrude said, 'It's so sad, I thought Anne would be with us at Christmas time, I thought of Christmas with you and me and Anne and Peter, and now she won't be there.'

Tim said, 'Let's not play chess. Let's go to bed.'

'Yes, my darling. Do you know, I've been thinking. Perhaps I'll try to write a novel, I always thought I could.'

'Oh dear,' said Tim anxiously, 'will you put me in it?'

They went to bed.

'Have you got a cold?' said Mrs Mount to Manfred.

'No.'

'I think you have, you got it from Janet, you always conceal your colds.'

'I have no cold. I forgot to tell you, Balintoy is coming back.'

'Oh *good*. But why just when the skiing is starting? He must have run out of money.'

'I gather he's heard a rumour that his mother intends to marry!'

'Then no wonder. I expect she started the rumour herself. Of course you never met his mother.'

'No.'

'She's a gorgon. They don't make them like that any more, even in Ireland. But where on earth does Balintoy get the cash, do you give it to him?'

Manfred smiled.

He and Veronica Mount were drinking brandy in Manfred's flat. It was late in the evening. Outside the pavements sparkled with frost. Snow was forecast. But inside Manfred's flat all was warm and soft.

The room they sat in was large and high-ceilinged, painted a pallid yellow which Manfred had not bothered to change when he moved in some years ago. In the subdued light of a few lamps, set about the simulacrum of a fire, it looked cosy enough. Manfred and Mrs Mount (they had dined out) were sitting at either end of a long shadowy sofa covered with small embroidered cushions, upon a pile of which Veronica kept peevishly trying to rest her elbow. A handsome silky rug at their feet depicted ornate mauve men in pursuit of ornate mauve breasts. Beyond, upon the pale darkened walls, hung prints and water colours, trophies of Manfred's casual taste. He was on the whole, careless of his surroundings, even oblivious, though sometimes, possessed by an idea, he would take pleasure in bringing home some visual treasure.

Manfred, turning his large bland face to his guest, was formally dressed as usual in a dark suit, white shirt, and darkish silk tie upon which some red asterisk-like forms were discreetly deployed. Veronica Mount was equally formal, unambitious, in a midnight-blue woollen dress into whose neck a ruffled scarf of pale blue silk had been thrust with careful abandon. Her restless elegant legs were tucked up onto the sofa. Her shiny expensive shoes dated from the far past.

Veronica went on, 'The Count will be glad to see Balintoy.'

'These are great days for the Count.'

'Yes, what with Gertrude and the Pope.'

'What has Gertrude done to him? Something wonderful.'

'What she has done,' said Veronica, 'she has done very easily, she has stretched out her hand and tweaked him inside the magic circle of her love.'

'It was a merciful act.'

'You are tediously unsuspicious. It was a self-interested act. She simply didn't want the Count to get away. Why should she lose a slave?'

'Well, I suppose that's all right,' said Manfred, 'so long as he doesn't mind. I think she needed to preserve, close by, his good opinion of her.'

'Yes—'

'She couldn't bear that the Count should go away carrying a blackened image of her inside his head.'

'That's true. And of course a blackened image is soon refurbished by a little petting. But if I were Tim I'd be a bit uneasy.'

'I wouldn't. There's something childish in Tim that absolutely captivates Gertrude—'

'She's virginal and he's raffish, as you see it.'

'Yes. Even perhaps it releases her after all those years with Guy.'

'Guy was *above* her. She married above herself. We all thought so at the time.'

'Did we, Veronica? No, Tim is safe. He's lucky actually, if he were hijacked he'd never be the one to get shot.'

'He'd toady up to the hijackers.'

'No, he's just lucky, like a drunk man. He may even be glad that there's someone like the Count to amuse Gertrude when he's not there.'

'Someone so honourable you mean! Yes, the Count is the soul of honour.'

'And he and Tim like each other.'

'All right, Tim is safe, but is she?'

'You mean — ?'

'Don't you think he'll run off again to that mistress?'

'No, why should he, he's happy, he's in love.'

'Don't be soppy, Manfred. It's all too good to be true.'

'I suppose Ed Roper has told everybody that story.'

'About the mistress? Well, he told *you*.'

'Yes, but I didn't spread it.'

'Oh you are so boringly discreet! It certainly had an electrical effect on Gertrude. What *did* happen exactly? I suppose we can't ask.'

'No. But whatever it was it's over.'

'Someone said Tim is going into business with Ed Roper, mugs or matches or something. Is that true?'

'Yes, I'm even involved in a remote financial sense.'

'I wouldn't invest a penny in Tim Reede.'

'Ed will see to it, he's no fool.'

'We've never had any evidence that Tim can paint.'

'We've never looked for any.'

'I knew you'd say that. Gertrude is planning a marvellous studio for him to play in, when they move to Hammersmith or Chiswick or whatever low-lying spot they're crazy about now. I wouldn't live beside that smelly river for anything. Guy not dead a year, and she's in bed with another man discussing wallpaper! I'm sorry Gertrude's leaving Ebury Street. It's the end of an era.'

'She's even distributing the ancestral pictures,' said Manfred.

'Is she? She hasn't offered me one.'

'She's going to give me that Sargent head of great aunt Judith.'

'It's rather small.'

'It's the most valuable. I've been telling her for years how much I like it.'

'You're incorrigible. I suppose it's conscience-money, this picture distribution. She's paying us off, we can't expect any more. Do you think Gertrude will really go back into teaching?'

'I think she'll try to.'

'She's bought a lot of learned books which I bet she won't read.'

'She's no scholar, but she's probably a good teacher.'

'She was going on about how they'd both be working. Pure romance I thought. She seems to think Tim will actually earn money.'

'Why not? He did before.'

'He's more likely to get rid of Gertrude's.'

'He seems less addicted to material possessions than the rest of us.'

'He'll learn to spend. But seriously, Manfred, you wouldn't be pleased to see Gertrude's money melting stupidly away?'

'It is true,' said Manfred, 'that I would be sad to see that money vanishing for which our great grandfather worked so intelligently and so hard.'

'And some of us got some and some of us didn't! At least Joseph always said he didn't get a bean. I wonder if it was true, considering what he squandered on that bitch, and I never knew what happened to the Strad.'

'Let's not have Joseph today, Veronica. Guy was so deplorably unambitious with his money.'

'At least he didn't lose it.'

'Unambitious,' said Manfred sadly. 'He never took my advice. More cognac?'

'Thanks. I wonder where it'll go if Tim doesn't spend it. Do you think they'll have any children? I know Gertrude can't, but they might adopt.'

'They might, when they get over the shock of being married. I see Tim as a father.'

'Do you? Janet will be so cross. So you are at least interested in the money?'

'Gertrude's?'

'Though you've got plenty of your own.'

'When has that ever stopped a man from wanting more? It is only poor people who don't want money, they lack the concept.'

'So you might have gone after that, even if you didn't want her.'

'What depths of cynicism you attribute to me, Veronica.'

'I suspect you are insincere. You *did* want her. Not just the money.'

'You keep urging me to admit it.'

'It's true that you didn't try very hard.'

'What could I do with you and Janet against me?'

'You jest. At least you would have had some sense of responsibility and kept the money for the family.'

'And increased it, so Janet would have done better with me.'

'Of course Janet and I had quite different motives—'

'In chaperoning me everywhere and never leaving me alone with Gertrude for a moment!' said Manfred. 'All the same, if I had wanted to pay court to Gertrude I imagine I could have managed it somehow.'

'Janet simply wanted to prevent Gertrude from marrying.'

'*A cause des chères têtes blondes* as you said.'

'Because of the children, yes.'

'Whereas you, my dear Veronica—'

'Whereas I—'

'But didn't you go a little far in sending that anonymous letter to the Count?'

Mrs Mount smiled and shifted her handsome silky legs. She sipped the cognac, then looked at Manfred. In the dim light she looked young, her face smooth, her dark eyes glowing.

'How did you know?'

'The Count showed me the letter and I recognized your typewriter.'

'Cunning old you.'

'What I couldn't make out was your motive.'

'You know my motive.'

'I mean your calculation. How was it supposed to help you to expose Tim's fling with Gertrude?'

'I reckoned the sudden publicity would force their hand. If it had stayed secret it would have been easier to dismantle if there were second thoughts. But confronted with us all Gertrude would be determined to go through with it.'

'Not bad reckoning,' said Manfred, 'and of course I'm flattered, but you played a risky hand, Veronica. I gather you also obligingly informed Gertrude that Guy and I were life-long enemies. Untrue incidentally.'

'How do you know I said that?'

'Gertrude told the Count who artlessly told me, only he didn't put it quite like that.'

'Nor did I quite.'

'I can see the working here. But it could have misfired. It was likely to attract Gertrude's attention to me. And it might have worked the other way and set off some deep anti-Guy particle in her of which we know nothing.'

'Do you think there is such a particle?'

'No. But one can't be sure.'

'I reflected on that, but I thought it more likely to put Gertrude off you.'

'You are very thorough, Veronica.'

'One must fight for one's life.'

'You exaggerate as usual.'

'No.'

'Then writing to tell Tim to try again, that was child's play.'

'It had a certain obviousness, and it worked.'

'Tim quites loves you now I'm told.'

'He imagines I feel a sentimental fondness for him, and that's always endearing. I let him think so. Why miss an ally? And if Tim and I are dear friends I can monitor the marriage.'

'Oh—my dear Veronica—!'

'You would have said something. It was too interesting to keep mum about.'

'About Tim and Gertrude? I don't know.'

'What made you so sure in France that they were having an affair, apart from their agitation?'

'Gertrude said Tim had just arrived, but I looked at his drawings and there were too many local ones, he must have been there several days.'

'So you think it'll stick? After Guy, it's so very odd.'

'Not really,' said Manfred. 'A bereaved woman often falls quickly in love with a quite different man. And as you said yourself, Gertrude is a person who must love somebody. It was a terrible bereavement and she couldn't bear it alone. She had to run to someone for consolation.'

'To someone. It's just as well I forced myself into your car on that occasion.'

'No force was necessary.'

'Well, I know you are a man who never does what he doesn't want to do, that's why I feel so safe with you. All right, you did what you pleased. But if Gertrude had come on to Rome instead of staying in France she might have fallen in love with you and not with Tim.'

'And what would I have done then I wonder.'

'I hate to think. You've always wrapped yourself in mystery. I feel I've had a narrow escape.'

Manfred smiled his bland smile. He said, 'You've had a narrower escape than you realize, my dear.'

'You mean that if Gertrude—'

'Nothing to do with Gertrude.'

'What then?'

'I fell in love.'

'What?'

'This summer I fell terribly in love.'

'Oh my God,' said Mrs Mount. She sat up straight, putting her feet on the rug. 'Who in heaven's name with?'

'Anne Cavidge.'

'No!' Mrs Mount was silent, taking it in. Then she said, 'An unfrocked nun. You would.'

'You are taking it sensibly.'

'Were you *afraid* of how I'd take it? That's some consolation. But I'm not taking it sensibly. I'm shattered, I'm terrified. Are you still in love?'

'I got nowhere.'

'*Are you still in love?*'

'Very considerable discomfort remains. But it will pass. She is gone. I got nowhere.'

'Oh—poor—old—you—But did you try?'

'Discreetly. I was soon aware of a major difficulty.'

'What?'

'Her affections were engaged elsewhere.'

'Gertrude.'

'No, the Count.'

'*Really?* I had quite set her down as being of the other persuasion. Surely Gertrude was her whole point, the object of her affections, the occasion of her departure?'

'No doubt she loves Gertrude too,' said Manfred, 'but she was madly in love with our Pierre. She *wanted* him.'

'So you hadn't a chance.'

'I hoped.'

486

'But why should she run and not fight? Or did you somehow wreck it?'

'I did nothing. Unlike you, Veronica. I am not prepared to stoop in order to obtain what I want.'

'You accept the homage.'

'I'm touched. You like living dangerously.'

'Anyway, you did nothing. Gertrude acted.'

'As you said, she simply reached out her hand and secured the Count.'

'I suspect he was ready to vanish and Gertrude knew it. But was the Count aware of the passion he had inspired in that chaste bosom?'

'No, I'm sure he had no idea. He loved Gertrude and he classified Anne.'

'And Gertrude didn't know?'

'No. She might have cursed but she would have held back.'

'I must say, I hardly noticed Anne at all, I couldn't *see* her—'

'Yes. A nun's invisibility. I worshipped it.'

'Still, it's strange that I missed the whole business—'

'Considering how relentlessly you watch. I thought the less you knew the better, dear Veronica. *Je te connais.*'

'Ah, if I had known it all—'

'As for Anne not fighting, consider how the poor thing was placed, loving both of them. What could she do? She had to give the Count a clear field. She probably felt she ought to *help* him to secure Gertrude.'

'She never thought much of Tim.'

'Then when Tim came back—'

'The Count didn't put up much of a fight either.'

'No. The Count is a moral oddity and so is Anne. They were made for each other, but alas it was not to be.'

'I think they're a spineless pair. Couldn't she have made *some* effort once Tim was back?'

'The Count was obsessed. I think she hoped to win him by silent patient love. And she didn't foresee Gertrude's move.'

'Then she's a fool. I would have done. All right, don't comment. Anyway, she waited and then hey presto it was too late.'

'She realized how much it meant to Gertrude to have the Count eternally around the place.'

'And to the Count to survive as Gertrude's slave. I find it all curiously digusting. So Anne didn't try, she ran away. But how do you know all this? She can't have told you?'

'*Good heavens* no!' said Manfred.

'The sharp eye of love?'

'I was present when the Count came to Ebury Street soon after Gertrude got back from the north. He was shuddering with emotion. Anne was patently annoyed.'

'That could have been for the other reason.'

'I considered that. She may have felt possessive about Gertrude. But when I began to watch there were plenty of other signs. The way she looked at him and —'

'Yet it remains a supposition?'

'No, I was very sure. I had the final proof on that Polish Pope evening. The Count and Gertrude were suddenly like young lovers. Anne saw what had happened. She had a look of death in her face.'

'She always had that look, she looked like a ghost, transparent. But when did you begin to love the cold pale creature?'

'She impressed me very much on that first occasion when we met her at Ebury Street just after she arrived. She seemed to be something amazing, she had an authority which touched me directly. That was love. Only I didn't realize it at once.'

'She still smelt of the convent. But you soon realized?'

'Yes . . . it gradually . . . became . . . an obsession. . . .'

'Oh dear. Oh dear, oh dear. But you said nothing and she didn't guess? I mean how did you get to know her at all, or did you?'

'I talked to her quite a lot *dans le cercle*.'

'But, heavens, were you ever alone with her?'

'Yes, once.'

'When, where?'

Manfred shook his head.

'Did anything happen?'

'No.'

'You fool!'

'It was all so amazing,' said Manfred. 'I became a different person, I lived in a different world where everything was huge and bright, but all my ordinary judgments left me. It was as if my mind was drained clean and I had a new mind, beautiful and clear but unfamiliar and hard to manage. All the dull old usual reactions were gone. I didn't know how to proceed. I felt alienated and awkward and I was so afraid of making a mistake. I was terrified of giving her any shock or hurt and then seeing her draw back. It was wonderful at first that she took me for granted as someone she could easily talk to. I hoped for some miracle of communication, some moment—It was all so precious, so—'

'So unlike the mediocre scene you usually put up with.'

'When I was driving her and Gertrude to Cumbria—it became extreme—'

'Oh *God*! I didn't come because I thought Anne was chaperoning Gertrude!'

'It was the other way round. I had Anne sitting next to me part of the way. I nearly went mad.'

'Your shoulders touched. I can't bear it!'

'I hoped she might take some notice. We talked quite a lot, and watching a man drive can interest a girl.'

'I fell in love with you when you were driving. But then I've loved you since the world began, since the big bang or whatever Gerald now thinks was the first thing.'

'Come Veronica, you've loved others.'

'Bagatelles.'

'You loved Guy once.'

'I don't remember.'

'I wanted Anne to drive the car. I had a bet with myself that if she drove the car everything would come out right. I knew that as soon as I saw her driving the car I would be uncontrollably in love and perhaps inspired—'

'But she didn't?'

'No.'

'Nor coming back?'

'No. But I was in a different mood then.'

'Less in love?'

'More in love, but more patient. I was making plans.'

'You didn't secretly go to see her in Cumbria—?'

'No, no, I didn't want to intrude on her when she was obsessed with looking after Gertrude. And I felt—not that she was fragile, I think she's the strongest thing I've ever met—but that she was new and strange and a bit lost. She was so much from elsewhere. I thought I had plenty of time, and I thought I was the only one who could *see* her, like you said, about her being invisible. I wasn't aware of any special danger, except of course the final one of her simply not wanting me, and this was somehow still, I can't quite express it, all wrapped up in the wonderful totality of her. I just didn't want to put a foot wrong. And, all the time, she was away in the north, I was so happy, just thinking of her safe up there in that place beside the sea—'

'Yes. I can recall your happiness. I thought it had another source.'

'Then when she got back—'

'You realized you had a rival. But if you had declared yourself she would have succumbed, how could she not.'

'She loved someone else. And why should she love me? I'm not irresistible.'

'Aren't you? I heard you offering to take her home from the Polish Pope party. Would you have kissed her in the car?'

Manfred was silent.

'And this migraine you suddenly developed—'

'Fictional. I was looking for something in common. We could have swopped pills.'

'How furious Gertrude would have been, she would have fallen in love with you directly. Do you know you share your passion with Ned Openshaw? He fell totally in love with Anne.'

'Discerning boy.'

'I hope she *has* left the country?'

'Yes.'

'And it's really over?'

'Yes—it's really over.'

'Don't you want to chase her now the Count's out of the way—or are you sure you'd fail? I know you hate failure.'

'You see—I think she's become a nun again—not in a formal sense, but—I'd never get her, never.'

'Too worldly? An attractive man is never too worldly for a lonely woman. However, don't think I'm trying to persuade you!'

'I've lost her,' said Manfred. 'And I have . . . made up my mind . . . to that.'

'It's not like you not to seize what you want. I conclude you did not love her enough.'

Manfred was silent.

'Now you're angry with me. I feel alienated from you. And you've been—you know— and that was why.'

'Yes.'

'Well, I endure your moods. I always have, it's part of the treaty.'

'I am grateful.'

'Pah! Now you regret having told me. You know my discretion, where you are concerned, is absolute.'

'Sometimes I feel sick to death of myself and everything about my life. But I recover.'

'My loving you is part of what you're sick of. But you recover. My love is a bond and a burden to you.'

'A burden sometimes, a bond never.'

'All right. You'd be off like a flash if you fancied someone.'

'Well, I'm still here.'

'I wish I had the magic to make you happy. I haven't. Yet here we are.'

'Here we are.'

Veronica looked at Manfred's profile. She did not make any move towards him. She tucked up her feet and narrowed her eyes.

Manfred said, 'I'm sorry you put it about that Guy and I were enemies. I loved Guy.'

'You said he was cold to you near the end. I wonder if he saw you married to Gertrude.'

'No, that would have been impossible, and I'm sure Guy knew it, it would have been incestuous.'

'Because Guy was a father to you.'

'In any case I could never have viewed Gertrude in that light.'

'I wish you'd made that clearer earlier. I suppose you were throwing dust in my eyes.'

'It was your idea, and it kept you occupied.'

'It kept me thoroughly unhappy.'

'I'm still sorry we didn't say Kaddish for Guy.'

'You would never have found a quorum *parmi les cousins et les oncles*.'

'I suppose not.'

'Your persistent secret sentimentality about our old religion amazes and touches me. Guy never felt like that, he wouldn't have thanked you for your prayers.'

'How can one be sure? When he was dying, I heard him talking to the ancestors.'

'What?'

'On one of those curious evenings I came through the hall and heard him talking Yiddish.'

'I didn't know Guy knew Yiddish.'

'He was all alone—'

'Perhaps it was the inspiration of death. I shall be there myself tomorrow. Chattering Yiddish in Abraham's bosom.'

'Veronica, I wish you wouldn't always pretend to be so old.'

'Protective colouration.'

'At least you don't have to pretend with me. How old *are* you?'

'Older than you think, younger than you think. When we travel together people say "he's so kind to the old dear". This used to amuse me, it doesn't any more. But I tell you one thing, on the day when you really go off with someone else I shall become a hundred in an hour like someone in a fairy tale.'

'Oh don't be so—'

'Vulgar is the word. I sometimes think you fear vulgarity more than evil.'

'Vulgarity is evil.'

'You must admit that no one has the faintest idea about *cosa nostra*.'

'No, thank God.'

'That leaves you free.'

'All right, all right—'

'Everyone thinks you're queer, and that helps of course.'

'Veronica, please—'

'I wish you were queer, I could bear your loving boys.'

'Oh don't start that again.'

'Sometimes I feel, like my own pain, how very very sad you are inside.'

'I have no inside.'

'I have. I live with fear. I have nothing in my life except my addiction and that fear. Sometimes I wish a friendly cancer would end it all, or that cosmic catastrophe Gerald keeps hinting at.'

The bell rang.

'Damn!' said Veronica.

'Who can it be at this hour?' Manfred went to the house telephone. 'Hello? Who's there?' He turned to Mrs Mount. 'It's Balintoy!'

'Oh *good*! Let him in, my darling.'

'I've still got that bottle of Power's whisky!'

They ran to the door of the flat to welcome the Irishman.

Balintoy came bounding in. His weather-beaten face looked to them older, but his eyes were a radiant piercing dark blue, a little moist now from the cold outside. Tiny snow flakes sparkled upon his overcoat and upon his curly well-tended shock of brown hair. They laughed and made much of him and settled him down with his whisky. And Balintoy, who knew more about them than they imagined, looked happily and affection-ately from one to the other, and stroked them with his outstretched hand. 'Now, my dears, tell me all the news!'

Anne Cavidge was sitting in the Prince of Denmark with Perkins on her knee. Outside it was snowing. Inside it was warm and smoky and noisy and rather dark. Anne had been there for some time, moving from one seat to another until she had got herself into a corner from which she could survey the whole bar. She was looking for Daisy.

Her aeroplane ticket to Chicago, dated tomorrow, was in her handbag. She had been deliberately vague, even mystifying, about her day of departure. Gertrude would probably reckon now that she had been gone over a week. She had seen, for her farewells, no one else; and she and Gertrude had tacitly avoided any 'last scene'. 'I expect you'll be off soon.' 'Yes, haven't quite fixed.' They shunned each other's eyes. Anne said she would ring, then did not ring. She sent a hasty note saying 'Just leaving'. Gertrude would understand.

She had left her flat and had moved into a hotel. No one knew where she was. No one had especially asked, since it was quickly assumed that she had left the country. Only Ned Openshaw made some vain attempts to find her, cheering his failure by a mystical certainty that they were bound to meet again. In fact, Anne was at the hotel where she had intended to stay when she arrived in London a year ago. She was wearing the blue and white dress which she had hastily bought in the village to put on when she took off her black robes forever. She touched the aeroplane ticket in her bag. She touched a grey stone which was in there too.

Anne had, in her final quest, now visited 'the old Prince' several times. Tonight was her last night in London and she did not now think that she would find Daisy. She had got used to spending evenings in the Prince, it was an occupation. No one spoke to her. No one, she felt, saw her. She looked and listened. She could not now think how it had not been clear to her that she ought to have looked for Daisy as soon as she returned from France, as soon as it was plain that Tim had returned to his wife. She should have done so at once instead of fretting about her own fate. Her unbroken pride had separated her from

494

Gertrude, her vanity had nearly drowned her in Cumbria, could not at least some vestige of professional smartness have prompted her not to lose *this* trick? Why had she not imagined Daisy's loneliness, her possible plight, her possible despair? Anne had been too absorbed in her own hopes; and earlier when she had visited Daisy she had been too high-mindedly concerned with organizing the defeat of those hopes to have any thought to spare for catastrophes which her selfless masochistic morality might be bringing about in Daisy's life.

Only later did she take to picturing that room with its chaos of clothes and its smell of drink. She recalled her own coldness, her inquisitorial hostility. She remembered Daisy's friendliness, then her anger. She thought suddenly, supposing Daisy were to kill herself? Everyone was busy surviving, seeking their own, arranging to be happy. No one seemed to have given a thought to Daisy, as if she had never been an actor in the drama at all. Daisy was an inconvenient embarrassing fading memory. Anne, sitting in her chilly hotel room, thought these thoughts quietly, then had leapt up in a sudden frenzy. She ran from the hotel and took a taxi to Daisy's flat in Shepherds Bush. Someone replied to the bell and Anne mounted the stairs. Daisy was gone. Her successor, a pleasant young girl, told Anne she was sorry, she had no idea where Miss Barrett was, she had left no address. Anne looked over her shoulder into a clean tidy bright room full of books. After that Anne took to going to the Prince of Denmark.

About the Count Anne felt deep awful pain but, although she continued to speculate, her speculations did not disturb her present plans and motives. Sometimes she felt that this 'falling in love' was an illness which had to come to her on her return to the world and which would before too long be cured. Or could she conceivably have combined duty and interest by securing the Count by ministering to his religious need? He had vaguely expressed such a need, but she had not been interested in his interest in Christ, only in his interest in her. Should she not have preached to him more fervently? Sometimes she obsessively relived past times, wondering, if I had only told him *then*, or *then*. . . ? When he had spoken of suicide she should have seized him in her arms instead of offering him rational arguments. Proper scruples, reasonable prudence, self-punishing masochism, or that demonic pride which so many years 'inside' had not seemed to have diminished one iota? She felt that she would have died of a rebuff. She thought, I lived on 'perfect moments' with Peter, moments like that wonderful telephone call at night. 'Goodnight, dear Peter.' 'Goodnight, dear Anne.' That was the pure honey of love, of hope. I was afraid to move on with him into the horrors of history. Now she had the torment of 'if only. . . .' It was a consolation to think here of Gertrude and of what Anne had come to view as Gertrude's *rights* in the matter. Anne's monstrous love would have shocked the Count and perhaps impaired whatever happiness he might now achieve as Gertrude's *cavaliere servente*. It would also certainly have upset Gertrude and perhaps made her 'acquisition' of the Count an impossibility. I have no place, no rights, thought Anne. Gertrude, always the princess, had to have whatever she wanted; and was it not proper that she should, as she herself had said, being secure in marriage, proceed to love everybody and be beautifully loved in return? 'It's so simple to love everyone and be loved by them. It's like a sheepfold with the sheep gathered in.' Ought Anne to have been magnanimous enough to be a sheep? She could even wonder whether she were not actually leaving, as Gertrude had expressed it, 'in a huff' and meanly depriving her friend of the perfection of happiness in 'having Anne as well'.

Anne at least did not delude herself by imagining that it was her duty to abstain from Peter because of the imminent failure of Tim. She saw Gertrude and Tim as secure. She even endeavoured now to appreciate Tim; and she reflected, as she had reflected in the case of Daisy, upon her own failure to feel, when she should have felt it, pity. She recalled the conversation, perhaps momentous, in which she had pictured Tim's corrupted future and told the Count that Tim ought to leave Daisy. How impure her judgment had been at that moment, how little sympathy she had really felt for the banished 'scapegoat'. Of course her scrupulous mind could even see that little outburst as a 'slip', a failure to observe her 'policy' of ignoring her own interests. And it was a curious thought that perhaps her own censorious coldness at that moment had somehow given strength to the Count's plea to Tim to return, or at least to separate himself from Daisy. How strangely interlaced all these histories

496

were. Seeing it this way Anne wondered if, here at least, she had not acted half-consciously on her own behalf, but she soon dismissed such speculations as trivial.

Sometimes more simply she thought that she had been a coward and would pay a coward's price. That was one way of looking at it. She should have played a bolder and more positive role, questioned the Count, not respected his secrecy and his reserve. What, in these reflections, she tried at all costs to avoid was the terrible love-yearning, the *I want him, I want him, I shall die without him* which kept returning and rising up in her heart. To this hot desire Anne opposed herself, and was cold, cold. That way indeed madness lay, an impure profitless suffering which at least she could spare herself. She could not yet banish him however, and saw again and again those pale eyes, that thin clever touchable face, and the awkward thin tall figure filling some enchanted separated area of space like the apparition of a holy saint. She saw him transfigured, saw his beauty which she was sure so few could see, and her body ached for him and she mourned. She reflected too upon his heroism, which she could not match. He loved Gertrude so much that he would stay beside her forever and see her belonging to another.

But I have to survive, Anne said to herself, and survive on my own terms. To stay, that would be heroism, yes: but I don't want to be that sort of hero. And she recalled Gertrude's words, in order to survive a terrible loss one has to become another person, it may seem cruel, survival itself is cruel, it means leading one's thoughts away from the one who is gone. Yes, thought Anne, and with a strangely fresh pang she remembered the deaths of her mother and her brother, when she was still at school, her father's death later when she was already a nun. How rarely she thought in detail about those loved ones now, though a certain consciousness of them, especially of her father, travelled always with her. How had she manged to survive those deaths? And now, with a swift dart of memory, she thought she could recall how even in the moment of hearing that Dick was dead, fallen from a cliff face in the Cairngorms, she had instinctively closed herself against pain, instinctively peered ahead into a time when she would be someone else who could be conscious of this loss without anguish. So, Gertrude too had survived, the healthy still youthful strength of her happiness-seeking being had reached out instinctively and found new consolations and satisfactions. Anne pictured her first arrival at Ebury Street and how, mixed with her sympathy and concern, she had felt suddenly safe, pleased with her warm well-appointed bedroom and with her sense of being in the right place. It couldn't *anyway* have been like that, thought Anne. She was only just now receiving the full shock waves of her departure from the convent, the full violence of that amazing act, itself like a kind of bereavement, whose full consequences remained still so obscure. And she thought, I have got to survive that too. And she thought that perhaps later on she would see her mad love for Peter as only one incident in some large pattern of change.

They had said 'once a nun always a nun'. They had said that they needed this thought of her as being, in their midst, still dedicated and holy. She had been so wise not to tell her love. If one syllable had passed her lips, if one gesture had escaped her, it would have changed the world, as Gertrude had said it could in seconds be utterly changed. I would be a different person, thought Anne, and that's what's important. Some great necessary integrity, some absolute availability, some eternal aloneness would have been lost by that revelation. She had kept her mouth shut, she had never told her love, and that at least was for her salvation. She was still 'empty and clean', transparent and invisible, although the voice that said this was still the voice of her pride. And she was homeless and free. She had left the convent because it was a home. Foxes have holes, but the Son of Man . . . only now, after the safety of her service to Gertrude, was she facing the void which she had chosen.

But was not the idea of 'void' itself an illusion, something 'romantic' as Guy might say? How soon she might fill up that void with all sorts of rubbish! Shall I jumble it all again, she wondered, seek refuges, fall stupidly in love? Can I really be an anchoress in the world, and what ever does it mean? Life was so full of chances. She might have drowned in Cumbria before Gertrude's eyes, she might have set off some new and awful causal chain by taking hold of Peter's hand. Now she was completely free to put herself in bondage, but what would the bondage be? Marriage? Anne was sure that that folly at least she could avoid. She would never marry, she was not made for the particular safety of married life, and it seemed to her that she had always known this. The Poor Clares were simply a stepping stone, a starting point. Or would she perhaps stay there forever, just *at* the starting point, a shadowy helper, a servant, without even the dignity of being 'inside'? Or would she go on to find her cell, her hermitage in a little white wooden house in a little lost senseless American town? Or work in prisons and find out herself as an eternal prisoner? Or maybe become a doctor, as her father had wished? Or would she perhaps end up after all as a priest in another church? At least she knew that she must now seek solitude, innocence and the silence of being totally uninteresting. 'To him that hath shall be given, and from him that hath not shall be taken away even that which he hath.' Anne gave her own sense to this saying. She knew that her salvation from a corruption which she well understood was to have not, and to be with those that have not. And she thought all these thoughts together with a full and gloomy realization that perhaps all that awaited her 'over there' was muddle and confusion and messy nasty moral failure.

At one time Anne would have put this self-analysis in terms of: only God can be perfectly loved. Human love, however behovable, is hopelessly imperfect. This hard truth had sent her into the convent. It had also in the end driven her out. Happiness sought anywhere but in God tends to corruption. This, which had once been doctrine for her, she held to now simply as a personal showing. She had been right after all, and the events of the last year had confirmed it, to think that she had been irrevocably spoilt for the world by God. And spoilt, and rightly spoilt, even though she no longer believed in Him. St Augustine had prayed by repeating simply again and again *My Lord and my God, my Lord and my God*. Anne felt now that she too could pray so in her utmost need, calling upon the name of the non-existent God.

Anne's hand returned to her handbag and she touched with her finger the elliptical grey stone, slightly chipped at one end, which her Visitor had shown to her and left behind him as a sign. The dense hardness of the stone was very cold at all times.

Instinctively she touched it with her damaged finger, the finger which had been scorched when she reached out to touch his garment. She could still feel the slightly rough texture of the cloth. The little scar had not healed. Victor, to whom on Gertrude's insistence she had displayed it, had been puzzled. He prescribed antibiotics. The scar showed no sign of going septic, but it persisted. Anne felt it now against the hard cold surface of the stone: the stone in whose small compass her Visitor had made her to see the Universe, everything that is. And if it is so small, thought Anne, beginning thus a sentence which she was never able confidently to finish.

There was no God, but Christ lived, at any rate her Christ lived, her nomadic cosmic Christ, uniquely hers, focused upon her alone by all the rays of being. He was defeated, she thought, the way to Jerusalem was not a triumphal progress. He was a failure, a pathetic deluded disappointed man who had come to an exceptionally sticky end. And yet: 'Weep not for me but for yourself.' Could she, knowing what she knew of him, of all his failure, all of it, tread that way after him? Could she relive his journey and his passion while knowing that he was after all not God? And she remembered the 'wonderful answer' which had made her Visitor laugh and call her 'witty', when she had said, 'Love is my meaning'. And she remembered too in an odd way something which the Count had said once about his own love and its object. 'I did it all, I enacted both sides of the relation, and this could be done because she was inaccessible.' And Anne cried out in her heart to her living Christ, 'Oh Sir, your yoke is heavy and your burden is intolerable.' And she was answered in his words, 'The work is yours.'

The work was hers; and as she measured its fearful ambiguity she seemed to see before her Guy's glittering eyes and his wasted face, and hear words spoken a year ago, of which she could not tell now whether they were her words or his. We want our vices to suffer but not to die. Purgatorial suffering is a magical story, the transformation of death into pain, happy pain whose guaranteed value will buy us in return some everlasting consolation. But there are eternal partings, all things end and end forever and nothing could be more important than that. We live with death. With pain, yes. But really . . . with death.

500

With a mental gesture as if dodging a blow Anne turned aside from these thoughts. They would go with her and there would be times when they would enter bodily into her flesh. Of this sort of corporal reality of thoughts the convent had taught her something. At least she thought it is possible to help people, to make them happier and less anxious, and this is somehow, I can't at the moment think how, both possible and necessary *because* of all those final endings. She had helped Gertrude. Gertrude had said, 'I was possessed by a devil and you saved me.' How much did I really do for her, thought Anne, how far did I really crucially help that great survivor to survive? At the very beginning, yes, I soothed her pain. Anne could not think of anyone else whom she had helped since her 'liberation'. Oh yes, she had helped Sylvia Wicks. She had met Sylvia and heard her story on one day when Sylvia, in final desperation, had come to Ebury Street seeking Gertrude. Gertrude was absent and Sylvia poured it all out to Anne, who kept it to herself. She agreed to talk to Sylvia's son (Paul) and then to the girl (Mary) whom he had made pregnant. Soon after this the young people pulled themselves together and took charge of their weeping raving parents. They decided to have the baby and to do their exams and then to get married. Meanwhile Sylvia would help them to look after the child. The child (a boy, they called him Francis) arrived in July. He was baptised (Anne was godmother) and the grandparents, transformed, vied for his affection. In fact, Mary's father was a widower, and, once he stopped shouting, a person of great rationality and charm. He and Sylvia became very fond of each other, to the joyful amusement of their children. Sylvia's life was totally transformed, she had never been happier, and could hardly now believe that a year ago she had felt suicidal despair. She told Anne that it was 'all her doing'. Well, thought Anne, I did something.

Anne met Manfred once at Sylvia's house. Manfred, to do him justice, knowing nothing of Anne's connection with her, rang Sylvia up out of his usual casual benevolence to find out if she needed money or anything, and he did in fact later on solve Sylvia's financial problems for her. He was rewarded and electrified to learn by telephone that Anne was actually with Sylvia at that moment. He raced for his car and arrived plausibly before she left; and this time Anne let him drive her back to her flat. This was the one occasion when he was alone with her. Manfred, driving unusually slowly, wondered if he should stop the car in some convenient side street and take her in his arms, at least make some passionate declaration. It was one of the most agonizing moments of his life. He decided that if he did so Anne would be startled, embarrassed, distressed, annoyed, and would ask him to desist. (This prediction of Manfred's was in fact correct, and he was of course also right in thinking that Anne never guessed his love.) His pride, equal in this respect to hers, could not have born the shock. He did not risk it. And in just this sense Mrs Mount was perhaps right to say that he did not love her enough.

Stroking Perkins, Anne began now to listen to the sounds round about her to which she had been oblivious. A group of people at the next table were having an animated conversation. Suddenly Anne was rigid with attention.

'Daisy Barrett's gone, you know.'

'Yes, to America.'

'She's gone to join some women friends, Libbers you know.'

'Where?'

'California, where else! Santa Barbara or something.'

'That should suit her.'

'She led a pretty crazy life here.'

'You don't know the half of it.'

'At any rate she got rid of that awful red-headed creep who was always after her.'

'I can't think how she stood that chap so long.'

'You heard what happened to him?'

'What?'

'He married a merry widow.'

'Rich?'

'Of course.'

'Daisy was too good for him.'

'Yes, Daisy's *someone*, she's a *real person*, if you know what I mean.'

'Well, God bless her, wherever she is. The sight of her boozy old painted face always made me feel better.'

'She hadn't an ounce of spite in her, she shouted and screamed but she forgave everybody and everything.'

'The Prince won't be the same without her.'

'What did she do with all those awful potted plants?'

'Gave them to Marje.'

'Oh, yes of course.'

'Did she tell you about the ghastly nun who was chasing her?'

'Daisy would be chased by a nun!'

'She was an unfrocked nun, actually.'

'What's more exciting, an unfrocked nun or an unfrocked priest?'

'Beautiful word, "frock".'

'Apparently this nun was a raving lesbian and had been chucked out of her convent for seducing the novices.'

'Darling, have you got her address?'

'How was Daisy when you saw her?'

'Oh in fine form. She said she was going off in search of her innocence.'

'Perhaps we should all do that.'

'But not tonight. Let's have another round. It's Piglet's turn.'

Anne stroked Perkins who was now purring, gently stroking the cat's black nose where the fur grew downward. Perkins looked up at Anne with her intense sinless passionless green eyes. For the first moment Anne felt shock and distress at the image of her which had escaped somehow and was wandering abroad, bandied about over the drinking glasses. Then she relaxed and smiled. It was funny really. And by what privilege could she be exempt from so general a human fate? We are all the judges and the judged, victims of the casual malice and fantasy of others, and ready sources of fantasy and malice in our turn. And if we are sometimes accused of sins of which we are innocent, are there not also other sins of which we are guilty and of which the world knows nothing?

So Daisy had gone to America, she had preceded Anne into the New World. She is another wanderer, she thought. Well, I shall follow after and carry my cross and my Christ with me. She had found, in that scrap of conversation, the relief of anxiety for which she craved. Daisy had set off 'in fine form'. Anne agreed that Daisy was 'someone'. And so she was seeking innocence. It was a quest suited to human powers. Perhaps after all, Goodness was too hard to seek and too hard to understand. Anne did not now feel it her duty to search further. But she thought in an odd way that if Daisy ever terribly needed her they would perhaps meet again.

Anne put Perkins down gently on the floor. She finished up her glass of wine and began to pull on her overcoat. Suddenly there was a commotion at the other end of the bar.

'Look, look who's here!'

'It's Barkiss, Barkiss is back!'

'I just opened the door and he walked in!'

Anne's neighbours leapt up and ran towards the shouting. People crowded round.

'It's Barkiss, he's come back to us!'

'Look how thin he is!'

'Quick, a ham sandwich for Barkiss!'

'He's been away a whole year!'

'Look at his poor old paws, he must have walked from Land's End!'

'I just opened the door and he walked in!'

'Good old Barkiss, dear old Barkiss, he's come back to the Prince of Denmark.'

Peering, Anne saw a big yellow Labrador frisking and wagging its tail amid the cries of joy. She watched for a little, smiling, then left the pub.

'*Time, please. Closing time. Time, gentlemen, please.*'

Outside, the shock of the cold blanched her face and the cold finger of her indrawn breath reached down into her shrinking body. She buttoned up her coat and pulled on her gloves.

It was still snowing and the roads and pavements were dark with running water and brown slush. The whitened cars moved slowly with a soft hissing sound. Anne looked upward. The snow, illuminated by the street lamps, was falling abundantly, against the further background of the enclosing dark. The big flakes came into view, moving, weaving, crowding, descending slowly in a great hypnotic silence which seemed to separate itself from the sounds of the street below. Anne stopped and watched it. It reminded her of something, which perhaps she had seen in a picture or in a dream. It looked like the heavens spread out in glory, totally unrolled before the face of God, countless, limitless, eternally beautiful, the universe in majesty proclaiming the presence and the goodness of its Creator.

Anne stood there for a while. Then she began to walk through the snowy streets at random, feeling lightened of her burdens. Tomorrow she would be in America.